"Anthony Horowitz is the lion of children's literature." Michael Morpurgo

"Horowitz has become a writer who converts boys to reading."
The Times

"A first-class children's novelist."
TES

EX LIBRIS

Anthony

Marchant

THE DIAMOND BROTHERS IN...

The Blurred Man

AND

I Know What You Did Last Wednesday

More wickedly funny books

by Anthony Horowitz

The Devil and His Boy

Groosham Grange

Return to Groosham Grange

The Switch

More Bloody Horowitz

The Diamond Brothers books:

The Falcon's Malteser

Public Enemy Number Two

South by South East

The Blurred Man

The French Confection

I Know What You Did Last Wednesday

The Greek who Stole Christmas

THE DIAMOND BROTHERS IN...

The Blurred Man

AND

I Know What You Did Last Wednesday

ANTHONY HOROWITZ

WALKER
BOOKS

This is a work of fiction. Names, characters, places and incidents are either the product of the author's imagination or, if real, are used fictitiously. All statements, activities, stunts, descriptions, information and material of any other kind contained herein are included for entertainment purposes only and should not be relied on for accuracy or replicated as they may result in injury.

First published individually as *The Blurred Man* (2002) and
I Know What You Did Last Wednesday (2002) by Walker Books Ltd
87 Vauxhall Walk, London SE11 5HJ

This edition published 2015

2 4 6 8 10 9 7 5 3 1

This book has been typeset in Sabon

Printed in Germany by GGP Media GmbH

British Library Cataloguing in Publication Data:
a catalogue record for this book is available from the British Library

ISBN 978-1-4063-6478-1

www.walker.co.uk

CONTENTS

TIM DIAMOND INC.
23 THE CUTTING, CAMDEN TOWN, NW1

Dear Reader,

It's been a while since I had lunch with the chairman of Walker Books. He's an old man now. Most of his hair's gone white and the rest of it's just gone. He wears bi-focal glasses but he doesn't really need them. He's forgotten how to read. He'd forget his own name if it wasn't written on his Zimmer frame.

And yet I still remember the day he took me out – just the two of us, face to face, though with a face like his I wouldn't have bothered. We met at the poshest restaurant in London ... then crossed the road to the café on the other side. He ordered two bacon sandwiches without the bacon. He was a vegetarian. And that was when he tried to sweet-talk me into writing an introduction for this collection of stories. But it takes more than a bag of sweets to get Tim Diamond on your side, so I told Walker to take a walk.

A few days later he came tiptoeing round my flat with a bag of books: a bit like Santa Claus without the beard, the laughter or (it was the middle of June) Christmas. This was his deal. Three dozen adventures of Maisy mouse and an old Where's Wally? annual in return for a couple of pages by me. But as far as I was concerned, there was still one book missing. The Walker cheque book ... preferably autographed. Unfortunately, when I pointed this out, the chairman just scowled. That was the sort of man he was: small, hard-edged and leathery. Just like his chair.

"I need an introduction!" he cried.

"All right. How do you do, I'm Tim Diamond," I said.

"No, no, no. For the book!"

"Why do you need an introduction?" Nick – my kid brother – asked. "You probably won't sell any copies anyway."

Actually, in the end, it was Nick who talked me into writing this. He reminded me it's only thanks to Walker that I've become known as England's sharpest, most successful private eye, the sort of detective that makes Hercule Poirot look like a short Belgian with a funny moustache! I have to admit that Walker have been behind me all the way. About thirty miles behind me.

They launched this book with a slap-up dinner at the Ritz. The service was so slow, the waiters deserved to be slapped. Twelve journalists came, but only eleven left. That was how bad the food was.

At the same time, they took out a full-page ad in British Airways "High Life" magazine. They were hoping the books would fly off the shelves and the funny thing is, they did. Maybe it was the new covers that had been specially designed to stop people noticing the new price. It certainly couldn't have been the title. The last time I got the four of diamonds in a high class poker game, I went home without my clothes. If they are going to name a book after a playing card, they could have at least chosen a king.

Anyway, here's the introduction. I'm not quite sure how to begin. Introducing the introduction is always the hardest part. I'm glad I'm not a writer. And if you met the guy who does the writing for me, you'd be glad too.

His name is Anthony Horowitz – and I use him to put my adventures down on paper. Let me tell you a bit about him. A lot of people have compared him to JK Rowling. They say he's not as good. He has a wife, two sons, a stuffed dog and a word processor, and the word processor is the only one that doesn't want to leave home. You ever see "Foyle's War", "Midsomer Murders" or "Collision" on TV? Me neither – but he wrote them all. They're the only programmes people fast-forward through to see the advertisements. He also writes a lot of books. About thirty of them at the last count. Enough books to immobilise a mobile library.

I met him just after I'd cracked the case that became known as "The Falcon's Malteser". I don't think his career was doing too well just then. How many other writers tap-dance outside Harrods in their spare time? Anyway, I told him my story, he began to write – and the rest was history. Actually, nobody wanted history. They wanted an adventure. So he had to write it a second time. But it worked. "The Falcon's Malteser" sold twenty-seven copies in Waterstone's the day it was published and I only bought twenty-six of them. Soon we were right at number one in the Bookseller chart. OK – it was the remainders chart but you've got to start somewhere. "The Times" critic said the book was "hysterical" and she should know.

Since then, I've cracked more cases than the entire baggage-handling department at Heathrow Airport, and Horowitz has written them all. "Public Enemy Number Two", "South by South East" – one day maybe he'll come up with a title that somebody actually understands. I had a pretty hairy time in Australia recently and he says that'll come out in a book too. Apparently the title is going to be: "The Radius of the Lost Shark".

Which brings me to the book you are now holding in your hand (unless you didn't buy it, in which case it's still on the shelf ... a bit like my editor). The two stories in this book all happened to me in the space of one year and all I can say is, I'm glad it wasn't a leap year. One extra day would have been the death of me.

Why do so many people want to kill me? I was nearly shot in "The Blurred Man" and the next time I go on the Millennium Wheel, I want to be sure I'm going to make it the whole way round. There were so many murders in "I Know What You Did Last Wednesday" that it's a miracle I wasn't one of them.

You may have noticed that this edition is printed on special cheap paper and as for the glue ... all I can say is, don't leave it out in the sun. The book is also carbon neutral. A forest in Norway was cut down to produce it but the good news is that another one was planted ... in England. The Norwegians have got too many anyway. You might like to know, ten per cent of every copy sold goes to a very worthwhile charity. Me. I have an overdraft and a hungry kid brother to support.

One last thing. Remember that this book comes with a MONEY BACK GUARANTEE. If for any reason you don't like it, Walker guarantee they won't give you back your money.

All the best,

Tim Diamond

THE BLURRED MAN

THE PEN PAL

I knew the American was going to mean trouble, the moment he walked through the door. He only made it on the third attempt. It was eleven o'clock in the morning but clearly he'd been drinking since breakfast – and breakfast had probably come out of a bottle too. The smell of whisky was so strong it made my eyes water. Drunk at eleven o'clock! I didn't like to think what it was doing to him, but if I'd been his liver I'd have been applying for a transplant.

He managed to find a seat and slumped into it. The funny thing was, he was quite smartly dressed: a suit and a tie that looked expensive. I got the feeling straight away that this was someone with money. He was wearing gold-rimmed glasses, and as far as I could tell we were talking real gold. He was about forty years old, with hair that was just turning grey and eyes that were just turning yellow. That must have been the whisky. He took out a cigarette and lit it. Blue smoke filled the room. This man would not have been a good advertisement for the National Health Service.

"My name is Carter," he said at last. He spoke with an American accent. "Joe Carter. I just got in from Chicago. And I've got a problem."

"I can see that," I muttered.

He glanced at me with one eye. The other eye looked somewhere over my shoulder. "Who are you?" he demanded.

"I'm Nick Diamond."

"I don't need a smart-arse kid. I'm looking for a private detective."

"That's him over there," I said, indicating the desk and my big brother, Tim.

"You want a coffee, Mr Carver?" Tim asked.

"It's not Carver. It's Carter. With a 't'," the American growled.

"I'm out of tea. How about a hot chocolate?"

"I don't want a hot anything!" Carter sucked on the cigarette. "I want help. I want to hire you. What do you charge?"

Tim stared. Although it was hard to believe, the American was offering him money. This was something that didn't happen often. Tim hadn't really made any money since he'd worked as a policeman, and even then the police dogs had earned more than him. At least they'd bitten the right man. As a private detective, Tim had been a total calamity. I'd helped him solve one or two cases, but most of the time I was stuck at school. Right now it was the week of half-term – six weeks before Christmas, and once again it didn't look like our stockings were going to be full. Unless you're talking holes. Tim had just seven pence left in his bank account. We'd written a begging letter to our mum and dad in Australia but were still saving up for the stamp.

I coughed and Tim jerked upright in his chair, trying to look businesslike. "You need a private detective?" he said. "Fine. That's me. But it'll cost you fifty pounds a day, plus expenses."

"You take traveller's cheques?"

"That depends on the traveller."

"I don't have cash."

"Traveller's cheques are fine," I said.

Joe Carter pulled out a bundle of blue traveller's cheques, then fumbled for a pen. For a moment I was worried that he'd be too drunk to sign them. But somehow he managed to scribble his name five times on the dotted lines, and slid the cheques across. "All right," he said. "That's five hundred dollars."

"Five hundred dollars!" Tim squeaked. The last time he'd had that much money in his hand he'd been playing Monopoly. "Five hundred dollars…?"

"About three hundred and fifty pounds," I told him.

Carter nodded. "Right. So now let me tell you where I'm coming from."

"I thought you were coming from Chicago," Tim said.

"I mean, let me tell you my problem. I got into England last Tuesday, a little less than a week ago. I'm staying in a hotel in the West End. The Ritz."

"You'd be crackers to stay anywhere else," Tim said.

"Yeah." Carter stubbed his cigarette out in the ashtray. Except we didn't have an ashtray. The smell of burning wood rose from the surface of Tim's desk. "I'm a writer, Mr Diamond. You may have read some of my books."

That was unlikely – unless he wrote children's books. Tim had recently started *Just William* for the fourth time.

"I'm pretty well-known in the States," Carter continued. "*The Big Bullet. Death in the Afternoon. Rivers of Blood.* Those are some of my titles."

"Romances?" Tim asked.

"No. They're crime novels. I'm successful. I make a ton of money out of my writing – but, you know, I believe in sharing it around. I'm not married. I don't have kids. So I give it to charity. All sorts of charities. Mostly back home in the States, of course, but also in other parts of the world."

I wondered if he'd like to make a donation to the bankrupt brothers of dumb detectives, a little charity of my own. But I didn't say anything.

"Now, a couple of years back I heard of a charity operating here in England," he went on. "It was called Dream Time and I kind of liked the sound of it. Dream Time was there to help kids get more out of life. It bought computers and books and special equipment for schools. It also bought schools. It helped train kids who wanted to get into sport. Or who wanted to paint. Or who had never travelled." Carter glanced at me. "How old are you, son?" he asked.

"Fourteen," I said.

"I bet you make wishes sometimes."

"Yes. But unfortunately Tim is still here."

"Dream Time would help you. They make wishes come true." Carter reached into his pocket and took out a hip-flask. He unscrewed it and threw it back. It seemed to do him good. "A little Scotch," he explained.

"I thought you were American," Tim said.

"I gave Dream Time two million dollars of my money because I believed in them!" Carter exclaimed. "Most of all, I believed in the man behind Dream Time. He was a saint. He was a lovely guy. His name was Lenny Smile."

I noticed that Carter was talking about Smile in the past tense. I was beginning to see the way this conversation might be going.

"What can I tell you about Lenny?" Carter went on. "Like me, he never married. He didn't have a big house or a fancy car or anything like that. In fact he lived in a small apartment in a part of London called Battersea. Dream Time had been his idea and he worked for it seven days a week, three hundred and sixty-five days a year. Lenny loved leap years because then he could work three hundred and sixty-six days a year. That was the sort of man he was. When I heard about him, I knew I had to support his work. So I gave him a quarter of a million dollars. And then another quarter. And so on..."

"So what's the problem, Mr Starter?" Tim asked. "You want your money back?"

"Hell, no! Let me explain. I loved this guy Lenny. I felt like I'd known him all my life. But recently, I decided we ought to meet."

"You'd never met him?"

"No. We were pen pals. We exchanged letters. Lots of letters – and e-mails. He used to write to me and I'd write back. That's how I got to know him. But I was busy with my work. And he was busy with his. We never met. We never even spoke. And then, recently, I suddenly realized I needed a break. I'd been working so hard, I decided to come over to England

and have a vacation."

"Wouldn't you have preferred a holiday?" Tim asked.

"I wrote to Lenny and told him I'd like to meet him. He was really pleased to hear from me. He said he wanted to show me all the work he'd been doing. All the children who'd benefited from the money I'd sent. I was really looking forward to the trip. He was going to meet me at Heathrow Airport."

"How would you know what he looked like if you'd never met?" I asked.

Carter blushed. "Well, I did sometimes wonder about that. So once I'd arranged to come I asked him to send me a photograph of himself."

He reached into his jacket and took out a photograph. He handed it to me.

The picture showed a man standing in front of a café in what could have been London or Paris. It was hard to be sure. I could see the words CAFÉ DEBUSSY written on the windows. But the man himself was harder to make out. Whoever had taken the photograph should have asked Dream Time for a new camera. It was completely out of focus. I could just make out a man in a black suit with a full-length coat. He was wearing gloves and a hat. But his face was a blur. He might have had dark hair. I think he was smiling. There was a cat sitting on the pavement between his legs, and the cat was easier to make out than he was.

"It's not a very good picture," I said.

"I know." Carter took it back. "Lenny was a very shy person. He didn't even sign his letters. That's how shy he was. He told me that he didn't like going out very much. You see, there's something else you need to know about him. He was sick. He had this illness ... some kind of allergy."

"Was Algy his doctor?" Tim asked.

"No, no. An allergy. It meant he reacted to things. Peanuts, for example. They made him swell up. And he hated publicity. There have been a couple of stories about him in the newspapers, but he wouldn't give interviews and there were never any photographs. The Queen wanted to knight him, apparently, but sadly he was also allergic to queens. All that mattered to him was his work ... Dream Time ... helping kids. Anyway, meeting him was going to be the biggest moment of my life... I was as excited as a schoolboy."

As excited as a schoolboy? Obviously Carter had never visited my school.

"Only when I got to Heathrow, Lenny wasn't there. He wasn't in London either. I never got to meet him. And you know why?"

I knew why. But I waited for Lenny to tell me.

"Lenny was buried the day before I arrived," Carter said.

"Buried?" Tim exclaimed. "Why?"

"Because it was his funeral, Mr Diamond!" Carter lit another cigarette. "He was dead. And that's why I'm here. I want you to find out what happened."

"What did happen?" I asked.

"Well, like I told you, I arrived here at Heathrow last Tuesday. All I could think about was meeting Lenny Smile, shaking that man's hand and telling him just how much he meant to me. When he didn't show up, I didn't even check into my hotel. I went straight to the offices of Dream Time. And that was when they told me..."

"Who told you?" I asked.

"A man called Hoover. Rodney Hoover..."

"That name sucks," Tim said.

Carter ignored him. "He worked for Lenny, helping him run Dream Time. There's another assistant there too, called Fiona Lee. She's very posh. Upper-class, you know? They have an office just the other side of Battersea Bridge. It's right over the café you saw in that photo. Anyway, it seems that just a few days after I e-mailed Lenny to tell him I was coming, he got killed in a horrible accident, crossing the road."

"He fell down a manhole?" Tim asked.

"No, Mr Diamond. He got run over. Hoover and Lee actually saw it happen. If they hadn't been there, the police wouldn't even have known it was Lenny."

"Why is that?"

"Because he was run over by a steamroller." Carter shuddered. Tim shivered. Even the desk light flickered. I had to admit, it was a pretty horrible way to go. "He was flattened," the American went on. "They told me that the ambulance people had to fold him before they could get him onto a stretcher. He was buried last week. At Brompton Cemetery, near Fulham."

Brompton. That was where the master criminal known as the Falcon had been buried too. Tim and I had gone to the cemetery at the end of our first ever case*. We were lucky we weren't still there.

"This guy Rodney Hoover tells me he's winding down Dream Time," Carter went on. "He says it wouldn't be the same without Lenny, and he doesn't have the heart to go on without him. I had a long talk with him in his office and I have to tell you ... I didn't like it."

"You don't think it's a nice office?" Tim asked.

"I think something strange is going on."

Tim blinked. "What exactly do you think is strange?"

Carter almost choked on his cigarette. "Goddammit!" he yelled. "You don't think there's anything unusual in a guy getting run over by a steamroller? It happens in the middle

* See *The Falcon's Malteser*

of the night and just a few days before he's due to have a meeting with someone who's given him two million dollars! And the next thing you hear, the charity he'd set up is suddenly shutting down! You don't think that's all a little strange?"

"It's certainly strange that it happened in the middle of the night," Tim agreed. "Why wasn't he in bed?"

"I don't know why he wasn't in bed – but I'll tell you this: I think he was murdered. A man doesn't walk in front of a steamroller. But maybe he's pushed. Maybe this has got something to do with money … my money. Maybe somebody didn't want us to meet! I know that if I was writing this as a novel, that's the way it would turn out. Anyway, there are plenty of private detectives in London. If you're not interested, I can find someone who is. So are you going to look into this for me or not?"

Tim glanced at the traveller's cheques. He scooped them up. "Don't worry, Mr Carpark," he said. "I'll find the truth. The only question is – where do I find you?"

"I'm still at the Ritz," Carter said. "Ask for Room 8."

"I'll ask for you," Tim said. "But if you're out, I suppose the room-mate will have to do."

We changed the traveller's cheques into cash and blew some of it on the first decent meal we'd had in a week. Tim was in a good mood. He even let me have a pudding.

"I can't believe it!" he exclaimed, as the waitress served us two ice-cream sundaes. The service in the restaurant was so slow that they were more like Mondays by the time they arrived. "Three hundred and fifty pounds! That's more money than I've earned in a month."

"It's more money than you've earned in a year," I reminded him.

"And all because some crazy American thinks his pen pal was murdered."

"How do you know he wasn't?"

"Intuition." Tim tapped the side of his nose. "I can't explain it to you, kid. I've just got a feeling."

"You've also got ice-cream on your nose," I said.

After lunch we took the bus over to Fulham. I don't know why Tim decided to start in Brompton Cemetery. Maybe he wanted to visit it for old times' sake. It had been more than a year since we'd last been there, but the place hadn't changed. And why should it have? I doubted any of the residents had complained. None of them would have had the energy to redecorate. The gravestones were as weird as ever, some of them like Victorian telephone boxes, others like miniature castles with doors fastened by rusting chains and padlocks. You'd have needed a skeleton key to open them. The place was divided into separate areas: some old, some more modern. There must have been thousands of people there but of course none of them offered to show us the way to Smile's grave. We had to find it on our own.

It took us about an hour. It was on the edge of the cemetery, overshadowed by the football stadium next door. We might never have found it except that the grave had been recently dug. That was one clue. And there were fresh flowers. That was another. Smile had been given a lot of flowers. In fact, if he hadn't been dead he could have opened a florist's. I read the gravestone:

LENNY SMILE
APRIL 31st 1955 – NOVEMBER 11th 2001
A WONDERFUL MAN, CALLED TO REST.

We stood in silence for a moment. It seemed too bad that someone who had done so much for children all over the world hadn't even made it to fifty. I glanced at the biggest bunch of flowers on the grave. There was a card attached. It was signed in green ink, *With love, from Rodney Hoover and Fiona Lee*.

There was a movement on the other side of the cemetery. I had thought we were alone when we arrived, but now I realized that there was a man, watching us. He was a long way away, standing behind one of the taller gravestones, but even at that distance I thought there was something familiar about him, and I found myself shivering without quite knowing why. He was wearing a full-length coat with gloves and a hat. I couldn't make out his face. From this distance, it was just a blur. And that was when I realized. I knew exactly where I'd seen him before. I started forward, running towards him. At that moment he turned round and hurried off, moving away from me.

"Nick!" Tim called out.

I ignored him and ran through the cemetery. There was a gravestone in the way and I jumped over it. Maybe that wasn't a respectful thing to do but I wasn't feeling exactly religious. I reached the main path and sprinted forward. I didn't know if Tim was following me or not. I didn't care.

The northern gates of the cemetery opened onto Old Brompton Road. I burst out and stood there, catching my breath. It came as a shock, coming from the land of the dead into that of the living, with buses and cabs roaring past. An old woman, wrapped in three cardigans, was selling flowers right next to the gate. Business can't have been good. Half the flowers were as dead as the people they were meant for. I went over to her.

"Excuse me..." I said. "Did someone just

come out through this gate?"

The old woman shook her head. "No, dear. I didn't see anyone."

"Are you sure? A man in a long coat. He was wearing a hat..."

"People don't come out of the cemetery," the old woman said. "When they get there, they stay there."

A moment later, Tim proved her wrong by appearing at the gate. "What is it, Nick?" he asked.

I looked up and down the pavement. There was nobody in sight. Had I imagined it? No. I was certain. The man I had seen in Joe Carter's photograph had been in the cemetery less than a minute ago. Once I'd spotted him, he had run away.

But that was impossible, wasn't it?

If it was Lenny Smile that I had just seen, then who was buried in the grave?

DEAD MAN'S FOOTSTEPS

We began our search for Lenny Smile the next day – at the Battersea offices of the charity he had created.

I knew the building, of course, from the photograph Carter had shown us. Dream Time's headquarters were above the Café Debussy, which was in the middle of a row of half-derelict shops a few minutes' walk from the River Thames. It was hard to believe that a charity worth millions of pounds could operate from such a small, shabby place. But maybe that was the point. Maybe they didn't want to spend the money they raised on plush offices in the West End. It's the same reason why Oxfam shops always look so run down. That way they can afford another ox.

But the inside of Dream Time was something else. The walls had been knocked through to create an open-plan area with carpets that reached up to your ankles and leather furniture you couldn't believe had started life as a cow. The light fittings looked Italian. Low lighting at high prices. There were framed pictures on the walls, of smiling children from around the world: Asia, Africa, Europe and so on. The receptionist was smiling too. We already knew that the place was being shut down, and I could see that she didn't have a lot to do. She'd just finished polishing her nails when we walked in. While we were waiting she started polishing her teeth.

At last a door opened and Fiona Lee walked in. At least, I guessed it must be her. We'd rung that morning and made an appointment. She was tall and slim, with her dark hair tied back in such a vicious bun that you'd expect it to explode at any moment. She had the looks of a model, but I'm talking the Airfix variety. All plastic. Her make-up was perfect. Her clothes were perfect. Everything about her was perfect, down to the last detail. Either she spent hours getting ready every morning, or she slept hanging in the wardrobe so that she didn't rumple her skin.

"Good morning," she said. Joe Carter had been right about her. She had such a posh accent that when she spoke you heard every letter. "My name is Fiona Lee."

We introduced ourselves.

She looked from Tim to me and back again.

She didn't seem impressed. "Do come in," she said. She spun round on her heel. With heels like hers I was surprised she didn't drill a hole in the floor.

We followed her down a corridor lined with more smiling kids. At the end was a door that led to an office on a corner, with views of Battersea Park one way and the Thames the other. Rodney Hoover was sitting behind a desk cluttered with papers and half-dead potted plants, talking on the telephone. An ugly desk for a very ugly man. Both of them looked like they were made of wood. He was running to fat and might have been a little less fat if he'd taken up running. He had drooping shoulders and jet black hair that oozed oil. He was wearing an old-fashioned suit that was too small for him and glasses that were too big. As he finished his call, I noticed that he had horrible teeth. In fact the last time I'd seen teeth like that, they'd been in a dog. Mrs Lee signalled and we sat down. Hoover hung up. He had been speaking with a strong accent that could have been Russian or German. I noticed he had bad breath. No wonder the potted plants on his desk were wilting.

"Good morning," he said.

"This is Tim Diamond, Mr Hoover," Mrs Lee said. She pronounced his name *Teem Daymond*. "He telephoned this morning."

"Oh yes. Yes!" Hoover turned to Tim. "I am

being sorry that I cannot help you, Mr Diamond." His English was terrible, although his breath was worse. "Right now, you see, Mrs Lee and I are closing down Dream Time, so if you have come about your little brother..."

"I don't need charity," I said.

"We helped a boy like you just a month ago," Fiona Lee said. She blinked, and her eyelashes seemed to wave goodbye. "He had always wanted to climb mountains, but he was afraid of heights."

"So did you buy him a small mountain?" Tim asked.

"No. We got him help from a psychiatrist. Then we paid for him to fly to Mount Everest. That little boy went all the way to the top! And although he unfortunately fell off, he was happy. That is the point of our work, Mr Diamond. We use the money that we raise to make children happy."

"And take the case of Billy!" Hoover added. He pointed at yet another photograph on the wall. If Dream Time had helped many more kids, they'd have run out of wall. "Billy was a boy who wanted to be a dancer. He was being bullied at school. So we hired some bullies to bully the bullies for Billy and now, you see, Billy is in the ballet!"

"Bully for Billy," I muttered.

"So how can we be of helping to you, Mr Diamond?" Hoover asked.

"I have some questions," Tim said. "About a friend of yours called Lenny Smile."

Both Rodney Hoover and Fiona Lee froze. Hoover licked his teeth, which can't have been a lot of fun. Fiona had gone pale. Even her make-up seemed to have lost some of its colour. "Why are you asking questions about Lenny?" she asked.

"Because that way people give me answers," Tim replied. "It's what I do. I'm a private detective."

There was an ugly silence. I had to say that it suited Rodney Hoover.

"Lenny is dead," he said. "You know very well that he's lying there in Brompton Cemetery. Yes? What could you possibly want to know about him?"

"I know he's dead," Tim said. "But I'd be interested to know exactly how he died. I understand you were there."

"We were there," Fiona said. A single tear had appeared in the corner of her eye and began to trickle down her cheek. "Poor, poor Lenny! It was the most ghastly, horrible moment in my life, Mr Diamond."

"I don't suppose it was a terrific moment for him either," I muttered.

She ignored me. "It was about eleven o'clock. Mr Hoover and myself had gone to see him. He didn't like to come out of his flat, so we often went round there to tell him how much money we had raised and how the charity was progressing. We talked. We had a glass of wine. And then we left."

"Lenny said he would come down with us to the car," Hoover continued. "It was a very beautiful night. He wanted to have some of the fresh air ... you know? And so, we left the flat together."

"Lenny was a little bit ahead of us," Fiona Lee explained. "He was a fast walker. Mr Hoover stopped to tie his shoelaces and I waited for him. Lenny stepped into the road. And then..."

"The steamroller was going too fast." He swore quietly in a foreign language. Fiona sighed. "But the driver was on his way home. He was in the hurry. And he ran over Lenny!" He shook his head. "There was nothing, nothing we could do!"

"Do you know the driver's name?" Tim asked.

"I believe it is Krishner. Barry Krishner."

"Do you know what happened to him?"

"He is in a hospital for the hopelessly insane in north London ... in Harrow," Fiona said. "You can imagine that it was a dreadful experience for him, running over a man with a steamroller. But it was his fault! And because he was speeding, he killed one of the most wonderful men who ever lived. Lenny Smile! I had worked for him for twenty years. Mr

Hoover too."

"You'd only worked for him for two years?" Tim asked.

"No. I worked with him also for twenty years," Hoover said. "But are you telling me, please, Mr Diamond. Who hired you to ask these questions about Lenny Smile?"

"I never reveal the names of my clients," Tim replied. "Joe Carter wants to remain anonymous."

"Carter!" Hoover muttered. He gave Tim an ugly look. It wasn't difficult. "I could have guessed this. Yes! He came here, asking all his questions as if Fiona and me..." He stopped himself. "There was not one thing suspicious about his death, Mr Diamond. It was an accident. We know. Why? Because we were there! You think someone killed him? Poppycock! Who would wish to kill him?"

"Maybe he had enemies," Tim said.

"Everybody loved Lenny," Fiona retorted. "Even his enemies loved him. All he did his whole life was give away money and help young people. That man built so many orphanages, we had to advertise for orphans to fill them."

"What else can you tell us about him?" I asked.

"It's hard to describe Lenny to someone who never met him."

"Try. Where did he live?"

"He rented a flat in Welles Road. Number seventeen. He didn't buy anywhere because he hated spending money on himself." She took out a tiny handkerchief and dabbed the corner of her eye. "It is true that he liked to be on his own a lot."

"Why?"

"Because of his allergies."

I remembered now. Carter had said he was sick.

"What was he allergic to?" I asked.

"Many, many things," Hoover replied. "Chocolate, peanuts, yoghurt, animals, elastic bands, insects..."

"If he was stung by a wasp, he would be in hospital for a week," Fiona agreed.

"He was also allergic to hospitals. He had to go to a private clinic." Hoover stood up. Suddenly the interview was over. "Lenny Smile was a very unique man. He was – as you say – one in a million. And you have no right ... no right to come here like this. You are wrong! Wrong with all your suspiciousness."

"Yes." Fiona nodded in agreement. "His death was a terrible accident. But the police investigated. They found nothing. Mr Hoover and I were there and we saw nothing."

"You can say to your 'anonymous' client, Mr Carter, that he should go back to Chicago," Hoover concluded. "And now, please, I think you should leave."

We left. The last thing I saw was Rodney Hoover standing next to Fiona Lee. The two of them were holding hands. Were they just co-workers, friends ... or something more? And there was something else. Hoover had said something. I wasn't sure what it was, but I was certain he had told me something that in fact he didn't want me to know. I tried to play back the conversation but it wouldn't come.

Tim and I left the offices of Dream Time together. Rodney Hoover and Fiona Lee had given us both the creeps. Neither of us said anything. But we both looked very carefully before we crossed the road.

At least Fiona had given us Smile's address, and as it wasn't far away that was where we went next.

Welles Road was round the back of Battersea, not far from the famous dogs' home. The tall, red-bricked buildings were all mansion flats ... not as big as mansions, but certainly smarter than your average flat. There were a dozen people living in each block, with their names listed on the front door. It turned out that Smile had lived at 17A – on the fifth floor. We rang the bell, but there was no answer so we tried 17B. There was a pause, then a woman's voice crackled over the intercom.

"Who is it?"

"We're friends of Lenny Smile," I shouted

back before Tim could come up with a story of his own.

"The fifth floor!" the voice called out. There was a buzz and the door opened.

With its faded wallpaper and worn carpets, the building seemed somehow tired inside. And so were we by the time we got to the fifth floor. The lift wasn't working. The whole place smelled of damp and yesterday's cooking. I thought you needed to be rich to live in Battersea (unless, of course, you happened to be a dog). But anyone could have lived here if they weren't fussy. The fifth floor was also the top floor. The door of 17B was open when we arrived.

"Mr Smile is dead!"

The woman who had broken the news to us so discreetly was about eighty, with white hair that might have been a wig and a face that had long ago given up trying to look human. Her eyes, nose and mouth all seemed to have run into each other like a melting candle. Her voice was still crackling, even without the intercom system. She was dressed in a pale orange dress decorated with flowers; the sort of material that would have looked better on a chair. There were fluffy pink slippers on her feet. Her legs – what I could see of them – were stout and hairy and made me glad that I couldn't see more.

"Who are you?" Tim asked.

"My name's Lovely."

"I'm sure it is," Tim agreed. "But what is it?"

"I just told you, dear. Lovely! Rita Lovely! I live next door to Mr Smile. Or at least ... I used to."

"Have you moved?" Tim asked.

Mrs Lovely blinked at him. "No. Don't be daft! Mr Smile is the one who's moved. All the way to Brompton Cemetery!"

"We know that," Tim said. "We've already been there."

"Then what do you want?"

"We want to get into his flat."

"Why?"

I decided it was time to take over. "Mr Smile was my hero," I lied. I'd put on the little-boy-lost look that usually worked with very old women. And also, for that matter, with Tim. "He helped me."

"He gave you money?" She looked at me suspiciously.

"He saved my life. I had a rare disease."

"What disease?"

"It was so rare, it didn't have a name. Mr Smile paid for my medicine. I never got a chance to thank him. And I thought, if I could at least see where he lived..."

That softened her. "I've got a key," she said, taking it out of her pocket. "I was his neighbour for seven years and I used to look after the place for him when he was away. You seem a nice boy, so I'll let you in, just for a few minutes. This way..."

It seemed to take her for ever to reach the door, but then she was very old. At last we were in. Mrs Lovely closed the door behind us and sat down to have a rest.

Smile's flat was small and ordinary. There was a living-room, but it was so neat and impersonal that it was hard to believe anyone had done any living there at all. There was a three-piece suite, a coffee table, a few ornaments. The pictures on the wall were even less interesting than the walls they hung on. It was the same story in the other rooms. The flat told us nothing about the person who had lived there. Even the fridge was empty.

"How often did you see Mr Smile?" I asked.

"I never saw him," Tim replied.

"I know, Tim. I'm asking Mrs Lovely."

"I hardly ever saw him," Mrs Lovely said. "He kept himself to himself, if you want the truth. Although I was here the night that he got run over."

"Did you see what happened?"

"Not really, no." She shook her head vigorously and then readjusted her hair and teeth. "But I did see him go out. There were two people with him, talking to him. They seemed to be helping him down the stairs."

"Helping him?"

"One on each side of him. A man and a woman..."

That would have been Rodney Hoover and Fiona Lee.

"After they'd gone, I heard the most terrible noise. It was a sort of rumble and then a scrunching. At first I thought it was my indigestion, but then I looked out of the window. And there they were! The two of them and the driver—"

"Barry Krishner..."

"I don't know his name, young man. But yes, the driver of the steamroller was there. He was looking as sick as a parrot. Hardly surprising!"

"What happened to the parrot?" Tim asked.

"There was no parrot!"

"You mean ... it got so sick it died?"

"There was the driver, the two people I had seen on the stairs and blood all over the road!" Mrs Lovely sighed. "It was the worst thing I have ever seen, and I've lived through two world wars! Blood everywhere! Lots and lots and lots of blood..."

"Thank you," Tim interrupted, going pale.

"Were there no other witnesses?" I asked.

"Just one." Mrs Lovely leant forward. "There was a balloon-seller on the other side of the road. He must have seen everything. I've already been asked about him once, so before you ask me again let me tell you that I don't know his name or where he had come from. He was an old man. He had a beard and about fifty helium balloons. Floating above his head."

"Why was his beard floating over his head?" Tim asked.

"The balloons, Tim!" I growled. I turned to Mrs Lovely. "Is there anything else you can tell us?" I asked. "Anything about Lenny Smile?"

"No. Not really." Suddenly there were tears in the old woman's eyes. She took out a handkerchief and blew her nose loudly. "I will miss him. It's true I hardly ever saw him, but he was a gentleman. Look at this note he sent me. It was my ninety-first birthday last week and he slipped it under the door."

She produced a crumpled sheet of paper, torn out of an exercise book. There were a couple of lines written in green ink:

Dear Mrs Lovely,
I hope you have a lovely birthday.
L.S.

That was all. The note couldn't have been less interesting or informative. And yet even so I thought there was something strange about it, something that didn't quite add up. I handed it back.

"Nobody else remembered my birthday," Mrs Lovely sighed. "I didn't get any cards. But then, most of my friends were blown up in the war..." She wiped her eyes. "I couldn't have asked for a more quiet neighbour," she said. "And now that he's gone, I'll really miss him."

How could she miss him when she had hardly ever met him? And why had Lenny Smile taken so much care not to be seen? I was beginning to realize that it wasn't just Carter's photograph that had been blurred. The same thing could be said for everything in Lenny Smile's life.

We found Barry Krishner, the steamroller driver, easily enough. There was only one institute for the hopelessly insane in Harrow. Well, two if you count the famous public school which was just a little further down the road. The hospital was a big, Victorian building, set in its own grounds with a path leading up to the front door.

"Are you sure this is the right place?" Tim asked.

"Yes," I said. "They've even got crazy paving."

I have to say, I was a bit worried about going into a mental asylum with Tim. I wondered if they'd let him out again. But it was too late to back out now. One of the doctors, a man called Eams, was waiting for us at the entrance. He was a short man, bald with a little beard that could have been bought at a joke shop. We introduced ourselves and he led us out of the winter sunlight into the gloomy heart of the building.

"Krishner has responded very well to treatment," he said. "Otherwise I would not let you speak with him. Even so, I must ask you to be extremely careful. As I am sure you can imagine, running someone over with a steamroller would be a very upsetting experience."

"For Lenny Smile?" Tim asked.

"For the driver! When Krishner first came here, he was in a state of shock. He ate very little. He barely spoke. Every night he woke up screaming."

"Bad dreams, Dr Eams?" Tim asked.

"Yes. But we have given him a lot of therapy and there has been considerable improvement. However, please, Mr Diamond, try not to refer to what happened. Don't mention any of the details – the steamroller, the accident itself. You have to be discreet!"

"Discreet is my middle name!" Tim nodded.

"And also please bear in mind, he is not a lunatic. He is here as my patient. So don't say anything that would make him think he is mentally ill."

Tim laughed. "I'd be mad to do that!" He nudged the doctor. "So, where's his padded cell?"

Barry Krishner was sitting in a small, old-fashioned room that could just as easily have belonged to a seaside hotel as an asylum. A large window looked out onto the garden and there were no bars. He was a small, grey-haired man, dressed in an old sports jacket and dark trousers. I noticed his eyes blinked a lot behind his spectacles, and he kept on picking his nails. Otherwise it would have been impossible to tell that he had, until recently, been in shock.

"Good afternoon, Barry," Dr Eams said. "These people want to ask you some very important questions about Lenny Smile." Krishner twitched as if he had just been electrocuted. Dr Eams smiled and continued in a soothing tone of voice. "You have nothing to worry about. They're not going to upset you." He nodded at Tim.

"It must have been a crushing experience," Tim began.

Krishner whimpered and twisted in his chair. Dr Eams frowned at Tim, then gently took hold of Krishner's arm. "Are you all right, Barry?" he asked. "Would you like me to get you a drink?"

"Good idea," Tim agreed. "Why not have a squash?"

Krishner shrieked. His glasses had slipped off his nose and one of his eyes had gone bloodshot.

"Mr Diamond!" Eams was angry now. "Please could you be careful what you say. You told me you were going to ask Barry what he saw outside Lenny Smile's house."

"Flat," Tim corrected him.

Krishner went completely white. I thought he was going to pass out.

Dr Eams stared at Tim. "For heaven's sake…!" he rasped.

"OK, doc." Tim winked. "I think it's time we got to the crunch…"

Krishner began to foam at the mouth.

"I really want to crack this case. Although I have to say, the clues are a bit thin on the ground…"

Barry Krishner screamed and jumped out of the window. Without opening it. Alarms went off all over the hospital and, two minutes later, Tim and I were being escorted off the premises with the gates locked securely behind us.

"They weren't very helpful," Tim muttered. "Do you think it was something I said?"

I didn't answer. We had spent the whole day following in a supposedly dead man's footsteps. They had led us nowhere.

So where did we go now?

A NIGHT AT THE CIRCUS

The next day was a Saturday. Tim was in a bad mood when he came in for breakfast. He'd obviously got out of bed the wrong side: not a good idea, since he slept next to the window. At least there was food in the fridge. The money that Joe Carter had paid us would last us a month, and that morning I'd cooked up eggs, bacon, tomatoes, sausages and beans. The papers had arrived – the *Sun* for me, the *Dandy* for Tim. An hour later the two of us were so full we could barely move. There's nothing like a great British breakfast for a great British heart attack.

But the truth is, we were both down in the dumps – and this time I don't mean the flat. We were no nearer to finding the truth about Smile. Rodney Hoover and Fiona Lee, the pair who ran Dream Time, were obviously creepy. According to Mrs Lovely, the next-door neighbour, they had half-carried Smile downstairs just before his fatal accident. Had he been drunk? Or drugged? They could have thrown him in front of the steamroller – but if so, why? As Tim would doubtless have said, they'd have needed a pressing reason.

Barry Krishner, the driver of the steamroller, hadn't been able to tell us anything. After his encounter with Tim, it would probably be years before he talked again. He might babble and jibber, but I guessed talking would be a little beyond him. The police had presumably investigated and found nothing. Maybe there was nothing to find.

And yet...

Part of me still wondered if Lenny Smile really was dead. I remembered the man I had glimpsed in Brompton Cemetery. He had looked remarkably like the man I had seen in the photograph, and had certainly taken off fast enough when I spotted him. But if Lenny wasn't dead, where was he? And who was it who had disappeared under the steamroller?

"I give up!" Tim exclaimed.

He seemed to be reading my mind. "This isn't an easy case," I agreed.

"No!" He pointed. "I'm talking about this crossword in the *Dandy!*"

I ignored him and flicked over the page in my newspaper. And that was when I saw it. It was on the same page as the horoscopes. An advertisement for a circus in Battersea Park.

Direct from Moscow
THE RUSSIAN STATE CIRCUS
Starring
The Flying Karamazov Brothers
Karl "On Your" Marx – The Human Cannon-ball
The Fabulous Tina Trotsky
Three Sisters on Unicycles
And much, much more!

There was a picture showing a big top, but it was what was in front that had caught my eye. It was a figure in silhouette. A man selling balloons.

"Look at this, Tim!" I exclaimed, sliding the newspaper towards him.

Tim quickly read the page. "That's amazing!" he said. "I'm going to meet an old friend!"

"What are you talking about?"

"My horoscope. That's what it says…"

"Not the horoscopes, Tim! Look at the advertisement underneath!"

Tim read it. "This is no time to be going to the circus, Nick," he said. "We're on a case!"

"But look at the balloon-seller!" I took a deep breath. "Don't you remember what Mrs Lovely said? There was a witness when Lenny Smile was killed. It was a man selling balloons. I thought that was odd at the time. Why should there have been a balloon-seller in Battersea Park in the middle of the night?"

"He could have been lost..."

"I don't think so. I think he must have been part of the circus. There's a picture of him here in the paper. Maybe the balloon-seller was advertising the circus!"

"You mean ... on his balloons?"

"Brilliant, Tim! Got it in one."

Tim ripped the page of the newspaper in half. He must have accidentally caught hold of the tablecloth, because he ripped that in half too. He folded the paper into his top pocket. "It's your turn to do the washing-up," he said. "Then let's go!"

In fact we didn't go back to Battersea until that evening. According to the advertisement, there was only one performance of the circus that day – at seven thirty – and I didn't see any point in turning up before. If the balloon-seller really was part of the big top, he'd probably be somewhere around during the performance. We would catch up with him then.

I don't know what you think about circuses. To be honest, I've never been a big fan. When you really think about it, is there anybody in the world less funny than a clown? And what can you say about somebody who has spent half their life learning how to balance thirty spinning plates and an umbrella on their nose?

OK. It's clever. But there simply have to be more useful things to do with your time! And, for that matter, with your nose. There was a time when they used to have animals – lions and elephants – performing in the ring. They were banned and I have to agree that was a good idea. But for my money they could ban the rest of the performers too, and put everyone out of their misery. I'm sorry. I've heard of people who have run away to join a circus, but speaking personally I'd run away to avoid seeing one.

But that said, I had to admit that the Russian State Circus looked interesting. It had parked its tent right in the middle of the park and there was something crazy and old-fashioned about the bright colours and the fluttering flags all edged silver by a perfect November moon. Four or five hundred people had turned out to see the show, and there were stilt-walkers and jugglers keeping the lines amused as they queued up to get in. As well as the tent itself there were about a dozen caravans parked on the grass, forming a miniature town. Some of these were modern and ugly. But there were also wooden caravans, painted red, blue and gold, that made me think of Russian gypsies and Russian palm-readers – old crones telling your future by candlelight. Tim had had his palm read once, when we were in Torquay. The palm-reader had laughed so much she'd had to lie down … and that was only the contents of one finger on his left hand.

We bought tickets for the show. Tim wanted to see it, and having come all this way across London, I thought why not? We bought two of the last seats and followed the crowd in. Somehow the tent seemed even bigger inside than out. It was lit by flaming torches on striped, wooden poles. Grey smoke coiled in the air and dark shadows flickered across the ring. The whole place was bathed in a strange, red glow that seemed to transport us back to another century. The top of the tent was a tangle of ropes and wires, of rings and trapezes, all promises of things to come, but right now the ring was empty. There were wooden benches raked up in a steep bank, seven rows deep, forming a circle all round the sawdust. We were in the cheapest seats, one row from the back. As a treat, I'd bought Tim a stick of candyfloss. By the time the show started, he'd managed to get it all over himself as well as about half a dozen people on either side.

A band took its place on the far side of the ring. There were five players, dressed in old, shabby tailcoats. They had faces to match. The conductor looked about a hundred years old. I just hoped the music wouldn't get too exciting – I doubted his heart would stand it. With a trembling hand, he raised his baton and the band began to play. Unfortunately, the players all began at different times and what followed was a tremendous wailing and screeching as they all raced to get to the end first. But the conductor didn't seem to notice and the audience loved it. They'd come out for a good time and even when the violinist fell off his chair and the trombonist dropped his trombone they cheered and applauded.

By now I was almost looking forward to seeing the show ... but as things turned out, we weren't going to see anything of the performance that night.

The band came to the end of its first piece and began its second – which could have been either a new piece or the same piece played again. It was hard to be sure. I was glancing at the audience when suddenly I froze. There was a man sitting in the front row, right next to the gap in the tent where the performers would come in. He was wearing a dark coat, a hat and gloves. He was too far away. Or maybe it was the poor light or the smoke. But once again his face was blurred. Even so, I knew him at once.

It was the man from the Brompton Cemetery.

The man in the photograph at the Café Debussy.

Lenny Smile!

I grabbed hold of Tim. "Quick!" I exclaimed.

"What is it?" Tim jerked away, propelling

the rest of his candyfloss off the end of his stick and into the lap of the woman behind him.

"There!" I pointed. But even as I searched for Lenny across the crowded circus, I saw him get up and slip out into the night. By the time Tim had followed my finger to the other side of the tent, he had gone.

"Is it a clown?" Tim asked.

"No, Tim! It's the blurred man!"

"Who?"

"Never mind. We've got to go..."

"But the circus hasn't even begun!"

I dragged Tim to his feet and we made our way to the end of the row and out of the big top. My mind was racing. I still didn't know who the man in the dark coat really was. But if it was the same person I had seen at the cemetery, what was he doing here? Could he perhaps have followed us? No – that was impossible. I was sure he hadn't seen us across the crowded auditorium. He was here for another reason, and somehow I knew it had nothing to do with spinning plates and custard pies.

We left the tent just as the ringmaster, a tall man in a bright red jacket and black top hat, arrived to introduce the show. I heard him bark out a few words in Russian, but by then Tim and I were in the open air with the moon high above us, the park eerie and empty and the caravans clustered together about thirty metres away.

"What is it?" Tim demanded. He had forgotten why we had come and was disappointed to be missing the show.

Quickly I told him what I had seen. "We've got to look for him!" I said.

"But we don't know where he is!"

"That's why we've got to look for him."

There seemed to be only one place he could have gone. We went over to the caravans, suddenly aware how cold and quiet it was out here, away from the crowds. The first caravan was empty. The second contained a dwarf sipping sadly at a bottle of vodka. As we made our way over to the third, a man dressed in a fake leopard skin walked past carrying a steel girder. Inside the tent I heard the ringmaster come to the end of a sentence and there was a round of applause. Either he had cracked a joke or the audience was just grateful he'd stopped talking. There was a drum roll. We approached the fourth caravan.

Lenny Smile – if that's who it was – had disappeared. But there was another dead man in Battersea Park that night.

I saw the balloons first and knew at once whose caravan this was. There were more than fifty of them, every colour imaginable, clinging together as if they were somehow alive and knew what had just happened. The strange thing was that they did almost seem to be cowering in the corner. They weren't touching the ground. But the balloon-seller was. He was stretched out on the carpet with something silver lying next to his outstretched hand.

"Don't touch it, Tim!" I warned.

Too late. Tim had already leaned over and picked it up.

It was a knife. The blade was about ten centimetres long. It matched, perfectly, the ten-centimetre deep wound in the back of the balloon-seller's head. There wasn't a lot of blood. The balloon-seller had been an old man. Killing him had been like attacking a scarecrow.

And then somebody screamed.

I spun round. There was a little girl there in a gold dress with sequins. She was sitting on a bicycle which had only one wheel, pedalling back and forth to stop herself falling over. She was pointing at Tim, her finger trembling, her eyes filled with horror, and suddenly I was aware of the other performers appearing, coming out of their caravans as if this was the morning and they'd just woken up. Only it was the middle of the night and these people weren't dressed for bed! There was a clown in striped pants with a bowler hat and (inevitably) a red nose. There was a man on stilts. A fat man with a crash helmet. Two more sisters on unicycles. The strong man had come back with his steel girder. A pair of identical twins stood like mirror images, identical expressions on their faces. And what they were all looking at was my big brother Tim, holding a knife and hovering in the doorway of a man who had just been murdered.

The little girl who had started it screamed once more and shouted something out. The strong man spoke. Then the clown. It all came out as jibberish to me but it didn't take a lot of imagination to work out what they were saying.

"Boris the balloon man has been murdered!"

"Dear old Boris! Who did it?"

"It must have been the idiotic-looking Englishman holding the knife."

I don't know at what precise moment the mood turned nasty, but suddenly I realized that the people all around me no longer wanted to entertain us. The clown stepped forward and his face was twisted and ugly ... as well as being painted white with green diamonds over his eyes. He asked Tim something, his voice cracking with emotion and his make-up doing much the same.

"I don't speak Russian," Tim said.

"You kill Boris!"

So the balloon man really was called Boris. The clown was speaking English with an incredibly thick accent, struggling to make himself understood.

"Me?" Tim smiled and innocently raised a hand. Unfortunately it was the hand that was still holding the knife.

"Why you kill Boris?"

"Actually, I think you mean 'why *did* you kill Boris,'" Tim corrected him. "You've forgotten the verb..."

"I don't think they want an English lesson, Tim," I said.

Tim ignored me. "I kill Boris, you kill Boris, he killed Boris!" he explained to the increasingly puzzled clown.

"I didn't kill Boris!" I exclaimed.

"They killed Boris!" the clown said.

"That's right!" Tim smiled encouragingly.

"No, we didn't!" I yelled.

It was too late. The circus performers were getting closer by the second. I didn't like the way they were looking at us. And there were more of them now. Four muscle-bound brothers in white leotards had stepped out of the shadows. The ringmaster was staring at us from the edge of the tent. I wondered who was entertaining the audience. The entire circus seemed to have congregated outside.

The ringmaster snapped out a brief command in Russian.

"Let's go, Tim!" I said.

Tim dropped the knife and we turned and fled just as the performers started towards us. As far as they were concerned, Tim had just murdered one of their number, and this was a case of an eye for an eye – or a knife wound for a knife wound. These were travelling performers. They had their own rules and to hell with the country in which they found themselves.

Tim and I took off across the park, trying to lose ourselves in the shadows. Not easy with a full moon that night. Something huge and solid sailed across the sky, then buried itself in the soft earth. The strong man had thrown his girder in our direction. We were lucky – he was strong, but he obviously had lousy aim. The girder would be found the next day sticking out of the grass like a bizarre, iron tree. Half a metre to the right and we'd have been found underneath it.

But I quickly realized that this was only the start of our troubles. The entire circus troupe had abandoned the performance in order to come after us. Word had quickly got round. We had killed old Boris and now they were going to kill us. There was a dull *whoomph!* and a figure shot through the air. It was the man in the crash helmet. This had to be Karl "On Your" Marx, the human cannon-ball. They had fired him in our direction, and I just had time to glimpse his outstretched fists as he soared through the night sky before I grabbed hold of Tim and threw him onto the grass. Marx whizzed past. We had been standing in front of an oak tree and there was a dull crunch as he hit the trunk, ending up wedged in a fork in the branches.

"Do you think he's OK?" Tim asked.

"I don't think he's oak anything!" I replied. "Come on!"

We scrabbled to our feet just as the clown set off across the grass, speeding towards us in a tiny, multicoloured car. I looked ahead with a sinking heart. We really were in the middle of nowhere, with grass all around, the river in the far distance and nobody else in sight. Anybody who had come to the park at that time of night would now be in the circus, watching the show.

"Run, Tim!" I gasped.

The clown was getting nearer. I could see his face, even less funny than usual, the grease paint livid in the moonlight. In seconds he would catch up with us and run us down. But then there was an explosion. The bonnet of the car blew open, the wheels fell off, water jetted off the radiator and smoke billowed out of the boot. The clown must have pressed the wrong button. Either that, or the car had done what it was designed for.

"Which way?" Tim panted.

I turned and looked back. For a brief, happy moment, I thought we had left the circus folk behind us, but then something whizzed through the darkness and slammed into the bark of another tree. It was a knife – but thrown from where? I looked up. There was a long telephone wire crossing the park, connected to a series of poles. And, impossibly, a man was standing, ten metres above the ground, reaching for a second knife. It was a tightrope walker. He had followed us along the telephone wires and was there now, balancing effortlessly in mid-air. At the same time, I heard the sudden cough of an engine and saw a motorbike lurch across the lawn. It was being driven by one of the brothers in white leotards. He had two more brothers standing on his shoulders. The fourth brother was on top of the other two brothers, holding what looked horribly like an automatic machine-gun. The motorbike rumbled towards us, moving slowly because of the weight of the passengers. But as I watched, it was overtaken by the three sisters on their unicycles. The moonlight sparkled not only on their sequins but on the huge swords which one of the other performers must have given them. All three of them were yelling in high-pitched voices, and somehow I knew that I wasn't hearing a Russian folk song. The man on stilts came striding towards us, moving like some monstrous insect, throwing impossibly long shadows across the grass. Somehow he had got ahead of us. And finally, to my astonishment, there was a sudden bellow and a full-sized adult elephant came lumbering out of the trees with a girl in white feathers sitting astride its neck. This would have to be the lovely Tina Trotsky. And despite the law, the Russian State Circus did have an animal or two hidden in its big top.

They had an elephant! Did they also, I wondered, have lions?

Tim had seen it too. "They've got an elephant!" he exclaimed.

"I've seen it, Tim!"

"Is it African or Indian?"

"What?"

"I can never remember which is which!"

"What does it matter?" I almost screamed the words. "It won't make any difference when it stamps on us!"

The circus performers were closing in on us from all sides. There was a rattle from the machine-gun and bullets tore into the ground, ripping up the grass. The dwarf I had seen in the caravan had woken up. It now turned out he was a fire-eating dwarf … at least, that might explain the flame-thrower he had strapped to his back. We had the elephant, the motorbike and the unicycles on one side. The dwarf and the stilt man were on the other. The tightrope walker was still somewhere overhead. The human cannon-ball was disentangling himself from the tree.

Things weren't looking good.

But then a car suddenly appeared, speeding across the grass. It raced past one of the unicyclists, knocking her out of the way, then curved round, snapping the stilt man's stilts in half. The stilt man yelled and dived head first into a bank of nettles. The elephant fell back, rearing up. Tina Trotsky somersaulted backwards, feathers fluttering all around her. The car skidded to a halt next to us and a door swung open.

"Get in!" someone said, and already I knew that I recognized the voice.

"Are you a taxi?" Tim asked. I think he was worrying about the fare.

"It doesn't matter what it is, Tim," I said. "Just get in!"

I pushed Tim ahead of me and dived onto the back seat. There was another rattle of machine-gun fire, a burst of flame and a loud thud as a second knife slammed into the side of the door. But then the car was moving, bouncing up and down along the grass. I saw a bush blocking the way, right in front of us. The driver went straight through it. There was a road on the other side. A van swerved to avoid us as our tyres hit concrete, and a bus swerved to avoid the van. I heard the screech of tyres and the even louder screech of the drivers. There was the sound of crumpling metal. A horn blared.

But then we were away, leaving Battersea Park far behind us.

It's like I said. I'd never liked the circus. And the events of the night had done nothing to change my mind.

THE REAL LENNY SMILE

"Well, well, well. This is a very nasty surprise. The Diamond brothers! Having a night at the circus?"

It was the driver of the car, the man who had saved us, who was speaking. He had driven us directly to his office at New Scotland Yard. It had been a while since we had last seen Detective Chief Inspector Snape. But here he was, as large as life and much less enjoyable.

It had been Snape who had once employed Tim as a police-constable. He had been no more than an inspector then – and he'd probably had far fewer grey hairs. He was a big, solid man who obviously worked out in a gym. Nobody got born with muscles like his. He had small blue eyes and skin the colour of raw ham. He was wearing a made-to-measure suit but unfortunately it had been made to measure somebody else. It looked as if it was about to burst. His tie was crooked. So were his teeth. So were most of the people he met.

I had never known his name was Freddy but that was what was written on the door. He had an office on the fourth floor, overlooking the famous revolving sign. I had been involved with Snape twice before: once when we were on the trail of the Falcon, and once when he had forced me to share a cell with the master criminal, Johnny Powers*. He wasn't someone I'd been looking forward to meeting a third time – even if he had just rescued us from the murderous crowd at the Russian State Circus.

His assistant was with him. Detective Superintendent Boyle hadn't changed much since the last time I'd seen him either. *His* first name must have been "Push". That was what was written on his door. Short and fat with curly black hair, he'd have done well in one of those BBC documentaries about Neanderthal man. He was wearing a black leather jacket and faded jeans. As usual he had a couple of medallions buried in the forest of hair that sprouted up his chest and out of his open-necked shirt. Boyle looked more criminal than a criminal. He wasn't someone you'd want to meet on a dark night. He wasn't someone you'd want to meet at all.

"This is incredible!" Tim exclaimed. He turned to me. "You remember the horoscope

* See *Public Enemy Number Two*

in the newspaper! It said I was going to meet an old friend!"

"I'm not an old friend!" Snape exploded. "I hate you!"

"*I'd* like to get friendly with him," Boyle muttered. He took out a knuckleduster and slid it over his right fist. "Why don't you let the two of us go somewhere quiet, Chief...?"

"Forget it, Boyle!" Snape snapped. "And where did you get the knuckleduster? Have you been in the evidence room again?"

"It's mine!" Boyle protested.

"Well, put it away..."

Boyle slid the contraption off his hand and sulked.

Snape sat down behind his desk. Tim and I were sitting opposite him. We'd been waiting for him in the office for a couple of hours but he hadn't offered either of us so much as a cup of tea.

"What I want to know," he began, "is what the two of you were doing at the circus tonight. Why were the performers trying to kill you? And what happened to Boris the balloon-seller?"

"Someone killed him," I said.

"I know that, laddy. I've seen the body. Someone stuck a knife in him."

"Yeah." I nodded. "The circus people thought it was us."

"That's an easy enough mistake to make

when you two are involved." Snape smiled mirthlessly. "We went to the circus because we wanted to talk to the balloon-seller," he explained. "Luckily for you. But why were you interested in him? That's what I want to know."

"I wanted to buy a balloon," I said.

"Don't lie to me, Diamond! Not unless you want to spend a few minutes on your own with Boyle."

"Just one minute," Boyle pleaded. "Thirty seconds!"

"All right," I said. "We were interested in Lenny Smile."

"Ah!" Snape's eyes widened. Boyle looked disappointed. "Why?"

"We're working for a man called Joe Carter. He's American..."

"He thinks Lenny Smile was murdered," Tim said.

Snape nodded. "Of course Smile was murdered," he said. "And it was the best thing that ever happened to him. If I wasn't a policeman, I'd have been tempted to murder him myself."

Tim stared. "But he was a saint!" he burbled.

"He was a crook! Lenny Smile was the biggest crook in London! Boyle and I have been investigating him for months – and we'd have arrested him if he hadn't gone under that steamroller." Snape opened a drawer and took out a file as thick as a north London telephone directory. "This is the file on Lenny Smile," he said. "Where do you want me to begin?"

"How about at the beginning?" I suggested.

"All right. Lenny Smile set up a charity called Dream Time. He employed two assistants ... Rodney Hoover, who comes from the Ukraine. And Fiona Lee. She's from Sloane Square. We've investigated them, and as far as we can see they're in the clear. But Smile? He was a different matter. All the money passed through his bank account. He was in financial control. And half the money that went in, never came out."

"You mean ... he stole it?" I asked.

"Exactly. Millions of pounds that should have gone to poor children went into his own pocket. And when he did spend money on children, he got everything cheap. He provided hospitals with cheap X-ray machines that could only see halfway through. He provided schools with cheap books full of typing errors. He took a bunch of children on a cheap adventure holiday."

"What's wrong with that?"

"It was in Afghanistan! Half the children still haven't come back! He bought headache pills that actually gave you a headache and food parcels where the parcels tasted better than the food. I'm telling you, Diamond, Lenny Smile was so crooked he makes an evening with Jack the Ripper sound like a nice idea! And I was this close to arresting him." Snape held his thumb and forefinger just millimetres apart. "I already had a full-time police officer watching his flat. It's like I say. We were just going to arrest him – but then he got killed."

"Suppose he isn't dead," I said.

Snape shook his head. "There were too many witnesses. Mrs Lovely, the woman who lived next door, saw him leave the flat. Hoover and Lee were with him. There was Barry Krishner, the driver. And Boris..."

"Wait a minute!" I interrupted. "Mrs Lovely didn't actually see anything. Barry Krishner has gone mad. I'm not sure Hoover and Lee can be trusted. And someone has just killed Boris." I remembered what Mrs Lovely had told us. "Mrs Lovely said that someone had been asking questions about the balloon-seller," I went on. "I thought she was talking about you ... the police! But now I wonder if it wasn't someone else. The real killer, for example!" Snape stared at me. "I think Boris saw what really happened," I concluded. "And that was why he was killed."

"Who by?" Snape demanded.

"By Lenny Smile!"

There was a long silence. Snape looked doubtful. Boyle looked ... well the same way Boyle always looks.

"What do you mean?" Snape demanded at

length.

"It all makes sense. Lenny Smile knew that you were after him. You say you had a policeman watching his flat?"

Snape nodded. "Henderson. He's disappeared."

"Since when?"

"He vanished a week before the accident with the steamroller…"

"That was no accident!" I said. "Don't you get it, Snape? Smile knew he was cornered. You were closing in on him. And Joe Carter was coming over too. Carter wanted to know what had happened to all the millions he'd given Dream Time. So Smile had to disappear. He faked his own death, and right now he's somewhere in London. We've seen him! Twice!"

That made Snape sit up. "Where?"

"He was at the circus. He was in the crowd. We saw him about a minute before Boris was killed. And he was at the cemetery. Not underground – on top of it! I followed him and he ran away."

"How do you know it was Smile?" Snape asked.

"I don't. At least, I can't be sure. But I've seen a photograph of him and it looked the same."

"We don't know much about Smile," Snape admitted. "Henderson was watching the flat, but he only saw him once. We know when he was born and when he died. But that's about all..."

"He didn't die. I'm telling you. Dig up the coffin and you'll probably find it's empty!"

Snape looked at Boyle, then back at me. Slowly, he nodded. "All right, laddy," he said. "Let's play it your way. But if you're wasting my time ... it's your funeral!"

"There was no funeral," I said. "Lenny Smile isn't dead."

"Let's find out..."

I'll tell you now. There's one place you don't want to be at five past twelve on a black November night – and that's in a cemetery. The ground was so cold I could feel it all the way up to my knees, and every time I breathed the ice seemed to find its way into my skull. There were the four of us there – Snape, Boyle, Tim and myself – and now we'd been joined by another half-dozen police officers and workmen, two of whom were operating a mechanical digger that whined and groaned as it clawed at the frozen earth. Tim was whining and groaning too, as a matter of fact. I think he'd have preferred to have been in bed.

But maybe it wasn't just the weather that was managing to chill me. The whole thing was like a scene out of *Frankenstein*. You know the one – where Igor the deformed

Hungarian servant has to climb into the grave and steal a human brain. Glancing at Boyle, I saw a distinct physical resemblance. I had to remind myself that two days ago I had been enjoying half-term and that the following day I would be back at school, with all the fun of double geography and French. In the meantime I had somehow stumbled into a horror film. I wondered what was going to turn up in the final reel.

The digger stabbed down. The earth shifted. Gradually the hole got deeper. There was a clunk – metal hitting wood – and two of the workmen climbed in to clear away the rest of the soil with spades. Snape moved forward.

I didn't watch as the coffin was opened. You have to remember that I was only fourteen years old, and if someone had made a film out of what was going on here I wouldn't even have been allowed to see it.

"Boyle!" Snape muttered the single word and the other man lowered himself into the hole. There was a pause. Then…

"Sir!"

Boyle was holding something. He passed it up to Snape. It was dark blue, shaped a bit like a bell, only paper thin. There was a silver disc squashed in the middle. It took me a few seconds to work out what it was. Then I realized. It was a police-constable's helmet. But one that had been flattened.

"Henderson!" Snape muttered.

There had been a police-constable watching Smile's flat. He had disappeared a week before the accident. His name had been Henderson.

And now we knew what had happened to him.

"Don't you see, Tim? It was Henderson who was killed. Not Lenny Smile!"

The two of us were back at our Camden flat. After our hours spent in the cemetery, we were too cold to go to bed. I'd made us both hot chocolate and Tim was wearing two pairs of pyjamas and two dressing-gowns, with a hot-water bottle clasped to his chest.

"But who killed him?"

"Lenny Smile."

"But what about Hoover? And the woman? They were there when it happened."

For once, Tim was right. Rodney Hoover and Fiona Lee must have been part of it. Snape had already gone to arrest them. The man they had helped down the stairs must have been Henderson. I had been right about that. He had been drugged. They had taken him out of the flat and thrown him into the road, just as Barry Krishner turned the corner on his way home…

And yet it wasn't going to be easy to prove. There were no witnesses. And until Smile was found, it was hard to see exactly what he could do. Suddenly I realized how clever Smile had been. The blurred man? He had been more than that. He had run Dream Time, he had stolen all the money, and he had remained virtually invisible.

"Nobody knew him." I said.

"Who?"

"Smile. Mrs Lovely never spoke to him. Joe Carter only wrote to him. We went to his flat and it was like he'd never actually lived there. Even Rodney Hoover and Fiona Lee couldn't tell us much about him."

Tim nodded. I yawned. It was two o'clock, way past my bedtime. And in just five and a half hours I'd be getting ready for school. Monday was going to be a long day.

"You'll have to go to the Ritz tomorrow," I said.

"Why?"

"To tell Joe Carter about his so-called best friend."

Tim sighed. "It's not going to be easy," he said. "He had this big idea about Lenny Smile when all the time he was someone else!"

I finished my hot chocolate and stood up. Then, suddenly, it hit me. "What did you just say?" I asked.

"I've forgotten." Tim was so tired he was forgetting what he was saying even as he said it.

"Someone else! That's exactly the point! Of

course!"

There had been so many clues. The note in the cemetery. Mrs Lovely and the card Lenny had sent her. The gravestone. The photograph of Smile outside the Café Debussy. And Snape…

"We know when he was born…"

But it was only now, when I was almost too tired to move, that it came together. The truth. All of it.

The following morning, I didn't go to school. Instead I made two telephone calls, and then later on, just after ten o'clock, Tim and I set out for the final showdown.

It was time to meet Lenny Smile.

THE BIG WHEEL

The tube from Camden Town to Waterloo is direct on the Northern line – which was probably just as well. I'd only had about five hours' sleep, and I was so tired that the whole world seemed to be shimmering and moving in slow motion. Tim was just as bad. He had a terrible nightmare in which he was lowered, still standing up, into Lenny's grave – and woke up screaming. I suppose it wasn't too surprising. He'd fallen asleep on the escalator.

But the two of us had livened up a little by the time we'd reached the other end. The weather had taken a turn for the worse. The rain was sheeting down, sucking any colour or warmth out of the city. We had left Waterloo station behind us, making for the South Bank, a stretch of London that has trouble looking beautiful even on the sunniest day. This is where you'll find the National Theatre and the

National Film Theatre, both designed by architects with huge buckets of prefabricated cement. There weren't many people around. Just a few commuters struggling with umbrellas that the wind had turned inside out. Tim and I hurried forward without speaking. The rain lashed down, hit the concrete and bounced up again, wetting us twice.

I had made the telephone call just after breakfast.

"Mrs Lee?"

"Yes. Who is this?" Fiona Lee's clipped vowels had been instantly recognizable down the line.

"This is Nick Diamond. Remember me?"

A pause.

"I want to meet with Lenny Smile."

A longer pause. Then, *"That's not possible. Lenny Smile is dead."*

"You're lying. You know where he is. I want to see the three of you. Hoover, Lenny and you. Eleven o'clock at the London Eye. And if you don't want me to go to the police, you'd better not be late."

You've probably seen the London Eye, the huge Ferris wheel they put up outside County Hall. It's one of the big surprises of modern London. Unlike the Millennium Dome, it has actually been a success. It opened on time. It worked. It didn't fall over. At the end of the millennium year they decided to keep it, and suddenly it was part of London – a brilliant silver circle at once huge and yet somehow fragile. Tim had taken me on it for my fourteenth birthday and we'd enjoyed the view so much we'd gone a second time. Well as they say, one good turn deserves another.

Not that we were going to see much today. The clouds were so low that the pods at the top almost seemed to disappear into them. You could see the Houses of Parliament on the other side of the river and, hazy in the distance, St Paul's. But that was about it. If there was a single day in the year when it wasn't worth paying ten pounds for the ride, this was it, which would explain why there were no crowds around when we approached: just Rodney Hoover and Fiona Lee, both of them wearing raincoats, waiting for us to arrive.

There was no sign of Lenny Smile, but I wasn't surprised. I had known he would never show up.

"Why are you calling us?" Hoover demanded. "First we have the police accusing us of terrible things. Then you, wanting to see Lenny. We don't know where Lenny is! As far as we know, he's dead..."

"Why don't we get out of the rain?" I suggested. "How about the wheel?" It seemed like a good idea. The rain was still bucketing down and there was nowhere else to go.

"After you, Mr Hoover..."

We bought tickets and climbed into the first compartment that came round. I wasn't surprised to find that there would only be the four of us in it for this turn of the wheel. The doors slid shut, and slowly – so slowly that we barely knew we were moving – we were carried up into the sky, into the driving rain.

There was a pause as if nobody knew quite what to say. Then Fiona broke the silence. "We already told that ghastly little policeman ... Detective Chief Inspector Snape. Lenny was with us that day. He was killed by the steamroller. And it is Lenny buried in the cemetery."

"No it isn't," I said. "Lenny Smile is right here now. He's on the big wheel. Inside this compartment."

"Is he?" Tim looked under the seat. "I don't see him!"

"That's because you're not looking in the right place, Tim," I said. "But that was the whole idea. You said it yourself last night. We all thought Lenny Smile was one thing, but in fact he was something else."

"You are not making the lot of sense," Hoover said. His face, already dark to begin with, had gone darker. He was watching me with nervous eyes.

"I should have known from the start that there was something strange about Lenny Smile," I said. "Nothing about him added up. Nobody – except you – had ever seen him. And everything about him was a lie."

"You mean … his name wasn't Lenny Smile?" Tim asked.

"Lenny Smile never existed, Tim!" I explained. "He was a fantasy. I should have known when I saw the details on the gravestone. It said that he was born on 31st April 1955. But that was the first lie. There are only thirty days in April. 31st April doesn't exist!"

"It was a mistake…" Fiona muttered.

"Maybe. But then there was that photograph Carter showed us of 'Lenny' standing outside the Café Debussy. You told us that he was allergic to a lot of things, and one of those things was animals. But in the photograph there's a cat sitting between his feet – and he doesn't seem to care. The allergy business was a lie. But it was a clever one. It meant that he had a reason not to be seen. He had to stay indoors because he was ill…"

Centimetre by centimetre, the big wheel carried us further away from the ground. The rain was hammering against the glass. Looking out, I could barely see the buildings on the north bank of the river. There was Big Ben, but then the rain swept across it, turning it into a series of brown and white streaks.

Tim gaped. "So there was no Lenny Smile!" he exclaimed.

"That's right. Except when Hoover *pretended* to be Lenny Smile. Don't you see? He rented the flat even though he never actually lived there. Occasionally he went in and out to make it look as if there was someone there. And of course it was Hoover who wrote that letter to Mrs Lovely."

"How do you know?"

"Because it was written in green ink. The message we saw in the card on Lenny's grave was also written in green ink – and it was the same handwriting. I should have seen from the start. It was Hoover we saw at the circus. And he was also there at Brompton Cemetery the day we visited the grave. I should have known it was him as soon as we met him at the Dream Time office."

"Why?" Tim asked.

"Because Hoover had never met us – but somehow he knew we'd been to Brompton Cemetery. Don't you remember what he said to us? 'You know very well that he's lying there in Brompton Cemetery.' Those were his exact words. But he only knew we knew because he knew who we were, and he knew who we were because he'd seen us!"

Tim scratched his head. "Could you say that last bit again?"

Fiona looked at me scornfully. "You're talking tommy-rot!" she said.

"Was Tommy part of this too?" Tim asked.

"Why would Rodney and I want to invent a man called Lenny Smile?" she continued, ignoring him.

"Because the two of you were stealing millions of pounds from Dream Time. You knew that eventually the police would catch up with you. And there was always the danger that someone like Joe Carter would come over from America to find out what was happening to his money. You were the brains behind the charity. You were the 'big wheels', if you like. But you needed someone to take the blame and then disappear. That was Lenny Smile. Henderson – the policeman – must have found out what was going on, so he had to die too. And that was your brilliant idea. You'd turn Henderson into Lenny Smile. He went under the steamroller and, as far as you were concerned, that was the end of the matter. Smile was dead. There was nothing left to investigate."

The pod was still moving up. There were a few pedestrians out on the South Bank. By now they were no more than dots.

"But now the police think Lenny Smile is alive," I went on. "That's why the two of you aren't in jail. They're looking for him. They don't have any proof against you. So the two of you are in the clear!"

Hoover had listened to all this in silence but now he smiled, his thin lips peeling back from his teeth. "You have it exactly right," he said. "Fiona and I are nobodies. We were just working for Lenny Smile. He is the real crook. And, as you say, they have no proof. Nobody has any proof."

"Hoover dressed up as Lenny Smile..." Tim was still trying to work it all out.

"Only once. For the photograph that Joe Carter requested. But he was wearing the same coat and the same gloves when we saw him – which is why we thought he was Lenny Smile. Both times, he was too far away for us to see his face. And, of course, in the photograph the face was purposely blurred." I turned to Rodney. "I'd be interested to know, though. What were you doing in the cemetery?"

Hoover shrugged. "I realized that the bloody fool of an undertaker had made a mistake with the date on the gravestone. I went there to put it right. When I saw you and your brother at the grave, I knew something was wrong. I have to admit, I panicked. And ran."

"And the circus...?"

"Mrs Lovely told us there had been a witness. I had to track him down and make sure he didn't talk."

"But it wouldn't have mattered if he'd talked," Tim said. "He was Russian! Nobody would have understood."

"I don't believe in taking chances," Rodney said. His hand had slid into his coat pocket. Why wasn't I surprised, when it came out, to see that it was holding a gun?

"He's got a gun!" Tim squealed.

"That's right, Tim," I said.

"You've been very clever," Hoover snarled. "But you haven't quite thought it through." He glanced out of the window. We had reached the top of the circle, as high up as the Ferris wheel went. Suddenly Hoover fired. The glass door smashed. Tim leapt. The rain came rushing in. "An unfortunate accident!" Hoover shouted above the howl of the wind. "The door malfunctioned. Somehow it broke. You and your brother fell out."

"No we didn't!" Tim whimpered.

"Anyway, by the time they've finished wiping you off the South Bank, Fiona and I will have disappeared. The money is in a nice little bank in Brazil. We'll move there. A beach house in Rio de Janeiro! We'll live a life of luxury."

"That money was meant for sick children!" I shouted. "Don't you have any shame at all?"

"I cannot afford shame!" He gestured with the gun, pointing at the shattered glass and the swirling rain. "Now which one of you is going to step out first?"

"He is!" Tim pointed at me.

"No, I'm not," I said. I turned back to Hoover. "It won't work, Hoover. Why don't you take a look in the next pod?"

Hoover's eyes narrowed. Fiona Lee went over to the window. There were about twenty people in the pod above us on the London Eye.

All of them were dressed in blue. "It's full of policemen!" she exclaimed. She went over to the other side. "And the one below us! That's full of police too!"

"It must be their day out!" Tim said.

"Forget it, Tim." It was my turn to smile. "You've been set up, Hoover. Every word you've said has been recorded. The pod's bugged. Your confession is on tape right now, and as soon as the ride is over you and Fiona will have another ride. To jail!"

Fiona had begun to tremble. Hoover's eyes twitched. His grip tightened on the gun. "Maybe I'll kill you anyway," he said. "Just for the fun of it..."

And that was when the helicopter appeared – a dark-blue police helicopter, its blades beating at the rain outside the broken window. It had come swooping out of the clouds and now hovered just a few metres away. I could see Snape in the passenger seat. Boyle was in the back, dressed in a flak jacket, cradling an automatic rifle. I just hoped he was pointing it at Hoover, not at Tim.

"Why do you think the police released you?" I shouted above the noise of the helicopter. "I rang Snape this morning and told him what I'd worked out and he asked me to meet you. You walked into a trap. He knew you'd feel safe up in the air, just the four of us. He wanted you to confess."

A second later there was a crackle and Snape's voice came, amplified, from the helicopter. "Put the gun down, Hoover! The pod is surrounded!"

Hoover swore in Ukrainian, and before I could stop him he had twisted round and fired at the helicopter.

I threw myself at Hoover.

He fired a second time. But his aim had gone wild. The bullet hit Fiona in the shoulder. She screamed and fell to her knees.

Hoover, with my hands at his throat, crashed into the window. This one didn't break. I heard the toughened glass clunk against his untoughened skull. His eyes glazed and he slid to the ground.

I turned to Tim. "Are you all right, Tim?" I asked.

"Yes, I'm fine." He pointed past the helicopter. "Look! You can see Trafalgar Square!"

It took another fifteen minutes for the pod to reach the ground. At once we were surrounded by uniformed police officers. Hoover and Lee were dragged out. They'd spend a few days in hospital on their way to jail. The helicopter with Snape and Boyle in was nowhere to be seen. With a bit of luck a strong gust of wind would have blown it out of London and maybe into Essex. The trouble with those two was that no matter how many times we helped them, they'd never thank us. And I'd probably end up with a detention for missing a day of school.

"We'd better go to the Ritz," I said.

"For tea?" Tim asked.

"No, Tim. Joe Carter..."

The American was still waiting to hear about his best friend, Lenny Smile. I wasn't looking forward to breaking the bad news to him. Maybe I'd leave that to Tim. After all, discreet was his middle name.

It had stopped raining. Tim and I walked along the South Bank, leaving the London Eye behind us. There were workmen ahead of us, shovelling a rich, black ooze onto the surface of the road. On the pavement, a tramp stood with an upturned hat, playing some sort of plinky-plonk music on a strange instrument – a zither, I think. I found a pound coin and dropped it into the hat. Charity. That was how this had all begun.

"Ta!" the tramp said.

"Tar? Don't worry," Tim said. "I've seen it..."

We crossed the river, the sound of the zither fading into the distance behind.

I KNOW WHAT YOU DID LAST WEDNESDAY

AN INVITATION

I like horror stories – but not when they happen to me. If you've read my other adventures, you'll know that I've been smothered in concrete, thrown in jail with a dangerous lunatic, tied to a railway line, almost blown up, chased through a cornfield dodging machine-gun bullets, poisoned in Paris … and all this before my fourteenth birthday. It's not fair. I do my homework. I clean my teeth twice a day. Why does everyone want to kill me?

But the worst thing that ever happened to me began on a hot morning in July. It was the first week of the summer holidays and there I was, as usual, stuck with my big brother Tim, the world's most unsuccessful private detective. Tim had just spent a month helping with security at the American Embassy in Grosvenor Square and even now I'm not sure how he'd decided that there was a bomb in the ambassador's car. Anyway, just as the ambassador was about to get in, Tim had grabbed hold of him and hurled him out of the way – which would have been heroic if there had been a bomb (there wasn't) and if Tim hadn't managed to throw the unfortunate man in front of a passing bus. The ambassador was now in hospital. And Tim was out of work.

So there we were at the breakfast table with Tim reading the morning post while I counted out the cornflakes. We were down to our last packet and it had to last us another week. That allowed us seventeen flakes each but as a treat I'd allowed Tim to keep the free toy. There was a handful of letters that morning and so far they'd all been bills.

"There's a letter from Mum," Tim said.

"Any money?"

"No..."

He quickly read the letter. It was strange to think that my mum and dad were still in Australia and that I would have been with them if I hadn't slipped off the plane and gone to stay with Tim. My dad was a door-to-door salesman, selling doors. He had a house in Sydney with three bedrooms and forty-seven doors. It had been two years now since I had seen him.

"Mum says you're welcome to visit," Tim said. "She says the door is always open."

"Which one?" I asked.

He picked up the last letter. I could see at

once that this wasn't a bill. It came in a square, white envelope made out of the sort of paper that only comes from the most expensive trees. The address was handwritten: a fountain-pen, not a biro. Tim weighed it in his hand. "I wonder what this is," he said.

"It's an envelope, Tim," I replied. "It's what letters come in."

"I mean … I wonder who it's from!" He smiled. "Maybe it's a thank-you letter from the American ambassador."

"Why should he thank you? You threw him under a bus!"

"Yes, but I sent him a bunch of grapes in hospital."

"Just open it, Tim," I said.

Tim grabbed hold of a knife, and – with a dramatic gesture – sliced open the mysterious envelope.

After we'd finished bandaging his left leg, we examined the contents. First, there was an invitation, printed in red ink on thick white card.

Dear Herbert, it began. Tim Diamond was, of course, only the name he called himself. His real name was Herbert Simple.

It has been many years since we met, but I would like to invite you to a reunion of old boys and girls from St Egbert's Comprehensive, which will take place from Wednesday 9th to Friday 11th July. I am sure you are busy but I am so keen to see you again that I will pay you £1,000 to make the journey to Scotland. I also enclose a ticket for the train.

Your old friend,
Rory McDougal

Crocodile Island, Scotland

Tim tilted the envelope. Sure enough, a first-class train ticket slid out onto the table.

"That's fantastic!" Tim exclaimed. "A first-class ticket to Scotland." He examined the ticket. "And back again! That's even better!"

"Wait a minute," I said. "Who is Rory McDougal?" But even as I spoke, I thought the name was familiar.

"We were at school together, in the same class. Rory was brilliant. He came first in maths. He was so clever, he passed all his exams without even reading the questions. After he left school, he invented the pocket calculator – which was just as well, because he made so much money he needed a pocket calculator to count it."

"McDougal Industries." Now I knew where I'd heard the name. McDougal had been in the newspapers. The man was a multi-Mcmillionaire.

"When did you last see him?" I asked.

"It must have been on prize-giving day, about ten years ago," Tim said. "He went to university, I joined the police."

Tim had only spent a year with the police but in that time the crime rate had doubled. He didn't often talk about it but I knew that he had once put together an identikit picture that had led to the arrest of the Archbishop of Canterbury. He'd been transferred to the mounted police but that had only lasted a few weeks before his horse resigned. Then he'd become a private detective – and of course, *he* had hardly made millions. If you added up all the money Tim had ever made and put it in a bank, the bank wouldn't even notice.

"Are you going?" I asked.

Tim flicked a cornflake towards his mouth. It disappeared over his shoulder. "Of course I'm going," he said. "Maybe McNoodle will offer me a job. Head of Security on Alligator Island."

"Crocodile Island, Tim." I picked up the invitation. "What about me?"

"Sorry, kid. I didn't see your name on the envelope."

"Maybe it's under the stamp." Tim said nothing, so I went on, "You can't leave me here."

"Why not?"

"I'm only fourteen. It's against the law."

Tim frowned. "I won't tell if you won't tell."

"I will tell."

"Forget it, Nick. McStrudel is my old

schoolfriend. He went to my old school. It's my name on the envelope and you can argue all you like. But this time, I'm going alone."

We left King's Cross station on the morning of the 9th.

Tim sat next to the window, looking sulky. I was sitting opposite him. I had finally persuaded him to swap the first-class ticket for two second-class ones, which at least allowed me to travel free. You may think it strange that I should have wanted to join Tim on a journey heading several hundred miles north. But there was something about the invitation that bothered me. Maybe it was the letter, written in ink the colour of blood. Maybe it was the name – Crocodile Island. And then there was the money. The invitation might have sounded innocent enough, but why was McDougal paying Tim £1,000 to get on the train? I had a feeling that there might be more to this than a school reunion. And for that matter, why would anyone in their right mind want to be reunited with Tim?

I was also curious. It's not every day that you get to meet a man like Rory McDougal. Computers, camcorders, mobile phones and DVD players ... they all came stamped with the initials RM. And every machine that sold made McDougal a little richer.

Apparently the man was something of a

recluse. A few years back he'd bought himself an island off the Scottish coast, somewhere to be alone. There had been pictures of it in all the newspapers. The island was long and narrow with two arms jutting out and a twisting tail. Apparently, that was how it had got its name.

Tim didn't say much on the journey. To cheer him up, I'd bought him a *Beano* comic and perhaps he was having trouble with the long words. It took us about four hours to get to Scotland and it took another hour before I noticed. There were no signs, no frontier post, no man in a kilt playing the bagpipes and munching haggis as the train went past. It was only when the ticket collector asked us for our tickets and Tim couldn't understand a word he was saying that I knew we must be close. Sure enough, a few minutes later the train slowed down and Tim got out. Personally, I would have waited until the train had actually stopped, but I suppose he was over-excited.

Fortunately he was only bruised and we managed the short walk down to the harbour where an old fishing boat was waiting for us. The boat was called the *Silver Medal* and a small crowd of people were waiting to go on board.

"My God!" one of them exclaimed. "It's Herbert Simple! I never thought I'd see *him* again!"

The man who had spoken was fat and bald,

dressed in a three-piece suit. If he ate much more, it would soon be a four-piece suit. His trousers were already showing the strain. His name, it turned out, was Eric Draper. He was a lawyer.

Tim smiled. "I changed my name," he announced. "It's Tim Diamond now."

They all had a good laugh at that.

"And who is he?" Eric asked. I suddenly realized he was looking at me.

"That's my kid brother, Nick."

"So what are you doing now ... Tim?" one of the women asked in a high-pitched voice. She had glasses and long, curly hair and such large teeth that she seemed to have trouble closing her mouth. Her name was Janet Rhodes.

Tim put on his "don't mess with me" face. Unfortunately, it just made him look seasick. "Actually," he drawled, "I'm a private detective."

"Really?" Eric roared with laughter. His suit shuddered and one of the buttons flew off. "I can't believe Rory invited you here too. As I recall, you were the stupidest boy at St Egbert's. I still remember your performance as Hamlet in the school play."

"What was so stupid about that?" I asked.

"Nothing. Except everyone else was doing Macbeth."

One of the other women stepped forward. She was small and drab-looking, dressed in a mousy coat that had seen better days. She was eating a chocolate flake. "Hello ... Tim!" she said shyly. "I bet you don't remember me!"

"Of course I remember you!" Tim exclaimed. "You're Lisa Beach!"

"No I'm not! I'm Sylvie Binns." She looked disappointed. "You gave me my first kiss behind the bike shed. Don't you remember?"

Tim frowned. "I remember the bike shed..." he said.

There was a loud blast from the boat and the captain appeared, looking over the side. He had one leg, one eye and a huge beard. All that was missing was the parrot and he could have got a job in any pantomime in town. "All aboard!" he shouted. "Departing for Crocodile Island!"

We made our way up the gangplank. The boat was old and smelly. So was the captain. The eight of us stood on the deck while he pulled up the anchor, and a few minutes later we were off, the engine rattling as if it was about to fall out of the boat. It occurred to me that the Silver Medal was a strange choice of boat for a multi-millionaire. What had happened to the deluxe yacht? But nobody else had noticed, so I said nothing.

Apart from Eric, Janet and Sylvie, there were three other people on board: two more women and another man, a fit-looking black guy dressed in jeans and a sweatshirt.

"That's Mark Tyler," Tim told me as we cut through the waves, leaving the mainland behind us. "He came first at sport at St Egbert's..."

I knew the name. Tyler had been in the British Olympic athletics team at Atlanta.

"He used to run to school and run home again," Tim went on. "He was so fast, he used to overtake the school bus. When he went cross-country running, he actually left the country, which certainly made the headmaster very cross. He's a brilliant sportsman!"

That just left the two other women.

Brenda Blake was an opera singer and looked it. Big and muscular, she had the sort of arms you'd expect to find on a Japanese wrestler – or perhaps around his belly.

Libby Goldman was big and blonde and worked in children's TV, presenting a television programme called *Libby's Lounge*. She sang, danced, juggled and did magic tricks ... and all this before we'd even left the quay. It was a shame that in real life we couldn't turn her off.

The journey took about an hour, by which time the coast of Scotland had become just a grey smudge behind us. Slowly Crocodile Island sneaked up on us. It was about half a mile long, rising to a point at what must have been its "tail", with sheer cliffs sweeping down into the sea. There were six jagged pillars of rock at this end, making a landing impossible. But at the other end, in the shelter of the crocodile's arm, someone had built a jetty. As the boat drew in, I noticed a security camera watching us from above.

"Here we are, ladies and gentlemen," the captain announced from somewhere behind his beard. "I wish you all a very pleasant stay on Crocodile Island. I do indeed! I'll be coming back for you in a couple of days. My name is Captain Randle, by the way. Horatio Randle. It's been a pleasure having you lovely people on my boat. You remember me, now!"

"Aren't you coming with us?" Eric demanded.

"No, sir. I'm not invited," Captain Randle replied. "I live on the mainland. But I'll be back to collect you in a couple of days. I'll see you then!"

We disembarked. The boat pulled out and headed back the way it had come. The eight of us were left on the island, wondering what was going to happen next.

"So where's old Rory?" Brenda asked.

"Maybe we should walk up to the house," Sylvie suggested. She was the only one of them who didn't have a full-time job. She had told Tim that she was a housewife, and was carrying three photographs of her husband and three more of her house.

"Bit of a cheek," Eric muttered. From the

look of him, walking wasn't something he did often.

"Best foot forward!" Janet said cheerily. Apparently she worked as a hairdresser, and her own hair was dancing in the wind. As indeed was Libby.

We walked. Sylvie might have called it a house but I would have said it was a castle that Rory had bought for himself on his island retreat. It was built out of grey brick: a grand, sprawling building with towers and battlements and even gargoyles gazing wickedly out of the corners. We reached the front door. It was solid oak, as thick as a tree and half as welcoming.

"I wonder if we should knock?" Tim asked.

"To hell with that!" Eric pushed and the door swung open.

We found ourselves in a great hall with a black and white floor, animal heads on the walls and a roaring fire in the hearth. A grandfather clock chimed four times. I looked at my watch – it was actually ten past three. I was already beginning to feel uneasy. Apart from the crackle of the logs and the ticking of the clock, the house was silent. It felt empty. No Rory, no Mrs Rory, no butler, no cook. Just us.

"Hello?" Libby called out. "Is there anyone at home?"

"It-doesn't-look-as-if-there's-anyone-here," Mark said. At least, I think that's what he said.

Speaking was something else that he did very fast. Whole sentences came out of his mouth as a single word.

"This is ridiculous," Eric snapped. "I suggest we split up and try and find Rory. Maybe he's asleep upstairs."

So we all went our separate ways. Mark and Eric headed off through different doors. Libby Goldman went into the kitchen. Tim and I went upstairs. It was only now that we were inside it that I realized just how big this house was. It had five staircases, doors everywhere and so many corridors that we could have been walking through a maze. And if it looked like a castle from the outside, inside it was like a museum. There was more furniture than you'd find in a department store. Antique chairs and sofas stood next to cupboards and sideboards and tables of every shape and size. There were so many oil paintings that you could hardly see the walls. Rory also seemed to have a fondness for ancient weapons – I had only been in the place a few minutes but already I had seen crossbows and muskets and flintlock pistols mounted on wooden plaques. On the first floor there was a stuffed bear holding an Elizabethan gun ... a blunderbuss. The stairs and upper landing were covered in thick, red carpet which muffled every sound. In the distance I could hear Janet calling out Rory's name but it was difficult to say if she was near or far away.

Suddenly we were lost and very much on our own.

We reached a corner where there was a suit of dull silver armour standing guard; a knight with a shield but no sword.

"I don't like it," I said.

"I think it's a very nice suit of armour," Tim replied.

"I'm not talking about the armour, Tim," I said. "I'm talking about the whole island. Why isn't there anyone here to meet us? And why did your friend send that old fishing boat to pick us up?"

Tim smiled. "Relax, kid," he said. "The house is a bit quiet, that's all. But my sixth sense would tell me if there was something wrong, and right now I'm feeling fine..."

Just then there was a high-pitched scream from another part of the second floor. It was Brenda. She screamed and screamed again.

"How lovely!" Tim exclaimed. "Brenda's singing for us! I think that's Mozart, isn't it?"

"It's not Mozart, Tim," I shouted, beginning to run towards the sound. "She's screaming for help! Come on!"

We ran down the corridor and round the corner. That was when we saw Brenda, standing in front of an open bedroom door. She had stopped screaming now but her face was white and her hands were tearing at her hair. At the same time, Libby and Sylvie appeared, coming up the stairs. And Eric was also there, pushing his way forward to see what the fuss was about.

Tim and I reached the doorway. I looked inside.

The room had a red carpet. It took me a couple of seconds to realize that the room had once had a yellow carpet. It was covered in blood. There was more blood on the walls and on the bed. There was even blood on the blood.

And there was McDougal. I'm afraid it was the end of the story for Rory. The sword that had killed him was lying next to him and I guess it must have been taken from the suit of armour.

Brenda screamed again and pulled out a handful of her own hair.

Eric stood back, gasping.

Libby burst into tears.

And Tim, of course, fainted.

There were just the eight of us, trapped on Crocodile Island. And I had to admit, our reunion hadn't got off to a very good start.

AFTER DARK

"It was horrible," Tim groaned. "It was horrible. Rory McPoodle ... he was in pieces!"

"I don't want to hear about it, Tim," I said. Actually, it was too late. He'd already told me twenty times.

"Why would anyone *do* that?" he demanded. "What sort of person would do that?"

"I'm not sure," I muttered. "How about a dangerous lunatic?"

Tim nodded. "You could be right," he said.

We were sitting in our bedroom. We knew it was the bedroom that McDougal had prepared for us because it had Tim's name on the door. There were seven bedrooms on the same floor, each one of them labelled for the arriving guests. This room was square, with a high ceiling and a window with a low balcony looking out over a sea that was already grey and choppy as the sun set and the evening drew in. There was a four-poster bed, a heavy tapestry and the sort of wallpaper that could give you bad dreams. There was also something else I'd noticed and it worried me.

"Look at this, Tim," I said. I pointed at the bedside table. "There's a telephone socket here – but no telephone. What does that tell you?"

"The last person who slept in this room stole the telephone?"

"Not exactly. I think the telephone has been taken to stop us making any calls."

"Why would anyone do that?"

"To stop us reporting the death of Rory McDougal to the police."

Tim considered. "You mean ... someone knew we were coming..." he began.

"Exactly. And they also knew we'd be stuck here. At least until the boat came back."

It was a nasty thought. I was beginning to have lots of nasty thoughts, and the worst one was this: someone had killed Rory McDougal, but had it happened before we arrived on the island? Or had he been killed by one of the people from the boat? As soon as we had arrived at the house, we had all split up. For at least ten minutes nobody had known where anybody else was, which meant that any one of us could have found Rory and killed him before the others arrived.

Along with Tim and myself, there were now six people on the island ... six and several halves if you counted Rory. Eric Draper, Janet Rhodes, Sylvie Binns, Mark Tyler, Brenda Blake and Libby Goldman. Tim hadn't seen any of them in ten years and knew hardly anything about them. Could one of them be a crazed killer? Could one of them have planned this whole thing?

I looked at my watch. It was ten to seven. We left the room and went back downstairs.

Eric Draper had called a meeting in the dining-room at seven o'clock. I don't know who had put him in charge but I guessed he had decided himself.

"He was head boy at school," Tim told me. "He was always telling everyone what to do. Even the teachers used to do what he said."

"What was Rory McDougal like as a boy?"

"Well … he was young."

"That's very helpful, Tim. I mean … was he popular?"

"Yes. Except he once had a big row with Libby Goldman. He tried to kiss her in biology class and she attacked him with a bicycle pump."

"But she wouldn't kill him just because of that, would she?"

"You should have seen where she put the bicycle pump!"

In fact Libby was alone in the dining-room when we arrived for the meeting. She was sitting in a chair at the end of a black, polished table that ran almost the full length of the room. Portraits of bearded men in different shades of tartan looked down from the walls. A chandelier hung from the ceiling.

She looked up as we came in. Her eyes were red. Either she had been crying or she had bad hay fever – and I hadn't noticed any hay on Crocodile Island. She was smoking a cigarette – or trying to. Her hands were shaking so much she had trouble getting it into her mouth.

"What are we going to do?" she wailed. "It's so horrible! I knew I shouldn't have accepted Rory's invitation!"

"Why did you?" I asked. "If you didn't like him..."

"Well ... he's interesting. He's rich. I thought he might appear on my television programme – Libby's Lounge."

"I watch that!" Tim exclaimed.

"But it's a children's programme," Libby said.

Tim blushed. "Well ... I mean ... I've seen it. A bit of it."

"I've never heard of it," I muttered.

Libby's eyes went redder.

Then three of the others came in: Janet Rhodes, Mark Tyler and Brenda Blake.

"I've been trying to call the mainland on my mobile phone," Janet announced. "But I can't get a signal."

"I can't get a signal either," agreed Mark,

speaking as quickly as ever. He sort of shimmered in front of me and suddenly he was sitting down.

"There is no signal on this island."

"And no phone in my room," Janet said.

"No phone in any room!" The singer was looking pale and scared. Of course, she was the one who had found the body. Looking at her, I saw that it would be a few months before she sang in a concert hall. She probably wouldn't have the strength to sing in the bath.

Somewhere a clock struck seven and Eric Draper waddled into the room. "Are we all here?" he asked.

"I'm here!" Tim called out, as helpful as ever.

"I think there's one missing," I said.

Eric Draper did a quick head count. At least everyone in the room still had their heads. "Sylvie isn't here yet," he said. He scowled. You could tell he was the sort of man who expected everyone to do exactly what he said. "We'll have to wait for her."

"She was always late for everything," Janet muttered. She had slumped into a chair next to Libby. "I don't know how she managed to come first in chemistry. She was always late for class."

"I saw her in her room a few moments ago," Mark said. "She was sitting on the bed. She looked upset."

"I'm upset!" Eric said. "We're all upset!

Well, let's begin without her." He cleared his throat as if we were the jury and he was about to begin his summing up. "We are clearly in a very awkward situation here. We've been invited to this island, only to discover that our host, Rory McDougal, has been murdered. We can't call the police because it would seem that there are no telephones and none of our mobiles can get a signal. Unless we can find a boat to get back to the mainland, we're stuck here until Captain Randle – or whatever his name was – arrives to pick us up. The only good news is that there's plenty of food in the house. I've looked in the kitchen. This is a comfortable house. We should be fine here."

"Unless the killer strikes again," I said.

Everyone looked at me. "What makes you think he'll do that?" Eric demanded.

"It's a possibility," I said. "And anyway, 'he' could be a 'she'."

I noticed Libby shivered when I said that – but to be frank she'd been shivering a lot recently.

"Did Rory invite you here too?" Mark asked.

"Not exactly. He invited Tim, and Tim couldn't leave me on my own at home. So I came along for the ride."

Eric scowled for a second time. Scowling suited him. "I wouldn't have said this place was suitable for children," he said.

"Murder isn't suitable for children," I agreed. "But I'm stuck here with you and it seems to me that we've all been set up. No phones! That has to be on purpose. All the rooms were prepared for us, with our names on the doors. And now, like you say, we're stuck here. Suppose the killer is here too?"

"That's not possible," Brenda whispered. But she didn't sound like she believed herself.

"Maybe Rory wasn't murdered," Tim suggested. "Maybe it was an accident."

"You mean someone accidentally chopped him to pieces?" I asked.

Janet glanced at the door. She was looking nervous. A hairdresser having a bad hair day. "Perhaps we should go and find Sylvie," she suggested.

Nobody said anything. Then, as one, we hurried out of the room.

We went back upstairs. Sylvie's room was halfway down the corridor, two doors away from our own. It was closed. Tim knocked. There was no reply. "She could have fallen asleep," he said.

"Just open the door, Tim," I suggested.

He opened it. Sylvie's room was a similar size to ours but with more modern furniture, an abstract painting on the wall and two single beds. Her case was standing beside the wall, unopened. As my eyes travelled towards her, I noticed a twist of something silver lying in the middle of the yellow carpet. But I didn't have time to mention it.

Sylvie was lying on her back, one hand flung out. When I had first seen her I had thought her small and silent. Now she was smaller and dreadfully still. I felt Mark push past me, entering the room.

"Is she…?" he began.

"Yes," Tim said. "She's asleep."

"I don't think so, Tim," I said.

Eric went over to her and took her wrist between a podgy finger and thumb. "She has no pulse," he said. He leant over her. "She's not breathing."

Tim's mouth fell open. "Do you think she's ill?" he asked.

"She's dead, Tim," I said. Two murders in one day. And it wasn't even Tim's bedtime.

Libby burst into tears. It was getting to be a habit with her. At least Brenda didn't scream again. At this close range, I'm not sure my eardrums could have taken it.

"What are we going to do?" someone asked. I wasn't sure who it was and it didn't matter anyway. Because right then I didn't have any idea.

"It might have been a heart attack," Tim said. "Maybe the shock of what happened to Rory…"

Darkness had fallen on Crocodile Island. It had slithered across the surface of the sea and thrown itself over the house. Now and then a full moon came out from behind the clouds and for a moment the waves would ripple silver before disappearing into inky blackness. Tim and I were sitting on our four-poster bed. It looked like we were going to have to share it. Two posters each.

Maybe it had been a heart attack. Maybe she had died of fright. Maybe she'd caught a very bad case of flu. Everyone had their own ideas … but I knew better. I remembered the twist of silver I had seen on the carpet.

"Tim, what can you tell me about Sylvie Binns?" I asked.

"Not a lot." Tim fell silent. "She was good at chemistry."

"I know that."

"She used to go out with Mark. We always thought the two of them would get married, but in the end she met someone else. Mark ran all the way round England. That was his way of forgetting her."

Mark Tyler had been the last person to see Sylvie alive. I wondered if he really had forgotten her. Or forgiven her.

"Maybe she was ill before she came to the island," Tim muttered.

"Tim, I think she was poisoned," I said.

"Poisoned?"

I remembered my first sight of Sylvie, on the quay. She had been eating a chocolate flake.

"Sylvie liked sweets and chocolate," I said.

"You're right, Nick! Yes. She loved chocolate. She could never resist it. When Mark was going out with her, he took her on a tour of a chocolate factory. She even ate the tickets." Tim frowned. "But what's that got to do with anything?"

"There was a piece of silver paper on the floor in her room. I think it was the wrapper off a sweet or a chocolate. Don't you see? Someone knew she couldn't resist chocolate – so they left one in her room. Maybe on her pillow."

"And it wasn't almond crunch," Tim muttered darkly.

"More likely cyanide surprise," I said.

We got into bed. Tim didn't want to turn off the lights, but a few minutes later, after he had dozed off, I reached for the switch and lay back in the darkness. I needed to think. Sylvie had eaten a poisoned chocolate. I was sure of it. But had she been given it or had she found it in her room? If it was already in the room, it could have been left there before we arrived. But if she had been given it, then the killer must still be on the island. He or she might even be in the house.

There was a movement at the window.

At first I thought I'd imagined it, but propping myself up in the bed, I saw it again. There was somebody there! No – that was impossible. We were on the first floor. Then I remembered.

There was a terrace running round the outside of the house, connecting all the bedrooms.

There it was again. I stared in horror. There was a face staring at me from the other side of the glass, a hideous skull with hollow eyes and grinning, tombstone teeth. The bones glowed in the moonlight. Now I'll be honest with you. I don't scare easily. But right then I was frozen. I couldn't move. I couldn't cry out. I'm almost surprised I didn't wet the bed.

The skull hovered in front of me. I couldn't see a body. It had to be draped in black. It's a mask, I told myself. Someone is trying to frighten you with a joke-shop mask. Somehow, I managed to force back the fear. I jerked up in bed and threw back the covers. Next to me, Tim woke up.

"Is it breakfast already?" he asked.

I ignored him. I was already darting towards the window. But at that moment, the moon vanished behind another cloud and the darkness fell. By the time I had found the lock and opened the window, the man – or woman, whoever it was – had gone.

"What is it, Nick?" Tim demanded.

I didn't answer. But it seemed that whoever had killed Rory McDougal and Sylvie Binns was still on the island.

Which left me wondering – who was going to be next?

SEARCH PARTY

Janet Rhodes didn't make it to breakfast.

There were just the five of us, sitting in the kitchen with five bowls of Frosties and a steaming plate of scrambled eggs that Brenda had insisted on cooking but which nobody felt like eating. Libby had another cigarette in her mouth but everyone had complained so much that she wasn't smoking it. She was sucking it. Eric was still in his dressing-gown, a thick red thing with his initials – ED – embroidered on the pocket. Mark was wearing a track suit. A security camera winked at us from one corner of the room. There were a lot of security cameras on the island. But none of us felt even slightly secure.

"What are we going to do?" Brenda asked. I got the feeling that she hadn't slept very much the night before. There were dark rings under her eyes and although she'd put on lipstick, most of it had missed her lips. "This island is haunted!" she went on.

"What do you mean?" Eric asked.

"Last night ... my window ... it was horrible."

"I've got quite a nice window," Tim said.

"I mean ... I saw something! A human skull. It was dancing in the night air."

So she'd seen it too! I was about to chip in, but then Eric interrupted. "I don't think it's going to help, sharing our bad dreams," he said.

"I didn't dream it," Brenda insisted.

"We've got to do something!" Mark cut in. "First Rory, then Sylvie. At this rate, there won't be any of us left by lunch-time."

"I don't want any lunch," Libby muttered.

"We need to talk about this," Eric said. "We need to work something out. But there's no point starting until we're all here." He glanced at the clock. "Where the hell is Janet?"

"Maybe she's in the bath," Tim suggested.

"In the water or underneath it?" Eric growled.

The minute hand on the kitchen clock ticked forward. It was nine o'clock. Suddenly Mark stood up. "I'm going upstairs," he announced.

"You're going back to bed?" Tim asked.

"I'm going to find her."

He left the room. The rest of us followed

him, tiptoeing up the stairs and along the corridor with a sense of dread. Actually, Eric didn't exactly tiptoe. He was so fat that it must have been quite a few years since his toes *had* tips. Mark Tyler had moved quickly, taking the stairs four at a time as if they were hurdles and he was back at the Olympic games at Atlanta. He was outside the door when we arrived.

"She's overslept," Tim said to me. "She's fine. She's just overslept."

Eric knocked on her door. There was no answer. He knocked again, then turned the handle. The door opened.

The hairdresser had overslept all right, but nothing was ever going to wake her up again. She had been stabbed during the night. She was lying on her back on a four-poster bed like the one in our room, only smaller. The bed was old. The paint had peeled off the posts and there was a tear in the canopy above her. In fact the whole room looked shabby, as if it had been missed out by the decorators. Maybe I noticed all this because I didn't want to look at the body. You may think I'm crazy, but dead people upset me. And when I did finally look at her, I got a shock.

Whoever had killed her hadn't used a knife. There was something sticking out of her chest and at first I thought it was some sort of rocket. It was silver, in the shape of a sort of long pyramid, with four legs jutting out. Then, slowly, it dawned on me what I was looking at. It was a model, a souvenir of the building that I had climbed up with Tim only the year before.

It was incredible. But true. Janet Rhodes had been stabbed with a model of the Eiffel Tower.

"The Eiffel Tower!" Tim muttered. His face was the colour of sour milk. "It's an outrage. I mean, it's meant to be a tourist attraction!"

"Why the Eiffel Tower?" I asked.

"Because it's famous, Nick. People like to visit it."

"No – I don't mean, why is it a tourist attraction. I mean, why use it as a murder weapon? It's certainly a strange choice. Maybe someone is trying to tell us something."

"Well, they certainly told Janet something," Tim said.

We were back at the breakfast table. The scrambled eggs were cold and congealed and looked even less appetizing than before. All the Frosties had gone soggy. But it didn't matter. There was no way anybody was going to eat anything today. The way things were going, I wondered if any of us would ever eat anything again.

Nobody was talking very much. I knew why. But it was Brenda who put it into words.

"Do you realize…" she began, and for once

her voice was hoarse and empty. "Do you realize that the killer could be sitting here, at this table."

Tim looked around. "But there's only us here!"

"That's what she means, Tim," I said. "She's saying that the killer could be one of us!"

Brenda nodded. "I know it's one of us. One of us got up last night and went down the corridor." She shuddered. "I thought I heard squeaking last night..."

"That was Tim," I said. "He snores."

"No. It was a floorboard. Somebody left their room..."

"Did anyone else hear anything last night?" Eric asked.

There was a pause. Then Libby nodded. "I have the room next to Mark," she said. She turned to look at him. "I heard your door open just after midnight. I heard you go into the corridor."

"I went to the toilet," Mark replied. His dark face had suddenly got darker. He didn't like being accused.

"You went to the toilet in the corridor?" Tim asked.

"I went to the toilet which is across the corridor, opposite my room. I didn't go anywhere near Janet."

"What about the skull?" Brenda whispered.

Eric scowled. He had forgotten about the dancing skull. "I know you say it's a dream, Eric," she went on. "But that's typical of you. You never believed anything I said, even when we were at school. Well, believe me now..." she took a deep breath. "Maybe it wasn't a ghost or a monster. Maybe it was someone in a mask. But they were there! I was awake. I jumped out of bed and went over to the window but by the time I got there, seconds later, they'd gone. Vanished into thin air..."

"It wasn't a dream," I said. "I saw it too."

"You?" Eric sneered at me.

I nodded.

"I didn't see anything," Tim said.

"You were asleep, Tim. But it was definitely there. It came out of nowhere ... like a magic trick. A rabbit out of a hat!"

"You saw a rabbit too?" Tim asked.

We all ignored him. "Any one of us could have climbed out onto the terrace," Brenda said. "Any one of us could have killed Janet. And Rory. And Sylvie! How do we know that she wasn't strangled or poisoned or something?"

"I think she *was* poisoned," I said.

Everyone looked at me so I told them about the sweet wrapper and Sylvie's love of chocolate. It was strange. Everyone in the room was ten years older than me but suddenly I was in control.

Not for long, though. Eric Draper, the ex-head boy, raised his hands. "Ladies and gentlemen," he announced. "I don't think we should jump to conclusions. Why would any of us sitting at this table want to kill Rory or Sylvie or Janet?"

"Mark used to go out with Sylvie," Libby said. She was staring at him. "When she broke up with you, you told me you wanted to kill her."

"That was ten years ago!" Mark protested. He jerked a finger at Libby. "Anyway, what about *you*? You nearly *did* kill Rory with that bicycle pump..."

"Yes. And what about you!" Tim pointed at Eric. "You say your name's Eric, so why are you wearing a dressing-gown that belongs to Ed?"

It took Eric a few seconds to work out what Tim was getting at. "Those are my initials, you idiot!" he snapped. He took a deep breath and raised his hands. "Look," he went on. "There's no point arguing amongst ourselves. We have to stick together. It could be our only hope."

The others fell silent. I had to admit, Eric was speaking sense. Blaming each other wouldn't help.

"Both Brenda and ... Tim's little brother saw somebody last night," he went on. I didn't know why he couldn't call me by my name.

"Now that could have been one of us, dressing up to frighten the others. But remember, we were all inside the house ... and this thing, whatever it was, was outside. So maybe it was someone else. Maybe it was someone we don't know about."

"You mean ... someone hiding on the island?" Mark said.

"Exactly. We know we can't call the police. We know we're stuck here. But it seems to me that the first thing we have to do is find out if there's anyone else here."

"We've got to organize a search party," I said.

Tim shook his head. "This is no time for a party, Nick," he muttered.

"You're right, Eric," Libby said. "We've got to go over the island from head to tail."

"But at the same time, I think we should keep an eye on each other," Brenda said. "I'll feel safer that way."

Eric went upstairs to get changed. Mark went with him. From now on, we were going to do everything in pairs. Brenda and Libby cleared the breakfast things. I'd already noticed that most of the food in the house was in tins – which was just as well. Even the cleverest killer couldn't tamper with a tin, so at least we wouldn't starve. At half past nine we all met in the hall. Then we put on our coats and went outside.

The search began back at the jetty, right at the head of the crocodile. The idea was that we could cover the entire island, working like the police searching a wood when someone has gone missing. That is, we kept ten metres apart, always in sight of one another, moving across the island in a line. It was a beautiful day. The sun was shining and the sea was blue, but even so I could feel a chill breeze on Crocodile Island. And there was something else. I couldn't escape the feeling that I was being watched. It was weird. Because it was obvious that there wasn't anybody in sight … not even so much as a sheep or a cow.

It only took us an hour to cover the island. There really wasn't very much there. Most of it was covered in gorse that only came up to the knee, which no killer could have hidden behind – unless, of course, he happened to be extremely small. There were a few trees but we checked the branches and Tim even climbed one to see if anyone was hiding at the top. Then I climbed up to help Tim down again and we moved on. We came to a couple of ruined outbuildings. I went inside. There was nobody there – but I did see something. Another security camera, fixed to the brickwork. Of course, a rich man like Rory would have had to be careful about security. I remembered the camera I had noticed in the kitchen. He had probably covered the whole island. Was that why I had felt we were being watched?

We went past the house and continued towards the crocodile's tail. The ground rose steeply up, finally arriving at a narrow point at least twenty metres above the sea. This was what I had seen from the boat. Six great rocks, steel grey and needle-sharp, rose out of the water far below. Looking down made my head spin. I wondered briefly if there might be a cave somewhere, perhaps tucked underneath the lip where we were standing. But then a wave rolled in, crashing against the cliff face. If there was a killer down there, he'd be soaking wet. And anyway, as far as I could see, there was no way down.

We moved away, retracing our steps. There was nobody outside the house, but how about inside? Starting in the hall, we went from room to room: the library, the dining-room, the conservatory, the hall and so on. We looked behind curtains, under tables, in the fireplaces and up the chimneys. Tim even looked in the grandfather clocks. Maybe he thought he'd find somebody's grandfather. We covered the ground floor and then went up to the first. Here were the bedrooms, with our names still attached to the doors. We went into every one of them. There was nobody there ... apart from the three very dead bodies. It wasn't easy searching those particular rooms, but we made ourselves ... although I think Tim was wasting his time doing it with his eyes tightly shut.

Nobody in the rooms. Nobody in the corridors. We found the attic but all that was there was a water tank. Tim dipped his head in and I made a mental note not to drink any more water. Not with his dandruff. Eventually, we gave up. We had been everywhere. There was nowhere else to look.

We started to go back down to the kitchen but had only got halfway there when Libby let out a little gasp.

"What is it?" Eric demanded.

"There." She pointed at the wall at the end of the corridor. "I don't know why I didn't see it before!"

What she had seen was a black-and-white photograph in a silver frame. It was hanging right in the middle of the wall with enough space around it to make it stand out. The question was – had Rory hung it there? Or had it been someone else? Was this something we were meant to see?

The photograph showed nine teenagers, all of them wearing the same uniform. It's funny how people change in ten years – but I recognized them at once: Eric Draper, Janet Rhodes, Mark Tyler, Brenda Blake, Sylvie Binns, Libby Goldman, Rory McDougal and Tim. Tim looked the weirdest of them all. He'd had long hair then, and spots. Lots of spots. Of course, I wouldn't have looked too great myself when the picture had been taken – but then I would only have been four years old.

There was one face, however, that I didn't know. He was standing at the edge of the group, slightly apart; a thin, gangly teenager with curly hair and glasses. He was wearing an anorak and had the sort of face you'd expect to see on a train-spotter. "Who's he?" I asked.

"That's Johnny!" Brenda replied. "Johnny Nadler. He was one of my best friends..."

"And mine," Libby agreed. "Everyone liked Johnny. We used to hang out with him in the yard." She walked closer to the photograph. "I remember when this was taken. It was prize-giving day. He came second in geography. I came first."

"Wait a minute," I interrupted. "Everyone in this photograph is here on Crocodile Island. Everyone except Johnny Nadler!"

"You're right!" Mark agreed. "Why wasn't he invited?"

"Because he's the killer!" Eric snapped. "He's got to be!"

"But why would Johnny want to kill Rory?" Brenda asked. "The two of them were friends. And every day after school he used to catch the bus with Sylvie – even though it took him eight miles in the wrong direction. That's how much he liked her."

"He let Janet cut his hair," Libby went on. "She accidentally cut a chunk out of his ear, but he didn't mind. In fact he laughed all the way to the hospital. Johnny wouldn't hurt anyone."

"What else can you tell me about him?" I asked.

"He came second in history as well as geography," Eric said. "He was really clever."

"He was always playing with model planes and cars," Mark added. "He used to build them himself. We always said he'd be an inventor when he left school but in fact he ended up working at Boots. I saw him there once, when I went in to get some ointment." He blushed. "I had athlete's foot."

"Did any of the rest of you ever see him again?" I asked.

Everyone shook their heads. I looked at the photograph again. It did seem strange that he was the only one in the picture who hadn't been invited to Crocodile Island. But did that make him the killer? And if so, where on earth was he? We had searched the entire island and we were certain now that we were the only ones who were there.

Eric looked at his watch. It was half past twelve. "I suggest we continue this meeting downstairs," he said.

"I need to change," Brenda said.

"Me too," Libby agreed.

Everyone started to move in different directions.

"Hold on a minute!" I said. "I thought we were all going to stick together. I think we should all stay in this room."

"Don't be ridiculous!" Eric snapped. "We have to eat something. It's lunch-time. And anyway, we've just searched the island. We know there's nobody else here."

"Well, I'm staying with Tim," I said.

"How do you know I'm not the killer?" Tim demanded.

Because whoever killed Rory and the others is brilliant and fiendish and you still have trouble tying your shoelaces. That was what I thought, but I didn't say anything. I just shrugged.

"I don't want to be near anyone," Libby said. "I feel safer on my own."

"Me too." Brenda nodded. "And I'm certainly not having anyone in the room with me while I'm changing."

"We can meet in ten minutes," Eric said. "We're inside the house. We know there's nobody else on the island. We'll meet in the dining-room at twenty to one."

He was wrong of course. This was one little group that was never going to meet again. But how could we know that? We were scared and we weren't thinking straight.

Tim and I went back to our room. Tim scratched his head, which was still damp from the water tank. "Johnny could be hiding on the island," he said. "What if there's a secret room?"

The same thought had already occurred to me, but I'd tapped every wall and every wooden panel and nothing had sounded hollow. "I don't think there are any secret rooms, Tim," I said.

"But you can't be sure..." Tim began to tap his way along the wall, his eyes half-closed, listening for a hollow sound. A few moments later, he straightened up, excited. "There's definitely something on the other side here!" he cried.

"I know, Tim," I said. "That's the window."

I left him in the bedroom, drying his hair, and went back downstairs. I was going to join the others in the dining-room. But I never got that far. I was about halfway down when I heard it. A short, sudden scream. Then a crashing sound. It had come from somewhere outside.

I ran down the rest of the way, through the hall and out the front door. Mark Tyler appeared, running round the side of the house.

"What was it...?" he demanded. He was trying not to sound scared but it wasn't working.

"Round the back?"

We went there together, moving more slowly now, knowing what we were going to find, not wanting to find it. The kitchen door opened and Brenda Blake came out. I noticed she was breathing heavily.

This time it was Libby Goldman. I'm afraid she had recorded her last episode of *Libby's Lounge* and for her the final credits were already rolling. Why had she gone outside? Maybe she'd decided to light up one of her cigarettes – in which case, this was one time when smoking certainly had been bad for her health. Fatal, in fact. But it hadn't been the tobacco that had killed her. Something had hit her hard on the head: something that had been dropped from above. I looked up, working out the angles. We were directly underneath the battlements. Behind them, the roof was flat. It would have been easy enough for someone to hide up there, to wait for any one of us to step outside. Libby must have come out to get a breath of fresh air before the meeting. Air wasn't something she'd be needing again.

There were footsteps on the gravel. Eric and Tim had arrived. They stared in silence. Mark stretched out a finger and pointed. It took me a minute to work out what he was pointing at. That was how much his finger was trembling.

And there it was, lying in the grass. At first I didn't recognize the object that had been dropped from the roof and which had fallen right onto Libby Goldman. I mean, I knew what it was – but I couldn't believe that that was what had been used.

It was a big round ball: a globe. The sort of thing you find in a library. Maybe it had been in Rory's library before the killer had carried it up to the roof. The United States of America was facing up. It was stained red.

I looked at Eric Draper. His mouth had dropped open. He looked genuinely shocked. Mark Tyler was standing opposite him, staring. Brenda Blake was to one side. She was crying.

One of them had to be faking it. I was certain of it. One of them had to have climbed down from the room after watching Libby fall. There was nobody else here. One of them had to be the killer.

But which one?

MORE MURDER

Eric Draper? Brenda Blake? Or Mark Tyler?

It was early evening and Tim and I had gone for a walk – supposedly to clear our heads. But the truth was, I wanted to be alone with him and somehow I felt safer away from the house. It struck me that all the deaths had taken place inside or near the building. And if we stayed too close to the house something else might strike me – a falling piano or a model of the Taj Mahal, for example.

I glanced down at the piece of paper I was holding in my hand. I had made a few notes just before we left:

RORY McDOUGAL – Killed with a sword.
SYLVIE BINNS – Poisoned.
JANET RHODES – Stabbed with an Eiffel Tower!

LIBBY GOLDMAN – Knocked down with a globe.

There was a pattern in there somewhere but I just couldn't see it. Maybe some fresh air would help after all.

"I've got an idea!" Tim said.

"Go ahead, Tim," I said.

"Maybe I could swim back over to the coast and get some help."

We were sitting on the jetty. Today the sea was flat, the waves caught as if in a photograph. I could just make out the mainland, a vague ribbon lying on the horizon. The sun was setting fast. How many of us would see it rise again?

I shook my head. "No, Tim. It's too far."

"It can't be more than five miles."

"And you can't swim."

"Oh yes. I'd forgotten." He glanced at me. "But you can."

"I can't swim five miles!" I said. "The water's too cold. And there's too much of it. No. Our only hope is to solve this before the killer strikes again."

"You're right, Nick." Tim closed his eyes and sat in silence for a minute. Then he opened them again. "Maybe we could get one of the others to swim..."

"One of the others *is* the killer!" I said. "I saw someone out on the terrace, wearing a skeleton mask. I don't know how they managed to disappear so quickly – but I wasn't imagining it. Brenda saw them too."

"Maybe it was Mark! He's a fast mover."

"And just now ... when Libby Goldman was killed. Someone must have climbed up onto the roof." I thought back. "Brenda was out of breath when she came into the garden..."

"She could have been singing!"

"I doubt it. But she could have been running. She drops the globe, then runs all the way downstairs..."

A seagull flew overhead, crying mournfully. I knew how it felt. I almost wanted to cry myself.

"What's missing is the motive," I went on. "Think back, Tim. You were at school with these people. There are only three of them left – Brenda, Mark and Eric. Would any of them have any reason to kill the rest of you?"

Tim sighed. "The only people who ever threatened to kill me," he said, "were the teachers. My French teacher once threw a piece of chalk at me. And when that missed, he threw the blackboard."

"How did you get on with Mark Tyler?"

"We were friends. We used to play conkers together." He scratched his head. "I did once miss his conker and break three of his fingers, but I don't think he minded too much."

"How about Brenda Blake?"

Tim thought back. "She was in the school choir," he said. "She was also in the rugby team. She used to sing in the scrum." He scratched his head. "We used to tease her a bit but it was never serious."

"Maybe she didn't agree."

The waves rolled in towards us. I looked out at the mainland, hoping to catch sight of Horatio Randle and his boat, the *Silver Medal*. But the sea was empty, darkening as the sun dipped behind it. What had the old fisherman said when he'd dropped us? *"I'll be back in a couple of days."* It had been Wednesday when we arrived. He might not return until the weekend. How many passengers would there be left waiting for him?

"How about Eric Draper?" I asked.

"What about him?"

"He could be the killer. It would have to be someone strong to carry the globe up to the roof in the first place. Can you remember anything about him?"

Tim laughed. "He was a great sport. I'll never forget the last day of term when the seven of us pulled off his trousers and threw him in the canal!"

"What?" I exclaimed. "You pulled off his trousers and threw him in the canal? Why?"

"Well, he was the head boy. And he'd always been bossy. It was just a bit of fun. Except that he nearly drowned. And the canal was so polluted, he had to spend six months in hospital."

"Are you telling me that the seven of you nearly killed Eric?" I was almost screaming. "Hasn't it occurred to you that this whole thing could be his revenge?"

"But it was just a joke!"

"You almost killed him, Tim! Maybe he wasn't amused."

I stood up. It was time to go back to the house. The other three would be waiting for us … if they'd managed to survive the last half-hour.

"I wish I'd never come here," Tim muttered.

"I wish you'd never come here," I agreed.

"Poor Libby. And Sylvie. And Janet. And Rory, of course. He was first."

We walked a few more steps in silence. Then I suddenly stopped. "What did you say, Tim?" I demanded.

"I didn't say anything!"

"Yes, you did! Before you weren't saying anything, you were saying something."

"I asked which side of the bed you wanted."

"No. That was yesterday." I played back what he had just said and that was when I saw it, the pattern I'd been looking for. "You're brilliant!" I said.

"Thanks!" Tim frowned. "What have I done?"

"Tell me," I said. "Did Libby come first in

anything at school? And was it ... by any chance ... geography?"

"Yes. She did. How did you know?"

"Let's get back inside," I said.

I found Eric, Mark and Brenda in the drawing-room. This was one of the most extraordinary rooms in the house – almost like a chapel with a great stained glass window at one end and a high, vaulted ceiling. Rory McDougal had obviously fancied himself as a musician. There was even a church organ against the wall, the silver pipes looming over us. Like so many of the other rooms, the walls were lined with old weapons. In here they were antique pistols; muskets and flintlocks. All in all, we couldn't have chosen a worse house to share with a mass murderer. There were more weapons than you'd find in the Tower of London and I just hoped that they weren't as real as they looked.

The three survivors were sitting in heavy, leather chairs. I stood in front of them with the organ on one side and a row of bookshelves on the other. Everyone was watching me and I felt a bit like Hercule Poirot at the end of one of his cases, explaining it to the suspects. The only trouble was, this wasn't the end of the case. I was still certain that I was talking to the murderer. He or she had to be one of the people in the room.

Somewhere outside, a clock chimed the

hour. It was nine o'clock. Night had fallen.

"Seven of you were invited to Crocodile Island," I began. "And I see now that you all have something in common."

"We went to the same school," interrupted Tim.

"I know that, Tim. But there's something else. You all got prizes for coming first. You've already told me that Rory was first in maths. Libby was first in geography..."

"What's this got to do with anything?" Eric snapped.

"Don't you see? Libby was first in geography and someone dropped a globe on her head. Someone told me that Sylvie Binns came first in chemistry and we think she was poisoned."

"Janet came first in French..." Mark murmured.

"...which would explain why she was stabbed with a model of the Eiffel Tower. And Rory McDougal came first in maths."

"He was stabbed too," Eric said.

"He was more than stabbed. He was divided!"

There was a long silence.

"That's the reason why Johnny Nadler wasn't invited to the island," Brenda said. "He never came first in anything. He was second..."

"But that means..." Eric had gone pale. "I came first in history."

"I came first in sport," Mark said.

Brenda nodded. "And I came first in music."

We all turned to look at Tim. But he couldn't have come first in anything ... could he? I noticed he was blushing. He licked his lips and looked the other way.

"What did you come first in, Tim?" I asked.

"I didn't..." he began, but I could tell he was lying.

"We have to know," I said. "It could be important."

"I remember..." Brenda began.

"All right," Tim sighed. "I got first prize in needlework."

"Needlework!" I exclaimed.

"Well ... yes. It was a hobby of mine. Just for a bit. I mean..." He was going redder and redder. "I didn't even want the prize. I just got it. It was for a handkerchief..."

The idea of my sixteen-year-old brother winning a prize for an embroidered hanky made my head spin. But this wasn't the time to laugh. Hopefully I'd be able to do that later.

"Wait a minute! Wait a minute!" Eric said. He looked annoyed. Maybe it was because I was ten years younger than him and I was the one who'd worked it out. "I came first in history – and you're saying I'm going to be killed ... *historically?*"

"That's what it looks like," I said.

"But how...?"

I pointed at the wall, at the flintlock pistols on the wooden plaques. "Maybe someone will use one of those," I said. "Or there are swords, arrows, spears ... that bear upstairs is even holding a blunderbuss. This place is full of old weapons."

"What about me?" Brenda whispered.

"You're not an old weapon!" Tim said.

"I came first in music." Brenda glared at the organ as if it was about to jump off the wall and eat her.

"But who's *doing* this?" Mark cut in. "I mean ... it's got to be someone in this room. Right? We know there's nobody else on the island. There can't be anybody hiding. We've searched everywhere."

"It's him!" Brenda pointed at Eric. "He never forgave us for throwing him in the canal. This is his revenge!"

"What about *you?*" Eric returned. "You once said you were going to kill us all. It was in the school yard. I remember it clearly!"

"That's true!" Mark said.

"You used to bully me all the time," Brenda wailed. "Just because I had pigtails. And crooked teeth."

"And you were fat," Tim reminded her.

"But I didn't mean it, when I said that." She turned to Mark. "You said you were going to kill Tim when he broke all your fingers with that conker!"

"I only broke three of them!" Tim interrupted.

"I didn't much like Tim," Mark agreed. "And you're right. I would have quite happily strangled him. Not that it would have been easy with three broken fingers. But I never had any argument with you or with Eric or any of the others. Why would I want to kill you?"

"It's still got to be one of us," Eric insisted. He paused. "It can't be Tim," he went on.

"Why not?" Tim asked.

"Because this whole business is the work of a fiendish madman and you're not fiendish. You're just silly!"

"Oh thanks!" Tim looked away.

"I know it's not me..." Eric went on.

"That's what you say," Brenda sniffed.

"I know it's not me, so it's got to be Brenda or Mark."

"What about Sylvie?" Tim suggested.

"She's already dead, Tim," I reminded him, quietly.

"Oh yes."

"This is all irrelevant," Mark said. "The question is – what are we going to do? We could be stuck on this island for days, or even weeks. It all depends on when Captain Randle comes back. And by then it could be too late!"

"I'd like to make a suggestion," I said. Everyone stopped and looked at me. "The first thing is, we've all got to keep each other in sight."

"The kid's right," Mark agreed. "So long as we can see each other, we're going to be safe."

"That's true!" Tim exclaimed. "All we have to do is keep our eyes open and everything will be fine." He turned to me. "You're brilliant, Nick. For a moment there I was getting really worried."

Then all the lights went out.

It happened so suddenly that for a moment I thought it was just me. Had I been knocked out or somehow closed my eyes without noticing? The last thing I saw was the four of them – Eric, Brenda, Mark and Tim – sitting in their chairs as if caught in a photograph. Then everything was black. There was no moon that night and even if there had been the stained glass window would have kept most of the light out. Darkness came crashing onto us. It was total.

"Don't panic!" Eric said.

There was a gunshot. I saw it, a spark of red on the other side of the room.

Tim screamed and for a horrible moment I wondered if he had been shot. I forced myself to calm down. He'd come first in needlework. Nobody would be aiming a gun at him.

"Tim!" I called out.

"Can I panic now?" he called back.

"Eric...?" That was Mark's voice.

And then there was a sort of groaning sound, followed by a heavy thud. At the same time I heard a door open and close. I stood up, trying to see through the darkness. But it was hopeless. I couldn't even make out my own hand in front of my face.

"Tim?" I called again.

"Nick?" I was relieved to hear his voice.

"Eric?" I tried.

Silence.

"Brenda?"

Nothing.

"Mark?"

The lights came back on.

There were only two people alive in the room. I was standing in front of my chair. One more step and I'd have put my foot through the coffee table. Tim was *under* the coffee table. He must have crawled there when the lights went out. Eric was on the floor. He had been shot. There was a flintlock pistol, still smoking, lying on the carpet on the other side of the room. It must have been taken off the wall, fired and then dropped. At least, that's what it looked like. Brenda was sitting in her chair. She was dead too. One of the organ pipes – the largest – had been pulled down on top of her. That must have been the thud I had heard. Brenda had sung her last opera. The only music she needed now was a hymn.

There was no sign of Mark.

"Are you all right, Tim?" I demanded.

"Yes!" Tim sounded surprised. "I haven't been murdered!" he exclaimed.

"I noticed." I waited while he climbed out from underneath the coffee table. "At least we know who the killer is," I said.

"Do we?"

"It's got to be Mark," I said. "Mark Tyler..."

"I always knew it was him," Tim said. "Call it intuition. Call it experience. But I knew he was a killer even before he'd done any killing."

"I don't know, Tim," I said. It bothered me, because to be honest Mark was the last person I would have suspected. And yet, at the same time, I had to admit ... it would have taken a fast mover to push the globe off the roof and make it all the way downstairs in time and Mark was the fastest person on the island.

"Where do you think he went?" Tim asked.

"I don't know."

We left the room carefully. In fact, Tim made me leave it first. The fact was that – unless I'd got the whole thing wrong – it was just the three of us now on the island; Mark could be waiting for us anywhere. Or waiting for Tim, rather. He had no quarrel with me. And that made me think. Tim had come first in needlework. Following the pattern of the other deaths, that meant he would probably be killed with some sort of needle. But what would that mean? A sewing needle dipped in poison? A hypodermic syringe?

Tim must have had the same thought. He was looking everywhere, afraid to touch anything, afraid even to take another step. We went out into the hall. The fire had died down and was glowing red. The front door was open.

"Maybe he went outside," Tim said.

"What would be the point?" I asked.

Tim shuddered. "Don't talk about points," he said.

We went outside. And that was where we found Mark. He had come first in sport but now he had reached the finishing line. Somebody had been throwing the javelin and they'd thrown it at him. It had hit him in the chest. He was lying on the grass, doing a good impersonation of a sausage on a stick.

"It's … it's … it's…" Tim couldn't finish the sentence.

"Yeah," I said. "It's Mark." There were a few leaves scattered around his body. That puzzled me. The nearest trees were ten metres away. But this wasn't the time to play the detective. There were no more suspects. And only one more victim.

I looked at Tim.

Tim looked at me.

We were the only two left.

NEEDLES

Tim didn't sleep well that night. Although I hadn't said anything, not wanting to upset him, even he had managed to work out that he had to be the next on the killer's list. He also knew that his own murder would have something to do with needlework. So he was looking for needles everywhere.

By one o'clock in the morning we knew that there were no sewing needles in the room, no knitting needles and no pine needles. Even so, it took him an hour to get into bed and several more hours to get to sleep. Mind you, nobody would have found it easy getting to sleep dressed in a full suit of medieval armour, but that still hadn't stopped Tim putting it on.

"There could be a poisoned needle in the mattress," he said. "Or someone could try and inject me with a syringe."

Tim didn't snore that night; he clanked.

Every time he rolled over he sounded like twenty cans of beans in a washing machine. I just hoped he wasn't planning to take a bath in the suit of armour the following morning. That way he could end up rusting to death.

At four-thirty, he woke up screaming.

"What is it, Tim?" I asked.

"I had a bad dream, Nick," he said.

"Don't tell me. You saw a needle."

"No. I saw a haystack."

I didn't sleep well either. I got cramp and woke up in the morning with pins and needles. I didn't tell Tim, though. He'd have had a fit.

We had breakfast together in the kitchen. Neither of us ate very much. For a start, we were surrounded by dead bodies, which didn't make us feel exactly cheerful. But Tim was also terrified. I'd managed to persuade him to change out of the armour but now he was worrying about the food. Were there going to be needles in the cereal? A needle in the tea? In the end, I gave him a straw with a tissue sellotaped over the end. The tissue worked as a filter and he was able to suck up a little orange juice and a very softly-boiled egg.

I have to say that for once I was baffled. It was still like being in an Agatha Christie novel – only this time I couldn't flick through to the last page and see who did it without bothering to read the rest. Personally, I had always thought Eric had been the killer. He seemed to have the strongest motive – being half-drowned on the last day of school. It was funny really. All eight of the old boys and girls of St Egbert's had disliked each other. But someone, somewhere, had disliked them all even more. The whole thing had been planned right down to the last detail. And the last detail, unfortunately, was Tim.

But who? And why?

Tim sat miserably at his end of the table, hardly daring to move. Why had he had to come first in *needlework* of all things? How was I supposed to find the needle that was going to kill him? I knew now that the only hope for me was to solve this thing before the killer struck one last time. And a nasty thought had already occurred to me. Would the killer stop with Tim? I wasn't meant to be part of this. I had never gone to St Egbert's. But I was a witness to what had happened and maybe I had seen too much.

I went over what had happened last night. We had always assumed that there was nobody else on the island, but thinking it through I knew this couldn't be true. We had all been sitting down: Brenda in front of the organ, Eric opposite her, Mark nearest the door and Tim and me on the sofa. But none of us had been anywhere near the light switch, and someone had most certainly turned off the lights – not just in the drawing-room but throughout the entire house. Somewhere down in the basement, there would be a main fuse switch. But that led to another question. If the killer had been down in the basement, then how had he or she managed to appear in the room seconds later to shoot Eric and push the organ pipe onto Brenda?

At the time, I had assumed that Mark had committed the last two murders. There had been a shot, then a thud, then the opening and closing of a door. But a few seconds later, Mark had himself been killed. And what about the leaves that I had seen lying next to his body? How had they got there?

I thought back to the other murders. Rory first. We had all been on the island and we had all separated. Any one of us could have attacked him and, immediately afterwards, left the chocolate on the bed for Sylvie to find. That was the night I had seen the face at the window. A face that had appeared and disappeared – impossibly – in seconds. And then we had found Janet. I remembered her lying in her bed, stabbed by a model of the Eiffel Tower. Her room had been shabby. There had been a tear in the canopy ... I had remarked on it at the time. Why had it caught my eye?

Libby Goldman next. The television presenter had been knocked down with a model globe. There was something strange about that, too. Someone must have carried it up to the roof and dropped it on her when she came out of the front door. But now that I thought about it, I hadn't seen the globe in any of the rooms when we had been searching the house. And that could only mean one thing. It had been on the roof from the very start, waiting for her...

Maybe you know how it is when you've been given a particularly nasty piece of homework – an impossible equation or a fiendish bit of physics or something. You stare at it and stare at it, but it's all just ink on paper and you're about to give up when you notice something and suddenly you realize it's not so difficult after all. Well, that was what was happening to me now.

I remembered the search party, slowly criss-crossing the island. We had seen security cameras everywhere and from the day I had arrived, I had felt that I was being watched. There was a security camera in the kitchen. I looked up. It was watching me even now. Were there cameras in other rooms, too?

At the same time, I remembered something Mark had said, when we had found the old photograph of St Egbert's. And in that second, as quickly as that, I suddenly knew everything.

"I've got it, Tim!" I said.

"So have I, Nick!" Tim cried.

I'd been so wrapped up in my own thoughts, that I hadn't noticed Tim had been thinking too. Now he was staring at me with the sort of look you see on a fish when it's spent too long out of water.

"You know who did it?" I asked.

"Yes."

"Go on!"

"It's simple!" Tim explained. "First there were eight of us on the island, then seven, then six, then five..."

"I know," I interrupted. "I can count backwards."

"Well, now there are only two of us left. I know it wasn't me who committed the murders." He reached forward and snatched up a spoon. Then he realized what he'd done, put it down and snatched up a knife. He waved it at me. "So the killer must be you!" he exclaimed.

"What?" I couldn't believe what I was hearing.

"There's only us left. You and me. I know it wasn't me so it must have been you."

"But why would I want to kill everyone?" I demanded.

"You tell me!"

"I wouldn't! And I didn't! Don't be ridiculous, Tim."

I stood up. That was a mistake.

"Don't come near me!" Tim yelled, and suddenly he sprang out of his chair and jumped out of the window. This was an impressive feat. The window wasn't even open.

I couldn't believe what had happened. I knew Tim was stupid but this was remarkable even by his standards. Maybe sleeping in a suit of armour had done something to that tiny organism he called his brain. At the same time, I was suddenly worried. I knew who the killer was now and I knew who was lined up to be the next victim. Tim was outside the house, on his own. He had made himself into a perfect target.

I had no choice. I went after him, jumping through the shattered window. I could see Tim a short distance away, running towards the tail of Crocodile Island. I had no idea where he was going. But nor of course did he. He was panicking – just trying to put as much distance between the two of us as he could. Not easy considering he was trapped on a small island.

"Tim!" I called.

He didn't stop. I ran after him, following the path as it began to climb steeply up towards the cliffs. This was where the island tapered to a point. I slowed down. Tim had already reached the far end. He had nowhere else to go.

The wind blew his hair around his head as he turned to face me. He was still holding the knife. I noticed now that it was a butter knife. If he stabbed me with all his strength he might just manage to give me a small bruise. His face was pale and his eyes were wide open and staring. The last time I had seen him like this was when they had shown *Jurassic Park* on TV.

"Get back, Nick!" he yelled. It was hard to hear him above the crash of the waves.

"You're crazy, Tim!" I called back. "Why would I want to hurt you? I'm your brother. Think about all the adventures we've had together! I've saved your life lots of times." I thought of telling him that I loved him but he'd have known that wasn't true. "I quite like you!" I said. "You've looked after me ever since Mum and Dad emigrated to Australia. We've had fun together!"

Tim hesitated. I could see the doubt in his eyes. He lowered the butter knife. A huge wave rolled in and crashed against the rocks, spraying us both with freezing, salt water. I looked past Tim at the rocks, an idea forming in my mind. There were six iron grey rocks, jutting out of the sea. I had noticed them the day we had searched the island. And of course, rocks like that have a name. Long and slender with pointed tops, standing upright in the water…

They're called needles.

I'm not exactly sure what happened next but I do know that it all happened at the same time.

There was a soft explosion, just where Tim was standing. The earth underneath his feet seemed to separate, falling away.

Tim screamed and his arm jerked. The butter knife spun in the air, the sun glinting off the blade.

I yelled out and threw myself forward. Somehow my hands managed to grab hold of Tim's shirt.

"Don't kill me!" Tim whimpered.

"I'm not killing you, you idiot!" I yelled. "I'm saving you!"

We rolled back together, away from the edge of the cliff ... an edge that was now several centimetres closer to us than it had been seconds before. I was dazed and there was grass in my mouth, but I realized that the killer had struck again. There had been a small explosive charge buried in the ground at the end of the cliff. Someone had detonated it and if I hadn't managed to grab hold of Tim, he would have fallen down towards to the sea, only to crash onto the needles fifty metres below.

We lay on the grass, panting. The sun was beating down on us. It was difficult to see. But then I became aware of a shadow moving towards us. I rolled over and looked up at the figure, limping towards us, a radio transmitter in one hand and a gun in the other.

"Well, well, well," he said. "It looks as if my little plan has finally come unstuck. And just when everything was going so well, too!"

Tim stared at the man. At his single eye, his

single leg, his huge beard. "It's … it's…" he began.

"It's Horatio Randle," I said. "Captain of the *Silver Medal,* the boat that brought us here."

"You got it in one, young lad!" he said.

"But that's not his real name," I went on. "Randle is an anagram. If you switch around the letters, you get…"

"Endral!" Tim exclaimed.

"Nadler," I said. "I think this must be Johnny Nadler. Your old school friend from St Egbert's."

The captain put down the radio transmitter. He had used it, of course, to set off the explosive charge a few moments before. He didn't let go of the gun. With his free hand, he reached up and pulled off the fake beard, the wig and the eye patch. At the same time, he twisted round and released the leg that he'd had tied up behind his back. It only took a few seconds but at once I recognized the thin-faced teenager I had seen in the photograph.

"It seems you've worked it all out," he muttered. His accent had changed too. He was no longer the jolly captain. He was a killer. And he was mad.

"Yes," I said.

"But it's impossible!" Tim burbled. "He couldn't have killed all the others. We looked! There was nobody else on the island!"

"It was Nadler all along," I said. I glanced

at him. The wind raced past and the waves crashed down.

He smiled. "Do go on," he snarled.

"I know what you did," I said. "Last Wednesday, you met us all at the quay, disguised as a captain. You'd sent everyone invitations to this reunion on the island and you even offered to pay a thousand pounds to make sure that they'd all come. Rory McDougal had nothing to do with it, of course. You'd killed him before we even set sail."

"That's right," Nadler said. He was smiling now. There was something horrible about that smile. He was sure this was one story I wouldn't be telling anyone else.

"You killed Rory and you left the poisoned chocolate for Sylvie. Then you dropped us on the island and sailed away again. There was no need for you to stay. Everything was already prepared."

"Are you saying ... he wasn't here when he killed everyone?" Tim asked. He was still lying on the grass. There was a buttercup lodged behind his ear.

"That's right. Don't you remember what Mark told us when we were looking at the picture? He said that Johnny Nadler wanted to be an inventor when he left school. He said he was always playing with planes and cars." I glanced at the transmitter lying on the ground just a few feet away. "I assume they were radio-controlled planes and cars," I said.

"That's right!" Tim said. "He was brilliant, Nick! He once landed a helicopter on the science teacher's head!"

"Well, that's how he killed everyone on the island – after he'd finished with Rory McDougal and Sylvie Binns." I took a deep breath, wondering if there was anything I could do. Tim was right next to the edge of the cliff. I was a couple of metres in front of him. We were both lying down. Nadler was standing over us, aiming with the gun. If we so much as moved, he could shoot us both. I had to keep talking and hope that I might somehow find a way to distract him.

"Janet Rhodes was stabbed with an Eiffel Tower," I went on. "But I noticed that there was a tear in the canopy above her bed. I should have put two and two together and realized that the Eiffel Tower was always there, above the bed. It must have been mounted on some sort of spring mechanism. Nadler knew that was where she'd be sleeping. All he had to do was press a button and send the model plunging down. He was probably miles away when he killed her."

"That's right!" Nadler giggled. "I was back on the mainland. I was nowhere near!"

"But what about the face you saw?" Tim asked. "The skull at the window! Brenda saw it too!"

"You've already answered that one, Tim," I said. "A remote control helicopter or something with a mask hanging underneath. Nadler controlled that too. It was easy!"

"But how could he see us?"

I glanced at Nadler and he nodded. He was happy for me to explain how it had been done.

"The whole island is covered in cameras," I said. "That was Rory's security system. We've been watched from the moment we arrived. Nadler knew where we were every minute of the day."

"Right again!" Nadler grinned. He was pleased with himself, I could see that. "It was easy to hack into McDougal's security system and redirect the pictures to my own TV monitor. I was even able to watch you in the bath!"

"That's outrageous!" Tim was blushing. He knew that Nadler would have seen him playing with his plastic duck.

"Nadler had positioned the globe up on the roof," I went on. "If we'd gone up and looked we'd probably have found some sort of ramp with a simple switch. He waited until Libby Goldman came out of the front door and then he pressed the button that released the globe. It rolled forward and that was that. She never had a chance. He killed Eric and Brenda the same way. First he turned out the lights. Then he fired a bullet and brought down an organ pipe ... both by remote control." I paused.

"How about Mark Tyler?" I asked.

"The javelin was hidden in the branches of a tree," Nadler explained. "It was on a giant elastic band. Remote control again. It was just like a crossbow." He giggled for a second time. "Only bigger."

Well that explained the leaves. Some of them must have travelled with the javelin when it was fired.

"And that just left you, Tim," I said. "Nadler had to wait until you came out here. Then he was going to blow the ground out from beneath your feet and watch you fall onto the needles below. And with you dead, his revenge would be complete."

"Revenge?" Tim was genuinely puzzled. "But why did he want revenge? We never did anything to him!"

"I think it was because he came second," I said. I turned to Nadler. "You came second in every subject at school. And the boat you picked us up in. It was called the *Silver Medal*. I guess you chose the name on purpose. Because that's what you're given when you come second."

"That's right." Nadler nodded and now his face had darkened and his lips were twisted into an expression of pain. His finger tightened on the trigger and he looked at me with hatred in his eyes. "I came second in maths, second in chemistry, second in French, second in geography, second in history, second in music and second in sport. I even came second in needlework, even though my embroidered tea towel was much more beautiful than your brother's stupid handkerchief!"

"It was a lovely handkerchief!" Tim said.

"Shut up!" Nadler screamed and for a moment I was afraid he was going to shoot Tim then and there. "Do you have any idea how horrible it is coming second?" he went on. Saliva flecked at his lips. The hand with the gun never moved. "Coming last doesn't matter. Coming fifth or sixth ... who cares? But when you come second, everyone knows. You've just missed! You've missed getting the prize by just a few marks. And everyone feels sorry for you. Poor old Johnny! He couldn't quite make it. He wasn't quite good enough."

He took a deep breath. "I've been coming second all my life. I go for jobs and I get down to the last two in the interviews but it's always the other person who gets it. I went out with a girl but then she decided to marry someone else because as far as she was concerned, I was Number Two. When I've tried to sell my inventions, I've discovered that someone else has always got there first. Number Two! Number Two! Number Two! I hate being Number Two...!

"And it's all your fault!" He pointed the gun at Tim and now the fury was back in his eyes. "It all started at St Egbert's! That hateful school! That was where I started coming second and that was why I decided to have my revenge. You all thought you were clever beating me at everything. Well, I've showed you! I've killed the whole lot of you and I've done it in exactly the way you deserve!"

"You haven't killed me!" Tim exclaimed.

I didn't think it was a good idea to point this out. Nadler steadied the gun. "I'm going to do that now," he said. "Your body will still end up smashing into the needles so everything will have worked out the way it was meant to." He nodded at me. "I'll have to kill you too, of course," he continued. "You weren't meant to be here, but I don't mind. You sound too clever for your own good. I'm going to enjoy killing you too!"

He took aim.

"No!" I shouted.

He fired at Tim.

"Missed!" Tim laughed and rolled to one side. He was still laughing when he rolled over the side of the cliff.

"Tim!" I yelled.

"Now it's your turn," Nadler said.

I closed my eyes. There was nothing I could do.

There was a long pause. I opened them again.

Nadler was still standing, but even as I watched he crumpled to the ground. Eric

Draper, the fat solicitor, was standing behind him. There was blood all over his shirt and he was deathly pale. But he was still alive. He was holding the blunderbuss, which he must have taken from the bear. He hadn't fired it. He had used it like a club and knocked Nadler out.

"He only wounded me..." he gasped. "I woke up this morning. I came to find you..."

But I wasn't interested in Eric Draper, even if he had just saved my life. I crawled over to the cliff edge and looked down, expecting to see Tim, smashed to pieces, on the rocks below.

"Hello, Nick!" Tim said.

There was a gorse bush growing out of the side of the cliff. He had fallen right onto it. I held out a hand. Tim took it. I pulled him to safety and we both lay there in the sun, exhausted, glad to be alive.

We found the *Silver Medal* moored at the jetty and I steered it back towards the mainland. Eric was slumped on the deck. Johnny Nadler was down below, tied up with so much rope that only his head was showing. We weren't taking any chances after what had happened. We had already radioed ahead to the police. They would be waiting when we got to the mainland. Tim was standing next to me. We had left six dead bodies behind us on Crocodile

Island. Well, I warned you that it was going to be a horror story.

"I'm sorry I thought you were the killer," Tim said. He was looking even more sheepish than ... well, a sheep.

"It's all right, Tim," I said. "It's a mistake anyone could have made." He swayed on his feet and suddenly I felt sorry for him. "Do you want to sit down?" I asked. "It's going to take us a while to get back."

Tim shook his head. "No." He blushed. "I can't!"

"Why not?"

"That bush I fell into. It was very prickly. My bottom's full of..."

"What?"

"...needles!"

I pushed down on the throttle and the boat surged forward. Behind us, Crocodile Island shimmered in the morning mist until at last it had disappeared.

READ OTHER GREAT BOOKS BY ANTHONY HOROWITZ...

THE ALEX RIDER SERIES

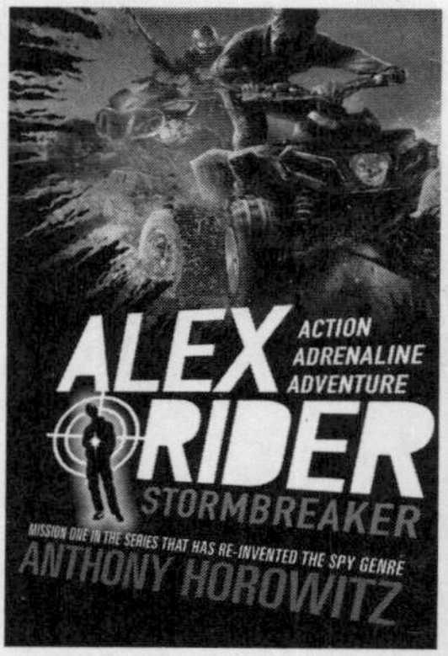

Alex Rider – you're never too young to die…

High in the Alps, death waits for Alex Rider…

Sharks. Assassins. Nuclear bombs. Alex Rider's in deep water.

Alex Rider has 90 minutes to save the world.

Once stung, twice as deadly. Alex Rider wants revenge.

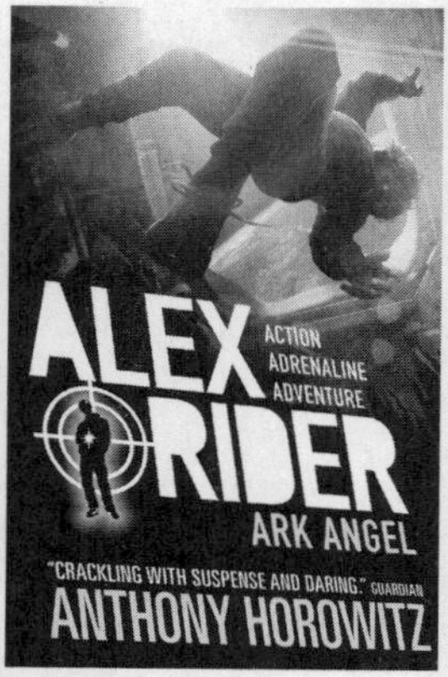

He's back – and this time there are no limits.

WELCOME TO THE DARK SIDE OF ANTHONY HOROWITZ

THE POWER OF FIVE

BOOK ONE

He always knew he was different.
First there were the dreams.
Then the deaths began.

BOOK TWO

It began with Raven's Gate.
But it's not over yet. Once
again the enemy is stirring.

BOOK THREE

Darkness covers the earth.
The Old Ones have returned.
The battle must begin.

BOOK FOUR

An ancient evil is unleashed.
Five have the power to defeat it.
But one of them has been taken.

BOOK FIVE

Five Gatekeepers.
One chance to save mankind.
Chaos beckons. Oblivion awaits.

LOOKING BACK, Henry Parker could honestly say that he had never wanted to hurt anyone. Certainly, it had never occurred to him that he would one day plan and then execute the perfect murder of an internationally well-known children's author … even if that was what actually happened. To begin with, all Henry wanted to do was write…

Photograph © Jon Cartwright

Anthony Horowitz is the author of the number one bestselling Alex Rider books and The Power of Five series. He has enjoyed huge success as a writer for both children and adults, most recently with the latest adventure in the Alex Rider series, *Russian Roulette*, and the highly acclaimed Sherlock Holmes novel, *The House of Silk*. His latest novel, *Moriarty*, is also set in the world of Sherlock Holmes and was published in October 2014. Anthony was also chosen by the Ian Fleming estate to write the new James Bond novel which will be published this year. Anthony has won numerous awards, including the Bookseller Association/Nielsen Author of the Year Award, the Children's Book of the Year Award at the British Book Awards, and the Red House Children's Book Award. In 2014 Anthony was awarded an OBE for Services to Literature. He has also created and written many major television series, including *Injustice*, *Collision* and the award-winning *Foyle's War*.

You can find out more about Anthony and his work at:
www.alexrider.com
@AnthonyHorowitz

"Anthony Horowitz is the lion of children's literature." Michael Morpurgo

"Horowitz has become a writer who converts boys to reading."
The Times

"A first-class children's novelist."
TES

THE DIAMOND BROTHERS IN...

The French Confection

AND

The Greek Who Stole Christmas

More wickedly funny books

by Anthony Horowitz

The Devil and His Boy

Groosham Grange

Return to Groosham Grange

The Switch

More Bloody Horowitz

The Diamond Brothers books:

The Falcon's Malteser

Public Enemy Number Two

South by South East

The Blurred Man

The French Confection

I Know What You Did Last Wednesday

The Greek who Stole Christmas

THE DIAMOND BROTHERS IN...

The French Confection

AND

The Greek Who Stole Christmas

ANTHONY HOROWITZ

WALKER
BOOKS

This is a work of fiction. Names, characters, places and incidents are either the product of the author's imagination or, if real, are used fictitiously. All statements, activities, stunts, descriptions, information and material of any other kind contained herein are included for entertainment purposes only and should not be relied on for accuracy or replicated as they may result in injury.

First published individually as *The French Confection* (2002), and *The Greek Who Stole Christmas* (2007) by Walker Books Ltd
87 Vauxhall Walk, London SE11 5HJ

This edition published 2015

2 4 6 8 10 9 7 5 3 1

This book has been typeset in Sabon

Printed in Germany by GGP Media GmbH

British Library Cataloguing in Publication Data:
a catalogue record for this book is available from the British Library

ISBN 978-1-4063-6477-4

www.walker.co.uk

CONTENTS

TIM DIAMOND INC.
23 THE CUTTING, CAMDEN TOWN, NW1

Dear Reader,

It's been a while since I had lunch with the chairman of Walker Books. He's an old man now. Most of his hair's gone white and the rest of it's just gone. He wears bi-focal glasses but he doesn't really need them. He's forgotten how to read. He'd forget his own name if it wasn't written on his Zimmer frame.

And yet I still remember the day he took me out – just the two of us, face to face, though with a face like his I wouldn't have bothered. We met at the poshest restaurant in London ... then crossed the road to the café on the other side. He ordered two bacon sandwiches without the bacon. He was a vegetarian. And that was when he tried to sweet-talk me into writing an introduction for this collection of stories. But it takes more than a bag of sweets to get Tim Diamond on your side, so I told Walker to take a walk.

A few days later he came tiptoeing round my flat with a bag of books: a bit like Santa Claus without the beard, the laughter or (it was the middle of June) Christmas. This was his deal. Three dozen adventures of Maisy mouse and an old Where's Wally? annual in return for a couple of pages by me. But as far as I was concerned, there was still one book missing. The Walker cheque book ... preferably autographed. Unfortunately, when I pointed this out, the chairman just scowled. That was the sort of man he was: small, hard-edged and leathery. Just like his chair.

"I need an introduction!" he cried.

"All right. How do you do, I'm Tim Diamond," I said.

"No, no, no. For the book!"

"Why do you need an introduction?" Nick – my kid brother – asked. "You probably won't sell any copies anyway."

Actually, in the end, it was Nick who talked me into writing this. He reminded me it's only thanks to Walker that I've become known as England's sharpest, most successful private eye, the sort of detective that makes Hercule Poirot look like a short Belgian with a funny moustache! I have to admit that Walker have been behind me all the way. About thirty miles behind me.

They launched this book with a slap-up dinner at the Ritz. The service was so slow, the waiters deserved to be slapped. Twelve journalists came, but only eleven left. That was how bad the food was.

At the same time, they took out a full-page ad in British Airways "High Life" magazine. They were hoping the books would fly off the shelves and the funny thing is, they did. Maybe it was the new covers that had been specially designed to stop people noticing the new price. It certainly couldn't have been the title. The last time I got the four of diamonds in a high class poker game, I went home without my clothes. If they are going to name a book after a playing card, they could have at least chosen a king.

Anyway, here's the introduction. I'm not quite sure how to begin. Introducing the introduction is always the hardest part. I'm glad I'm not a writer. And if you met the guy who does the writing for me, you'd be glad too.

His name is Anthony Horowitz – and I use him to put my adventures down on paper. Let me tell you a bit about him. A lot of people have compared him to JK Rowling. They say he's not as good. He has a wife, two sons, a stuffed dog and a word processor, and the word processor is the only one that doesn't want to leave home. You ever see "Foyle's War", "Midsomer Murders" or "Collision" on TV? Me neither – but he wrote them all. They're the only programmes people fast-forward through to see the advertisements. He also writes a lot of books. About thirty of them at the last count. Enough books to immobilise a mobile library.

I met him just after I'd cracked the case that became known as "The Falcon's Malteser". I don't think his career was doing too well just then. How many other writers tap-dance outside Harrods in their spare time? Anyway, I told him my story, he began to write – and the rest was history. Actually, nobody wanted history. They wanted an adventure. So he had to write it a second time. But it worked. "The Falcon's Malteser" sold twenty-seven copies in Waterstone's the day it was published and I only bought twenty-six of them. Soon we were right at number one in the Bookseller chart. OK – it was the remainders chart but you've got to start somewhere. "The Times" critic said the book was "hysterical" and she should know.

Since then, I've cracked more cases than the entire baggage-handling department at Heathrow Airport, and Horowitz has written them all. "Public Enemy Number Two", "South by South East" – one day maybe he'll come up with a title that somebody actually understands. I had a pretty hairy time in Australia recently and he says that'll come out in a book too. Apparently the title is going to be: "The Radius of the Lost Shark".

Which brings me to the book you are now holding in your hand (unless you didn't buy it, in which case it's still on the shelf ... a bit like my editor). The two stories in this book all happened to me in the space of one year and all I can say is, I'm glad it wasn't a leap year. One extra day would have been the death of me.

Why do so many people want to kill me? I could have been plastered all over Paris in "The French Confection". And as for "The Greek Who Stole Christmas" ... well, next year I'm giving that particular holiday season a miss. Tinsel, turkeys and gift-wrapped hand grenades? No thanks.

You may have noticed that this edition is printed on special cheap paper and as for the glue ... all I can say is, don't leave it out in the sun. The book is also carbon neutral. A forest in Norway was cut down to produce it but the good news is that another one was planted ... in England. The Norwegians have got too many anyway. You might like to know, ten per cent of every copy sold goes to a very worthwhile charity. Me. I have an overdraft and a hungry kid brother to support.

One last thing. Remember that this book comes with a MONEY BACK GUARANTEE. If for any reason you don't like it, Walker guarantee they won't give you back your money.

All the best,

Tim Diamond

THE FRENCH CONFECTION

THE FRENCH FOR MURDER

Everybody loves Paris. There's an old guy who even wrote a song about it. "I love Paris in the springtime...", that's how it goes. Well, all I can say is, he obviously never went there with my big brother, Tim. I did – and it almost killed me.

It all started with a strawberry yoghurt.

It was a French strawberry yoghurt, of course, and it was all we had in the fridge for breakfast. Tim and I tossed a coin to decide who'd get the first mouthful. Then we tossed the coin to see who'd keep the coin. Tim won both times. So there I was sitting at the breakfast table chewing my nails, which was all I had to chew, when Tim suddenly let out a great gurgle and started waving his spoon in the air like he was trying to swat a fly.

"What is it, Tim?" I asked. "Don't tell me! You've found a strawberry!"

"No, Nick! Look...!"

He was holding up the silver foil that he'd just torn off the yoghurt carton and looking at it, and now I understood. The company that made the yoghurt was having one of those promotions. You've probably seen them on chocolate bars or crisps or Coke cans. These days you can't even open a can of beans without finding out if you've won a car or a holiday in Mexico or a cheque for a thousand pounds. Personally, I'm just grateful if I actually find some beans. Anyway, the yoghurt people were offering a whole range of prizes and there it was, written on the underside of the foil.

Congratulations from Bestlé Fruit Yoghurts! You have just won a weekend for two in Paris! Just telephone the number printed on the carton for further details and ... Bon Voyage!

"I've won, Nick!" Tim gasped. "A weekend for two...!" He stopped and bit his thumb. "Who shall I take?" he muttered.

"Oh thanks a lot, Tim," I said. "It was me who bought the yoghurt."

"But it was my money."

"If it hadn't been for me, you'd have spent it on a choc-ice."

Tim scowled. "But Paris, Nick! It's the most romantic city in Europe. I want to take my girlfriend."

"Tim," I reminded him. "You haven't got a girlfriend."

That was a bit cruel of me. The truth was, Tim hadn't been very lucky in love. His first serious relationship had ended tragically when his girlfriend had tried to murder him. After that he'd replied to one of those advertisements in the lonely hearts column of a newspaper, but he can't have read it properly because the girl had turned out to be a guy who spent the evening chasing him round Paddington station. His last girlfriend had been a fire eater in a local circus. He'd taken her out for a romantic, candlelit dinner but she'd completely spoiled it by eating the candles. Right now he was on his own. He sometimes said he felt like a monk – but without the haircut or the religion.

Anyway, we argued a bit more but finally he picked up the telephone and rang the number on the yoghurt carton. There was no answer.

"That's because you've telephoned the sell-by date," I told him. I turned the carton over. "This is the number here..."

And that was how, three weeks later, we found ourselves standing in the forecourt at Waterloo station. Tim was carrying the tickets. I was carrying the bags. It had been more than a year since we'd been abroad – that had been to Amsterdam on the trail of the mysterious assassin known as Charon – and that time we had gone by ferry. Tim had been completely seasick even before he reached the sea. I was relieved that this time we were going by train, taking the Channel Tunnel, although with Tim, of course, you never knew.

We took the escalator down to the international terminal. Ahead of us, the tunnel was waiting: a thirty-two mile stretch linking England and France, built at a cost of twelve billion pounds.

"You have to admit," Tim said. "It's an engineering marvel."

"That's just what I was thinking," I said.

"Yes. It's a fantastic escalator. And so much faster than going down the stairs..."

We had two seats next to each other right in the middle of one of the carriages. The train was pretty full and soon we were joined by two other passengers opposite us. They were both travelling alone. The first was from Texas – you could tell just from his hat. He was chewing an unlit cigar (this was a non-smoking compartment) and reading a magazine: *International Oil*. The other passenger was a very old lady with white hair and skin so wrinkled I was amazed it managed to stay on. I wasn't sure if she had huge eyes or extremely powerful spectacles but every time she looked at me I thought I was about to be hit by a pair of grey and white golf balls. I looked out of the window. The platform was already empty, sweeping in a graceful curve beneath the great glass canopy. Somewhere a door slammed.

The train left exactly on time at ten minutes past ten. There was no whistle. No announcement. I wouldn't have known we had moved if it hadn't been for the slight shudder – and even that was Tim, not the train. He was obviously excited.

About an hour later there was an announcement on the intercom and we dipped into the tunnel carved out underneath the sea. That was a non-event too. A car-park, a sign advertising hamburgers, a white cement wall and suddenly the outside world disappeared to be replaced by rushing blackness. So this was the engineering miracle of the last century? As far as Eurostar was concerned, it was just a hole in the ground.

Tim had been ready with his camera and now he drew back, disappointed. "Is this it?" he demanded.

I looked up from my book. "What were you expecting, Tim?" I asked.

"I thought this train went under water!" Tim sighed. "I wanted to take some pictures of the fish!"

The other passengers had heard this and somehow it broke the silence. The old lady had been knitting what looked like a multi-coloured sack but now she looked up. "I love taking the train," she announced, and for the first time I realized that she was French. Her accent was so thick you could have wrapped yourself in it to keep warm.

"It sure is one hell of a thing," the Texan agreed. "London to Paris in three and a half hours. Great for business."

The Texan held up his magazine. "I'm in oil. Jed Mathis is the name."

"Why do you call your oil Jed Mathis?" Tim asked.

"I'm sorry?" Jed looked confused. He turned to the old lady. "Are you visiting your grand-children in Paris?" he asked.

"Non!" the lady replied.

Tim dug into his pocket and pulled out a French dictionary. While he was looking up the word, she continued in English.

"I have a little cake shop in Paris. Erica Nice. That's my name. Please, you must try some of my almond slices." And before anyone could stop her, she'd pulled out a bag of cakes which she offered to us all.

We were still hurtling through the darkness. Tim put away his dictionary and helped him-self. At the same time, a steward approached us, pushing one of those trolleys piled up with sandwiches and coffee. He was a thin, pale man with a drooping moustache and slightly sunken eyes. The name on his badge was Marc Chabrol. I remember thinking even then that he looked nervous. A nervous traveller, I thought.

But then, why would a nervous traveller work on a train?

Jed produced a wallet full of dollars and offered to buy us all coffee. A free breakfast and we hadn't even arrived. Things were definitely looking up.

"So what do you do?" Erica Nice asked, turning to Tim.

Tim gave a crooked smile. It was meant to make him look smart but in fact he just looked as though he had toothache. "I'm a private detective," he said.

The steward dropped one of the coffee cups. Fortunately, he hadn't added the water yet. Coffee granules showered over the KitKats.

"A private detective?" Erica trilled. "How very unusual!"

"Are you going to Paris on business?" the Texan asked.

Now of course the answer was "no". We were on holiday. Tim hadn't had any business for several weeks and even then he had only been hired to find a missing dog. In fact he had spent three days at Battersea Dogs' Home where he had been bitten three times – twice by dogs. The trouble was, though, he was never going to admit this. He liked to think of himself as a man of mystery. So now he winked and leaned forward. "Just between you and me," he drawled, "I'm on a case." Yes. A nutcase, I thought. But he went on.

"I've been hired by Interplop."

"You mean Interpol," the Texan said.

"The International Police," Tim agreed. "It's a top-secret case. It's so secret, they don't even know about it at the top. In other words..." He gestured with his almond slice, spraying Jed with crumbs, "...a case for Tim Diamond."

The steward had obviously heard all this. As he put down the first cup of coffee, his hands were shaking so much that the liquid spilled over the table. His face had been pale to begin with. Now it had no colour at all. Even his moustache seemed to have faded.

"Where are you staying in Paris?" the old lady asked.

"It's a hotel called The Fat Greek," Tim said.

"Le Chat Gris," I corrected him. It was French for "grey cat" and this was the name of the hotel where Bestlé Yoghurts had booked us in for three nights.

The name seemed to have an electric effect on the steward. I'd been watching him out of the corner of my eye and actually saw him step backwards, colliding with the trolley. The bottles and cans shook. Two packets of gingerbread biscuits rocketed onto the floor. The man was terrified. But why?

"Paris is so beautiful in the spring," the old lady said. She'd obviously seen the effect that

Tim was having on the steward and perhaps she was trying to change the subject before the poor man had a heart attack. "You must make sure you take a stroll on the Champs Elysées … if you have the time."

"How much do I owe you for the coffee?" the American asked.

"Four euros, monsieur…" The steward reached down and picked up the biscuits. The way he took the money and moved off, he could have been trying to get to Paris ahead of the train. I guessed he wanted to get away from us as fast as he could. And I was right. He didn't even stop to offer anyone else in the carriage a coffee. He simply disappeared. Later, when I went to the loo, I saw the trolley standing on its own in the passageway.

Twenty minutes after we'd entered the tunnel, the train burst out again. There was nothing to show that we'd left one country and entered another. The French cows grazing in the fields looked just the same as the English ones on the other side. An official came past, looking at passports. Erica Nice looked at Tim as if puzzled in some way and went back to her knitting. Jed returned to his magazine. We didn't speak for the rest of the journey.

We arrived at the Gare du Nord about an hour later. As everyone struggled with their luggage, Tim gazed at the name. "When do we arrive in Paris?" he asked.

"Tim, this is Paris," I told him. "The Gare du Nord means north station. There are lots of stations in the city."

"I hope you have a lovely time," Erica Nice said. She had an old carpet-bag. It was big enough to hold a carpet – and maybe that was what she had been knitting. She winked at Tim. "Good luck with the case, mon ami!"

Meanwhile, the Texan had grabbed a leather briefcase. He nodded at us briefly and joined the queue for the exit. Tim and I retrieved our two bags and a few moments later we were standing on the platform, wondering which way to go.

"We'd better find the Metro," I said. Bestlé had given us some spending money for the weekend but I didn't think it would be enough for us to travel everywhere by taxi.

Tim shook his head. "Forget the metro, Nick," he said. "Let's take the tube."

I didn't even bother to argue. I knew a little French – I'd been learning it from a little Frenchman who taught at our school – and I knew, for example, that Metro was the French word for tube train. On the other hand, I didn't know the French for idiot, which was the English word for Tim. I picked up the bags and prepared to follow him when suddenly we found ourselves interrupted.

It was Marc Chabrol. The French steward had reappeared and was standing in front of us, blocking our way. He was terrified. I could see it in his bulging eyes, the sweat on his cheeks, the yellow and black bow tie which had climbed halfway up his neck.

"I have to talk to you, Monsieur," he rasped. He was speaking in English, the words as uncomfortable in his mouth as somebody else's false teeth. "Tonight. At eleven o'clock. There is a café in the sixth *arrondisement*. It is called La Palette..."

"That's very nice of you," Tim said. He seemed to think that Chabrol was inviting us out for a drink.

"Beware of the mad American!" The steward whispered the words as if he were too afraid to speak them aloud. "The mad American...!"

He was about to add something but then his face changed again. He seemed to freeze as if his worst nightmare had just come true. I glanced left and right but if there was someone he had recognized in the crowd, I didn't see them. *"Oh mon Dieu!"* he whispered. He seized Tim's hand and pressed something into the palm. Then he turned and staggered away.

Tim opened his hand. He was holding a small blue envelope with a gold star printed on the side. I recognized it at once. It was a sachet of sugar from the train. "What was all that about?" Tim asked.

I took the sugar and examined it. I thought

he might have written something on it – a telephone number or something. But it was just a little bag of sugar. I slipped it into my back pocket. "I don't know..." I said. And I didn't. Why should the steward have left us with a spoonful of sugar? Why did he want to meet us later that night? What was going on?

"Funny people, the French," Tim said.

Ten minutes later, we were still at the Gare du Nord. The money that Bestlé had given us was in English pounds and pence. We needed euros and that meant queuing up at the Bureau de Change. The queue was a long one and it seemed to be moving at a rate of one euro per hour.

We had just reached the window when we heard the scream.

It was like no sound I had ever heard, thin and high and horribly final. The station was huge and noisy but the scream cut through the crowd like a scalpel. Everybody stopped and turned to see where it had come from. Even Tim heard it. "Oh dear," he said. "It sounds like someone has stepped on a cat."

Tim changed thirty pounds, and taking the money we moved in the direction of the Metro. Already a police car had arrived and several uniformed gendarmes were hurrying towards the trains. I strained to hear what the crowd was saying. They were speaking French, of course. That didn't make it any easier.

"What's happened?"

"It's terrible. Somebody has fallen under a train."

"It was a steward. He was on the train from London. He fell off a platform."

"Is he hurt?"

"He's dead. Crushed by a train."

I heard all of it. I understood some of it. I didn't like any of it. A steward? Off the London train? Somehow I didn't need to ask his name.

"Tim," I asked. "What's the French for murder?"

Tim shrugged. "Why do you want to know?"

"I don't know." I stepped onto the escalator and allowed it to carry me down. "I've just got a feeling it's something we're going to need."

LE CHAT GRIS

Le Chat Gris was in the Latin quarter, a dark, busy area on the south side of the River Seine. Here the streets were full of students and the smell of cheap food. It was a small, narrow building, wedged between an art gallery and a café. A metal cat, more rusty than grey, hung over the main entrance and there were brightly coloured flowers in the front windows. On closer inspection they turned out to be made of plastic.

The reception area was so small that if you went in too quickly you'd be out the other side. There was a receptionist standing behind the desk which was just as well as there wasn't enough room for a chair. He was an old man, at least sixty, with a crumpled face and something terribly wrong with his eyes. When he looked at our passports he had to hold them up beside his ear. He took our names, then sent us to a room on the fifth floor. Fortunately there was a lift but it wasn't much bigger than a telephone box. Tim and I stood shoulder to shoulder with our cases as it creaked and trembled slowly up. Next time, I decided, I'd take the stairs.

The truth was that Bestlé hadn't been too generous with the accommodation. Our room was built into the roof with wooden beams that sloped down at strange angles. It made me think of the Hunchback of Notre Dame. You needed a hunched back to avoid hitting your head on the ceiling. There were two beds, a single window with a view over the other rooftops, a chest of drawers and a bathroom too small to take a bath.

"Which bed do you want?" I asked.

"This one!" Tim threw himself onto the bed next to the window. There was a loud "ping" as several of the springs snapped. I sat down, more carefully, on the other bed. It felt like the duvet wasn't just filled with goose feathers, but they'd also left in half the goose.

We dumped our luggage and went out. This was, after all, Thursday morning and we only had until Sunday afternoon. Back in the reception area, the receptionist was talking to a new arrival. This was a square-shouldered man with narrow eyes and black, slicked-back hair. He was wearing an expensive, charcoal grey suit. Both of them stopped when they saw us.

I dropped the key with a clunk.

"Merci," I said.

Neither of the men said anything. Maybe it was my accent.

There was a mirror next to the front door and but for that I wouldn't have noticed what happened next. But as Tim and I made our way out, the man in the grey suit reached out and took my key, turning it round so that he could read the number. He was interested in us. That was for sure. His eyes, empty of emotion, were still scrutinizing us as the door swung shut and we found ourselves in the street.

First the death of the steward on the train. Then the last whispered warning: *"Beware the mad American!"* And now this. There was a nasty smell in the air and already I knew it wasn't just French cheese.

"Which way, Nick?" Tim was waiting for me, holding a camera. He had already taken three photographs of the hotel, a streetlamp and a post-box and he was waiting for me in the morning sunlight. I wondered if he had remembered to put in a film.

I thought for a moment. I was probably being stupid. We were here in Paris for the weekend and nothing was going to happen. I couldn't even be sure that it really was Marc Chabrol who had fallen under the train. "Let's try down there," I said, pointing down the street.

"Good idea," Tim agreed as he turned the other way.

What can I tell you about Paris? I'm no travel writer. I'm not crazy about writing and I can't usually afford to travel. But anyway...

Paris is a big city full of French people. It's a lot prettier than London and for that matter so are the people. They're everywhere: in the street-side cafés, sipping black coffee from thimble-sized cups, strolling along the Seine in their designer sunglasses, snapping at each other on the bridges through eighteen inches of the latest Japanese lens. The streets are narrower than in London and looking at the traffic you get the feeling that war has broken out. There are cars parked everywhere. On the streets and on the pavements. Actually, it's hard to tell which cars are parked and which ones are just stuck in the traffic jams. But the strange thing is that nobody seems to be in a hurry. Life is just a big jumble that moves along at its own pace and if you're in a hurry to leave then maybe you should never have come there in the first place.

That first day, Tim and I did the usual tourist things. We went up the Eiffel Tower. Tim fainted. So we came down again. We went to the cathedral of Notre Dame and I took a picture of Tim and another of a gargoyle. I just hoped that when I got them developed I'd remember which was which. We went up the Champs Elysées and down the Jardin des Tuileries. By lunch-time, my stomach was rumbling. So, more worryingly, were my feet.

We had an early supper at a brasserie overlooking another brasserie. That's another thing about Paris. There are brasseries everywhere. Tim ordered two ham sandwiches, a beer for him and a Coke for me. Then I ordered them again using words the waiter understood. The sandwiches arrived: twenty centimetres of bread, I noticed, but only ten centimetres of ham.

"This is the life, eh, Nick?" Tim sighed as he sipped his beer.

"Yes, Tim," I said. "And this is the bill."

Tim glanced at it and swallowed his beer the wrong way. "Ten euros!" he exclaimed. "That's ... that's...!" He frowned. "How much is that?"

"A euro's worth about seven old francs," I explained. "It's about seventy pence. So the bill is about seven quid."

Tim shook his head. "I hate this new money," he said.

"I know," I agreed. "Because you haven't got any."

We were walking back in the direction of the hotel when it happened. We were in one of those quiet, antique streets near the Seine when two men appeared, blocking our way. The first was in his forties, tall and slim, wearing a white linen suit that was so crumpled and dirty, it hung off him like a used paper bag. He was one of the ugliest men I had ever seen. He had green eyes, a small nose and a mouth like a knife wound. None of these were in quite the right place. It was as if his whole face had been drawn by a six-year-old child.

His partner was about twenty years younger with the body of an ape and, if the dull glimmer in his eyes was anything to go by, a brain to match. He was wearing jeans and a leather jacket and smoking a cigarette. I guessed he was a body-builder. He had muscles bulging everywhere and a neck that somehow managed to be wider than his head. His hair was blonde and greasy. He had fat lips and a tiny beard sprouting out of the middle of his chin.

"Good evening," White Suit said in perfect English. His voice came out like a whisper from a punctured balloon. "My name is Bastille. Jacques Bastille. My friend's name is Lavache. I wonder if I might speak with you."

"If you want to know the way, don't ask us!" Tim replied. "We're lost too."

"I'm not lost. Oh, no." Bastille smiled, revealing teeth the colour of French mustard. "No. But I want to know what he told you. I want to know what you know."

Tim turned to me, puzzled.

"What exactly do you mean?" I asked.

"The steward on the train. What did he tell you?" There was a pause. Then … "Lavache!"

Bastille nodded and his partner produced what looked like a little model of that famous statue, the Venus de Milo. You know the one. The naked woman with no arms that stands somewhere in the Louvre.

"No thank you," Tim began. "We're not…"

Lavache pressed a button and ten centimetres of razor-sharp metal sprang out of the head of the statue. It was a neat trick. I don't think the real statue ever did that.

Tim stared at it.

"Where is it?" Bastille demanded.

"Your friend's holding it in his hand!" Tim gasped.

"Not the knife! *Sacré bleu!* Are all the English such idiots? I am talking about the object. The item that you were given this morning at the Gare du Nord."

"I wasn't given anything!" Tim wailed.

"It's true," I said, even though I knew that it wasn't.

Bastille blinked heavily. "You're lying."

"No, we're not," Tim replied. "Cross my heart and hope to…"

"Tim!" I interrupted.

"Kill them both!" Bastille snapped.

They really did mean to kill us there and then in that quiet Paris street. Lavache lifted the knife, his stubby fingers curving around the base, a bead of saliva glistening at the corner of his mouth. I glanced back, wondering if we could run. But it was hopeless. We'd be cut down before we could take a step.

"The older one first," Bastille commanded.

"That's him!" Tim said, pointing at me.

"Tim!" I exclaimed.

The knife hovered between us.

But then suddenly a party of American tourists turned the corner – about twenty of them, following a guide who was holding an umbrella with a Stars and Stripes attached to the tip. They were jabbering excitedly as they descended on us. There was nothing Bastille and Lavache could do. Suddenly they were surrounded, and realizing this was our only chance I grabbed hold of Tim and moved away, keeping a wall of American tourists between us and our attackers. Only when we'd come to the top of the street where it joined the wide and busy Boulevard St Michel did we break away and run.

But the two killers weren't going to let us get away quite so easily. I glanced back and saw them pushing their way through the crowd. Bastille shoved out a hand and one of the tourists, an elderly woman, shrieked and fell backwards into a fountain. Several of the other tourists stopped and took photographs of her. Bastille stepped into the road. A car swerved to avoid him and crashed into the front of a restaurant. Two lobsters and a plateful of mussels were sent flying. Someone screamed.

It still wasn't dark. The streets were full of people on their way to restaurants, too wrapped up in their own affairs to notice two English visitors running for their lives. I had no idea where I was going and I wasn't going to stop and ask for directions. I grabbed Tim again and steered him up an alleyway with dozens more restaurants on both sides. A waiter in a long white apron, carrying several trays laden with plates and glasses, stepped out in front of me. There was no way I could avoid him. There was a strangled cry, then a crash.

"Excusez-moi!" Tim burbled.

Fortunately, I didn't know enough French to understand the waiter's reply.

The alleyway brought us back to the Seine. I could see Notre Dame in the distance. Only a few hours before we had been standing on one of its towers, enjoying the view. How could our holiday have become a nightmare so quickly?

"This way, Tim!" I shouted.

I pulled him across a busy street, cars screeching to a halt, horns blaring. A gendarme turned round to face us, a whistle clenched between his teeth, his hands scrabbling for his gun. I swear he would have shot us except that we were already on the other side of the road and a few seconds later Bastille had reached him, brutally pushing him out of the way. The unfortunate gendarme spun round and collided with a cyclist. Both of them collapsed in a tangle of rubber and steel. The last I saw of the gendarme, he had got back to his feet and was shouting at us, making a curious, high-pitched noise. Evidently he had swallowed his whistle which had now got lodged in his throat.

The river was now right in front of us with a pedestrian bridge leading over to the other side. Bastille and Lavache were already crossing the road, blocked for a moment by a bus that had slipped in between them and us.

"The river!" I said.

Tim reached into his pocket and took out his camera.

"No!" I yelled. "I don't want you to photograph it! I want us to cross it!"

We ran onto the bridge, but I hadn't taken more than a few steps before I saw that we'd made a bad mistake. The bridge was closed. There was a tall barrier running across the middle of it with a MEN AT WORK sign – but no sign at all of any men actually at work. They had left their tools, though. There was a wheelbarrow, a pile of steel girders, a cement mixer ... even if we could have climbed over the fence it would have been hard to get through.

"We've got to go back!" I shouted.

But it was too late. Bastille and Lavache had already arrived at the entrance to the bridge and were moving more slowly, both of them smiling. They knew they had us trapped. Lavache had his knife out. It was difficult to hear with the noise of the traffic, but I think he was humming.

We couldn't go back. We couldn't climb the fence. If we jumped over the side, we'd probably drown. This was only March and the water would be ice-cold. Just twenty metres separated us from the two Frenchmen. There was nothing we could do.

And that was when I saw the boat. It was what they called a Bateau Mouche, one of those long, elegant boats with glass windows and ceilings that carry tourists up and down the river throughout the day and night. This one was full of people enjoying a dinner and dance. I heard the music drifting up to us. They were playing a waltz, the "Blue Danube". A strange choice considering they were on the Seine. Already the boat was slipping under the bridge. Another few seconds and it would have disappeared down towards the Eiffel Tower.

"Jump, Tim!" I ordered.

"Right, Nick!" Tim jumped up and down on the spot.

"No. I mean – jump off the bridge!"

"What?" Tim looked at me as if I was mad.

Bastille was only five steps away from us now. I ran to the edge of the bridge, hoisted myself up and jumped. Tim did the same, a few seconds behind me. I caught a glimpse of Bastille, staring at us, his face twisted between anger and amazement. Then I was falling through space with the river, the bridge and the boat corkscrewing around me. I thought I might have mistimed it but then my feet hit something and I crashed onto the deck. I was lucky. I had hit the front of the boat where there was a sheet of tarpaulin stretched out amid a tangle of ropes. It broke my fall.

Tim was less fortunate. He had jumped a few seconds after me, allowing the boat to travel a few metres further forward. I heard the glass shatter as he went feet first through the glass roof. There were more screams and the music stopped. I pulled myself up and gazed groggily through a window. Tim had landed on one of the tables and was lying there, sprawled out, surrounded by broken plates and glasses and with what looked like a whole roast duck in his lap.

"Que fais-tu? Qu'est-ce que se passe?"

A man in a blue uniform had appeared on the deck. He was staring at me in horror. It was the captain of the Bateau Mouche. There were a couple of waiters with him. I didn't even struggle as the three of them grabbed hold of me. I wondered if they were going to lock me up or throw me over the side. Certainly it didn't look as if they were going to invite me in for a dance and something to eat.

I twisted round and took one last look back at the bridge. Bastille and Lavache were leaning over the side, watching, and as I was dragged inside they vanished, swallowed up in the gathering gloom.

DOWN AND OUT

You won't meet many thirteen-year-olds who have been locked up in prisons on both sides of the Channel, but I'm one of them. I did time in Strangeday Hall, sharing a cell with Johnny Powers, England's public enemy number one*, and here I was in prison in Paris, this time with Tim. It was half past nine in the evening. We'd been given dinner – bread and water – but the fact that it was French bread and Perrier didn't make it taste any better.

Miraculously, neither Tim nor I had been hurt jumping from the bridge. The captain had locked us both up in the kitchen on board the ship and by the time we docked, the police were already waiting. I suppose he must have radioed on ahead. I hadn't tried to argue as we were thrown into the back of a van and driven at high speed through the streets of Paris.

* See *Public Enemy Number Two*

Nobody spoke English and even if they had they wouldn't have believed us. I assumed they'd call the British consul or someone. I would leave the explanations until then.

Neither of us had said anything for a while but at last Tim broke the silence. "That's the last time I buy a Bestlé yoghurt," he muttered.

"It wasn't their fault, Tim," I said, although I knew how he felt. We hadn't even been in Paris one day and we'd witnessed one murder, been chased by two killers and were now locked up ourselves. It was probably just as well that we weren't planning to stay a whole week. "I just wish I knew what it was all about," I added.

"They tried to kill us, Nick," Tim explained. "They nearly *did* kill us!"

"I noticed, Tim. But why?"

Tim thought for a moment. "Perhaps they don't like foreigners?" he suggested.

"No. They were looking for something. Something they thought we had." I already knew it had to be tied in with Marc Chabrol, the steward we had met at the Gare du Nord, and the sachet of sugar he had given us. But what could be so important about a packet of sugar? It was still in my back pocket. I reached in and took it out. "This is what they were after," I said.

"Sugar?"

"Unless there's something else inside..."

I was about to open it there and then but at that moment the door opened and a young policeman with close-cropped hair and glasses walked in. I slipped the sachet back into my pocket. I could always examine it later.

"This way, please," the policeman said.

He led us back out and down a corridor, then into an interrogation room that smelled of cigarette smoke. There was a table and three chairs but nothing else, not even a window. A naked light bulb hung on a short flex from the ceiling. The policeman gestured and we all sat down.

"You are English," he said.

"That's right," I said. The man obviously had a first-class brain.

"This is an outrage!" Tim exclaimed. "You can't keep us here. I demand to speak to the British ambassador! If the British ambassador is busy, I'll speak to his wife."

The policeman leaned forward. "First of all, monsieur, I can keep you here for as long as I wish," he said. "And secondly, I doubt very much that the British ambassador would be interested in you. Or his wife!"

"Why wouldn't he be interested in his wife?" Tim asked.

The policeman ignored him. "You and your small brother have caused great damage to one of our Bateaux Mouches," he went on. "It is most fortunate that nobody was injured. I wish to know why the two of you jumped off the bridge. You were trying to commit suicide, perhaps? Or could it have been a joke?"

"It was no joke," I said. "There were two men trying to kill us…"

The policeman looked at me in disbelief.

"It's true," I went on. "They said their names were Bastille and Lavache. They had a knife…"

"Tell me your names," the policeman commanded. He took out a notebook and prepared to write.

"I'm Tim Diamond," Tim said. "You may have heard of me."

"No, monsieur…"

"Well, I'm a well-known detective back in London." Tim pointed at the notebook. "That's the capital of England," he added, helpfully.

The policeman paused and took a deep breath. He was getting older by the minute. "I am aware of that," he said. "May I ask, what is your business here in Paris?"

"Of course you can ask!" Tim said.

The policeman groaned. "What is your business?" he demanded.

"We're on holiday," I told him. "We only arrived today. We're staying in Le Chat Gris in the Latin quarter…"

The policeman looked at me strangely, as if he were seeing me properly for the first time.

"Le Chat Gris..." he repeated. He closed the notebook. "Could you please wait here for a minute."

He stood up and left the room.

In fact it was ten minutes before he returned. The moment he walked in, I noticed there was something different about him. He was brisk, emotionless. And when he spoke, he did his best not to meet our eyes. "I have spoken with my superior officer," he said. "And he says that you are free to go!"

"How can we be free to go when we're locked up in here?" Tim asked.

"No, no, no, monsieur. He says that you may leave."

"They're unlocking the door and letting us out," I explained.

"As far as we are concerned, this incident is closed." The policeman did the same to his notebook.

"What about Bastille and Lavache?" I asked.

"We have no record of these men. It is our view that they do not exist!"

"What?"

"You jump off the bridge for a joke or maybe as a game and you make up the story of the killers to explain your actions. That is the view of my Superintendent."

"Well, he can't be as super as all that," I growled.

But there was no point arguing. For whatever their reasons, the French police had decided to let us go. As far as I was concerned, I just wanted to get out of jail. And out of Paris too, for that matter. I'd only been there for a day but so far our visit had been less fun than a French lesson – and twice as dangerous.

"Let's go, Tim," I said.

And we went.

It was almost eleven o'clock by the time we got back to the Latin quarter, but the night wasn't over yet. Tim wanted to stop for a beer and I was still anxious to open the packet of sugar that was burning a hole in my back pocket. We looked for a café and quite by coincidence found ourselves outside an old-fashioned, artistic sort of place whose name I knew. It was La Palette, the very same café where the train steward, Marc Chabrol, had asked us to meet.

He wasn't there, of course. Right now, if Chabrol was sipping coffee, it was with two wings and a halo. But there was someone there that we recognized. He was sitting out in the front, smoking a cigar, gazing into the night sky. There was no way I'd forget the hat. It was Jed Mathis, the businessman we had met on the train.

Tim saw him. "It's Ned," he said.

"You mean Jed," I said.

"Why don't we join him?"

"Forget it!" I grabbed Tim and we walked forward, continuing towards our hotel.

"But Nick! He paid for the drinks on the train. Maybe he'd buy me a beer."

"Yes, Tim. But think for a minute. What's he doing at La Palette?" I looked at my watch. It was eleven o'clock exactly. "It could just be a coincidence. But maybe he's waiting for someone. Maybe he's waiting for us! Don't you remember what Marc Chabrol said?"

"He asked us if we wanted to buy a KitKat."

"Yes. But after that. In the station, he warned us about someone who he called 'the mad American'. Jed Mathis is American! He said he was from Texas."

"You think Mathis killed Chabrol?"

"Mathis was on the train. And Chabrol ended up underneath it. I don't know. But I don't think we should hang around and have drinks with him. I think we should go home!"

We hurried on. Le Chat Gris loomed up ahead of us, but before we got there I noticed something else.

There was a man standing opposite the hotel. It was hard to recognize him because he was holding a camera up to his face, taking a picture. I heard the click of the button and the whir as the film wound on automatically. He wasn't a tourist. That much was certain. Not unless his idea of a holiday snap was two

English tourists about to check out. Because the photograph he had taken had been of us. There could be no doubt about it. I could feel the telephoto lens halfway up my nose.

He lowered the camera and now I recognized the man. He had been standing in the reception area that morning when we left: a dark-haired man in a grey suit.

Marc Chabrol, the steward.

Bastille and Lavache.

And now this.

Just what was happening in Paris and why did it all have to happen to us?

A car suddenly drew up, a blue Citroën. The man with the camera got in and a moment later they were roaring past us. I just caught a glimpse of the driver, smoking a cigarette with one hand, steering with the other. Then they were gone.

Tim had already walked into the hotel. Feeling increasingly uneasy, I followed him in.

We took the key from the squinting receptionist and took the stairs back to the top of the hotel. There were a lot of them and the stairway was so narrow that the walls brushed both my shoulders as I climbed. Finally we got to the last floor. Tim stopped for breath. Then he unlocked our door.

Our room had been torn apart. The sheets had been pulled off the bed and the mattress slashed open, springs and enough hair to cover a horse tumbling out onto the floor. Every drawer had been opened, upturned and smashed. The carpet had been pulled up and the curtains down. Tim's jackets and trousers had been scattered all over the room. And I mean scattered. We found one arm on a window-sill, one leg in the shower, a single pocket under what was left of the bed. Our suitcases had been cut open and turned inside out. We'd need another suitcase just to carry the old ones down to the bin.

Tim gazed at the destruction. "I can't say I think too much of room service, Nick," he said.

"This isn't room service, Tim!" I exploded. "The room's been searched!"

"What do you think they were looking for?"

"This!" I took out the packet of sugar. Once again I was tempted to open it – but this wasn't the right time. "This is the only thing Chabrol gave us back at the station. It must be the object that Bastille was talking about." I slid it back into my pocket, then thought again. It seemed that Bastille was determined to get his hands on the sugar. I wouldn't be safe carrying it. It was better to leave it in the hotel room. After all, they'd already searched the place once. It was unlikely they'd think of coming back.

I looked around, then slid the sugar into the

toilet-roll in the bathroom, inside the cardboard tube. Nobody would notice it there and the police could pick it up later. Because that was the next step.

"We've got to call the police," I said.

"We've just come from the police," Tim reminded me.

"I know. But if they see our room, they've got to believe us. And as soon as they're here, I'll show them the packet. Maybe they'll be able to work the whole thing out."

I looked for the telephone and eventually found it – or what was left of it. You'd have to be an expert at electronics or at least very good at jigsaws to use it again.

"Why don't we talk to the man downstairs?" Tim asked.

I thought of the squinting receptionist. Only that morning he'd been talking to the man in the grey suit, the one who'd just taken our photograph.

"I don't trust him," I said. At that moment I wouldn't have trusted my own mother.

Tim held up a short-sleeved shirt. It had been a long-sleeved shirt when he had packed it. He looked as if he was going to burst into tears. At least he could use the rest of the shirt as a handkerchief if he did.

"Let's go back down, Tim," I said. "We can call the police from the lobby. I noticed a phone booth."

"What's the French for 999?" Tim asked.

"17," I replied. I'd seen it written next to the phone.

But the phone in the hotel was out of order. There was a sign on the window reading *"Hors de service"*. I translated for Tim and he went over to the receptionist. "We want to call the police," he said.

"Please?" The receptionist narrowed his eye. I think he would have liked to have narrowed both his eyes, but the one on the left wasn't working.

"No," Tim explained. "Police." He saluted and bent his knees, doing an imitation of a policeman. The receptionist stared at him as if he had gone mad.

"Les flics," I said.

"Ah!" The receptionist nodded. Then he leant forward and pointed. "You go out the door. You turn left. Then you take the first turning left again," he growled. He actually spoke pretty good English even if the words had trouble getting past his throat. "There's a police station just at the next corner."

We left the hotel, turned left and then immediately left again. We found ourselves in a narrow alleyway that twisted its way through the shadows before coming to a brick wall.

"This is wrong," I said.

"You don't want to go to the police anymore?" Tim asked.

“No, Tim. I still want to go to the police but this is the wrong way. It’s a dead-end.”

“Maybe we have to climb over the wall.”

“I don’t think so…”

I was getting worried. After everything that had happened to us so far, the last place I wanted to be was a dead-end … or anywhere else with the word “dead” in it. And I was right. There was a sudden squeal as a van appeared racing towards us. The squeal, incidentally, came from Tim. The van was reversing. For a moment I thought it was going to crush us, but it stopped, just centimetres away. The back doors flew open. Two men got out.

Everything was happening too quickly. I couldn’t even tell who the men were or if I had seen them before. I saw one of them lash out and Tim spun round, crumpling to the ground. Then it was my turn. Something hard hit me on the back of the head. My legs buckled. I fell forward and one of the men must have caught me as I felt myself being half-pushed, half-carried into the back of the van.

Tim was next to me. “Some holiday!” he said.

Then either they hit me again or they hit him. Or maybe they hit both of us. Either way, I was out cold.

PARIS BY NIGHT

I knew I was in trouble before I even opened my eyes. For a start, I was sitting up. If everything that had happened up until now had been a horrible dream – which it should have been – I would be lying in my nice warm bed in Camden with the kettle whistling in the kitchen and maybe Tim doing the same in the bath. But not only was I sitting in a hard, wooden chair, my feet were tied together with something that felt suspiciously like parcel tape and my hands were similarly bound behind my back. When I did finally open my eyes, it only got worse. Tim was next to me looking pale and confused ... by which I mean even more confused than usual. And Bastille and Lavache were sitting opposite us, both of them smoking.

The four of us were in a large, empty room that might once have been the dining-room of a grand château but was now empty and dilapidated. The floor was wooden and the walls white plaster, with no pictures or decorations. A broken chandelier hung from the ceiling. In fact quite a lot of the ceiling was hanging from the ceiling. Half of it seemed to be peeling off.

I had no idea how much time had passed since they'd knocked us out and bundled us into the back of a delivery van. An hour? A week? I couldn't see my watch – it was pinned somewhere behind me, along with the wrist it was on – so I twisted round and looked out of the window. The glass was so dust-covered that I could barely see outside, but from the light I would have said it was early evening. If so, we had been unconscious for about fifteen hours! I wondered where we were. Somewhere in the distance I thought I heard singing, the sound of a choir. But the music was foreign – and not French. It sounded vaguely religious, which made me think of churches. And that made me think of funerals. I just hoped they weren't singing for us.

"Good evening," Bastille muttered. He hadn't changed out of the dirty linen suit he had been wearing when we met him the day before. It was so crumpled now that I wondered if he had slept in it.

"What time is it?" Tim asked.

"It is time for you to talk!" Bastille blew a cloud of smoke into Tim's face.

Tim coughed. "You know those things can damage your health!" he remarked.

Not quickly enough, I thought. But I said nothing.

"It is *your* health that should concern you, my friend," Bastille replied.

"I'm perfectly well, thank you," Tim said.

"I mean – your health if you fail to tell us what we want to know!" Bastille's green eyes flared. He was even uglier when he was angry. "You have put us to a great deal of trouble," he went on. "We've searched you and this morning we searched your room. Are you going to tell us where it is?"

"It's on the top floor of the hotel!" Tim exclaimed.

"Not the room!" Bastille swore and choked on his cigarette. "I am talking about the packet that you were given by Marc Chabrol."

"The ex-steward," Lavache added. He giggled, and, looking at his ape-like hands, I suddenly knew how Chabrol had managed to "fall" under a train.

I'd said nothing throughout all this. I was just glad that I'd decided not to bring the packet with us. The two men must have searched Tim and me while we were unconscious. They had found nothing and it looked like they weren't going to go back and search the hotel room a second time.

"He gave us a cup of coffee," Tim was

saying. "But we drank it. Unless you're talking about ... wait a minute..."

"Who *are* you people?" I cut in. I didn't want him to say any more. So long as we had the sachet, they wouldn't kill us. They needed to know where it was. But the moment they heard it was hidden in the toilet, we were dead. That much was certain. I would just have to keep them talking and hope for the best. "Look..." I went on. "The steward didn't give us anything. We're just here on holiday."

"*Non, non, non!*" Bastille shook his head. "Do not try lying to me, *mon petit ami*. I know that your brother is a private detective. I also know that he was sent to Paris by Interpol. I know that he is working on a special assigment." His face turned ugly, which, with his face, wasn't difficult. "Now I want you to tell me how much you know and who gave you your information."

"But I don't know anything!" Tim wailed.

He'd never spoken a truer word in his life. Tim knew nothing about any special assignment. He'd have had trouble telling anyone his own shoe size. And he also hadn't realized that this was all his fault. If only he'd kept his mouth shut on the train! He'd told Jed Mathis and the old woman that he was working for Interpol. Could one of them have passed it on? Jed Mathis...?

Beware the mad American...

It was too late to worry about that. I realized that Tim was still talking. He had told them everything. The competition on the yoghurt pot. The free weekend. The truth.

"He's right," I admitted. "We're just tourists. We're not working for anyone."

"It was a strawberry yoghurt!" Tim burbled. "Bestlé yoghurts. They're only eighty calories each..."

"We don't know anything!" I said.

Bastille and Lavache moved closer to each other and began to mutter in low, dark voices. I couldn't understand a word they were saying, but somehow I didn't like the sound of it. I tried to break free from the chair but it was useless. Things weren't looking good. By now they must have realized that they were wrong about us, that we were exactly what we said. But they weren't just going to order us a taxi and pretend the whole thing had never happened. As they're always saying in the old movies ... we knew too much. I still had no idea who they were or what they were doing, but we knew their names and had seen their faces. That was enough.

The two men straightened up. "We have decided that we believe you," Bastille said.

"That's terrific!" Tim exclaimed.

"So now we are going to kill you."

"Oh!" His face fell.

Lavache walked to the far side of the room

and I strained my neck to watch him. He reached out with both hands and suddenly a whole section of the wall slid to one side. I realized now that it wasn't a wall at all but a set of floor-to-ceiling doors. There was another room on the other side, filled with activity, and at that moment I realized what this was all about. Perhaps I should have guessed from the start.

Drugs.

The other room was a laboratory. I could see metal tables piled high with white powder. More white powder being weighed on complicated electronic scales. White powder being spooned into plastic bags. There were about half-a-dozen people working there, young men and women with dirty faces but pristine laboratory coats. They were handling the white powder in complete silence, as if they knew that it was death they were carrying in their hands and that if it heard them it would somehow find them out.

Lavache lumbered into the room, vanishing from sight. When he reappeared, he was holding something which he handed to Bastille. Right then I was more scared than I've ever been in my life, and you know me ... I don't scare easily. But suddenly I remembered that I was thirteen years old, that I hadn't started shaving yet and that my mother (who'd been shaving for years) was thousands of miles away. I was so scared I almost wanted to cry.

Bastille was holding a bottle of pills.

He approached Tim first. "These are super-strength," he said. "I think five of them will be enough."

"No, thank you," Tim said. "I haven't got a headache."

"They're not headache pills, Tim," I said.

Bastille grabbed hold of Tim and forced his mouth open. He had counted five pills into the palm of his hand and I watched, powerless, as he forced them down Tim's throat. Then he turned and began to walk towards me.

"They don't taste very nice!" I heard Tim say, but then I'd gone crazy, rocking back and forth, yelling, kicking with my feet, trying to tear apart the parcel tape around my wrists. It was useless. I felt Lavache grab hold of my shoulders while at the same time, Bastille took hold of my chin. I don't know what was worse. Feeling his bony fingers against my face or knowing there was nothing I could do as he forced my mouth open. His right hand came up and the next moment there were four or five pills on my tongue. They had an evil taste. I drew a breath, meaning to spit them out, but his hand was already over my mouth, almost suffocating me. I screamed silently and felt the pills trickle down the back of my throat. I almost felt them drop into the pit of my stomach. Then Bastille pulled his hand clear and my head sank forward. I said nothing. I thought I was dead. I thought he had killed me.

Things happened very quickly after that. It seemed to me that the lights in the room had brightened and that somebody had turned up the heating. My eyes were hurting. And then the walls began to revolve, slowly at first, like the start of a ride at a funfair. But there was nothing fun about this. Drugs are poison and I was sure I had just been given a lethal overdose. I was sweating. I tried to speak but my tongue refused to move; anyway, my mouth was too dry.

I heard the parcel tape being ripped off and felt my hands come free. Lavache was standing behind me. I tried to look at him, but my head lolled uselessly. He pulled me off the chair and carried me outside. Bastille followed with Tim.

There was a white van waiting for us in an enclosed courtyard – we could have been anywhere. I looked back at the house we had just left. It was a grey building, three storeys high. Most of its paint had flaked off and there were scorch marks, as if it had been involved in a fire. About half the windows were shattered. Others had been bricked in. The place looked derelict. I guessed it was supposed to.

I was bundled into the van and the next moment the engine started up, roaring at me like a mechanical beast. I almost expected it to come bursting through the floor, to gobble me up. The noise hammered at my ears and I groaned. Tim was thrown in next to me. The doors slammed. My stomach heaved. We were off.

There was a small window set in the door and I managed to stagger over to it and pull myself onto my knees to look out. But it was hard to see anything. The world was spinning faster now, tilting from side to side. I just made out a series of letters in red neon, but it seemed to take me for ever to work out the three words they formed:

THE FRENCH CONFECTION

The van turned a corner and I lost my balance. Before I fell, I caught a glimpse of a blue star ... on a flag or perhaps on the side of a building. Then the sound of the van's engine rose up again and swallowed me. The floor hit me in the face. Or maybe it was me who had hit the floor. I no longer knew the difference.

The journey took an hour ... a month ... a year. I no longer had any idea. What was the stuff they had given me? Whatever it was, it was taking over, killing me. I could feel it happening, an inch at a time. The van stopped. Hands that no longer belonged to bodies pulled us out. Then the pavement slapped me in the face, there was another scream from the engine and suddenly I knew that we were alone.

"Tim...?" I gasped the word. But Tim was no longer there. He had turned into some horrible animal with sixteen eyes, tentacles and...

I forced myself to concentrate, knowing that it was the drug that was doing it to me. The image dissolved and there he was again. My brother.

"Nick..." He staggered to his feet. All three of them. Things weren't back to normal yet.

The sky changed from red to blue to yellow to green. I stood up as well.

"Must get help," I said.

Tim groaned.

We were back in the centre of Paris. It was late at night. And Paris had never looked like this before.

There was the Seine but the water had gone, replaced by red wine that glowed darkly in the moonlight. It was twisting its way underneath the bridges, but now that I looked more closely, I saw that they had changed too. They had become huge sticks of French bread. There was a sudden buzzing. A Bateau Mouche had suddenly sprouted huge blue wings and legs. It leapt out of the water and onto one of the bridges, tearing a great chunk out with a hideous, hairy mouth before spiralling away into the night.

The ground underneath my feet had gone

soft and I realized I was sinking into it. With a cry I lifted one foot and saw that the tar had melted and was dripping off my trainer. Except the tar was yellow, not black.

"It's cheese!" I shouted. And it was. The entire street had turned into cheese – soft, ripe, French cheese. I gasped for air, choking on the smell. At the same time, the cheese pulled me into it. Another few seconds and I would be sucked underneath the surface.

"Nick!" Tim called out.

And then the cheese was gone as he pointed with an arm that was now a mile long. There was a snail coming down the Boulevard. No … not one snail but a thousand of them, each one the size of a house, slithering along ahead of the traffic, leaving a grey, slimy trail behind them. At one corner, the traffic lights had gone red and all the snails were squeaking at each other, a fantastic traffic jam of snails. At the same time, I heard what sounded like a gigantic burp and a frog, the size of a bus, bounded across my vision, leaping over a building. But the frog was missing its legs. It was supporting itself on giant crutches.

The world twisted, heaved, broke up and then reformed with all the pieces in different positions: a jigsaw in the hands of a destructive child.

Suddenly we were surrounded by grinning stone figures, jabbering and staring at us with empty stone eyes. I recognized them: the gargoyles from Notre Dame. There must have been a hundred of them. One of them was sitting on Tim's shoulder like a grey chimpanzee. But Tim didn't seem to have noticed it.

Light. Car lights. Everywhere. A horn sounded. I had stepped into the road – but it didn't matter because the cars were the size of matchboxes. They were all Citroëns. Every one of them. And they were being followed by cyclists. The Tour de France had come early that year. All the cyclists were smoking cigarettes.

Tim was clutching a streetlamp. Now he was wearing a striped jersey and a beret and there was a string of onions hanging from his side. *"Je suis,"* he said. *"Tu es, il est..."*

I opened my mouth to reply.

Crash! Crash! Crash!

I saw it before he did. Perhaps he didn't see it at all. Even now, with the drug pumping through my body, I knew that it wasn't real, that I was hallucinating. But it made no difference. As far as I was concerned, everything I saw was real. And if it was real, it could kill me. It could step on me. It could crush me.

The Eiffel Tower! On our first day in Paris we had crossed the city to visit it. Now the Eiffel Tower was coming to visit us. There it was, walking across Paris, swinging one iron foot, then the next, moving like some sort of giant, four-legged crab. One of its feet came down in a pancake stall. Wood shattered. Pancakes flew in all directions. Somebody screamed.

The cheese was getting softer. I was sinking into a boulevard of Brie, a dual carriageway of Camembert. The squirming yellow slipped round my waist, rose over my shoulder and twisted round my neck. I didn't even try to fight. I'd had enough. I waited for it to pull me under.

I thought I was going to die and if I'd waited another minute I might well have. But just then I heard what I thought was an owl, hooting in my ear. At the same time, I found myself staring at a face I knew. A dark-haired man in a grey-coloured suit. I became aware of a blue flashing light which either belonged to a dragon or a police car. I looked up and saw something driving out of the moon, flying through the sky towards me. An ambulance.

"Don't go to sleep!" a voice commanded. "Don't go to sleep! Don't go to sleep!"

But it was too late. I went to sleep.

For ever.

THE MAD AMERICAN

"You're lucky to be alive," the man said.

It was two days later. I don't want to tell you about those two days. I'd spent both of them in hospital in Paris and all I can say is, if you've ever had your stomach pumped, you'll know there are plenty of things you can do that are more fun. I don't remember much about the first day. The next day, I felt like a spin-drier that's been left on too long. All I'd eaten in the entire time was a little bread and water. Fortunately, the water didn't have bubbles. I don't think I could have managed the bubbles.

And now, here I was in the headquarters of Sûreté, the French police force. It's funny how police stations are the same the whole world over. This may have been grander and smarter than New Scotland Yard. The curtains were velvet and the pictures on the wall showed some grey-haired Frenchman in a suit rather than our own grey-haired Queen in a crown. But it still smelled the same.

Tim was sitting next to me. He was the colour of the yoghurt that had brought us here in the first place, with eyes like crushed strawberries. His hair was dishevelled and he looked like he hadn't slept in a month. I was going to say something but decided against it. I probably looked just as bad.

We were in the office of the Chief of Police – a man called Christien Moire. I knew because I'd seen the name and title on the door. It was on his desk too. Maybe he was worried he was going to forget it. He was the man in the grey suit whom I'd seen standing outside Le Chat Gris, the man who had been talking to the receptionist and who had later taken our photograph. Things were beginning to add up even if I still had no idea of the sum total.

"Another one hour and it would have been too late," Moire went on. He spoke English as if he had no idea what he was saying, lingering on every word. He had the sort of accent you get in bad television plays: *Anuzzer wan our an' eet would 'ave bin too late*. I hope you get the idea. "You were very lucky," he added.

"Sure," I muttered. "And we'd have been even luckier if you'd arrived a couple of hours before."

Moire shrugged. "I'm sorry," he said. But

his dark, empty eyes looked about as apologetic as two lumps of ice. "We had no idea you had been taken," he went on.

"Who are you?" Tim demanded. "You call yourself the Sûreté. But what exactly are you sure about?"

"The Sûreté," Moire repeated, "is the French police force. I am the head of a special unit fighting the traffic in ..."

"...drugs." I completed the sentence.

"*Exactement.* I have to say that you and your brother seem to have turned up in the wrong place at the wrong time. If I hadn't been watching you..."

"You were at the hotel," I said. "I saw you outside. You had a camera..."

"Is that your hobby?" Tim asked. "Photography?"

Christien Moire stared at Tim through narrow eyes. He obviously hadn't ever met anyone like him before. "Le Chat Gris has been under surveillance," he said. "Perhaps I should explain..."

"Perhaps you should," I said.

Moire lit a Gauloise. It's a funny thing about the French. Not only do they all smoke, but they smoke the most horrible cigarettes in the world. Forget about the health warning on the packet. The smoke from Moire's cigarette was so thick, you could have printed it on that.

"For some time now," he began, "we have

been aware of a drug-smuggling operation. Somebody has been moving drugs to London … using the trains under the channel. We still don't know how they're doing it. We have searched the trains from top to bottom but we have found nothing. Worse still, we do not know who they are."

"Is there anything you *do* know?" I asked.

Moire glanced at me with unfriendly eyes. "We know only the code-name of the man behind the operation," he replied.

"The Mad American," I said.

That surprised Moire, but he tried not to show it. "The drugs arrive from Marseilles," he went on. "They are weighed and packaged somewhere in Paris. Then the Mad American arranges for them to be sent to London. We've been working with the English police to try to stop them. So far we have had no success in London. But in Paris we had one lucky break."

"Le Chat Gris," I said.

"Yes, we learned that the hotel is sometimes used by the Mad American. When dealers arrive from London to buy his drugs, that is where they stay. He meets them there. They pay him the money and then his two associates – Jacques Bastille and Luc Lavache – arrange for the drugs to be sent on the train."

"So *that's* why you photographed us!" I said. "You thought we'd come to Paris to buy drugs!"

"I know it sounds unlikely," Moire said. "An English kid and his idiotic brother –"

"Nick isn't idiotic!" Tim protested.

"We became interested in you the moment you reported that Bastille and Lavache had attempted to kill you," Moire went on. "I ordered the photograph to be taken so that we could check you against our criminal files."

"But if you thought we were criminals, why did you let us go in the first place?" I asked. It had puzzled me at the time, the policeman suddenly changing his mind and telling us we could leave.

"The answer to that is simple," Moire said. "We still had no idea what part you had to play in all this, but you had mentioned Le Chat Gris and that was enough. It was important that the Mad American should not be aware that the police were involved. I personally ordered your release, and at the same time I made sure that we kept you under – how do you say? – surveillance. This was very lucky for you, considering how things turned out."

"You were following us."

"Yes. I saw you go back to the hotel, and minutes later I saw the van with the two men who knocked you out and kidnapped you. We followed the van but unfortunately lost it in traffic..."

"...so you don't know where we were taken."

"No. But I knew that you were in danger and I had every gendarme in Paris looking out for you. One of them saw you and radioed HQ. By that time they had pumped you with enough drugs to kill a horse."

"Why would they want to kill a horse?" Tim asked.

Moire ignored him. "We only got to you in the nick of time. Another ten minutes, and the two of you would now be in Père Lachaise."

"You mean, another hotel," Tim said.

"No. Père Lachaise is a cemetery."

"OK. You saved us, Monsieur Moire," I said. "But now, if you don't mind, I'm heading back to the hotel, packing and leaving for London."

"That's right, Monsieur Loire," Tim agreed. "We're out of here!"

"I'm afraid not." Moire hadn't raised his voice. If anything, he had done the exact opposite. But that's the thing about the French. When they're being really nasty, they don't shout. They whisper. "You realize that I could have you arrested?" he asked.

I almost laughed. "What for?" I demanded.

"You were found in the middle of Paris, full of drugs," the police chief explained. He sounded almost reasonable. "Two English tourists who decided to experiment with these forbidden substances..."

"That's a complete lie!" I exclaimed.

"Yes!" Tim agreed. "We're not tourists!"

"And then there is the matter of the Bateau Mouche..." Moire continued. "You jumped off a bridge, endangering the lives of the people on the boat. This could also prove to be drug-related."

"What do you want, Moire?" I demanded.

Moire leaned forward. His face could have been carved out of stone. Even the cigarette smoke seemed to have solidified. "There are two things we wish to find out," he said. "First, who is the Mad American?"

"Why don't you ask Bastille and Lavache?" I demanded.

"They wouldn't tell us anything. And if we did arrest them, it would only let their boss know that we were getting close ... and that would ruin everything. The second thing we wish to know is, how are they smuggling the drugs across the Channel? As I have told you, we have searched the train many times ... but with no success. These packets of white powder – they must be somewhere. But..." He smacked his forehead with the palm of his hand. "It is infuriating!"

"What do you want us to do?" I asked.

"I want you to go back to the hotel," Moire replied. "It will be as if nothing has happened."

"Why?"

"Because you can be useful to me ... on the

inside. My men will continue to watch you. You'll be completely safe. But maybe you can find the answers to the questions. And if there is anything to report..."

"Forget it!" I snapped.

"Right!" Tim nodded. "Bestlé only paid for four days. We can't possibly afford it."

"Bestlé?" For the first time Moire looked puzzled. "Who is Bestlé?"

"It doesn't matter," I replied. "We're British citizens. You can't blackmail us!"

"You don't think so?" Moire almost smiled. "You are Europeans now, my friend. And if you don't do exactly as I tell you, let me assure you that you will be spending a great deal of time inside a European jail."

I wanted to argue, but I could see there was no point. The last person to argue with Christien Moire probably found himself with a one-way ticket to Devil's Island.

He knew he'd beaten me. "Go back to Le Chat Gris and wait for further instructions," he said. "Don't worry about the bill. I will see to it."

"And what if we get killed?" I asked.

"My department will pay for the funeral too."

I sank back in my chair. There was nothing I could say. Not in French. Not in English. It really wasn't fair.

* * *

And that was how we found ourselves, a few hours later, back in our room at Le Chat Gris. As I'd walked back into the hotel, I'd known how those French aristocrats must have felt as they took their last steps towards the guillotine. The receptionist had almost fallen off his chair when he saw us and he'd been on the telephone before we'd reached the lift. The Mad American would have presumed we were dead. Now he'd know he was wrong. How long would it take him to correct his mistake?

Tim sat down on the bed. He was actually looking quite cheerful, which made me feel even worse. "Maybe this isn't so bad, Nick," he said.

"Tim!" I cried. "How bad can it get?"

"We're working for the French police now," he said. "This could be good for business! *Tim Diamond Inc ... London and Paris.* That'll look good on the door."

"It'll look even better on your gravestone," I said. "Don't you understand, Tim?" We're not working for anyone! Christien Moire was lying through his teeth!"

"You mean ... he isn't a policeman?"

"Of course he's a policeman. But he doesn't want us to work for him. He's using us!" I'd taken a guidebook of Paris out of my case. Now I sat down next to Tim. "Moire wants to find out the identity of the Mad American," I explained. "What's the best way to do that?"

"Just ask for Tim Diamond..."

"Just *use* Tim Diamond. He's sent us back here because he knows that our turning up again will panic the Mad American. He's already tried to kill us twice. He's certain to try again – and this time Moire will be watching. He's using us as bait in a trap, Tim. The Mad American kills us. Moire gets the Mad American. It's as simple as that."

I opened the guidebook. "I'm not sitting here, waiting to be shot," I said.

"Where do you want to be shot?" Tim asked.

"I don't want to be shot anywhere! That's why I'm going to find the Mad American before he finds us." I started to thumb through the pages. I still didn't know what I was looking for, but I had a good idea. "After we were knocked out, we were taken to the Mad American's headquarters," I said.

"But we were knocked out!" Tim said. "We didn't see anything."

"We didn't see much," I agreed. "But there were some clues. A blue star. Some words in a shop window – THE FRENCH CONFECTION. And when we were tied up, I heard something. Music. Singing."

"Do you think that was the Mad American?"

"No, Tim. It was coming from a building nearby." I stopped, trying to remember what I had heard. "It wasn't French singing," I said. "It was different... It was foreign."

Sitting next to me on the bed, Tim was making a strange noise. I thought for a moment that he had stomach-ache. Then I realized he was trying to hum the tune.

"That's right, Tim," I said. "It was something like that. Only a bit more human."

Tim stopped. I tried to think. How had the singing gone? It had been sad and somehow dislocated. A choir and a single male voice. At times it had been more like wailing than singing. Remembering it now made me think of a church. Was that it? Had it been religious music? But if so, what religion?

I'm not sure what happened first. The thought seemed to come into my mind at exactly the same moment as I found myself looking at the words *The Jewish Quarter* in the guidebook in my hands.

"Jewish music!" I exclaimed.

"Jewish?"

"The music that we heard, Tim. It was coming from a synagogue!"

Tim's eyes lit up. "You think we were taken to Jerusalem?"

"No, Tim. We were in Paris. But there's an area of Paris that's full of synagogues." I waved the book at him. "Le Marais. That's what it's called. The Jewish sector of Paris..."

"But how big is it?" Tim asked.

I read the page in front of me:

Originally a swamp, the Marais has grown to become one of the most fashionable areas of Paris. Its narrow streets are filled with shops and boutiques including some of the city's most elegant cafés and cake shops. The Marais is home to the Jewish quarter with numerous synagogues and kosher restaurants based around the Rue des Rosiers.

There was a map showing the area. It only had a couple of dozen roads. "It doesn't look too big," I said. "And at least we know what we're looking for. The French Confection."

"But what *is* The French Confection, Nick?"

"I think it must be a shop. Maybe it sells cakes or sweets or something. But once we've found it, we'll know we're right next to the factory. Find the sign and we'll have found the Mad American."

"And then?"

"Then we call Moire."

We slipped out of Le Chat Gris down the fire escape, dodging past Moire's men who were waiting for us at the front of the hotel. Then we dived into the nearest Metro station and headed north.

It was a short walk from the station to the start of Le Marais – the Place Vendôme, one of those Paris squares where even the trees manage to look expensive. From there we headed down towards a big, elegant building that turned out to be the Picasso museum. I'd studied Picasso at school. He's the guy who painted women with eyes in the sides of their necks and tables with legs going the wrong way. It's called surrealism. Maybe I should have taken Tim in, as he's pretty surreal himself. But we didn't have time.

We backtracked and found ourselves in a series of long, narrow streets with buildings rising five storeys on both sides. But I knew we were on the right track. There was no singing, but here and there I saw blue stars – the same stars I had glimpsed as I was bundled into the van. I knew what it was now: the six-pointed Star of David. There was one in every kosher food store and restaurant in the area.

We'd been following the Rue des Rosiers – the one I'd read about in the guidebook – but with no sign of the building where we'd been held. So now we started snaking up and down, taking the first on the right and the next on the left and so on. It was a pretty enough part of Paris, I'll say that for it. Tim had even forgotten our mission and stopped once or twice to take photographs. We'd been chased and threatened at knife-point. We'd been kidnapped, drugged and threatened again – this time by the French police. And he *still* thought we were on holiday!

And then, suddenly, we were there.

It was on one of the main streets of the area – the Rue de Sevigny. I recognized it at once: the burnt face of the building, the broken windows, the ugly chimney stacks… And there was the archway that we had driven through. There was a courtyard on the other side which was where the white van had been parked. I stood there in the sunlight, with people strolling past on the pavements, some carrying shopping bags, others pushing prams. And none of them knew. The biggest drug factory in Paris was right in front of them, just sitting there between a café and a cake shop, right in the middle of the Marais. I couldn't believe I had found it so easily. It was hard to believe it was there at all.

"Nick…!" Tim whispered.

I grabbed hold of him and pulled him down behind a parked car as Bastille and Lavache appeared, coming out of the front door and walking across the courtyard. Each of them had a heavy box in their hands. Another shipment on its way out! It made me angry that anyone should be dumb enough to want to buy drugs and angrier still that these two grim reapers would be getting richer by selling them.

"What do we do now?" Tim whispered.

"Now we call Moire," I said.

"Right!" Tim straightened up. "Let's ask in there!"

Before I could stop him he had walked across the pavement and into the cake shop. There was the sign in the window that I had seen from the van. THE FRENCH CONFECTION. Why did the name bother me? Why did I feel it was connected with something or someone I had seen? It was too late to worry about it now. Tim was already inside. I followed him in.

I found myself in a long, narrow shop with a counter running down one wall. Everywhere I looked there were cakes and croissants, bowls of coloured almonds and tiny pots of jam. The very air smelt of sugar and flour. On the counter stood one of the tallest wedding cakes I had ever seen: six platforms of swirly white icing with a marzipan bride and groom looking air-sick up on the top. There was a bead curtain at the back and now it rattled as the owner of the shop passed through, coming out to serve us. And of course I knew her. I'd met her on the train.

Erica Nice.

She stopped behind the counter, obviously as surprised to see us as we were to see her.

"You...!" she began.

"Mrs Nice!" Tim gurgled. I wondered how he had managed to remember her name. "We need to use your telephone. To call the police."

"I don't think so, Tim," I said.

Even as I spoke I was heading back towards the door. But I was already too late. Erica's hand came up and this time it wasn't holding an almond slice. It was the biggest gun I'd ever seen. Bigger than the wrinkled hand that held it. Its muzzle was as ugly as the smile on the old woman's face.

"But ... but ... but..." Tim stared.

"Erica Nice," I said. "I suppose I should have guessed. Madame Erica Nice. Say it fast and what do you get?"

"Madamericanice?" Tim suggested.

"Mad American," I said. "She's the one behind the drug racket, Tim. When we met her, she must have been checking the route. That's why she was on the train. And that's how Bastille and Lavache knew we were in Paris."

Erica Nice snarled at us. "Yes," she said. "I have to travel on the train now and then to keep an eye on things. Like that idiot steward – Marc Chabrol. He was scared. And scared people are no use to me."

"So you pushed him under a train," I said.

She shrugged. "I would have preferred to stab him. I did have my knitting needles, but unfortunately I was halfway through a woollen jumper. Pushing was easier."

"And what now?" I asked. I wondered if she was going to shoot us herself or call her two thugs to finish the job for her. At the same time,

I took a step forward, edging my way towards the counter and the giant wedding cake.

"Those idiots – Jacques and Luc – should have got rid of you when they had the chance," Erica hissed. "This time they will make no mistakes."

She turned to press a switch set in the wall. Presumably it connected the shop with the factory next door.

I leapt forward and threw my entire weight against the cake.

Erica half turned. The gun came up.

The door of the shop burst open, the glass smashing.

And as Erica Nice gave a single shrill scream and disappeared beneath about ten kilograms of wedding cake, Christien Moire and a dozen gendarmes hurled themselves into the shop. At the same time, I heard the blare of sirens as police cars swerved into the road from all directions.

I turned to Moire. "You followed us here?"

Moire nodded. "Of course. I had men on all sides of the hotel."

Erica Nice groaned and tried to fight her way out of several layers of sponge, jam and butter cream. Tim leaned forward and scooped up a fragment of white icing. He popped it into his mouth.

"Nice cake," he said.

THE WHITE CLIFFS

The next day, Christien Moire drove us up to Calais and personally escorted us onto the ferry. It would have been easier to have taken the train, of course. But somehow Tim and I had had enough of trains.

It had been a good week for Moire. Jacques Bastille and Luc Lavache had both been arrested. So had Erica Nice. The drug factory had been closed down and more arrests were expected. No wonder Moire wanted us out of the way. He was looking forward to promotion and maybe the Croix de Guerre or whatever medal French heroes get pinned to their right nipple. The last thing Moire needed was Tim and me hanging around to tell people the part we had played.

Moire stopped at the quay and handed us our tickets as well as a packed lunch for the crossing. "France is in your debt," he said, solemnly, and before either of us could stop him he had grabbed hold of Tim and planted a kiss on both cheeks.

Tim went bright red. "I know I cracked the case," he muttered. "But let's not get too friendly..."

"It's just the French way," I said. Even so, I made sure I shook hands with Moire. I didn't want him getting too close.

"I wish you a good journey, my friends," Moire said. "And this time, perhaps you will be careful what you say while you are on the ship!"

"We won't be saying anything," I promised. I'd bought Tim a Tintin book at the harbour bookstall. He could read that on the way home.

Moire smiled. *"Au revoir,"* he said.

"Where?" Tim asked. I'd have to translate it for him later.

We were about halfway home, this time chopping up and down on the Channel, when Tim suddenly looked up from the Tintin book. "You know," he said. "We never did find out how Erica Nice was smuggling the drugs on the train."

"Haven't you guessed?" I sighed and pulled out the blue sugar sachet that had started the whole thing. It was the sachet Tim had been given at the Gare du Nord. Somehow I'd never quite got round to opening it. I did so now.

There was a spoonful of white powder inside.

"Sugar?" Tim muttered.

"I don't think so, Tim," I replied. "This is just one sachet. But Erica Nice was transporting thousands of them every day on the train. A little parcel of drugs. One dose, already weighed and perfectly concealed." I tore open the packet and held it up. The powder was caught in the wind and snatched away. I watched it go, a brief flurry of white as it skimmed over the handrail and disappeared into the grey water of the English Channel.

"Do you think we ought to tell Moire?" Tim asked.

"I expect he's worked it out for himself," I said.

In the distance I could see the white cliffs of Dover looming up. We had only been away for a week but somehow it seemed a lot longer. I was glad to be home.

Tim was still holding the packed lunch that Moire had given us. Now he opened it. The first thing he took out was a strawberry yoghurt.

"Very funny," I said.

The yoghurt followed the drugs into the channel. Then we went downstairs to order fish and chips.

THE GREEK WHO STOLE CHRISTMAS

DEATH THREAT

I knew it was going to be a bad Christmas when I walked past the charity shop and the manager ran out and tried to offer me charity. It seemed that everyone in Camden Town knew I was broke. Even the turkeys were laughing at me. On the last day of term, the teachers had a whip-round for me … not that I really needed a whip, but I suppose it's the thought that counts. Christmas was just a few weeks away and the only money I had was a ten-pound book token that my parents had sent me from Australia. I tried to swap it for hard cash at my local bookshop, but the manager – a thin-faced woman in her forties – was completely heartless.

"I need to eat," I explained.

"Then buy a cookery book."

"I can't afford the ingredients!"

"I'm sorry. You can only use a book token to buy books."

"What's the point of buying books if I'm too faint to read?"

She smiled sadly at me. "Have you tried Philip Pullman?"

"No. Do you think he'd lend me some money?"

I couldn't believe my parents had sent me a book token for Christmas, but then of course they had no idea about anything. My dad had moved them to Sydney a few years before – he was a door-to-door salesman, selling doors, and he must have been doing well because this year he'd printed his own Christmas card. HAVE AN A-DOOR-ABLE CHRISTMAS, it said on the cover. There was a picture of a kangaroo with a red hat on, looking out of an open door. I was still laughing as I ripped it to pieces. My parents had two new kids of their own now: Doreen and Dora. Two sisters I'd never met. That made me sad sometimes. They weren't even two years old and they probably had more spare cash than me.

I was thinking about Australia as I walked home from the bookshop. My mum and dad had wanted to take me with them when they emigrated, and maybe it had been a mistake to slip off the plane before it took off. While it was taxiing down the runway, I was running away to find a taxi – and they hadn't even noticed until they were thirty-five thousand feet above France. Apparently my mum had hysterics. And my dad had my lunch.

I'm still not sure it was a smart decision. They say that London is like a village, and I certainly enjoyed living there. The only trouble was, I'd moved in with the village idiot. I'm talking, of course, about my big brother, Herbert Timothy Simple. But that wasn't what he called himself. He called himself Tim Diamond, Private Detective – and that's what it said in the Yellow Pages, along with the line: "No problem too problematic." He'd written that himself.

Tim was the worst private detective in England. I mean ... he'd just spent two weeks working in a big department store in the West End. He was supposed to be looking out for shoplifters but I don't think he'd kept his eye on the ball. In fact, the ball was the first thing that got stolen. After that, things went from bad to worse. The store had twenty-three departments when he started but only sixteen when he left. He was fired, of course. The dummies in the window probably had a higher IQ than Tim. He was lucky he had me. I solved the crimes, Tim got the credit. That was how it worked. If you've read my other stories, you'll know what I'm talking about. If you haven't, go out and buy the books. If you like, I'll even sell you a ten-quid book token. You can have it for nine quid.

Anyway, right now Tim was out of work. And November had arrived like a bad dog, snapping at everyone in the street and sending them hurrying home. As usual, it wasn't going to snow – but the pipes were frozen, the puddles had iced over and you could see people's breath in the air.

They were playing a Christmas carol on the radio as I let myself in. Tim was sitting at his desk wrapped in a blanket, trying to open a tin of sardines that was so far past its sell-by date he'd probably have more luck selling it as an antique.

I threw myself into a chair. "Any news?" I asked. "I don't suppose anyone has offered you a job?"

"I just don't get it," Tim replied. "You'd think someone, somewhere would need a private detective. Why is no one hiring me?"

"Maybe it's because you're no good," I said.

"You might be right," Tim nodded sadly.

"There are police dogs that have solved more crimes than you."

"Yes," Tim agreed, "but at least I don't have fleas."

I got up and turned the radio off. Tim had managed to get the tin open and the room was suddenly filled with the smell of twenty-seven-year-old sardines. And it was just then that there was a knock on the door.

I looked at Tim. Tim looked at me. We had

a client and we also had a room that looked like a rubbish tip and smelled like the River Thames during the Great Plague.

"One minute!" Tim shouted.

In that one minute, we raced around like two people in a speeded up commercial for Fairy Liquid. Papers went into drawers. Plates went into the kitchen. The sardines went into the bin and the bin went out the window. Sixty seconds later, the office looked more like an office and Tim was sitting behind his desk with a straightened tie and a crooked smile. I took one last look around and opened the door.

A man walked in. I guessed he was in his forties: short and fat, smoking a cigar. The cigar was short and fat too. He was dressed in a nasty suit. The pattern was so loud you could almost hear it coming. He had black, greasy hair, thick lips and eyes that would have been nicer if they'd matched. His shoes had been polished until you could see your face in them – though with his face I wouldn't have bothered. There was a gold signet ring on his finger. The way it squeezed the flesh, I doubted it would ever come off.

"You always keep your clients waiting outside?" he demanded as he came in and took a chair.

"We were filing," Tim explained.

He looked around. "I don't see no filing cabinets." He spoke like an American but he wasn't one. He was just someone who spent too much time on planes.

"We were filing our nails," I said.

He helped himself to one of Tim's business cards from the desk. "Are you Tim Diamond?"

"Yeah. That's me." Tim narrowed his eyes. He always does that when he's trying to look serious. Unfortunately it just makes him look short-sighted. "I'm a private eye."

"I know," the man growled. "That's why I'm here. My name is Jake Hammill and I want to hire you."

"You want to hire me?" Tim couldn't believe it. He leant forward. "So what can I do for you, Mr Camel?"

"Not Jay Camel. I'm Jake Hammill. You want me to spell it for you?"

"N-O," Tim said.

"I work in the music industry. As a matter of fact, I'm the manager of a woman who's a very famous pop singer."

Tim scowled. "If she's so famous, how come I've never heard of her?"

"I haven't told you her name yet."

"Maybe it would help if you did."

Hammill glanced at me. He was obviously suspicious. He turned back to Tim. "Can you keep a secret?" he asked.

"I'm not going to tell you," Tim replied.

"All right." Hammill nodded. "Her name is Minerva."

I have to admit, I was surprised. Hammill looked pretty small-time to me, but Minerva was one of the biggest names in the business. She was a multimillionaire pop singer and a movie actress. I doubted there was anyone in the world who hadn't seen her videos. She was the woman with the golden voice and the silver-plated breasts. Her clothes were outrageous – like the rest of her lifestyle. She had been born in Greece but now she lived most of the time in New York. The fact that she was visiting London had made the front page of every newspaper ... even the *Financial Times*.

"The thing is," Hammill said, "I've got a serious problem..." He twisted his signet ring nervously around his finger like he was trying to take it off. "Listen to me," he went on. "Minerva has been invited over here for Christmas. Tomorrow she's turning on the Christmas lights in Regent Street. And on Thursday at midday she's opening the Santa Claus grotto at Harrods department store in Knightsbridge. There's going to be a lot of press. A lot of TV. It's great publicity. But this is the problem..." He drew a breath. "I think she's in danger."

"What makes you think that?" I asked.

"Well, yesterday she received an anonymous letter."

"An anonymous letter!" Tim exclaimed. "Who from?"

Hammill scowled. "I don't know. It was anonymous. But it threatens her with death."

"So where is this letter, Mr Hubble?" Tim asked.

"It was sent to Minerva. She's got it. I'd like you to come and meet her at her hotel and she'll take you through it."

"She'll take me through the hotel?"

"No. She'll take you through the letter." He leant forward and already I could see the doubt in his face. "I have to say, Mr Diamond, I need to be sure you're the right man for this job. I wanted to go to the police, but Minerva's husband insisted that a private detective would be better. I understand you advertise in the Yellow Pages."

"Yeah," I muttered. "They match his teeth."

"I take it you know how to look after yourself," Hammill said.

Tim looked puzzled. "But I'm not ill!" he muttered.

Hammill rolled his eyes. Maybe I was imagining things but I could have sworn they went in opposite directions. "I'm not asking about your health," he said. "I need someone to stay close to Minerva while she's in London, and that may mean getting into a fight. So what I'm asking you is – do you know judo or karate?"

"Sure!" Tim nodded. "Judo, karate and

origami. When do you want me to start, Mr Rubble?"

It was obvious to me that Hammill was having second thoughts about Tim. And maybe third and fourth thoughts too. For a moment he bit his fingernail, deep in thought. Maybe he had plans to bite all the way down to the signet ring. Then he came to a decision. "All right," he said. "Minerva is staying at the Porchester hotel, which is in Hyde Park. That's highly confidential information by the way."

"What do you mean?" Tim demanded. "Everyone knows that the Porchester hotel is in Hyde Park."

"Sure. But nobody knows she's staying there. Otherwise we'd have fans all over the place."

"That would help with the ventilation..."

"Minerva likes her privacy. She's booked in under the name of Mrs Smith. Room sixteen. I want you to visit her this evening. Say, seven o'clock?"

"Seven o'clock," Tim said obediently.

"That's right. I'll let her take a look at you and if she thinks you're up to it, you're hired."

Tim nodded. I knew what was coming next. He was sitting back in his chair with his feet resting on his desk, trying to look every inch the private detective. The fact that he had a hole in one of his shoes didn't help. As far as he was concerned he was back in business.

And he was determined to prove it. "What about my fee?" he demanded.

"You're not hired yet," Hammill reminded him.

"OK, Mr Rabble. But I'd better let you know now, I'm not cheap. The only thing that goes cheap in this office is my budgerigar, and I don't think your superstar wants a bodyguard with feathers."

Hammill tried to make sense of this, decided it wasn't worth trying and stood up. "I'll see you this evening," he said. One last twist of the ring. It wasn't going anywhere, but he was. He walked out of the office, slamming the door behind him.

There was a moment's silence.

I went over to the cupboard and searched through the CDs. I knew we'd have a Minerva recording somewhere and, sure enough, there it was – her third album, *Think Pink*. I looked at the face on the cover: the blonde hair, the green eyes, the lips that looked like they could suck in a horse. Not for the first time I wished we had a CD player, but Tim had pawned it months ago. Along with just about everything else. That was another sad thought. When I walked into the Camden Town pawn shop, I felt more at home than I did at home.

But maybe our luck was going to change. All Tim had to do was protect her for a couple of days and there'd be a handsome cheque at the end of it. He might even end up taking a bullet for her. If so, I just hoped they'd pay him extra. And whatever happened, it might be fun to hang out with one of the biggest entertainers on the planet.

"I can't believe it!" I said. "We're going to meet Minerva!"

"It's even better than that," Tim replied. "She's opening the grotto at Harrods. Maybe we'll meet Father Christmas!"

I slid the CD back into the cupboard.

Minerva had just received a death threat and her husband had hired Tim Diamond. That was like getting her a knitted cardigan when what she really needed was a bullet-proof vest. Well, one thing was certain: this was going to be a Christmas to remember. I just wondered if Minerva would still be around to see in the New Year.

SUITE SIXTEEN

The Porchester was in the middle of London's Park Lane, a five-star hotel that cost the earth. The sort of place I wouldn't be able to stay in a blue moon. You could tell it was expensive: I spotted two celebrities in the revolving doors and by the time I'd reached the reception desk I'd passed three more. There was enough fur and jewellery in that place to fill a store. And that was just the men.

The reception area was all glass and marble, including the receptionist's dress. That's fashion for you. Tim and I had arrived half an hour early to drink in the atmosphere – and looking at the prices in the hotel bar we certainly weren't going to be drinking anything else. A glass of water here cost the same as a glass of wine anywhere else, and for a glass of wine you needed to take out a loan. Nothing cost peanuts here … not even the peanuts.

That's the thing about the super-rich. They don't mind when things are crazily expensive. It just reminds them how rich they are.

We went over to the reception desk and asked to see "Mrs Smith". The receptionist was a slinky-looking girl with long fingernails. She had perfect teeth but she didn't smile and she spoke through her nose, so I guessed she didn't like showing them. She picked up a telephone and dialled a number with a fingernail that was a little longer than her finger. She spoke for a few seconds, then put the phone down. Her earrings jangled. So did my nerves.

"The second floor," she said, barely moving her lips. Maybe she was training to be a ventriloquist. "It's suite sixteen."

So Minerva had a suite, not a single room. We took the lift to the second floor and I have to admit I enjoyed the journey. It's the only lift I've ever seen with solid gold buttons and a chandelier. I could see Tim staring at everything as if he'd just died and gone to heaven. He'd insisted on putting on a suit, which he'd found at the bottom of the wardrobe. It was just a shame that the moths had found it first. Still, so long as nobody wondered why the jacket had seventeen buttonholes but only seven buttons, he'd be fine.

The lift door opened and we found ourselves in a corridor with about a mile of pink carpet, more chandeliers and the sort of wallpaper that seemed wasted on a wall. Suite sixteen was about halfway down – a double wooden door with gold numbers on.

Tim raised his hand, about to knock. And that was when we heard it. A sudden, loud crack from the other side. A gunshot? I wasn't so sure but Tim had no doubt at all. His eyes widened and he threw himself at the door – shoulder-first – obviously intending to smash it down, climb through the wreckage and rescue Minerva from whoever was taking pot shots at her. It didn't budge. Tim howled as he dislocated his shoulder. I reached out and opened the door. It was unlocked anyway.

We ran in. The door led straight into a plush living room. There were three people there. One of them was Jake Hammill, the manager who had come to our office that afternoon. The other was an older man dressed in a velvet jacket with a silk cravat around his neck. He had one of those permanent suntans that give your skin the colour of a peach but the texture of a prune. The third was Minerva. I recognized her at once with that strange buzz of excitement you get when you find yourself face to face with someone really famous. She was holding half a Christmas cracker. The tanned man was holding the other half. Well, that explained the bang we had just heard.

"Who the hell are you?" the older man asked.

"I'm Tim Diamond." Tim shrugged and I heard a loud click as his shoulder blade somehow managed to slip back into place. Well, that was something. Minerva looked as if she was about to call the police. At least she wouldn't have to ask for an ambulance too.

"So what do you mean just bursting in here?" the man continued. "Haven't you ever heard of knocking?"

"Wait a minute! Wait a minute!" Hammill interjected. "This is the private detective I was telling you about. The one you told me to see. Tim Diamond."

"What about the kid?" the man asked.

"I'm his little brother, Nick," I said.

"Yeah, well ... you'd better sit down."

Minerva had been watching all this with a mixture of puzzlement and disbelief. I sat down on the sofa next to her, thinking that a million kids would have given their right arm to be where I was right now and wondering what she'd do with a million right arms. She was dressed simply in expensive jeans and a white shirt, but even so she was one of the most beautiful women I'd ever seen. She had long, blonde hair, eyes that were somewhere between blue and green and the sort of body that made me wish I was older than fourteen. Maybe she was smaller than I'd imagined but then I don't have much imagination. And looking at her, I didn't need it. She was the real thing and she was right there next to me.

Meanwhile, Tim had sat down in a chair. I could tell he fancied Minerva too. As far as I know, Tim has never had a steady girlfriend. He just simply hasn't had any luck finding a woman who's attracted to a twenty-eight-year-old with no money and no brains. To be fair to Tim, he's not that unattractive. I mean, he's slim and he's dark and he's reasonably fit. And it seemed to me that Minerva was definitely interested in him. Mind you, if the old, wrinkled guy was her husband, I wasn't that surprised. How did a world-famous sex symbol end up married to her grandfather?

"So – how can I help you?" Tim asked with a lazy smile. He crossed one leg over the other and his foot caught a lamp, sending the shade flying.

"I told you," Hammill growled. "Minerva needs a bodyguard."

"With a body like that I'm not surprised!" Tim agreed.

"Hold on!" the old man interrupted. "That's my wife you're talking about."

"And who are you?" Tim asked.

"I'm her husband!" He was perched on the arm of the sofa next to Minerva. "My name is Harold Chase." He lay a hand on Minerva's shoulder, and maybe I was wrong but I could have sworn she shuddered slightly. "I'm paying you to make sure nobody hurts my baby."

"You've got a baby?" Tim demanded.

"I'm talking about Minerva!"

"I don't need looking after," Minerva said. They were the first words she had spoken, and I could hear the faint Greek accent fighting to get out. I was also reminded that this was the voice that had sold a billion CDs. "I don't need looking after"; it almost sounded like the title of one of her songs.

"We've got to take control of this situation," Hammill cut in. "You read what that letter said. Show it to Mr Diamond."

Minerva thought for a moment, then pulled a white envelope out of her pocket. She held it for a moment. "This arrived yesterday," she said. "It was slipped under the door of my suite. It's from somebody who hates me."

Tim opened the letter and read aloud:

"DEAR MINERVA, YOU ARE A MONSTER. I CANNOT FOREGIVE YOU FOR WHAT YOU DID IN TROPOJË LAST SUMMER. HOW COULD YOU DO THAT? I WILL NEVER FORGET IT AND VERY SOON I AM GOING TO KILL YOU. YOUR LIFE WILL COME TO AN END IN LONDON. THIS WILL BE YOUR LAST CHRISTMAS!"

Tim lowered the letter. "What makes you think that whoever wrote this hates you?" he asked.

Minerva stared at him. "I'm sorry?" she quavered.

"Well, he does call you *dear* Minerva..."

I snatched up the letter. It was straight out of a computer: blue ink on a plain sheet of paper. I noticed that whoever had written it couldn't spell "forgive". The envelope was addressed: Minerva, Suite 16.

"What happened in Tropojë?" I asked.

"Nothing happened in Tropojë," Harold replied.

"It's the concert," Hammill cut in. "It's gotta be!"

"Forget it, Jake."

"No, Harry. They might as well know." Hammill turned to us. "It was just one of those things," he explained. "It happened last summer, like the letter says. Minerva was going to give a big charity concert in Albania. It was to benefit OAK."

"What's OAK?"

"Overweight Albanian Kids. It tries to help kids who watch too much TV and eat too many McDonald's. Some of them have to wear elasticized clothing. Many of them are in wheelchairs. They can walk – they're just too lazy. Anyway, they were really looking forward to the concert, but at the last moment Minerva had to pull out."

"Why?" I asked.

"I had a headache," Minerva replied. Obviously the overweight kids of OAK had never given her much cause for concern. Until now.

"You upset a lot of fans, Minerva," Jake said.

"And you think one of the fans is out to get her?"

"That's what it looks like."

I wasn't so sure. The idea of an oversized Albanian TV addict travelling all the way to England to kill Minerva sounded a bit far-fetched to me. On the other hand, there was that spelling mistake: English clearly wasn't their first language. But there was something about the letter I didn't like – and I don't just mean the death threat. I knew there was something wrong. Something didn't add up. But I hadn't yet had time to work out what it was.

"My own feeling is that we should just get out of London," the husband said. "I can't sleep with the thought of you being in danger."

"Harold – you're exaggerating!" Minerva shook her head. "This trip is great publicity. Turning on the lights and opening the grotto is a big deal. I'm not going to run away just because some freak writes me a stupid letter." She turned to Tim. "I've got a single coming out on December twenty-fifth," she said.

"What's it called?" I asked.

Tim sighed. "It's called Christmas Day,

Nick," he said. "Everyone knows that."

"I mean – what's the single called?"

"It's a song about cowboys," Minerva said. "The title is 'Like a Virginian'." She fell silent for a moment and then she really surprised me. "If you boys are going to work with me, you might as well know that I hate this goddamn country and I hate Christmas."

"Minerva—" Harold began.

"Shut up, Harold! I just want to put my cards on the table."

"Your Christmas cards?" Tim asked.

"I don't have any. Those stupid pictures of angels and three wise men. If they were so wise, what was all that business with the gold, frankincense and myrrh? You think a baby's got any use for that sort of stuff?" She shook her head. "I hate everything about Christmas. Those stupid Christmas trees that drop needles all over the carpet. Those boring carols that go on and on. Santa Claus with his stupid beard."

"What about Christmas presents?" I asked.

"Why would I care about Christmas presents? I've got everything I want already." She realized she was still holding the half-cracker that she had pulled with her husband when we came in. "And I don't like these stupid crackers either," she went on. "They were sent up to the room by some fan or someone and all they've given me is a headache. As far as I'm concerned, the best thing to do with Christmas would be to forget the whole thing."

She threw down the cracker. A silver acorn and a slip of paper rolled out onto the table.

I don't know what it was that made me pick up the piece of paper. Maybe after Minerva's little speech I needed a laugh. Or maybe there was something about it that whispered to me that actually it didn't belong in a cracker. Anyway, I unfolded it and sure enough there was the same blue ink as the letter, the same typeface. There were just two lines.

WHEN MINERVA SEES THE LIGHTS
THAT'S WHEN I'LL HAVE HER IN MY SIGHTS

I read it out.

"I don't get it," Tim said. "It's not very funny..."

"It's not a joke, Tim!" I exclaimed. "It's another death threat."

"But that's impossible!" Harold seized the piece of paper and held it with a shaking hand. "How did this get inside the cracker?" he demanded. He stared at Jake Hammill. "You brought them up here!" he continued accusingly. "What's going on?"

"I just picked them up from reception!" Hammill replied. "They said they'd been left in your name by a fan."

"What does it mean?" Minerva asked. Her voice had gone quiet.

Nobody spoke – so I did. "It must mean tomorrow," I said. "When you turn on the Christmas lights." I picked up the acorn. It was heavy – solid silver, maybe. "And look at this," I said.

"An acorn..." Tim was puzzled.

"Off an *oak* tree, Tim," I said. "They're telling you who it came from."

"Of course!" Harold Chase stood up. He was shaking so much, I was worried something was going to fall off. "That's it," he said. "We're not going to turn on the lights. Forget it. We're not going anywhere near them."

"Harold..." Hammill began.

"I mean it, Jake."

"Forget it, Harold!" Minerva had also got to her feet. "Look – I've already promised. I'm going to turn on these stupid lights. I've got to be there: the Mayor of London is coming. All the press will be out. It's going to be a big event."

"It'll be an even bigger event if someone shoots you," I muttered.

Tim turned to me. "That's a terrible thing to say, Nick!" He thought for a moment. "Anyway, they might not shoot her. They might run her over or blow her up or possibly fix the wires so she gets electrocuted..."

Minerva had gone a little pale. "Do you think you can protect me, Mr Diamond?" she asked.

Tim smiled. "I'm the private eye who never blinks," he replied. "And from this moment I'm not going to let you out of my sight. I'm going to walk with you, eat with you and go to bed with you—"

"Hey! Wait a minute! I'm in the bed!" Harold interrupted.

"We have a four-poster," Minerva said.

"That's great," Tim said. "We can have one post each."

Jake Hammill stepped forward. "I think Minerva will be safe enough while she's here at the Porchester hotel," he said. "Suppose Mr Diamond joins us tomorrow evening on the way to Regent Street?"

Minerva nodded. "I'm staying in all day tomorrow. That'll be fine."

"That just leaves the question of your fee, Mr Diamond," Hammill continued.

"No question about it," Tim said. "I want one."

"Of course." Hammill blinked uncertainly. "We'll pay you two hundred pounds a day. But let's get one thing straight. If anyone takes a shot at Minerva, we'll expect you to step in front of the bullet."

"Don't worry!" Tim jerked a thumb at me. "That's what he's for."

So there it was, signed and sealed. I still wondered why Minerva hadn't gone straight to the police – but maybe it wouldn't suit her being surrounded by the men in blue. I wanted to tell her that Tim would offer her about as much protection as a paper umbrella in the rain, but two hundred pounds was two hundred pounds. I watched as Jake Hammill counted out the money, and it occurred to me that the only time I'd been expecting to see the Queen that Christmas had been on her TV broadcast. But here were twenty little portraits sliding into Tim's outstretched hand. I almost wanted to kiss her. Or him.

We took the bus home. We could have afforded a cab but we'd already decided to blow a big chunk of the money on a three-course meal at our local Italian. I was already dreaming of a twelve-inch pizza on an eleven-inch plate. Extra cheese and pepperoni. And maybe extra pizza too. But even so, I couldn't get Minerva out of my mind. I went over what had happened in the suite. I was still certain something was wrong.

"If you ask me, Tim, there's something strange about this," I said.

Tim looked around him. "It's just a bus, Nick," he said.

"I'm not talking about the bus. I'm talking about Minerva. Those death threats! Whoever heard of a death threat inside a Christmas cracker?"

"Yeah," Tim nodded. "And there was no sign of a paper hat."

I shook my head. "I wouldn't be surprised if they weren't making the whole thing up … the three of them. You heard what she said. All she wants to do is sell her CDs. Maybe the whole thing's just a publicity stunt."

Tim shook his head. "I don't think so, Nick. I think she's in real danger. Don't ask me why – I've just got an instinct for this sort of thing. A sixth sense."

"Sure," I muttered. "It's just a shame you missed out on the other five."

I looked out of the window. It had got dark a while ago and it looked as if it was going to snow. There were a few flakes dancing in the wind. As we turned a corner, I noticed a man standing on the pavement with a sandwich board. He was handing out leaflets about the end of the world. London is full of people like that. Maybe it's the city that drives them mad or maybe they're mad before they arrive and it's the city that attracts them. Anyway, this man had three words in red paint across his chest:

DEATH WILL COME

He seemed to catch my eye as we went past. And I found myself wondering. Was he just a harmless crank trying to sell religion to anyone who would listen?

Or did he know something I didn't?

REGENT STREET

Everyone makes a fuss about the Christmas lights on Regent Street and maybe there was a time when they were actually worth travelling in to see. I remember when I was small, my mum would take me into town and the lights would flicker and flash and sparkle and people would cross the road with their necks craned, staring at them in wonderment, and they wouldn't even complain when they were run over by the 139 bus.

But that was then. Nowadays the lights are more or less the same as they are on any other high street at Christmas. Worse than that, they're paid for by big business, so you don't just get Santa, stars or whatever. You get the latest characters from a Disney movie. Or "Harry Christmas" from J.K. Rowling. Or whatever.

Even so, turning on the lights is still a big

deal. If it isn't a member of the royal family, it's a pop star or a Hollywood actor. All the newspapers and TV stations record the moment when the button gets pressed, and the next day you can read all about it on page one: MINERVA LIGHTS UP LONDON. And just for one day the earthquakes and the wars and the dirty politics are left to page two.

We were driven to Regent Street in a stretch limo. The chauffeur was a tall, slim man in a grey uniform and I couldn't help wondering if someone hadn't stretched him too. Minerva and her husband sat on the back seat. For the first time I noticed he was wearing a hearing aid, but he didn't need it because no one was talking to him. She was gazing out of the window. It was made from special glass so that no one could look in. Her manager, Jake Hammill, had the next seat to himself. Tim and I were closest to the front – and furthest from the bar. The three of them were drinking champagne but all we'd been offered was a glass of iced water. Well, we were staff. Official security and its younger brother.

As usual Minerva was in a bad mood, but I had to admit that from where I was sitting she looked fabulous. She was wearing a bright red number with white fur trimmings. Think Father Christmas only thirty years younger and after major cosmetic surgery. Her lips were bright red too, shaped like a perfect kiss.

It would have been hard to believe that this was the woman who hated Christmas. She'd done herself up like the sort of present every man in London would want to open. I glanced at Tim and saw that he was drooling. I just hoped it wouldn't stain the carpet.

"Now, remember!" Harold Chase said to his wife. She turned round slowly and looked at him without a lot of interest. "You pose for the cameras. You make a little speech. You turn on the lights. And then we get the hell out of there."

"What's the big worry?" Minerva drawled.

"The big worry?" Harold's eyes bulged. For a nasty minute I thought they were going to fall out of his face. "There could be a killer out there, baby. You're going to be out in the open, exposed. Anyone could take a shot at you." He leant forward and turned to Tim. "You'd better keep your eyes open, Mr Diamond," he said.

"You don't have to worry, Mr Cheese," Tim assured him. "I've had my eyes on your wife all evening."

"Well, you'd just better make sure nothing goes wrong."

"What could possibly go wrong with me around?" Tim exclaimed. He threw his hands back in a gesture of surprise, emptying his glass of iced water over the driver.

The car drew to a halt. It was just coming

up to six o'clock on a cold, dry Tuesday evening, but the shops were still open and there were Christmas shoppers everywhere. We got out and suddenly the night seemed to explode in a thousand flashes. They came so thick and fast that I found myself blinded. It was as if I had entered an electrical storm that signalled the end of the world.

Of course, it was nothing so dramatic. Minerva was being photographed by a huge pack of press photographers, all of them holding up great, chunky cameras with lenses that were definitely pleased to see her. For a few seconds Minerva seemed to be frozen, half in the car and half out of it. Then she came to her senses and began to smile and wave; the silent, bad-tempered woman who had been sitting opposite me was instantly replaced by the perfect star that she was as the lights flashed all around her. And at that moment I got an idea of what it must be like to be a celebrity – loved not because of what you are but because of what the cameras want you to be.

At the same time, I was puzzled. Minerva had received two death threats. Even if she had decided not to take them seriously, her husband and manager had been worried enough to hire Tim and me. And yet here she was completely surrounded by photographers. It occurred to me that any one of them could have a gun. There were a few police around, but right now killing Minerva would be the easiest thing in the world. I said nothing. I could only stand there as she turned and smiled and smiled and turned while the photographers shouted at her from every side.

"Over here, Minerva!"

"Give us a smile, Minerva!"

"This way, Minerva!"

Tim nudged me. He was standing with his back to the car, blinking in the flashlights, but I could see that he was suddenly alert. I followed his eyes and saw a rather shabby-looking man in a suit hurrying towards us and suddenly I knew what was going to happen.

"Leave this to me..." Tim muttered.

"No, Tim!" I began.

But it was too late. Tim charged forward and grabbed hold of the man, then spun him around and threw him onto the bonnet of the limousine.

"That's far enough!" Tim exclaimed.

"I... I... I..." The man was too shocked to speak.

"What do you want with Minerva?" Tim demanded.

"I'm the Mayor of London!" the man exclaimed.

Tim looked suspicious. He was still pinning him down. "If you're the Mayor of London, where's your red cloak and pointy hat?"

"I'm not that sort of mayor," the man

growled. "I think you've been watching too many pantomimes."

"Oh no I haven't!" Tim replied.

By now, two policemen had appeared and had pulled Tim away, helping the Mayor to his feet. Because it *was* the Mayor, of course. I'd recognized him instantly – his bald head, his brightly coloured cheeks and his entirely colourless moustache. Jake Hammill had seen what had happened. He hurried over and placed himself between the Mayor and Tim.

"I'm so sorry!" he said. "We've hired private security and I guess he was a little jumpy."

"It's an outrage," the Mayor exclaimed. He had a whiny voice.

"Come and meet Minerva, Mr Mayor. She's been longing to say hello."

The thought of shaking Minerva's hand – or indeed any part of her – must have cheered the Mayor up because he seemed to have forgotten that he had just been attacked by Tim. Hammill took him over to his client, who was still posing for the cameras. "Minerva … this is the Mayor!" he said.

"How lovely to meet you, Mr Mayor!" Minerva sounded so genuine, I almost believed her myself. She kissed him on the cheek and night became day again as the photographers captured the moment for the morning's head-lines. "Where do we go to turn on the lights?" she asked.

“This way…” The Mayor had gone red.

We made our way to a raised platform that had been constructed at the side of the road. There must have been four or five hundred people all around us, many of them waving autograph books and flashing cameras of their own. A Salvation Army band was playing carols. They finished “Away in a Manger” and began a version of “Silent Night” that was anything but.

Minerva climbed the stairs and I couldn’t stop myself thinking of gallows and public hangings. I remembered the warning inside the cracker. Was someone really about to have a crack at her? I tried to think where I would hide myself if I were a sniper. I looked up at the rooftops. It was hard to see anything in the darkness but there didn’t seem to be anyone there. How about an open window? All the windows in the street were closed. Then perhaps in the crowd…

By now Minerva had reached the top of the stairs. Was she being brave or stupid? Or was it just that she refused to take any of this seriously?

Jake Hammill was certainly looking nervous. So was Harold Chase. He was standing to one side, his hands in his pockets, pulling his black cashmere coat around him like he was trying to hide in it. His eyes were darting left and right. Even if nobody took a shot at his wife, I'd have said a major heart attack was a strong possibility. He didn't look like he'd last the night.

So there we all were on the platform: Minerva and the Mayor at the front, the rest of us grouped behind. There was a single red button, mounted on a wooden block, and a microphone. Minerva stepped forward. The crowd fell silent. The Salvation Army players came to the end of a verse and stopped – unfortunately not all at the same time.

"Ladies and gentlemen!" It was the Mayor speaking. His voice whined the full length of Regent Street and it wasn't just the fault of the microphone. "I'd like to welcome you all here and I hope you've all remembered to pay the congestion charge! We've had some great stars turn on the lights in Regent Street. But this year, if you ask me, we've got the biggest star of all. Please welcome … Minerva!"

Everyone clapped and cheered.

"Thank you. Thank you so very much!" Minerva's voice echoed after the Mayor's. "I'm so thrilled to be here, at Christmas. It's such a wonderful time of the year – the birth of baby Jesus and of course my new CD is about to be released. So Happy Christmas to everyone, and here goes…"

She lifted her finger.

And that was when it happened.

There were two gunshots. They sounded

incredibly close and there could be no doubt that Minerva was the target. At once the entire atmosphere changed. There was a single second of frozen silence and then screams as the crowd panicked and began to scatter, people pushing each other to get out of the way. The band was swept away in the stampede. I saw someone fall into the big drum. The cymbal player was knocked off her feet with a final crash. On the platform, the Mayor had been the first to dive for cover. Minerva hadn't moved, as if unsure what to do. I couldn't see if she had been hit or not. With that bright red dress, it was hard to tell.

Then Tim leapt into action. I have to hand it to him – at least he was braver than the Mayor, who had curled into a ball in the corner of the platform with his head buried in his hands. Tim had been hired to protect Minerva and that was what he was going to do – even if the shots had already been fired. Even if she was already dead.

"Get down!" he shouted.

He lunged forward and I guessed that he meant to throw himself on top of Minerva – which, I had to admit, was quite an attractive idea. Unfortunately, Minerva had already stepped aside. Tim missed and landed, with his arms outstretched, on the red button.

At once, ten thousand light bulbs burst into multi-coloured life. This year the Regent Street lights had been sponsored by McDonald's. They depicted stars and Christmas trees decorated with twinkling hamburgers and fries. At the same time, a specially arranged Christmas carol – "We Wish You a McMerry Christmas" – boomed out of the speakers.

The Mayor opened one eye. "You idiot!" he screamed. "You've turned on the Christmas lights instead of Minerva!"

I'm not sure what would have happened next. Perhaps Tim would have ended up being murdered himself. But then Harold Chase stepped forward and pointed. "There!" he yelled. "There he is!"

He was pointing at the rooftops and now, with all the extra bulbs burning below, the darkness had become a sea of red and blue and yellow and white. And sure enough, high above one of the department stores, I could make out a short, plump figure half hidden behind a chimney stack. He was staring down at us and, although I couldn't see what it was from this distance, there was definitely something in his hand. A gun? He certainly would have had a clear shot at Minerva from where he was standing – but not any more. Half a dozen policemen had already reached the platform and they had all grabbed a piece of her. Jake and Harold were also grabbing at her. Tim had crawled off the red button and was trying to climb on top. The entire platform looked like a training session for the All Blacks with Minerva in the middle of the scrum.

The figure on the roof didn't seem to be moving and that was when I decided to take action. I didn't really know what I was doing. Part of me was asking questions. Why hadn't I seen the sniper earlier? Why hadn't he made a faster escape – or at least tried to fire off a few more shots? Was that a gun in his hand? And part of me knew that I wouldn't find the answers hanging around on Regent Street. I had to go and look for them myself.

I leapt down from the platform, pushed my way through what was left of the crowd and plunged into the nearest shop. It was a huge place selling clothes that I couldn't possibly afford and – one glance told me – that I wouldn't want to buy if I could. Blue blazers and red cravats have never been my style. There was a lift opposite the front door and I was lucky. The doors were just closing as I arrived. I ran in and pressed the top button – the sixth floor. I was lucky again. The lift didn't stop on the way up.

The sixth floor seemed to be devoted to Christmas presents for people you don't like: really nasty golfing jumpers, oversized umbrellas and multicoloured shoes. There weren't too many shoppers around as I burst out of the lift and made for the nearest fire door. Sure enough, a flight of concrete stairs led up to the roof. I took them two at a time and it only occurred to me now that I was unarmed and about to come face to face with a would-be assassin who probably wouldn't be too pleased to see me. But it was too late to go back. And, I figured, he couldn't be more deadly than those golfing jumpers.

I reached a door marked FIRE EXIT and slammed into it ... which, incidentally, set off all the fire alarms and the sprinkler system on the seven floors below. But now I was on the roof: a strange landscape of chimneys, satellite dishes, water tanks and air-conditioning units. I stopped for a moment and let my eyes get used to the darkness. Not that it was exactly pitch black. The Regent Street lights were still glittering below me and, looking down, I could see the scattered crowds, the police, what was left of the Salvation Army band.

Something moved. And there he was, the man that Harold Chase had seen from below. He was only about fifteen metres away from me, cowering on the other side of the roof. He didn't look like your typical assassin. He was short and very fat – almost spherical – with white, curly hair. I wondered if he was one of the overweight Albanians. It was Minerva's absence at a concert in Albania that had started all this.

The man looked at me with something between horror and dismay. He raised a hand as if to prevent me moving forward.

"No!" he shouted. "I d-d-didn't..."

Then he turned and ran.

I chased after him and that was when I discovered that I had miscalculated. I had run into the wrong store and there was a three-metre gap between his roof and mine. But I hadn't come this far to let an impossible jump and a probable fall to my death seven floors below worry me. I picked up speed and threw myself off the edge.

For a moment I hung in the air and I could feel the ground a very long way beneath me. The cold night air was rushing into me and – for a nasty moment – so was the pavement. The other roof was too far away. I wasn't going to make it. Suddenly I was angry with myself. Who did I think I was? Spider-Man? If so, I'd forgotten to pack a web.

But I didn't fall. Somehow my outstretched hands caught hold of the edge of the other roof and I winced as my stomach and shoulders slammed into the brickwork. I could taste blood and dust in my mouth. I'd cut my lip and maybe loosened a couple of my teeth. Using what little strength I had left, I managed to pull myself up and roll to safety. Painfully, I got to my feet. I wasn't surprised to see that the little fat man had gone.

He had left something behind. I saw them – three small silver objects on the asphalt. At first I thought they were bullets, but as I walked towards them, I realized they were too big. People down in the street were pointing up at me and shouting as I dropped to one knee and scooped them into my hand.

Three oak leaves. That was what the sniper had left behind. The acorn in the cracker and now this. He was definitely trying to tell me something and I'd got the message loud and clear.

DINNER FOR TWO

When I woke up the next morning, we were right back where we'd started. Which is to say, we were in Camden Town, in the office, and once again Tim was out of work. It turned out that nobody had been particularly impressed by my death-defying leap when all I'd got to show for it was grazed arms, bruises and a handful of silver oak leaves. I'd given the police a description of the man I'd seen on the roof – not that it added up to much. Small and fat. The curly hair could have been a wig. And although he had spoken, he hadn't said enough for me to be sure whether he had an Albanian accent or not.

As I'd sat in the bath that night, I'd gone over his words a dozen times. *No! I d-d-didn't…* Had he been scared or did he always stammer like that? And what had he meant? The police had decided that he was angry – that he was telling me he hadn't shot Minerva in the sense that he had missed. To me it seemed simpler than that. "I didn't do it. It wasn't me." That was what he had been trying to say. But then why had he left the oak leaves behind? Maybe they were the symbol of the society for Overweight Albanian Kids. And finally, where was the gun? I thought I'd seen something in his hand but he hadn't had it when I reached the roof.

Anyway, the case was over as far as we were concerned. Now that the police knew Minerva was in real danger, they had taken over protection duties – and looking at some of those officers leering at her on Regent Street, I could see that plenty of them were going to be putting in for overtime. The good news was that we still had about seventy pounds of the two hundred Jake Hammill had given us. That would buy us a Christmas turkey, Brussels sprouts, roast potatoes and chestnut stuffing. It was just a shame that Tim had sold the oven.

I found him at breakfast with a bowl of cornflakes and the morning newspaper. He wasn't looking too pleased and I soon saw why. He'd made the front page. There was a picture of him spread out on his stomach just after he had accidentally turned on the Christmas lights.

"Have you seen this?" he wailed as I sat down. "And look at this!"

He tapped the caption underneath the picture:

DIM DIAMOND ASSAULTS MAYOR AND TURNS ON THE LIGHTS

"It must be a misprint," he said.

"Are you sure?" I asked.

Tim sighed – and suddenly he was looking sad. "You know, Nick," he began. "Recently, I've been thinking."

"Did it hurt?" I muttered.

He ignored me. "Maybe I should think about getting another job. I mean, look at me! I'm twenty-eight. I never have any money. I'm six months behind on the rent. I can't remember the last time you and I had a square meal."

"We had pizza the night before last," I reminded him.

"That was circular. And whenever I do get a job – like this business with Miranda – it always seems to go wrong." He sighed again. "She told me I was the most stupid person she'd ever met."

"Maybe she was joking."

"She spat at me and tried to strangle me!"

"Well … she's Greek."

Tim shook his head. "As soon as the New Year begins, I'm going to find myself a proper job," he said. "It shouldn't be too difficult. I've got qualifications."

I fell silent. I didn't have the heart to remind

him that he only had two A levels – and one of them was in embroidery.

It looked as if we were going to have a pretty glum Christmas. But as you'll probably know by now, nothing in our lives ever turns out quite how we expect. A second later there was a knock at the door and before either of us could react, Minerva walked in. I was so surprised, I almost fell off my chair. Tim was so surprised he actually did fall off his.

She was on her own and she was trying to look inconspicuous dressed in jeans and a black jersey with a one-thousand-dollar pair of sunglasses hiding her eyes. But Minerva was Minerva. She couldn't look inconspicuous if she covered herself in mud and sat in a swamp.

"Minerva!" Tim gasped as he picked himself up.

"I didn't want to see you," Minerva said, taking off her sunglasses so she could see him better. "I didn't want to come here," she went on. "But I had to. Last night I behaved like a cow."

"You ate grass?" Tim asked.

"No. I behaved disgracefully towards you. I spat at you. I tried to strangle you. But this morning, when I woke up, I realized I'd got it all wrong." She sat down. "Harold brought in the newspapers and I saw that we got every single front page. And part of that was thanks to you. *The Times* called you a maniac. The

Mail said you were idiotic. The *Guardian* thought you were a banker."

"That *was* a misprint," I said.

Minerva ignored me. "If I'd just turned on those ridiculous lights, the most I would have got would have been the front page of the evening paper. But the way things turned out, I got more publicity than I could have dreamed of. Harold is certain my new CD is going to go straight to number one."

"How is Harold?" I asked.

"He had a very lucky escape last night," Minerva said. "One of those bullets missed him by a centimetre. It even burnt a hole in the side of his coat."

"You mean ... it could have hit his pace-maker?" I exclaimed.

"It was a near miss. But I'm not here to talk about Harold." She turned to Tim. "I want to make it up to you, Timothy," she said. "I want to invite you to dinner. I've already reserved a table for two."

"Isn't two a little early for dinner?" Tim asked.

"For just the two of us, I mean!" Minerva smiled but I wasn't entirely convinced. I'd met sharks with friendlier teeth. "At eight o'clock this evening," she went on. "There's a restaurant I go to. It's called The Gravy." She giggled mischievously. "I thought we might have a little tête-à-tête."

"I'm not that crazy about French food," Tim muttered.

"You'll like this," Minerva simpered. "Make sure you dress up smart. You should put on that suit of yours with seven buttons and seventeen buttonholes."

And with that she was gone.

I went over to the window and looked out as she left the building. There was a police car waiting for her. It was true, then. The men in blue had now taken over Tim's job.

"They're giving her round-the-clock protection," I said.

"They think someone's going to kill her near a clock?"

Tim looked slightly dazed. I could see that he was already imagining himself in some swanky restaurant, drinking champagne with the rich and famous. It was time to bring him down to earth.

"You're not going," I said.

"Why not?" Tim replied.

"She's not interested in you, Tim. If she's invited you out, it's only for the publicity. That's all she cares about."

"Maybe she's got a soft spot for me."

"I don't think she's got a soft spot for anyone except herself. Anyway, she's a married woman."

"Listen, kid." Tim leant back in his chair. "You don't understand the female mind.

Maybe she's looking for something rough and a little bit dangerous."

"Then she can buy herself a yak."

"She likes me!"

"She's using you, Tim."

"She's invited me to dinner!"

"Well, if you're going, I'm going too."

Tim stared at me as if I'd just slapped him in the face – and I can't say I wasn't tempted. "Forget it, Nick," he said. "You heard what she said. This is a dinner for two. I don't need you there. I'm going on my own. And this time, my decision is final!"

The Gravy was one of London's most exclusive restaurants, reserved for celebrities and millionaires. It was so exclusive, even the waiters had trouble getting in, and the name was written in tiny letters as if it didn't want anyone to notice. It was tucked away in a quiet street near Covent Garden with a doorman sizing up everyone who came close. He looked at Tim and me with an expression of complete disgust. But this was the sort of place where even the doormat didn't say WELCOME. It preferred to say GO AWAY.

Why had I come? Part of the answer was that I was worried about Tim. I still didn't know what Minerva was up to, but I didn't trust her and I wanted to be there if things took a turn for the worse. But also, I quite fancied dinner at The Gravy. The food was said to be so good that the chef actually cried when you ate it. The house speciality was a leg of lamb cooked in Armagnac – and no matter that it cost you an Armagnac and a leg. Even a glass of water at The Gravy was expensive. It probably came out of a gold-plated tap.

The head waiter showed us to the best table, and there was Minerva looking stunning in a white silk dress that hugged her tight in all the right places and tighter still in some of the wrong ones. Her face fell when she saw me but she didn't protest as a couple of waiters hastily added a third setting to the table. It was only as we sat down that she muttered, "I'm surprised you brought your little brother, Timothy. Couldn't you find a babysitter?"

"I'm no baby, Minerva," I said.

"I was hoping to be alone with your big brother. I want to get to know him a little better."

"Just pretend I'm not here."

And that's exactly what she tried to do for the rest of the meal. The waiter came over with three menus but she chose only for the two of them, leaving me to decide for myself. That suited me. I went for the straightforward steak and chips, leaving the fancy stuff with the French names to her and Tim. If I've got one rule in life, it's never eat anything you can't translate.

"So tell me, Timothy," Minerva said, winking at him. "How would you like a little bubbly?"

Tim looked awkward. "Actually, I had a bath before I came."

"Bollinger!" she exclaimed.

"No. Really. I did!"

Minerva ordered a bottle of Bollinger. I asked for a Coke. The way she was making eyes at Tim, it really did seem that she had designs on him and I couldn't understand it. I mean, he was fifteen years younger than her and about fifty thousand times poorer. What could she see in him? I watched him as he opened the champagne for her. There was an explosive pop, followed by a scream from the other side of the room.

"The head waiter?" Tim asked.

"No," I said. "Just a waiter's head."

Minerva didn't seem to mind. She snuggled up close to him. "I love a man who makes me laugh," she said. "Can I ask you something, Timothy? Do you have a girlfriend?"

"Not at the moment," Tim answered.

"There's nobody waiting for you in bed tonight?"

"It's just Tim and his Paddington Bear hot-water bottle," I told her.

Tim glared at me.

"I fill it for him every night."

The waiter arrived with the first course:

soup for me, caviar for Tim and Minerva. Personally, I've never understood caviar. I mean, when I order eggs, I don't expect them to turn up tiny, black and fifty quid a mouthful. But she seemed happy enough. I wondered who would pick up the bill.

I could see that Tim was already well out of his depth. He was looking more and more uncomfortable the closer Minerva got, and she was already close enough. Any closer and she would be on his lap.

"Timothy ... I think you and I were meant for each other," she breathed.

"What about your husband?" Tim squeaked.

She sniffed. "Let's not talk about Harold. He's half the man you are."

"Which half are you talking about?"

I couldn't help chipping in again. "If you dislike him so much," I asked, "why did you marry him?"

To my surprise, Minerva looked me in the eye for the first time and I knew at once that she was going to be completely honest. "Why do you think?" she replied coldly. "I married Harold for his money. That was at the start of my career. I'd just left Athens and I had nothing. He promised to help me – and he did. Of course, all that's changed now. Now I'm worth millions!"

"So why are you still with him?"

"I can't be bothered to divorce him. Anyway, it's more fun the way things are."

"Does he know where you are tonight?"

Minerva laughed. "Of course he knows. You should have seen his face when I told him I was going out with Timothy. I thought he was going to have a heart attack!"

So that was why she had invited Tim to The Gravy. I should have seen it from the start. Minerva loathed her husband – that much had been obvious when we first met them at their suite at the hotel – and she amused herself by humiliating him. And what better way than to be seen out in public with someone like my big brother, Tim?

At that moment I disliked her as much as anyone I had ever known. More than Charon, the four-fingered assassin we met in Amsterdam. More than my homicidal French teacher, Monsieur Palis. The thing about Minerva was that she was beautiful, rich and loved by millions. But she had the heart of a snake.

Somehow we got through to the next course. My steak was fine but I didn't like the look of the grey, jelly-like dish that Minerva had ordered for herself and Tim. It came in a yellow sauce with rice and beans.

Tim wasn't sure either. He had eaten about half of it when he stopped and looked up. "What did you say this was?" he asked.

"*Cervelles de veaux au beurre.*"

He took another mouthful. "It tastes interesting," he said. "What does that mean?"

"Grilled calves' brains in butter."

Two minutes later we were standing outside on the pavement with the doorman glowering at us, glad to see us go.

"That was a nice evening," I said.

"Do you think Minerva enjoyed it?" Tim asked.

"Well, you may have spoiled it a bit when you were sick on her." I looked around for a bus or a taxi.

"I want to go home," Tim groaned. He was still looking very green.

"To Paddington Bear?"

"Just get us a cab!"

But as it turned out, we weren't going to need a bus or a cab. Because just then a car came screeching to a halt in front of us and two men leapt out.

"It's a police car!" Tim exclaimed.

That was particularly brilliant of him and I wasn't sure how he'd worked it out. Maybe it was the blue uniforms the men were wearing. Or it could have been the car with its flashing lights and the word POLICE emblazoned on the side. But he was right. I thought they'd come to look after Minerva – but it was the two of us they made for.

"Are you Tim Diamond?" one of them asked.

"Yes..."

"Get in the car. You're coming down to the station."

"What's going on?" I demanded. "What's happened? And how did you know we were here?"

They ignored me.

The policeman was examining Tim. "We want to talk to you," he said.

"What about?" Tim quavered.

The policeman smiled but without a shred of warmth or humour. It was the sort of smile a doctor might give you before he explained you only had a week to live. "You're wanted, Mr Diamond," he said. "For murder."

THE DEAD MAN

I don't like police stations. They're full of violent and dangerous characters who need to be kept away from modern society ... and I'm not talking about the crooks. A lot of people say the British police are wonderful, but I'd have to disagree. I was only fourteen but I had been arrested so often, it couldn't be long before they gave me my own set of personalized handcuffs. I even spent a month in prison once – and I hadn't done anything wrong! When I look back on it, there's only one word to describe the way I've been treated. Criminal.

This time they drove us to a police station in Holborn, about ten minutes' drive from The Gravy. Tim had gone very pale and quiet in the back of the car. *Cervelles de veaux au beurre* and now this! We stopped and the two policemen led us in through a door and down the usual corridor with white tiles on the walls and hard neon lighting above ... the sort of corridor that can only take you somewhere you don't want to be. There was an interrogation room at the end: four chairs, one table and two detectives. The furniture was hard and unattractive but that was nothing compared to the men.

Detective Chief Inspector Snape and Detective Superintendent Boyle. They were old friends and, like most of Tim's old friends, they hated us. Why was it that whenever we got into trouble, the two of them always seemed to show up? Surely the Metropolitan Police could have found two new officers to molest us? Anyway, put an ape and a Rottweiler in suits and you'll get a rough idea of Snape and Boyle. Snape was the older of the two and the one less likely to have rabies. He was looking old, I thought. But he'd probably looked old the day he was born.

"Well, this really is the perfect end to a horrible day," Snape began as we sat down. It didn't look as if he was going to offer us a cup of tea. "Tim Diamond! The only detective in London with no brains."

Tim went a little green.

"I wouldn't mention brains unless you know a good dry cleaner," I said.

"I want to go to bed!" Tim moaned.

"You're not going anywhere, Diamond," Snape cut in. "I'm investigating a murder and right now you're my only suspect."

"Can I hit him?" Boyle asked hopefully.

"No, Boyle."

"Can I hit his little brother?"

"No!"

"But they were resisting arrest, sir!"

"We haven't arrested them yet, Boyle." Snape shook his head and sighed. "I've just sent Boyle on an anger-management course," he told us.

"Did it work?" I asked.

"No. He got angry and hit the manager so they sent him back again."

"Well you're wasting your time," I said. "We haven't murdered anyone."

Snape looked at me with disdain. "What can you tell me about a man called Reginald Parker?" he said.

"I can't tell you anything, Snape," I said. "We've never met him."

"What's happened to him?" Tim asked.

"He's been murdered," Snape replied. "He was strangled this afternoon. He lived at 27 Sparrow Lane and his neighbour heard the sound of a fight. She called us and we found the body."

"What makes you think it's got anything to do with us?" I asked.

Snape nodded at Boyle. "Show them!"

Boyle leant down and produced a car battery connected to a tangle of wires with clamps on the end. He placed it on the table and glanced unpleasantly at Tim. Snape raised his eyes. "I don't mean that! I want you to show them the evidence!"

Boyle scowled. He opened a drawer and this time he produced a transparent evidence bag with something inside it. I recognized it at once. *No problem too problematic*. It was Tim's business card.

"We found this next to the body," Snape said. "How do you explain that?"

"A coincidence?" Tim suggested.

Snape's face darkened. "Of course it's not a coincidence, you idiot! It's a clue! Was Reginald Parker a client of yours? That wouldn't surprise me. Anyone stupid enough to hire you would almost certainly wind up dead."

I shook my head. "I told you, Chief Inspector. We've never seen him."

"How can you be so sure of that? I haven't even told you what he looked like."

Boyle opened the drawer a second time and produced a black and white photograph.

You can always tell when the police have taken a picture of someone after they're dead. They don't smile for the camera. In fact, they don't do anything. And the black and the white somehow seems to suit them. All the colour has already gone. The photograph showed a short, plump man with curly hair, lying on his back in the mess that had once been the room where he lived. I gasped. Because the truth was that I did know him. I had seen him once and only briefly, but it wasn't a face I was going to forget.

Reginald Parker was the man who had tried to shoot Minerva. He was the man on the roof above Regent Street.

"Did you find a gun in his room?" I asked.

Snape shook his head. "No. I told you. He was strangled."

"How about a handful of silver acorns? Or anything to do with oak trees?"

Boyle leant over the table and grabbed me by the collar. I felt myself being dragged to my feet. My feet left the floor. One of my shirt buttons went shooting over my shoulder. "Are you taking the mickey?" he demanded.

"No!" I gurgled. "I'm trying to help you. I did meet this man. I just didn't know his name."

Boyle turned to Snape, still holding me in the air. "Shall I wire him up to the car battery, sir?"

"Certainly not, Boyle!" Snape looked offended. "He's going to tell us everything anyway."

"I know that, sir. But this way he'll tell us quicker."

"Just put him down!"

Boyle looked on the edge of tears but he dropped me back into my seat. And then I told them everything that had happened since Jake Hammill had walked into our office. The meeting at the hotel. The events in Regent Street. Snape nodded when I talked about that. He must have seen Tim on the news.

"You're sure it was Parker on the roof?" he asked.

"It's the same face, Chief Inspector," I said.

"And you think he was a member of this organization – Overweight Albanian Kids?"

"He was certainly overweight." I nodded at the photograph.

"But as far as we know, he wasn't Albanian."

"Maybe he lived in Albania when he was young."

"We'll check it out."

"Does this mean you're letting us go?" Tim asked, getting to his feet.

"Not so fast, Diamond!"

"All right." Tim sat down, then got up more slowly.

Snape glowered. "I'll see you two again!" he said.

"Yeah. And I'll be waiting." Boyle was standing there holding one of the electrical contacts in his hand. The other was on the table. I passed it to him.

"Don't forget this," I said.

He took it in the other hand.

We could still hear Boyle screaming as we raced back down the corridor and out onto the street. But that's the modern police for you. Shocking.

When Tim and I had breakfast the next morning, I could see he was deep in thought. He didn't even react when he upturned the cereal packet and got the plastic toy.

"I just don't get it," he said at length.

"What's that, Tim?"

"Well … this guy … Archibald Porter."

"I think you mean Reginald Parker."

"He tried to kill Minerva and now somebody has killed him. But that doesn't make any sense. Nobody knew who he was. So why kill him? If they wanted to protect Minerva, they could have just reported him to the police."

He frowned but then his eyes brightened. "Maybe it was just another coincidence!" he exclaimed. "Maybe his death was an accident!"

"It's quite tricky to get strangled by accident," I pointed out.

Tim nodded. "I wonder how he got my business card?"

"That's exactly what we're going to find out…"

We were lucky that Snape had given us Parker's address. As soon as Tim had finished breakfast, we looked up Sparrow Lane in Tim's *A–Z*. Actually, it was an *A–W*. He'd got it cheap. Then we took a bus to the other side of

London and a narrow street of terraced houses not far from the old meat market. Number 27 was halfway down and looked exactly the same as numbers 25 and 29 – apart, that is, from the policeman on duty and the blue and white POLICE LINE: DO NOT CROSS taped over the front door.

To be honest, I'd forgotten that Snape would have left someone on duty and I could see at a glance that we weren't going to get past the policeman at the door. He had the sort of face that if he ever decided to join the dog unit, he wouldn't need a dog. Ignoring him, I went straight to the house next door and rang the bell, hoping the owner would be in.

She was. The door opened and a huge, cheerful Caribbean woman in a brilliantly coloured dress appeared on the doorstep, the great slabs that were arms folded across her ample breast. "Yes, me darlings? How can I help you?" she boomed out.

I nudged Tim.

"I'm Tim Diamond," Tim said.

"Yes?" The woman was none the wiser.

"My brother is a private detective," I told her. "He wants to ask you some questions about the guy who lived next door."

"That's right," Tim explained. "And if he lived next door, then I'd imagine he must have been your neighbour."

"That's brilliant, Tim," I muttered. "How did you work that one out?"

It turned out that the woman was called Mrs Winterbotham and had lived at number 25 for almost as many years. Her husband was out, working at the meat market, and she invited us into her kitchen and gave us tea and coconut biscuits. She had already told the police everything but she was going to enjoy telling us again.

"Reginald was an actor," she said, then looked left and right and lowered her voice as if he might be listening from beyond the grave. "But he wasn't a very good one. Oh no! He was out of work most of the time. He was in *The Cherry Orchard* last May, playing one of the cherries. And last year he appeared at the Unicorn Theatre in a one-man show."

"Was it popular?" I asked.

"No. Only one man came." Mrs Winterbotham dropped three sugar cubes into her tea and helped herself to another biscuit. "Reginald was a nice man. But, you know, I'm not sure it really helped his career, his having a stutter."

I remembered now. Parker had stuttered when he was on the roof. So it hadn't been because he was afraid.

"I said to him that he ought to be a mime artist," Mrs Winterbotham went on. "That way he wouldn't have had to talk. But I don't think people would have paid to see him. He didn't have the figure for it. To be honest with you, I've seen more attractive figures hanging up in the meat market."

"When was his last job?" I asked.

"Well..." She put down the biscuit and leant forward conspiratorially. "That's what I told the police. He always got a job at Christmas. He worked in a department store. But this year something very unusual happened. He got paid for a one-night appearance in the West End! He didn't tell me what it was but I do know that it was a lot of money."

"Who paid him?"

"He never said. But I don't think it can have worked out because when I saw him the next morning, he was very upset."

"How do you know he was upset?" Tim asked.

"He was crying."

"You're sure they weren't tears of happiness?"

"Oh no, Mr Diamond. He was completely miserable. And then that afternoon, someone came to the house. I heard this banging and crashing and I went round to the garden to see what was happening. Then there was silence. I knocked on the door but I got no answer. So I called the police."

"Just one last question, Mrs Winterbotham..." I began.

"Please. Call me Janey!"

"Was Reginald Parker Albanian?"

"No. As far as I know, he'd never been to Albania. In fact, he never went anywhere. He couldn't afford it. Most of the time he just sat at home and watched TV." She sighed and I got the idea that maybe she'd been his only friend in the world. "And now he's dead. I can't believe it. Now, how about a nice piece of banana cake?"

We didn't have the cake.

Because suddenly, even as Mrs Winterbotham had been talking, everything had made sense. Suddenly I was back on the roof, hearing Reginald Parker as he called out across the gap. *I d-d-didn't...* I saw the cracker with the acorn and the death threat and knew what it was that was wrong with the letter Minerva had been sent. I thought about Regent Street and the bullet that had come so close it had drilled a hole in Harold Chase's coat. I knew exactly what job Reginald had been hired for – it could only be one job – and I also knew what was going to happen at twelve o'clock that day. I looked at my watch. It was five past eleven. We had less than one hour left.

"We have to get to Harrods, Tim!" I said.

Tim shook his head. "This is no time for Christmas shopping, Nick."

"We're not going shopping. We have to find Minerva."

"Why?"

A taxi drove by. I reached out and flagged it down.

"She's going to be murdered, Tim. And I know who by."

KILLER WITH A SMILE

We were on the wrong side of town. We had to cross the whole of London to reach Knightsbridge, and with Christmas just weeks away the traffic could hardly be worse. As we sat in a traffic jam on the edge of Hyde Park I could feel the minutes ticking away. Worse than that, I could see them. The taxi meter was running and Tim was staring at it in dismay, watching as the last of his earnings disappeared.

We finally made it with about five minutes and ten pounds to spare, but even so it was going to be tight. Harrods was a huge place and the grotto was right up on the fourth floor. Worse than that, the entire store was heaving – not just with shoppers but with the usual crowd of fans and policemen who had turned out to see or to protect Minerva. There were security men on all the doors and more photographers waiting in the street, although you'd have thought by now the papers would have had enough of her. I certainly had.

And what nobody knew was that the killer was already inside the building. He would smile at Minerva and he would murder her ... and she wouldn't even know it had happened until she woke up dead.

"This way, Tim!"

We had plunged off the street and into women's handbags, then into cosmetics, then food. Harrods was every Christmas present you could ever imagine – more presents than anyone in the world could ever want. It was Christmas gone mad: hundreds of miles of tinsel; thousands of glittering stars and balls; enough Christmas trees to repopulate a forest. Don't get me wrong. I love Christmas and I'll tear open as many presents as I can get my hands on. But as I ran for the escalators, past the groaning shelves and the grinning sales assistants, I couldn't help but feel there had to be something more to it than this. Maybe something less, if you know what I mean.

We reached the escalators and began to fight our way up. I had a strange sense of déjà vu as I went. Suddenly I was in another department store in a different part of London almost two years before. I'd been running then too – to escape from two German assassins who'd been trying to make sure that the only way I saw Boxing Day was from inside a box. But that was another time and another story and if you want to know about it, I'm afraid you're going to have to buy another book.

We got to the fourth floor and there was a sign pointing towards Santa's grotto, "Jingle Bells" blaring out of the speakers and little kids everywhere, dragging their mothers to see the man in red.

I stopped, panting. "I hope we're not too late," I gasped.

"Yes," Tim agreed. "Santa may not have any presents left!"

Sometimes I think Tim doesn't belong in the real world. Maybe he'd be more comfortable in a nice white room with padded walls. But this was no time to argue. It was twelve noon exactly. Somewhere in the clock department down below, a thousand clocks would be chiming, bleeping or shooting out cuckoos. The grotto had just been opened by Minerva. And the way ahead was blocked.

There were toys everywhere. Vast Lego castles, cuddly toys, jigsaw mountains and Scalextric cars buzzing round in furious circles. Children were pulling and pushing in every direction. In the far distance I could see the green, plastic entrance to a green, plastic cave with a long line of people waiting to go in. That was where we had to be. But our path had been closed off by a sixteen-stone store security guard with the body of a wrestler and the face of a boxer at the end of a particularly vicious fight. At least, I assumed he was a security guard. It was hard to be sure. He was dressed as an elf.

"You can't go this way!" he told me. "You have to go to the back of the queue." So he *was* a security guard. I should have known. How many elves do you see carrying truncheons?

"Where's Minerva?" I demanded. I was afraid I was already too late – and this brute in green tights was only making things worse.

"She's in with Santa Claus, opening the grotto. You'll have to wait in line if you want her autograph."

"I don't want her autograph. I want to save her life!"

But it was no good. I might as well have argued with Rudolph the Red-Nosed Reindeer (there was a mechanical version next to the cave). I had to stop myself pulling out my hair. I was expecting a gunshot at any moment and here I was trying to reason with an elf. I looked around me, wondering if I could bribe him with a cuddly toy – or if not, hit him with one. That was when I saw Detective Chief Inspector Snape, standing grim-faced with Boyle next to him, the two of them surrounded by Barbie dolls.

"Snape!" I shouted out, and before the

security guard could stop me I had run over to the two men.

"What are you doing here, Diamond?" he snapped the moment he saw me.

Boyle curled his lip and looked ugly – which in his case wasn't very difficult. Once again he lumbered forward and grabbed hold of me.

"Don't worry, Boyle!" I said. "I haven't come here to steal your Barbie doll."

"Then why are you here?" Snape demanded.

"You've got to find Minerva," I began. "She's in danger."

"I know she's in danger," Snape replied. "Boyle and I are on special duty. We're looking after her."

"You don't understand..."

How could I tell them what I knew? There wasn't enough time and with all the noise in the place – the children screaming, the music playing, Rudolph singing and all the rest of it – I'd have been hoarse before I got to the end. But just then Minerva appeared, coming out of the grotto with her manager, Jake Hammill, next to her. There was no sign of her husband, but somehow I wasn't surprised.

I twisted out of Boyle's grip, and with Tim right behind me I ran over to her. As usual, Minerva was looking drop-dead gorgeous in a slinky, silver number, and despite everything I was glad that I had arrived in time and that she hadn't, after all, dropped dead. She was holding a present, about the size and shape of a shoe box. Santa must have just given it to her.

She saw me. "You!" she snapped – and unless that's Greek for Happy Christmas, she wasn't too pleased to see me.

I stood in front of her, my eyes fixed on the box. I didn't want to touch it. To be honest, I didn't want to be anywhere near it. I had a good idea what was inside.

"Did Santa give you that?" I demanded.

"Yes." She nodded.

"Do you know what it is?"

Minerva shrugged. She didn't really care. She was only here for the publicity. "No," she said.

"I think it's a clock," Tim chimed in.

"Why?"

"Well ... I can hear it ticking."

Snape leant forward and took the box. "What's all this about?" he demanded.

"Chief Inspector," I said, and suddenly my mouth was dry. "I'd be very careful with that unless you want to spend this Christmas in six different parts of London all at the same time."

"What are you talking about?" Hammill demanded.

"There's probably an oak leaf or two in there and maybe some acorns. But I'll bet you any money that the rest of it is a bomb."

Maybe I said the word too loudly. Somehow the crowd caught on to what was happening and suddenly the entire department was filled with hysterical mothers dragging their screaming kids off to the nearest escalator. I ignored them. I just wanted to know if Snape was going to believe me. And to be fair to him, just this once he gave me the benefit of the doubt. Very gently, he lowered the box to the ground, then turned to Boyle. "Have you got a knife?" he asked.

Boyle reached into his pocket and took out first a cut-throat razor, then a bayonet and finally a flick knife. He pressed a button and ten centimetres of ugly steel leapt out to join in the cheerful Christmas atmosphere. Snape took it. Very carefully, he cut a square in the side of the parcel and peeled the cardboard back. He looked inside.

"He's right!" he said.

He didn't need to tell me. Looking over his shoulder, I could just make out part of an alarm clock, some loops of wire and something that could have been Plasticine but definitely wasn't.

Snape looked up. "Plastic explosive," he whispered. "It's connected to an alarm clock. It'll blow up when the bell goes." He squinted through the square he had cut out. Then, very slowly, he handed the package to Boyle. "All right, Boyle," he said. "This is timed to go off in forty minutes. You'd better get it down to the bomb disposal squad."

"Where's that?" I asked.

"It's a forty-five-minute drive away."

Boyle stared at him.

"See if you can find a short cut," Snape advised.

Boyle disappeared – in a hurry. Snape turned to me. "So what's this all about?" he demanded.

"Santa just gave me that!" Minerva rasped. She was standing there dazed.

"Have you been a bad girl this year?" Tim asked.

"It's not Santa!" I said. "Come on..."

The five of us – me, Tim, Minerva, Jake Hammill and Snape – dived into the grotto. Out of the corner of my eye I saw the security guard talking into his radio, presumably calling for reinforcements. There was nobody else left on the fourth floor – as far as I knew, there was nobody left in Knightsbridge. White plastic snow crunched underfoot as we followed the path into the cave. White plastic stalactites hung down and white plastic stalagmites pointed up – or maybe it was the other way round. I can never remember. We passed a couple more mechanical singing reindeer and arrived just in time to see a familiar red figure, about to leave by a back exit.

"Hold it right there, Santa!" I shouted.

Santa froze, then slowly turned around.

"It's ... it's ... it's...!" Tim exclaimed. He stopped. He had no idea who it was, and with the red hood, the white beard and the golden-framed spectacles, I couldn't blame him. His own mother wouldn't recognize him. His own wife hadn't.

I walked forward and pulled off the beard. And there he was.

"Harold!" Minerva exclaimed.

"Harold?" Hammill quavered.

"That's right," I said. "Harold Chase."

There could be no doubt about it. The old man reached up and lowered the hood, revealing more of his face, his silver hair and his hearing aid. He had concealed his permanent suntan with make-up. But there could be no disguising the venom with which he was looking at his wife.

Snape took over. "You just gave Minerva a bomb," he said.

Harold Chase said nothing.

"That's a very original present," Tim commented.

"Not really, Tim," I said. "He was trying to kill her."

It was the word "kill" that did it. The bomb had been taken away. But Harold Chase exploded. "I hate her!" he screamed. "You have no idea what it's been like living with her! I know why she married me. She wanted my money! But now that she's so big and so famous she doesn't need me. And so she humiliates and belittles me. She's made my life hell!"

He took a step towards us. Tim took three steps back.

"But that's not the worst of it," Harold went on. "She's a hypocrite. She smiles at the crowds on Regent Street when secretly she despises them. She hates Christmas too – and every year she's ruined it for me. No carols, no presents, no tinsel, no fun. She's stolen Christmas from me and that was a good enough reason to want to see her dead."

By now, he was frothing at the mouth and I almost wished Boyle was there to deal with him. Fortunately the security guard disguised as an elf had appeared with two colleagues, and the three of them dragged Harold out. He was still screaming as he went.

The five of us went back downstairs to a champagne bar on the ground floor. It was somewhere quiet and we had a lot to talk about. Minerva paid for champagne for herself and the others. I got a glass of lemonade. I had to admit she seemed very shaken by what had happened. Her face was pale. Her eyes were thoughtful. And even her silver-plated breasts seemed to have lost their sparkle.

"All right, Diamond," Snape said, emptying his glass. "Spit it out!"

"He hasn't drunk anything yet," Tim said.

"I want you to tell me what's been going on. How did you know about Harold Chase and how did you figure out his plan?"

"I worked it out when we visited Janey Winterbotham," I explained.

"The next-door neighbour?" Snape sniffed. "I spoke to her. She didn't tell me anything."

"She told me that Reginald Parker was an out-of-work actor but that he had a job in a department store every Christmas," I said. "What else could he have been but a department store Santa? That was when it all fell into place."

"Why don't you start at the beginning?" Jake Hammill suggested.

"All right." I drew a breath. "This is the way I see it. Harold Chase hated Minerva for all the reasons he just told us. His hatred had obviously driven him mad and he decided to kill her. But the trouble was, it was too obvious. If Minerva died, he would be the main suspect. Everyone knew how badly she treated him."

"A lot of people would die to be married to me," Minerva sniffed.

"He was married to you – and you were the one he wanted to die," I reminded her. "Anyway, Harold couldn't kill you himself. He'd be arrested at once. But then he had an idea. He realized that the best way to get rid of you was to create someone who didn't exist: a crazy fan. He used that concert you cancelled – for Overweight Albanian Kids – and pretended that someone was out to get revenge."

"You mean ... it was Harold who wrote that anonymous letter?" Hammill asked.

"Exactly. He even put a fake spelling mistake in it – but if he couldn't spell 'forgive', how come he could spell 'forget' a few lines later? The whole thing felt fake to me."

"And what about the cracker?"

"That was another clue. I thought at the time that there was something weird about it, but it was only later that I realized what it was." I turned to Hammill. "You'd booked Minerva into the Porchester hotel under a false name."

"Right," he said.

"But the box of crackers was addressed to her. Whoever sent it even knew the number of the suite where she was staying. It had to be an inside job."

"But wait a minute," Snape interrupted. "If it was Chase all the time, what was Reginald Parker doing on the roof at Regent Street?"

"Reginald Parker had been paid by Chase," I explained. "His neighbour told us he got a lot of money for a job in the West End. She probably thought it was a job in theatre. My guess is that Chase paid him to leave the silver oak leaves on the roof. Parker had no idea what he was doing. He didn't have a gun or anything. I saw him carrying something, but it could have been a camera. After all, he knew Minerva was there. He was a complete innocent. That's what he tried to tell me when I went up there. 'I didn't...' That was all he managed. But what he wanted to say was, 'I didn't do it!' He must have been horrified when he heard the shots."

"So who did shoot at me?" Minerva asked. She poured herself some more champagne. I wondered what she was celebrating. Maybe it was the fact she was still alive.

"That was Harold," I said. "Again, I'm only guessing, but I'd say he fired two blank shots from a gun he had inside his pocket. When we were on the platform, the shots sounded very close. He fired twice and then pointed to Reginald up on the roof – because, of course, he knew he'd be there. You see, he was creating the illusion of a killer ... someone who didn't really exist. The only snag is, the gun burnt a hole in his coat." I glanced at Minerva. "You thought he'd almost been hit. In fact, he'd fired the shots himself."

"I don't get it," Minerva exclaimed. "He wanted to protect me! It was Harold who persuaded me to get a bodyguard!"

"He did that to throw off any suspicion. At the same time, he made sure you hired the worst private detective in London. Someone too stupid to get in the way of his plan."

"And who was that?" Tim asked.

"Have some more champagne, Tim," I said.

"And then Harold Chase killed Reginald Parker," Snape said.

"You've got it in one, Chief Inspector. Chase had chosen Parker because he knew he was going to be the Santa Claus at Harrods. First of all he hired him to go on the roof. Then he killed him and took his place. Tim's business card must have fallen out of his pocket during the fight. It was when I saw the card that I put two and two together..."

"You did your maths homework?" Tim asked.

"No, Tim. I cracked the case."

There was a long silence. Either I'd been talking too slowly or they'd been drinking too quickly but all the champagne was gone. And I hadn't even touched my lemonade.

Jake Hammill put an arm around Minerva. "Baby, I'm so sorry," he said. "What a terrible experience for you!"

Minerva shrugged. "It wasn't so bad," she said. "I've got rid of Harold. I'm going to get lots of publicity. And my CD's certain to go to number one." She got to her feet. I thought she was going to leave, but she took one last look at me. "You're quite smart for a scruffy fourteen-year-old," she said. Then she flicked her eyes towards Tim. "As for you, you're just an utter loss."

She walked out.

"What did she mean?" Tim wailed.

I thought for a moment. "Justanutterloss. It's Greek for sensational," I said.

"Really?" Tim's eyes lit up.

"Sure, Tim," I said. Well, after all, it was Christmas.

There are a few things to add.

Two weeks later, Tim and I got a surprise in the post – and this time it wasn't a bomb, an unpaid bill or a poison pen letter. It was a note from Jake Hammill. It seemed that he wasn't so bad after all. We had just saved his most famous client from a murder attempt that would have been not only the end of her career, but – even worse – the end of his percentage. And as a token of his gratitude, he'd decided to send us a cheque for ten thousand pounds. I'll never forget the sight of Tim holding it between his hands. The last time he had seen that many zeros, it had been in his school report.

We talked a lot about what to do with the money. Of course, we were going to have a proper Christmas lunch. Tim was going to pay off the rent. I was finally going to get a new school uniform – the last one had so many patches in it, it was more patches than uniform. But that would still leave us with several thousand pounds, which was just about the most money we'd ever had.

I forget who suggested it first, but that was when we decided to fly out to Australia to be reunited with our parents. It had been years since we'd seen them, and sometimes I thought it was unnatural for a young lad to be living without his mother, often crying himself to sleep, having to be tucked in every night and cheered up by his brother. Not that I minded doing all that for Tim, but even so I thought it would do us all good to be a family again, just for a while.

And the next day we bought two British Airways tickets to Sydney. We were going to travel out as soon as the Easter term ended, and maybe one day I'll write down what actually happened when we got there. *The Radius of the Lost Shark*. That's the title I've got written down in my notebook. It's another story I've got to tell.

What else is there? Harold Chase got life in jail for attempted murder, but looking at him I didn't think that would be too many years. Snape took the credit for the arrest, of course. They actually put his face on the front cover of the monthly police journal, *Hello, Hello, Hello* magazine. Reginald Parker's remains were scattered in the River Thames, in front of the National Theatre – as he'd requested in his will. It can't have been pleasant, though. He hadn't been cremated.

And what about Minerva? She may have got to number one, but I didn't care. I never listened to her music again. She may have had everything, but without a heart you're just nothing. She was like a December without Christmas – and at the end of the day, what's the point of that?

READ OTHER GREAT BOOKS BY ANTHONY HOROWITZ...

THE ALEX RIDER SERIES

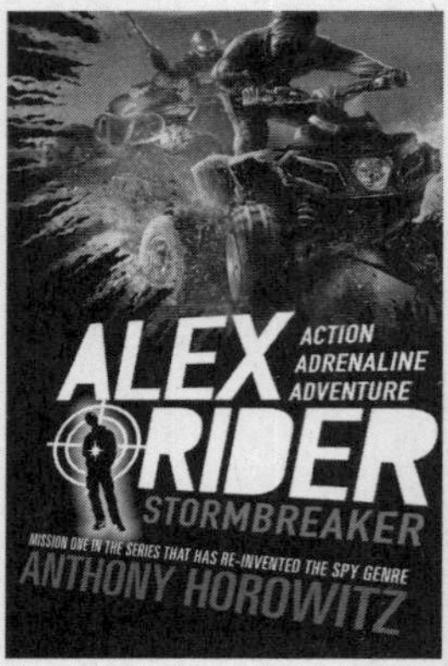

Alex Rider – you're never too young to die…

High in the Alps, death waits for Alex Rider…

Sharks. Assassins. Nuclear bombs. Alex Rider's in deep water.

Alex Rider has 90 minutes to save the world.

Once stung, twice as deadly. Alex Rider wants revenge.

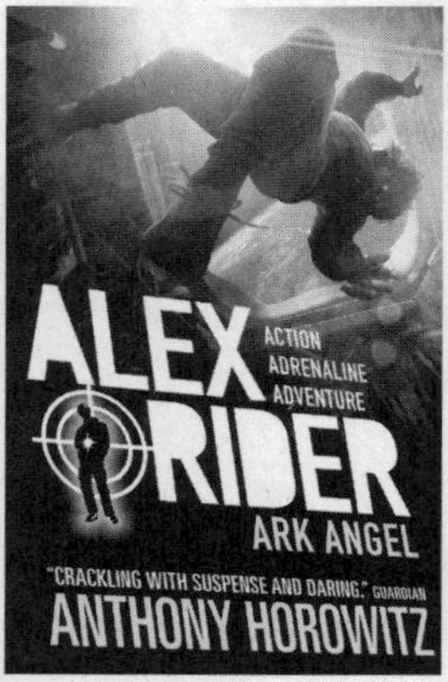

He's back – and this time there are no limits.

WELCOME TO THE DARK SIDE OF ANTHONY HOROWITZ

THE POWER OF FIVE

BOOK ONE
He always knew he was different.
First there were the dreams.
Then the deaths began.

BOOK TWO
It began with Raven's Gate.
But it's not over yet. Once
again the enemy is stirring.

BOOK THREE
Darkness covers the earth.
The Old Ones have returned.
The battle must begin.

BOOK FOUR
An ancient evil is unleashed.
Five have the power to defeat it.
But one of them has been taken.

BOOK FIVE
Five Gatekeepers.
One chance to save mankind.
Chaos beckons. Oblivion awaits.

Anthony Horowitz is the author of the number one bestselling Alex Rider books and The Power of Five series. He has enjoyed huge success as a writer for both children and adults, most recently with the latest adventure in the Alex Rider series, *Russian Roulette*, and the highly acclaimed Sherlock Holmes novel, *The House of Silk*. His latest novel, *Moriarty*, is also set in the world of Sherlock Holmes and was published in October 2014. Anthony was also chosen by the Ian Fleming estate to write the new James Bond novel which will be published this year. Anthony has won numerous awards, including the Bookseller Association/Nielsen Author of the Year Award, the Children's Book of the Year Award at the British Book Awards, and the Red House Children's Book Award. In 2014 Anthony was awarded an OBE for Services to Literature. He has also created and written many major television series, including *Injustice*, *Collision* and the award-winning *Foyle's War*.

You can find out more about Anthony and his work at:
www.alexrider.com
@AnthonyHorowitz

THE SWITCH

More wickedly funny books

by Anthony Horowitz

The Devil and His Boy

Groosham Grange

Return to Groosham Grange

The Switch

More Bloody Horowitz

The Diamond Brothers books:

The Falcon's Malteser

Public Enemy Number Two

South by South East

The Blurred Man

The French Confection

I Know What You Did Last Wednesday

The Greek who Stole Christmas

THE SWITCH

ANTHONY
HOROWITZ

WALKER
BOOKS

This is a work of fiction. Names, characters, places and incidents are either the product of the author's imagination or, if real, are used fictitiously. All statements, activities, stunts, descriptions, information and material of any other kind contained herein are included for entertainment purposes only and should not be relied on for accuracy or replicated as they may result in injury.

First published 1996 by Walker Books Ltd
87 Vauxhall Walk, London, SE11 5HJ

This edition published 2015

2 4 6 8 10 9 7 5 3 1

This book has been typeset in ITC Veljovic

Printed in Germany by GGP Media GmbH

British Library Cataloguing in Publication Data:
a catalogue record for this book is available from the British Library

ISBN 978-1-4063-6476-7

www.walker.co.uk

For Jill, with love

CONTENTS

INTRODUCTION

I'm often asked which is my favourite book and, outside the Alex Rider series, this is probably it.

The Switch was one of the last books that were directly inspired by my own childhood – the others were *Groosham Grange* and *Granny*. All three of them have a lot of the same ingredients: rich parents, unhappy heroes, peculiar nannies, horrible schools and lots of bizarre jokes.

Spurling, the chauffeur in the book, is based on a rather dangerous-looking man called Bob who used to drive my father around. Mitzy, the housekeeper, is a jokey version of my own nanny whose name was Miss FitzGerald but who was always called Fitzy. My mother had a really savage and unpleasant German Shepherd called Major. He appears here as Vicious. And Snatchmore Hall, though exaggerated, is based on the house where I was brought up – White Friars in Stanmore.

I suppose that makes Tad Spencer, whose underpants snap during the headmaster's speech, a version of ... me! Re-reading the book, I notice that he has black hair and brown eyes. He eats too much. He plays Scrabble with his mother. It's all horribly accurate and if I hadn't written it myself, I'd sue.

But then the story was inspired by a feeling that I often had when I was about eleven years old. Stuck in the misery of north London's very own Guantanamo

Bay – a particularly nasty boarding school called Orley Farm – I often used to dream of running away and there were many, many moments when I would wish I was someone else.

This is what happens to Tad at the start of the story. The only difference is that – through a mechanism that is never properly explained – in his case it actually happens.

The Switch is a body-swap book and I should say at once that it's not an entirely original idea. There was a famous film when I was young called *Vice Versa* in which a father swaps bodies with his son ... it was later remade as *Freaky Friday*. People have swapped bodies in books, on television and even in graphic novels.

I'd wanted to do a body-swap story for a long time but I knew I couldn't write one until I came up with a completely original angle. And then one day, I happened to pass one of those trendy "green" cosmetic shops – selling soaps, perfumes, candles and all the rest of it – and I noticed a sign in the window. NONE OF OUR PRODUCTS ARE TESTED ON ANIMALS. At that moment, the whole rest of the book popped into my head and I knew I had to sit down and write it.

The reason why I like the book so much, and what makes it different from anything I'd written before, is the character of the two boys – Tad Spencer and Bob Snarby. I love everything about Bob from his dishonesty and his unhygienic lifestyle to his completely revolting parents ... there are very few parents in my books but Eric and Doll strike me as a perfect couple and I was determined not to kill them off in the end. One of the things you may notice in this book is that all the good people are villains and all the villains are actually quite nice – which I suppose is also part of the "switch".

But Tad and Bob are harder to pin down. Both of them change during the story and both of them discover that there are huge advantages to not being themselves. In a strange way, I don't think I could have ever created Alex Rider without writing *The Switch* first. Because as the story progresses, and despite all the fantastic things, the two boys become more and more real. Look at the scene in Chapter 8 when they finally meet. I think they're my first believable heroes and the last chapter – "Together" – has a real sadness and seriousness about it. It suggested to me that I could write a completely new, more emotional book if I wanted to. And the one that I wrote next was *Stormbreaker*.

It's strange to think that I wrote *The Switch* more than twelve years ago. So much has happened since then. But as I began by saying, it's still one of my favourites and I'm very glad that you've bought it. At least, I assume that you've bought it. If you're just reading this in the shop, it'll cost you less than a packet of Eric Snarby's cigarettes and it won't give you bad breath or cancer – so give it a try!

Anthony Horowitz

BEAUTIFUL WORLD

The white Rolls Royce made no sound as it sped along the twisting country road. It was the middle of summer and the grass was high, speckled with wild poppies and daisies. Sunlight danced in the air. But the single passenger in the back of the car saw none of it. His head was buried in a book: *My 100 Favourite Equations*. As he flicked a page, he popped another cherry marzipan chocolate into his mouth, the fourteenth he had eaten since Ipswich. The automatic window slid open and yet another chocolate wrapper was whipped away by the wind. It twisted briefly in the air, then fell. By the time it hit the ground, the Rolls was already out of sight. And Thomas Arnold David Spencer was a little nearer home.

Thomas Arnold David – Tad for short – was

thirteen years old, dressed in grey trousers that were a little too tight for him, a striped tie and blue blazer. He had short black hair, rather too neatly combed, and deep brown eyes. He was returning home from Beton College on this, the first day of the summer holidays. It was typical of Tad that he should have started his homework already. Tad loved homework. He was only sorry he hadn't been given more.

The Rolls Royce paused in front of a set of wrought-iron gates. There was a click and the gates began to open automatically. At the same time, a video camera set on a high brick wall swivelled round to watch the new arrival with a blank, hostile eye. Beyond the gates, a long drive stretched out for almost half a mile between lawns that had been rolled perfectly flat. Two swans circled on a glistening pond, watching the Rolls as it continued forward. It passed a rose garden, a vegetable garden, a croquet lawn, a tennis court and a heated swimming pool. At last it stopped in front of the fantastic pile that was Snatchmore Hall, home of the Spencer family. Tad had arrived.

The chauffeur, a large, ugly man with hooded eyes, crumpled cheeks and a small, snub nose, got out of the car and held the door open for Tad. "Glad to be home, Master Spencer?"

"Yes, thank you, Spurling." Tad's voice was flat, almost emotionless. "Rather."

"I'll take your cases to your room, Master Spencer."

"Thank you, Spurling. Just leave them on the bed."

Tad went over to the swimming pool, where a bored-looking woman was lying on a sunlounger, gazing at herself intently in a small mirror. This was his mother, Lady Geranium Spencer.

"Good afternoon, Mother," Tad said. He knew not to kiss her. It would have ruined her make-up.

"Oh hello, dear." His mother sighed. "Is it the holidays already?"

"Yes."

"Oh. I thought it was next week. What do you think of the nose?"

"It's jolly good, Mother. They've moved it a little, haven't they?"

"Yes. Just a teensy-weensy bit to the left." Lady Spencer had visited no fewer than six plastic surgeons that summer and each one of them had operated on her nose, trying to give her the exact look she required. Now she was sure she had at last got it right. The only trouble was that she wasn't allowed to sneeze until Christmas. "How was school, darling?" she asked, putting the mirror away.

"It was fine, thank you, Mother. I came first in French, English, Chemistry, Maths and Latin. Second in Ancient Greek and Geography. Third in..."

"Ah! Here's Mitzy with the tea!" his mother interrupted, stifling a yawn. "Just what I fancied. A teensy-weensy tea."

The front door of the house had opened and a trolley,

piled high with cakes and sandwiches, had appeared, seemingly moving by itself. As it drew closer, however, a tiny woman could be seen behind it, wearing a black dress with a white apron. This was Mitzy, the family's servant for the past forty years.

"Hello, Master Tad!" she gurgled breathlessly as she heaved the trolley to a halt. It was so heavy it had left deep tyre-tracks across the lawn.

"Hello, Mitzy." Tad smiled at her. "How are you?"

"I can't complain, Master Tad."

"And Bitzy?" This was Mitzy's husband. His real name was Ernest but he had been given his nickname after he'd been blown to pieces by a faulty gas main.

"He's still in hospital." Mitzy sighed. "I'm seeing him on Sunday."

"Well, do give him my regards," Tad said cheerfully, helping himself to a smoked salmon roll.

Mitzy limped back to the house while Tad ate. Lady Spencer cast a critical eye at her son. "Have you put on weight?" she asked.

"Just a little, Mumsy. I'm afraid you're going to have to buy me a completely new uniform for next term. This one's much too tight."

"What a bore! That's the third this year."

"I know. The elastic on my underpants snapped during the headmaster's speech. It was rather embarrassing..."

Just then there was a loud bark and a dog bounded across the lawn towards Tad and his mother. It was a

Dalmatian – you could easily tell that from its black and white coat – but it was like no Dalmatian you had ever seen.

For a start it was huge. Its teeth were incredibly sharp and its mouth, instead of grinning in the friendly way ordinary Dalmatians do, was twisted in an ugly frown. The reason for all this was that the Spencers had taken the unfortunate dog to a vet who had turned it into a killing machine, filing down both its teeth and its claws until they were needle-sharp. The last burglar who had tried to break in had needed 107 stitches when Vicious had finished with him. In the end the police surgeon had run out of thread and had been forced to use glue.

But Vicious recognized Tad. Panting and whimpering, the dog sat down and raised a paw, its eyes fixed on the tea trolley.

"Hello, Vicious. How are you?" Tad reached out with an éclair. The dog leapt up and half of Tad's arm disappeared down its throat as Vicious sucked the éclair free.

"You spoil that dog," his mother remarked.

After tea, Tad went up to his room, taking the elevator to the third floor. Spurling had carried his cases up and Mrs O'Blimey, the Irish housekeeper, had already unpacked them. Tad sat down on his four-poster bed and looked around him contentedly. Everything was where it should be. There were his two computers and fourteen shelves of computer games.

There was his portable television plugged into his own video recorder and satellite system. His favourite books (Dickens and Shakespeare) bound in leather and gold, stretched out in a long line over his butterfly collection, his stereo and interactive CD system and his tank of rare tropical fish. Then there were nine wardrobes containing his clothes and next to them a door leading into his private bathroom, sauna and Jacuzzi.

Tad stretched out his arms and smiled. He had the whole summer holiday to look forward to. As well as the country house in Suffolk, there was the villa in the South of France, the penthouse in New York and the mews house in Knightsbridge, just round the corner from Harrods. He unbuttoned his jacket and took it off, letting it fall to the floor. Mrs O'Blimey could pick it up later. It was time for dinner. And soon his father would be home.

In fact Sir Hubert Spencer didn't get in until after nine o'clock. He was a large, imposing man with wavy silver hair and purple blotches in his cheeks, nose and hands. He was dressed, as always, in a plain black suit cut from the very finest material. As he strode into the room and sat down he pulled out an antique pocket watch and glanced at the face.

"Good evening, Tad," he said. "Good to see you. Now. I can give you nine and a half minutes..."

"Gosh! Thank you, Father."

Tad was delighted. He knew that his Father was a

busy man. In fact, business ruled his life. Ten years ago, Sir Hubert Spencer had set up a chain of shops that now stretched across England, Europe and America. The shops were called simply "Beautiful World" and sold soaps, shampoos, body lotions, sun creams, vitamins, minerals, herbs and spices ... everything to make you feel beautiful inside and out. What made these shops special, however, was that the ingredients for many of the products came from the Third World – yak's milk from the mountain villages of Tibet, for example, or crushed orchids from the tropical rain forests of Sumatra. And all the shops carried a notice in large letters in the window:

NONE OF OUR PRODUCTS ARE TESTED ON ANIMALS

Sir Hubert had realized that people not only wanted to look good, they wanted to feel good too. And the better they felt, the more they would spend and the richer he would become.

Sir Hubert never stopped. He was always developing new products, finding new ingredients, dreaming up new advertising ideas, selling more products. It was said that while he was being knighted by the queen, two years before, he had managed to sell her ten gallons of face-cream and a lifetime's supply of Japanese seaweed shampoo. He had appeared on the front page of all the newspapers after that. Because, despite his great wealth, Sir Hubert was very popular. "Good old Sir Hubert!" people would shout out if they saw him in the street. "He may be stinking rich, but he's all right."

The reason for this popularity – and also for his knighthood – was his charity work. At about the same time that he had set up Beautiful World he had started a charity called ACID. This stood for The Association for Children in Distress and was based in London. ACID aimed to help all the young people who had run away or been abandoned in the city, giving them shelter and providing them with food or clothes. Tad himself had donated two pairs of socks and a Mars bar to the charity. He was very proud of his father and dreamed of the day when, maybe, he would be knighted too.

"Sorry I'm late," Sir Hubert announced now as he sat himself down in his favourite armchair beside the fire with Vicious curled up at his feet. "We've got problems with our new Peruvian cocoa-leaf bubble bath. Not enough bubbles. We may have to do more tests..." He turned to Spurling, who was standing beside him. "Have you poured me a brandy, Spurling?"

"Yes, Sir Hubert."

"Have you warmed it for me?"

"Yes, Sir Hubert."

"Well, you can drink it for me too. I haven't got time."

"Certainly, Sir Hubert." Taking the glass, the chauffeur bowed and left the room.

Sir Hubert turned to Tad, who was playing Scrabble with Lady Spencer. Tad was a little annoyed. He had a seven-letter word but unfortunately it was in Ancient Greek. "So, Tad," he exclaimed. "How was school?"

"Jolly good, Father. I came first in French, English, Chemistry, Maths and Latin. Second in..."

"That's the spirit!" Sir Hubert interrupted. "Now. What have you got planned for the summer holiday?"

"Well, I was thinking about going on safari in Africa, Father."

"Didn't you do that last holidays?"

"Yes. But it was rather fun. One of the guides got eaten by a tiger. I got some great photos."

"I thought you wanted to go to the Red Sea."

"We could do that afterwards, Father."

"Oh – all right." Sir Hubert turned to his wife. "You'd better take the boy to Harrods and get him some tropical clothes," he said. "Oh – and some scuba-diving lessons."

"And there is one other thing, Father."

"What's that, Tad?" There was a jangling sound from Sir Hubert's top pocket and he pulled out one of his mobile phones. "Could you hold the line, please," he said. "I'll be with you in ninety-three seconds."

Tad took a deep breath. "Rupert said he'd come up this week. You know – he's my best friend. And we thought we might go to Maple Towers together."

"Maple Towers?"

"It's that new theme park that's just opened. It's

got an amazing new ride – the Monster. Apparently it's almost impossible to go on it without being sick..."

"A theme park?" Sir Hubert considered, then shook his head. "No. I don't think so."

"What?" Tad stared at his father. Perhaps unsurprisingly "no" was his least favourite word.

"No, Tad. These theme parks seem very vulgar to me. Why don't you go horse-racing at Ascot?"

"I'll do that too, Father."

"What about flying lessons? You've hardly touched that two-seater plane I bought you..."

"I will, Father, but..."

"No. I don't want you going on those rides. They're dangerous and they're noisy. And all those people! You're a sensitive boy, Tad. I'm sure they're not good for you."

"But, Father! Mother...!"

"I have to agree with your father," Lady Spencer said. She looked at her Scrabble letters which she had been studying for the past ten minutes. "Is Zimpy a word?" she asked.

Tad was in a bad mood when he went to bed. Dressed in his brand new silk pyjamas, he flicked off the light and slid himself between the crisply laundered Irish linen sheets. The trouble was that he was a boy who had everything. And he was used to having everything. He expected it.

"It's not fair," he muttered. His head sank back into his goose-feather pillow. Moonlight slid across the wall and onto his pale, scowling face. "Why can't I go to the theme park? Why can't I do what I want to do?"

Suddenly Snatchmore Hall seemed like a prison to him. His parents, his great wealth, his school and his surroundings were just the shackles that bound him and he wanted none of it.

"I wish I was somebody else," he muttered to himself.

And 127 million light years away, a star that had been burning white suddenly glowed green, just for a few seconds, before burning white again.

But Thomas Arnold David Spencer hadn't seen it. He was already asleep.

THE CARAVAN

Tad knew something was wrong before he'd even opened his eyes.

First there was the sound, a metallic pattering that seemed to be all around him: frozen peas falling on a tin plate. That was what had woken him up. At the same time he became aware of the smell. It was a horrible smell – damp and dirty – and the worst thing was that it seemed to be coming from him. He moved slightly and that was when he knew that something had happened to the bed too. The sheets were wrinkled and rubbed against his skin like old newspaper. And the pillow...?

Tad opened his eyes. His face was half buried in a pillow so utterly disgusting that he was almost sick. It was completely shapeless, stuffed with what felt like old rags. It had no cover and, though it might once have been white, it was now stained with dried-up puddles of sweat and saliva, various shades of yellow and brown. Tad pushed it off his face, gasping for air.

He looked up, staring through the grey light. But what he saw made no sense. His brain couldn't take it in. He lay there, unable to move.

Instead of the chandelier that should be hanging over his bed, there was a neon tube with a tangle of naked wires twisting out of a broken plastic fitting. The sound of the frozen peas, he now realized, was rain hitting the walls and the ceiling. He was lying in a small bed in the corner of a small room in ... it had to be a caravan. He could tell from the shape of the walls. There was a window with no curtains but he couldn't see out because the glass was the frosted sort that you sometimes get in bathrooms or toilets. The room was very cold. Tad drew his legs up and the bed creaked and groaned.

The room was only a little larger than the bed itself, divided from the rest of the caravan by a plastic-covered wall with a door. Somebody had left some clothes crumpled in a heap on the floor. A pair of torn and soiled jeans poked out from a tangle of T-shirts, socks and underwear. There were also some comics, a battered ghetto-blaster and a few toys, broken, missing their batteries.

How had he got here? Tad tried to think, tried to remember. He had gone to bed like he always did. Nothing had happened. So how...? There could only be one answer. He had been kidnapped. That had to be it. Someone had broken into Snatchmore Hall getting past the wall, the moat, the security system and the dog, had drugged him while he was asleep and kidnapped him. He had read about this sort of thing happening. His father would have to pay some money – a ransom – but that was no problem because Sir Hubert had lots of money. And then he would be allowed to go home.

The more Tad thought about it, the more relieved he became. In fact, it was almost exciting. He'd be on the television and in all the newspapers: MILLIONAIRE'S SON IN RANSOM DEMAND, BOY HERO RETURNS HOME SAFE. That would certainly be something to tell them when he got back to school! And when the kidnappers were finally caught (as of course they would be), he would have to go to court. He would be the star witness!

Tad glanced at his watch, wondering what time it was. The watch was gone. That didn't surprise him. It was a Rolex, solid gold, with built-in calendar, calculator and colour TV. His mother had given it to him a year ago to thank him for tidying his room when Mrs O'Blimey was off sick. The wretched kidnappers must have taken it. (They also seemed to have taken his silk pyjamas – he was wearing only pants and a black T-shirt that was several sizes too big.) Tad lowered his hand – then raised it again. Was he going mad ... or was his wrist thinner than it had been? With an uneasy feeling in his stomach, he closed his third finger and his thumb in a circle around where his watch had once been. They met.

Tad began to tremble. How long had he been in the caravan? Could it have been weeks – even months? How had he managed to lose so much weight?

Cautiously, he swung himself out of the bed. His bare feet came to rest on a carpet so old and dirty that it was impossible to tell what colour it had once been. The smell of stale cigarette smoke hung in the air. Tip-toeing, one step at a time, he crossed the room, making for the door.

His hand – the hand was thinner too, just like his wrist – closed round the doorknob and slowly he turned it. The door was unlocked. Tad opened it and stepped into a second room, larger than the first and shrouded in darkness.

This room was dominated by a large, fold-down bed – he could just make out its shape as his eyes got used to the gloom – and now he realized there were two people inside it, buried beneath a blanket that rose and fell as they breathed. One of the figures was snoring loudly. Tad was sure it was a woman. Her breath was rattling at the back of her throat like a cat-flap in the wind. The man next to her muttered something in his sleep and turned over, dragging the cover with him. The woman, still asleep, groaned and pulled it back again. Tad stepped forward, his foot just missing an empty whisky bottle on the floor. The wall on the other side of the room was nothing more than a ragged curtain, hanging on a rail. He had to get to it before the two people – his kidnappers – woke up.

He forced himself to take it slowly, making no sound. He was helped at least by the rain. It was coming down more heavily now, striking the metal skin of the caravan and echoing throughout, the noise masking the sound of his own footsteps as he edged round the bed. At last he reached the curtain. He padded at the material until he found a gap and, with a surge of relief, passed through.

He found himself now in the third and last section of the caravan. It was without doubt the most disgusting part of all.

It was a kitchen, shower and toilet combined, with all the different articles of those rooms jumbled up together. There were dirty pots and pans stacked up in the shower and used, soggy towels next to the sink. A roll of toilet paper had unspooled itself over the oven and there were two grimy bars of soap, a razor and a toothbrush on the hob. Unwashed plates, thick with food from supper the night before, lay waiting on a shelf over the toilet while the oven door hung open to reveal two flannels, a sponge shaped like a duck and a hairbrush that was matted with curling black hair. All the walls and the ceiling were coated with grease and there were pools of water and more hair on the floor. Tad was amazed that anyone could live like this. But it wasn't his problem. He just wanted to get out.

And there was the front door! He was amazed that it was as easy as this. All he had to do was get out the door and run. He would make it to the nearest telephone and call the police. Tad took one step forward. And that was when he saw the other boy.

The boy was thin and pale and about a year younger than Tad. He had long fair hair that hung in greasy strands over a rather sickly looking face dotted with acne. His right ear was pierced twice with a silver ring and a stud shaped like a crescent moon. The boy could have been handsome. He had bright blue eyes, full lips and a long, slender neck. But he looked hungry and dirty and there was something about his expression that was pinched and mean. Right now he was standing outside the caravan, staring at Tad through a small window.

Tad opened his mouth to cry out. The boy did the same.

And that was when Tad knew, with a sense of terror, that he wasn't looking at a window. He was looking at a *mirror*. And it wasn't a boy standing outside the caravan. It was his reflection!

It was him!

Tad stared at himself in the mirror, watched his mouth open to scream. And he did scream – a scream that wasn't even his voice. His hands grabbed hold of his T-shirt and pulled it away from him as if he could somehow separate himself from the body that was beneath it.

His body.

Him.

Impossible!

"Whass all this racket, then? Whass going on?"

Tad spun round and saw that the curtain had been pulled back. Before him stood a man, wearing a pair of stained pyjama trousers but no top. His naked stomach was dangling over the waistband, a nasty rash showing round the belly button. The man's face was pale and bony and covered with a gingery stubble that matched what was left of his hair. His eyes were half-closed. One of them had a sty bulging red and swollen under the lid. There was a cigarette dangling from his lips and Tad realized with a shiver of disgust that he must have slept with it there all night.

"Who are you?" Tad gasped.

"Whaddya mean who am I? What the devil are you talking about?"

"Please. I want to go home..."

The man stared at Tad as if trying to work him out. Then suddenly he seemed to understand. A slow, nasty smile spread across his face, making the cigarette twitch. "You been at the glue again," he muttered.

"What?" Tad's legs were giving away beneath him. He had to lean against the wall. Then a voice called out from the other side of the curtain. "Eric? What is it?" It was a woman's voice, loud and shrill.

"It's Bob. 'e's been sniffing the glue again. I reckon 'e's 'ad an 'ole tube full. And now 'e doesn't know 'oo 'e is or where 'e is."

"Well, slap some sense into 'im and throw 'im in the shower," the voice cried out. "I want my breakfast."

"I'm not Bob," Tad whimpered. "There's been a mistake."

But before he could go on, the man had grabbed hold of him, one hand closing around his throat. "There was a mistake all right!" the man snarled. "And what was it? Bostik? Araldite? Well, you'd better get your head in order, you little worm. 'cos it's your turn to wash up and make the breakfast!" And with that, the man threw Tad roughly into the corner, spat out the cigarette and went back into the bedroom, drawing the curtain behind him.

Tad stayed where he was for a long time. His heart was racing so fast that he could hardly breathe. He looked at his hands again, his stomach, his legs. With trembling fingers, he touched his cheeks, his eyebrows, his hair, tugged at the two pins in his right ear. He let his hands fall and gazed at his palms. He knew, even without understanding why, that he had never seen those hands before. They weren't his hands.

Somehow, something horrible had happened. He had gone to sleep as Tad. *But he had woken up as Bob.*

A few minutes later the curtain was drawn back and a woman came out.

She was one of the ugliest women Tad had ever seen. For a start, she was so fat that the caravan rocked when she moved. Her legs, swathed in black stockings, were thin at the ankles but thicker than tree-trunks by the time they disappeared into her massive, exploding bottom. She had arms like hams in a butcher's shop and as for her face, it was so fat that it seemed to have swallowed itself. Her squat nose, narrow eyes and bright red lips had sunk into flabby folds of flesh. Her hair was black and tightly permed. She wore heavy plastic earrings, a wooden necklace and a variety of metal bangles, brooches and rings.

She took one look at Tad and shook her head. The earrings rattled. "Gawd's truth!" she muttered to herself. Then suddenly she lashed out with her foot. Tad cried aloud as her shoe caught him on the hip. "All right, you," the woman exclaimed. "If you're not going to 'elp, you can clear out. Go out and be sick or something. That'll sort you out."

"Please..." Tad began, getting to his feet.

"I told you that glue was no good for you. But would you listen? No! You get yourself dressed..." The woman snatched a handful of clothes from the top of the fridge and threw them at Tad. "Now get out, Bob. I don't wanna see you again until you got yourself sorted."

"No. You don't understand..."

But the woman had clenched her fist and Tad realized she didn't want to know. Clutching the clothes, he scrabbled for the door, found the handle and turned it. Behind the woman, the man had appeared, now wearing a knitted shirt and jeans and smoking a fresh cigarette. He saw what was happening and laughed. "You show 'im, Doll!" he called out.

"Shut up!" his wife replied.

Tad fell through the door and into his new world.

THE FUNFAIR

Tad was standing in the middle of a fair that had been set up on a patch of lumpy ground near a main road. There were about a dozen rides and the usual shooting galleries and sideshows. But everything was so old and broken down, with flaking paint and broken lightbulbs, that it didn't look fun at all. The fair was completely encircled by a cluster of caravans and trucks, some with electric generators. Thick cables snaked across the ground, joining everything to everything in a complicated tangle. There was nobody in sight.

Although the rain had eased off, it was still drizzling and this, along with the grey light of early morning, only made the scene more wretched. Tad felt the water dripping down his arms and legs and remembered that he was almost naked. Hastily he sorted out the clothes the woman had thrown him; a pair of jeans, faded and torn at the knees, a jersey, socks and trainers. Holding them up in front of him, Tad knew at once that they were much too small. There was no way they could possibly fit him. But when he did finally pull them on, they did!

Tad looked back at the caravan. It was one of the largest in the fair. Once it had been white but rust had eaten away most of the paintwork and dirt covered what little was left. The door was still firmly shut but there was a buzzer next to it and below that a slip of paper under a plastic cover. It read:

ERIC AND DOLL SNARBY

Doll. That was what the man had called the woman. Next to the name-plate somebody had added three letters, gouging them into the side of the caravan.

BOB

Tad ran his finger along it and swallowed hard. Bob Snarby. Was that who he was?

"I am not Bob Snarby! I'm Tad Spencer!"

But even as he spoke the words, he knew that they weren't true. Like it or not, something had happened and, for the time being anyway, he was this other boy. He was also very hungry. The smell of bacon was seeping out under the caravan door. He could almost hear it sizzling in the pan. He had no money and no idea where he was. But breakfast was cooking on the other side of the door. What choice did he really have?

Tad opened the door and went back in.

Doll Snarby was sitting, wedged behind the table with a mountain of eggs, bacon, sausages and toast in front of her. As Tad came into the room she pronged a whole fried egg on her fork and slipped it into her mouth, a trickle of grease dribbling down her chin. Eric Snarby was at the stove, a new cigarette between his lips. He had a bad cough. In fact he was spluttering as much as the bacon in the pan.

"So you come back in, 'ave you," Eric coughed. "Just like you to shove off when it's your turn to do the cooking."

"Don't be cruel to the boy," Doll Snarby shouted. She reached out and jabbed Tad hard in the ribs. "That's *my* job!"

"I suppose you want some bacon," Eric asked.

"Yes, please," Tad said.

"Oh! *Please!*" Eric sang the word in a falsetto voice. "'aven't we got airs and graces today." He coughed again, spraying the bacon with spittle. "'e'll be saying *thank you* next an' all!"

"Leave the little maggot alone," Doll said. She slid an empty plate in front of Tad.

Tad looked down. The plate was coated in grease and dried gravy from the night before. "This is dirty," he said.

Doll scowled. "Well, there's no point washing it, is there!" she said, reasonably. "You're only going to put more food on it."

Eric Snarby slid two lumps of bacon, a fried egg and a piece of fried bread onto Tad's plate. Doll picked up two pieces of toast, emptied half a jar of marmalade between them and pressed them into a sandwich. Eric had made himself a cup of tea and sat next to his wife.

She sniffed at him. "You smell!" she exclaimed.

"So what?" he replied, the eye with the sty twitching indignantly.

"Why don't you 'ave a barf?" his wife complained.

"Because we don't 'ave a barf," Eric Snarby replied. "And I'm not going in the shower. Not 'til you take out your knickers!"

Tad tried not to listen to any of this but instead concentrated on his breakfast. He had never seen food like it. Back home at Snatchmore Hall breakfast would have been freshly squeezed orange juice and a croissant, perhaps lightly scrambled eggs on a square of wholemeal toast and three pork sausages from Fortnum & Mason. This food was disgusting. Tad was sure he would only be able to manage a few mouthfuls and he was amazed to find himself eating it all. After that he drained a whole mug of tea and only felt a little queasy when he found a cigarette end nestling in the dregs at the bottom.

"Feeling better?" Eric Snarby asked.

"A bit." Tad had almost said "thank you" but stopped

himself at the last minute. Doll Snarby shifted on her seat and the next moment there was an explosion as she let loose a jet of stale air. Tad was horrified but Eric just grinned. "Cor!" he exclaimed. "That nearly put out my cigarette!"

Doll grunted with satisfaction. She wiped her mouth on the sleeve of her dress and stood up. "All right," she said. "Let's get to work."

"Work?" Tad blinked.

"Don't you start, Bob," Doll yelled, casually striking the back of Tad's head with her hand. "You pull your weight or you don't eat."

"Come on! Get off your backside." Eric slapped him again from the other direction. "Let's get stuck in."

It turned out that the Snarbies ran the Lucky Numbers stall at the fair and Tad spent the rest of the morning helping to rig it up. First there were the prizes to be set out: large stuffed gorillas hanging comically from one hand with a half-peeled banana in the other. Then the stall itself had to be washed down, the electric light bulbs hung and a few loose planks of wood hammered into place. The work was easy enough – but not for Tad. He had never done anything like this before and found it almost impossible. He got a stiff neck from carrying the toys, a handful of splinters from washing the stall and had only managed two bangs with the hammer before he had caught his thumb and gone off howling. Eric Snarby watched Tad with disgust. At midday, he shook his head, rolled another cigarette and went back into the caravan. There he found Doll, reading *The Sun* and munching a packet of chocolate digestive biscuits.

"What is it?" Doll wasn't pleased to see him.

"It's the boy. Bob." Eric lit the cigarette and sucked in smoke. "There's something about 'im. 'e's not 'imself."

Doll blew her nose noisily, then looked around for a handkerchief. "Of course he's not himself!" she exclaimed. "What do you expect with 'alf a tube of Araldite inside 'im!"

Eric Snarby nodded and bit his lip. He seemed about to go but then he stopped and looked up and suddenly there was fear in his eyes. "What 'appens if Finn wants him again?" he asked.

"Finn." Now it was Doll's turn to go pale. Even as she spoke the word, she seemed to shrink into herself, her rolls of flesh quivering.

"Suppose Finn wants the boy?" Eric persisted.

Both the Snarbies were silent now. Eric's cigarette was so close to his lips that it was actually burning them but he didn't seem to notice. Smoke crept up the side of his face like a scar. Doll Snarby was clutching the last chocolate digestive. Suddenly it exploded in her hand, showering her husband with crumbs.

"Bob'll be all right," she said. "Finn's not due back for a couple of days. By the time he gets here, Bob'll be fine." She took a deep breath and lashed out with one hand, catching her husband by the ear. As he squealed in pain, she drew him close. "Just keep 'im away from the glue," she hissed. "The Bostik, the Araldite, the Pritt Stick, the lot! And Finn won't notice a thing!"

The fair was busy that night. The rain had stopped and the people had come out, milling round the stalls and queuing for the rides. By then, Tad had learnt two things, overhearing the conversation of the other stall owners.

First it was Friday. Less than twenty-four hours had passed since he had gone to bed at Snatchmore Hall as Thomas Arnold David Spencer. And second, the fairground had been set up in a place called Crouch End, not too far from his parents' second London home. Tad could run away. Surely he would be able to find his way home.

But what would he do when he got there? If he knocked on the door, his parents wouldn't even open it – not to a scruffy, fair-haired kid who probably looked like he'd come to steal the silver. They might even set Vicious on him! The thought of the Dalmatian dog with its razor-sharp teeth was enough to make Tad tremble. He had nothing to prove that he was telling the truth. He didn't even have his own voice!

The more he thought about it, the more he realized he had no choice but to stay where he was – at least for the time being. Perhaps when he woke up the next day he would find he had switched back again. Perhaps Spurling would turn up in the Rolls Royce and drive him home. Perhaps...

The truth was that Tad wasn't used to making decisions for himself. He didn't know what to do and even if he had known he would have been too afraid to try.

A movement caught his eye. Tad turned. And that was when he began to think he really had gone mad.

There was a man standing on the other side of the funfair, partly hidden in the shadows. Or was it a man? He was less than four feet tall with hair reaching down to his shoulders. He had dark skin and wore a tunic that left his legs and arms bare. There were two streaks of blue paint on his cheekbones and a leather collar round his neck. He was an Indian, Tad realized. Some sort of pygmy.

The man was staring at Tad. Tad could see the lights of the funfair reflected in his dark eyes. Now he gestured with his head and walked slowly, deliberately, away. The message was clear. He wanted Tad to follow him.

Tad stepped forward, pushing through the crowd. He passed close to a hot dog stall and caught the sweet, heavy smell of frying meat. The Indian had stepped out of sight and Tad quickened his pace, stepping over the cables and leaving the brightly lit centre of the funfair. It was only now, in the darkness outside the ring of caravans, that he wondered if this was a good idea. Perhaps he was being led into some sort of trap. Perhaps the Indian had something to do with what had happened to him.

The chimes of the merry-go-rounds and the clatter of the other rides seemed suddenly very distant. The Indian had completely disappeared. Tad was about to turn round and go back when he noticed a caravan, set apart from the others. It was a proper, old-fashioned gypsy's caravan, lavishly painted with silver and gold leaf. Above the door hung a sign:

Doctor Aftexcludor —
Your future In The Stars.

The Indian was standing in the doorway, three steps above ground level. He was lit now by a yellow glow that came from within. He nodded at Tad again, then turned and moved inside. Tad thought for a moment. Then he crossed the grass and gravel and walked up to the caravan.

The door was still open but there was nobody in sight.

"Hello...?" Tad called out.

Far away, the merry-go-round started up again. There was a snap and a clang from an air rifle aimed at a metal plate. A shout of laughter from the other side of the darkness.

Tad made his decision.

He climbed the three steps to the caravan door and went in.

DOCTOR AFTEXCLUDOR

It was like being inside some strange church or temple. Tad looked around him wondering just how much more could happen to him today.

The walls of the caravan were covered with thick material, like a tapestry. The floor was richly carpeted. Even the ceiling was hidden by folds of what looked like silk. There were no windows and hardly any furniture. Cushions were scattered on the carpet round a low wooden table on which stood a gleaming crystal ball. There were old, leather-bound books piled up in crooked towers but there were no shelves. Dozens of joss-sticks poked out of strange bronze holders, their tips glowing, filling the room with smoke. The only other light came from a row of candles, perilously close to the wall. Sneeze and the whole place will go up in flames, Tad thought.

The owner of the caravan was sitting crosslegged on one of the cushions, smoking a long pipe. He was wearing a red silk dressing gown with a heavy collar and a strange black hat, a bit like a fez. The man had brown skin, deep black eyes and a pointed nose and chin. His hair was silver. Tad would have said he was about sixty or seventy. He had the look of a statue that has been left out in the open – not just weather-beaten but somehow timeless. His was a very odd face and a rather unsettling one.

"Good evening," the man said in a slightly sing-song voice. "Would you mind closing the door?"

Tad did as he was told, instantly cutting out all the sounds of the fair. The man waved a languid hand. "Please sit down."

Tad looked for a chair, couldn't see one, so sat down on a cushion. "Who are you?" he demanded.

"They call me Dr Aftexcludor," the man said.

"Dr Aftexcludor?" Tad thought for a moment. "That's a stupid name," he said. "I don't believe it's your real name at all."

The man sighed. "What are names?" he asked. "They're labels. Things people use to make us into what they want us to be." He fell silent for a moment. "And what of your name?" he demanded. "Bob Snarby." He spoke the two words with a smile.

"That's not my name!" Tad looked more closely at the old man. "But you know that, don't you. You know who I am!"

Dr Aftexcludor nodded slowly. "Yes. I do know what has happened to you. At least, I think I can guess."

"What *has* happened to me? I insist you tell me. If you don't tell me, I'm going to the police! It's horrible and unfair and I'm fed up with it. This funfair, the Snarbies, having to work! I want my mother. I want my Rolls Royce. I want to go home!"

Dr Aftexcludor chuckled. "Well, you certainly don't sound like Bob Snarby," he muttered.

Just then a curtain parted and the Indian reappeared, holding a tray. Tad hadn't realized that the caravan had two sections but looking over the Indian's shoulder he saw what seemed to be a corridor extending some way into the distance. But that was impossible. The corridor was longer than the caravan itself. The curtain fell back and the Indian moved forward. On the tray were two steaming glasses of tea.

"I haven't introduced you," Dr Aftexcludor said. "This is Solo."

"Solo?"

"That's not his real name either. I call him that because there's only one of him left."

"What do you mean?"

"He's from Brazil. An Arambayan Indian – but he's the last of the tribe. I met him in Rio de Janeiro and brought him with me to Europe..." Dr Aftexcludor turned to the Indian and muttered a few words in a language that sounded a little like Spanish, a little like a dog barking. The Indian nodded and withdrew. "I won't tell you his story now," he said. "You're not ready for it."

"What do you mean?" Tad snapped. There was something about Dr Aftexcludor he didn't like. Maybe it was that the old man seemed to know so much but explained so little.

Dr Aftexcludor picked up his tea. "Perhaps we should begin with you," he said. "Tad Spencer. That's your real name, if I'm not mistaken."

"How do you know my name?" Tad demanded.

"It's my job!" The old man nodded at the table and for the first time Tad noticed the crystal ball. He looked into it and saw the inside of the caravan, the doctor, himself, all twisted into a swirl of colours, trapped inside the brilliant glass. "Your future in the stars," Dr Aftexcludor explained. "Two pounds fifty and I tell people everything they want to know. Although, of course, most people don't know what they want to know and what they do want to know isn't what they ought to want to know." He shook his head as if trying to make sense of this. "Anyway," he went on, "telling their name is the easy bit."

"What's happened to me?" Tad demanded. He forced himself to look away from the crystal ball.

"That's not so easy. Obviously you've switched places with Bob Snarby..."

"You mean he's in my body with my parents in my house!" The thought hadn't occurred to Tad until this moment.

"I'm afraid so. But the real question is, how has this happened?" Dr Aftexcludor smiled to himself and for just one moment Tad wondered if he knew more than he was letting on. "I would say, if you want a professional opinion, that you've been hit by a wishing star."

"A what?"

"A wishing star. They're an extremely rare phenomenon and they have to be in exactly the right position at exactly the right time. Let me see..." Dr Aftexcludor reached out and took one of the books. He opened it and Tad saw that it was an old book of astronomy, the heavy pages (handwritten, not printed) filled with diagrams of stars and planets and their possible alignments. "Yes. Here we are." He pointed to one of the pictures. "In the Andromeda Galaxy. This little star here – Janus, its name is. That's Latin, although of course I wouldn't need to tell you that. Janus moved into the right orbit for about thirty seconds last night. That would have been around about ten o'clock. And the simple fact is that if you had made a wish at exactly that moment, the wish would have come true."

Tad stared at the picture, trying to think back. Then he remembered. "I wished I was somebody else," he said, slowly.

"Well, there you are then," Dr Aftexcludor said. "That's just what you are. Somebody else. Perhaps you'd better have a sip of tea."

Tad blinked. "Wait a minute," he spluttered. "You're telling me ... I wished. And my wish came true?"

"Evidently."

"But then ... I can wish again! Why can't I wish myself back the way I was?"

"Well, of course you can," Dr Aftexcludor said. "But the one snag is that you'll have to wait for the same star, Janus, to return to the same orbit."

"When's that?" Tad was excited now. For the first time he could see a way out of this nightmare.

Dr Aftexcludor opened the book at another page and ran a long, skeletal finger down a column of figures. He flicked back a few pages, closed his eyes as he worked it all out, then slammed the book shut. "January 13th," he said.

"January 13th!" Tad almost burst into tears. "But that's seven months away!"

"Rather more, I'm afraid," Dr Aftexcludor muttered. "I'm talking about January 13th in the year 3216."

"But that's ... that's..."

"One thousand, two hundred and twenty years from now. Yes. I know. You'll be one thousand, two hundred and thirty-three years old."

And then Tad did begin to cry, more than he had ever cried in his life. Dr Aftexcludor looked at him sadly. "I'm sure it's not that bad," he said.

"Of course it's bad!" Tad wailed. "It's terrible! It's the worst thing that's ever happened."

The doctor handed Tad a handkerchief and Tad

blew his nose. "What am I going to do?" he asked miserably.

"I'm not sure there's anything you *can* do," Dr Aftexcludor replied. "You are Bob Snarby now – whether you like it or not." He reached out and patted Tad on the shoulder. Tad looked up and once again he wondered if the old man wasn't hiding something. It was there in his eyes. Dr Aftexcludor was doing his best to look sympathetic but Tad knew that deep down he was enjoying this. "I can give you one bit of advice though."

"What's that?"

"Well. I know it won't look that way at the moment, but perhaps you might end up actually enjoying being Bob Snarby. Or to put it another way, maybe you can do a better job of being Bob Snarby than Bob Snarby ever did."

"But I'm not Bob Snarby!"

"That's just my point."

Tad had had enough. He threw down the handkerchief and stood up. "I don't know what you're talking about," he said. "And I don't believe you anyway. I've never heard of wishing stars. I don't believe they exist. I think it's all just a lot of lies and when I wake up tomorrow I'll be back to myself and that will be that. I'm not interested in you or your stupid servant. In fact I never want to see either of you again." Tad stormed out of the caravan, slamming the door behind him. Dr Aftexcludor watched him go.

"Goodbye, Tad," he muttered. "Or should I say ... hello, Bob?"

Tad spent the rest of the evening hiding and crept back into the Snarbies' caravan only when the fair had closed for the night. He had begun to feel ill and wondered if he had caught a cold when he had been sent out, half-naked, into the rain. One moment he was too hot, the next he was shivering with cold. There was a heavy thudding in his head.

Eric and Doll were not pleased to see him.

"Skived off all afternoon, 'ave we?" Eric complained. "Where've you bin then, Bob? 'aving a bit of a laugh? Breaking into cars, I'll bet. Or vandalizing old age pensioners again."

"I've been thinking," Tad said. He coughed loudly and shivered again.

"Thinking? Thinking?" Both the Snarbies burst into malicious laughter. "You never done no thinking in your life," Doll exclaimed. She had been holding a cream éclair and now she took a huge bite. Cream oozed out of her hand. "You was bottom of the class in everything at school," she went on with her mouth full. "Bottom in Maths. Bottom in History. Second to bottom in Geography – and that was only because you gave the other boy multiple stab wounds!"

"So what was you thinking about?" Eric Snarby asked. "Don't tell me!" He grinned. "It was Einstein's theory of electricity."

"It's relativity," Tad said. He found it hard to catch his breath. "Einstein invented the theory of relativity."

"Don't you contradict your father!" Doll exploded, grabbing hold of Tad's ear.

"That's right." Eric cried, grabbing hold of the other one.

"Wait a minute. Please. You don't understand..." Tad tried to get to his feet but suddenly the caravan seemed to be moving. He felt it spin round, then dive as if down a steep hill. He flailed out, trying to keep his balance. Then fell unconscious to the floor.

There was a long silence.

"Blimey!" Doll said, looking at the silent boy. "That's a bit of a shocker! Is 'e dead?"

"I don't fink so," Eric Snarby muttered. He leant down and put a hand to Tad's lips. "'e's still breathing. Just." He blinked nervously. "Wot we gonna do?" he went on. "I suppose we'd better call a doctor."

"No way! Forget it!" Doll snapped. "A doctor'll take one look at all them bruises we given the boy and then we'll have the social workers in and then the police."

Eric Snarby went over to an ashtray and rummaged inside it. A moment later he pulled out an old cigarette end, re-lit and screwed it into his lips. "So what are we going to do?" he asked again.

Doll Snarby thought for a long moment, twisting her wooden necklace with one pudgy hand. "We'll look after 'im ourselves," she said.

"But 'e looks awful!" Eric Snarby protested. "'e could

be full of glue, Doll. Maybe 'is 'eart and lungs 'ave got all stuck together and that's wot's doing it. What are we going to do if 'e dies?"

"He won't die..."

"But what if 'e does? What will we tell Finn?"

At the mention of Finn, Doll froze. "Don't talk to me about Finn," she rasped.

Eric Snarby went over to Tad, picked him up and carried him through to the bed. But for the faintest movement of the boy's chest as it rose and fell, he could have been dead already. Doll stared at him with bulging eyes, then threw a soiled blanket over him. "Go out and get 'im two Mars bars and a bottle of Lucozade," she rasped. "And don't worry! The boy's going to be fine!"

FINN

But Tad only got worse.

Wrapped in filthy sheets in the corner of the caravan, Tad seemed to be breathing more and more slowly as if he had found the one sure way out of his new body and was determined to take it. Eric Snarby sat watching over him while, in the next room, Doll Snarby blinked back the tears and tried on different hats for the funeral. But then, three days after Tad had fallen ill, there was a knock on the door. It was Solo, the Indian from Dr Aftexcludor's caravan.

"Blimey!" Doll exclaimed, staring at the tiny figure. "It's the last of the blooming Mohicans. What do you want, dearie?"

By way of an answer, Solo held out a curious bottle. It was circular in shape, fastened with a silver stopper.

It was half-filled with some pale green liquid.

"What is it?" Doll demanded.

Eric Snarby appeared at the door beside her. "Don't touch it," he muttered. "It's some sort of foreign muck." He waved at Solo. "'oppit!" he shouted. "Go on! Allez-vous! Push off!"

"Medicine." Solo muttered the single word and nodded at the bottle.

"What do you know about medicine?" Eric sneered.

Doll snatched the bottle from him. "Shut up!" she exclaimed. "That old geezer 'e works for ... Aftexcludor. 'e's a doctor, innee?"

"Medicine," Solo repeated.

"I 'eard! I 'eard!" Eric muttered, sourly. He turned to Doll. "'ow do they even know the boy's ill?" he whispered. "We didn't tell no one."

"What does it matter 'ow they knew?" Doll uncorked the bottle and smelled the contents. She wrinkled her nose. "It smells all right," she said. She nodded at Solo. "All right, you can shove off, shorty!" she said. "And tell your boss ta, all right?"

Whether Solo had understood or not he turned and walked away.

Doll turned to Eric. "Get me a glass!" she ordered. "And make sure you wipe it first with your sleeve."

Dr Aftexcludor's medicine was the first liquid that Tad had accepted since he fell ill. Even the smell of it seemed to revive him a little and he emptied the glass in one swallow. After that he slept again but his breathing seemed to have steadied and a little colour crept back into his face. Then, that evening, quite suddenly he woke up. The fever had broken.

"My baby!" Doll threw her arms round Tad and burst into tears.

"Be careful!" Eric muttered. "You're so fat you'll smother 'im!"

Eric and Doll Snarby were so relieved to have their son back with them that later that evening they went out and bought fish and chips for him – although Doll Snarby ate most of the chips as she carried them home. That night Tad ate properly for the first time. And when he slept again it was a normal, healthy sleep.

With the change in Tad's health came a change in the weather. The sun shone and the crowds came out, enjoying the first weeks of the summer holidays. When she was sure he wouldn't collapse on her, Doll Snarby set Tad to work on the Lucky Numbers stall.

It wasn't difficult to run. All Tad had to do was to sit in front of the stuffed gorillas holding a big basket of tickets. And as the crowds walked past, he would shout out a patter he had quickly learnt from his new father.

"Come on! Try your luck! Three tickets for a pound. If it ends in a five you're a winner! Lots of chances! Come on, sir! See if you can win a nice cuddly toy for the missus!"

This is what Tad did for the next four days. He felt safe in the stall, sitting on his own, and he even enjoyed the work, sitting out in the sun, watching the crowds go by. There was one thing that puzzled him to begin with. Not one single ticket that he sold actually ended in a five and soon he was surrounded by hundreds of coloured scraps of paper – torn up and thrown away by the losers. The gorillas stayed where they were. But it didn't take him long to work out the answer. There *were* no fives. No fifty-fives, no sixty-fives, no hundred-and-fives. They had never even been printed. And the punters had as much chance of winning a cuddly toy for the missus as they did of waking up on the moon.

But Tad didn't mind. He didn't feel a twinge of guilt. Eric Snarby was giving him five pence out of every pound he made and the money was quickly mounting up. Tad felt better with coins in his pocket. He felt more like his old self.

Before he knew it, he had settled into a routine. The fair closed just after midnight and Tad shut up the stall and crawled into his bed at the back of the caravan after quickly swallowing down a meal. The Snarbies bought him take-away Chinese, take-away Indian, take-away fish and chips. And the cost of each meal they took away from his earnings. Bed was the worst time for him. Lying curled up on the lumpy mattress, he would think back to his life at Snatchmore Hall. He had been away from home for less than a week but somehow home had already become a distant memory. As he shivered in the damp air, Tad would remember his electric blanket, the chocolate that Mitzy placed on his pillow last thing at night, the Jacuzzi waiting for him in the morning. Could he go back? Tad doubted it. If he turned up at Snatchmore Hall looking the way he did now, talking the way he did, smelling the way he did ... they wouldn't even let him through the gate.

"You are Bob Snarby now – whether you like it or not."

That was what Dr Aftexcludor had told him and Tad believed him. He *was* Bob Snarby. He had no choice.

Another week passed and the fairground prepared to close. Eric and Doll Snarby were planning to travel north to join another, larger fair in Great Yarmouth. Tad had almost laughed when he heard that. Great Yarmouth was only forty miles from Snatchmore Hall. He was actually moving closer to home! But at the same time he knew that it might just as well have been four hundred miles for all the difference it would make.

He sold almost two hundred tickets on the last day. It was a Saturday afternoon and he had been left on his own. Eric and Doll had opened a bottle of wine at lunch-time and had gone back to the caravan to sleep it off. He had watched the caravan shaking on its wheels and had heard their screams of laughter as they chased each other round the bedroom but now it was silent and he imagined they were asleep. Tad picked up the bucket of tickets and shook them.

"Come on! Try your luck..." he began. Then stopped.

A man had limped up to the stall and was standing

in front of him, looking at him strangely. Tad's first impression was of a shark in human form; the man had the same black eyes and pale, lifeless flesh. Although he wasn't physically huge, there was a presence about him, something cold and ugly that seemed to reach out and draw Tad helplessly towards him. The man had grey hair, cropped short to match the grey stubble on his chin. He wore a shabby suit and a pair of perfectly round wire-frame spectacles.

And then he turned his head and Tad gasped. His face was normal on one side but the other was completely covered by a tattoo. Somebody had cut an immense spider's web into the man's white flesh. It stretched from his ear to his forehead to his nose, to the side of his mouth and down to his neck. The tattoo was livid black and – most horrible of all – it seemed to be eating its way into the man's flesh. Somehow it was almost more alive than the face on which it hung.

"Try your luck...?" Tad muttered but the rest of the words refused to come.

"Hello, Bobby-boy!" The man smiled wickedly, revealing a line of teeth riddled with silver fillings. He had more fillings in his mouth than teeth. "I hope you're well."

"I'm OK." Tad looked at the stranger warily.

"I asked if you was well," he said. "Are you one hundred percent? 'OK' is not good enough!"

"I'm fine," Tad answered, mystified.

"That's good. Because I hear – I'm reliably informed

– that you been ill," the man said.

"What about it?" Tad had learnt that the ruder he was, the more people would accept that he was Bob.

The man smiled again. He had been leaning on a black, silver-capped walking stick but now he leant it against the stall. "Glue was what I heard," he murmured.

"What about it?"

The man shook his head slowly. "You modern kids," he said. "When I was your age, you wouldn't have found me touching stuff like that. No. Gin was good enough for me. A half bottle of gin in my schoolbag, that's what got me through the day." He took out a cigarette and lit it. "Mind you," he went on, "gin could be a treacherous friend too. It's gin I got to thank for this..." He tapped the tattoo on the side of his face.

"What happened?" Tad asked, feeling queasy.

"I was drunk. Drunk as a lord. And some mates of mine took me down the tattooist for a laugh. When I woke up, this was what he'd done to me. The web and the spider." Tad glanced at the tattoo. The man laughed. "One day I'll tell you where he put the spider," he said. He blew out smoke. His eyes behind the round lenses were suddenly distant. "Anyway, I had the last laugh, so to speak. I went back to the tattooist and gave 'im what you might call a piece of my mind."

"You told him what you thought of him... " Tad said.

"I *wrote* him what I thought of him. That's what I

did. I tied him to a chair and wrote it all over his body. Used his own needles. Oh yes. I turned that man into a walking dictionary – and not the sort of words you'd want your mother to hear. He went mad in the end, I understand. He's in an institute now. An institute for the insane. The other inmates never talk to him. But sometimes they ... *read* him." The man broke off and laughed quietly to himself.

There was a commotion as the caravan door opened and Eric and Doll Snarby appeared, hurrying across the fairground towards them. Eric was half-dressed, his shirt out of his trousers and the sty under his eye throbbing in time with his breath. Doll was also a mess, her lipstick smeared and one earring missing. Tad had never seen them like this. They were, he realized, terrified.

"Finn!" Doll exploded. "What a pleasure to see you! What a joy!"

"We wasn't expecting you 'til later," Eric added. "Or naturally we would 'ave bin 'ere to welcome you."

"Please, my dear Snarbies!" The man called Finn positively beamed at them. "No need to get your underwear in a twist. I've had all the welcome I need, thank you." He nodded at Tad, and in that moment it was as if a conjuror had waved a silk over the man's face. Suddenly the smile was gone and in its place was a leer of such force and ugliness that Tad shivered. "The boy's not 'imself," he snapped. "What have you done to 'im?"

"We looked after him!" Doll wheezed. "You know how precious he is to us, Finn. He was ill..."

"...'e made 'imself ill!" Eric interjected.

"What are children coming to?" Doll Snarby trilled. "You beat them senseless and it doesn't do any good at all! I don't know..."

"He got at the glue?" Each word was a bullet, fired at the Snarbies.

"It wasn't our fault, Finn!" Eric had gone chalk white.

"Oh Gawd! Please, Finn...!" Doll tried to slide herself behind her husband but he pushed her away.

Finn thought for a moment. Then he relaxed and his face rippled back to what it had been before. "I'm taking him with me this evening," he explained in a gentler voice. "A little business engagement. A business enterprise. I need my partner."

His partner? Tad heard the word and swallowed.

"Is he ready?" Finn asked.

"Of course he's ready, Finn," Doll croaked. "We wouldn't let you down!"

"That's settled then," Finn said. "I'll be back for him at nine o'clock."

He picked up his stick and used it to unhook one of the gorillas. The gorilla slid down the length of the stick and into his hand. Finn smiled. "My lucky day!" he exclaimed. "It looks like I won!"

Holding the gorilla, he turned and limped away.

NIGHTINGALE SQUARE

There was a full moon that night. As Finn and Tad crossed the empty square, their shadows raced ahead of them as if searching for somewhere to hide. It was a few minutes after midnight. Tad had heard the church bells toll the hour. They had seemed far away, almost in another world. Here, everything was pale and grey, the buildings like paper cut-outs against the black night sky.

Nightingale Square was in Mayfair, one of the smartest areas of London. Tad had been here before and now recognized the square. Sir Hubert Spencer had friends here and had once brought Tad here for tea. Tad scanned the handsome Georgian houses with growing discomfort. He already had a nasty idea just what sort of "business" Finn had in mind. But what would he do if the chosen house was the very one where he had once been a guest?

Finn leant against a metal railing in the middle of the square and raised his stick. "That's the one," he whispered. "Number twenty-nine. That's my lucky number, Bobby-boy. It's the number of times what I been arrested."

Tad glanced at the house. It was tall and narrow with classical white pillars and wide marble steps leading up to the front door. It was on the corner of the square with an alleyway next to it leading, presumably, to a garden at the back. Thick ivy grew up one side of the house. Tad followed it with his eye. The ivy twisted past three windows and a balcony, stopping just short of the roof. At the very top there was a brightly coloured box with a name and a telephone number. A burglar alarm.

"It's the London home of a real milord," Finn explained. "A member of the harry stocracy. 'is name is Lord Roven."

At least it wasn't one of his father's friends. But Tad still couldn't relax. He listened with dread as Finn went on.

"I seen 'im in the papers, Bobby-boy. Lord Roven and his lovely wife, the two of them dripping with diamonds and gold and mink." Finn's eyes had gone dark now. A bead of sweat trickled down the side of his head. "It's not fair, is it?" he hissed. "Them so rich and us so poor. I never had no education, Bobby-boy. OK.

It's true. I did burn down the school. And maybe it was wrong of me to lock all the teachers inside it first. But I never 'ad a chance. Never! And that's why it's all right, you see. To break into 'is 'ouse and steal 'is things. Because he's got everything and we got nothing and stealing is the only way to make things change."

Breaking in. Stealing. Tad's worst fears had been realized. His mouth had gone dry and it took him a few moments to find his voice. "How do you know Lord Roven won't be in?" he asked.

"'e always goes out tonight," Finn replied. "Tonight is 'is bridge night. It'll be four in the morning before 'e gets home."

"And Lady Roven?"

"In the country."

Finn licked his lips, then pointed again with the stick. "There's the window, Bobby-boy. Up there by the alarm. You can get in there."

Now Tad understood why he had been chosen. A man wouldn't have been able to climb up. The ivy wouldn't hold him. He needed a boy. "How do you know the window will be open, Finn?" he asked. His mind was desperately searching for a way out of this nightmare.

"I arranged it."

"But what about the alarm...?"

The stick whistled down, missing Tad's head by less than an inch. "What's the matter with you?" Finn demanded.

"Nothing...!"

"Nuffing, Bobby-boy? Oh yes. There's something queer all right. Finn can smell a fish. A rotten fish." Finn rested the stick on Tad's shoulder and gazed into his eyes. "You been ill," he continued. "I can respect that. I've made lots of people ill myself. But you're acting like you never been on a job before. What's happened to you?"

"I'm all right, Finn. Nothing's changed."

"I wonder." Finn let the stick slide off Tad's shoulder. "But you better not let me down, Bobby-boy. Stuffed with nice things this 'ouse is. Nice pictures and candlesticks. Smart jewellery and antiques. And you got to get me in!" Finn looked left and right, then hurried across the road. Feeling sick and frightened, Tad followed. The last time he had come to Nightingale Square it had been for crumpets and tea. Now he was back as a thief in the night. It was impossible. When he had woken up in the Snarbies' caravan he had thought things were as bad as they could get. But this was far, far worse.

Finn had already reached the other side of the road and was crouching down. As Tad joined him, he straightened up and now he was holding what looked like a circular section of the pavement. Looking closer, Tad saw it was the cover of a manhole. Finn grunted and set it down, then pulled out a tangle of multicoloured wires which he began to examine.

"What are you doing?" Tad asked.

"What do you think I'm doing?" Finn shook his head and sighed. "The alarm's connected to the police." He pulled out a pair of wire-cutters, selected an orange-coloured wire and snipped it in two. "At least, it was."

"You've cut it!"

"Don't disappoint me, Bobby-boy." Finn glanced upwards and suddenly it seemed to Tad that he was holding the wire-cutters like a weapon. "You've seen it all before. You know the procedure. You know what's what."

"Of course, Finn."

"Good." Finn flipped the cutters over and put them away, then slid the manhole into place and stood up. "Fifteen minutes," he said. "That's how long we got before they'll send someone round to check." He gestured at the house. "I want the door open in five."

Tad stood staring at the house. A hundred excuses formed in his mind but died before they could reach his lips. He couldn't risk asking anything. Finn was already suspicious and if Tad asked something he was supposed to know ... he thought of the wire-cutters and hurried forward.

Gingerly he reached out and took hold of the ivy, testing it against his weight. He had been right about one thing. The twisting stems would never have taken the weight of a man but holding on tight he was able to lift himself off the ground. The ivy bent but held firm.

"Five minutes," Finn reminded him.

Tad began to scale the wall, pulling himself up a

few centimetres at a time. Finn stood below, keeping a look-out along the empty pavement. Somewhere a car door slammed and an engine started up. Tad froze. But the sound grew more distant and finally disappeared. Tad grunted and dragged himself up over the first window.

He had passed the balcony and was making his way up to the third floor when he made the mistake of looking back down. It was the worst thing he could have done. The ground seemed a very long way away and for a moment he couldn't move. This sort of thing might have been easy for Bob Snarby but Tad Spencer had always been afraid of heights. The whole house had begun to spin with him attached to it and he was certain he would have to let go. Already he could imagine the wind sailing past him, the crushing impact as he hit the concrete below. He wanted to shout out but he was too frightened even to draw breath.

There was a low whistle from the pavement. Finn. The sound snapped Tad out of his paralysis and he began to climb again. He was more afraid of Finn than he was of falling. It was as simple as that. He had to go on.

But the further up he went, the thinner the ivy became. It was bending now, pulling away from the wall. Tad heard the unmistakeable sound of a branch snapping and his left foot suddenly kicked out into space. For a ghastly moment, he hung there, feeling himself topple backwards away from the wall as the ivy came loose. Another branch broke. But then Tad lurched out and managed to grab a thicker clump. Carefully, he transferred his weight across. Then, gritting his teeth, he began to haul himself up further.

He was only half a metre from the window and was about to reach out to open it when there was a second, low whistle – this time a warning. A moment later, a car drove past, its headlights spilling out over the white front of the house. Instinctively, Tad stopped and pressed himself against the brickwork, not moving, not turning round. The car continued through the square and darkness fell like a curtain behind it. Finn whistled an "all clear". Tad began again.

He pressed his hand against the window and almost shouted with relief as it began to open inwards. It wasn't locked! At least Finn had been right about that. The strange thing was that Tad wasn't frightened any more. The truth was, he felt almost pleased with himself. At school he had never been any good at sports. He had never managed to get more than ten centimeters up a rope and the parallel bars had made him feel sick. He had been excused football and rugby – his parents thought they were too dangerous – and had even cheated at cross country running by getting a taxi to wait for him around the first corner.

And now he had climbed fifteen metres up the side of a building and he wasn't even out of breath! Tad didn't want to admit it but it was true. He was proud of himself. He was pleased.

Letting go of the ivy with one hand, he reached out for the window. This was the difficult part but he knew he had to keep moving. At least three minutes had passed since he had begun the climb. Finn had given him five. The police would be here in fifteen. Carefully, he swung his weight from the ivy onto the window sill. Then he pulled himself up and in.

It was only at the very last moment that he lost his balance. Half in the house, half out of it, he suddenly found himself flailing at the air, his centre of gravity hopelessly lost. Even then, some instinct saved him. He knew that he could topple backwards and down or throw himself forwards and in. He took the second option, twisted in mid-air and dived forwards. His shoulders passed neatly through the window. Unable to stop himself, he pitched forward, then fell to the floor with a crash. The noise seemed deafening, but nobody came. Nobody had heard. So Finn was right again. It seemed that there was nobody in the house.

The window had opened into a box room, stacked high with suitcases and tea chests. Tad could just make out a door in the half-light and crept over to it. The door led out to a corridor with, straight ahead of him, a flight of stairs going down. Tad tip-toed out.

Someone had left a light on in the hall. Tad hurried down four flights of thickly carpeted stairs past paintings by Rubens and Picasso. A huge chandelier hung over him and a gold-framed mirror reflected his image as he scuttled over to the front door. Tad was certain now that the house was empty. It had that feel. His own feet rapped out a brittle sound on the marble slabs in the hall. A grandfather clock ticked. But nothing else stirred.

He reached the front door and slid off the security chain and drew back the bolts. The door opened and there was Finn, standing in front of him, his spectacles two brilliant white discs as they caught the streetlight.

Finn lifted his walking stick and pushed Tad aside. He hurried into the house and closed the door behind him. There was a sheen of sweat on his forehead and a vein in his neck was throbbing rapidly. The spider's web was pulled taut.

"What the devil happened?" he hissed.

"What do you mean...?" Tad began.

"You made the devil of a racket at the window, Bobby-boy. An 'orrible racket. I'd have heard you three blocks away."

"I fell," Tad replied. "Anyway, what does it matter? The house is empty. You said so yourself."

Finn half-smiled. "Got a tongue in your head, have you?" he snarled. "That sounds more like my old Bob." He glanced at his watch. "Seven minutes," he said. "We'd better move."

"Where are we going?"

"We'll start with the safe. On the second floor." Leaning on his stick, Finn hurried towards the stairs and began to climb. Tad followed, saying nothing.

They had reached the first landing when the door opened.

Finn saw it first and stopped. He was on a landing about five steps below the level of the door with Tad just behind him. A man in a blue silk dressing gown and leather slippers stepped out. He was in his sixties with silver hair and a gaunt face and Tad didn't need to ask his name. It had to be Lord Roven. The owner of the house was looking down at them, clutching a heavy silver candlestick as a weapon in his hand.

"Stop there!" he said in a cultivated voice. "I heard you come in the window and I've already called the police. You might as well wait where you are and make it easier on yourselves."

Finn looked over his shoulder at Tad and snarled at him with the cob-webbed side of his face. "You little fool!" he hissed. "You little idiot! I told you, didn't I? All that blooming noise!"

Tad took a step back. Everything was swimming again. He felt sick. He just wanted to disappear.

Finn turned back to Lord Roven. "What are you doing here?" he demanded. "Wednesdays is your bridge night."

Lord Roven frowned. He shook his head slowly. "It's Thursday..." he said.

"Thursday!" Finn almost shouted the word. A tic had appeared at one of his eyes, making the cobweb dance. "Thursday?" he whimpered again. "Then it's not my fault, is it? It was a perfect plan. Perfect! I just got the day wrong, that's all!"

Then everything seemed to collide with itself. Tad

would never be quite sure what happened – or when.

The shrill sound of a siren cut through the night. Finn took a step forward. Lord Roven moved towards him, reaching out as if to grab him. Finn dropped his ebony walking stick – or part of it. When Tad looked again, he was still holding the handle but the rest of the stick had fallen away and an ugly length of steel protruded from his hand. A sword stick, Tad realized. But Lord Roven hadn't seen it. Whether Finn lifted the sword or whether his victim walked onto it, Tad couldn't say. But the next thing he knew, Finn had laughed out loud, a single cry that danced in his throat. At the same time, Lord Roven groaned and fell to the floor. Then there was a screech of tyres. A blue light flashed on and off through a downstairs window. A hand hammered at the door.

"The kitchen!" Finn hissed, snatching up the rest of his walking stick. "We can get out the back way!"

"You've killed him!" Tad whispered.

Finn swore and then grabbed Tad by the throat. For a moment their faces were pressed so close that they touched and Tad could feel the stubble of the man's beard rubbing against his own skin. "I'll kill you too if you don't move!" he snarled. "Now – come on!"

The thumping on the door continued, harder now, and a second police siren echoed across the square. Finn ran down the stairs – five steps at a time – and slid across the marble hallway. Tad followed. He could just make out a uniformed shape through the stained glass next to the front door but he ignored it, twisting round to follow the passage back past the grandfather clock. Then Finn grabbed hold of him and pulled him through an open doorway even as a booted foot crashed into the front door, splintering the wood and smashing the first of the locks.

Tad found himself in the kitchen, a long, narrow room all white and silver with French windows leading into a garden at the end. Finn was already trying the handles but they were securely locked.

"Stand back!" he ordered. As Tad obeyed, he raised his walking-stick, then brought it whistling through the air into the glass. The window shattered at exactly the same moment as the front door was kicked in. Tad heard the falling wood, the sound of voices shouting in the hall. "Move!" Finn commanded.

Tad followed Finn into the garden. The lamps on the police cars were still flashing and the bushes and trees loomed up on him, flickering blue against the night sky. The garden was surrounded by a low wall with other gardens on each side.

"Split up!" Finn hissed. "Confuse 'em. We got more chance that way. Meet back at the caravan..." Then before Tad could stop him, he hoisted himself over the wall and disappeared down the other side.

Tad swung round. Two policemen had stepped out of the kitchen and were standing in the garden. Slowly, they began to approach, and Tad realized they were afraid of him.

"All right..." one of them began.

Tad turned his back on them and ran. He felt his feet first on the grass, then in the soft earth of the flower-beds. His scrabbling hands found the garden wall and he pulled himself up, half-expecting the two policemen to grab him and pull him back. But he had been too fast for them. He twisted over the top of the wall and fell, squirming down the other side.

"There goes one of them! Round the other side!"

A heap of garden rubbish had broken his fall. Tad stood up and brushed some of it away. There were more whistles, more shouts. Lights had gone on in the adjoining houses, illuminating the gardens that ran along the back. Tad looked one way, then another, then began to run. He reached another garden wall and threw himself over it. Then another. He had forgotten all about Finn, didn't care if he had been caught or not. Tad couldn't stop. A window opened in one of the houses and somebody shouted. He came to a garden fence, kicked out at it with his foot and broke through.

He found himself in a narrow alleyway. Down one end he could see flashing lights and hear voices. The other end was dark and silent. That was the direction he chose.

Tad never knew how he got away without being arrested. But the alleyway led to a main road and suddenly he was in the clear with no policemen in sight and the chaos of Nightingale Square far behind him. He ran for an hour and only stopped when he could run no more.

He had escaped from Finn. He had escaped from the Snarbies. But now he was on his own and wanted for murder. He had little money, nowhere to go. Tad found an entrance to an office and slipped inside, burying himself in the shadows. He was still there six hours later when the first of the traffic hit the streets and the city of London woke to another day.

HOME

"Bacon sandwich and a cup of tea, please."

Tad had found his way to a run-down café in a Soho back street. He was the only customer. He paid for his breakfast using the last of his money and chose a table in the furthest corner. He had bought a late edition of the morning paper and now he opened it, thumbing through the pages.

He found the murder of Lord Roven in a single column on page four. There was a photograph of the house in Nightingale Square and a headline that read: BRUTAL MURDER IN LONDON'S MAYFAIR. The report concluded that the police had chased two intruders, a man and a boy, but both had escaped. So Finn hadn't been arrested either! Tad didn't know whether to be pleased or sorry. If Finn was free, he couldn't lead the police to Tad. On the other hand, he would almost certainly be looking for Tad himself. After the disaster of the failed break-in, Tad didn't like to think what would happen if he were found.

Tad bit into his sandwich and actually found himself enjoying it. He should have been terrified or in despair but the truth was that he was neither. He felt confident ... even calm. As he sat in the café with his elbows on the table and his long hair falling over his eyes, Tad wondered if he was changing in some way that he couldn't understand.

A couple more people came into the café and ordered coffees. Neither of them even glanced in his direction. Cupping his hands round his tea, feeling the warmth, Tad tried to work out his options.

He was a thirteen-year-old, on his own in London, wanted by the police. He knew that he had been seen at Lord Roven's house and it surely wouldn't be hard to track him down. And what then? The fact was that it had been Tad who had broken into the house and let Finn in. He was as responsible for the old man's death as if he had held the sword himself. If the police caught him, he would go to prison. It was as simple as that.

He had to get out of London. He knew that. But with no money in his pocket, it wasn't going to be easy.

Briefly, he considered going back to the fun-fair. Whatever he thought of them, Eric and Doll Snarby would look after him. And they'd take him with them when they moved to the fair at Great Yarmouth. But if he went back to the Snarbies, he would be going back to Finn. Tad remembered the look on Finn's face as he stabbed forward with the sword. He shivered and took a sip of tea. He couldn't go back to Finn. There had to be another way.

And that was when the idea came to him.

Go home.

Not to the Snarbies but to his real parents and his own home. Sir Hubert Spencer had a house in Knightsbridge – only an hour's walk from where he was sitting now. It was his only chance. He had considered it before, when he was at the fair at Crouch End. But things had been different then. He had been too frightened to think straight, too frightened to act. Tad had come a long way since then. He was certain now that he could make his parents believe what had happened to him. After all, he knew everything about them. He could describe things that only their true son would know. All he had to do was talk to them.

He finished his breakfast and set off, up through Green Park and on towards the heart of Knightsbridge. He followed the road past Harrods Department Store and thought sadly of the times he had visited it with his mother. Lady Geranium used to take him there on his birthday and let him choose his own present. One year it had been a grand piano (although he had never played it). The next he had chosen the entire chocolate department. But now, of course, they wouldn't even have allowed him through the door.

The Spencers' London home was in a quiet street on the other side of Harrods. Number One, Wiernotta Mews was a pale blue house on three floors with a kitchen and dining-room in the basement. Tad had a bedroom on the second floor and slept there whenever the family was visiting London. He wondered if they would be there now.

It was eleven o'clock and the mews was empty. The other house owners were probably all at work. Tad crossed the cobbled surface and reached for the bell. It was only then that he had second thoughts. If the Spencers were at home and he rang the bell, Spurling would probably come to the door. And what would the chauffeur see? A dirty, dishevelled boy whom he wouldn't recognize. The door would be slammed before Tad had a chance to explain.

Tad sighed. It would be much easier to explain things once he was *inside* the house. But how was he to get in? Break in – for the second time in twenty-four hours? Then he remembered. His mother always left a spare key in one of the baskets of flowers that hung on either side of the front door. Tad quickly found it, opened the gate and followed the metal stairway down to the kitchen entrance.

As quietly as he could, he slipped the key into the lock and turned it. The house was silent. Tad stepped inside.

He stood for a few seconds in the quarry-tiled kitchen. His heart was pounding in his chest and he had to remind himself that he wasn't a thief. He wasn't breaking in. This was his house. He lived here. Even so, when he moved forward it was on tip-toe and his ears were pricked for the slightest sound.

He passed through the kitchen and crept upstairs. The first floor consisted of a single, open-plan room with leather sofas, Turkish carpets and a huge, wide-screen TV. A spiral staircase led upwards and he followed it to the second floor, where his own bedroom was located. He stopped in front of a door, tapped gently and went in.

The room was just as he had left it – evidently nobody had been there in the last few days. His bed, with its duvet patterned like a giant dollar bill, was freshly made. His London toys, books and computers were exactly where he had left them. Tad ran his hand over one of the surfaces, taking it all in. He had come home! Quickly he stripped off his clothes and went through into the adjoining bathroom. He didn't care if anyone heard him now. He turned on the shower and stood for ten minutes in the hot, jetting water. It was as if the shower were washing away not just the dirt but all the memories of the past week. He dried himself in one of his own American towels. He had never appreciated how soft and warm they really were.

Outside, he heard a car draw up. A door slammed and a voice called out. He recognized it at once. It was his mother! His parents had arrived.

He felt a surge of excitement. In just a few moments

he would see them again, talk to them, tell them what had happened. They would be shocked, of course. But once they understood, they could all begin again. The nightmare would finally be over.

Moving quickly, Tad pulled some clothes out of the cupboard and tried to get dressed. It was only now that he realized he had a problem. The pants he was holding were obviously several sizes too big. The trousers were the same. Reluctantly, he picked up Bob Snarby's clothes and put them back on. At least they fitted and, washed and groomed, he felt a bit more like an ordinary boy, less like a street urchin. Even so he was nervous. What if his parents refused to listen to him? What if they simply threw him back out on the street?

He could hear footsteps coming up the stairs. Tad thought for a moment, then went over to a drawer beside the bed, opened it and pulled out a cheque book. It was his own cheque book, and he was certain that he would still be able to sign Tad Spencer's signature. There was over ten thousand pounds in his current account; his pocket money for the past six months. Whatever happened, that money was now his.

He had just shoved the cheque book in his pocket when the door to the bedroom opened. Tad stared. He wasn't sure what he had been expecting but, whatever it was, it certainly wasn't this.

A short, fat, dark-haired boy in a ginger-and-brown checked suit had just walked in and was staring at Tad with the same shocked expression with which Tad was staring at him. Tad tried to speak. He felt the bed pressing against the back of his legs and he sat down. The other boy smiled.

And that was when Tad knew. He had thought at first that he was looking at himself and in a way, of course, he was. It was his own body that had just walked into the room but there was somebody else inside it. And the suddenly narrowed eyes – the cruel smile – told him who that somebody was.

"Bob Snarby!" he whispered.

"Tad Spencer!" the other boy replied. "I been expecting you."

FACE TO FACE

Bob Snarby closed the door and moved into the room. Tad watched him with a sense of wonderment. His first thought was how fat this boy was, how arrogant he looked with his puffed-out cheeks and slicked back hair. But then he remembered that he was actually looking at himself! Bob was wearing one of his own favourite suits. The Rolex watch that his mother had bought him was on the other boy's wrist. Tad realized that he was jealous, that he disliked Bob Snarby on sight.

But it wasn't Bob Snarby. It was him! Tad rested against a chair, thoroughly confused.

For a long minute the two boys stared at each other; Bob Snarby in Tad's body and Tad Spencer in Bob's body. At last Tad spoke.

"Do I call you Bob or Tad?" he asked.

The fat boy smiled. "I suppose you can call me Bob," he said. "You know that's who I am."

"What happened?" Tad demanded. "How did you turn yourself into me?"

"I didn't," Bob replied. "I didn't have nothing to do with it."

"You're lying!"

Bob moved further into the room. "I'll tell you what happened," he said. "But you'd better not get nasty with me. Spurling's downstairs and one shout from me and you'll be out on your ear. Know what I mean?"

Tad nodded.

"All right." Bob sat down on the bed. "I'd had an 'orrible day at the funfair. Up in Crouch End. Moving in is always the worst part and I was dog tired ... only if I was a dog they'd 'ave put me out of my misery. Mum and Dad were out at the pub. I went to bed."

"What time?"

"It must have been about half ten. Anyway, I fell asleep and woke up in your place. That's all there was to it. One minute I was in the van, the next..." Bob shook his head. "It gave me a nasty turn, I can tell you. Waking up in that bed! It was so big it took me a while just to find my way out."

"So what did you do?" Tad asked.

"I couldn't believe it at first. There I was, surrounded by all this gear – CDs and computer games and the rest of it. You know what my first thought was?"

"I can guess," Tad said.

"Bob, my boy, I thought, you've got to nick as much of this stuff as you can carry. You can ask questions later. But right now you've got to get out of here before someone comes and throws you out." Bob sighed. "That was when I caught sight of meself in the mirror." He paused. "I mean, *myself*, don't I. I've got to learn how to talk proper, haven't I! Anyway, that was when I started screaming the place down. It was like a horrible dream – only I knew I was awake."

"That's more or less what happened to me," Tad muttered.

"I bet. You must have been sick waking up with Eric and Doll! I wish I could have seen your face!"

"You've got my face!" Tad retorted, angrily.

"Let's not make it any more confused, shall we?" Bob Snarby said. "Where was I? Oh – right. I'm screaming my head off when the door flies open and this old biddy comes rushing in. I didn't know who the hell she was but then she starts calling me 'Master Tad' and tries to get me to calm down..."

"It was Mrs O'Blimey," Tad said.

"That's right. The housekeeper. Well, I got back into bed and the old lady fussed over me but I kept my mouth shut. You see, I knew something strange was going on and I didn't want to queer my own pitch, like. You know? I could smell the money and I was thinking to myself – Bob, old mate, I don't know what's going on 'ere. It's a right mystery and no mistake. But you could do yourself quite nicely out of all this. Just take your time. Try and work it all out..."

Bob Snarby pulled a bar of chocolate out of his pocket and broke a piece off. "I never used to like this stuff," he said, half to himself. He offered the bar to Tad. "You want some?"

Tad shook his head.

"Well, I did manage to work it out in the end," Bob continued, munching the chocolate. "Somehow – Gawd knows how – I'd switched bodies with a fat, posh boy called Tad Spencer. It was like something out of a comic. Or maybe a film. I once saw a film on telly where something like that happened. I don't know. Anyway, as I lay there in that great big bed, surrounded by all that lovely stuff, I realized it had happened to me and after a bit I stopped worrying about how or why and just decided to ... go with it."

"But how could you persuade them?" Tad thought back to his own experiences with the Snarbies and with Finn. "My mother and father would never have believed you were me. You're much too common. You don't know anything. You never been to public school."

"You mean – 'You never *went* to public school'" – Bob corrected him. "It's true what you're saying, although if you don't mind me saying so, Tad, you're not exactly in a position to be snobbish." He smiled. "But all right, I admit it. There were a lot of things I didn't know that I ought to if I really was going to be you. I knew that."

"So what did you do?"

"In the end it was easy. I hadn't said much yet so they didn't know anything was wrong. The old woman – Mrs O'Blimey – thought I'd just been having a bad dream. And that afternoon, Spurling asked me if I'd like to go out riding. I said yes – I thought he was talking motorbikes or something. I didn't realize he meant on a horse! No, ta very much, I thought. But then, as I said, I had this idea. I got on the horse and the two of us trotted along for a bit. And then I fell off." Bob rubbed his backside. "I didn't have to fake that bit, I can tell you. Your mum saw me fall. She had the horse shot immediately – but this is the good part." He winked at Tad. "I told her I'd banged my head when I fell and I wasn't seeing things straight. You know ... like I had amnesia or something."

"Amnesia..." Tad almost admired Bob despite himself. The idea couldn't have been simpler.

"Right." Bob broke off another piece of chocolate. "Well, of course your mum was worried sick. She called in a whole army of doctors and I told them I wasn't sure who I was and that I'd forgotten all my Ancient Greek and Latin and all that stuff and they said that I was definitely concussed. I had to stay in bed while they did all these tests and they only let me out a couple of days ago. Now your mum – or I should say my mum – has brought me down to London to go shopping. We're going on holiday in a couple of weeks..."

"A safari in Africa," Tad said, gloomily.

"That's right! First class flights. Five star hotel. It's

like winning the blooming pools!" He finished the chocolate and dropped the wrapper on the floor. "How about you?" he asked. "What have Eric and Doll had to say about the new Bob Snarby?"

"They think I've been sniffing glue," Tad said.

Bob thought about this for a moment, then threw his head back and laughed. "I bet they have!" he said. "Yeah. That'd explain everything. "

Tad moved closer to the bed. "Listen to me, Bob," he pleaded. "We've got to sort this out..."

"What do you mean?"

"We've got to tell them what's happened. Your parents and my parents. If we both tell them, they'll have to believe us and maybe they'll be able to find a way to turn us back into ourselves."

Bob stared at Tad as though he were mad. "But why should I want to do that?" he demanded.

"What?" Tad felt something cold reach out and touch the back of his neck.

"Why should I want to change back?" Bob said.

"Because you've got to!" Tad cried. "I can't be you and you can't be me. We've got our own parents and our own lives. We've got to put things back the way they were."

"Forget it!" Bob exclaimed. "I'm better off now than I've ever been in my entire life and if you imagine I'm going to let you spoil it, you've got another think coming."

"It's all wrong...!" Tad began.

"It's perfect!" Bob shouted the words. "I never had a chance. I never had anything. Not from the day I was born. Eric and Doll, they made me what I was and I was stuck with it. And do you know what made it worse? All around me, in the newspapers, on the TV, in the shops, I saw all the things I could never, ever have. Computer games and hi-fi. Smart clothes. TVs and videos. I'd never have them – not in my whole life – just because of who I was..."

"That's not true..."

"It is true! But you wouldn't understand that. You had it all, didn't you. It was all just given to you on a plate. Yeah – well now you're finding out what it's like on the other side of the fence and I'm not surprised you want to switch back again. Only you can't. Because I won't let you."

"You must!"

"I won't!"

Something inside Tad snapped and before he knew what he was doing he had thrown himself on to Bob Snarby, his fists flailing, his face twisted with anger and hatred. He expected the other boy to defend himself but Bob just fell backwards onto the bed with Tad on top of him, not even trying to push him off. Tad hit him, again and again, but his fists seemed to make no impact, slapping against the skin and sinking into the soft folds of flesh. He only realized now that Bob was shouting, calling for help. Suddenly the door crashed open. Out of the corner of his eye Tad saw a great bulk in a blue and grey uniform descending on him. Two hands reached out and grabbed him; one round his neck, the other under his arm. He was pulled off Bob and into the air as easily as if he were nothing more than a set of empty clothes.

"Are you all right, Master Tad...?"

"Yes, Spurling. Thank you." Bob got unsteadily to his feet. His shirt was rumpled and there were tears welling up in his eyes.

"Spurling..." Tad twisted round in mid-air, his feet ten centimetres off the ground. As much as he squirmed and struggled, he couldn't free himself from the chauffeur's grip.

"Who are you?" Spurling demanded. "What are you doing here?"

Tad opened his mouth to answer but, before he could speak, before he could find the right words, Bob moved forward. "He was here when I came in," he sobbed. "He was searching the room. I think he was looking for something to steal."

"Tad, darling?" The voice came from outside the room and the next moment Lady Geranium Spencer appeared. She took one look at Tad and her face paled. "How frightful!" she exclaimed. "It's a burglar!"

"Mummy....!" Bob Snarby ran into Lady Geranium's arms. "He attacked me!" he wailed.

"Spurling! Call the police immediately," Lady Geranium snapped. She pushed Bob away from her. "Do be careful, darling," she continued. "You're going to rumple Mummy's hair."

"Wait a minute!" Tad shouted. "You're not his mother! You're my mother!"

"I'm nothing of the sort!" Lady Geranium replied. "Oh, Spurling! Take him downstairs. I think I'm going to have one of my turns."

"Yes, ma'am."

Tad opened his mouth to speak again but Spurling shook him so hard that all the breath went out of him. There was nothing he could do as he was carried out of the room, half-across the chauffeur's massive shoulders.

Spurling carried Tad back downstairs, threw him into a cupboard and locked the door. Suddenly everything was black, apart from a tiny chink of light coming through the keyhole. Tad pounded at the door, then, realizing it was useless, sank to his knees. He heard something outside. He pressed one eye against the keyhole. Spurling was on the telephone, waiting to be connected. There was a movement and Lady Geranium appeared, hand-in-hand with the boy she thought was her son.

"We're going out, Spurling," she snapped.

"Yes, ma'am."

"Come along, Tad!"

Inside the cupboard, the real Tad watched Bob Snarby turn round and gaze directly at him. Bob's lips twisted in a cruel, triumphant smile.

And then he was gone.

ACID

The office was small and square with a desk, two chairs, a filing cabinet and a low coffee table. There was no carpet. A single window looked out over a tangle of railway lines with King's Cross Station in the far distance. Tad was sitting on his own. He had been here now for twenty minutes but he still had no idea where he actually was.

After Bob Snarby had left with his mother, Spurling had unlocked the cupboard door. Of course, Tad had tried to speak, to explain who he was, but after just two words the chauffeur had cut him off.

"You don't talk to me. I don't want to know. Keep your mouth shut – or else!"

Tad had known Spurling all his life. Only two weeks before the man had been collecting him from school, carrying his suitcases for him. But it was a completely different creature who had pulled him out of the cupboard and who towered over him now. Behind the smart uniform, the brightly polished buttons and the chauffeur's cap, the man was a thug. He had the same lifeless eyes as Finn. Tad didn't try to speak again. But he found himself wondering what such a man was doing working for his father.

With his arm twisted painfully behind him, Tad had been led out of the house and thrown into the back of a black Volkswagen Estate. It must have been Spurling's own car. Tad had never seen it before. They had driven in silence for about half an hour, passing King's Cross Station. Then Spurling had suddenly swerved off the road, through an archway and into an office car park. Tad hadn't had time to see what the office was. They had gone in through a side door, up two flights of stairs. Tad had glimpsed one large room, full of people talking on telephones, tapping at computers, shuffling papers amongst themselves. But the chauffeur had led him away from here, along a corridor and into the room where he found himself now. As soon as Spurling had gone, Tad had tried the door. It was locked.

He wasn't in a police station. At least, he didn't think so. There had been no police cars near the building and anyway it didn't have that sort of smell. But if it wasn't a police station, what was it? Tad looked around him, searching for clues.

The desk and the filing cabinet were locked, like

the door, and told him nothing. There were two posters on the wall. One showed a syringe with the line: SAY NO TO DRUGS. The other was an advertisement for the Samaritans. Tad gazed out of the window as a train trundled past. King's Cross ... somehow that meant something to him but he couldn't remember what.

Then there was the click of a key turning in a lock. The door opened and a young woman came in, carrying a file.

"Hello," she said. "My name is Marion Thorn. Please sit down."

As Tad moved away from the window, he examined the new arrival. Marion Thorn was tall and slender with long, black hair and dark skin. She was wearing a grey jacket and trousers with a brooch, her only jewellery, pinned at the lapel. Her manner was businesslike but she had a pleasant smile with the perfect, white teeth of a film star.

Growing more puzzled by the minute, Tad sat down.

"I expect you're wondering who I am," Marion said. "The first thing is to assure you – I'm not the police."

Tad was relieved but said nothing.

"What's your name?" Marion asked.

Tad thought for a moment. "Bob Snarby," he said.

"Bob Snarby." Marion opened the file and wrote the name down. "You do realize," she went on, "that Sir Hubert Spencer could have pressed charges. Breaking into his house, attacking his son ... these are very serious offences."

"It wasn't like that..." Tad began.

Marion held up a hand. "You're very lucky, Bob. Sir Hubert is a very unusual man. A very kind man. He's dedicated a lot of his life to helping young people like you. That's why he decided to pass you over to us."

"Us...?" But suddenly Tad knew where he was. Suddenly it all made sense.

"This office belongs to a charity," Marion explained. "We're called ACID."

"The Association for Children in Distress," Tad muttered.

"You've read about us?" Marion asked.

Tad almost wanted to laugh. How could he tell her that he had known about ACID all his life? "I read about you in the papers," he said.

Marion Thorn nodded. "ACID was founded by Sir Hubert Spencer," she explained. "We have a terrible situation in London. Children ... out on the streets, some of them as young as eleven and twelve. They have nowhere to go. And there are terrible temptations." She nodded in the direction of the poster. "Drugs. Crime. And nobody cares about them. Nobody wants to know."

She paused and Tad was amazed to see real tears in her eyes. Marion took out a handkerchief and blew her nose. "We go out and find these children," she said. "We search the railway stations, the back streets, the amusement arcades ... and we bring them in. We help them and we want to help you, Bob. But first we have to ask you some questions. Do you mind?"

Tad shook his head. "Go ahead..."

Suddenly Marion Thorn was businesslike again. She spread the file on the desk and sat with pen poised. "How old are you?" she asked.

"Thirteen."

"How long have you been in London?"

"A couple of weeks."

"Are you homeless?"

"Yes." Tad hesitated. He didn't want to lie but there was no way he could tell the whole truth. "I ran away from home."

"Your mum and dad must be very worried about you." Marion's voice was reproachful now.

"They don't care about me," Tad replied. "I bet they haven't told anyone I'm missing."

"Can you give me their address?"

"They don't have an address. They live in a caravan. They were in Crouch End when I left but they could be anywhere now. I think they've gone north."

"So nobody knows where you are. You have no friends or relatives? No social workers? Nobody to look after you?"

"I'm all on my own," Tad said, feeling miserable.

"Good! Good!" Marion muttered.

Tad glanced at her. There was something in her voice that hadn't been there before. She sounded almost hungry. And her face seemed to have changed too. Her dark eyes were gleaming as she made a hurried note at the bottom of the file. She looked up and saw Tad staring at her. At once she relaxed. "What I mean is ... it's good that we found you," she explained. "ACID is always interested in young people with no families. That's where we do our best work."

"What exactly do you have in mind?" Tad asked.

Marion glanced at him curiously, as if there was something about him that didn't quite add up. But whatever was in her mind, she dismissed it. "All we want to do is to get you off the street," she said. "That means somewhere to live, a good meal inside you and a chance to earn some money to support yourself. ACID has a centre just outside London where we run education programmes for boys like you. That's what it's called ... the Centre. I'd like to take you there now."

For some reason that he couldn't understand, Tad was uneasy. Perhaps it was the look he had seen in Marion's eyes a moment before. "What if I don't want to come?" he asked.

And there it was again. A sudden hardness behind that smiling, beautiful face. "Then we'd have no choice but to hand you over to the police, Bob. The break-in at Sir Hubert's was a very serious matter. I'm afraid it's us or it's prison."

Tad considered. Marion reached out and clasped his hand. Her fingers were long, her nails perfect. "We only want to help, Bob," she said. "Have you got anywhere else to go?"

And suddenly Tad was angry with himself. This was his parents' charity! What was there to worry about? For the first time since the switch had taken place someone was actually trying to help him, and instead of being grateful, he was almost being rude. He sighed. "I haven't got anywhere else to go," he said. "And I'm glad I was brought to you. You can take me to the Centre."

Marion smiled. She closed the file. "Good," she said. "We'll leave at once."

There was a black van waiting for Tad in the car park behind the building. As Tad walked across the tarmac towards it, he felt a sudden chill. The evening was drawing in but it was still warm and he paused, wondering what was wrong. Marion Thorn was next to him and she rested a hand on his arm. "It's half an hour to the Centre," she said. "You can sit in the back."

Tad looked at the van. It had no windows at the back, not even a small panel set in the door. Nor did it have any logo on the side. Its colour made him think of a hearse.

"Is something wrong, Bob?"

Tad remembered the moment in the office, the chill in Marion's eyes. Then he dismissed it. ACID was his parents' charity. ACID was going to look after him. "No. I'm fine."

He got into the van. There was a bench along one side, metal with no cushions. A sheet of metal separated the back from the driving compartment. When Marion closed the door, Tad found himself entombed in a metal box which would have been pitch black but for a single bulb burning behind a metal grille in the ceiling. He heard Marion walk round the side. A driver must have turned up for there was a brief exchange. Two doors slammed shut and the engine started.

It was only then that Tad realized that – apart from Marion – nobody had seen him since he had left the Knightsbridge house. He had seen nobody. If anybody came searching for him now, it would be as if he had vanished off the face of the earth.

He had put himself completely in the power of ACID and its staff. As the van moved off, picking up speed, Tad wondered if he hadn't made a terrible mistake. ACID was a charity. ACID wanted to help him. Everything was going to be all right. Tad sat back and waited for them to arrive.

THE CENTRE

Tad, washed and dressed in pale blue dungarees that reminded him uncomfortably of prison uniform, followed Marion Thorn down a seemingly endless corridor, lit by a line of tiny, halogen lights. Video surveillance cameras swivelled to follow them as they walked and a hidden air-conditioning system whispered all around them. Tad glanced through a large, plate-glass window where test tubes and bottles, glass pipes and burners fought for desk-space with computers and CD Rom and machines so complicated that he could only guess at their use. A man and a woman, both in white coats, came down the corridor the other way and passed them without speaking. Somewhere an intercom called out: "Dr Eastman to Room 113, please. Dr Eastman to Room 113."

He had barely glimpsed the Centre as he had been led out of the van and into the nearest building. From the outside it looked like an ordinary industrial estate: a cluster of dull, redbrick buildings with frosted glass windows allowing no view in or out. True, it was surrounded by a high wire fence with an electric security barrier permanently manned by a uniformed guard. But there was nothing unusual about that. People who lived nearby (and the Centre was surrounded by ordinary houses) probably thought it was a small factory. If they ever thought about it at all.

Marion Thorn had reached a door and was punching in a combination number on the electronic panel next to it. Tad stopped. "Where are we?" he demanded. "What's going on?"

There was a buzz and the door clicked open. "In here, please, Bob," she said.

The room was a surgery. If Tad had been uneasy before, he was now positively alarmed. But, following Marion's pointing hand, he sat down on a narrow bed. A second door opened and two men came in. Both were short and round with curly black hair and wide, loose mouths. Both were bearded. It took Tad a second to realize that they were identical twins. He grimaced, wondering if he were dreaming. Tweedledum and Tweedledee in white coats with stethoscopes! What next?

That question was soon answered as the two men began a medical examination that started at Tad's head and went inch by inch all the way to his toes. The doctors – if that's what they were – seemed particularly interested in his hair, his teeth, his eyes and his skin.

"Excellent condition."

"Unusually good. Yes. Good dermatology..."

"Yes..."

They spoke to each other in short, clipped sentences. But never did they say a word to Tad. Lying on the bed, he felt like a piece of meat in a butcher's shop and he was relieved when it was finally over.

One of the doctors nodded at Marion. "You can take him down."

"Down where?" Tad demanded. He was angry now.

"This way, Bob." Marion opened the door.

Tad didn't speak as Marion led him back down the corridor to a wide area with a series of lifts. Various thoughts were turning over in his mind and none of them were very pleasant. If ACID really wanted to help him, they had an odd way of going about it. He wondered if his father had any idea what went on in the Centre. This place was beginning to turn his stomach – and he decided to get out the first moment he could.

The lift arrived and he and Marion got in.

"Up?" Tad asked.

"Down," Marion replied. Tad glanced at the panel beside the door. The lift didn't have any buttons. The doors closed and it began to descend as if with a mind of its own.

"Where are we going, exactly?" Tad demanded.

"You'll find out, Bob." Marion's voice was as calm as ever. "We're going to help you. But first we want you to help us..."

The lift stopped. The doors opened. Tad stepped out and stared.

He was in a huge, vaulted chamber. It could have been an underground health club, a hospital or a television studio... Tad's first impressions were of all three. First there were the showers and baths with steam rising into the air. Then there were what looked to be orderlies, doctors and scientists, dressed in white, bustling about with trolleys piled high with bottles, basins, bandages and the occasional syringe. And finally there were the television monitors flickering on steel gantries and, high overhead, the banks of brilliant arc lamps, flooding the scene with a hard, unnatural light.

And then he noticed the other children.

Marion Thorn had told him that ACID collected children off the streets of London. What she hadn't told him was what happened to them next.

One boy was dressed only in swimming trunks, standing in an elaborate shower cubicle. The floor was slowly turning and as the boy rotated he was sprayed by different-coloured jets of water. An elderly woman was watching him closely and every few minutes she took a Polaroid photograph, clipping the results to a wall-chart nearby.

Opposite him, a black youth of about eighteen

was lying on a bed, completely covered in some sort of pale silver grease. The grease started at his ankles and went all the way to his neck. His eyes were hidden behind a large pair of goggles, obviously designed to protect him from the glowing neon tubes that hung only inches from his skin. Two men in white coats were watching him. Tad recognized the twins who had just examined him.

There were girls there as well. One was strapped to a high-backed chair, her feet immersed in a large bucket that buzzed and vibrated beneath her. A few metres away from her, a second had been hung upside down with wires attached to her ears and nose. Opposite her, in a partly screened-off area, another boy was being slowly spun in what looked like a giant washing machine, while next to him a girl of about twenty sat in a bath, with green foam bubbling around her neck.

Laboratory rats!

Tad felt something – a shiver or a scream – rising to his throat and had to force himself to hold it back. He had never seen anything like it in his life. He had had no idea what experiments were being conducted in this dreadful, secret place. But they were being conducted on children.

How had it happened? Somebody must have taken over ACID and twisted it to their own, evil purposes. Even as he stared at the incredible activity all around him, Tad knew that he had to get out of here. He had to let his father know what was happening. Sir Hubert

Spencer had powerful friends. Once he knew the truth, he would put an end to it.

A hand clamped down on Tad's arm and he looked up to see a blank-faced man dressed as a security guard. "This way," the man said in a voice that didn't allow for argument.

"Wait a minute..." Tad began.

But then Marion Thorn was at his side. "Don't worry, Bob," she said. "We're not going to hurt you..."

"What's going on here?" Tad began to struggle. The security man's grip tightened. "It's just tests," Marion explained. "On your hair. On your skin. Your nails and your eyes. You did say you wanted to help us, Bob."

"But I didn't mean..."

Marion nodded at the security guard. "Take him to Area Seven."

Before Tad could say another word, the guard had jerked him forward, dragging him by the shoulder. Tad was shouting now, using words that he didn't even know he knew. Even then as he was pulled further into the chamber, Tad realized that he didn't only look like Bob Snarby: he was beginning to sound like him too.

"Prepare experimental Area Seven!" This voice came from a set of hidden loudspeakers and boomed in the air. Tad tried to dig his heels in. He passed a boy, lying asleep on a bed. The boy's hair had gone a brilliant shade of pink. Two more men were seeing to a second boy, helping him out of the washing machine.

"Amazing! He's been washed twenty-six times..."

"Yes. And he's hardly wrinkled at all!"

Tad yelled and dug his heels in. The security guard dragged him towards an empty bed.

Before he could do anything about it, he found himself thrown onto his back and firmly tied down with three straps over his neck, his ankles and his chest. The security guard moved away and for a minute Tad wriggled like a fish on dry land. But it was hopeless. He couldn't break free. He sank back and twisted his head – just in time to see another boy in what looked like a telephone box disappear in an explosion of mauve steam. Tad shut his eyes. It was horrible! It was impossible!

And what were they going to do to *him*?

It was only now as he lay still that he became aware of the smell in the air. Strong air conditioning had managed to get rid of most of it but now, lying in the middle of the chamber, he felt almost suffocated by the smell of crushed strawberries. The strange thing was, the smell meant something to him. It reminded him of something. But what?

There was a movement in the corner of his eye and Tad turned back as the twin doctors approached, one holding a page of notes, the other a plastic bottle.

"What are you...?" Tad began but stopped as his ear was given a sharp twist. Obviously the two men weren't in the mood to discuss things with him. Instead they muttered to each other.

"What's the active ingredient?"

"Very rare. Some sort of berry grown by the Arambayan Indians in Brazil. Just came in. The code is B/341."

Arambayan Indians. That meant something to Tad too. But, confused and frightened as he was, he couldn't remember where he had heard the words before.

One of the doctors opened the bottle and Tad recoiled, his skin crawling. One of the doctors called out and Marion Thorn approached, now wearing a white coat over her suit.

"Are you nervous, Bob?" she asked.

"Let me go!" Tad cried.

"There's nothing to worry about! We just want to rub something into your face. It's a special sort of cream. It's perfectly safe."

"Then why do you want to test it on me?"

Marion smiled again. "We know it's safe," she repeated. "And we know it's good for you. What we don't know, though, is how good it is for you. So that's why we want you to try it for us."

"Well, I don't want to." Tad pressed against the straps. "I want to go home!"

"You don't have a home, Bob," Marion replied, reasonably. "That's why we brought you here." She leaned down and brushed the hair out of his eyes. "Let's not forget that you're a crook, Bob. A house-breaker. It's either here or the police."

"I choose the police!"

"I'm sorry, Bob. It's too late now."

Marion nodded and one of the twins squeezed a bright yellow cream into his gloved hand. The cream looked a little like custard, only thicker and even at this distance it had a heavy, exotic smell. Positioning himself above Tad's head, the man rubbed some of the cream into his face and neck, being careful to avoid his eyes while the second man made notes. Soon Tad's face was completely coated. Marion Thorn walked away.

The cream was cool, not cold, and smelt of ... it wasn't quite lemon and it wasn't quite pineapple but something in between. Despite himself, Tad had to admit that it was a very pleasant smell and he didn't even mind when the first man opened his dungarees and attached a wire to his chest. The cream was smooth and the smell was delicious. He could feel it invading his nostrils and seeping into his brain. Pineapples and lemons say the Bells of St Clements. Next to him a machine began to bleep softly, in time with his heart.

"Slight dilation of the eyes," one of the twins muttered in a low voice. "How's his pulse?"

"Fast."

"This is nice," Tad said, slurring the words. "This is very, very nice."

"Loosen the straps," one of the men said. Or perhaps it was both of them. Tad's vision was beginning to blur.

"There's too much active ingredient."

"Moon-fruit?"

"Yes."

"Let's leave him and see..."

"Moon. Goon. Balloon. See you soon," Tad replied and giggled. Now that the straps had been loosened he could move his hands and he tried to wipe some of the cream off. But his arms wouldn't obey him.

After that, everything seemed to stretch out of shape. Tad was hardly aware of the chamber any more. He was floating, spinning, rocking, his mind far away. He thought the twins came back a couple of times. Once they wiped some of the cream off and added some cold liquid from a bottle. Another time they took his temperature. But he didn't care. He was above it all.

Somewhere an alarm went off and the boy who had been doused in the mauve steam was carried away, his skin a mass of bright spots. A girl was led into the telephone box in his place. Tad whimpered. The cream was less cool now. He could feel it burning his skin. But he was too weak and giddy to cry out. He twisted round on his bed, looking for Marion Thorn.

And then he saw a door open and a man step out. The man was far away, high up on a gantry and Tad wasn't sure at first if he was imagining things. It had to be the cream that was doing it to him. It couldn't be true.

But then Marion Thorn approached the man. The two of them exchanged a few words and Marion laughed. The man took out a cigar and lit it. And suddenly Tad knew.

He was looking at the man behind ACID, the man who had set up the Centre and who ran it.

Sir Hubert Spencer.

He was looking at his father.

BREAK-OUT

It was as if Tad had been plunged into freezing water. The strange, dream-like state that the cream had thrown him into was suddenly shattered and he was wide awake, struggling with his thoughts, trying to make sense out of what he knew to be true.

The products in the Centre. He knew what they all were and had known from the moment he had been brought in.

The boy under the lamps was coated in grapefruit and aloe sun-tan oil. The girl with her feet in the bucket was testing coconut corn remover. The girl in the green foam was trying out a cucumber and kiwi fruit bubble bath. The boy in the shower was being sprayed with body lotion made from different types of seaweed, while the one in the telephone box was being subjected to a beetroot and banana bodyrub.

They were all products sold by Beautiful World. He had been seeing and smelling products like them all his life.

Beautiful World.

NONE OF OUR PRODUCTS ARE TESTED ON ANIMALS

But they were tested. *On children!*

Tad was horrified. A sudden bleeping made him turn his head and he saw that the machine he was connected to had speeded up. It was a heart monitor – of course! He watched, fascinated as his heart, beating rapidly now, sent huge peaks across the screen. But at the same time he forced himself to calm down. The doctors had loosened his straps, believing him to be in a trance. If any of them looked at the machine, they would know otherwise and he would be strapped down again.

Tad lay back and closed his eyes. Gradually the heart monitor slowed and quietened. Could it be true? Beautiful World, owned by his parents, was taking kids off the street. and using them as laboratory rats to test the safety of their products! And the charity that actually went out and found them – ACID – had also been set up by Sir Hubert and Lady Geranium.

But that was impossible. That would make them...

Monsters.

Tad took a deep breath, then opened his eyes again.

BLEEP. BLEEP. BLEEP.

The heart monitor had almost exploded and there was nothing he could do to stop it. Sir Hubert Spencer had climbed down a metal staircase and was heading straight for him, Marion Thorn at his side. Now it took every ounce of Tad's will-power to bring himself back under control. He had to pretend to be drugged. It was his only chance.

"He's just over here, Sir Hubert..." Marion's voice reached his ears. Not trusting himself, Tad closed his eyes once again. Suddenly he felt the presence of the man standing right next to him.

His father.

His enemy.

No...!

"So this is the boy?" A wisp of cigar smoke crossed Tad's nostrils. "A nasty-looking piece of work. What's he testing?"

"The moon-fruit, Sir Hubert. B/341."

"Any adverse effects?"

"It's much too strong, Sir Hubert. As you can see, the subject is virtually unconscious. There's also a little burning around the ears. Do you see?"

Tad felt Marion's finger drawing a line down the side of his face. How he managed to stop his heart from giving him away he would never know. As she withdrew the finger, the bleeping quickened again and he groaned, pretending to be having a bad dream.

"The little viper broke into my house, you know,"

Sir Hubert snarled. It was his own father, talking about him! But it was as if Tad were hearing his voice for the first time. "I don't want to see him again. Do you understand me?"

"Absolutely, Sir Hubert. We'll be testing that new microwave sauna for the first time tomorrow morning. I'd have said that Master Snarby was perfect for it. What do you think?"

Sir Hubert laughed. "Let me know what happens," he said.

The two of them walked away. Left to himself, Tad let out a great sigh and listened as the heart monitor once again resumed a steady pace. Even as Sir Hubert had been speaking, he had resisted the temptation to cry out, to try and explain who he really was. It would have been no good. He was sure of it. Sir Hubert wouldn't have listened, and it would have destroyed the one chance he had to get out of here.

The straps were loose. He was wide awake. And nobody knew it.

Cautiously, Tad looked around him. Sir Hubert and Marion Thorn were already some distance away and there was no sign of the twins. It must have been getting towards the end of the night, as the chamber was emptying. There were certainly fewer staff than when he had arrived.

Tad knew what he had to do. The very mention of a microwave sauna had been enough to conjure up the most horrible images. He had to get out of here before he ended up like a television dinner and he had perhaps only seconds in which to do it. Marion Thorn would be coming back to check on him. So would the twins. It had to be now!

Tad slipped one arm out of the straps and quickly unfastened the buckles on his chest and neck. Finally he bent double and freed his ankles. So far so good. Nobody had seen him. There was a cloth nearby and he used it to wipe off the moon-fruit cream. Marion had certainly been right about one thing. The skin on his cheeks was puffed up and sore. The cloth felt as if it were made of iron wool. Now, how did he get out of here? There was a door at the far end of the chamber – Sir Hubert and Marion had just passed through it, but the thought of running into the two of them was too horrible to contemplate. Then there were the lifts. But Tad remembered that they had no controls. He wouldn't even know how to call them and anyway they were too far away. That just left the metal staircase which Sir Hubert had taken. It had to be the right way. The chamber was underground. Tad had to go up.

Tad checked again that no one was looking, then pulled the heart monitor off his chest. That was his only mistake.

The connections were no sooner free than the machine began to scream, sending an alarm signal that could be heard from one side of the chamber to the other. Everybody turned. The twins appeared from behind a screen and began to move towards him. At the far end of the chamber a group of security guards ran forward, looking around to see where the disturbance had come from.

Tad swung himself onto his feet and set off. The first of the twins reached him and grabbed hold of his arm. Tad twisted out of his grip and pushed as hard as he could. The twin was sent flying into a shelf of bottles that collapsed all around him, glass smashing and liquid splashing out. The twin screamed. One of the bottles must have contained acid. As Tad watched, the man's shoes began to dissolve.

Some of the other children were sitting up now, shouting encouragement. But the second twin had worked out where Tad was heading. The man, twice Tad's size, had positioned himself at the bottom of the stairs.

"All right," he began. "Don't move!"

There was a trolley loaded with bottles and test tubes and, as the second twin edged towards him, Tad grabbed it and propelled it forward. The trolley slammed into the man, glass falling and shattering all around. The twin was caught unprepared. The side of the trolley thumped into his stomach and at the same time his foot slipped. With a great shout he lost his balance and fell, crashing down onto his back. Tad leapt over him and onto the first step.

The other children were cheering him on, their cries echoing around the chamber. But the fastest of the security men had already reached the stairs, just behind Tad. Halfway up, Tad suddenly wheeled round and kicked out. His foot caught the man on the chin, knocking him over the banister and onto a work surface below. The security guard fell with a great cry, smashing into a row of test tubes and a Bunsen burner. The burner was still on. The jetting flame came into contact with the spilled chemicals and there was a satisfying "whumph" as a sheet of flame mushroomed to the ceiling. Immediately a bell began to ring. The sprinkler system came into operation and suddenly Tad found himself climbing through a tropical storm. He was grateful for the water. It would add to the chaos. And it would wash the last of the cream from his face.

Tad reached the top of the stairs. There was a short corridor, then a door. He scrabbled for the handle, almost crying out with relief when it turned. Not daring to look back at the chaos he had left behind him, he jerked the door open and ran through, colliding with some sort of secretary who was just coming in. He didn't apologize. The woman fell in a shower of graphs and typewritten sheets. Tad leapt over her and on down a wide, softly lit gallery.

He hadn't found a way out yet. This was some sort of storage area. One side of the gallery was lined by a series of large copper vats, each labelled: FACE CREAM, FOOT LOTION, AFTERSHAVE and so on. A pipe ran out of each of them, running up the wall to join a complicated network across the ceiling. The other side of the corridor contained a row of levers. Tad walked slowly past them. In front of him there was a double door. There was still nobody behind them.

He had almost reached the doors when they swung open and he found himself face to face with Marion Thorn.

She must have taken a second lift, leaving Sir Hubert somewhere on the surface. Then, when the alarm was raised, she must have doubled back. But Tad didn't stop to consider how she had got there. He stared at the woman who had met him when he had been taken to ACID, hardly able to recognize her. Then he had thought her beautiful and kind. Now her eyes were bulging, her mouth was twisted in a grimace of hatred and her hair seemed to stand on end.

"You stay there!" she cried in a high-pitched voice and, to his amazement, Tad saw that she had produced a gun and was pointing it at him. She steadied it with both hands. "If you move, I'll shoot you in the heart."

Tad looked left and right. Behind him he could hear the commotion in the main chamber, the jangle of the alarm bells, the hiss of the sprinkler system. He wondered how long it would be before the security guards burst through the door. He knew he wouldn't get a second chance. If they caught him he had a one-way ticket to the microwave. His eyes darted left and right. In a split second he had taken in the pipes, the levers, the position of the vats.

"I'm going to enjoy experimenting on you," the charity worker continued. She was confident now, enjoying her victory. "Sir Hubert warned me you were a nasty piece of work."

Tad looked down. "Please..." he muttered.

Marion Thorn threw back her head and laughed. It was what Tad had been waiting for.

He lunged to one side even as Marion lifted the gun and fired. The bullet missed him, passing over his head and ricocheting off a metal pipe. At the same moment, his hands found two of the levers. He pulled them. Marion aimed the gun again. But she was too late. The next moment there was a rush and a gurgle as two hundred gallons of bright red vanishing cream shot out of a pipe and crashed down onto the unfortunate woman.

Marion Thorn vanished.

Tad looked back. The door burst open and two more security guards appeared, both of them armed. Grateful now for the speed and agility he must have inherited from Bob Snarby, Tad twisted round and ran. There was an explosion and a bullet whistled past, smashing into a pipe close to Tad's head. A thin spray of pink ooze jetted into the air. Tad ran forward, vanishing cream licking at his ankles, and threw himself through the door.

And he was out! The cold night air embraced him and he ran into it with a sense of exhilaration. Quickly he took in the low, red-brick buildings that made up the compound and the tall wire fence that surrounded it. Already a klaxon had begun to let out its unnatural wail and, at the same time, brilliant spotlights suddenly sliced through the darkness, huge white circles gliding across the tarmac.

Tad ran on, but with every step he found himself slowing down, realizing the hopelessness of his situation. There was no way out of the Centre. The gate was too heavily guarded. The fence was unclimbable. And everywhere he looked there were more security guards, some on foot, some on motorbikes, making sure every centimetre of the compound was covered.

"Escape alert! Escape alert!" The inhuman voice rang out across the rooftops. Tad stumbled and come to a breathless halt.

On the other side of the fence he could see houses. In the distance there was a pub. He almost wanted to cry. The real world, ordinary people doing ordinary things, were only a few metres away. But he couldn't reach them. He would never see them again. There was no way out.

"There he is!"

It was a man's voice, coming from just behind him. To one side a jeep suddenly sprang forward, its headlights slanting down. Tad stood where he was. There was nothing more he could do.

And then it happened. At the last minute, just when he thought it was all over, there was the blare of a horn and a London taxi appeared out of nowhere, accelerating towards the fence. Tad watched as it burst through, snapping the wire, and hurtled towards him.

Meanwhile the jeep had also accelerated and suddenly the two vehicles were heading straight for one another in what had to be a head-on collision. It was the driver of the jeep who lost his nerve. With millimetres to spare, he wrenched the wheel. The jeep swerved, crashed into a building and disappeared in a pillar of flame. The taxi screeched to a halt in front of Tad and the back door opened.

"Get in!" a voice commanded.

Tad hesitated. But then there was a gunshot and a bullet hammered into the taxi's bodywork and, without any further prompting, Tad dived forward. His head and arms passed through the open door and he was full length on the back floor and the voice was yelling "Go! Go! Go!" The taxi leapt forward again, made a complete circle and shot through the hole in the fence. There were more shots. The back window shattered and fell inwards, covering Tad with glass. The driver cursed as the taxi mounted the pavement then rocketed into the road. But they were away! Round one corner and through a set of red traffic lights and they had left the Centre far behind.

Tad lay where he was, stretched out on the floor. He was bruised and exhausted and there was glass in his hair and all over his clothes. But he was safe.

"All right. You can sit up now."

Tad recognized the voice and felt the hairs on his neck prickle. A hand reached down and dragged him into the seat. Tad slumped back, the last of his strength draining out of him.

"Good evening, Bobby-boy," Finn said. "What a turn-up – eh! We been looking all over for you."

GREAT YARMOUTH

"Aren't you pleased to see me?" Finn demanded.

"And me!" The driver peered over his shoulder and grinned. It was Eric Snarby. He had a broken cigarette between his lips. In all the excitement he'd bitten it in half.

"Keep your eye on the road, Snarby," Finn snapped. "And your foot on the axe-hellerator. We got a long way to go!"

Tad turned to Finn. "How did you find me?" he asked.

Finn brushed broken glass off his shoulders. The whole of the window had fallen in but fortunately it was a warm night – and a dry one. "I been looking for you ever since that little business in Nightingale Square," he explained. "In fact I 'ad the 'ole network out. All over

London. The barrow-boys and the traffic wardens. The thieves and the beggars. The cleaners, the cabbies and the couriers. I was worried about you, you see, my boy. I was worried about what might 'appen to you."

"You mean, you were worried I'd be picked up by the police."

"I wanted to find you." They drove past a street lamp and for a moment the skin behind the spider's web glowed a horrible orange. "And you're lucky I did, Bobby-boy. If old Finn hadn't come looking for you, 'oo knows what would 'ave 'appened to you. Shampooed to death, perhaps. Or bubble-bathed 'til you was insane..."

Tad leant forward. "You know about the Centre!" he exclaimed.

Finn smiled. "There's nothing happens in London that Finn don't know about," he replied. "And the nastier it is, the sooner I hear..."

Tad twisted in his seat and looked out of the broken window. The street behind them was empty. "Where are we going?" he asked.

"You might as well lie back and get some kip," Finn replied. "We're going to the country. Life in town's a bit 'ot for old Finn at the moment. We're going to join the fair."

"Great Yarmouth!" Tad remembered the Snarbies talking about the move."

"That's right. Boring, snoring, rain-always-pouring Great Yarmouth. But we can lie low there and work out how to earn a dishonest penny or two."

"Your mum'll be glad to see you!" Eric crooned from the front seat.

"Shut up and keep your eye on the road!" Finn snapped. "And get a move on for Gawd's sake. You're only doing a hundred miles an hour!"

Eric Snarby slammed his foot onto the pedal and the taxi leapt forward, racing into the night.

The Pleasure Beach at Great Yarmouth was a true, permanent, old-fashioned funfair. It was more wood than plastic, more falling apart than thrilling. All in all there were about thirty rides, dominated by a huge roller coaster that stretched out parallel with the sea. There were dodgems, of course, a leaky water flume, a waltzer and a ghost train so old that it could have been haunted by the ghosts of people who had once ridden it. Its most recent attraction was a Mirror Maze, a circular building mounted with speakers so that anyone passing could hear the cries and laughter of the people inside. But the Mirror Maze, like the rest of the funfair, was closed. It was seven-thirty in the morning. And, as Tad gazed up at the highest loop of the roller coaster, he was utterly alone.

Eric Snarby had a caravan just across the road from the Pleasure Beach and he and Finn had gone in to get a few hours' sleep. Doll had not yet woken up. There wouldn't have been enough room for Tad, even if he had been tired. But he'd slept in the taxi. He was glad to be on his own.

He needed to think.

It was still so hard to believe. His parents, Sir Hubert and Lady Geranium Spencer, running a business that used children in experiments? The brains behind a charity that horribly exploited the young people who needed its help? It was impossible, unthinkable. His parents were decent people. His father had been knighted by the Queen! But as hard as he tried to persuade himself that his parents were somehow innocent, that they knew nothing, Tad couldn't make it work.

In the distance, the waves rolled and broke against the beach hidden behind the roller coaster. The sun had risen but the sky was still grey. Tad shivered and walked on.

What made it so difficult was that he wasn't even sure any more who he was. Was he Tad Spencer or was he Bob Snarby? He looked like Bob. He was beginning to talk like him and to think like him. And (it was only now that he realized it) he was even beginning to enjoy some aspects of being Bob. It was crazy but that was the truth. He liked being thin. He liked being fit, able to run without wheezing and to climb without trembling. It was true that he had lost all his wealth, his toys, his comfortable house and servants but in a strange way he felt almost relieved, as if it were a weight off his shoulders.

There wasn't a lot to admire about Bob Snarby or his background but at least he was free. Tad wasn't sure if he was Tad or if he was Bob but for the first time in his life he felt he was himself.

But what was he going to do?

He couldn't stay with Eric and Doll Snarby, not if that meant working for Finn. At the same time, he had nowhere else to go. And then there was the real Bob Snarby to consider. Tad remembered his meeting with the fat boy in Knightsbridge. Could he allow Bob Snarby to remain in his place? It didn't seem fair. It didn't seem right.

He looked up and blinked. Although he hadn't noticed it before, there was one caravan in the fair, an old-fashioned gypsy-style caravan that he would have recognized even without the sign above the door:

Doctor Aftexcludor —
Your future In The Stars.

Tad stared at it. The caravan was parked next to the ghost train and even at this early hour the door was open. Tad thought back to his last meeting with the caravan's peculiar owner. Dr Aftexcludor had known who he was. He had seemed – at least in part – sympathetic. And he had told some crazy story about wishing stars ... how they had caused the switch. False name, false story, Tad thought now. Perhaps this was the right time to find out the truth.

Tad went over to the caravan and looked inside. There was no sign of the doctor or his curious Indian friend, Solo. Tad climbed in.

The thick smell of incense filled his nostrils and he was once again amazed by how the caravan seemed so much bigger inside than out.

"Dr Aftexcludor...?" he called softly.

There was a book, lying open on the table, next to the crystal ball. Tad almost got the feeling that it had been left there for him to find. Moving forward, he turned a page. The paper was old and heavy and really not like paper at all. Tad looked down and began to read.

Two pages were exposed and there was a naked figure drawn on each one, two boys connected by a complicated series of arrows. The figures were surrounded by stars, planets and other astrological devices and some of the arrows pointed up towards these. The book was handwritten, the sentences tumbling into each other and slanting in different directions. Growing ever more uneasy, Tad realized what the book reminded him of. It was like something out of a fairy story. A book of spells.

There were two words written in red but the ink was so old that it had lost most of its colour. Tad ran a finger across them. "The Switch". Underneath, a line of writing twisted in a curve. "Janus. The star of change. Invoking its power. To effect the switch between two personalities..." Tad didn't understand all of it but he understood enough. Anger exploded inside him along with shock and disbelief. He picked up the ancient book and was about to throw it across the room when...

"Master Snarby! How nice to see you again."

Tad whirled round. He hadn't heard anyone come in but now Dr Aftexcludor was standing right behind him, dressed in a dark green velvet jacket and baggy pantaloons. The Indian, Solo, was with him, standing in the doorway, blocking it.

"I'm not Bob Snarby!" Tad snarled. "I'm Tad Spencer. You know that. You're the one who did it!"

"Did what?" Dr Aftexcludor looked the picture of innocence.

"You know!" Tad pointed at the open book. "All that stuff you told me about 'wishing stars' was nonsense and you know it! You're responsible. You're some sort of..."

Magician? Tad stopped himself before he actually uttered the word. It was ridiculous. Real magicians didn't exist, did they? Not real ones. But after what had happened to him, he suddenly realized, anything was possible.

"You did it," he repeated, weakly.

"Why should I have wanted to?" Dr Aftexcludor asked, reasonably.

"I don't know. But..." Tad remembered now. "There was something you were going to tell me. Something about Solo."

"Ah yes." Dr Aftexcludor moved forward and sat down, crosslegged at the table. He may have looked old but his movements were still somehow those of a younger man. "I was going to tell you a story," he said.

"You said I wasn't ready."

"Are you now, Tad? Do you want to hear it?"

"Yes."

Dr Aftexcludor nodded. "Yes. I think so. Draw closer, Tad, Bob, whatever you want to call yourself."

Tad sat opposite the old man. There was a crystal ball on the table and he found himself fixated by it, by the colours that seemed to swirl around inside it. Dr Aftexcludor muttered something in the strange language that he had used before and Solo retired. Tad glanced at him as he disappeared into the next room.

"You said Solo was an Arambayan Indian," Tad said.

"Yes. The last of the tribe."

Arambayan Indians. Moon-fruit. Suddenly Tad knew what this was all about.

His eyes were fixed on the crystal ball and he couldn't have broken away if he had tried to. And now it was as if shapes were forming themselves out of the colours. Maybe it was him. Maybe it was all the smoke in the room that was somehow sending him to sleep but it was as if he were looking through the reflection on a pool and into the world beneath. It was a forest. He had never seen so much green, believed there could be so many different shades. There were flowers, brilliant colours. He could smell them! And now he could hear the rushing of a great river as the images rose and drew him into them.

And all the time he heard the voice of Dr Aftexcludor, coming as from miles away, telling him the terrible story that he was seeing with his own eyes.

"The Amazon basin," he began. "The rainforest west of Manaus. Denser and wilder than anywhere in the world. There are not many places where man has not at some time trodden on this wretched planet, Tad, but not in the rainforests. The rainforests are the last great uncharted territory ... even if the bulldozers are doing their work and the lands are rapidly dwindling.

"There was a tribe of Indians here called the Arambayans. They were not even discovered by white men until 1947, Tad, just after the war. Westerners found them and for a time did them no harm. They were visited by missionaries. And they began to trade – for there was a fruit that grew in the Arambayans' land; a fruit that looked like a crescent moon and tasted of pineapples and lemon."

"The moon-fruit!" Tad exclaimed and saw it, hanging in clusters, brilliant yellow moons against a swathe of dark green leaves.

"The moon-fruit," Dr Aftexcludor repeated. "Now, all would have been well except that the fame of this new and delicious fruit spread across the globe. And a man heard about it. He tasted it. And he decided that he wanted to buy it. All of it."

"Who was this man?" Tad whispered.

"I'll come to that. The trouble is, the Arambayans were a very suspicious people. You see, they'd always been very happy just the way they were. They were peaceful. They just got on with their lives, raising their families and growing their fruit. They sold enough to meet their immediate needs. But their needs, you see, were small.

"They didn't trust this man-from-over-the-seas, and they didn't want anything to do with him. The more money he offered them, the less they trusted him. So when he offered to buy all their moon-fruit, they politely but firmly said no.

"Unfortunately the man wouldn't take no for an answer. He still wanted the moon-fruit. And so he did a terrible thing..."

The crystal ball had gone dark now. It was showing Tad a tropical night sky. But now he saw lights gliding through the darkness. A helicopter. It landed on a rough strip hacked out of the jungle. Tad knew that he was watching something secretive, something wrong. The blades of the helicopter began to slow down and the pilot stepped out. Tad recognized him. It was his father's chauffeur: Spurling.

"I said that the Arambayans didn't like war," Dr Aftexcludor continued, "but they did have enemies. There was a tribe on the edge of the territory who had always been jealous of them and it was to this tribe, the Cruel People, that the man-from-over-the-seas turned. Suppose they were to own the moon-fruit, would they sell it to him? And at a reasonable price? A deal was struck. And one dark night the Cruel People were given what they needed to take what wasn't theirs."

Spurling had heaved three wooden crates out of the helicopter. He was surrounded by black, painted faces now, their expressions ugly and menacing.

"He supplied them with guns. Oh – it's been done before, Tad! The Arambayans had blowpipes, bows and arrows, spears. But now their enemy, the Cruel People, had joined the twentieth century. They had guns. Automatic rifles. And fuelled by alcohol and greed, they fell on their poor neighbours."

Dr Aftexcludor fell silent but the crystal ball told its own story. He saw the Arambayan village, a circle of straw-covered huts on the edge of a river. He saw the women with their children, the men swimming and laughing in the clear water. Then there was a shot. It came from the edge of the forest. A young boy, barely older than Tad, was thrown wounded to the ground and then the Cruel People were on them, swarming over the village as more shots rang out and the flames rose from the first of the houses.

Tad covered his eyes. He couldn't take any more.

"It was my father," he muttered. "It was Sir Hubert Spencer and Beautiful World."

"Solo was one of the very few who escaped alive," Dr Aftexcludor went on. "You might say he's the last of the Arambayans. I've looked after him ever since but he has no real life..." His voice trailed away. "I'm sorry," he said at length. "But you said you wanted to hear. You said you were ready."

“I know.” Tad felt an intense sadness, deeper than anything he had experienced in his life. It was as if a river were running through him. “I had to know,” he said at last. “And ... I suppose ... I'm glad I know now.”

“Yes.”

Tad stood up. Suddenly he knew what he had to do. “Goodbye, Dr Aftexcludor,” he said. “Thank you.”

“Goodbye, Tad. And good luck.”

Tad paused at the door. “There is one thing,” he said. “Will I ... will you ever change me back into Tad Spencer?”

Dr Aftexcludor shook his head. “Only you can do that,” he said. “You can be what – and who – you want to be.”

Tad left. He never saw Dr Aftexcludor again.

When Tad got back to the caravan, Eric and Doll Snarby had finally woken up and were once again tucking into a mountainous breakfast, this time consisting entirely of kippers. Tad had never seen so many kippers slipping and slithering over each other on one plate. Finn was sitting in a corner, smoking a cigarette.

“My Bob!” Doll sobbed by way of greeting. “Back 'ome at last!” She picked up one of the kippers and used it to wipe her nose. “I been so worried about you!”

“It's true,” Eric added. “Your mum's been worrying 'erself to death. Some nights she's only managed nine pizzas.”

“My little boy!” Doll sniffed.

"And a dozen Mars bars. She 'ad a dozen Mars bars. But apart from that she couldn't eat a thing!"

"Shut up, the two of you," Finn snapped and the Snarbies fell silent. Finn leaned forward and held something up, a narrow book with a blue cover. His eyes locked into Tad's. "Where did you get this, you thieving vermin?" he demanded.

Tad recognized the cheque-book that he had taken from his own bedroom in Knightsbridge. His hand fell automatically to his back trouser pocket.

"It was in the back of the cab," Finn explained. "Must 'ave slipped out your back pocket."

"It's mine!" Tad said.

"Yours, is it? That's funny, 'cos it 'asn't got your name in it." Finn opened the cheque-book. "'Thomas Arnold David Spencer,'" he read. He scratched his cheek, his nails rasping against three days' stubble. "So who's he?" he demanded.

"Leave the boy alone, Finn," Doll said.

"You stay out of this, Doll, or by Heaven I'll pull your leg off and kick you with it." Finn turned back to Tad. "Who is he?"

"He's no one. Some rich kid. He's the son of Sir Hubert Spencer. You know..."

"Sir Hubert Spencer, Beautiful World?" Finn weighed the cheque book in his hand. "Pick-pocketed it, did you?"

"Yes."

"What did I tell you about stealing!" Eric Snarby

leant forward and slapped Tad hard on the side of his head. "If you're going to steal something, make sure you can sell it. A cheque-book's no blooming good! Why didn't you get 'is watch?"

"Wait a minute. Wait a minute..." Finn was thinking. You could almost see the thoughts passing one at a time across his eyes. "The Spencers, they got a place down near Ipswich," he muttered. "Snatchmore Hall or something..."

"What – you going to burgle it?" Doll asked.

"Not burgle it. No." Finn raised the chequebook to his nostrils and sniffed it. He let out a pleasurable sigh. "A rich kid with his own bank account, that's given old Finn a thought. Maybe burgling ain't the right game for us. Maybe there's an easier way..."

"What you got in mind, Finn?" Eric demanded.

"You wait and see," Finn replied. "Just you wait and see."

PRIME STEAK

Tad clung to the branch of the oak tree, his dangling feet only inches from the razor wire and broken glass below. Using all his strength, he swung one hand in front of another and passed over the garden wall. If he dropped onto the ground now he would break both his legs but, just as he remembered there would be, a great pile of grass clippings had been left, close to the wall. Tad gritted his teeth, then let go with both hands. He fell, hit the pile and sank to his waist in the cut grass. Fortunately, the weather had been dry. The grass was old and soggy, but not the porridge he had feared.

He stood up inside the grounds of Snatchmore Hall, the home that had once been his.

He made his way quickly towards the house, taking care not to be seen. As he drew closer, he ducked behind trees or ran crouching from bush to bush. At last he came to the edge of the lawns with the swimming pool to one side and the side entrance to the house just ahead. As he paused, catching his breath, there was a sudden movement and he ducked back out of sight. A car had started up and was rolling down the drive towards the main gate. Tad caught sight of Spurling behind the wheel. And where was the grim-faced chauffeur off to now, he wondered? Looking for more children to invite to the Centre? Or perhaps selling more weapons to wipe out another unco-operative Indian tribe?

The car passed through the electronic gates which swung smoothly shut behind it. At least that was one less danger to have to worry about. He had already seen Mrs O'Blimey leave the house to go shopping. Mitzy was on holiday. Lady Geranium Spencer would still be in bed.

That just left Bob Snarby. On his own.

Tad had to cross about a hundred metres of open ground to reach the safety of the house and he was once again grateful for this new body of his. He could cover the ground in less than a minute. He tensed himself, then darted forward.

And stopped.

Finn and he had planned all this carefully, taking into account the electronic gates, the wall, the video cameras and the trip-wires concealed in the garden. But they had forgotten the last security measure in the house – and now it was too late.

Vicious had sprung out as if from nowhere. The over-sized Dalmatian stood in front of him, its hackles rising, its lips pulled back to reveal its specially sharpened teeth. There was a savage hunger in its eyes as it padded forward, its paws barely seeming to touch the ground. Tad remembered the last intruder to come across Vicious, the 107 stitches the man had needed. When he had left hospital he had looked like a jigsaw puzzle.

Tad looked around. He was right out in the open with nowhere to run. If he turned and tried to make it back to the trees, the dog would be on him before he had taken three paces. It was about to spring. Every single part of the creature was poised for the attack. Tad closed his eyes and prepared for the worst.

"You can be what – and who – you want to be."

It was as if the words had been whispered in his ear. They were virtually the last words that Dr Aftexcludor had spoken to him and, remembering them now, Tad suddenly had an idea.

He opened his eyes and held out his hand, palm down, showing it to the dog.

"Vicious..." he muttered.

The dog growled again.

"Good old Vicious! Don't you know me, boy? It's Tad! You remember me!"

The dog looked at him blankly. And it didn't stop growling.

"You know it's me!" Tad insisted. He tapped his

chest. "I'm in here. I know it's not my body but it's still me. You're not going to hurt me, are you!"

And then the Dalmatian wagged its tail! It recognized him!

Tad let out his breath in a huge sigh of relief. Vicious was drooling now, expecting an éclair. Tad pointed with one finger. "Basket!" he commanded.

"Basket!" Tad said again.

The dog turned and ran into the house. Tad watched it go with a sense of elation. It wasn't just that he had survived the encounter. It was something more. Despite his new face, his new clothes, even his new smell, he now realized that deep down there *was* still a part of him that was Tad Spencer. And always would be.

With more hope and excitement than he had felt in weeks, Tad ran the rest of the way and went in through the kitchen door.

He had known it would be open. Mrs O'Blimey was always forgetting to lock it and, as Tad had suspected, the kitchen was empty. There was a second door on the other side and Tad went through it, passing into a small, bare room filled with television monitors, video recorders and other equipment; the security room of Snatchmore Hall.

Tad sat down in front of a console. Set in the panel opposite him was a colour television screen showing a wobbling image of the main gates. Next to it was a grid with ten numbered buttons and a microphone. Tad punched in a code: 1–10–8.

There was a buzz and the gates swung open.

Tad kept his eyes on the screen. A battered white van had appeared with IPSWICH ABATTOIRS – LOVELY FRESH MEAT painted on the side. Finn had stolen the van the day before and it was of course he who was behind the wheel. As he drove through the gates and onto the drive, he leaned out of the window and gave a thumbs-up sign to the closed-circuit camera. Tad pressed the buttons again and the gates closed.

He was waiting for Finn by the kitchen door when the van arrived. Finn killed the engine and got out. "Any trouble?" he demanded.

"No," Tad replied. "The chauffeur's out. There's no sign of the servants. And Mum ... I mean ... Lady Geranium must still be in bed."

"Good boy! Good boy!" Finn reached into the van and pulled out a sack. Perhaps it really had been used for carrying meat once, as it was old and stained and smelled horrible. "Right. Let's go," he said.

The two of them set off on tiptoe through the house. Everything felt unreal for Tad – just as it had done when he broke into the mews house in London. To be in his home yet at the same time an intruder, breaking the law ... it made him dizzy just to think about it. But he couldn't tell Finn that. In fact, it almost amused him, pretending that he was here for the first time.

"What a place! What a place!" Finn whispered as they crossed the main hall and made for the stairs.

There was a little antique table leaning against a wall and Finn stopped beside it. He picked up a silver cigarette box and held it to the light. "Worth a bob or two," he whispered.

"That's not what we're here for," Tad reminded him in a low voice.

"Shame to leave it though." Finn slipped the box into his pocket and crept on. The two of them climbed the stairs and started along a corridor, Finn softly opening each door he came to and peering into the room behind. The door they wanted was the fifth on the right. Tad could have found his way to it blindfolded. But once again, he said nothing. He would let Finn do it his way.

A bathroom. A sauna. An empty bedroom. A dressing-room. Finn reached the fifth door and opened it. The sound of snoring rose and fell in the half-light. Finn whistled softly and hitched up the sack. Tad followed him into what had once been his bedroom.

It was a wreck. The carpet was almost completely hidden by the sweet papers, crisp packets, biscuit boxes, crumpled comics, old socks and smelly underwear that covered it. The neat shelves of books and computer games (his books, his computer games!) had been torn apart and one of the computers had a broken screen and jam all over the keyboard. One wall had been covered by a zig-zagging line of spray paint. The whole room stank of cigarette smoke.

Finn took this all in and smiled. "He treats his room

just like you do, Bob," he muttered.

"Sssh!" Tad's eyes had been drawn to the bed, where the room's occupant lay, his stomach in the air, snoring heavily. Once again Tad had the strange sensation of realizing that he was looking at himself but this time he felt only disgust. The boy on the bed resembled nothing so much as a huge jelly-fish. His arms and legs were splayed out and his silk pyjamas had slipped down to reveal a great, swollen belly. Rolls of fat bulged underneath the pyjamas and as the boy breathed they moved – but in different directions. Bob Snarby had fallen asleep with his mouth wide open and there was a bead of saliva caught between his upper and lower lip which quivered each time he snored.

"Is this really me?" Tad muttered. "Was this me?"

"What?" Finn hissed.

"Nothing."

"What a slob!" Finn muttered. "I hope the sack's big enough!"

Tad and Finn crept forward right up to the sleeping boy. They exchanged a glance. "Now!" Finn said.

Together they pounced. Bob Snarby didn't even have time to open his eyes before he found himself grabbed and half-buried in the foul-smelling sack. As Finn hoisted him up, Tad pulled. The sack slid over Bob's head, down his body and over his feet. As the end came clear, Finn produced a length of rope and tied it in a tight knot. "Prime steak," he muttered and grinned at his own joke. "Now let's get him loaded up."

A few minutes later the gates of Snatchmore Hall opened for a second time and the white butcher's van rocketed out and veered off down the lane. Finn was gripping the wheel, staring out with wide, manic eyes. Tad was sitting next to him. The sack was kicking and squirming in the back.

Lady Geranium Spencer woke up at midday exactly, nicely in time for either a late breakfast or an early lunch. She had a slight headache and was feeling depressed after what had been a depressing evening. She and Sir Hubert had taken dear Tad to a performance of Shakespeare's *Comedy of Errors*. Tad should have loved it. It was his favourite play and, as this was a touring production from Athens, it was actually in Greek. But instead of being pleased, Tad had been ghastly. He had complained through Act One, slept through Act Two, eaten too much ice-cream in the interval and then been sick in Act Three. Lady Geranium groaned quietly. The truth was, Tad hadn't been the same since he fell off that horse. Not the same at all.

She got up and went into the bathroom. She paused in front of the mirror and gave a little scream. A hideous brown face stared back at her. Then she remembered. She had gone to bed with a mud pack on her face but she had been so tired she had forgotten to take it off.

Half an hour later, wrapped in a dressing gown, Lady Geranium walked down the corridor on her way to the breakfast room. She passed her son's bedroom and looked in. To her surprise there was no sign of the boy. The room was as horrible as ever ... after twenty-five years' loyal service, Mrs O'Blimey had put in her resignation a few days before and Mitzy still wasn't back following her nervous breakdown.

"Tad?" Lady Geranium called out.

There was no answer but then Lady Geranium noticed an envelope pinned to the door. It was addressed to: SIR HUBERT AND LADY GERANIUM SPENCER. SNATCHMORE HALL. But the words hadn't been written. They had been torn out of newspapers and magazines.

Puzzled and slightly alarmed, she took the envelope down and opened it. There was a single sheet of white paper inside and on it a message, also set down in words that had been cut out and glued into place.

We have your son. do
not call the police or
you will never see him
again. bring one million
pounds in a suitcase to
great yarmouth funfair at
midnight tonight. leave it
at the entrance to the big
dipper. no tricks. no police.
you have been warned.

Lady Geranium read the note three times. Then she ran to the telephone and rang Sir Hubert.

DARK THOUGHTS

Sir Hubert Spencer held the ransom note in his shaking hands and read it for the twenty-seventh time. His face, never handsome at the best of times, was taut and twisted with anger.

"It's an outrage!" he exclaimed – and not for the first time either. "They won't get away with it!"

"Taking our boy!" Lady Geranium sobbed.

"I'm not talking about the boy!" Sir Hubert exploded. "It's me I'm thinking about! How dare they try to threaten *me*? Don't they know who I am?"

Sir Hubert paced up and down the room like a tiger in a cage. His wife watched him anxiously. "Can you find the money?" she asked. "A million pounds! It seems an awful lot."

"Of course I can find the money," Sir Hubert

snapped. "The question is, do I want to?"

Lady Geranium stared at him. "What do you mean?"

"Well, the fact is, my dear ... I wonder if young Tad is actually worth it."

"What?"

"Ever since he fell off that damn horse he hasn't been the same. He's stupid. He's slovenly at the table. He doesn't speak French, German or Greek any more. He's messy. The truth of the matter is, I'm beginning to wonder if this kidnap business mightn't be a blessing in disguise."

Lady Geranium thought for a moment. "It is true," she said in a low voice. "He has changed. Do you think, if we don't pay ... they might just keep him?"

Just then there was a knock at the door.

"Come in!" Sir Hubert called.

The door opened and the chauffeur, Spurling, came in, looking as smart as ever in a freshly pressed uniform. But his eyes were dark and his face was grim. "Forgive me interrupting you, sir," he began.

"Go on, Spurling..."

The chauffeur coughed discreetly, like a doctor about to give bad news. "I've been studying the film, sir. The film taken this afternoon by the security camera at the gate. I think there's something you ought to see..."

The three figures stood, huddled together in the empty fairground, completely dwarfed by the great bulk of the roller coaster that towered behind them. Somewhere on the other side of it, lost in the darkness, the waves rolled in. They sounded slow and heavy. There was something wrong with the night. The air was too warm. There was no breeze at all. And the sky was tinted an unnatural shade of purple – as if it were in pain.

"There's going to be a storm," Eric Snarby said.

"It's a 'orrible night," his wife agreed.

"Shut up!" Finn hissed and glanced at his two companions, who pursed their lips and looked away.

Finn was holding a radio transmitter and now he pressed a black button on the side. "Testing, testing. One, two, three..."

"I can hear you, Finn. Loud and clear." Tad's voice came back thin and disembodied. He could have been anywhere but in fact he was on the other side of the road in the Snarbies' caravan.

"You all right, Bobby-boy?" Finn held the transmitter only inches from his lips. "'ow's our guest?"

"Trussed up like a Christmas turkey and twice as fat," came the reply. "I'm fine, Finn."

"All right. Robert and out." Finn clicked the transmitter off and grinned. "You know what this is?" he said. "This is the perfect plan!"

"You said that last time," Eric muttered.

"And the time before," Doll added.

"This time I got it all worked out. The Spencer kid is in the caravan with Bob – but nobody knows that. Only us. Now at midnight, I'll be at the roller coaster.

His lordship will come with the money. The two of you will be watching from the ghost train..."

"I don't like ghosts," Doll said.

"It's only plastic! It can't 'urt you!"

"Go on, Finn..." Eric rasped. He was looking pale and nervous. Perhaps it was just the heat of the night but there was a film of sweat on his forehead and cheeks and his sty was wet and glistening. His whole head looked like a rotten fruit.

"You'll 'ave a radio transmitter," Finn went on. "When I got the money and I know everything's all right, I'll signal you. That's when I 'op it. You signal Bob and tell 'im to bring the Spencer boy over. Then you leave too."

"What if it's a trick?" Doll asked. "What if it's the police what turn up?"

Finn shook his head. "They won't risk the police," he said. "These rich types – they treat their kids like spun glass. They wouldn't do nothing to hurt little Tad. No. I'll get the money and I'll be gone. You Snarbies'll 'ave plenty of time to get clear. And then we'll all meet in London and we'll be rich!"

"What about Bob?" Eric asked. "If 'e 'ands over the boy, they'll 'ave 'im!"

Finn smiled slowly, his silver fillings glinting in the night. "We don't need Bob any more," he said. "He's not the same any more. 'e 'asn't been the same since that business with the glue. 'e let me down badly in Nightingale Square and I been thinking ... maybe it's time 'e spent a bit of time with 'er Majesty."

"Prison?" Doll muttered.

"They'll only give 'im a few years. It'll do 'im good." Finn was friendly now, simpering at both the Snarbies. "You won't miss 'im, he added. "Another couple of years and 'e'd 'ave left 'ome anyway."

"That's true," Eric Snarby said.

Finn slid his walking-stick through his belt and took the Snarbies' arms in his hands. "A million quid!" he said. "And one less to share it with." He laughed quietly. "Now let's go and get a drink."

Tad put the transmitter down and drew back the curtain. Bob Snarby was lying on Eric and Doll's bed, his hands tied behind him, his ankles taped together and a gag drawn tight across his mouth. As soon as he saw Tad, he began to squirm, rocking his body back and forth and trying to shout out. But the gag cut off virtually any noise and all Bob could do was plead with the other boy with his eyes.

"I'll undo the gag," Tad said. "But if you shout out, I'll put it right on again. Do you understand?"

"Mmmmm!" Bob jerked his head up and down.

Tad went over to him and untied the gag. It was an old scarf of Doll's and he dreaded to think what it tasted like. As soon as the cloth fell free, Bob opened his mouth and drew in a great breath. Tad was tensed, ready to pounce on him – but Bob didn't shout. To Tad's astonishment, he simply burst into tears.

For the first time, Tad actually felt sorry for the other boy. Lying there with tears streaming down his pudgy cheeks, his smart clothes all wrinkled and disarrayed, he really looked pathetic. Bob Snarby probably hadn't cried since the day he was born. But it seemed that he had changed. It seemed that they both had.

"It's all right," Tad said. "No one's going to 'urt you."

"You already have hurt me!" the other boy replied. His voice was petulant. Tad had often used that voice when he couldn't get what he wanted.

"Do you want a cup of tea, Bob?" There was no reply.

"Would you prefer it if I called you Tad?"

"No..."

Tad gazed at his prisoner. "It seems to me that you *are* Tad now," he said. "And I *am* Bob. We really have switched!"

"Is that why you've done this?" the other boy cried. "You've kidnapped me because you're jealous that I've taken your place."

"No." Tad smiled. "You probably won't believe me, but I don't want to switch back any more." Even Tad was surprised by what he had just said. It was as if he'd only just realized it himself. But now he saw the boy he had been; a great, spoiled ball of flab in an expensive suit. He remembered how his parents had earned the money that had turned him into that. And he knew that it was true. He could never go back. Not to Snatchmore

Hall. Not to them. "I don't want to be Tad Spencer any more," he said. "I think I'm happier being you."

Bob tugged at his cords again but Finn had tied them and they stayed firm. "So why *have* you kidnapped me?" he asked.

"It was Finn who kidnapped you," Tad said. "He did it for the money and I didn't have any choice. But I been doing a bit of thinking and I've got a plan of my own."

"What plan?"

"That's my business." Tad smiled. "But you listen to me, Tad Spencer. You do exactly what I say, when I say it. And everything's going to be all right."

In the security room at Snatchmore Hall, Sir Hubert Spencer sat down in front of the television screen.

The cameras had caught a figure running from the edge of the shrubbery across the lawn. Spurling had frozen the image and now he closed in on it until a boy's face filled the screen. The image was hazy, distorted at the edges but still recognizable.

"I know him!" Lady Geranium exclaimed.

"We all know him!" Sir Hubert snarled. "He's the little brat you found at the mews house. The one you sent over to ACID."

"The one who escaped from the Centre!" Lady Geranium's face had gone white ... all of it apart from her nose. After so many operations, the nose seemed to have a life of its own. Sometimes it even blew itself when she wasn't expecting it. "So what was he doing here?" she asked.

"A very good question, my dear."

"Do you think it was a coincidence?"

"No. I don't."

Sir Hubert stared at the image on the screen. With a shaking finger he drew a line across Tad's face. "First the mews. Then the Centre. Now here." There was a long silence. "This boy – Bob Snarby – must know about us. Beautiful World. The experiments. Everything!"

Spurling coughed discreetly. "Would you like me to deal with him, sir?" he asked.

"Yes, Spurling. I would."

The chauffeur reached into his jacket and drew out a slim, black revolver: a Davis P-380 .38 automatic.

"What are you going to do?" Lady Geranium asked.

"Don't worry yourself, my dear," Sir Hubert said. "This kidnapping may be just what we need. Great Yarmouth funfair at midnight? That's where the boy will be ... along with his accomplices."

"If you want me to murder them all, sir, might I suggest the TEC-9 automatic machine gun?" Spurling said.

"No, Spurling." Sir Hubert smiled. "Your job is to get the boy. Just the boy." He reached out and picked up a telephone. "First of all we're going to call the police," he said. "When we go to Great Yarmouth, they'll come too. And of course they'll be armed."

"They'll shoot the boy!" Lady Geranium cried.

"Spurling will fire the first shot. It'll be dark. Nobody will know what's happening. And yes! The police will open fire. With luck everyone will be killed."

"Can you be sure, sir, that the police will oblige?" the chauffeur asked.

"No, Spurling. But you'll be there. And I want you to find the boy." Sir Hubert began to dial. "Whatever happens, you're to put a bullet between his eyes. Do you understand me?"

"Perfectly, sir." Spurling reached out and turned a switch below the television monitor.

The screen went black.

ROLLER COASTER

The first drops of rain began to fall at five to twelve. Fat and heavy, they exploded on impact like bursting tennis balls. From somewhere far away came a low, deep rumbling of thunder. It was a horrible night; close and sticky. The sky was streaked with mauve and throbbed as if it were about to burst.

Eric and Doll Snarby were waiting in the shadows of the ghost train, the two of them jammed into a single carriage that had been decorated to resemble a vampire bat. Neither of them looked happy.

"No good will come of it," Eric was saying. "I tell you, my dear. I've got a bad feeling about this."

"Me too," Doll moaned.

"You and me ... we was 'appier before we met Finn," Eric went on. "I mean, we was never in any trouble.

A bit of shop-lifting, maybe. There was always the smash-and-grabs, of course. We did thieve a couple of motor cars. A couple of dozen, now I think about it. And then there was the pick-pocketing. But apart from that we was honest people, you and me. Honest, decent people."

"We should never 'ave fallen in with 'im," Doll muttered. "'e's an 'orrible man and no mistake."

The subject of their discussion was pacing up and down with his walking-stick about a hundred metres away in front of the roller coaster. In fact, Finn was staggering as much as pacing. He had drunk half a bottle of gin – and the other half was still in his pocket. Another great ball of rain fell down, hitting him on the shoulder. Finn swore, wiping water away from his nose and chin. Somewhere in Great Yarmouth, a clock struck midnight. Finn peered through the darkness. A car had appeared at the entrance to the Pleasure Beach. A white Rolls Royce.

The car stopped and Sir Hubert Spencer got out, carrying an attaché case with a silver combination lock. The thunder rumbled again.

Sir Hubert closed the door behind him and walked through the funfair, passing between the silent machines. His feet rapped against the concrete, the sound all around him as if he were being followed by a crowd of invisible bodyguards. But he seemed to be on his own. As he passed in front of the ghost train, Eric and Doll Snarby shrank from sight, then quickly looked back the way he had come. The Rolls Royce was on its own in the street. Nothing was moving. Eric raised a hand with the thumb up. Finn saw the signal and nodded.

Neither Eric nor Finn had seen the figure who had been hiding in the back of the car. Neither of them was watching as the door slowly opened, then clicked shut again. But even as Sir Hubert Spencer walked the last few steps up to the roller coaster, Spurling slipped out of the car and hurried into the shadows. A street lamp glimmered on something metallic that he held in his hand. But a moment later he was gone, swallowed up by the darkness.

Sir Hubert Spencer walked up to Finn and stood, towering over him. Two more different men would have been hard to imagine. Sir Hubert was dressed in an expensive raincoat, his hair immaculate, his face grim and businesslike. Finn was as sly and as shabby as ever, leaning on his walking-stick, one eye blinking over the tattoo. The two of them were worlds apart and yet as they drew close their eyes connected and each seemed to recognize something in each other.

"Good evening, Sir Hubert," Finn began.

"Let's not waste words," Sir Hubert snapped. If he had noticed Finn's peculiar tattoo, he showed no reaction. "You have my son?"

"He's safe, Sir Hubert. And very near. Do you have the particulars?"

"The what?"

"The money!"

"Where's the boy?"

"The money first!"

There was a long pause. Sir Hubert seemed unwilling to open the attaché case and suddenly Finn was suspicious. "You do have the money?" he demanded. "You haven't tried anything fancy, I take it?"

"Of course I haven't," Sir Hubert replied. "What do you think I am?"

Finn's lips stretched in a sly smile, dragging the cobweb. "Oh, I think I know what you are, Sir Hubert," he murmured. "I'd say you're pretty much the same as me, although I dare say there aren't many who'd suspect it. You're wondering how I know? Well, it takes one to know one, as my old mum used to say before she went on the bottle. Oh yes – you got your fancy title. You got a position. But I can see what's what and I can smell it too and you're not going to try and tell me any different, are you!"

Sir Hubert laughed. "All right," he said. "Why not admit it? You're a rogue and so am I. But there is one difference between us, Mr..."

"Finn. Archibald Finn. What is the difference, Sir Hubert?"

"Only this." Sir Hubert's face twisted with contempt. "I am successful. Immensely, stupendously successful. But you're nothing. A petty criminal. That's the difference between us, Mr Finn. I've got away with it. But you've been caught!"

Sir Hubert raised his hand and Finn shrank away, lifting his own walking-stick as if in self-defence. But Sir Hubert wasn't going to hit him. The movement was only a signal. Finn saw it and understood its significance too late.

A shot rang out, astonishingly loud in the wet night air. Finn screamed as a bullet hammered into his shoulder, throwing him forward into Sir Hubert's arms. For a moment the two men stood there, locked together, their faces almost touching.

"You cheated me!" Finn whined.

"Of course I cheated you!" Sir Hubert smiled. "That's what I do!"

Desperately, Finn lunged for the attaché case and managed to rip it away from Sir Hubert's grasp. The case fell open and suddenly Finn was surrounded by hundreds of scraps of paper, tumbling and scattering around his feet. Newspaper. Sir Hubert hadn't brought a million pounds. He hadn't brought any money at all.

"No..." Finn whimpered. His shoulder was on fire, blood trickling round his neck.

Sir Hubert laughed a second time.

And then two searchlights exploded into life and there was the roar and clatter of engines as two police helicopters came in low, flying over the sea. Somewhere a whistle shrieked. There was another roll of thunder and immediately after it an amplified voice that could have come out of the clouds themselves.

"This is the police! Stay where you are! We are

armed! Do not attempt to move!"

But Finn was already moving. Cursing and weeping at his bad luck, he had stumbled away from Sir Hubert, dropping the worthless attaché case. He had dropped his walking-stick when the bullet hit him and his empty hand was clamped over the wound. Now he searched for a way out. But it was too late. Two police cars tore in from opposite directions, skidding to a halt outside the main gate. Uniformed police poured out of them whilst more men with dogs suddenly appeared at the edge of the fair and began to spread out in a line. Then the helicopter searchlights swung in on him and Finn froze. He was trapped by the light, blinded and flattened by it like a germ on a laboratory slide.

"Stay where you are!" the voice commanded again. It was coming from the first of the helicopters that now hovered over him, whipping up the dust and sending the blank paper notes flying. "We are armed!"

For a moment Finn was lost in a dust-cloud. He realized he had one chance and he took it. With a great shout he hurled himself over a low wall and onto the tracks of the roller coaster itself. And then he was away, staggering towards the corner and the first ascent. By the time the police had reached Sir Hubert, Finn had gone.

A thin, grey man in blue and silver uniform had marched up to Sir Hubert. This was the chief inspector in charge of the operation. His name was Jones. He was in his late fifties with the drawn, skeletal face of a man who never slept. "What happened?" he demanded. "Who fired the shot?"

"It was him!" Sir Hubert replied. "He had a gun. When he saw there was no money, he tried to kill me."

"But it looked to me like he was the one who was hit, sir," Jones said.

"Yes," Sir Hubert explained. "I managed to get hold of the gun. He pulled the trigger and he hit himself."

The chief inspector gazed at Sir Hubert. He was obviously puzzled by something. But he didn't speak.

"The man's getting away!" Sir Hubert shouted, pointing at the roller coaster. "Why don't you get after him?"

The chief inspector nodded. Three policemen jumped over the wall and began to run down the track. All of them were armed.

Meanwhile, Finn had reached the highest point of the roller coaster, a length of track that ran flat for just a few feet before plunging down again in what would have been the biggest thrill of the ride. For a few moments he stood there, swaying. The two helicopters buzzed around him, their searchlights sweeping across him without settling on him. Finn batted at them, a miniature King Kong. They were giving him a headache. He wanted them to go away.

Climbing the track had taken all his strength. He had lost blood. There were little pools of it behind him, every few steps. He looked at it, marvelling. A terrible, deafening burst of thunder came rolling in from the sea and he almost lost his balance. As he swayed on the metal track the night exploded, smashed by a massive bolt of lightning. The light danced in Finn's eyes and he sang out drunkenly.

"It's all over for you, Finn," he cried. "This time it's the end, old friend. There's nowhere for you to go now."

He glanced round, alerted by the sound of men climbing. The three policemen were already halfway up the track, using their hands as well as their feet to move forward on the rain-swept surface.

"Go away!" he shouted. "Leave me alone!"

The policemen squatted down, their guns aimed at Finn. "Throw down your weapon!" the nearest one shouted.

Finn threw back his head and laughed. "One last drink!" he shouted but the wind snatched away the words before they could be heard. "A toast to Sir Hubert lousy Spencer and his rotten, stinking son. And a toast to prison! Back to prison we go! Back to the old cell!"

He reached into his pocket.

The three policemen, believing he was going for his gun, opened fire as one.

For a moment Finn stood there on the track, his arms outstretched, his face twisted in a ghastly smile as if he were welcoming the storm and the night that was rushing in to take him. Then he plummeted forward.

Still hiding in the ghost train, Eric and Doll Snarby watched Finn as he seemed to dive into death. There was a last, high-pitched scream. The two of them covered their eyes. But months later they would still be unable to sleep, remembering the dreadful thud as the body hit the ground.

The ambulance came about twenty minutes later.

With the police still combing the Pleasure Beach, Finn was carried into the ambulance, his body covered by a blanket. Chief Inspector Jones watched the body go. It was half past twelve but the night seemed to have gone on forever. He sighed and shook water from his head as a younger policeman approached.

"Sir?"

"Yes!"

"There's still no sign of the Snarbies, sir. But we found this ... next to the ghost train." The policeman handed Jones a radio transmitter, dripping wet. "Apparently they've got a caravan, sir," the policeman went on. "Across the road."

Jones slid the transmitter into his pocket and nodded. "Then that's where we'll find Tad Spencer," he said.

Three minutes later, the chief inspector and his men had the caravan surrounded. Sir Hubert Spencer had followed them over and was watching with keen, narrowed eyes. The door to the caravan was closed but the lights were on behind the windows. Apart from the raindrops hitting the roof and bouncing off, there was no sign of movement. The rain was falling so hard now that it seemed almost solid, a single mass of water. The chief inspector drew his raincoat around him and shivered.

He gave a signal and about a dozen policemen hurried forward, their feet splashing down in puddles as they closed in on the caravan. But Jones wasn't taking any chances. He had guessed the kidnap victim was in the caravan but he still didn't know who might be with him. He lifted a megaphone and held it to his lips.

"This is the police!" Even amplified, his voice was almost drowned out by the rain. He turned up the volume. "The caravan's surrounded," he called out. "Open the door and come out with your hands up..."

The rain lashed down. The door of the caravan remained closed.

Jones sighed. He put down the megaphone and walked forward. There were just ten metres between him and the caravan. He didn't try to run.

With Sir Hubert and all the other policemen watching, he reached the door. He opened it. A dozen guns were raised. A dozen men waited to run forward.

Jones shook his head. The caravan was empty. There was nobody there.

And it was then that the radio transmitter that he had put in his pocket suddenly crackled into life. The chief inspector pulled it out and stared at it. It was the last thing they had expected.

"This is Bob Snarby," came a voice, and it was Bob

Snarby's voice even if it was Tad who really spoke. "I've got the kid and I've got a knife. I'll give 'im up ... but only to Sir Hubert Spencer. If 'e wants the kid back, 'e'll find 'im in the Mirror Maze. Back in the fair.

"We're in the Mirror Maze. But Sir Hubert's got to come alone. No tricks. I've got a knife and I'll use it. I want to see Sir Hubert and I want to see him alone."

THE MIRROR MAZE

Tad didn't have a knife.

He had guessed Sir Hubert would double-cross Finn and at ten minutes to twelve he had crept out of the caravan taking Bob Snarby – his hands still tied and his mouth gagged with him. The two boys had been in the funfair when Finn had fallen to his death. Afterwards, they had slipped into the nearest attraction to hide.

It was only when he was inside that Tad realized where he was. Flicking on the torch that he had brought from the Snarbies' caravan, he had been astonished by the sight of about a thousand reflections of himself, leaping out of the darkness. He swung the torch left and right and was dazzled by the thousand beams of light that shone back at him. And behind the torchlight, everywhere he looked, line after line of Tad Spencers stared back, an army of scrawny, fair-haired boys, standing there, their faces grim. And Bob Snarby was also there of course. Line after line of him, dripping wet and shivering, his hands securely tied.

He was inside the Mirror Maze.

Tad flicked off the radio transmitter and set it down, wondering how long it would take Sir Hubert to arrive. He had no idea what would happen to him when this was all over but he supposed he would end up in jail. He no longer cared. It seemed to him now that everything had led to this moment, a last meeting with the man who had almost had him killed. Tad knew that he couldn't go to the police. No matter how terrible his crimes, Sir Hubert was still his father. But there was one thing that he could do. Somehow he would make his father recognize him. He would tell him about the switch and everything that had happened since. He would tell him what he knew about ACID and Beautiful World.

And then he would turn his back on him and never see him again.

Outside the Mirror Maze, Sir Hubert had arrived.

He was walking with the chief inspector, shielding under an umbrella as the rain crashed down. The Mirror Maze was partly surrounded by the other police officers, all of them dripping wet. As far as they were concerned, the excitement was over. Finn was dead. There was only some crazy kid to deal with. They just wanted to get home to bed.

Jones paused outside the front entrance to the Mirror Maze. "Are you sure you're going to be all right, Sir Hubert?" he asked.

Sir Hubert shook rain off his umbrella. "Don't worry, Chief Inspector." He sniffed. "I'll talk to this wretched guttersnipe and see what he wants – if he even knows himself. I'll talk him out into the open and then you and your men can deal with him."

"He did say he had a knife, sir," Jones reminded him. "And there's still the matter of the gun."

"What gun?" Sir Hubert asked.

Jones looked at Sir Hubert curiously, as if he were trying to look through him. "The gun that you said Finn had, sir. Somebody fired a shot but we still haven't found the gun..."

Sir Hubert smiled. "I'm not afraid," he said. "If the boy's got a gun, so much the worse for him." He stepped forward eagerly. "Now let's get this over with. I've wasted enough time with this young street urchin already."

As Sir Hubert approached the entrance, another figure flitted out of the shelter of the dodgems and ran the few paces to the back of the Mirror Maze. Nobody saw him. The man worked quickly, using a screwdriver to prise three wooden planks away from the rear wall. This made a hole large enough to slip through even though this was an unusually large man.

Spurling. Sir Hubert's chauffeur.

He tore his uniform as he squeezed inside and for

a moment his arm hung outside in the rain with his sleeve caught on a nail. Water dripped off his hand and the cold metal barrel of the gun it was holding. Then he unhooked himself. He pulled the gun in. And turned to find the boy he had come to kill.

Sir Hubert let the door swing shut behind him and stood in utter darkness. He listened for any sound of movement but the rain beating down on the roof and walls would have muffled it anyway.

"Is there anybody there?" he called out. "Bob Snarby? I understand that's your name. Do you want to speak to me?"

Silence. The darkness unnerved him. But just before the door had closed he had noticed a bank of electric switches set to one side and now he groped for them. He flicked one of them on but there was still no light. Sir Hubert thought he heard something – a faint electronic whine – but against the pattering of the rain it was hard to be sure. He left the switch down and found another. This time a single red bulb came on, high above the mirrors.

It was enough. Sir Hubert found himself facing a corridor of glass that broke off immediately in three different directions. There were panels everywhere. Some were transparent, some were mirrors. If you moved forward too quickly you could easily crash into an invisible barrier – or into a reflection of yourself. The light that Sir Hubert had turned on wasn't strong enough to reach the outer walls of the Mirror Maze. The deep red glow spread out in a wide circle. But the mirrors, the sweeping corridors, seemed to go on for ever.

And everywhere he looked, Sir Hubert saw the faces of the three people who had finally come together.

One thousand Tad Spencers.

One thousand Bob Snarbies.

One thousand Sir Huberts.

Reflections of reflections of reflections.

"Bob Snarby," Sir Hubert said.

"I'm not Bob Snarby. I'm Tad. I'm your son."

Sir Hubert didn't understand. It was the rough-looking boy who had spoken, the one with the studs in his ear. His son couldn't speak. He was gagged.

"You tried to kill me," Tad said.

Sir Hubert said nothing. He would let the boy talk. A few more seconds and Spurling would be ready.

"When I was in the Centre ... I couldn't believe it was you. I didn't want to believe it! My own dad. Doing experiments on kids off the street. It was like I was seeing you for the first time – and what I saw ... it was horrible!"

"I'm not your father!" Sir Hubert snapped. He took a step forward and cried out loud as he banged into a sheet of glass. He spun round. The reflections watched him.

"I know about the Indians too," Tad went on. "The Arambayans." Dragging Bob with him, Tad made his way to the very centre of the maze. He felt safer here, with glass all around. "How could you do that, Dad?" he shouted. "Kill all those people just to make money! Didn't you have enough?"

"There's no such thing as enough!" Sir Hubert shouted back. "And why do you call me your father?"

"Because you are!"

"No. You have my son with you. This whole thing is ridiculous. Let him go and we can sort this all out. Nobody's going to hurt you." He took another step forward. All around, his reflections moved as well.

"Stay where you are!" Tad also moved and once again the patterns shifted, endless lines of men and lines of boys crossing and recrossing each other in the Mirror Maze. "Admit it!" he cried. "I admired you so much but it was all a lie. You're a criminal. Worse than Finn!"

And then Sir Hubert saw it. A fourth image had appeared in the mirrors, on the very edge of the red circle ... a huddled shape reflected round and around. Would the boy have seen him? Of course he would. But there was nothing he could do. Sir Hubert allowed himself a thin, cruel smile. Spurling was here. It was finally over.

"You want me to tell you the truth?" Sir Hubert called out. "It's my pleasure!" He slammed his hand against a mirror. A thousand hands thundered at a thousand reflections of Tad. "Yes – boy – you have learned rather too much about me. My little experiments in the Centre? How else can I be sure that my products are safe? The stupid public gets all upset when it's rabbits or mice or monkeys on the operating table but who cares about delinquent children dragged off the London streets? Homeless, hopeless children like you? So – yes – my charity, ACID, turned you into a laboratory rat as it has done a hundred children before you. It's all you deserve."

"And you kill people!" Tad cried, horrified and sickened by what he was hearing. "The Arambayans..."

"Primitives! Savages! Animals!" Sir Hubert laughed. "They wouldn't sell me what I wanted so of course I had them wiped out. Do you think anybody cares? When people pay seventeen pounds fifty for a bottle of Moonfruit Massage, they're not thinking of a tribe of Indians on the other side of the world! Nobody ever thinks of anybody else. That's what capitalism is all about!"

Once more the pattern changed. A thousand guns took aim.

"Kill him, Spurling!" Sir Hubert snapped. "He knows about me. I want him dead!"

"Kill him, Spurling! I want him dead!"

The words echoed all around the fairground just as every word had echoed ever since Sir Hubert had accidentally turned on the loudspeakers in the Mirror Maze. The police had heard everything. Sir Hubert Spencer had confessed to unspeakable crimes. Experimenting on children! Genocide! And now attempted murder.

The chief inspector was the first to react. While everyone else just stood there, as if in shock, he ran forward, heading for the entrance to the maze.

Inside, Spurling's finger tightened on the trigger. A single bead of sweat drew a careful line down his forehead. His target was only a few metres away from him. But which target? Where should he fire?

"Kill him!" Sir Hubert shouted again.

Tad was utterly surrounded by guns. They were in front of him, behind him, above him and below him. He spun round, trying to find a way out but now he realized that he too was trapped in the Mirror Maze. His fists struck out at the glass walls. They seemed to have closed in on him, boxing him in.

"Mmmm..." Bob Snarby shook his head from side to side and at last he managed to get his shoulder to the gag, dragging it off. The guns seemed to be pointing at him too and his eyes bulged with fear.

The chief inspector kicked open the door of the Mirror Maze and ran in. He shouted two words. "Sir Hubert!"

Spurling fired.

And everywhere mirrors smashed as, one after another, the bullet tunnelled through them, each tiny hole becoming a thousand tiny holes in the reflections as spidery cracks – millions of them – splintered out in all directions. At the same time there was one last great burst of thunder that smashed through the clouds and shook the entire building.

Tad cried out as the bullet hit him, throwing him off his feet. The pain was like nothing he had ever experienced. He felt every tiny millimetre of the bullet's progress as it passed through his skin, his flesh, his muscle and his bone. His shoulders hit the mirror behind him and he slid down, trailing blood behind him. The thunder pounded at his ears and there was a flash of lightning worse than any that had come before, slicing into his eyes, blinding him.

At the same instant, Bob Snarby screamed too.

Tad reached the ground, one leg bent under him, the other outstretched. And in the last few seconds before darkness came, he saw what had happened.

A uniformed policeman. Spurling with the gun. Sir Hubert, his eyes staring, photographed a thousand times.

Then a gunshot. Two more. Two thousand sparks of flame. Mirrors shattering. Spurling's reflection falling back and disappearing.

Suddenly there was no more pain. Tad closed his eyes. Suddenly there wasn't anything.

The boy with fair hair and two studs in his ear shivered and lay still.

TOGETHER

The Saint Elizabeth Institute for Juvenile Care was a plain, modern building in Sourbridge, on the outskirts of Birmingham. It didn't quite look like a prison – there were no bars on the windows – but it was just about as welcoming. The front was bare brick, the doors solid steel. The Institute had been built on the edge of a busy road but as the traffic thundered past nobody turned to look at it. It was the sort of place that had been designed not to be seen.

Three months after the shoot-out at Great Yarmouth Pleasure Beach, with the last of the summer hanging in the air, a boy stepped out of a door at the back of the Institute and stood in front of the fenced-in square of tarmac that was the football pitch, the exercise yard and the garden for those who lived inside. The boy was fourteen years old with short, black hair. Although he was dressed in the pale blue shirt and denim trousers that was the uniform of the St Elizabeth Institute, there was something about him that suggested he was used to more comfortable clothes.

The boy's name was Thomas Arnold David Spencer. He paused outside the door as if looking for someone. Then he started to walk forward.

There was a second boy sitting on a bench at the far end of the yard, also dressed in blue shirt and denims, his arm in a sling, chewing gum. This boy was much thinner than the other and had long, fair hair.

Hearing the footsteps approach, Bob Snarby turned round. He seemed to take a long time to recognize Tad and when he did finally speak his voice was unfriendly. "What are you doing here?"

"I've been sent here," Tad said.

"What? You're living here too?"

"Yes. I just got here today."

"So what happened to your mum and dad? Sir Hubert and Lady Money-bags. And what about Snatchmore Hall?"

"Snatchmore Hall's up for sale," Tad replied. "My parents are in jail."

And it was true. Tad Spencer was back in his own body. Bob Snarby was back in his. But everything in the lives of both boys had changed.

Tad still didn't know how he had switched places again – whether it was the storm or the shock of the bullet that had hit him. He even wondered if Dr Aftexcludor hadn't played a part in it. After all, with Sir Hubert's confession and subsequent arrest, the Arambayans had been revenged and hadn't that been the whole point?

He hadn't died in the Mirror Maze. What he had experienced was the jolting, terrible power of the switch as it fell on him a second time, sucking him out of Bob's body and sending him back to his own. He had thought he was dying. But seconds later, he had stood up, his arms tied behind him. He was unhurt.

It was Bob Snarby who had been rushed to hospital and emergency surgery and for the next week had remained in a critical condition. But Bob had always been tough. Slowly he had begun to recover and four weeks later the doctors were finished with him. He was allowed out of the hospital. Eric and Doll Snarby weren't there to greet him.

For the Snarbies had both disappeared. Although the police had discovered several cigarette ends and a cold steak and kidney pie in the ghost train, Eric and Doll had simply vanished into thin air. There had since been a few sightings of them in Ireland, a huge, fat woman and a balding little man, working as fish and chip sellers in a mobile van. Apparently there were never any chips, as the woman constantly ate them all. But since then they had moved on again. The police had given up hope of arresting them.

Spurling was dead. He had made the mistake of

turning his gun on the police and the chief inspector – who was also armed – had shot him in self-defence. The chauffeur had been buried a few days later in the same cemetery as Finn.

With the arrest of Sir Hubert and Lady Geranium Spencer, Beautiful World had collapsed. NONE OF OUR PRODUCTS ARE TESTED ON ANIMALS. When the truth about the tests had become known, the entire country had recoiled in horror. Several of the shops were actually burned down by furious, shouting crowds. The police had raided the Centre, freeing the children who were still there and making over a dozen arrests. Sir Hubert's knighthood had of course been withdrawn. He was now just plain Hubert Spencer: prisoner 7430909 in Wormwood Scrubs – where he was sentenced to remain for the next ninety years.

It had been one final twist of fate that had thrown the two boys together.

The police had decided to overlook Bob's part in the kidnapping and the break-in at the house of Lord Roven. He had, after all, been under Finn's influence and Finn had now paid for his crimes. It was quickly decided that Bob should be put into care. But Tad, too, had no parents and nowhere to go. His was a more difficult case in that he did have relatives who could look after him but unfortunately they had all disowned him, not wanting to be involved in the scandal. His file had been passed around from committee to committee but eventually he had been taken into care as well.

Both boys had been sent to the St Elizabeth Institute. They had arrived on the same day.

Now Tad waited for Bob to speak. Bob gazed at the other boy. His face was blank, neither hostile nor friendly. "You aren't so fat any more," he said.

Tad shrugged. "I've been doing more exercise. And I don't eat so much now."

"And you've 'ad your ear done."

"Yes." There was a silver stud in Tad's right ear. He rubbed it gently. "I got to like having one." He paused. "There were quite a lot of things I liked about being you, Bob."

"Well, you're not me any more," the other boy snapped. "So why 'ave you come looking for me? Come to 'ave a good laugh?"

"I've got nothing to laugh about," Tad replied. "I'm the same as you now. My parents are gone and it looks like I'm stuck here." He sighed. "Bob, I came to say I'm sorry."

"Sorry?"

"It was me who Spurling came to kill. And it was me who should have got shot. I suppose I did. But it was you who had all the pain, the hospital, all the rest of it. I didn't know we were going to switch back again..."

"It certainly couldn't 'ave happened at a worse time," Bob agreed. He swung round – but slowly. "So you're stuck here, are you?"

Tad nodded. "I don't care," he said. "I couldn't have gone back home anyway, even if Snatchmore Hall hadn't been sold."

"Didn't you 'ave uncles? Aunts?"

"They didn't want me." Tad looked around him and sighed. "I might as well stay here as anywhere," he said. "It's only for two years. Then I'll be sixteen and they'll have to let me out. And then I can start again."

Tad fell silent. There were a few trees near the yard, their leaves turning gold with the arrival of autumn. Behind them he could see the sun, already beginning to set.

"So what now?" Bob Snarby asked.

"I hoped we could be friends," Tad said.

"What? You 'n' me?"

"Why not?" Tad sat down next to Bob. "Nobody's ever known each other as well as you and I have. I mean, we've actually been each other."

"Did you ever tell anyone?" Bob Snarby asked.

"About the switch?" Tad shook his head. "No. I didn't think anyone would believe me."

"Me neither."

"It's only two years," Tad went on. "And then we'll be on our own. No parents. No Finn. Nobody to tell us what to do or turn us into what they want us to be. In some ways, maybe that's the best thing that ever happened to me."

"Yeah? And what then?" Bob wasn't convinced. "What do you think will happen to us then? You say you're the same as me now. Well, what chance do you think people like us ever have?"

"I think we can be anything we want to be," Tad replied. "If we stick together. And if we want it hard enough. With what you know and what I know ... together we can take on the world."

Bob smiled for the first time. "Listen to you!" he said. "I bet you was never like this before you was me."

"I bet you've changed too."

"Yeah. Maybe." Bob shrugged ruefully – the movement made him wince. "You know, in the end I didn't much like being you," he admitted. "It was lovely to start with. Like having Christmas every day. But can you imagine Christmas every day? How bored you'd get? I was beginning to feel like I was drowning. No wonder you were the way you were. You were spoiled rotten."

"Eric and Doll weren't great parents either."

"That's true."

Bob stood up. Tad helped him get to his feet, then held out a hand. "Friends?" he asked.

Bob Snarby took the hand. They shook.

A bell rang inside the Institute and together they began to walk back.

They had been each other and now they were themselves. But best of all they were together and as they slowly crossed the exercise yard, walking side by side, Tad was filled with hope and with happiness, knowing in his heart that the adventure of his life had only now begun.

READ OTHER GREAT BOOKS BY ANTHONY HOROWITZ...

THE ALEX RIDER SERIES

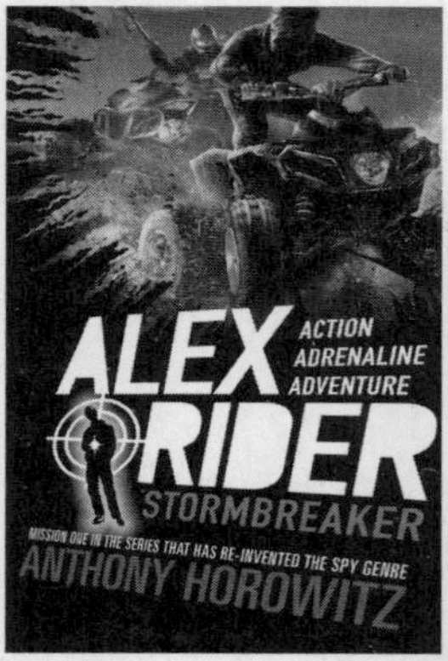

Alex Rider – you're never too young to die...

High in the Alps, death waits for Alex Rider...

Sharks. Assassins. Nuclear bombs. Alex Rider's in deep water.

Alex Rider has 90 minutes to save the world.

Once stung, twice as deadly. Alex Rider wants revenge.

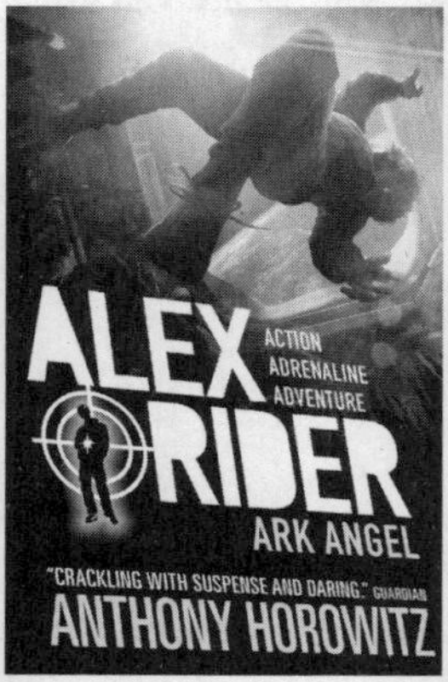

He's back – and this time there are no limits.

Alex Rider bites back…

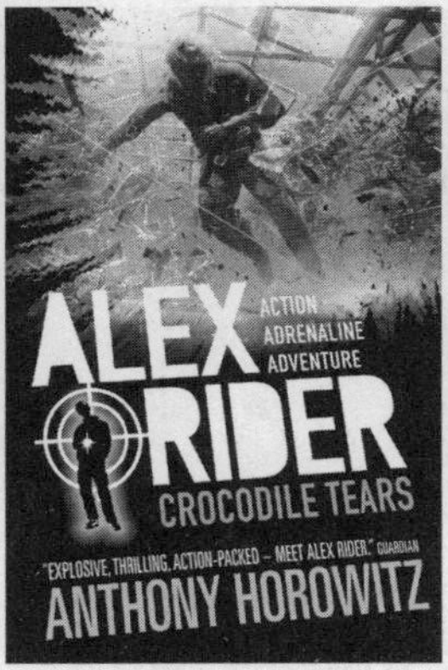

Alex Rider – in the jaws of death…

One bullet.
One life.
The end starts here.

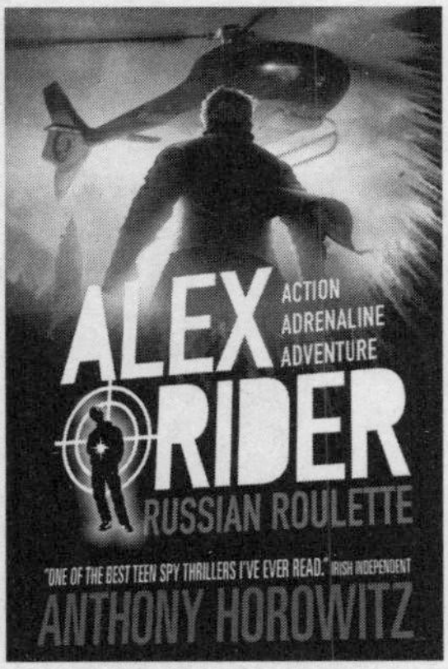

Get your hands on the deadly prequel

ALEX RIDER
ACTION
ADRENALINE
ADVENTURE

THE MISSION CONTINUES AT
alexrider.com

ACTION. ADRENALINE. ADVENTURE.

alexrider.com /alexrideruk

WELCOME TO THE DARK SIDE OF ANTHONY HOROWITZ

THE POWER OF FIVE

BOOK ONE

He always knew he was different.
First there were the dreams.
Then the deaths began.

BOOK TWO

It began with Raven's Gate.
But it's not over yet. Once
again the enemy is stirring.

BOOK THREE

Darkness covers the earth.
The Old Ones have returned.
The battle must begin.

BOOK FOUR

An ancient evil is unleashed.
Five have the power to defeat it.
But one of them has been taken.

BOOK FIVE

Five Gatekeepers.
One chance to save mankind.
Chaos beckons. Oblivion awaits.

LOOKING BACK, Henry Parker could honestl say that he had never wanted to hurt anyone. Certainly, it ha never occurred to him that he would one day plan and the execute the perfect murder of an internationally well-know children's author … even if that was what actually happened To begin with, all Henry wanted to do was write…

Photograph © Jon Cartwright

Anthony Horowitz is the author of the number one bestselling Alex Rider books and The Power of Five series. He has enjoyed huge success as a writer for both children and adults, most recently with the latest adventure in the Alex Rider series, *Russian Roulette*, and the highly acclaimed Sherlock Holmes novel, *The House of Silk*. His latest novel, *Moriarty*, is also set in the world of Sherlock Holmes and was published in October 2014. Anthony was also chosen by the Ian Fleming estate to write the new James Bond novel which will be published this year. Anthony has won numerous awards, including the Bookseller Association/Nielsen Author of the Year Award, the Children's Book of the Year Award at the British Book Awards, and the Red House Children's Book Award. In 2014 Anthony was awarded an OBE for Services to Literature. He has also created and written many major television series, including *Injustice*, *Collision* and the award-winning *Foyle's War*.

You can find out more about Anthony and his work at:

www.alexrider.com

@AnthonyHorowitz

GRANNY

More wickedly funny books

by Anthony Horowitz

The Devil and His Boy

Groosham Grange

Return to Groosham Grange

The Switch

More Bloody Horowitz

The Diamond Brothers books:

The Falcon's Malteser

Public Enemy Number Two

South by South East

The Blurred Man

The French Confection

I Know What You Did Last Wednesday

The Greek who Stole Christmas

GRANNY

ANTHONY
HOROWITZ

WALKER
BOOKS

This is a work of fiction. Names, characters, places and incidents are either the product of the author's imagination or, if real, are used fictitiously. All statements, activities, stunts, descriptions, information and material of any other kind contained herein are included for entertainment purposes only and should not be relied on for accuracy or replicated as they may result in injury.

First published 1994 by Walker Books Ltd
87 Vauxhall Walk, London, SE11 5HJ

This edition published 2015

2 4 6 8 10 9 7 5 3 1

This book has been typeset in ITC Veljovic

Printed in Germany by GGP Media GmbH

British Library Cataloguing in Publication Data:
a catalogue record for this book is available from the British Library

ISBN 978-1-4063-6475-0

www.walker.co.uk

For my sister, Caroline

CONTENTS

INTRODUCTION

Do you have a granny?

Grannies aren't the same as grandmothers. For a start, they don't even have to be women. They are just very old, very unpleasant and seem to cast a shadow that stretches out long before they enter the house. By and large, grannies hate young people. This is because young people have computer games, mobile phones, hair, teeth, good skin and the whole world ahead of them while grannies sit on their own in the darkness (to save electricity), knitting and complaining about how much worse everything has got since they were young. The truth is though that they never *were* young ... or if they were, they didn't notice.

The book you are now holding was inspired by my own granny, a truly dreadful woman called Esther Charatan who often visited when I was young. I could tell she was coming because my father would be in a terrible mood, my mother (her daughter) would develop a nervous twitch, the dogs would howl and the sun would go in. I was about eight years old when I realized that it was all her fault. It actually came as a great shock. I thought everyone liked her. I thought – because she was my grandmother – that she must be a nice person. In a way, I think I began to grow up the day I discovered that she was actually evil.

What do I mean by that? She never murdered anyone.

She didn't want to destroy the world. But I think there's another sort of evil that is often overlooked ... and it is this. Granny never did anything to help anyone else. She was rich and healthy (she lived into her nineties) but she was utterly selfish and complained all the time. I remember that she had an argument once with one of her own children – my Uncle Geoff – and didn't speak to him again for seventeen years! As far as I know, she never tried to make anyone happy ... and if you ask me, evil is a perfectly reasonable description of someone like that.

There are some who say you shouldn't be rude about old people and there is a certain amount of truth in that. I'd be the first person to help an old lady across the road, for example, even if she didn't want to go. But at the same time, we have to be careful. Being old doesn't necessarily make you right and there have been some very old people who have been very bad indeed. Look at Mr Mugabe, the President of Zimbabwe, who (at the time of writing) is 84 and about as horrible as it is possible to be. Do we need to be polite about him? Or what about Livia, the Roman Empress who poisoned her husband when she was 65? Or even Mr Burns in *The Simpsons*?

No. I see absolutely nothing wrong in poking fun at the elderly if they deserve it. And I would have poked a great deal more at my grandmother (sharp sticks, flaming torches) if I'd been given the chance.

In fact she died when she was 93 and I'm glad to

think that although she never made anyone laugh when she was alive – I never once heard her tell a joke – she has amused a lot of people as a character in this book. Because, despite my own feelings, *Granny* is supposed to be funny. It's always been my belief that the best way to weaken your enemies, whether they're bullies, politicians or unpleasant relatives, is to laugh at them.

Anyway, a lot of this book is based on truth. Thattlebee Hall is a version of White Friars in Stanmore, where I was brought up. The house had a huge garden and a very old gardener called Mr Lampy. Maud Warden is based on my mother who did play Chopin on the piano and bridge on Tuesdays. I really did have to eat those disgusting cream cheese teas when I went to visit my grandmother who lived in a horribly overheated flat in Mayflower Lodge ... I changed the name to Wisteria Lodge in the book. I often went on holidays to Bideford in Devonshire. And even Anthony Lagoon exists. I worked there in my gap year.

All I can say is that I hope you enjoy reading it more than I enjoyed living it. In all honesty, that shouldn't be too hard.

Anthony Horowitz

PROLOGUE:
HEATHROW AIRPORT

The storm broke early in the evening and by seven o'clock it looked as if Heathrow might have to shut down. Runway One had disappeared in the rain. Runway Two was a canal. Half the planes had been delayed and the other half were circling hopelessly above the clouds, waiting their turn to land. The wind had blown an Air France DC10 all the way to Luton while, in a jumbo jet from Tokyo, seventy-nine Japanese passengers had all been sick at the same time. It was a night no one would forget.

The green Mercedes reached the airport at exactly half past seven, skidding round a corner and spraying water over two traffic wardens, a porter and a visitor from Norway. Swerving across the road, it missed a taxi by inches and rocketed into the car park of Terminal

Three. The electric side window slid down and a hand with a signet ring and the initials GW entwined in gold reached out to pluck a parking ticket from the machine. Then the car jumped forward again, shot up three ramps with the tyres screaming and crashed into a wall. Ten thousand pounds' worth of metal and paintwork crumpled in on itself. The engine died. Steam hissed from beneath the bent and broken bonnet.

The doors of the car opened and three people got out. The driver was a short, bald man. Next to him was a woman in a fur coat. The back seat had been occupied by a twelve-year-old boy.

"You told me to park on the fourth floor!" the man screamed. "The fourth floor!"

"Yes, Gordon..." the woman muttered.

"But this car park's only got three floors!" the man moaned. He pointed at the wreck of his car. "And now look what's happened!"

"Oh, Gordon..." The woman's lips quivered. For a moment she looked terrified. Then she blinked. "Does it really matter?" she asked.

The man stared at her. "You're right!" he exclaimed. He laughed out loud. "It doesn't matter at all! We're leaving the car here! We'll never see it again...!"

The man and the woman rushed into each other's arms, kissed each other and then grabbed their luggage, which the boy had meanwhile taken out of the boot. They had only two suitcases between them and these looked as if they had been packed in a hurry. Part of a pink silk tie, a striped pyjama leg and a frilly shower cap were poking out of one side.

"Come on!" the man exclaimed. "Let's go..."

But just then there was a flash of lightning and an explosion of thunder and the three of them froze, alone in the middle of the dimly lit car park. A plane roared past overhead.

"Oh, Gordon..." the woman whimpered.

"It's all right," Gordon snapped. "She's not here. Keep your hair on. We're going to be all right. I'd keep my hair on except I packed it..."

"Come on. We've got to get the tickets," the boy said. And without waiting for his parents he began to walk towards the lifts.

Ten minutes later, the family was queuing up at the British Airways ticket desk. After the darkness of the storm, the building was unnaturally bright, like a television set with the colour turned up too much. There were people everywhere, milling around with their suitcases and carrier bags. A policeman with a machine gun patrolled the area. He was the only person smiling.

"Good evening, sir." The man at the ticket desk was in his early twenties with close-cropped hair and tired eyes. He had his name – OWEN – on a badge on his chest but in his tiredness he had pinned it on upside down. "Can I help you?"

"You certainly can, Nemo," the man said, squinting at the badge. "I want three flights..."

"Three flights, sir?" Owen coughed. He had never seen such nervous-looking passengers. They all looked as if they had just come off the worst fairground ride in the world. "Where to?" he asked.

"America," the man replied.

"Africa," the woman said at the same moment.

"Australia," the boy exclaimed.

"Anywhere!" the man said. "Just so long as it leaves soon."

"And it's got to be far away!" the woman added.

"Well, sir..." Owen swallowed. "It would help if you actually knew where you wanted to go..."

The man leaned forward, his eyes wild and staring. (They weren't staring in quite the same direction, which made him look even more wild.) His clothes were expensive – tailor-made – but the ticket salesman couldn't help noticing that he had dressed in a hurry. His tie was crooked and, more surprisingly, on the wrong side of his neck.

"I just want to go away," the man hissed, "before *she* gets here."

The woman burst into tears and tried to hide her face in her mink coat. The boy began to tremble. The ticket-seller's eyes flickered to the computer screen in front of him. The computer screen flickered back. "How about the nine o'clock flight to Perth?" he suggested.

"Scotland!" The man screamed the word so loudly that several passengers turned to look at him and the policeman dropped his machine gun.

"Australia," the ticket-seller said.

"Perthect!" the man exclaimed. He snapped a gold Visa card onto the counter. "We'll have two tickets first class and one in tourist for the boy. Ow!" The man cried out as his wife's elbow caught him on the side of his head. "All right," he said, rubbing a red mark above his eye. "We'll all go first class together."

"Certainly, sir." The ticket-seller picked up the credit card. "Mr Gordon Warden?"

"Yes. That's me."

"And the child's name?"

"Jordan Warden."

"Jordan Warden." The ticket-seller tapped the name into the computer. "And your wife...?"

"Maud N. Warden," the woman said.

"Gordon Warden. Jordan Warden. Maud N. Warden. Right..." He tapped some more buttons and waited as the machine spat out three tickets. "Check in at Desk 11. And it'll be Gate 6 for boardin' Mr Warden."

Five hours later, British Airways Flight 777 took off for Perth in Western Australia. As the plane reached the end of the runway and lurched upwards into the swirling night and rain, Gordon Warden and his wife sank back into their first class seats. Mr Warden began to giggle. "We've done it," he said in a quivering voice. "We've beaten her..."

"How do you know she's not on the plane?" his wife asked.

Mr Warden sat bolt upright. "Stewardess!" he called. "Bring me a parachute!"

Just across the aisle, Jordan strained in the soft half-light to get a sight of the other passengers. Had they really done it? Or were they going to see that terrible, wrinkled face turning slowly to leer at them in the crowded cabin?

The plane reached thirty thousand feet and turned south on the first leg of its journey across the world.

The events that had begun nine months before were finally over.

GRANNY'S FOOTSTEPS

Nine months before, the Wardens had been a wealthy and – to all appearances – happy family living in a large house in North London. The house was called Thattlebee Hall.

It was a huge place with eleven bedrooms, five living-rooms, three staircases and about a mile of thickly-carpeted corridors. You could have played tennis in one of the bathrooms – which was something Mr and Mrs Warden occasionally did, quite naked, using the soap as a ball. It was also very easy to get lost. One man – who had come to read the gas meter – actually stayed there for three days before anyone noticed him, and that was only because he had parked his gas van in the hall.

The family occupied the main body of the house.

There was a nanny, Mrs Jinks, with rooms on the top floor. The west wing was occupied by two Hungarian servants – Wolfgang and Irma. And there was even a smaller house at the bottom of the garden where the gardener, a very old man called Mr Lampy, lived with two cats and a family of moles that he had been too kind-hearted to gas.

Gordon Warden, the head of the family, was a short and rather plump man in his early fifties. He was of course extremely wealthy. "My suits are tailor-made, my private yacht is sailor-made and I drink champagne like lemonade." This was something he often liked to say. He smoked cigars that were at least eight inches long even though he could seldom get to the last inch without being sick. His wife, Maud, also smoked – cigarettes in her case. Sometimes, at dinner, there would be so much smoke in the room that they would be unable to see each other and guests would be gasping for fresh air by the time coffee was served.

They also saw very little of their only child. They were not cruel people but the fact was that there was no room for children in their world. To Mr Warden, children meant runny noses, illnesses and noise – which is why he employed a nanny, at great expense, to handle all that for him. Even so, he always made sure he spent at least five minutes with Jordan when he got home in the evening. He nearly always remembered his birthday. And he would smile pleasantly if he happened to pass his son in the street.

Mr Warden was a businessman but he never spoke about his business. This was because it was almost certainly illegal. Nobody knew exactly what he did but some things were certain. If Mr Warden saw a policeman approaching he would dive into the bushes, and he seldom went anywhere without a luxurious false moustache. Mr Warden loved luxury. As well as the made-to-measure suits, he had a liking for silk shirts and shoes made from endangered species. He had a gold tie, a gold signet ring and three gold teeth. He was particularly proud of the teeth and as a special sign of affection had left them to his wife in his will.

Maud Warden did not work. She had never worked, not even at school, and as a consequence could not read or write. She was however a very fine bridge player. She played bridge twice a week, went out to lunch three times a week, and went riding on the days that were left. To amuse herself, she had piano lessons, tennis lessons and trapeze lessons. Sometimes to please her husband she would play a Chopin nocturne or a Beethoven sonata. But he actually much preferred it when she put on her spangly leotard and swung in the air, suspended from the ceiling by her teeth.

The Wardens had one child and weren't even certain quite how they had ended up with him. Although he had been christened Jordan Morgan Warden, he liked to call himself Joe.

Joe did not like his parents. He didn't like the house, the garden, the cars, the huge meals, the cigarette smoke ... any of it. It was as if he had been born in a prison cell, a very comfortable one certainly, but a prison nonetheless. All day long he dreamed of escaping. One day he would be a trapeze artist in a circus, the next a flier in the Royal Air Force. He dreamed of running away to Bosnia and becoming a relief worker or hiking to the very north of Scotland and looking after sheep. He wanted to be hungry, to feel cold, to have adventures and to know danger and he was angry because he knew that so long as he was a child none of this would be his.

The strange truth is that many rich children have a much worse life and are much less happy than poor children. This was certainly the case for Joe.

To look at, he was a rather short boy with dark hair and a round face. He had brown eyes but when he was day-dreaming they would soften and turn almost blue. Joe had very few friends, and what friends he did have were unfortunately just like him, locked up in their own homes and gardens. The two people closest to him were Mrs Jinks, his nanny, and Mr Lampy, the gardener. Often he would go down to the bottom of the garden and sit in the old shed with the two cats and the family of moles and the strange smell of gin that always hovered in the air.

"Next week I'm going," he would say. "I'm really going. I'm going to join the Foreign Legion. Do you think they take twelve-year-olds?"

"I wouldn't join the Foreign Legion, Master Warden,"

the gardener would reply. "Too many foreigners for me."

"Don't call me 'Master Warden'! My name is Joe."

"That's right, Master Warden. That's what it is."

This, then, was life at Thattlebee Hall. But there was one other member of the family. She didn't live with the Wardens but she was somehow never far away. And the whole family, everything, would change with her coming. Even the sound of her footsteps approaching the front door would be enough to trigger it off. *Scrunch ... scrunch ... scrunch.* Suddenly the sun would seem to have gone in and the shadows would stretch out like a carpet unrolling to welcome the new arrival.

Granny.

She always came to the house by taxi and she never gave the driver a tip. She was a short woman and every year she seemed a little shorter. She had wiry silver hair which looked all right from a distance – only when you got closer could you see right through to the speckled pink surface of her skull. Her clothes, even on the hottest summer day, were thick and heavy, as were her spectacles. These were enormous with bright gold frames and two different sorts of glass. Once, just for a joke, Joe tried them on. He was still bumping into things two weeks later.

Her real name was Ivy Kettle (she was Mrs Warden's mother) but nobody had called her that since she had turned seventy. From that time on she had simply been Granny. Not Grandma. Not Grandmother. Just Granny.

Somehow it suited her.

There was a time when Joe had liked his granny and had looked forward to her visits. She seemed to take a real interest in him – more so than his own parents – and she was always winking and smiling at him. Often she would give him sweets or fifty pence pieces. But as he grew older, he had begun to notice things about his granny that he had not noticed before.

First there were the physical details: the terrible caves in her wrists where the skin seemed to sag underneath the veins, the blotchy patches on her legs, the whiskers on her upper lip and the really quite enormous mole on her chin. She had no dress sense whatsoever. She had, for example, worn the same coat for *twenty-seven years* and it had probably been second-hand when she bought it. Granny was very mean to everyone. But she was meanest to herself. She never bought any new clothes. She never went to the cinema. She said she would prefer to wait and see the films on video even though she was far too mean to buy a machine to play them on. She had a pet cat which she never fed. Tiddles was so thin that one day it was attacked by a budgerigar and that was the last time it was ever seen. As for the money and sweets that she gave Joe, Mrs Warden had actually slipped them to her when she arrived. It was simply an arrangement to make Joe like Granny more.

Then there were her table manners. Although it's a sad thing to say, Granny's table manners would have made a cannibal sick. She had a large mouth framed by some of the yellowest teeth in the world. These teeth were stumpy and irregular, slanting at odd angles, and actually wobbled in her gums when she laughed. But how hard they worked! Granny would eat at a fantastic rate, shovelling food in with a fork, lubricating it with a quick slurp of water and then swallowing it with a little sucking noise and a final hiccup. Sitting at the table, she would remind you of a cement mixer at a building site and watching her eat was both fascinating and repulsive at the same time.

Another aspect of her bad table manners was her tendency to steal the silver. After lunch with Granny, Mr Warden would insist on a spoon count. Wolfgang and Irma would spend hours in the pantry checking off the pieces that remained against the pieces that had been laid and then writing down a long list of what would have to be replaced. When Granny left the house at half past four or whenever, her twenty-seven-year-old coat would be a lot bulgier than when she arrived, and as she leaned over to kiss Joe goodbye, he would hear the clinking in her pockets. On one occasion, Mrs Warden embraced her mother too enthusiastically and actually impaled herself on a fruit knife. After that, Mr Warden installed a metal detector in the front door which did at least help.

But nobody in the family ever mentioned this – either to each other or to anyone else. Mr Warden was never rude to his mother-in-law. Mrs Warden was always pleased to see her. Nobody acted as if anything was wrong.

Joe became more and more puzzled about this – and more confused about his own feelings. He supposed he loved her. Didn't all children love their grandparents? But *why* did he love her? One day he tackled Mrs Jinks on the subject.

"Do you like Granny, Mrs Jinks?" he asked.

"Of course I do," his nanny replied.

"But why? She's got wrinkled skin. Her teeth are horrible. And she steals the knives and forks."

Mrs Jinks frowned at him. "That's not her fault," she said. "She's old..."

"Yes. But..."

"There is no but." Mrs Jinks gave him the sort of look that meant either a spoonful of cod-liver oil or a hot bath. "Always remember this, Joe," she went on. "Old people are special. You have to treat them with respect and never make fun of them. Just remember! One day you'll be old too..."

LOVE FROM GRANNY

If Joe had doubts about Granny, the Christmas of his twelfth year was when they became horrible certainties.

Christmas was always a special time at Thattlebee Hall: specially unpleasant, unfortunately. For this was when the whole family came together and Joe found himself surrounded by aunts and uncles, first cousins and second cousins – none of whom he particularly liked. And it wasn't just him. None of them liked each other either and they always spent the whole day arguing and scoring points off each other. One Christmas they had actually had a fight in the course of which Aunty Nita had broken Uncle David's nose. Since then, all the relations came prepared and as they trooped into the house, the metal detector would bleep like crazy, picking up the knives, crowbars and knuckle-dusters that they had concealed in their clothes.

Joe had four cousins who were only a few years older than him but who never spoke to him. They were very fat, with ginger hair and freckles and pink legs that oozed out of tight, short trousers, like sausages out of a sausage machine. They were terribly spoiled of course, and always very rude to Joe. This was one of the reasons he didn't like them. But the main one was that Joe realized that if his parents had their way, he would end up just like them. They were reflections of him in a nightmare, distorted mirror.

But the star of Christmas Day was Granny. She was the head of the family and always came a day early, on Christmas Eve, to spend the night in the house. Joe would watch as the house was prepared for her coming.

First the central heating would be turned up. It would be turned up so high that by eleven o'clock all the plants had died and the windows were so steamed up that the outside world had disappeared. Then her favourite chair would be moved into her favourite place with three cushions – one for her back, one for her neck and one for her legs. A silver dish of chocolates would be placed on a table, carefully selected so only the soft centres remained. And a large photograph of her in a gold frame would be taken out of the cupboard under the stairs and placed in the middle of the mantelpiece.

This had been happening every year for twelve years. But this year Joe noticed other things too. And he was puzzled.

First of all, Irma and Wolfgang were both in a bad mood. At breakfast, Irma burned the toast whilst Wolfgang spent the whole morning sulking, muttering to himself in Hungarian, which is a sulky enough language at the best of times. His parents were irritable too. Mrs Warden bit her nails. Mr Warden bit Mrs Warden. By midday they had consumed an entire bottle of whisky between them, including the glass.

Joe had seen this sort of behaviour before. It was always the same when Granny came to visit. But it was only now that he began to wonder. Were they like this *because* Granny was coming? Could it be that they didn't actually want to see her at all?

It was seven o'clock on the evening of Christmas Eve when Granny finally arrived. She had told Mr Warden that she would be coming at lunch and Wolfgang had been dutifully waiting at the door since then. When the taxi did finally draw up, the unfortunate man was so covered in snow that only his head was showing and he was too cold to announce she was there. It was a bad start.

"I've been waiting out here for ten minutes," Granny muttered as Mrs Warden opened the door after just two. "Really, dear. You know this weather doesn't agree with me. I'm going to have to go to bed straight away – although goodness knows I won't sleep. This house is far too cold."

"What are you thinking of, Wolfgang?" Mrs Warden sighed, gazing at the blue nose and forehead which was just about all she could see of her faithful Hungarian servant.

Granny stepped into the house, leaving her luggage on the drive where the taxi driver had dumped it.

"A little brandy?" Mrs Warden suggested.

"A large one."

Granny stood in the hall waiting for someone to help her off with her coat and at the same time examining her surroundings with a critical eye. Mr Warden had recently bought a new Picasso of which he was very proud. It hung by the door and she noticed it now. "I don't think very much of that, dear. Too many squiggles and it doesn't go with the wallpaper."

"But Mummy, it's a Picasso!"

"A piano? Don't be ridiculous. It doesn't look anything like a piano." Granny could be deaf when she wanted to be. At other times she could hear a pin drop half a mile away. She moved towards the living-room then suddenly stopped and pointed. "But I like that very much," she said. "How original! And what a lovely colour!"

"But Mummy. That's not a painting. That's a damp patch."

Joe had watched all this from the first floor landing but hearing Mrs Jinks opening a door behind him, he realized he had to show himself. Quickly he stood up and went down the stairs.

"Hello, James!" Granny cooed. "You've put on a lot of weight!"

"My name's Joe, not James," Joe said. He was sensitive about his name. And his weight.

"No, it's not. It's Jordan," his mother said. "Really Jordan! Joe is so common!"

"Jordan? That's what I said," Granny interjected. "Haven't you grown, Jordan! What a big boy you are! What a big boy!" And with these words, Granny went into a "spread".

Joe shuddered. The spread was the word he used to describe what Granny was doing now. It was the one thing he dreaded most.

The spread was the position Granny took when she wanted to be kissed. She widened her legs and crouched down slightly with her arms open as if she wanted him to jump onto her knees and maybe even onto her shoulders. Of course, if Joe had done this, Granny would have broken into several pieces as she was over ninety years old and very frail. And with the spread came the terrible words... "Aren't you going to give your grandma a kiss, then?"

Joe swallowed hard. He was aware that his mother was watching him and that he had to be careful what he did. But at the same time he hated what he knew he had to do.

Kissing Granny was not a pleasant experience. First there was the smell. Like many old ladies, she wore an expensive perfume that was very sweet and very musty and, if you got too close to it, made you feel a little sick. There were no labels on her perfume bottles but this one might have been called "Decomposing Sheep". Then there was her make-up. Granny wore a lot of make-up. Sometimes she put it on so thickly that you could have drawn a picture in it with your thumbnail. Her lipstick was the worst bit. It was bright blood red and no matter how carefully Joe tried, he always came away with a glowing mirror-image of Granny's lips on his cheek. Nobody knew what make of lipstick Granny used, but Mrs Jinks could only get it off him with a Brillo pad.

But worst of all was her skin. As well as kissing her grandson, Granny insisted on his kissing her and her skin was as withery as a punctured balloon. No words could describe the feel of her skin against his lips, actually flapping slightly between the upper and the lower lip at the moment of kissing. One night Joe had woken up screaming. He had just had a nightmare in which he had kissed Granny too enthusiastically and had actually swallowed her whole.

Smack! Granny kissed Joe.

Smeruberry smack! Joe kissed Granny.

Then, with a satisfied smile, she continued into the living-room. Outside, Irma was pouring hot water over Wolfgang to thaw him so that he could carry in the cases. Mr Warden was nowhere to be seen. This was something else that had puzzled Joe – how his father was never around when Granny arrived. The year before, Joe had found him hiding inside the grand piano and he was there now. He could tell from the cigar smoke coming out of the keyboard.

Granny sat down in the chair that had been chosen for her. It was one of those old-fashioned wing chairs and she always sat in it even though her legs couldn't touch the ground, with the result that you could see straight up her dress. Not that you would look. Your eyes would stray up to her bulging knees wrapped in what looked like surgical stockings, and then beyond to the yellowing flesh of her thighs. And that would be enough. Her legs were like a set out of *Dr Who*.

Mrs Warden had poured a large brandy. Granny swallowed it in a single gulp. "Where's Gordon?" she asked, glancing suspiciously at the piano.

"I don't know..." Mrs Warden faltered.

"I can see him, Maud darling. I'm not blind you know..."

Mr Warden came out of the piano, hitting his head on the lid with an echoing thud. "I was tuning it," he explained.

"I'll have another brandy please, dear. And do you have anything other than this cooking brandy?"

"Cooking brandy?" Mr Warden exploded. "That's Remy Martin. From Harrods."

"And I'm sure the Arabs love it," Granny replied, either mishearing him or pretending to. "But it burns my throat."

Nobody slept well that night. The trouble was, Granny was a terrible snorer. At dinner she had complained of a touch of indigestion and an upset stomach after having been kept waiting in the cold and so she was only able to manage three portions of lamb stew, two portions of lemon mousse and half a bottle of wine. Finally she had tottered off to bed and ten minutes later her snores were resounding through the house. Even in the vast surroundings of Thattlebee Hall there was no escaping it. Joe went to sleep with his head buried under five pillows. Mrs Warden finally managed to drop off after squeezing a wax candle into each ear. Mr Warden didn't sleep at all. In the morning there were huge bags under his eyes – and even huger ones on the bedroom floor, which he was busily packing. It took Mrs Warden half an hour and a fountain of tears to persuade him not to move into a hotel.

But it was Christmas Day: the snow sparkled in the garden and the church bells rang. Santa Claus had visited, the smell of turkey wafted through the house and everyone was in a good mood. Even the arrival of all the relations and the terrible crash as Uncle Michael's Volvo accidentally reversed into Uncle Kurt's Rover couldn't completely spoil the scene. The Wardens always waited for everyone to arrive before they opened their presents. Now the whole family repaired to the Christmas tree. Wolfgang, Irma and Mrs Jinks came in to join them and Mr Warden served champagne and orange juice – champagne for his wife and himself, orange juice for everyone else. It was a happy moment. Even Granny was smiling as she tottered out of the breakfast room and took her place in her favourite chair.

Joe found himself sitting between his Uncle David and one of his cousins. There were about fifteen people in the room but as he looked around, he found himself concentrating only on Granny. She was sitting in her usual place, smiling, her legs dangling a few inches above the carpet. Joe gazed at her. Was he imagining it, or was there something strange about Granny's smile? It was as if she were enjoying some secret joke. He had thought at first that she was looking out of the window but now he realized that her eyes were fixed on him. Occasionally her lips quivered and as the presents were handed out she couldn't hold back a soft and high-pitched giggle.

"This is for you, Jordan."

His father had handed him a present from under the tree. Joe flipped open the label on the top and immediately recognized the large, spidery handwriting.

TO JORDAN. LOVE FROM GRANNY.

Now although there were many presents for Joe under the tree, this was one he was particularly looking forward to and, holding it in his hands, he suddenly felt ashamed. A moment ago he had been looking at his granny as if she were ... what? Some sort of monster!

But he couldn't have been more wrong. She was just a kind old lady, surrounded by her family, enjoying the day. And she loved him. The proof of it was in his hands.

Joe loved science fiction. He had seen *Star Wars* three times and had dozens of books about aliens and space travel on his bedroom shelves. But what he liked best of all was robots – and when Granny had asked him what he wanted for Christmas that was what he had said. He had actually seen one in Hamley's – about half a metre high and packed with all the latest Japanese micro-circuitry. You had to assemble it yourself – and that was the challenge – but when it was finished it would walk, talk, lift and carry ... all by radio-control. And there it was now in front of him. Joe recognized Granny's gift-wrap at once. It was actually wedding paper – she was always economizing like that. It was a large, rectangular box, just the size it should have been. As his fingers tore through the paper he could feel the cardboard underneath. Then the paper was off. The box was open. And his heart and stomach shrank.

The robot was the sort of thing you might give to a two-year-old. It was made of brightly coloured plastic with a stupid, painted face and the name, HANK, written in large letters on its chest. Radio control? It had a key sticking out of its back. Wind it up and it would stagger a few inches across the carpet and fall over, whirring and kicking its legs uselessly. Suddenly Joe realized that everyone was looking at him: his aunts and uncles, Wolfgang, Irma, Mrs Jinks. His four cousins were nudging each other and sniggering. They were all thinking the same thing.

A baby toy! What a baby!

"Do you like it, dear?"

He heard his granny's voice and looked up. And that was when he finally knew. There was something in her face that he had never seen before and now that he had noticed it he would never be able to see her any other way again. It was like one of those optical illusions you sometimes find in cereal packets. You look at a picture one way but then you suddenly notice something different and you can never see it again the same way.

He was right.

She had done it on purpose.

She knew exactly what he wanted and she had gone out and deliberately chosen this baby toy to humiliate him in front of the entire family. Of course, his mother would try to explain that Granny meant well and that she hadn't understood what he wanted. He would be made to write a thank you letter and every lying word would hurt him. But at that moment, looking at her, he knew the truth. He could see it in the wicked glimmer in her eyes, in the half-turned corner of her mouth. And it was so strong, so horrible that he shivered.

She was *evil*. For reasons that he did not yet understand, Granny hated him and wanted to hurt him in any way she could.

Joe shivered.

He knew the truth about Granny even if nobody else in the room could see it. But that wasn't what frightened him.

What frightened him was that Granny knew he knew. And she didn't care.

Maybe she knew that whatever Joe said, nobody would believe him. Or maybe it was something worse. Watching her, hunched up in the middle of the Christmas gauze and glitter, her eyes sliding slowly from left to right, he realized she was planning something. And that something included him.

TEA WITH GRANNY

A few weeks later, Granny invited Joe to tea. She always used to do this towards the end of the holidays but curiously neither Mr nor Mrs Warden were ever available. Mr Warden was at work. And Mrs Warden – who was now having lessons in Chinese cookery – was at wok. And so Mrs Jinks was the only one left to take him.

Up until now, Joe would have quite looked forward to seeing his Granny. But not any more. He knew now, and even the thought of her filled him with dread.

"I don't want to go," he told Mrs Jinks as she got into the car.

"Why ever not, Jordan? You know how your granny looks forward to seeing you."

Yes. Like a fox looks forward to seeing chickens,

Joe thought. "I don't like her," he said.

"That's a cruel thing to say."

"I think *she's* cruel..."

"Now that's quite enough of that!" Mrs Jinks sniffed. "I suppose you're still thinking about that silly Christmas present. It was a misunderstanding, that's all."

Joe had set fire to the misunderstanding. He had taken the toy robot to the bottom of the garden and poured lighter fuel over it and then put a match to it. He and old Mr Lampy had watched as it melted, the plastic bubbling and blistering and the colours running into each other so that for a moment it did look like some alien creature before it shrivelled into a black and sticky puddle.

The old gardener had shaken his head. "You shouldn't ought to have done that, Master Warden."

"Why not?"

"It should've gone to a charity shop or a hospital. I'm sure there was someone somewhere who'd have wanted it."

And Joe had felt a twinge of guilt. But it was too late. The robot was gone.

Granny lived in a flat in a tall, modern block called Wisteria Lodge. This was what the estate agents would have called a purpose-built block, although they might not be able to say what its purpose actually was. Perhaps it was simply to house grannies, as hardly anyone in the building was under seventy years of age. Everything in Wisteria Lodge happened in slow motion. The lift had been specially adapted to go so slowly that you couldn't feel it moving. On one occasion it broke down and Mr and Mrs Warden stood in it for three-quarters of an hour before they realized what had happened.

Granny's flat was on the sixth floor with views over a small field and the traffic on the North Circular Road. Once she had lived in a comfortable house in a tree-lined avenue but when that had got too much for her to handle, her daughter had moved her here. It was actually a very pleasant flat with silk curtains, thick carpets, antique furniture and chandeliers but if you asked her about it Granny would shrug and sigh, "Well, I have to put up with it. I don't have any choice, do I? Oh dear, oh dear. I don't know..." And she would look so sorry for herself that you would forget that there were thousands of old people in far smaller places with no heating and no real comfort who would have given their right arm to live here.

"Hello, Jack. How lovely to see you! Come in. Make yourselves comfortable!"

Waves of pure heat shimmered in the air as Jordan stepped unwillingly into the flat, Mrs Jinks gently pushing him from behind. The central heating was on full all the time. Granny had once been given a six-inch cactus by Mr Warden after a business trip to the Sahara and obviously the intense heat suited it for it was now over eleven feet high, dominating the room with brilliant flowers and vicious spikes.

"Come in, Mrs Jinks. What an unusual hat!"

"I'm not wearing a hat, Mrs Kettle."

"Then if I were you, I'd change my hairdresser."

Granny moved forward and stooped over Jordan. "So how are you, my dear?" She reached out with a gnarled finger and prodded his cheek. "Healthy skin. Healthy colour. Full of vitamins?" She winked at Mrs Jinks.

"He gets plenty of vitamins," Mrs Jinks replied. Granny's comment about the hat had annoyed her, Joe could see.

"And how are his enzymes?" Granny asked.

"His what?" Mrs Jinks enquired.

"His enzymes! Has he got healthy enzymes? What about his cytoplasm?"

Mrs Jinks shook her head. "I'm sorry, Mrs Kettle," she said. "I don't know what you're talking about."

"Oh, come in!" Granny snarled briefly and jerked a finger into the room.

The table had already been laid for tea and Joe sat down with Mrs Jinks next to him. Briefly, he scanned the food that lay before him. There it was, the same as always. It was incredible. How could a tea possibly be so vile?

First, there were egg mayonnaise sandwiches, but the eggs had been left out so long that the yellows had taken on a greenish tint and they had so much salt in them that they made your eyes water. Then there was herring on a plate – raw and slippery and soused in some sort of particularly sharp vinegar. Granny's homemade cakes were dry and heavy, guaranteed to glue the top of your mouth to the bottom of your mouth with little taste in between. Even the biscuits were horrible: round, colourless things with neither chocolate nor cream but decorated with almond flakes and bits of desiccated cherry that got caught in your teeth.

But by far the worst item on the table was Granny's cream cheese special. Joe caught sight of it and felt his mouth water unpleasantly and his stomach shrivel as if trying to find somewhere to hide. Granny's cream cheese special consisted of just one thing: cream cheese. That was all it was: a big bowl of cream cheese – and he knew that he would be expected to eat it all.

And he couldn't refuse it – that was the worst of it. It was part of his upbringing. Mr Warden insisted that children shouldn't be allowed to leave the table until they had finished everything they had been given. After all, food cost money and the money was his. As a child, Mr Warden had once remained at the table for an astonishing forty-six hours before he had finally given in and agreed to eat a plate of bread-and-butter pudding that his father had given him. The fact of the matter is that the worst thing about parents is often their parents. That's certainly where they get their most rotten ideas.

"I'll just get some serviettes..."

Granny hobbled off into the kitchen and Joe quickly turned to Mrs Jinks.

"I can't eat this," he said.

"Of course you can," Mrs Jinks replied. But she didn't sound convinced.

"No! Can't you see? She's done it on purpose. She's chosen all the things I can't stand and she's put them here because she knows you'll make me eat them. She's torturing me!"

"Joe – you're going to get a big smack if you go on like this."

"Why won't you believe me?" The whole conversation had taken place in whispers but these last words rasped in his throat. "She hates me!"

"She loves you. She's your granny!"

Then Granny returned from the kitchen carrying some faded paper serviettes. "Not started yet?" she croaked, grinning at Joe.

She put the serviettes down and picked up a green porcelain bowl, filled to the brim with thick cream cheese. Then she forked out a raw herring and laid it on the top. "That'll give it extra taste," she cackled. Finally she slid the whole thing towards him and as she did so Joe saw the trembling half-smile on her lips, the rattlesnake eyes that pinned him to his seat. Her long, knobbly fingers with their uneven, yellow nails were scratching at the tablecloth with sheer excitement. Her whole body was coiled up like a spring.

"Now, eat it all up, dear!"

Joe looked at Mrs Jinks but she turned away as if unwilling to meet his eyes. He looked at the cream cheese, slooping about in the bowl with the herring lying there like a dead slug. Suddenly his mind was made up.

He pushed the bowl away.

"No, thank you," he said. "I'm not hungry."

"What?" Granny gurgled. She had been taken off guard and jerked in her seat as if she had just sat on a drawing pin. "But..." Her mouth opened and shut. "What's the matter...? Mrs Jinks...!"

This was what Joe had been most afraid of. Whose side would Mrs Jinks take? And Mrs Jinks herself seemed unsure.

"Aren't you hungry?" she asked.

"No," Joe said.

"Can't you manage a little bit?"

"I'm not feeling well."

"Well, in that case..." Mrs Jinks turned apologetically to Granny. "If he's not well..." she began.

Granny's face shimmered. It was like looking at a reflection in the sea. One moment there was a look of absolute rage and hatred, the sort of look soldiers must have seen before they were bayoneted by the enemy. But then, with a huge effort, Granny managed to wipe it away, replacing it with a look of hurtful sadness. Huge crocodile tears welled up in her eyes. Her lips drew back and puckered like a healing wound.

"But darling," she said. "I spent the whole morning

getting it ready. It's your favourite."

"No, it's not," Joe said. "I don't like it."

"But you've always liked it! Have you been eating chocolate and crisps? Have you spoiled your appetite? Is that it? Mrs Jinks..."

What was happening at the table was completely unheard of. It was like that moment in *Oliver Twist* when Oliver asks for more – only in reverse as Joe was asking for less. And normally all hell would have broken loose. But Mrs Jinks had seen the look on Granny's face, the full force of her hatred. Like Joe, she had glimpsed behind the mask – and now she was taking Joe's side.

"Joe's not hungry," she said.

"Have a drink!" Granny trilled. "I've got some hot Ribena in the kitchen."

"No, thank you." Joe only liked Ribena cold. For some reason, once it was heated up it went all sweet and sticky.

"How about a nice lemon and honey milkshake?"

"No," Joe insisted.

"I could sprinkle some nutmeg on the top!"

"No, thank you."

"I think I'll take Joe home," Mrs Jinks said. She wasn't as clever as Granny at hiding her emotions. It was obvious that she wanted to get away.

Granny saw it too. Slowly the anger crept back into her cheeks. Her little eyes widened and there was a soft yellow glow in what should have been their whites.

"This is your fault, Mrs Jinks," she hissed.

"Mine?" Mrs Jinks was indignant.

"You're not bringing the boy up properly. Filling him up with sweets and biscuits..."

"I did no such thing, Mrs Kettle."

"Then why won't he eat? Why won't he eat?" Granny gesticulated with a trembling fist. The edge of her wrist caught one of the bowls of cream cheese and it flew off the table, landing with a loud plop in her lap. "Now look what you've made me do!" She got up and took two steps back from the table. It was a mistake. She had forgotten the cactus. "Aaaagh!" Granny leapt three feet in the air as she came into contact with the spikes, then collapsed in a heap on the floor. Her dress was covered in cream cheese. Her face was quite purple with anger.

Joe had never seen anything like it. It was wonderful and terrifying at the same time. What was Granny going to do? Was she going to mutter the magic words that would turn Mrs Jinks into a spotted toad? Or – more likely – was she merely going to succumb to a massive heart attack?

In the end, she did neither. She got to her feet, took a deep breath and shrivelled back into an old, defeated woman.

"All right," she muttered with a sigh. "Take him home. Leave me here on my own. I don't mind. I'll just sit by myself and maybe do some knitting."

Granny had never knitted anything in her life.

Except, maybe, her brow.

And so they left. Mrs Jinks hurried Joe out of the flat and into the lift – although of course that meant the two of them had to spend another ten minutes standing in awkward silence before they reached the ground. Mrs Jinks was flushed and looked worried. And she had every reason to be.

After they had gone, Granny went to the drinks cabinet and grabbed a bottle of brandy. She pulled the cork out with her teeth (although she very nearly pulled her teeth out with the cork) and took a large swig. Then, feeling better, she went over to the telephone and dialled a number. The phone rang many times before it was answered.

"Hello?" came a thin, quavering voice from the other end.

"Is that Mrs Bucket?"

"Yes. This is Elsie Bucket."

"This is Ivy Kettle speaking."

"Yes, Ivy, dear. How very nice to hear from you." But the voice at the other end sounded faintly bored.

"Listen!" Granny spat the word into the receiver. "I've just had the boy here in my flat. My grandson..."

"Jeremy?" now the voice was a little more interested.

"His name's John! Now listen, Mrs Bucket. I've been thinking about Bideford and I've decided. I'm going to bring him along. For you..."

"How delightful of you, my dear Ivy." The voice

dripped with icy charm.

"There is just one problem..." Granny went on.

"What problem, Ivy?"

"He's got a nanny. A wretched spiteful nanny. I think she may get in our way."

"Then you'll have to deal with her, my dear. Or do you need help?"

"I don't need help, thank you, Mrs Bucket!" Granny scowled and chewed air. A lump of cream cheese slithered off her dress and dripped onto her shoes. "I'll deal with Mrs Jinks," she said at last. "And then the boy will be yours..."

GRANNY VS NANNY

Mrs Jinks liked to say that she belonged to "the old school" which was strange because she had never actually been to school in her life. She had been Joe's nanny for five years – but the truth is that she would never have taken the job in the first place if it hadn't been for a mistake.

Before she had come to Thattlebee Hall, Mrs Jinks had earned her living by dancing. A plump, blonde-haired woman with shapely legs, she worked at a Soho club where she performed exotic dances with a snake called Anna. The owner of the club had a stutter and introducing the snake – "Anna, an anaconda" – sometimes took him three-quarters of an hour. For this reason Mrs Jinks decided to get a new job and this was when the mistake was made.

She applied to be a dancer at another club, The Blue Balloon in Battersea, but in her haste she dialled the wrong number and got through to Mrs Warden. Now, as it happened, Mrs Warden had placed an advertisement in the newspaper that very day. Her current nanny, Miss Barking, had just handed in her notice in order to go and fight in the Gulf War and she herself was about to go on holiday. So she needed somebody fast.

Ten minutes later Mrs Warden had hired Mrs Jinks in the belief that she was a nanny and Mrs Jinks had taken the job in the belief that it was as a dancer. By the time the two of them had realized the mistake it was too late. Mr and Mrs Warden had left for a four-week safari in South Africa. And Mrs Jinks was on her own at home with Joe.

For his part, Joe was quite delighted by the error. Aged seven at the time, he had endured six and a half years of Miss Barking – a woman so tough and so muscular that he had often wondered if she was really a woman at all. There was something very attractive about Mrs Jinks. Maybe it was her round, cheerful face, her loud laugh and her generally unsuitable appearance. Maybe it was her pet snake. But she was unquestionably different.

So in the next four weeks Joe taught her everything he knew about nannying – and the fact is that at the end of the day children know more about nannying than nannies themselves. He took her to the library and together they browsed through books such as

Childcare Made Easy and *Tips for Top Nannies*. He took her through such activities as bathing, dressing and tidying. He even showed her how to tell him off.

The result was that when Mr and Mrs Warden returned from their safari, they found the house more organized and tidier and Joe cleaner and quieter than ever before and the two of them decided to forget how entirely unsuitable the new nanny was.

As for Mrs Jinks, she had soon decided that life as a nanny was much more pleasant than life as an exotic dancer. She smartened her appearance and became a little more severe and soon it was impossible to tell that it was not she who had taught Joe but Joe who had instructed her.

When she had been with the family for one year, Mrs Jinks took a two-week holiday in the Amazon basin where, one evening, she quietly returned her anaconda to the wild. She never spoke about the snake again. But she always kept a photograph of it in a frame beside her bed.

Joe only ever mentioned the tea with Granny once – and that was the following day.

"What's an enzyme?" he asked Mrs Jinks, remembering the word Granny had used.

"I don't know," Mrs Jinks replied, a frown on her face. She sighed. "We'd better look it up."

And so they did. They went to the library and looked up the word in a medical dictionary and this is what it said:

Enzymes. The organic substances which accelerate chemical processes occurring in living organisms. Enzyme mechanisms are the key to all biological processes.

"What does that all mean?" Joe asked.

Mrs Jinks slammed the book. "It doesn't matter," she said. "I don't think your granny knew what she was talking about. We won't mention it again."

But Mrs Jinks was never quite the same after this particular encounter with Granny. There was a worried look in her eyes. Loud noises – a slamming door or a car backfiring – jolted her. Joe got the impression that she was walking a tightrope and was afraid of falling off at any time.

And then the thefts began.

It was the second week in February and Granny had come for lunch. Joe hadn't seen her since the tea and he had been dreading it, but in fact she couldn't have been more pleasant. She gave him a smaller-than-usual kiss and a larger-than-usual present of one pound which hadn't even been given to her by her daughter in the usual way. She ate her lunch without complaining, complimented Irma (who immediately dropped all the dishes) and left all the knives and forks on the table.

It was only as she was leaving, as Wolfgang handed her her twenty-seven-year-old coat, that she let out a sudden scream.

"My cameo brooch!" she exclaimed. Tears welled in her eyes. "My beautiful cameo brooch. It's gone!"

"Are you sure you were wearing it, Mummy?" Mrs Warden asked.

"Of course I'm sure. I put it on specially. It was on the lapel of my coat."

"Well, maybe it's dropped off."

"No, no," Granny wailed. "I pinned it quite securely." She turned to Mrs Jinks. "You didn't happen to see it, did you, Mrs Jinks?" she asked with a quizzical smile.

"No, Mrs Kettle," the nanny replied. Two pin-pricks of pink had appeared in her cheeks. "Why should *I* have seen it?"

"Well..." Granny couldn't have looked more innocent. "You have often admired my cameo brooch. And I did see you looking in the hall cupboard just before lunch."

"Are you suggesting...?" Mrs Jinks didn't know what to say. Her cheeks were now dark red with anger.

"I wasn't suggesting anything," Granny interrupted. She almost sang the words and her whole body was shaking with pleasure. Once again her lips slid away from her teeth in a yellowy smile. "I'm sure Wolfgang will find it in the garden."

But Wolfgang never did find the brooch and the next time Granny came for lunch, the whites of her eyes were quite red from weeping. In fact she was crying so much that instead of her usual tiny lace handkerchief she had brought along a tea towel.

"Never mind, Mumsy," Mrs Warden said. "I'll buy you another one. Don't be so upset. It's only a piece of jewellery."

That was the day that Mrs Warden found her diamond earrings had gone missing. She screamed the house down.

"My earrings, Gordon!" she screeched. "My lovely earrings. They matched my ears! How can they have gone? Oh no...!"

"Someone get her a tea towel," Mr Warden muttered. He was trying to read the *Financial Times*. "And put it in her mouth."

"Were they your diamond earrings, darling?" Granny asked. She was sitting in her usual chair, her face a picture of innocence.

"Yes," Mrs Warden sobbed.

"How sad. You know, Mrs Jinks was saying to me only the other day how much she liked those earrings. What a shame that they've suddenly disappeared..."

Joe was as puzzled as anyone by the thefts but already a nasty thought was forming in his mind. Two thefts. Both had taken place on days when Granny was in the house. And twice Granny had pointed the finger at Mrs Jinks...

That night, Joe got out of bed and crept downstairs. The hall was dark but he could see light spilling out underneath the door of the living-room. He pressed his ear against the wood. As he had thought, his parents were inside.

"Someone must have taken them," Mrs Warden was saying. "They can't have just walked out of the drawer."

"But who?" That was Mr Warden's voice.

"Well, Mummy was saying that Mrs Jinks..."

"Mrs Jinks would never...!"

"I don't know, Gordon. First Mummy's brooch. Now my earrings. And Mrs Jinks *was* in the cupboard."

Joe was half-crouching in the darkness, trying to hear the words through the thick wood. A floorboard creaked just behind him and he spun round as a hand reached out and touched his arm. For a horrible moment he had thought it was Granny, but in fact it was Mrs Jinks who had just come down the stairs. Joe opened his mouth to speak but she touched a finger to her lips and beckoned him back upstairs.

Mrs Jinks led him all the way to the top of the house. Only when she was back in her room with the door shut did she speak.

"Really, Joe!" she scolded him. "I'm sure I've told you something about listening at doors."

Joe sighed. "I was only..."

"I know what you were doing. And it doesn't matter. Sit down."

Joe sat down on the bed. Mrs Jinks sat beside him.

"Listen, my dear," she began. "I don't want to worry you but I think we ought to have a little talk – and I'm not sure if I'll have another opportunity."

"You're not leaving, are you, Mrs Jinks?"

"No, no, no. Not unless I have to. But I wanted to have a word with you about your granny. Just in case..."

Mrs Jinks took a deep breath.

"Did I ever tell you about my time in the Amazon basin?" she asked at last. "That time when I went to release my snake back into the wild?"

"Anna, an anaconda!" Joe exclaimed. Mrs Jinks had often spoken of her snake.

"That's right. Well, I wanted to release her as far away from civilization as I could. People are funny about snakes and I couldn't bear to think of her ending up as a handbag or a pair of shoes or something. So I went to the town of Iquitos, which is on the Amazon river, and paid a fisherman to take me by canoe into the Amazon jungle.

"We sailed for three days, Anna, me and the fisherman. I can't begin to describe that jungle to you. I've never seen anything like it before – so green and so heavy and so silent. You could feel it pressing in on you on all sides. All that vegetation! Only a river as mighty as the Amazon could have managed to find a way through.

"On the third day we turned off into a tributary. By now the town was a long way behind us. There were no huts or anything and I was certain that Anna would be safe. So I took her out of her basket, gave her a kiss, and released her—"

"But what's this got to do with Granny?" Joe asked.

"You'll find out if you don't interrupt!" Mrs Jinks paused. "Anna had gone," she went on, "and I was sitting there in the middle of a clearing feeling rather sorry for myself when suddenly…" She swallowed. "Suddenly the biggest crocodile you've ever seen burst out of the undergrowth and lurched towards me. It must have been at least five metres long. Its scales weren't green (like they are in some of your old picture books) but an ugly grey. And it had the most terrible teeth. Razor sharp and quite revolting. Obviously it had never seen a dentist in its life and if it had it had probably eaten him."

"How come it didn't eat you?" Joe asked.

"Oh, it tried to. But fortunately I was holding my umbrella and managed to force it into the creature's mouth, between its upper and its lower jaw. But that's not the point."

Mrs Jinks drew Joe closer to her.

"I have never forgotten that crocodile's eyes, the way it looked at me. And not long ago I saw another pair of eyes just like them. Exactly the same. And I'm ashamed to say, Joe, that it was your granny's eyes at that tea party of hers. I saw them and quite frankly I would have preferred to have been sitting down with the crocodile."

"So you believe me!" Joe whispered.

"I'm afraid I do."

"But what can we do?"

"There's nothing I can do," Mrs Jinks said, "except to warn you to look after yourself. And remember this, Joe. In the end, the truth will always come out, no matter how long it takes."

Joe pulled away. "You're talking as if you're not going to stay!" he cried.

Mrs Jinks looked at him tiredly. "1 don't know," she said. "I really don't know. But I had to talk to you, Joe. Before it was too late..."

The next theft took place on the following Sunday. This time it was Mr Warden who was the victim. He had dozed off in his chair after lunch and when he woke up he knew at once that something was wrong. And it was. Someone had stolen two of his gold teeth.

"It'th a thcandal!" he cried out, whistling at the same time. There was a large gap at the front of his mouth. "Thith ith a matter for the polithe!"

Granny, of course, was there. As Mr Warden raged and whistled, she shook her head as if she were utterly confused. "Who would want to take two gold teeth?" she asked. "Although now I think about it, Mrs Jinks was telling me how very much she admired them..."

After that, things happened very fast.

The police arrived in two police cars and an unmarked van. This, when it was opened, revealed two of the most ferocious dogs Joe had seen in his life. They were Alsatians, long-haired with thin, angular bodies and evil black eyes. Their tongues were drooling as they began to pad around the house, sniffing suspiciously.

"There's no meat out, is there?" the dog handler asked.

"Meat? No!" Mrs Warden replied.

"Good. It's just that Sherlock and Bones here haven't eaten for five days. It keeps them keen. But I can't let them get a smell of meat."

"Please, officer," Mrs Warden gestured. "My husband is in here..."

The policemen followed her through into the living-room. Irma and Wolfgang went back to the west wing leaving Joe and Mrs Jinks in the hall. Mrs Jinks was looking rather pale.

"I think I'll go and sit outside," she said. "I need the fresh air."

As she moved away, Joe heard a door softly close. Had someone been watching them? Granny? Suddenly worried, without knowing why, he opened the door and followed the passage on the other side all the way down to the kitchen.

There was someone there. Afraid of being seen, he peered round the corner just in time to see Granny climbing down from a cupboard with something in her hand. Now she was moving rapidly towards him and Joe ducked into the larder to hide. He heard a swish of material and caught a whiff of Decomposing Sheep as she passed but then she was gone. What was she doing? What had she taken?

Joe waited until he was sure she had gone before he went back out into the hall but now there was no sign of her. In the living-room, he could hear his father talking to one of the policemen.

"Yeth, offither. They were thtolen when I wath

athleep!"

He went back to the front door and looked out. Mrs Jinks was sitting on a bench at the side of the house and as he watched her, Joe heard a window open on the first floor. He wanted to call out to her but suddenly the two police dogs appeared, lumbering across the lawn, and he shrunk back.

But not before he had seen...

Something was drifting onto Mrs Jinks. At first Joe thought it was raining. But whatever it was was brown. And it was some sort of powder. Mrs Jinks hadn't noticed. She was sitting quietly, deep in thought. The powder sprinkled onto her shoulders, her lap, her hair.

And then the police dogs stopped, their bodies rigid. As Joe stared in horror, their eyes lit up and the hair on their backs began to bristle. The one called Sherlock began to growl. The other one – Bones – was panting; short, quick breaths that rasped in its throat.

Slowly, silently, the two of them closed in on Mrs Jinks.

"Hello, doggies..." Mrs Jinks had seen them. She stood up, noticing for the first time the brown powder that covered her arms and legs. She smelled it. And that must have been when she knew. The colour drained out of her face. Then she screamed, turned and ran.

"Sherlock! Bones!" The police dog handler had seen what was happening but too late. Like two bolts fired from a crossbow, the dogs took off after Mrs Jinks who had already sprinted across the lawn, through an ornamental pond, and who was now making for the bushes.

"Heel!" the police dog handler cried.

One of the police dogs bit Mrs Jinks's heel. Mrs Jinks screamed again and disappeared into the bushes. With a terrible snarling and snapping the dogs fell on top of her.

Joe had watched all this in horror and the rest was just a whirl. He vaguely remembered the policemen racing across the lawn when it was already far too late. He heard them all shouting as they blamed each other for what had happened. Someone must have called an ambulance, for a few minutes later one arrived, but then the stretcher bearers refused to get out until the dogs had been chained and muzzled. He saw Sherlock and Bones being led back to the police van, their heads hanging in disgrace, and saw, with a wave of despair, that they looked a lot fatter than they had been when they arrived.

Later on, he heard – and somehow he wasn't surprised – that the cameo brooch, the earrings and the two gold teeth had all been found in Mrs Jinks's room. They had, however, found nothing of Mrs Jinks apart from a few blood-stained scraps of clothing.

But for Joe, the very worst memory of the day, the one that would keep him awake all of that night and most of the next was of something he had seen in the middle of all the activity. As he stood in the hall he had heard something and had turned round just in time to see Granny coming down the stairs. At that moment, with just the two of them there, the mask was off again and the crocodile smile that Mrs Jinks had described was there for him to see.

But it wasn't the smile that frightened Joe. It was what Granny was holding in her hand, what she had taken from the kitchen a few minutes before.

It was a box of Bisto gravy powder. Without saying a word, Granny hurried past him and went into the kitchen to put it back.

GRANNY MOVES IN

Nobody felt the death of Mrs Jinks more keenly than Joe. It was as if he had lost his only friend – which, in a way, he had. And not only was she dead but she had been branded a thief and that hurt him all the more. "The truth will always come out." That was what she had said to him. But how could he go to his parents or the police and tell them that it was Granny who had taken the jewellery and the gold teeth and that it was she who had killed Mrs Jinks by pouring gravy powder over her when the police dogs were near because ... because... What reason could there possibly be? They would think he was mad.

Every day when he got home from school, Joe found himself on his own. He took to walking down to the bottom of the garden where Mr Lampy would be waiting for him and the two of them would sit together next to a burning brazier with the family of moles watching them through the window of the shed.

"I'm going to run away," he would say. "I'll go to China and work in a paddy-field."

"I don't know, Master Warden," Mr Lampy would reply. "China's a long way away. And who's this Paddy you're talking about?"

Meanwhile, Mr and Mrs Warden had problems of their own. The summer holiday was about to start and that meant the departure of Wolfgang and Irma. Every year the cook and her husband went home to Hungary although, as they only owned a caravan just outside Budapest, Mr Warden would have much preferred it if the home had come to them. What it meant was that for three weeks there would be no cook and no butler. Worse still, Mrs Warden had been unable to find a new nanny to look after Joe even though she'd advertised. The fact that the last nanny had just been eaten by two dogs probably didn't help.

"We've got to find someone to look after Jordan," Mrs Warden said the night after Wolfgang and Irma had gone.

"What? What did you say?" Mr Warden was lying in bed, smoking a cigar and reading *The Economist*.

Mrs Warden pivoted round upside down. She had recently begun a course in escapology and as well as being hand-cuffed, straitjacketed and sellotaped, she was also tied by one foot to the chandelier. "I said we've got to find someone to look after Jordan."

"Oh yes. But who?"

"I was thinking about Mr Lampy."

"Mr Lampy? He's just the gardener. And he's over eighty. Completely senile..."

Mrs Warden tugged with her teeth at one of the ropes that bound her. It wouldn't give. "We could ask Mabel Butterworth. She's an angel."

"You're absolutely right," Mr Warden said. "She died two years ago."

"Did she?" Mrs Warden blinked. "No wonder she hasn't been returning my calls." She considered for a moment. "How about Barbara Finegold? She always says how much she likes kids."

"But she means goats," Mr Warden said. "She's always had a fondness for goats. She keeps two of the brutes as pets."

"Well, there must be someone."

"How about you?" Mr Warden suggested. "After all, you are the boy's mother."

"I hadn't thought of that," Mrs Warden muttered. "I suppose it is an idea... I mean, I could look after him for a few days."

Mrs Warden twisted round again, trying to release a hand from the straitjacket without dislocating her shoulder. Nothing happened.

"This isn't working," she sighed. "I'm sorry, Gordon, but I'm afraid you're going to have to untie me. Gordon? Gordon...?"

But Mr Warden had fallen sound asleep.

The next day did not begin well. Mrs Warden had a headache (from sleeping upside down) and had no wish to be left alone with Joe. Mr Warden had left early for the office even though – as Mrs Warden realized an hour after he was gone – it was Saturday. Joe was waiting for her in the kitchen, studying a map of China.

"Good morning, Jordan," she said.

Joe looked up. He had been thinking about life in Chwannping.

"Now," Mrs Warden went on. "I'm just going to make you some breakfast. Then I'm afraid I have a hair appointment and then my bridge lesson with Dr Vitebski. This week we're learning about suspension bridges. So will you be all right on your own until lunch?"

Joe nodded.

"Good." Mrs Warden was in a hurry. She threw a spoonful of coffee granules into her mouth and sipped some boiling water from the kettle. "I'd love to have lunch with you," she went on, "but I'm meeting Jane for elevenses and as she's always late it's bound to be twelveses. The poor dear is all at sixes and sevens! Maybe I'll buy her some After Eights."

Joe had lost count trying to work this out but his mother went on anyway. "I'm going shopping this afternoon," she said. "I thought I'd go to the spring sales. The sofa in the living-room needs some new springs. Then tea at the Ritz and I should be home in time for supper."

"Do you want me to make the supper?" Joe asked.

"I don't think so, darling!" Mrs Warden giggled. "Leave that to me!"

But in fact she was so exhausted after her day's shopping that she quite forgot to cook. That evening, Mr Warden and Joe sat at the table staring gloomily at three tins of pink salmon. Mrs Warden was even gloomier. She couldn't find the tin opener.

"This house is going to the dogs!" Mr Warden muttered. "And I'm going to a hotel!"

Mrs Warden burst into tears. "It's not my fault," she wept. "I've been so busy! How can I be expected to do everything?"

"Well, is there *no* food in the house?" Mr Warden asked.

"There was a chicken and some peas."

"You could at least have cooked the peas," Mr Warden growled.

"I tried to. But the chicken ate them. And then I tried to cook the chicken but it ran away."

The days without Wolfgang and Irma crawled slowly by. Mrs Warden filled the house with ready meals. Mr Warden spent longer and longer at the office. And Joe began to teach himself Chinese. But quite rapidly things began to fall apart.

On Tuesday night the dishwasher broke down, much to the horror of Mrs Warden, who hadn't washed a dish herself since 1963 (and then she had only rinsed it). The next day she went out and bought a hundred paper plates which were fine with the main courses and puddings but caused problems with the soup. On Wednesday, Mr Warden attempted to dry his shoes by placing them in the microwave. His feet were actually glowing as he took the tube to work and he caused a bomb scare at Charing Cross. On Thursday, the toaster exploded when Mr Warden tried to light it with a match. On Friday it was the Hoover. Mrs Warden only just escaped a terrible injury when she tried to use it to blow-dry her hair.

You may think it pathetic that Mr and Mrs Warden were so incapable of looking after themselves but you'd be surprised how true this is of the very rich. They've been looked after by servants for so long that they don't know how to do anything for themselves. Ask the Queen what a Brillo pad is and she'd probably tell you it was a lovely place to live.

Anyway, as the week progressed, the house became dustier and dirtier and more broken down. Joe for the most part avoided his parents and spent most of his time with Mr Lampy. Chinese had proved impossible to learn so he was thinking now about volunteering for the American shuttle to Mars.

And then, on Saturday, Granny came to lunch.

"You know, Maud, darling," she said, munching on a mouthful of Marks and Spencer's Instant Saturday Lunch, "you and Gordon look terribly tired."

"I am tired!" Mr Warden muttered.

"Don't you usually go to the south of France at this time of the year?"

"We can't, Mumsy," Mrs Warden sighed.

"Why ever not?" Granny had hardly glanced at Joe, sitting opposite her at the table, but he was suddenly suspicious. Granny knew perfectly well that his parents had a flat in Cannes. She also knew that the flat only had one bedroom.

"What about Jordan?" Mrs Warden said.

"I'm sure he'd love to go with you."

"There's no room," Mr Warden muttered.

"Well..." There was a pause. "I could look after him while you were away."

Joe's mouth went dry. One after another the hairs on the back of his neck stood up. Alone with Granny? He'd prefer to be alone with a sabre-toothed tiger.

"I could move in, if you wanted me to," she went on. Her whole face had gone rubbery and there was a sweetness in her voice. But Joe could see her eyes. They were still sly. "Joe would love it. Wouldn't you, dear?"

"Aaagh!" Joe yelled. For even as Granny had spoken the words, he had felt a terrible explosion of pain. Under the table, a leathercapped shoe had just come into hard contact with his knee.

"I'm sorry, dear?" Granny gazed at him enquiringly.

"You can't!" Joe gasped.

"What?" Mr Warden was furious. "Your granny offers to look after you and that's all you can say?"

"I mean... I mean, it isn't fair on Granny." Joe was

blushing now. Could he tell the truth? That was what Mrs Jinks had advised but looking at his parents now he knew it was impossible. He forced himself to think. "I'd love to be with Granny," he went on. "But wouldn't it be too much work for her? It might make her ill."

"Oh, silly me!" Granny trilled. "I've dropped my fork!" She disappeared under the table.

"Wait a minute..." Joe began.

"What is the matter with you, Jordan?" his mother asked.

A second later, Joe jerked upright in his seat as three metal prongs buried themselves in his thigh. He had been holding a glass of water but now he cried out, his hand jerked and the water sprayed over his father, putting out his cigar.

"Have you gone mad?" Mr Warden demanded.

"No, father, I..." Joe put down the glass and reached under the table. There were three holes in his trousers – not to mention in his leg.

"I'll look after him." Granny was already back in her seat. For someone so old, she had moved incredibly fast. "It would only be for a few weeks. I'm sure we'd have a lot of fun..."

Joe stared at her. Granny leaned forward and picked up the bread knife: thirteen inches of serrated steel. She looked at him and smiled. Joe shrank back into his chair. When he spoke, his voice was thin and high-pitched. "What about Mr Lampy?" he quavered.

"What about him?" his mother said.

"He's a lot younger than Granny. Couldn't he look after me? That way, you and father could have your holiday, Granny wouldn't have to bother about me and everyone would be happy."

Across the table, Granny was gripping the bread knife so tightly that her fingers had gone white and the veins were wriggling under her skin like worms. Joe held his breath, his eyes fixed on the knife.

"I did suggest Mr Lampy," Mrs Warden said.

"Maybe it's not such a bad idea," Mr Warden muttered.

"I think it's a very good idea..."

Granny put down the knife. Her lips had gone all wobbly and there were tears brimming in her eyes like rainwater in the folds of a tent. "Well, if you don't want me," she burbled. "If you don't like me..."

"Of course he likes you, Mummy," Mrs Warden said. "Jordan was just worried about you, that's all."

"I certainly was," Joe agreed.

"Well, all right." Granny forced herself to cheer up. "You two get your tickets then and have a lovely time." But then her eyes narrowed and the next words were aimed directly at Joe. "And if anything terrible happens to Mr Lampy, if he's unlucky enough to have a dreadful accident in the next few days, just you let me know."

"Now don't you worry about me, Master Warden," Mr Lampy said.

It was the morning before Mr and Mrs Warden were

about to leave. Mr Lampy had just come out of the shed carrying a canister of petrol. He had been cutting back the shrubbery at the bottom of the garden and was about to light a bonfire.

"You and me ... we're going to get along all right."

"That's not what I'm worried about," Joe replied. "It's Granny..."

"You and your granny!" Mr Lampy set the canister down and rubbed the small of his back. "Ooh!" he exclaimed. "I been to see the doctor today and he goes on about someone called Arthur Itis. Arthur Itis? I never heard of him."

"Please, Mr Lampy..."

Mr Lampy smiled. He was a very old man and when he smiled his face folded into a hundred creases. He had spent his whole life out of doors. In ten years in the Navy he had never once gone below deck – all the more remarkable when you consider that he served on a submarine. "I haven't seen your granny and I don't intend to see her," he went on. He leaned down and picked up the petrol canister. "I reckon she'll be leaving the two of us alone."

Joe watched as Mr Lampy walked away. He wasn't convinced but there seemed to be no point in arguing any more. The last thing he saw of Mr Lampy was the old gardener leaning over a great pile of wood-cuttings and leaves, sprinkling it with petrol from the canister. He didn't see Mr Lampy light the match.

The explosion could be heard thirty miles away

and at first the police thought it was a terrorist attack. Like Mrs Jinks before him, nothing was found of Mr Lampy – which was hardly surprising. He had blown a crater five metres deep in the earth. Four trees, the rockery, the garden shed and the moles went with him, blown into so many pieces that it was quite impossible to say what belonged to what. One question puzzled everyone. How had Mr Lampy managed to sprinkle nitroglycerine on his bonfire? And how had it got into what should have been a canister of petrol?

The investigation led nowhere. One witness did come forward claiming that he had seen a figure climbing over the fence into the garden of Thattlebee Hall. But as the witness had been on his way back from the pub and as he insisted that the figure he had seen had been a woman, and one who was over ninety years old, his evidence was discounted.

A few days later, Mr and Mrs Warden left for their flat in the south of France.

The same day, Granny moved in.

GATHERING OF THE GRANNIES

Breakfast was cream cheese.

Lunch was cream cheese.

Tea was more cream cheese.

After just one day, Joe was the colour of cream cheese. The house had never felt so big and he had never felt so small. His parents were away in another country. Mrs Jinks and Mr Lampy were dead. There was just Joe and Granny and he knew with a horrible sick feeling in the pit of his stomach that he was completely in her power.

Of course, Granny was enjoying every minute of it, moving round the house, warbling to herself like a sick canary as she glued shut the windows and turned up the heating. By lunch-time Joe was sweating.

"You look ill, dear," Granny trilled.

"I'm hot."

"It must be the flu. You'd better have two spoonfuls of cod-liver oil. Better still, I'll go to the fishmongers and buy you a whole cod's liver."

That afternoon, Mr and Mrs Warden telephoned from the south of France. Although Joe was in the room, they didn't ask to speak to him. Instead, Mrs Warden gabbled down the phone to Granny at twice her usual speed. She always did this to save money on long-distance calls.

"Are you sure everything's all right, Mumsy?" she asked.

"Don't you worry, dear. Jasper and I are having a wonderful time. He's no trouble at all!"

"There is one thing, Mummy. Could you put an advert in *The Lady* for a new nanny? We'll have to have one when we get back."

"Oh, Jack won't be needing a new nanny..."

Joe heard the words. They sent a shiver down his spine.

"Mummy...?"

Granny was holding the telephone in a clawlike hand. She smiled into it. "Lovely talking to you, dear. Must go!" The smile evaporated. Granny hung up.

Granny made a number of telephone calls after that but Joe was pretty certain that none of them were to *The Lady*. She was careful to close the door before she began but Joe did manage to hear her checking train times with British Rail and so assumed that she

– and presumably he with her – was about to go away.

This was confirmed at the end of the day. Joe had eaten his supper on his own and was settling down to watch television when the door opened and Granny came in.

"Bedtime, Jane, dear!"

"I'm Joe! And it's only eight o'clock. I never go to bed before nine."

"Don't argue with Granny. Granny knows best!"

"But I'm watching *The Bill*!"

"So am I, dear." Granny flicked the television off. "The electricity bill – and that should save a bit! Now up to bed!"

But the torment didn't even stop there. Although it was a warm night, Granny had insisted on his wearing a vest as well as his pyjamas, a dressing-gown as well as a vest and two extra blankets on top of everything else.

"We don't want your flu to get any worse, do we, dear," she said when she came into his room.

"I can't sleep like this," Joe said. "I feel like a sausage roll!"

"You can't have a sausage roll now, dear," Granny replied. "But maybe I'll get you one tomorrow." And with a soft giggle, she switched off the light and went out.

Joe lay in bed for a long time. He was too hot to sleep and also too angry. As he lay in the half-darkness, he began to think about how unfair life was. He was twelve (almost thirteen) years old. He could read, write, add up, speak French, swim, juggle and name over a thousand characters in science fiction books and films. But did he have any life of his own? No! His every movement was controlled and organized by adults with less imagination than him. His parents, the teachers at his posh prep school – they were all the same, passing him around as if he were no more than a tin of sweets. Of course, it wouldn't be so bad if the grown-ups had more sense. But nobody had to be qualified to be a parent. And his parents were not only unqualified, they had quite happily handed him to a woman who hated him and who in the last few weeks had just killed his two best friends. But who would believe him? Nobody!

If he hadn't been so hot and angry, maybe he would have slept. But he was still awake at nine o'clock when the doorbell rang. He was awake at ten past nine when it rang again. And he had given up any idea of sleeping by half past when it rang for a third time.

As the evening dragged on, Joe began to hear strange sounds coming from downstairs. The hiss of a can being opened and a peal of high-pitched laughter. A clink of glasses and the slam of a cupboard door. More laughter. There seemed to be four or five women downstairs. The muffled sound of arguing and then another cackle of laughter drifted up to his room. In the end he couldn't bear it any longer. He got up and went downstairs.

The hall was dark but the door to the living-room was half open which was how the sounds had escaped. Thankful for his bare feet and the thick carpets, Joe tiptoed forward and peeped in. An extraordinary sight met his eyes.

There were five grannies in the room, playing poker. They had assembled a green baize card table and had two decks of cards scattered over the surface, on the floor and – in at least two instances – up their sleeves. The room was thick with smoke. Two of the grannies were smoking cigarettes while a third had helped herself to one of Mr Warden's cigars. They had opened half a dozen cans of beer and a bottle of whisky. There were glasses everywhere. Granny had also provided food. There was a bowl of popcorn, some bright pink hot dogs with fried onions and American mustard, a plate of pickled cucumbers, two boxes of Fortnum and Mason chocolates, some salt beef sandwiches and several packets of chewing gum. Joe wasn't at all surprised that there wasn't an ounce of cream cheese in sight.

But what made the spectacle so bizarre as well as so revolting was the old ladies themselves. Their combined ages must have added up to well over four hundred. Joe had once seen a few minutes of a video called *Revenge of the Killer Zombies*. It had given him nightmares for a week. Well, this was far, far worse.

Granny One was a small, shrivelled woman, no more than four feet high. Her head barely came over the edge of the table and she was blinking at the cards in her hand with small, pink eyes. She seemed to be finding it difficult to balance on her chair – perhaps because of the enormous amount of jewellery she was wearing and the bulging handbag she was clutching to her chest. This granny's hands were everywhere at once: holding her cards (and trying to stop her neighbour seeing them), guarding her bag, tilting her whisky glass towards her lips and poking her nose and ears. Look quickly, and you might think she had four arms. Her name was Granny Anne.

Granny Two was wearing what looked like a pair of curtains – but they were curtains you would draw at your peril. For this granny was immensely fat. She was so fat that she seemed to have partially melted into her chair. She was obviously a careful poker player as she was keeping her cards close to her chin – or rather, chins, for she had three of them. The third of these was crowned with a wispy beard. Granny Two was sucking a hot dog. She couldn't eat it as, for extra comfort, she had removed her false teeth and placed them in front of her on the table. Her name was Granny Smith.

The first things Joe noticed about Granny Three were her quite horrible eyes. She was wearing a heavy pair of spectacles which, over the years, had stretched her ears and sunk into her nose. In fact her entire face was lop-sided and she hadn't helped it by putting on too much lipstick – at the same time missing her lips. Her eyeballs, magnified by what looked like inch-thick glass, were a milky shade of white with one a little higher than the other. Granny Three was smoking, eating, drinking and talking all at the same time. And all the time she was watching. Her eyes, darting about in her drooping sockets, missed nothing. She answered to the name of Granny Adams.

Granny Four, shovelling enormous handfuls of popcorn into her mouth, was a vulture. She had the same long neck, bald head and cruel eyes. And she was wearing a flowing green cloak mounted with feathers which added to the illusion. This was the granny who was smoking the cigar. She was using it to point with and as Joe watched, the glowing tip caught Granny Smith on the chin. Granny Smith cried out and fell backwards, two aces tumbling out of her jacket. Granny Adams threw a glass of beer at her and screamed with laughter while Granny Anne pounded the table and chewed gum. This last granny was called Granny Lee.

Dominating the table was Granny herself, looking almost royal in a billowing dress with flouncy neck and sleeves. She was sitting with her arms and legs apart and a scowl on her face. Suddenly she threw her cards down.

"A full house. Kings high. Beat that!" She announced.

"I've got a pair of twos," Granny Anne exclaimed in a quavering voice.

Granny Smith grabbed them and tore them up. "You lose, Anne. Two twos aren't worth anything."

"Well, I've got another two in my bra," Anne

exclaimed.

"Cheat! Cheat! Cheat!" Granny Adams screeched with laughter. "I haven't got anything," she added and threw her cards in a shower over her head.

"Well, I've got a royal flush," the vulture granny snapped. "Ace, king, queen, knave, ten." She spread the cards on the table.

"How did you do that?" Granny scrabbled at the cards, examining them as if they were forgeries. Her face had gone dark red. "You've been cheating as well, haven't you, Lee?"

"Of course I've been cheating," Granny Lee replied. "We've all been cheating. But I've just been cheating better than you."

"Well, how much do I owe you?" Granny was sulking now, her lip jutting out and her shoulders slumped.

"Let me see..." Granny Lee scribbled a few figures on a sheet of paper. "That's two shillings and fourpence."

"How much is that in new money?" Granny Anne asked nervously.

"We don't have nasty new money here, Anne," Granny replied. She brought her elbow up sharply, catching the little granny in the eye. "Two shillings and fourpence is just what it says it is."

"Oh! Lovely old money!" Granny Smith sighed, her three chins rising and falling in perfect unison. "It used to be worth something once, money did. I could buy dinner for three people with two shillings and fourpence."

"Yes," Granny Lee snapped. "But the trouble was, you'd eat it all yourself!" And her whole body shook as she laughed uncontrollably.

Meanwhile Granny had gathered in the torn and crumpled cards and was once again shuffling the pack.

"So tell me, Ivy," Granny Anne asked. "What's the news about that grandson of yours?"

At the door, Joe froze.

"Yes!" Granny Adams rubbed her hands together. Her eyes rolled like two worms in walnut shells. "How are his enzymes?"

"Enzymes! Enzymes!" Granny Lee and Granny Anne chorused.

Granny held up a hand. "You'll find out soon enough," she rasped. "I'm taking him with me tomorrow."

"What?" The other grannies stared in amazement and delight.

"Can you?" Granny Smith asked. "What about his parents?"

"They're not here," Granny replied. "Anyway, they don't care a jot about him. They won't even notice."

"Do you mean..." Granny Lee twisted her neck until the bones clicked. "You've got him all to yourself?"

Granny nodded. "Yes. I've had quite a bit of fun at his expense, I can tell you." She licked her lips and began to deal. "But maybe I'm getting old. I feel I haven't quite made him miserable enough!"

Joe felt the hairs on the back of his neck prickle.

If only he could have tape-recorded this conversation – his parents would have had to believe him. He'd guessed that Granny hated him. Now he had the proof of it. But all that talk of enzymes worried him. What were they planning? Where was he going to be taken?

"How I hate children!" the vulture granny moaned.

"Me too!"

"I can't stand them."

"I detest them!"

All the grannies were nodding so vigorously that Joe wouldn't have been surprised if their heads had come loose from their necks and rolled across the surface of the card table.

"You know what I hate about them?" Granny Smith said. "I hate their perfect skin. It's all pink and shiny and smooth. I hate their hair, so thick and wavy. But most of all I hate their teeth." She gazed at her own on the table in front of her. "Do you know where children keep their teeth? In their mouths! It isn't fair."

"I hate children because they're so healthy," Granny Anne went on. "They're always shouting and playing and having fun and running about. I haven't run anywhere since 1958 and that was only for a bus."

"I hate them because of everything they've got," Granny Adams muttered. "We never had computers and pop music and T-shirts and mountain bikes. But they have. I fought in two world wars but nobody ever gave me a skateboard. Oh no!"

"Children smell," Granny Lee announced. "They're

too small and they make too much noise. Why can't they be more like us?"

"Yes. With arthritis!"

"And swollen knees."

"Hard of hearing!"

"What?"

"And wrinkly."

"Horrid! Horrid! Horrid! Horrid! Horrid!" All five grannies were chorusing together now and pounding their fists on the table at the same time. Joe couldn't believe what he was seeing. It seemed that the five old ladies had gone quite mad.

At last Granny stopped them.

"But we can at least get our revenge," she said. "There are so many ways to upset a grandchild."

"Oh, yes!" Granny Adams giggled. Her glasses jumped up and down on her nose. "When I see my grandchildren, I always poke them a lot. I do find that children hate being poked."

"I don't just poke them," the little granny said. "I pat them on their heads and fiddle with their clothes. It does annoy them so, although of course they're not allowed to complain."

"And don't forget the kiss!" Granny Smith said. "The wet kiss on the cheek makes them squirm like frogs in a pond!"

"What about presents?" Granny asked. "Presents are a marvellous way of spoiling any child's day."

"Oh, yes! A boring book token!"

"Talcum powder!"

"Something you know they've already got!"

"What I do," Granny said, "is buy them something that's too young for them. Something that will make them feel babyish. They feel so ashamed. It's hilarious."

(At the door, Joe remembered the toy robot and found that his face was burning once again. But this time it wasn't with embarrassment. It was anger.)

"I have a much better idea," Granny Lee said. "I buy my grandchildren hideously unsuitable clothes. I've managed to find some of the most ghastly pullovers in the world."

"I knit them myself," Granny Anne muttered.

"The children *have* to wear them," Granny Lee went on. "And you should see them! I always take them out to tea and watch their faces as they walk out in their horrible, huge, brightly-coloured jumpers..."

"I've got a much better idea," Granny Adams interjected. "My grandchildren are a little overweight. So guess what I buy them – chocolates! I get them a whole box and of course they eat them and that just makes them fatter and spottier and when they go back to school they're terribly teased and all thanks to me. You should try the chocolate wheeze! The little brats can never resist a chocolate."

"It seems to me that you should combine the two ideas," Granny said. "Give them the chocolates. And give them a jersey that's a little too small. Then, when their tummies are bulging it will really show."

The other four grannies thought about this and then all shrieked with laughter. More glasses of whisky were poured. More beer cans were cracked open. The fat granny was laughing so much that her whole body was convulsing and her face had gone bright red.

Joe couldn't bear any more. He took three steps away from the door, shrinking into the shadows of the hall. But even as he went he heard his name once again being bounced around the card table.

"So you're going to take the boy?"

"Oh, yes. He's coming. I've had my eye on him for a long time."

"Which eye, dear? The real one or the glass one?"

"Have you spoken to ... Elsie Bucket?" This was Granny Lee's voice. She had spoken the name with awe.

"Oh, yes. I spoke to Elsie. She's delighted."

"Delighted!"

"Excited!"

"Enzymes!"

"Hee hee hee..."

The five of them were like witches. Add a cauldron and a few frogs and there would have been no difference. Joe turned and tiptoed back the way he had come. The voices followed him as he made his way back to bed.

THE GOLDEN GRANNY AWARDS

"Pack your bags, Judas. We're going on holiday."

It was breakfast the following day and Joe had just come downstairs to find Granny tucking into a plate of eggs, bacon, sausage, tomatoes, fried bread and black pudding. She had prepared a half grapefruit topped with a small amount of cream cheese for him.

"Where are we going?" Joe asked. He knew she was always getting his name wrong on purpose and decided not to correct her.

"To Bideford in Devonshire. It's a delightful town. I spent many happy years there in the war."

"The Crimean War, Granny?"

"There's no need to be rude, dear." Granny lashed out with a curiously powerful fist. If Joe hadn't ducked at the last moment she would have broken his chin.

Even so he felt the air as it punched past him. "It was the Second World War. Ah, what happy days those were. Rationing and bombs and dried eggs for breakfast. Your grandfather got blown to smithereens in the Second World War. Such happy days!"

"I don't want to go to Bideford," Joe said, sitting on the edge of his chair in case he had to duck a second blow.

"I'm sure you don't, dear," Granny simpered. "But you're twelve and I'm ninety-four. So you don't really have any choice."

"I could ring Mum and Dad..."

"And drag them all the way back from France? I don't think they'd be very pleased. Anyway, I've already told them I'm taking you." She smiled unpleasantly.

"Why are you doing this, Granny?" Joe demanded. "What do you want?"

Granny paused with her fork inches from her mouth. Egg white dangled greasily in front of her lips. Suddenly she was innocent again. "I want to look after you," she said. "Just like any granny would."

The taxi dropped them at Paddington Station and the driver scowled as Granny counted out the fare in one, two and five-penny pieces. It took her ten minutes to pay by which time the driver was covered in coins.

"Seven pounds twenty pence?" she demanded. "There you are! That's seven pounds twenty-one. Keep the change!"

Joe grabbed the suitcases and Granny grabbed Joe and together they made their way through the station concourse. As they walked, Joe saw something rather strange. A woman had got out of the taxi just behind them – he had noticed her out of the corner of his eye because he had thought he recognized her – and now she seemed to be following them. Nervously, he glanced over his shoulder. She was still there, her face almost completely hidden by a scarf over her mouth and a pair of dark glasses over her eyes. A lock of blonde hair poked out from under a voluminous hat and she walked with a pronounced limp. Where had Joe seen her before?

But maybe he was imagining the whole thing. For when he looked around again a few moments later, the mysterious woman had gone.

Granny checked her ticket and pointed at a train. There was a guard standing beside it, leaning against it with one hand splayed out on the metal surface and the other hand in his pocket. The guard hadn't shaved that morning. There was a cigarette behind his ear.

"Excuse me..." Granny said.

The guard looked at her with a syrupy smile and almost at once Joe recognized the sort of man he was. He was just like his Uncle David, the sort of man who believes that all old people are like children, that they don't understand anything except simple words spoken loudly. Joe had always hated that sort of behaviour but now his interest was aroused. How would Granny react?

"Yes, my love. How *are* you today?" The guard shouted out the words. He was leaning over Granny, nodding his head at her.

Granny's lips tightened. "Is this the train for Bideford?" she snapped.

"No, dear!" The guard was still shouting and he shook his head vigorously for good measure. "There's no *station* at Bideford, darling. There hasn't been for twenty years! You have to go to *Barnstaple* and get a bus!"

"Is this the train for Barnstaple?" Granny demanded.

"Yes!" Now he nodded like a thirsty duck. He was showing all his teeth (and several fillings) in a wide smile. "Can you get on all right, dear? Got a *ticket*, have you?"

"Of course I've got a ticket!"

"Good! Good! Now you change at Exeter, all right. Do you think you can remember that?"

"Yes."

"That your grandson, is he? *He'll* look after you! Don't you worry, love. You'll be all right."

The guard hadn't noticed but Granny's cheeks had gone a dark red and her lips were so tight they could have been sewn together. She didn't say anything more but got on the train with Joe and found her seat. Then she looked at her watch.

"We've got ten minutes," she muttered, as much to herself as him. "You wait here. I'll be right back..."

As soon as Granny had gone, Joe slipped out of his seat and went over to the open door. He was curious. What was she going to do? He saw her scuttling across the concourse to the newsagent and a minute later she came out clutching something in her hand. Now she was hovering, waiting for something. Joe followed her eyes and saw the guard, still leaning against the train with his palm flat on the surface. Suddenly making up her mind, Granny moved towards him. She was going to do something, Joe was sure of it. But then a crowd of tourists appeared and for a minute, Joe's vision was blocked.

When he looked again, Granny was past the guard and walking back towards the train. The guard had been distracted by something but now he took his cigarette out, lit it and once again leaned against the train. Joe hurried back to his seat. He was sitting back with his eyes half-closed when Granny joined him.

Three minutes later, the train left.

Granny had brought a magazine with her but she didn't read it. She was smiling to herself with that odd, dangerous light in her eyes.

Joe glanced at her handbag, which lay halfopen on the seat beside her. There was a torn carton inside. What was it she had bought in the newsagent? Joe read one single word and shuddered.

SUPERGLUE.

They were delayed for one hour at Reading while they prised the guard off the train. He had run the whole way from Paddington, one hand glued to the side of the carriage. He was taken to hospital by ambulance to be treated for exhaustion, multiple blisters and shock. Granny watched through the window as the ambulance left.

"I hate being patronized," she said.

"Yes, Granny."

For the rest of the journey, Joe kept his mouth firmly shut.

Bideford was pretty enough, stretched out along a harbour with a few fishing boats moored on the other side of the parking meters. The taxi had brought Joe and Granny all the way from Barnstaple and as it cruised along the High Street he noticed two things. The first was that every single shop in the town sold Devonshire clotted cream. And the second was that there seemed to be an unusually large number of elderly ladies in the street – all of them with knitted hats and shopping trolleys.

"No wonder it's called Bideford," Joe thought to himself. "The place is full of old biddies."

The taxi turned right and followed a narrow, twisting road up a steep hill. At the top it stopped and Joe saw the hotel where they were staying.

It was a tall, double-fronted house, four floors high but with extra rooms built into the roof. The house was old but the owners had tried to modernize it with a revolving door (which looked ridiculous) and a white marble forecourt. The hotel advertised forty-five rooms "all with hot and cold running water" except that someone had crossed out the "and" and replaced it with "or". Apparently they had plumbing problems. It was called The Stilton International.

Granny paid the driver and she and Joe went in. The reception area was surprisingly large – the whole hotel seemed bigger inside than out.

While Granny checked in for both of them, Joe wandered between the artificial leather sofas and the wilting pot plants – the hotel was as hot as Granny's flat – and went over to a large sign on the opposite wall. It was made up of plastic letters, although some of the alphabet was evidently missing, and it read:

THE STILTON INTERNATIONAL
welcoMes grannies
TonigHt at 10.00pm in the
Elsie Bucket Conference Room
THe GOLDeN GRANNY AWARDS

"The Golden Granny Awards..." Joe muttered the words to himself and, looking around him, he suddenly realized – with a lurch in his stomach – that the hotel was occupied entirely by grannies. There were half a dozen of them sitting in the reception area reading magazines or nodding off to sleep. The lift arrived and three more grannies got out, whispering among themselves. Two grannies met on the forecourt and

Joe heard them greet each other.

"Gladys!"

"Evelyn! I haven't seen you since ... 1942!"

"Fifty-two years ago, Gladys! You haven't changed..."

"Haven't I, Evelyn, dear?"

"No! You're still wearing the same dress."

A coach had drawn up and another fifteen grannies got out and formed a queue at the reception, chatting excitedly among themselves. They were all carrying shopping trolleys and old, heavy suitcases. But now Joe noticed something else. It was very strange, but they had brought what looked like scientific equipment along with them too.

One granny had a large test tube. Another had a Bunsen burner. A third granny had a series of twisting glass pipes while the granny behind her had some sort of electrical apparatus complete with copper wires, magnetic switches and complicated micro-circuitry. The last granny in the line was completely bowed down by something that could have come straight out of one of his science fiction books: it was like a glass and steel tuba with a whole series of levers and buttons and flashing lights. One of the other grannies was admiring it.

"You got an electro-static de-energizer!" she exclaimed. "How lovely! Where did you find it?"

"My grandson's a nuclear physicist," the other granny explained. "He made it for me."

"Did you tell him what it was for?"

"No. And fortunately he didn't ask."

Not one single granny had looked at Joe. He was aware that he was the only person in the building under seventy (even the receptionist was white-haired). Normally he would have expected the grannies to tussle his hair or tug at his clothes. But it was as if they were actually avoiding him. He felt their eyes settle momentarily on him but then dart away. Nobody spoke to him. They seemed almost afraid of him.

Something poked Joe in the ribs and he spun round to find Granny dangling a key in front of him. "Here you are, Jasper," she said. "You've got room 45. Go and unpack and I'll see you at dinner. And you be a good boy, now!"

Joe took the key and as his hand came into contact with the cold metal a shiver ran down his whole body. Granny's eyes had locked into his and for a moment he could see the hunger in them. He felt her eyes sucking him dry and at the same time the words "electro-static de-energizer" echoed in his mind. What did it do? What was it for?

And why was he so sure that it had something to do with him?

Room 45 was at the very top of the hotel, built into the roof with slanting walls and a small, low window. Joe quickly unpacked then set out to explore the Stilton International. He had never been anywhere quite like it in his life.

In the basement there was a swimming-pool, but the water was so hot that the entire room was filled with steam and he could hardly see anything. But there were grannies there. He couldn't see them but he could hear them, cackling eerily in the steam and pattering across the tiled surface like ghosts.

Near the swimming-pool there was a beauty parlour and Joe stared through the open door as one of the grannies lay back in what looked like a dentist's chair. The beauty specialist was a small, foreign-looking man with a wig and a moustache that didn't quite match. The granny he was working on already had two cucumber slices on her eyes, two straws up her nose and a thick white cream on her lips.

"Oh yes, Mrs Grimstone," he was saying. "To bring out the beauty of the skin, to give it back its youth, it requires the natural products only." He produced a bucket and scooped out a handful of something brown and steaming. "That is why I use only the finest quality buffalo dung. Rich in minerals and vitamins. High in protein. It will draw out the natural colour."

Joe moved away as the beauty specialist slapped the first handful of the stuff on Mrs Grimstone's cheek.

There was a fashion shop on the ground floor where Joe watched grannies trying on all sorts of brilliantly coloured clothes. One granny was standing in front of a mirror having squeezed herself – with great difficulty – into an impossibly tight leopard-skin leotard with a black top and brilliant red head-band which now matched her brilliant red face.

"Gorgeous, Mrs Hodgson," the shop assistant was crooning. "Quite gorgeous! You don't look a day over eighty-five!"

Next to the fashion shop was a health food shop. The window was filled with pills and bottles, strange roots and powders ... all of which were designed to make whoever swallowed them feel young again.

"I particularly recommend raw garlic and seaweed cocktail," the owner was saying. "Just two mouthfuls and I guarantee you'll find yourself running..."

"...running for the loo," Joe thought to himself and went on his way.

In the next twenty minutes, he covered the entire hotel and came to two inescapable conclusions.

The Stilton International had been built by grannies, for grannies and was run by grannies. And everyone who came there wanted to be young again. They were obsessed with it.

So where, he wondered, did that leave him?

The thought was still on his mind as he joined Granny for dinner. This was served in a large room with ten round tables, each seating eight or nine grannies. Joe was joined by the four grannies he recognized from the card game at Thattlebee Hall – Granny Anne, Granny Smith, Granny Adams and Granny Lee – as well as two other grannies he didn't know. None of them spoke to him although Granny Adams spent several minutes examining him through her inch-thick spectacles until the first course was served.

The first course was quail's eggs. The grannies fell on them like wolves.

Joe remembered an old phrase he had once heard. "You can't teach Grandma to suck eggs." He could certainly see it was true now as the ninety grannies in the room grabbed the miniature eggs, smashed the shells against their plates, the tables or indeed each other and then sucked out the contents. Soon the whole room was filled with the sound of slurping as the balls of glistening white were vacuumed. Granny Smith – the fat granny – was enjoying hers so much that she wasn't even bothering to remove the shells. Joe wondered if there might be a prize for the granny who sucked the most eggs, and that made him think of the Golden Granny Awards he had seen advertised.

He turned to Granny. "What are the Golden Granny Awards?" he asked.

Granny looked at him suspiciously. "Never you mind," she snapped. "They've got nothing to do with you."

"Past your bedtime," Granny Smith added, picking a piece of eggshell out of her teeth.

"When is his bedtime?" Granny Lee asked.

Granny looked at her watch. "Now!"

"But..." Joe began. He glanced at the kitchen door, which had just opened. A waiter was carrying in a vast silver dish of poached eels with mashed potato. Joe blinked. "Maybe you're right," he said. "I am a bit tired."

Joe got up and left the room. As he went he felt himself being followed by a hundred and eighty eyes (three of them glass). He saw one granny nudge another and point, heard a soft chuckle as his name was whispered. "Jordan ... that's the boy ... Ivy Kettle's boy..."

The first eels were being served as he left. Netted, boiled and stretched out on a plate... Joe knew exactly how they felt.

Of course, he didn't go to sleep.

At ten o'clock exactly he crept back downstairs, avoiding the lift in case the noise gave him away. The hotel was in half-darkness, the front doors locked, the reception area empty. The receptionist was still behind the desk, but she had fallen asleep.

10.00 p.m. The Elsie Bucket Conference Room...

Although Joe hadn't been inside the room on his tour of the hotel, he found it easily enough, following the sign out of the reception area and past the health food shop. As he padded along the thickly carpeted corridor towards a pair of heavy wooden doors, he heard a woman's voice, amplified by a microphone system but still muffled by the wall.

"And welcome, ladies and ladies, to the annual Golden Granny Awards..."

There was a round of applause.

Taking his courage – and the handles – in both hands, Joe opened the doors and quickly stepped inside. He would never forget the sight that met his eyes.

The Elsie Bucket Conference Room was enormous. It was a long, low-ceilinged room with a wooden floor and a stage at the far end. It had seats for about two hundred and fifty people and every one was taken. Joe realized that as well as the grannies in the hotel other grannies must have travelled from all over the country to be here. There were grannies in every seat – two to a seat in places. There were more grannies standing at the sides and yet more grannies hunched up on the floor in front of the stage.

The stage itself was decorated with a rippling wall of gold in front of which hung a sign: THE GOLDEN GRANNY AWARDS. The awards themselves – little statuettes of golden tortoises – were arranged on a nearby table. There was a granny sitting at a piano whilst an elderly man addressed the audience. Joe thought he recognized him as someone who had once done magic tricks or something on television – but that had been about five years ago. His name was Dan Parnell and he was wearing a red dinner jacket and a silver bow tie.

Joe had entered the room at the very back. He slid behind a row of spotlights and watched with bated breath.

"As you know," Dan Parnell said, "every year we give out these awards to the grannies who have most distinguished themselves in certain fields."

"I've never been in a field!" someone shouted from

the back and all the other grannies screeched with laughter.

"The tortoise lives for many, many years," the man went on. "And this is why our awards take the form of a tortoise. Do you know, ladies, that the combined ages of everyone in this room add up to twenty-two thousand, five hundred!"

This news was greeted by a huge round of applause, cat-calls and stamping feet. Joe watched nervously as the spotlights trembled and shook. Dan Parnell held up a hand for silence.

"Nobody wants to be old," he went on. "Let's face it! Being old is beastly. And it's not just the wrinkles and the false teeth." He pulled open his mouth to show his own which glinted in the light. "It's not just the aches and the nasal hair. What hurts is having to stand by and watch young people take over. That's what I hate. That's what we all hate."

There was another explosion of applause which went on a full ten minutes.

"But we can have our revenge!" Dan Parnell continued at last. "We can get in their way. We can upset them. We can do all sorts of things if we set our minds to it – and we can have a lot of fun. That's what these awards are about and without any more ado, let's get on with the presentation."

Joe peered out as Dan Parnell went over to the row of tortoises. The granny at the piano played a few dramatic chords. The grannies in the audience clapped and punched at the air with clenched fists.

"The first award is for the longest time getting on a bus. This award has been won this year by Rita Sponge who managed to take a staggering three-quarters of an hour getting on a 19 bus at Piccadilly Circus!" There was a burst of applause, but Dan held up a hand for silence. "And – wait for it – she then managed to spend another twenty-three minutes looking for her bus pass! An amazing one hour eight minutes in total!"

This time the applause was loud and sustained as Granny Sponge – a tall, drooping woman with wet, red eyes – came onto the stage to collect her award.

"The second award is for the longest queue in a post office. Again, another record, ladies and ladies. Forty-five people kept waiting for over half an hour in the Bath post office. And the man behind her actually had a nervous breakdown! Step forward Doreen Beavis!"

Granny Beavis was small and lively. She was so excited by her award that, having snatched it, she actually fell off the stage. But this only delighted the other grannies all the more.

"And now we come to the Elsie Bucket Difficult Shopper award. A very close result this year. Congratulations to Enid Crabb who spent the whole day in Harrods and had every single video recorder demonstrated to her three times without actually buying one. Also congratulations to Betty Brush for buying half an ounce of every single meat on display at her local supermarket, a performance that took three hours and kept sixty-one people waiting. But I'm afraid you were both pipped to the post by this year's winner, Nora Strapp, who spent so long complaining about a Biro she had bought at Woolworth's that the manager eventually committed suicide. Well done, Nora!"

Everyone applauded (apart from Enid Crabb and Betty Brush). Nora Strapp picked up her award and pranced off the stage.

Joe watched, unbelieving, as the other awards were presented. There was an award for the most unnecessary visits to a doctor and an award for the most absurd reason for telephoning the police. One granny picked up an award for causing the worst scene at a wedding whilst another was unable to pick up her award for causing the most violent argument in a family as she was still in hospital.

Joe's granny didn't win anything but Granny Smith got an honourable mention for the most damage caused when trying to be helpful.

An hour later, the last award had been given and Dan Parnell had left the room to huge applause. Joe was just preparing to sneak back to his bedroom when another granny took the stage. She was older than anyone in the room. Looking at her, at the hundreds of wrinkles on her face, at the white hair reaching down to her shoulders and her trembling, claw-like hands, Joe would have said she was well over a hundred. There were terrible blotches on her cheeks. Her eyes were completely empty.

"And now... " she screeched – she had a terrible, sandpaper voice – "the moment we have all been waiting for! But before I go on, I must introduce our uninvited guest!"

Our uninvited guest...

Somehow Joe knew who the old woman was talking about and he went hot and cold at exactly the same time. She was gazing at him now, her eyes as welcoming as a shark's. He took one step back.

A huge net fell over his head, reaching down all the way to his feet. He looked up and realized that there was a balcony running along the back of the hall, that there were another ten grannies up there and that he had been observed from the moment he had come in. It had been they who had dropped the net. Now another four grannies ran forward and seized the corners. He tried to struggle but it was hopeless. He had been netted like a north Atlantic cod.

Joe squirmed and kicked, only entangling himself all the more. Somewhere in his mind he swore never to eat another fish-finger. But it was too late for that.

"Bring him forward!" the old woman cried.

With the cackling of the grannies all around him, Joe was dragged onto the stage.

THE GRANNYMATIC ENZYME EXTRACTOR

"You all know me," the oldest granny exclaimed.

Joe was on the stage beside her, struggling and straining. The grannies had not only tied him up – that would have been bad enough. They had also fastened him into a straitjacket which they had evidently knitted themselves as it was made out of pink wool.

"My name is Elsie Bucket," the woman went on, "and I am the oldest granny in Great Britain. One hundred and six years old today! "

There was loud applause from the audience but Elsie Bucket did not smile. She held up a grey, skeletal hand for silence.

"Yes," she said. "I have received seven telegrams from the Queen. Seven telegrams! But have I so much as received one single present? Not on your nelly!" She sniffed. "So much for the Queen!"

She walked slowly to the front of the stage.

"I am old and like you, fellow grannies, I do not wish to be old. All my life I have thought about this. I was so afraid of being old that I never actually enjoyed being young. Fortunately, however, I was a brilliant scientist. It was I, for example, who invented the telephone. I can't tell you how angry I was when my sister rang me to tell me it had already been invented. Even so, I managed to invent the telephone bill. From there I went on to invent the electricity meter, the television licence and, later, the wheel-clamp.

"However, my greatest invention has taken me sixty years. It is here tonight. You, dear grannies, have all brought with you one component – as I asked you to in this very room last year. What a wonderful achievement! From a simple light bulb to an electrostatic de-energizer, from a long-life battery to a teaspoon of nuclear fuel, you have all brought exactly what I asked of you. But here I must say a special 'thank you' to Ivy Kettle." Joe stopped struggling and glowered at his granny who was sitting in the third row with a smug look on her face. Elsie Bucket gestured at her. "It was Ivy who provided us with the single most important – and potentially the most difficult – component of all. He may be small and rather unhygienic. But he's real. He's alive (for the time being). And he's here. She brought us a boy!"

"A boy! Oh joy! A boy!"

The grannies had all gone into ecstasies like very religious people at a prayer meeting. Joe felt the blood rush into his face as they all gazed at him, screeching and clapping, pointing and grinning. One granny had become so excited that she had gone red in the face and keeled over in her chair – but everyone ignored her in the general chaos. Joe was certain that at any moment he would wake up in bed. It was all a nightmare. It had to be. To be tied up in a pink strait jacket in a Devonshire hotel with over five hundred grannies hooting at you – that sort of thing just couldn't possibly happen in the real world.

Except that it had. This was no dream.

"And so, fellow grannies, no more talk! No more waiting! Let us do what we have so looked forward to doing. And let me show you my invention. Grannies – I give you ... the Grannymatic Enzyme Extractor!"

There was a hush in the room as the gold curtain slid back and even Joe gasped when he saw what had been constructed there at the back of the stage.

At first he thought it was an electric chair. An ordinary wooden chair was indeed part of it with coils and wires twisting round the legs and vanishing under the seat. But there was much more to it than that. A maze of glass pipes and tubes zigzagged and spiralled away into a line of bottles, some of them empty, some of them filled with a dark green liquid. A circular gauge reading EMPTY in blue and FULL in red hung from a tangle of wires with a golden arrow waiting to travel the distance between the two. The object that looked like a glass and steel tuba – Joe had seen it briefly in the reception area – was now suspended above the machine. Joe realized it could be lowered onto the head of whoever sat there. It in turn was connected to a complicated metal structure surrounding the chair and – Joe swallowed hard when he saw this – there were no fewer than thirteen large hypodermic syringes pointing inwards, attached to it at different levels. Joe imagined himself sitting in the chair (somehow it wasn't very hard to do) and saw that there would be two needles pointing at his ankles, two at his knees, two at his thighs, one at his stomach, one at the small of his back, two at his elbows, two at his neck and one – the highest – at the centre of his forehead. The syringes, big enough to inject a horse, were built into gold, magnetic coils. All of them were wired up to work automatically.

The whole ghastly contraption was connected to a control desk a few feet away. This was made up of the usual array of dials and gauges, flashing lights and buttons that he had seen on every episode of *Star Trek*. The only difference was that it had also been decorated with a small lace cloth and a flower in a pot. There was a comfy armchair behind it for the operator to sit on.

"Take him!" Elsie Bucket commanded.

Joe lashed out as the four grannies who had captured him fell on him again, giggling and wheezing. But he was helpless. As old and as weak as they were there were four of them and he was pinioned by the straitjacket. They pulled him, dragging his heels across the stage, and tied him into the chair. Two leather straps went over his legs, two more across his chest, one on each arm and a final one around his throat. There was nothing he could do.

He sat, facing the audience, half-blinded by the spotlights that were trained on him. He could just make out the small round heads staring at him like so many coconuts behind the glare but he was aware only of the thirteen needles pointing towards him. His hand grappled for a wire or a circuit he could pull ... anything to sabotage the machine. But he had been tied too tightly and the chair had been too well designed. Gritting his teeth, he slumped back. Now he could only wait.

"The Grannymatic Enzyme Extractor!" Elsie Bucket announced, moving into the light. "Last year, you will recall, we tested my elixir of life, the secret potion that would make me and all my dear granny friends young again. Over one hundred ingredients had gone into my elixir of life! Avocado oil, ginseng, yoghurt, royal jelly, raw oysters, ox blood, iron oxide, zinc, milk of magnesia, yak's milk, cactus juice, the yolk of an ostrich egg and much, much more. But it didn't work. And why didn't it work? Because there was one missing ingredient.

"Enzymes are the stuff of life. Without enzymes there can be no life. And this boy's enzymes, added to my wonderful elixir, will turn back the clock and instantly return us to our glorious, wonderful youth! And what about this glorious, wonderful youth?" Elsie Bucket pointed at Joe. "Sadly, the operation will kill the child. But I am sure even he won't mind when he knows how happy he will be making all of us."

"I do mind!" Joe shouted.

Elsie Bucket ignored him. "In a minute I shall flick the switch," she said. "The machine will do the rest. His enzymes will be sucked out of him. They will travel down these pipes here..." She pointed them out. "They will be thoroughly disinfected and then added to my elixir here." She tapped on one of the jars of green liquid. "From just one boy I estimate we can make five hundred doses, enough for everyone here! By the time the process is over," she added almost as an afterthought, "the boy will be as shrivelled as an overcooked cocktail sausage. If you find this disturbing, I suggest you don't look."

"I find it disturbing!" Joe cried out. But Elsie Bucket was already leaning over him, lowering the tuba-contraption onto his head. "A little electro-massage," she whispered to him. "Very painful, but it helps the enzymes flow."

"You're mad!" Joe spat out the words.

"How dare you talk to an old lady like that!" Elsie Bucket smiled, her face close to his, and Joe saw her grey tongue loll out of her mouth like a dying slug, then curl back to lick her ancient, discoloured teeth and suddenly he was more sick than afraid.

"Now!" Elsie Bucket sang out the word.

"Now!" the grannies chorused.

"No!" Joe strained with every muscle but the straps that held him were too thick.

Elsie Bucket capered over to the control desk and sat down in the armchair. She raised her hands and flexed her fingers as if she were a concert pianist. Joe heard the bones clicking against each other.

Then she stabbed down.

The machine hummed and whirred into life. The green liquid bubbled. The light bulbs blinked and flickered. The leather straps around him seemed to tighten but perhaps that was his own body tensing up as it all began. Electricity buzzed through the tuba-helmet which began to grow hot against his head. Joe clawed at the arms of the chair as slowly, one after another, the hypodermic needles shivered and then began to move forward. The arrow on the EMPTY and FULL gauge trembled excitedly. The whole thing was rattling and shaking, as indeed were all the watching grannies.

The hypodermic syringes slid forward.

Elsie Bucket yanked at a lever, her eyes bulging, her whole face twitching with delight.

The green liquid in the bottles surged and boiled. Electricity flickered. The needles moved again.

Joe opened his mouth to scream.

And then all the lights went out and everything stopped.

For a long moment nobody did anything. Then Joe heard Elsie Bucket's voice calling out of the darkness. "Don't panic, grannies! It's only a fuse. We'll have it mended in a moment!"

But even as she spoke, Joe was aware of someone close by him. He felt warm breath on his cheek. A pair of hands reached out to undo first the strap around his throat, then the ones on his arms. And at the same time a voice spoke to him. It was a voice he recognized, a woman's. But he still couldn't see.

"Run for it, Joe," the voice whispered. "Get out of here and get back to London. You can do it!"

The remaining straps fell away. The knitted strait-jacket was cut through with a single stroke. There was a pause and Joe realized that his mysterious rescuer had gone and that he was once more on his own. He stood up.

The lights came back on. The Grannymatic Enzyme Extractor shuddered back into life.

Elsie Bucket stood inches away, staring at him, her face twisted with fury. "Stop him!" she screamed in a voice that could have broken glass. "He's getting away!" At the same time she reached out to grab Joe herself.

Joe did the only thing he could. He twisted to one side and pushed Elsie Bucket away. Elsie gave a small, despairing gurgle and fell backwards into the seat of the Extractor just as the thirteen needles jerked forward like angry snakes. Joe didn't see what happened next. He was already running towards the edge of the stage, searching for a way out. But he heard Elsie Bucket's final scream as she was thoroughly punctured. He heard the great wail from the grannies in the audience. And he heard the sucking and bubbling as the Grannymatic Enzyme Extractor did what it had been built for.

Elsie Bucket had received her last royal telegram. The machine had attempted to extract her enzymes but having failed to find any had extracted everything else. There was nothing left of the granny apart from her clothes, punctured in thirteen places. These were now draped over the wooden seat with a few wisps of black smoke curling upwards into the light. At the same time a horrible grey ooze travelled along the tangle of pipes and spat itself out into the waiting bottles.

In the audience, the grannies moaned, yelled and bit each other, uncertain what to do next. The machine had finished with Elsie Bucket and was now vibrating dangerously, trying to tear free of the stage. A few yards away, Joe found a fire exit and, taking a deep breath, reached for the handle. He felt the cold steel under his hand and pushed. Mercifully, the door was unlocked. He felt the handle give and the door open and then he was out, tumbling into the night air.

And at that precise moment, the Grannymatic Enzyme Extractor exploded. Joe felt a fist of hot air punch him in the back. He was thrown forward, somersaulting twice and landing in a bed of flowers. He tried to stand up, then winced and covered his head as bricks, tiles, windows, wigs and false teeth showered down all around him. It seemed to go on for ever but at last everything was silent again and slowly, painfully, he got up.

The Stilton International had been partially destroyed. There was nothing left of the Elsie Bucket Conference Room. Nor could he make out a single surviving granny. It was like pictures he had seen of the Second World War – jagged broken walls, thick smoke, fires burning in the wreckage. Already the fire brigade and ambulance service had been alerted. He could hear their sirens in the far distance.

And then somebody moved, limping painfully through the smoke, coughing and spluttering. Joe tried to run but he had sprained his ankle and he could only wait there as the figure approached.

It was Granny.

Somehow Joe wasn't surprised that she had survived. But the explosion had not left her unharmed. She had lost a large clump of her hair and all her remaining teeth. Her arms and legs were covered in cuts and bruises and her twenty-seven-year-old coat hung off her in ribbons.

The two of them stood gazing at each other in the debris. At last Granny spoke.

"Are you all right, Jamie, my dear?"

"My name is Joe – and I'm not your dear!"

"Oh, yes you are." Granny's eyes flickered over to what had been the Elsie Bucket Suite. "We're very lucky," she said. "We seem to be the only survivors of an unfortunate accident..."

"An accident?"

"Oh, yes. It must have been the gas. Of course, that's what it was. Somebody must have left the oven on."

"I'm going to tell the truth!" Joe snarled.

Granny just smiled. "You could try telling your version of the truth, but do you really think anyone would believe you? A twelve-year-old boy? They'd think you were mad, Jeffrey. They'd lock you up."

Joe glanced at the wreckage of the hotel and realized that she was right. There would be nothing left of the Grannymatic Enzyme Extractor – and even if they managed to find a few tubes and valves, what expert would be able to work out what they were really for? Even as he watched, the flames leaped up, finding a way through the bricks and rubble.

Granny took a step nearer. Joe stood his ground. "Maybe you're right," he said. "But you can't hurt me any more. I know about you. And one day..."

"One day what?" Joe had been too kind, even now, to say what he was thinking. But now Granny said it for him. "One day I'll be dead? Is that what you're thinking?" She smiled toothlessly in the moonlight. Smoke from the ruined building curled around her legs. "Oh, yes. Even I won't live for ever. But don't you see, Joe, you'll never be rid of me. Because, you see, when I die, I'll come back. I'll come back and haunt you and there's nothing you'll be able to do."

"You're lying," Joe whispered. The fire engines

were getting nearer. He could hear the engines now, racing up the hill.

"Oh, no! The grave won't keep me lying down for long. I'll come back, you'll see. Just when you least expect it..." Her eyes blinked, black in the white light of the moon. "And then ... oh yes, what fun we'll have."

Half a minute later the firemen arrived with the police right behind them. They found one old lady waiting for them in the garden. She was standing next to a twelve-year-old boy lying flat out on the grass.

"You'd better look after my grandson," she said in a feeble, tearful voice as they wrapped a blanket round her and led her away. "He seems to have fainted. I suppose it must have been the shock."

GOODBYE, GRANNY

Mr and Mrs Warden returned from the south of France a few days later. They had not had a good holiday. Mr Warden had fallen asleep in the sun and was horribly burned. The top of his bald head was a glowing red and three layers of skin had peeled off his nose. He couldn't sit down without crying. Mrs Warden had been bitten by three hundred mosquitoes. Attracted by her body spray, they had invaded her bed and bitten every inch from her ankles to her ears. Her face in particular was dreadfully swollen. When Mr Warden had woken up beside her the following morning, he had actually screamed.

Wolfgang and Irma returned from Hungary the day after. They had enjoyed their holiday so much that in the four weeks they had been away they had forgotten how to speak English. They had brought everyone souvenirs of Hungary: a beetroot for Mr Warden, a book of Hungarian poetry for Mrs Warden and furry hats for Joe and Granny.

As for Granny herself, Joe had seen little of her after the events in Bideford. They had been released from hospital after one night's surveillance and had travelled back to London on the first train. The police had asked them a lot of questions but both of them had pretended they were asleep when the hotel exploded. Joe had hated doing it but he knew he had no choice. He was only twelve. Nobody would have believed him.

Even so, he got grim amusement from reading the newspapers the following day. He had always suspected you couldn't believe half the things you read in the papers but now he knew it was all a pack of lies.

300 GRANNIES PERISH IN HOTEL HORROR

FAULTY FUSE BLAMED FOR BIDEFORD BANG

BRITAIN GRIEVES FOR GRANNIES –

QUEEN MUM SENDS MESSAGE

He had stayed with Granny at Thattlebee Hall for five days but in that time he had barely seen her. When his parents got home, she had left without saying goodbye.

However, she had managed to play one last mean trick on him.

On Sunday, a new nanny arrived. Apparently

Granny had interviewed and selected her personally before she had gone. The new nanny was a short, plain woman wearing no make-up and a dress that seemed to have been fashioned out of a potato sack. Her hair was grey, as indeed was the rest of her. Her name, she said, was Ms Whipsnade.

"Miss Whipsnade," Wolfgang announced as he opened the door to her.

"I said Ms," the new nanny exclaimed, dropping her suitcase on Wolfgang's foot.

It turned out that Ms Whipsnade had worked for sixteen years as a social worker before going into politics. She was a communist and had stood for Parliament seven times. At the last election she had got four votes against the winner's twenty-six thousand, five hundred and eighty. Even so, she had demanded a recount. Ms Whipsnade was also a strict vegetarian and actually wept when she saw Joe's leather shoes. Neither Mr Warden nor his wife were entirely sure about the new arrival but as Granny had already offered her the job, there wasn't much they could do. And so Ms Whipsnade was shown to her room – which she promptly declared a nuclear-free zone. She also tore off all the wallpaper in the mistaken belief that it had been printed in South Africa.

On the following Monday, much to his relief, Joe went back to school. He had hardly slept at all since that night in Bideford and there were dark rings around his eyes. It wasn't just the horror of the Grannymatic

Enzyme Extractor. That had almost faded in his mind. Much, much worse was his last encounter with Granny, outside in the wreckage. Her words seemed to hang like cobwebs in the darkness and her beady eyes and twisted mouth were somehow always there – just out of sight. He realized now that he was more afraid of Granny dead than he was of her alive.

And that of course was exactly what she had intended. Alone in his room, Joe counted the hours until daylight and the days until he would be back at school. There at least he would be surrounded by young, happy, normal people. He felt safer with other children. Other children were all right. Anybody old – the headmaster, the dinner lady, the caretaker, the lollipop lady – now belonged to another, twilight world. Joe looked at them and he was afraid.

Time passed and for a while everything was all right.

Then Granny fell ill.

Joe first heard the news one afternoon at school. After lunch he was called into the headmaster's study. The headmaster, a white-haired man of about sixty, was called Mr Ellis. He had been a teacher for forty-four years even though he was allergic to children. He was sitting in a large leather chair when Joe came in. "Do sit down, Warden," he said. "Sit down."

That was when Joe knew it had to be bad news.

Mr Ellis sneezed. "I'm afraid I have some bad news for you, Warden. It's your grandmother..."

"She's not dead, is she?" Joe exclaimed.

"No! No!" The headmaster was surprised by the boy's alarm. He sneezed twice more and tried to shrink into his chair. "No. But it is quite serious. Pneumonia."

"She can't die!" Joe whispered. "She can't!"

Mr Ellis blinked. "I have to say, it's rare to find a boy so fond of his granny," he muttered. He pulled out a handkerchief and dabbed at his eye. "It does you credit, Warden. I'm sure she'll be all right. But in the meantime, perhaps it would be better if you went home."

Joe returned home that afternoon. The new nanny was in his room, painting pink triangles on his walls to show her support for the gay movement. She had also donated his bed and all his books to the Cuban miners.

"How's Granny?" Joe asked.

Ms Whipsnade blinked. "Her name is Ms Kettle," she snapped. "As a term, 'granny' is both sexist and, worse, ageist."

"How is she?"

"I haven't heard. For some reason your parents refuse to speak to me."

For the next few days there were a lot of comings and goings at Thattlebee Hall. Car doors slammed at all times of the day and night and Mr and Mrs Warden seemed to speak permanently in whispers. Nobody told Joe anything and the first inkling he had that things were really serious was when he saw his Uncles

David and Kurt arrive at the front door. The relations never came to the house unless it was for Christmas or a funeral and Christmas had been over long ago. Listening at the door, Joe learned that Granny's pneumonia had got worse and that her doctors had more or less given up hope. His uncles were already arguing about her will.

And then on Friday morning came the news. Granny had died in her sleep.

At breakfast, Wolfgang and Irma were both tearful. Meanwhile, Ms Whipsnade – imitating the burial customs of the Taramuhara Indians – danced in the garden and set fire to the summer house. Later that morning, as soon as the fire brigade had gone, Mrs Warden went to Harrods and bought herself a black Yves St Laurent dress with a crêpe tunic, silk veil and diamante trim. Mr Warden spent most of the time on the telephone. He then drank an entire bottle of champagne. Irma assumed he was drowning his sorrows but Joe wasn't so sure. Certainly his father was singing merrily enough when he was carried to bed.

The funeral took place on the Sunday. It was a terrible day. The weather had turned and the various relatives – the Wardens and the Kettles – had to battle their way into the cemetery against the howling wind and rain. It seemed that the entire family had turned out: Michael, David, Kurt and Nita were there along with Joe's four cousins (all in black shorts – the rainwater streaming in rivulets down their legs). But there were other relatives too: tiny Aunt Cissie, fat cousin Sidney and twitching Uncle Geoff. Then there was Uncle Fred who had flown all the way from Texas to be there and several other relatives whom Joe didn't recognize.

Wisely, the vicar kept the sermon short. The weather was just too horrible. After two minutes, Aunt Cissie was actually blown into the open grave by a particularly vicious gust of wind. The rain lashed down and all the colour ran out of Uncle Fred's suit – soon he was standing in a puddle of blue ink. About halfway through the service there was a great flash of lightning and Uncle David had an epileptic fit. The four cousins left early with chilblains. Even the vicar looked alarmed and managed to get most of the words wrong. All in all it was a dreadful affair.

But worse, in some ways, were the days that followed. Joe had been left out of everything – as if he were too young to understand funerals, deaths and the rest of it. As for Ms Whipsnade, she had been fired after she had told Mrs Warden that her mother had not died so much as been recycled. A great silence had descended on Thattlebee Hall. It wasn't that the house was in mourning. That would have been perfectly understandable. No. It was something altogether different and more difficult to explain.

For his part, Joe was terrified.

"I'll come back..."

What could he do? He couldn't sleep. He couldn't

even relax. He had lost so much weight that he had to look twice to find himself in the mirror. At any time he expected to see Granny return. How would it happen? Would she dig her way out of the grave and return, dripping mud and slime, to the house? Or would she come in the night, materializing suddenly above his bed and floating around the room? Not for a minute did he doubt that Granny would return. She had promised it and he had seen the certainty in her eyes.

Inevitably, Joe himself fell ill. His temperature shot up to one hundred and three and the sweat poured off him as he tossed and turned in his bed. He hadn't eaten anything for a week and his ribs were so pronounced that Wolfgang – much to everyone's amazement – was able to use them to demonstrate his skill as a xylophone player. Doctors were called in and, after listening to Joe's feverish cries, announced that he had been traumatized by his granny's death. It seemed more than likely that he was about to join her.

Joe did have moments when he was cool and rational. It was at these times that he tried to work out what to do. He knew he was afraid – that he was actually being scared to death by the memory of what Granny had said. And he also knew he had to tell someone about it. That was the only way to bring the nightmare to an end. Tell someone and they'd be able to face it together. But at the same time he knew there was no one. He couldn't go to his parents. Mrs Jinks and Mr Lampy were both gone. He was on his own.

And then the postcard came.

It was addressed to him, written in neat, block capitals. On the front was a picture of Bideford. On the back was a simple message:

THE TRUTH WILL ALWAYS COME OUT.

That was all. The card was unsigned.

Joe thought long and hard. He knew he had heard the words before but he couldn't remember where. The only clue seemed to be the picture of Bideford. He had often wondered who it was who had freed him from the Enzyme Extractor while the lights were out, and had played the voice in his mind over and over again. He had always assumed that it must have been one of the grannies who had taken pity on him and who had perished in the blast. But now, looking at the card, he wasn't so sure. "The truth will always come out." Who had said that to him and when?

From that time on, Joe began to recover. It wasn't just the fact that he knew that, after all, he did have a friend. It was also his belief in what the postcard said. The truth was important. The truth mattered. It mattered more than the fact that he was only twelve and that his story was completely preposterous. People like Granny, all bullies in fact, only managed to survive because they lived behind the truth. Once people knew them for what they were, they would be powerless.

One evening, a week after the funeral, Joe got out of bed and went downstairs. His parents were in the sitting-room, watching television. It was *The Money*

Programme, his father's favourite, but even so he pressed ahead.

Joe told them.

He turned off the television and told them everything that had happened since Christmas and the toy robot. He told them about the cream cheese tea, the death of Mrs Jinks and his suspicions about the death of Mr Lampy. Then he told them what had really happened in Bideford, what had caused the explosion and how he had escaped.

Mr and Mrs Warden listened to all this in complete silence but when he had at last finished, Mrs Warden stood up.

"Is that all?" she asked.

"Yes," Joe said. He cast his eyes down. The room was suddenly like a refrigerator. He could feel his mother's anger, chilling him.

"You do realize that's my mother you're talking about?"

"Yes."

Mrs Warden let out a single sob. "We'll discuss this in the morning," she said and walked out of the room with her nose in the air.

"Look where you're going!" Mr Warden shouted.

There was a loud clunk as Mrs Warden hit the corner of the door. Then she was gone.

"Now look what you've done," Mr Warden snapped. He did the same to his cigar even though it was only half-smoked. "Lost your marbles, have you?" he asked.

"Father..."

"I've heard some pretty daft stories in my time," he said. "But that one takes the biscuit. And on the subject of biscuits it's time for my hot milk. I'll talk to you in the morning, young man!"

Joe watched his father leave. For the first time in more years than he could remember he felt hot tears brimming on his eyelids. "I hate this house," he muttered. "I hate them all." He was still holding the mysterious postcard. Now he tore it into pieces. He didn't care who had sent it any more. Nobody would ever believe him. Nobody cared about him. He was nobody.

That was the truth.

Later that evening, Mr and Mrs Warden lay in bed. Mr Warden had decided against the hot milk and was sipping a glass of brandy instead. Mrs Warden was half-concealed under an icepack which was pressed against her face where the door had hit her.

"That story," Mr Warden muttered. "It was ridiculous."

"Ludicrous," Mrs Warden agreed.

"Outrageous."

"Monstrous."

"Your mother ... she would never have behaved like that!"

"Of course not!"

"No."

There was a long silence.

"She was rather horrible to me once or twice, though," Mr Warden murmured. "Of course, I adored her. She was your mother. But she could be ... difficult."

"I suppose so," Mrs Warden agreed.

"I mean, she never liked me," Mr Warden went on. "When I asked if I could marry you, she poured tea over me. And her wedding present to us. Twelve fish-fingers. That wasn't very generous."

"She could be worse," Mrs Warden murmured. "When I was a little girl, she made me share my room with two lodgers, one of whom – Mr Baster – had very unsavoury habits. And do you know, she never took me out once. Not in my whole life!"

"Really?" Mr Warden was genuinely surprised.

"Not even shopping. She never had any time for me. She once told me she didn't want children. She'd even tried to abandon me. She left me in a basket on the steps of a police station."

"Good lord! How distressing."

"It was very embarrassing. I was sixteen years old!"

Mr Warden reflected. "Your father adored her, though," he said.

"Yes. He did adore her. Only he forgot their anniversary once and she never spoke to him again."

"She was a hard woman."

"Oh, yes."

Both of them sat in silence again. Then Mr Warden scooped a cube out of his wife's ice-pack and added it to his brandy. "I suppose Jordan's story could be true, then," he muttered.

"Yes. I suppose so."

"I mean, she was a hard woman."

"Very hard."

On the mantelpiece, the clock struck ten although in fact it was half past nine. The clock had never worked properly since Granny, in a moment of anger, had stamped on it.

"Of course," he went on, "it's very sad, your mother passing away like that."

"It's devastating," Mrs Warden agreed.

"Tragic."

"Terrible."

"Too, too awful! I'll miss her..." Mr Warden took a large gulp of brandy.

"Will you?" Mrs Warden asked.

"Well, I will a bit." Mr Warden swallowed. "But to tell you the truth, my love, I wasn't a hundred per cent fond of her."

"Not a hundred per cent?"

"No."

"Fifty perhaps?"

"Well ... not even fifty." Mr Warden frowned. "I know it's a horrible thing to say, my angel. But no. If you really want the truth, I wasn't very fond of her at all."

Mrs Warden slid the ice-pack off her head. Most of it had melted now anyway. "Nor was I," she whispered.

"What?"

"Oh, Gordon! It's dreadful of me. She was my mother. But I have to admit it. It's true. I really didn't love her."

"I never looked forward to her visits," Mr Warden said.

"I dreaded them."

"I hated them!"

"I loathed them!"

Mr and Mrs Warden looked at each other. And in that moment – perhaps the first true moment they had shared together in twenty years of marriage – they understood many things.

The first was that they had lied to each other. The second was that they had lied to themselves. That was what was so odd and uncomfortable about this period of mourning. They weren't really mourning at all. They weren't glad that old Mrs Kettle was dead. They would never have thought that about anyone. But they couldn't honestly say that they would miss her – which was what they had been saying. That was all a lie.

Their marriage was full of lies too. They could see that now, sitting in bed with Mrs Warden's ice-pack dripping onto the electric blanket. And without saying anything they knew they had come to a crossroads. Mrs Warden was beginning to wonder if perhaps, just possibly, she hadn't treated her only child just a little bit like her mother had always treated her. And Mr Warden too was asking himself what sort of father he had really been. For that matter, what sort of husband had he been? What sort of man was he? Everything had been poisoned by lies.

And then both Mr and Mrs Warden had the same thought at the same time.

"That business about her ... coming back," Mr Warden said.

"She won't," Mrs Warden muttered. "I mean, let's be adult about this, Gordon, dearest. It's not possible."

"It's absurd."

"Nonsensical."

"Out of the question."

Mr and Mrs Warden edged closer to each other in bed. Mr Warden put his arms around Mrs Warden. Mrs Warden put her arms around Mr Warden. There was a sudden fizz, a flash and all the lights in the house went out as the electric blanket short-circuited. The two parents were plunged into blackness.

"She won't come back," Mr Warden's voice quavered in the dark. "She can't..."

But they were still clinging onto each other when dawn finally broke and the first fingers of light announced the next day.

GRANNY COMES BACK

Curiously, Granny wasn't actually dead. This is what had happened.

She had indeed been taken ill with a bad cold and, before she had even sneezed twice, she had telephoned for an ambulance to take her to hospital. By the time the ambulance men had arrived, she had decided she was too ill even to walk and had insisted on being carried to the waiting vehicle. It was then that something very unfortunate had taken place.

As the ambulance men carried her out of the block of flats a neighbour had chanced to walk past and asked them if they knew the time. Both ambulance men had lifted their wrists to look at their watches. In doing so, they unwittingly tilted the stretcher. This was a bad mistake. Granny gave a little scream and rolled off the stretcher, falling straight into a large puddle. The result was that by the time she arrived at the hospital, Granny's cold really had developed into a mild form of pneumonia and she had to be given a bed.

Even so, her illness was not life-threatening. The doctors were sure she would be able to go home in a day or two and left her quite happily sitting up in bed with a furry knitted jacket and the latest copy of *Hello!* magazine.

Now, Granny had been placed in an ordinary public ward – in the geriatric wing. There were eight beds there and each one was occupied ... indeed one bed actually had two elderly people in it, lying head-to-foot and foot-to-head – as ever, the National Health Service was finding it hard to cope. But despite the crowding, the nurses and doctors were as cheerful as possible, working long hours into the night, and nobody complained.

Nobody, that is, except for the woman in the bed next to Granny.

Her name was Marjory Henslow and she was a retired headmistress. Having spent her whole working life telling people what to do, she hadn't allowed retirement to stop her. She treated the nurses, the cleaners and her fellow patients like children, her face frozen in a permanent sneer of disapproval. She was a woman with opinions about everything and expressed them at all times of the day and night.

"Mrs Thatcher? A wonderful woman! She showed

them in the Gulf War. That's what the train drivers need. A few Exocet missiles would soon show them what's what! I'd blow them all up. And the miners! I say we should close all the pits down. What's wrong with nuclear energy? Let's drop nuclear bombs on the miners and the teachers and the train drivers. Bing! Bang! Boom! When I was a headmistress I used to flog everyone. It never did them any harm. I even used to flog the other members of staff. And I flogged dead horses! Why not? A bit more flogging would put the Great back in Britain..."

This went on twenty-four hours a day (Mrs Henslow even talked in her sleep). It was hardly surprising that she alone in the ward had no flowers or grapes. Nobody visited her. Nobody liked her.

One evening she got talking to Granny.

"This is a horrible place," she said. "I wouldn't come here if I wasn't ill. These nurses! Some of them are coloured, you know. Not that I'm a racist. But, well, the Nazis did have *some* good ideas..."

"I suppose so," Granny agreed.

"This ward is so drab and uncomfortable." Mrs Henslow leant towards Granny. "Well, tomorrow I'm moving to a different hospital."

"Are you?" Granny quavered.

"Oh, yes. You see, I have private medical insurance. Well, there was some sort of mixup and it's taken them a few days to sort it out. But tomorrow I'm off to a private hospital outside London. And I won't miss this place, I can tell you!"

"Lucky you," Granny scowled. It had to be said that the ward wasn't the most comfortable of places.

"I am lucky. Tomorrow I'll have my own private room with a colour television and a nice view. The food there is absolutely delicious, I'm told. Brought in fresh from Harrods' Food Hall. You actually get a menu – not like here."

Granny thought back to her lunch that day. It had been battered fish. It had been served underneath a battered tin dish. It hadn't been very hot. And it hadn't been very nice.

"I've heard this hospital is so nice," Mrs Henslow went on, "that people actually make themselves ill to get in there. My neighbour's wife cut off her hand to be admitted and she said it was worth every finger!" Mrs Henslow smiled. "Of course I'm sure you'll get better *eventually* here. The NHS is wonderful really. If you're too poor to afford better."

By now Granny was dark red with anger – and when the doctor came round later, it was discovered that her temperature had gone up to one hundred and five. Everyone assumed of course that it was her pneumonia that had caused the rise. The doctor doubted she would even live to see the next day and this is what he had reported to Mr and Mrs Warden who in turn had called in all the relatives.

But as it turned out, it was Mrs Henslow who suddenly took a turn for the worse during the night and quite unexpectedly died. Granny was lying awake – she was too angry to sleep – and actually heard the other lady breathe her last.

And that was what gave her the idea.

Granny had been perfectly content in the public ward until Mrs Henslow had described the hospital she was being transferred to. Food from Harrods? Colour TV and a view? Why couldn't she go there? Why *couldn't* she? Granny gazed at the still and silent figure in the next bed. By chance, Mrs Henslow was wearing a very similar nightie to her own. She was about the same age. And it was true, was it not, that one very old lady in bed with the sheets drawn up to her chin looks very much like the next. Mrs Henslow had no relatives or visitors to give the game away. The nurses and doctors had for the most part avoided her. Nobody had examined her that closely.

So why not?

Why not indeed?

And so it was that Granny swapped beds with Mrs Henslow and the following morning it was Mrs Henslow's death that was reported to Mr and Mrs Warden while Granny, her eyes peeping out over the sheet, was carried into a waiting ambulance and transferred to the private hospital.

And for the next few days – while Mrs Henslow was buried in the raging storm – it was Granny who reclined on duck down pillows watching her own 22-inch colour television whilst popping grapes, lychees and other exotic fruits between her lips. It didn't even matter when she forgot to answer to the name of Mrs Henslow. She was old. She was ill. She was bound to be confused.

Nobody noticed. It had all gone exactly according to plan.

There was an awkward silence at breakfast the next day. Mr and Mrs Warden hadn't slept a wink and it showed. Mr Warden had eaten his muesli dry and then poured half a pint of milk over his toast and marmalade. Mrs Warden had cleaned her teeth with her husband's shaving foam and was quite literally frothing at the mouth. For his part, Joe hadn't intended to come down to breakfast. But he was fed up being ill and wanted to get back to school – which meant he had to start eating.

"Jordan..." Mr Warden said.

Irma, who happened to be passing at that moment, dropped her tray and gasped. In all the years she had been with the Wardens, she had never heard Mr Warden address his son at the breakfast table.

"It seems we have matters to discuss," Mr Warden went on. "I suggest we meet this evening."

"This morning!" Mrs Warden interrupted.

"I shall return early from work and we shall meet this afternoon," Mr Warden decided. "Half past four in the living-room. Irma will bake a cake. We shall have tea. As a family."

"As a family!" Irma exclaimed. "Are you feeling ill, Mr Warden, sir?"

"Yes. I am feeling extremely ill as a matter of fact," Mr Warden replied. "But that is what we shall do."

After breakfast, Mr Warden went to work. Mrs Warden went shopping. And Joe stayed at home. His thoughts were buzzing. He had seen the change in his parents. It was incredible. It was astounding. Could it be that...? Somehow, had they decided to believe him? Joe got dressed and went out feeling more alive than he had in weeks.

But neither Joe nor his parents had a particularly nice day.

"I'll come back..."

Mr Warden tried to concentrate on his work in his office but Granny's words echoed over and over in his head. Where would she pop up? Under his desk? In his filing cabinet? Outside the window ... even if it was twenty-seven floors up? He reached for a cigar and rolled it against his cheek, taking in the aroma of the tobacco. "You're being ridiculous," he muttered to himself.

Somebody touched him lightly on the shoulder. Mr Warden screamed and jumped three feet into the air. The cigar slipped and disappeared into his left ear. Then he saw who it was. It was his secretary. She was looking at him in dismay.

"Lock the doors," Mr Warden whimpered. "Lock the filing cabinets. Lock everything! I want to be on my own…"

"I'll come back…"

Mrs Warden was at the Brent Cross shopping centre. There wasn't anything she particularly needed but she often found that buying things cheered her up. Once, when she was particularly depressed she had bought three lampshades, a deck chair, an umbrella and two pairs of gloves without actually wanting any of them. She was in that sort of mood. She was thinking of buying a Swiss Army knife. It might come in useful if she ever decided to join the Swiss Army.

She was standing on the escalator, travelling up past the central fountain, when she saw the figure standing at the top, waiting for her. She blinked. The yellow cheeks, the crooked smile, the gleaming eyes … it couldn't be! Mrs Warden stared. The escalator carried her ever nearer. It was!

"No!" she screamed. "Go away, Mummy!"

Turning round, Mrs Warden clambered down the up escalator, pushing the other shoppers out of the way. People were shouting at her, trying to stop her, but she ignored them. She just had to get back down. She could feel the metal beneath her feet carrying her the other way. It was like her worst nightmare come true. "No!" she wailed again, shouldering her way past a pair of newly-weds and scattering parcels and packages everywhere. Then somehow her foot got tangled in the escalator, she dived forward, turned a somersault and landed spread-eagled on the marble floor.

"Is she all right?"

"I think she's had a fit."

"She went mad!"

Security men were running towards her from every direction. With a soft moan, Mrs Warden looked back up the escalator. And there it was. What had frightened her wasn't Granny at all. It was a full-size cardboard cut-out of a dinosaur. It stood outside a video store with a sign reading: FANTASIA – BUY IT HERE. How could she possibly have made that mistake? Was she going mad?

The first security guard had reached her. Everyone was looking at her. Mrs Warden slowly began to laugh.

"I'll come back..."

Joe saw Granny everywhere. During the course of the day she had popped out of the fridge, out of the toaster, out of the dustbin and out of the fireplace. She had risen, dripping water, out of the pond and clawed her way up through the lawn. The clouds had twisted themselves into Granny's shape. The birds in the trees had winked at him with her eyes. Twice, Irma had become Granny and even Wolfgang had momentarily borrowed her shadow.

It was all imagination, of course. The real horror was still to come.

That afternoon at four o'clock, Mr and Mrs Warden sat in the living-room with Joe and the tea that Irma had prepared. The Hungarian cook had decided that it was such an important occasion that she had gone quite mad. There were huge piles of sandwiches, home-made scones, sausage rolls, tea cakes, crumpets, cakes, biscuits and even a jelly. But no one was eating. Mrs Warden was a nervous wreck. Her hair was all over the place ... and not only on her head. Mr Warden had bitten all his nails and was now starting on his wife's. Even Joe was trembling.

"I have called this meeting," Mr Warden began, "because I have something important to say."

"Yes, that's right," Mrs Warden agreed.

Then the telephone rang.

Mrs Warden sighed. "I'll get it," she said.

She stood up and walked across the room. The telephone was standing on a little antique table. She picked up the receiver. "Hello? Maud N. Warden..." she said.

There was a moment's silence.

Then Mrs Warden let out a great scream and dropped the receiver as if it were a scorpion she had accidentally grasped. Everyone stared at her. Joe had never seen his mother like it. Her hair, already in disarray, was actually standing up on end, like in a cartoon. Her eyes were bulging. All the colour had drained out of her lips – including even the colour of her lipstick.

"It's her!" she screamed – but the sound came out as a hoarse, strangled whisper.

"That's nonsense!" Mr Warden muttered. "I mean. Really, Maud. It's not possible."

But Mrs Warden could only point at the telephone

with a wobbling finger. "It's her!" she groaned again.

"What did she say?" Mr Warden burbled. "She said ... she was coming back!"

"It's not possible." Mr Warden strode forward and snatched up the receiver. "Who is this?" he demanded.

Another pause. Joe waited silently. He hadn't breathed since the telephone rang.

Mr Warden's mouth fell open. Now he was holding the receiver away from him, as if it could suck him in down the wire. "No!" he shouted at it. "Go away! We don't want you!" And with that he hung up – so hard that he actually broke the telephone into several pieces.

"It was her!" Mrs Warden whimpered.

"It was her," Mr Warden agreed. "I'd know that voice anywhere."

"What did she say?" Joe asked.

"She said she was much better now and she'd be here in half an hour."

"Much better?" Joe shuddered. "How can you be much better when you're dead?" Somewhere in the back of his mind he knew that the whole thing was ridiculous. Ghosts didn't announce their arrival by telephone. But seeing his parents as terrified as they were he decided to go along with them. It was better than being left on his own.

"Half an hour..." Mrs Warden whispered. And that was when the full horror of it hit her. "Half an hour!" she screamed.

"Pack!" Mr Warden yelled.

Exactly twenty-nine minutes later, the front door of Thattlebee Hall burst open and the Wardens tumbled out grasping two hastily packed suitcases. Mrs Warden had thrown on her favourite fur coat. Mr Warden was clutching his wallet, the family passports and his eighteen favourite credit cards. His car – a green Mercedes – was waiting for them at the front.

"In!" Mr Warden yelled, wrenching open the door and catching his wife with it on the head.

"Aaagh!" Mrs Warden cried.

"And me!" Joe shouted, piling into the back. He was actually enjoying all this.

"Quickly!" Mr Warden stabbed forward with the ignition key, missed and tried again. This time it went in. He twisted and the Mercedes coughed into life.

At the same time, a taxi appeared, rumbling up the drive.

"There!"

"No!"

"Aaagh!"

"Mummy!"

"Help!"

Granny – the ghost of Granny – was in the back seat. There could be no mistaking her, sitting there, gazing out of the window – back from the dead! And this wasn't a dream. The entire family was seeing her at the same time.

Mr Warden wrenched the gear-stick and slammed his foot down on the accelerator. The car leapt forward.

Granny, sitting in the back of the taxi, frowned and pursed her lips. She had been released, fully recovered, from the hospital just half an hour before. She had of course telephoned to say she was coming and had been quite unable to understand the hysterical reactions of her daughter and son-in-law. And where were they going now? One moment the Mercedes was tearing down the drive, heading straight for the taxi. Then it had swerved to one side, ploughed across the lawn and then burst through a hedge onto the main road.

The taxi stopped and she got out.

"That'll be eighteen quid, love," the taxi driver said.

With a snarl Granny slammed the car door behind her, breaking both the window and the taxi driver's nose. She strode across the lawn, her hands on her hips, and gazed at the hole in the hedge. They had gone. Left her. How could they?

Granny fell to her knees, lifted her hands to the sky and howled.

The storm broke a few minutes later.

EPILOGUE: ANTHONY LAGOON

Anthony Lagoon was a cattle station in the middle of the Northern Territory of Australia. It consisted of a long, low wooden house with glass windows and a verandah which was the manager's house and four shacks for the workers. There was a water tower, a flaking metal cattle run and an airstrip. The nearest town, Mount Isa, was a two hour flight away. Nobody knew who Anthony was. But then the outback is full of people who prefer not to be remembered.

Mr Warden had bought Anthony Lagoon as soon as he had landed in Perth. He had seen it advertised for sale in the *Perth Exchange* and had made an instant decision.

"We'll be safe there," he said. "No roads. No telephones. No letters. She'll never find us."

And six days later, after driving all the way across Australia to Townsville, around the one-way system and then west again, they arrived.

There were four jackeroos working on Anthony Lagoon – all of them men on the run. Rolf had poisoned his wife. Barry and Bruce were wanted for armed robbery. And Les had been hiding for so long that he'd forgotten what it was he'd actually done although, as he frequently told the others, it must have been something brutal. These were tough, brutal men. Rolf had only one leg. He'd lost the other in a car accident and hadn't even noticed for a month. Bruce chewed live bullets and Barry scoured saucepans with his beard. Les could rip a cow in half with his bare hands. They were four of the ugliest, most violent men you could hope to meet. They only had one string vest between them and played poker to decide who would wear it.

You'd think Rolf, Barry, Bruce and Les would have made mincemeat out of the new owners of Anthony Lagoon but the surprising fact is that they quickly warmed to them. But then the Wardens had changed beyond all recognition.

Mr Warden had taken off his business suit and put on a pair of jeans, a brightly coloured shirt and a ten-gallon hat that came down to his nose. After only a week he had acquired an Australian accent. Having been stuck in an office all his life, he now found he loved the fresh air. Although there were over one hundred thousand head of cattle on the station, he had decided to get to know each and every one of them by name.

After all her riding lessons, Mrs Warden quickly impressed the jackeroos with her excellent horse riding. They decided they liked her as soon as she had galloped twice round the paddock blindfold and backwards. Then she set to work rebuilding the compound, repairing the fences, planting a garden, putting pretty lace curtains into Bruce and Barry's bedrooms and generally making the place more like home.

Mrs Warden also taught Joe how to ride (she never called him Jordan now). Following her example, the four jackeroos decided to lend a hand with Joe's education and soon Joe knew everything there was to know about managing cattle and, for that matter, robbing banks.

Joe loved his life on the cattle station. He had so often dreamed of running away – to a circus, to the Foreign Legion, to wherever – that it took him a long time to realize that this was what he had actually done ... even if his parents had rather surprised him by coming along too. But now every day was an adventure as he galloped across the paddocks under the hot Australian sun, dodging down to avoid the tree-spiders and surging, waist-deep, through the lagoons.

It was hard work. The day started at five when Joe rode out alone to get the horses in. Joe had never seen the dawn before and he marvelled at the thousand shades of red that shimmered over the horizon as the sun climbed up into the sky. He loved the smell of the air and the great silence of the plains and rapidly forgot Latin, Greek, Algebra, Geography and just about everything else he had been learning at school. Joe worked all day until sunset. There was no television on the station but he didn't miss it. He actually went to bed tired, not because he had to. And every ache, every pain, every cut and every blister was precious to him because it was part of the adventure.

Naturally, Joe lost weight. He grew tall and muscular with broad, suntanned shoulders. Once a month, Rolf, Barry, Bruce and Les took him with them to Mount Isa and he would stay up late into the night, drinking and gambling. That was the best thing. He was an equal. Nobody treated him like a child any more.

News has a strange way of travelling in Australia, crossing huge distances without the help of a stamp or a telephone line. And the happiness of the Wardens was completed one day by the arrival of someone who had heard they were there and had decided to join them. As soon as he saw who it was, Joe understood everything: the strange figure he had seen at Paddington Station, the last-minute rescue at the hotel and the anonymous postcard.

The new arrival was Mrs Jinks.

"I thought I was doomed when the police dogs came after me," she explained, "and indeed I was bitten quite badly. But I was very lucky. Just as I burst through the bushes, a large rabbit appeared. The dogs decided they preferred the taste of rabbit to me and attacked that instead. I managed to climb a tree and waited there until everyone had gone."

"But you kept your eye on me after that, didn't you, Mrs Jinks," Joe said.

"Well, yes. I couldn't reveal myself, unfortunately – I was still wanted for theft, after all. But I was frightened to leave you on your own and when your granny came to look after you I knew something was going on. I followed you to Bideford in disguise and I was there at the Stilton International when they tied you to that horrible device."

"And it was you in the dark." Joe shivered. "It was lucky the lights fused."

"That wasn't luck at all. That was me. I turned the power off at the main fuse box and then crept onto the stage to untie you."

"I got your card," Joe said.

"Yes. I thought it was time your parents knew the truth. Of course, I couldn't tell them myself. So I hoped a little nudge would do the trick."

Mr and Mrs Warden were delighted to see Mrs Jinks. They knew now that they had been deceived and couldn't apologize enough. They immediately invited her to stay with them at the cattle station and Joe was delighted when she agreed.

And so time passed at Anthony Lagoon which was a very pretty place now with a duck pond, a village green, two English sheepdogs, a willow tree and a beautiful croquet lawn. Often, when the day's work was done, Mrs Jinks would stroll out with Joe and they would talk about what had happened.

"Do you think she'll ever find us?" Joe asked one evening.

"Who, dearest?"

"Granny. The ghost of Granny."

Mrs Jinks looked past the verandah where Mr Warden was pushing Mrs Warden on a swing and beyond over the outback to the deep red glow where the setting sun marked the end of the world. "No," she said. "I don't think so."

"I hated her." Joe shuddered. "Old people are horrible."

"No," Mrs Jinks corrected him. "There's nothing wrong with being old. Don't forget – you'll be old one day. Nobody can avoid it."

"Well, I won't be like Granny," Joe said.

"Of course you won't," Mrs Jinks agreed. "If you're kind and cheerful when you're young, you'll be kind and cheerful when you're old ... only more so. Old age is like a magnifying glass. It takes the best and the worst of you and magnifies them. Granny was selfish and cruel all her life. But you can't blame her for being old."

"She could still find us here." Joe's eyes – older and more knowing – scanned the horizon. He shivered in the cool evening breeze.

"It doesn't matter any more," Mrs Jinks replied. "Even if she did find you ... you're ready for her now."

In fact Granny died two years later – this time for real.

After the Wardens had left she had found there was nobody to look after her and had rapidly gone into a decline. This was her tragedy. All the spitefulness of her life had caught up with her and suddenly she was alone.

Her hair had never grown again after the accident and although she had been given new false teeth, they didn't fit, with the result that she couldn't talk or eat solids. She was moved to an Old People's Home next to a cement factory and spent the next two years on her own, sipping porridge through a straw. In an attempt to cheer her up, the matron of the home gave her a parrot. The parrot bit her. The wound went septic. And that was what finally finished her off.

That was a year ago.

But Granny is not forgotten. Deep in the heart of the Australian outback, the aborigines gather around a huge camp fire. Their black bodies are painted and they sit quite naked apart from a twist of cloth around their loins. Then the music of the didgeridoo throbs and wails through the darkness and if the magic is working a figure appears, wrapped in a thick coat against-the desert chill. The aborigines see her scowling in the light of the fire, her eyes glowing, her mouth opening and closing as she chews on her invisible feast. They call her "old-woman-walk-by-night".

It is Granny. Looking for Joe.

But she hasn't found him yet.

READ OTHER GREAT BOOKS BY ANTHONY HOROWITZ...

THE ALEX RIDER SERIES

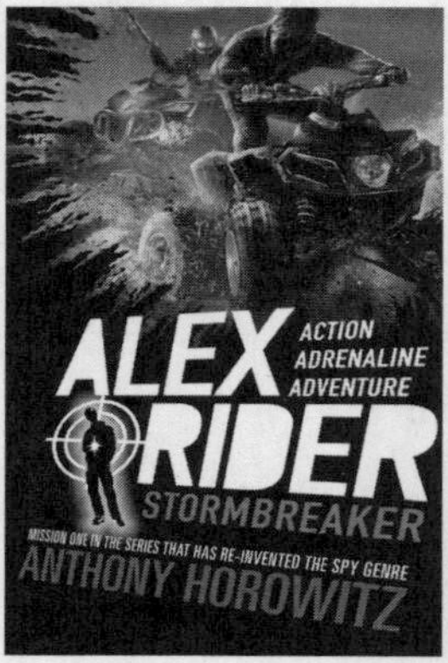

Alex Rider – you're never too young to die…

High in the Alps, death waits for Alex Rider…

Sharks. Assassins. Nuclear bombs. Alex Rider's in deep water.

Alex Rider has 90 minutes to save the world.

Once stung, twice as deadly. Alex Rider wants revenge.

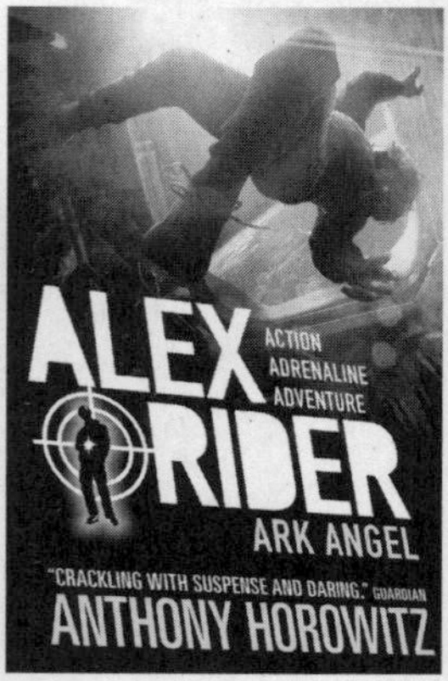

He's back – and this time there are no limits.

Alex Rider bites back…

Alex Rider – in the jaws of death…

One bullet.
One life.
The end starts here.

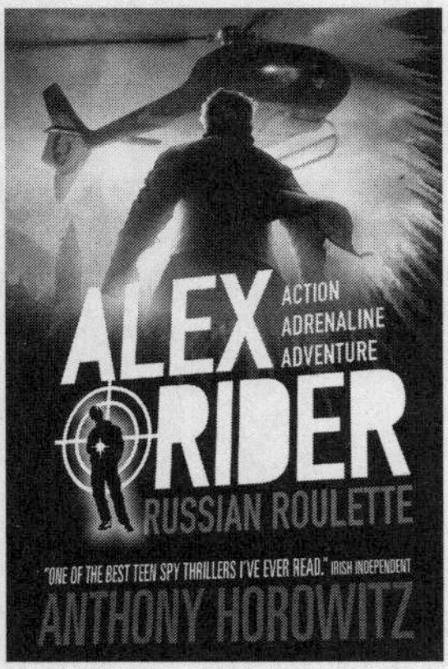

Get your hands on the deadly prequel

ALEX RIDER
ACTION
ADRENALINE
ADVENTURE

THE MISSION CONTINUES AT
alexrider.com

ACTION. ADRENALINE. ADVENTURE.

alexrider.com /alexrideruk

WELCOME TO THE DARK SIDE OF ANTHONY HOROWITZ

THE POWER OF FIVE

BOOK ONE

He always knew he was different.
First there were the dreams.
Then the deaths began.

BOOK TWO

It began with Raven's Gate.
But it's not over yet. Once
again the enemy is stirring.

BOOK THREE

Darkness covers the earth.
The Old Ones have returned.
The battle must begin.

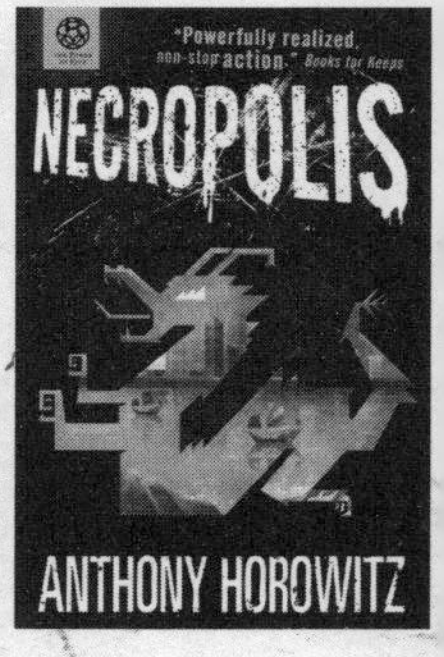

BOOK FOUR

An ancient evil is unleashed.
Five have the power to defeat it.
But one of them has been taken.

BOOK FIVE

Five Gatekeepers.
One chance to save mankind.
Chaos beckons. Oblivion awaits.

Anthony Horowitz is the author of the number one bestselling Alex Rider books and The Power of Five series. He has enjoyed huge success as a writer for both children and adults, most recently with the latest adventure in the Alex Rider series, *Russian Roulette*, and the highly acclaimed Sherlock Holmes novel, *The House of Silk*. His latest novel, *Moriarty*, is also set in the world of Sherlock Holmes and was published in October 2014. Anthony was also chosen by the Ian Fleming estate to write the new James Bond novel which will be published this year. Anthony has won numerous awards, including the Bookseller Association/Nielsen Author of the Year Award, the Children's Book of the Year Award at the British Book Awards, and the Red House Children's Book Award. In 2014 Anthony was awarded an OBE for Services to Literature. He has also created and written many major television series, including *Injustice*, *Collision* and the award-winning *Foyle's War*.

You can find out more about Anthony and his work at:

www.alexrider.com

@AnthonyHorowitz

The Devil and his Boy

More wickedly funny books

by Anthony Horowitz

The Devil and His Boy

Groosham Grange

Return to Groosham Grange

The Switch

More Bloody Horowitz

The Diamond Brothers books:

The Falcon's Malteser

Public Enemy Number Two

South by South East

The Blurred Man

The French Confection

I Know What You Did Last Wednesday

The Greek who Stole Christmas

The Devil and his Boy

ANTHONY
HOROWITZ

WALKER
BOOKS

This is a work of fiction. Names, characters, places and incidents are either the product of the author's imagination or, if real, are used fictitiously. All statements, activities, stunts, descriptions, information and material of any other kind contained herein are included for entertainment purposes only and should not be relied on for accuracy or replicated as they may result in injury.

First published 1998 by Walker Books Ltd
87 Vauxhall Walk, London, SE11 5HJ

This edition published 2015

2 4 6 8 10 9 7 5 3 1

This book has been typeset in ITC Veljovic

Printed in Germany by GGP Media GmbH

British Library Cataloguing in Publication Data:
a catalogue record for this book is available from the British Library

ISBN 978-1-4063-6479-8

www.walker.co.uk

For Wendy Boase

CONTENTS

INTRODUCTION

I hated history when I was at school.

This was largely the fault of my history teacher, Mr Evans, who was so old that we often used to think that he must have been alive when most of it was happening. I still remember his terrible, whining voice ... he used to speak as if he had dust at the back of his throat. And he never looked at us. To this day, I'm not sure if his eyes were real or made of glass, but as he sat, hunched up over his desk at the front of the classroom, he used to remind me of an exhibit in a museum. It really was as if someone had taken him to the taxidermist and got him stuffed before he was quite dead.

For Mr Evans, history was just a series of names and dates that we all had to learn by heart. So a lesson might go...

1605............................Gunpowder Plot
1618............................Thirty Years' War begins
1620............................Pilgrim Fathers
1642............................Civil War
1649............................Execution of Charles I

And on. And on. And on...

It wasn't until I had left school that I began to think that history might have been more fun than

Mr Evans had ever have imagined. Take another look at the list above. The Gunpowder Plot could be a really exciting story about a bunch of Spanish spies who tunnel underneath the Houses of Parliament in London and try to blow the whole place up. And what about the Pilgrim Fathers who crossed the Atlantic in the Mayflower and landed in America? For them, it must have been an amazing journey across a world that was completely unknown. What was it like? How many of them got seasick? And I'd have loved to have been present at the execution of poor King Charles. The whole of London turned out to watch ... but then in those days having your head chopped off was something of an entertainment.

By now you should be getting the general idea. *The Devil and His Boy* is a history story – but it's very much my sort of history. Basically, it's an adventure story that just happens to take place five hundred years ago.

I would have loved to have lived during the reign of Queen Elizabeth I. It was such a rude, noisy, dirty, dangerous, difficult time. London would have stank. There were no toilets and the sewage ran right down the middle of the streets. No wonder there were so many outbreaks of the plague. London was much, much smaller than it is now, surrounded by thick forests that were full of highwaymen – so even getting there safely was an achievement. And once you arrived, you couldn't expect to be welcomed with open arms. On the contrary, the Londoners were famous for their bad manners. Often they would thrown mud balls (or worse) at visiting tourists just because they felt like it. There were thieves and tricksters everywhere. They'd take your luggage and your life.

If you lived in London in the sixteenth century, you would have shared one room (and possibly one bed) and your mother, your father, your brothers and your sisters, and possibly a couple of pigs and a duck too. You almost certainly wouldn't go to school. And you might well be married before you were even thirteen. Not that it would be a long marriage. Most people died in their thirties ... maybe that was why life was so intense.

There would be no TV, no computer games, and no books like this one – hardly anyone could read so why bother? But you'd be able to kick a pig's bladder around in the street – the beginning of soccer – or perhaps pop out to a nice public hanging. You would never, ever have a bath. And you would wear the same clothes until they either rotted away or burst. What a laugh!

And at the same time, you would be a citizen of a country that ruled the world. At this time, America was hardly known at all (and there was certainly nothing united about the states). Britain was at war with much of Europe, but, thanks to heroes like Sir Walter Raleigh and Sir Francis Drake, we always seemed to be on the winning side. And then there was Shakespeare! The world's greatest playwright was alive and working on the south bank of the River Thames. How I wish I could have been at the first night of *Hamlet* or *Macbeth*. If only I could have got his autograph ... just think what it would be worth now!

Anyway, it's time to get on with the book. I loved writing it. And I still think it's a lot of fun ... even if it is history.

Anthony Horowitz

the stone of vision

It was just before midnight when Queen Elizabeth slipped out of bed and went in search of her magician.

Although she had allowed her Maids of Honour to lead her into the bedroom and help her undress more than an hour before, she hadn't even tried to sleep. Part of the trouble, of course, was being Queen of England. She could still feel the crown on her head even when she wasn't wearing it ... there was so much to think about, so much to do. But the real problem was her bed. It was a huge, four-postered thing with no fewer than five quilts. The first was silk, the next velvet, then there was a gold one and a silver one and finally, on top, a quilt embroidered with a rather gloomy picture of the Sermon on the Mount. The quilts had been given to her by the Spanish ambassador, the French ambassador, the Dutch ambassador, the German ambassador and the Archbishop of Canterbury and she had to use them all in case she gave offence to any one of them. The result was that even on the coldest winter nights she was always much too hot.

For a moment she stood in the middle of the room and glanced out of the window. There was a full moon that night which pleased the Queen. She knew that the magician would like it. Somehow his spells always worked better when there was a moon and this one seemed huge, a perfect white circle hanging in the darkness. Her eyes travelled down and she saw the Thames, ash white as it twisted through the city of London. Everything was silent. The Queen nodded. This was the right time.

She crossed the room to a tapestry which covered an entire wall. The tapestry showed a lion being hunted and, when she was young, the snarling face with its awful eyes had given her nightmares. But she was an elderly woman now. Sixty years old. And being Queen was often nightmare enough.

The tapestry was suspended from a rail and she pulled it aside to reveal a bare brick wall with no visible door or window. At the far end, over a bookshelf, there was a metal hook and without hesitating the Queen went over to it and turned it. There was a click and a whole section of the wall swung inwards on a hidden hinge to reveal a jagged opening and a spiral staircase leading down. Grey cobwebs hung in the air. A fat black spider, frightened by the light from the bedroom, tumbled down the brickwork and then scuttled along the floor, disappearing into the shadows.

The Queen lifted a candle from her room and started forward. After the warmth of the bedroom the stairs were very cold. A draft twisted round her ankles and slithered up her legs. The candle in her hand flickered and her shadow seemed to jump away, tugging at her as if it could pull her back upstairs. For a moment she wondered if this was a good idea. She could still turn back, go to bed and forget all about it. The Queen was afraid. But a single question had tormented her for more than forty years. She had to know the answer. She had to know it now.

She continued down. A moth, attracted by the light, flew into her face. Its feathery wings brushed against her lips and she gasped out loud. Her hand banged against the wall and she almost dropped the candle. She stopped for a minute, catching her breath, then, gripping the candle more tightly, she followed the stairs to their end, passing through an archway and along a corridor where the ceiling curved low over her head as if groaning under the weight of the great palace a hundred metres above.

She had reached a door made of thick planks of wood bound together with iron and so low that she had to bend to open it. It reminded her of the door of one of her own dungeons. Her hand found a silver ring and she turned it, the metal cold against her skin. On the other side, a warm yellow glow and the faint smell of rosemary welcomed her into a small, circular chamber. The door swung shut behind her as she went in.

"Good evening, Queen."

"You were expecting me, Wizard?"

"Oh yes. I knew you were going to come and visit me before you had decided it yourself. Sit down..."

Nobody else would have dared to talk to Queen Elizabeth in this way. For a start she should have been called "Your Royal Highness" or "Your Majesty". And nobody ever told her what to do – not even so much as to sit down. But the person seated in the high wooden-backed chair was no ordinary man.

Dr John Dee was sixty-six years old but looked much older, having a white moustache and a white beard that came to a point about halfway down his chest. He wore a long black robe and a black cap that could have been painted on to his head. His eyes were brown – a strange, watery brown, the colour of melted chocolate. There was a grey cat, half asleep, on his lap and he occasionally stroked it with a long, elegant finger. Dr Dee spoke with a Welsh accent. So, rather more remarkably, did the cat.

"So you know why I am here," the Queen said.

"Of course I do."

"Do you know everything, Wizard?"

Dr Dee shook his head. "I know many things, Queen. And my stone of vision tells me more. But only God knows everything and I am just a man."

"Can you tell me when I am going to die?" the Queen asked.

The magician hesitated. His eyes narrowed and he seemed unsure what to say. Then the cat arched its back, stretched its legs and suddenly opened its quite brilliant emerald eyes. "You'll die," the cat said, "when you stop breathing."

There was a silence in the room. For a long minute the Queen gazed at the cat. Then she smiled. "It's a good answer," she said.

"But that isn't the question you came to ask," Dee muttered.

"No." Suddenly the Queen was nervous. Her fingers closed on a gold locket she was wearing round her neck. She had taken all her other jewellery off for bed. But this locket never left her. It was part of her. "I have to know about him," she said.

"Why now?"

"Because I can't wait any longer. I think of him all the time, Wizard. I know I can never see him but I still wonder about him – whether he is dead or alive."

Dr Dee stroked the cat. "I can tell you what you want to know," he said. "But I have to warn you now, Queen. It might be better not to ask. Magic has a nasty way of changing things. You cast a spell, you ask for secret knowledge and before you know what you've done you've opened a barrel of worms ... or something worse than worms if you're unlucky."

"I still have to know," the Queen insisted. "Enough

of this, Wizard. You've known me long enough to know when my mind is made up. Do your magic. Tell me what you see."

"She's making a mistake!" the cat murmured.

"Hush!" Dr Dee stroked the cat, then lifted it up and set it to one side.

There was a low table between Dr Dee and the Queen, a number of objects scattered across the top. These were the tools of the magician's trade. There were three or four old books, so old that the words seemed to be sinking into the thick, yellowy pages. There were two candles and a tapering wand. Between them lay what looked like an ordinary piece of silvery-grey stone, about the size of a dinner plate. Dr Dee picked it up and cradled it in his hands.

"I will need something of his," Dee said in a low voice.

Once again the Queen's fingers reached for the locket round her neck but this time she took it and drew it over her head. Nestling it in the palm of one hand, she opened it with the other. Inside the locket was the miniature portrait of a man and opposite it, a lock of light brown hair. The Queen gazed at the hair for what seemed like an eternity, then she let it fall on to the table. "It's all I have," she said.

"You're prepared to lose it?"

There was a flicker of anger in the Queen's eyes. "Do what you have to," she said.

Dr Dee picked up the hair and laid it on the stone. His hands were still cupped round it but now he moved them away a little, his eyes fixed on the stone as if he were trying to look through it. The Queen leaned forward and as she did so, the lock of hair moved. She thought that it had been caught in a draught but then she realized that the stone had become hot and that it was the heat that was causing the effect. The air above the stone was shimmering. The colour of the stone was changing: from grey to white and then to metallic silver.

"No...!" The word escaped the Queen's lips as a whisper. The lock of hair had burst into flame. Now the flickering pieces rose into the air, twisted and disappeared. The surface of the stone was no longer rough or remotely stony. It had become a mirror but as Dr Dee looked into it, it did not show his reflection.

"His name was Robert." The magician's eyes were focused far away and the Queen knew that he was seeing things outside the room, outside and far away.

"Yes. Robert..." Even uttering his name was a knife-wound. She had never done it before. "Tell me, Wizard. Is he alive?"

A long silence. And then...

"No, Queen. He is dead."

The Queen fell back in her chair, covering her eyes with her hands. Somehow she had always expected it but like all bad news it had lost none of its power to hurt. But Dr Dee was still gazing into the mirror that had been a stone and there was a look of puzzlement on his face.

"What is it?" the Queen demanded.

"I don't know..." And then, as if a cloud had parted and the sun had broken through, the magician looked up. "He had a son," he said.

"What?"

"Robert is dead but his son is still alive."

The Queen gripped the sides of her chair. "Where is he? What is he called? What do you know about him?"

"He's far from here. I can't see his name." The stone was getting hotter and hotter. The very air inside the chamber was beginning to burn.

"Try! You must try!"

"No. All I can see is a castle and a pig. It's very difficult..." Dr Dee waved a hand over the stone, clearing the smoke. "The pig is outside the castle and over the boy."

"He's still a boy? How old is he?"

"Thirteen. The castle..." Dr Dee frowned. "They're building chimneys on the castle. Strange-looking chimneys. I can see the boy limping past the castle and he's looking at the chimneys and..."

"Why is he limping?"

"Because of the pig..."

"Why must your answers be so mysterious, Wizard? Where is the boy? If you can't tell me his name, at least tell me where he is!"

But before Dr Dee could reply, there was a sudden crackle as if something were short-circuiting. At the same time, the mirror shattered, a thousand cracks exploding across its surface. Then the cracks faded and a second later the stone was exactly as it had been, lying flat and ordinary on the table.

"That's all I can tell you, Queen." Dr Dee picked up the stone. It was quite cool to touch. "But you have spies and men of intelligence. It should be enough."

"A castle, strange chimneys and a pig. It's another of your wretched riddles, Wizard. Where do I even start?"

"Framlingham!" The cat – which had been quite forgotten during all this – leapt on to Dr Dee's lap. "They're building chimneys on Framlingham Castle."

"How do you know?" the Queen asked.

The cat shrugged. "A little bird told me," it remarked. "And then I ate the little bird."

"Framlingham ... in Suffolk." The Queen got to her feet. "Only four or five days from here. You've done well, Wizard. You have my thanks and will have much more!"

The Queen left, climbing back up the secret staircase to her bedroom. She was still awake when the sun rose above the thatched roofs and wooden houses of London and the first horses stumbled along the rough, pitted tracks that were the city's roads. The year was 1593. The Queen, of course, was Elizabeth I. And she was already planning the course of events that would change one boy's life for ever and with it the entire history of the country she ruled.

the pig's head

It was raining in Framlingham; a cold, grey, December rain that dripped and trickled into every corner and wiped away the colour of everything it touched. The streets were so full of puddles that there were more puddles than street, with only a few patches of brown mud here and there to remind you that the place had once been built on dry land. The two moats surrounding Framlingham Castle were full to overflowing. The town gardens and bowling green had disappeared.

The inn stood just outside the town, next to a large swamp. It was a squat, dark, evil-smelling place with rotting timbers and mouldy walls. It had few windows – glass was too expensive – but the noise of singing and the smell of roasting meat seeped through the thatched roof and chimney. An inn sign swung in the wind.

The sign showed the head of a pig, severed from its body, for that was the inn's name.

THE PIG'S HEAD, FRAMLINGHAM
PROPRIETORS: SEBASTIAN & HENRIETTA SLOPE

At about five o'clock in the afternoon a young boy came out of the inn carrying a bucket. Despite the weather, he was wearing only the lightest of clothes: a shirt open at the neck, a waistcoat that was too short for him, a pair of trousers that flapped around his ankles. He had neither shoes nor socks. His bare feet splashed in the mud as he went to draw water from the well.

The boy was about twelve or thirteen years old. Nobody knew or cared when exactly he had been born. He had long, reddish-brown hair, pale skin and bright, intelligent blue eyes. He was painfully thin – his rags seemed to hang off his shoulders without actually touching his body and there was a bruise on the side of his cheek, the size of a man's fist. He lowered the bucket into the well, gripping the handle that groaned rustily as it turned; his fingers were unusually long and slender. The boy's name was Thomas Falconer. That, at least, would be the name they'd carve on his gravestone when starvation or the plague carried him away. For now they simply called him Tom.

He was about to lift the bucket out of the well when a sound made him turn. A man had appeared, a traveller on horseback, his body lost in the folds of a dark cloak and his face hidden by his hat. The horse was a great black stallion with a white blaze on its chest. Steam snorted from its nostrils as it jerked forward, its hooves striking angrily in the mud. It came to a halt and the rider swung himself effortlessly down. Mud had splattered his leather boots and the bottom of his cloak. He had evidently been riding for some time.

"Boy!" The man called out.

Forgetting the bucket, Tom ran to obey. "Yes, sir?"

"Take the horse to the stable. See that he's watered and fed. If any harm comes to him, you'll answer for it."

The man dragged his luggage from behind his saddle and handed the reins to Tom. He was about to turn away but suddenly he stopped and for a moment Tom found himself being examined by two narrow, grey eyes in a dark, weathered face.

"What's your name, boy?" the man demanded.

"Tom, sir." Tom was surprised. People seldom took any notice of him.

"How long have you worked here, Tom?"

"All my life, sir. Ever since I was able to work."

The rider stared at Tom as if trying to read something in his face. "Your parents own this place?" he asked.

Tom shook his head. "My parents are dead," he said.

"Who were they? Do you know?"

It was one question too many. Travellers often passed through Framlingham on their way to the ports at Harwich and Ipswich, but they came as strangers and that was how they left. It was the unwritten law. In an uncertain world, it could be dangerous to give too much information about yourself.

Tom's lips clamped shut. The man seemed to understand. "Look after the horse, Tom," he said and walked into the inn.

The inn was crowded, the fire a distant red glimmer behind so many huddled bodies. Thick smoke coiled upwards from the hearth, from the tallow candles on the mantle and from pipes clenched in the teeth of men, and women too. Two more boys – older and better fed than Tom – were bustling in and out of the kitchen carrying wooden trenchers of meat and bread, somehow forcing their way through the great tangle to find the tables beyond. Someone somewhere was playing a fiddle but the sound was almost drowned out by the shouting, arguing, laughing and drunken singing of the guests.

The landlord noticed the new arrival the moment the door opened but then he had the sort of eyes that noticed everything. This was Sebastian Slope. He was a small, nervous man who had never quite recovered from the pox which had ravaged his skin and eaten away part of his nose. He had tried to grow a beard and moustache to hide the damage but unfortunately the hair – as well as being bright orange – was thin and uneven, sprouting in one part of his face but not in another with the result that he looked as if he had been horribly injured – perhaps by a musket at close range.

Rubbing his pale, white hands together he approached the new arrival who was standing there waiting, water dripping from his cloak.

"Good evening, my lord. Welcome. Welcome to The Pig's Head." Slope's teeth had long ago rotted away – all but a couple of them – and he now found it easier to speak through what was left of his nose. His voice was thin and high-pitched. If a rat could talk it would probably sound much the same. "What can I do for you, my lord? A pint of the finest ale? A delicious supper? A nice leg of mutton? Or perhaps the speciality of the house. A potato! Have you ever tried a potato, my lord? It is quite new and the most remarkable thing..."

"I need a room for the night," the traveller interrupted.

"Of course. Of course. We can provide you with the best linen sheets. And only six of our guests have slept on them since they were last washed..."

"I'll have a bed with clean sheets. And I'll eat some lamb. Yes. And a rabbit too. Mushrooms. Some cheese. And beer not ale."

"Beer. Yes. Yes. Will you eat in your chamber, my lord, or at the common table? It'll be sixpence downstairs and eightpence up, but if you have it up perhaps we could arrange for one of our kitchen maids to keep you company...?"

"I'll eat down here."

"You do us all a privilege, my lord." Slope twisted a smile on to his lips but at the same time a strange gleam had come into his eyes so that he looked both servile and sinister at the same time. "Have you come far, my lord?"

"From London," the stranger replied.

"And returning soon?"

"Tomorrow."

This was the information that the innkeeper had been angling for. He swallowed once, his adam's apple performing a somersault in his scrawny throat. "Henrietta!" he called out. "Henny!"

A moment later a tiny woman with grey, straggly hair hurried out of the smoke. This was Henrietta Slope and although to look at she could have been Sebastian's grandmother, she was in fact his wife. She too had caught the pox – in seventeen years' marriage it was the only thing her husband had given her. The disease had attacked her lips which had shrivelled away so that when she smiled she was forced to use her teeth.

"We have a guest," Sebastian said.

"A guest! How lovely! And a gentleman!" Henrietta curtsied twice. "Have you ordered food, my lord? The food here is a delight. We've only had nine cases of food poisoning since our new cook started!"

"I've ordered," the traveller muttered.

"He has indeed," Sebastian agreed. "Lamb. Mushrooms. Cheese. And rabbit..."

"Rabbit?" Henrietta grinned liplessly. "Fresh today. It couldn't be fresher. In fact, I strangled it myself."

"Thank you." The traveller seemed to be in a hurry

to get away from this odd couple but suddenly he leaned across the bar and drew them closer to him. "I was talking just now to that boy outside..." he began.

"Tom?" Sebastian's face darkened. "If he offended your lordship, I'll throw him down the well."

"That boy's useless!" Henrietta shrieked. "He's worse than useless. He's a drip. He's a damp patch. A dead worm!"

"He hasn't offended me," the traveller interrupted. "I'm merely interested in him. Where did you find him?"

Sebastian glanced at his wife then leered at the new guest. "Are you interested in buying him?" he asked.

"We might sell him," Henrietta simpered. "Although of course we'd miss him. He works very well for us. A very hard worker. Very fit..." She seemed to have completely forgotten what she had been saying only a few moments before.

"Where did you find him?"

"He was an orphan." Henrietta's eyes filled with tears. "I have two sons of my own, sir. I took him in out of the goodness of my heart." She tapped her chest which seemed too thin and hollow to contain any heart at all. "We look after him in return for a few light tasks about the house..."

"What of his parents?" the traveller asked, becoming more interested by the second.

"They worked up at the castle," Sebastian replied. "The father fell off a horse and broke his neck. The mother died giving birth to him. He came into the world with nothing and if it weren't for Mrs S and me, nothing is all he'd have now."

The traveller's eyes narrowed and for a moment he said nothing. He was obviously deep in thought. But then he shook his head and straightened up. "Send me my food as soon as possible," he said and went and sat at the nearest table.

Sebastian Slope watched the man as he took his place, then slipped through a door and into the kitchen. Here there was a second, huge fire with a rather angry-looking pig on a spit being turned by a fat, sweating cook with dirty hands and a runny nose. Henrietta had followed her husband in and now he drew her to one side, standing over a huge cauldron of soup that was slowly congealing.

"What do you think, my precious?" he asked.

"Rich," Henrietta murmured. "Definitely rich."

"That's what I thought." Sebastian tried to pick his nose, remembered it wasn't there and bit his nail absent-mindedly instead. "Did you notice the cloak – lined with velvet, my jewel? And the boots..."

Henrietta nodded. "I think this is one for Ratsey," she muttered.

"Yes," Sebastian said. "Ratsey will like this one. You'd better call the boy."

But at that very moment the outer door opened and Tom came back into the kitchen. It had begun to rain more heavily and water dripped out of his hair, running down the side of his neck. He was carrying the bucket, full now and heavy.

"Where have you been?" Sebastian swung a lazy arm and slapped the back of his hand across Tom's head.

"Lazing again, I'll be bound!" Henrietta did the same, only harder.

"I'm sorry!" Tom cried out. "A gentleman came. He told me to see to his horse."

"Yes." Sebastian leaned closer. Tom cowered away but the landlord was smiling. "What sort of a horse does he ride?"

"A stallion. Black with a white mark."

"Valuable?"

Tom hesitated. He knew what was about to happen and thought about lying but it was no good. The Slopes would know. They always did. "Yes," he said.

Sebastian grabbed him by the collar and drew him so close that his lips almost touched the boy's ear. "You're to go into the wood," he whispered. "Find Ratsey. Tell him we have a mark. The London road. Tomorrow..."

"But it's dark. It's raining..."

"Are you arguing with me?" Sebastian hadn't raised his voice but his grip had tightened and his eyes, dark to begin with, had gone almost black.

"No."

"Then be off with you. To the burnt oak. And if he isn't there, wait for him to come."

Tom ran out, slamming the door behind him. Sebastian and Henrietta Slope watched him go.

"You're too good to that child," Henrietta sighed.

"I'm too soft-hearted, I know it," Sebastian agreed.

"I wonder why our guest was so interested in him?" Henrietta scratched her head and sighed as a lump of hair fell into the soup. Her disease was definitely getting worse.

Sebastian considered for a moment. "I don't suppose we'll ever know," he replied.

Husband and wife kissed each other, grey lipless teeth on to grey pock-marked flesh. Then they left the kitchen and went back into the inn.

gamaliel ratsey

After he had left The Pig's Head, Tom climbed up the hill and back into the town centre. It had stopped raining and the clouds had parted enough to allow a slice of moonlight to cut through. Tom was grateful for it. Without the moon he would have had to make the journey in almost pitch blackness for the only other light came from the candles burning behind the windows of the houses and – with the high price of wax – there were few enough of them.

He passed through the market square, skirting an old, crooked building that stood in the middle. This was called the Market Cross and Tom knew that there was a schoolroom on the upper floor. Not that he had ever been inside it. He had never been to school, not even for a day. He had never learned to read or write anything more than the three letters of his own name.

Tom was an orphan who had never known his parents. He was beaten and bullied every day. He was half starved and owned nothing more than the rags he was wearing. And yet despite all this he wouldn't have described himself as unhappy. For a start he had never once been outside Framlingham so he had nothing with which to compare his own life. At the same time, he had listened to travellers staying at the inn and knew that there were poor people and hungry people all over England – so why should things be any different for him? At least he had a roof over his head – even if it was only a stable roof which leaked in the rain. He had plenty of scraps and leftovers to eat. The Slopes might beat him but so far they hadn't broken anything. All in all, things could be worse.

Ahead of him, Framlingham Castle loomed up, its walls dark and ancient against the night sky. Tom had heard about the great banquets and tournaments that had taken place there years ago. But that was all in the past. Now the castle was crumbling. Cracks had appeared in the brickwork and weeds had quickly sprouted in the cracks. The ridiculous, twisting chimneys which had been added to the battlements were just its final humiliation.

Tom hurried round it, keeping the town ditch on his left. The town seemed to end very suddenly. The road became a track. The track grew more and more uneven. And then he was walking across a bumpy field with a black, skeletal forest springing up ahead.

Most of the trees had lost their leaves. The forest in winter was a cold, forbidding place. As Tom continued, branches twisted and interlocked above his head while roots formed tangled knots beneath him. The glistening tree trunks were like huge bars. With every step he took he felt himself being swallowed up by a vast, living cage.

Somewhere, far away, an animal howled in the darkness. One of the dogs from the village? Or something worse? Tom knew that it was unlikely that wolves would come so far south at this time of year – but even so he found himself quickening his pace.

He had been this way many times and soon found what he was looking for. A tree shaped like a Y, a rough slope covered in white pebbles, a circular clearing and there on the far side, an old oak tree that had been hit by lightning, split in half and burned coal black. This was the burnt oak that Sebastian Slope had referred to. This was where Ratsey would be found.

Ratsey.

Tom realized that he was shivering and wondered if it was entirely due to the cold. He drew two fingers into his mouth and whistled a high-pitched note, then a lower one. It was a signal he had used often although he still had no idea how Ratsey heard it, where he came from, how he knew when someone was about to arrive. The sound should have echoed through the trees but on this damp, dreary night the whistle sounded very small. Tom lifted his fingers again, then hesitated as a second terrible howl ripped through the dark sky. It was a wolf. It couldn't be anything else.

"Tom, Tom, the piper's son..."

The voice was hushed, singing the words with a soft laugh. Tom turned round and almost cried out. A moment ago there had been no one there but now there was a man, dressed in a long leather coat with a sword at his waist. At least, he was man up to the neck. He had the head of some sort of horrible monster with bloodshot eyes that bulged out of their sockets, yellow teeth as thick as piano keys, swollen cheeks like over-ripe melons and a chin that curved round until it almost touched his nose.

The man finished his song. "Tom, Tom, the piper's son. Will he stay or will he run?"

Tom relaxed, recognizing the voice. "Ratsey!" he exclaimed.

"Did I scare you, Tom?"

"No..."

"A shame. I meant to."

Ratsey laughed, then reached up and grabbed hold of his chin. He pulled and his entire face came away – it was nothing more than an elaborate mask. The face underneath it was an unusually handsome one with black hair sweeping over the forehead and almost touching the man's shoulders. His eyes, alight with humour, were pale blue and the more he smiled, the brighter they seemed to shine. But for his sword, his leather coat (patched in so many places that there must have been very little of the original coat left) and his mud-spattered boots, you might have taken him for a priest or a choirboy. But then, if you had looked deeper into those eyes, you might have noticed how very black his pupils were and if at that moment he were to stop smiling you would realize that this was a man who would never come near a church – unless it was to burn it down.

"What do you think of the new mask?" he demanded. He held it up so that its pointed nose almost touched his own.

"It's horrible," Tom replied.

"Thank you." He set the mask down. "And now, I wonder what brings you out on this wet and wicked night?"

Tom swallowed. "There's a man," he said. "A traveller."

"Is he rich?"

"Master Slope says he might be."

"Might be?" Ratsey laughed and pulled a metal bottle from somewhere inside his coat. He unscrewed the lid, raised it to his lips and swallowed. "Tell me what you think, Tom-Tom! Is he rich?"

"I don't know, Ratsey."

Ratsey considered this statement for a moment. He lowered the bottle and smacked his lips. He sighed. He sucked his teeth. And then, before Tom could move, he lashed out, grabbing hold of the boy's ear and dragging him towards him with such force that Tom cried out with pain.

"I asked you a question," he said in a reasonable tone of voice. "When I ask a question I expect an answer. That's the whole point."

"He's rich!" Tom shouted. He could feel his ear coming away from his head. "He's got a good horse. Black, with white markings. His clothes are smart. He has money."

"Which way is he coming?"

"The London road!"

"Excellent!" Ratsey let go and Tom reeled back, clutching his ear. Ratsey gazed at him apologetically, then handed him the bottle. "Here you go, old chap," he said. "Have a swig of that. It'll take away some of the cold."

Tom hesitated but Ratsey gestured and he raised the bottle to his lips. It contained some sort of brandy.

"In a strange way, you remind me of me when I was young," Ratsey said. "Not of course that I was as scrawny and ragged as you. As a matter of fact, my father was a duke." He winked. "Strange to think that when I was your age I ate off gold plates and had servants to do everything for me."

"So what happened, Ratsey?"

Ratsey smiled. "I got bored and I ran away. I went to war." He reached out, took the bottle and drank. For a long moment he stared into the distance and Tom could see the moon reflected in his eyes. "Captain Ratsey – that was me. I fought for the Queen in Ireland. Good old Queeny! I saw her once, you know, Tom-Tom. She was as close to me as that tree over there." He nodded at the oak. "Glorious days! But then times got hard. No money. No food. No fun..." He jerked his head to one side as if shaking off the memory and suddenly he was business-like again. "Tell Slope that I'll be waiting," he said.

"Yes, Ratsey."

Ratsey gestured with his head and Tom set off at once, scrabbling across the clearing and back up the slope. When he reached the top, he stopped and turned round. But the clearing was already empty. Ratsey had vanished as quickly and quietly as he had appeared and the burnt oak stood solitary, dead in the pale glow of the moon.

It was still dark when Tom opened his eyes the following morning. In the summer months he would be woken by the sun breaking through the cracks in the walls of the stable where he slept but in the winter it was always the cold that did it.

As he set to work, Tom thought about Ratsey and about the traveller who would be leaving for London that day. He knew what was going to happen. The same thing had been going on for as long as he could remember. But there was nothing he could do about it. It was no business of his.

Tom had just finished cleaning out the hearth – the ashes thick with fat and grease – when he became aware of voices in the main room. The first, high-pitched in anger and indignation, he knew at once. It was Sebastian Slope.

"You can't take him!" he was saying. "I won't let you!"

"You'll hang if you try to stop me."

A moment later the door opened and the traveller stormed in, already dressed in his cloak and with his sword buckled at his waist. Sebastian Slope was right behind him. The innkeeper had obviously got up in a hurry. He was wearing a dirty vest, hanging outside his trousers. His eyes were bleary and his orange hair was even more dishevelled than usual.

The traveller ignored him. His attention was fixed on Tom, kneeling by the hearth. "Tom," he said, "do you have any possessions? Anything you call your own?"

"No, sir." Tom was too dazed to understand what was happening.

"Then you have nothing to pack. Come with me. We're leaving now."

"But ... my lord!" Slope's blustering hadn't worked so now he began to whine. "My wife and I ... where would we be without the boy? We've treated him like a son..."

"You've treated him like a slave and believe me, you will hear more of it."

"You don't want him, my lord!" Slope was actually

crying but – rather repulsively – the tears were coming out of what was left of his nose. "He's no good to you. He's a sneak. He's a sniveller. If it wasn't for Mrs S and me he'd have been hanged years ago."

"Tell me, boy..." he said – the traveller was standing firmly between Tom and the innkeeper – "do you want to stay with this man and his wife?"

Tom wasn't sure what to say. He certainly had no love for either of the Slopes, but to leave...? To step outside the small world of Framlingham? It was something he had never even for a minute considered.

"He wants to stay!" Sebastian Slope exclaimed. "He loves Mrs S and me. Like we was his own parents."

"No!" Tom was amazed to find himself saying it. "I don't want to stay."

"Then let's go."

With his back turned to him, the traveller didn't see the landlord snatch up a knife that had been lying on a table. Tom opened his mouth to call out a warning – but the traveller had no need of it. He must have heard something, for in less than a second his sword was out of its sheath. He spun round and slashed down twice. The first stroke gashed Slope's arm, drawing a thin line of blood. The second sliced across his stomach and for a horrible moment Tom was sure it had killed him. But the blade had only cut through the waistband of his trousers. As Sebastian Slope howled in pain, they slid down to his ankles, exposing a pair of knees like oversized conkers.

"This way, Tom."

Not sure if he was awake or asleep, Tom followed the traveller out into the yard and watched as he saddled and made ready his horse. It didn't take him very long. As he led the animal out of the stable, he smiled at Tom for the first time. "You've never ridden a horse," he said.

"No, sir."

"It's not difficult. You'll sit behind me and hold on to me. You'll soon get used to it."

"Where are you taking me, sir?"

"To London."

London!

London was a four-day ride away but for Tom it could have been on the other side of the planet ... on the other side of the moon even. London was a city, he knew, with a tower and a river and a cathedral so great that the church at Framlingham could fit inside it. He had heard it said that crowds of people lived there; not just dozens of people but hundreds, maybe even a thousand.

He tried to speak but couldn't find the words. In silence, he allowed the traveller to help him on to the horse and clung to the saddle, hardly daring to move. He was much higher than he had imagined and he was grateful when the traveller climbed up and sat before him.

"Say goodbye to it, Tom," the man said. "You're starting a new life."

But before they could move, there was a screech and Henrietta Slope emerged from the inn. Her husband was right behind her, holding up his trousers with his good hand.

"What are you doing?" she squealed. "You've no right! I'll have the law on to you."

"I am the law," the traveller replied. "And you have every reason to fear me. But although you don't deserve it, I'll play fair with you." He threw a handful of coins into the mud. "This is for my room and board. Now be silent and let us pass."

The traveller kicked with his feet and the horse trotted forward. At the same time, Henrietta threw herself in front of it. Tom wasn't sure what happened next. The horse reared up and he clung on for dear life. Henrietta fell back, losing her balance. With a great scream, she crashed to the ground, slap into the middle of a pile of soft and steaming horse manure. Sebastian tried to help her but, with his trousers in a knot, he was too slow.

The horse had left the courtyard. Tom and the traveller were gone. Henrietta Slope took her husband's hand and allowed him to pull her to her feet. She gazed down the road at the horse with its two figures already vanishing into the distance. "Are you all right?" Sebastian asked.

Henrietta wiped a hand across the back of her leg. "I stink!" she exclaimed.

"I know, my dear," Sebastian agreed. "But don't

worry. The horse manure will hide it." He held up his hand, blood trickling between his fingers. "He cut me!" he complained.

Henrietta looked at the blood, then back at the road. "It's nothing compared to what Ratsey will do to him," she muttered.

"Ratsey...!" Sebastian had forgotten but now an ugly light came into his eyes. He tore a piece off the bottom of his vest and wrapped it round his hand. "You think he'll find him?"

"He'll find him. Ratsey never misses." Henrietta's cheeks twitched as she tried to draw lips that weren't there into a triumphant smile. "We'll have the boy back – aye and that fine horse with him. And as for our brave traveller..."

"Dead meat, Mrs S."

"Dead and buried, my beloved."

And laughing softly to themselves, the innkeeper and his wife turned and began to scavenge for the coins in the mud where they'd been thrown.

the ambush

He was leaving Framlingham!

As he watched the last traces of the village disappear behind him, Tom still couldn't believe it was happening. He had been born in Framlingham. He had lived his whole life there. And he'd always assumed he would die there – probably quite soon. And not only was he leaving ... he was on a horse! The Slopes could never have afforded a horse like this, even with all the money they had stolen. The only animal they'd ever owned had been a dog and that had gone mad when they forgot to feed it.

It was the man who broke the silence.

"Tom," he said, "do you have a second name?"

"My father's name was Falconer, sir," Tom replied. "At least, that was what they put on his gravestone.

But I've only ever been Tom."

"And my name is Hawkins," the traveller said. "Sir William Hawkins." He smiled. "A hawk and a falcon. We make a good pair."

Hawkins pulled on the reins and the horse stopped. He twisted in the saddle and gazed at the boy behind him. His eyes narrowed. He reached out and brushed the hair out of Tom's eyes, his fingers stroking the boy's forehead. "It is most wonderful," he muttered. "You remind me of someone. I knew it the moment I first set eyes on you. But who? There's the mystery. Who indeed?"

He turned round and the horse moved off again.

"Are we really going to London?" Tom asked.

"We are."

"But why? What do you want with me?"

"It's not for me to answer your questions, Tom," Hawkins replied. "I was told to find you and that's what I've done. But for the rest of it ... you'll have to wait until we arrive."

Until we arrive.

But would they?

Ever since they had set out another fear had been stirring in Tom's mind. Gamaliel Ratsey was somewhere out there. Maybe he was watching them even now. Tom glanced around him. On one side there were fields, cut into narrow strips with rough trenches in between. On the other, trees were already beginning to thicken into a wood which would soon surround them. Hawkins had spoken of the road to London, but of course there was no real road. They were following a track that was so faint it was barely a track at all. There was nobody else in sight.

"Why are we going this way?" Tom asked.

"It's the way I came," Hawkins replied.

"Is this the only way to London?"

"It's the fastest way. Why, Tom? What's the matter?"

Tom wasn't sure how to answer. Part of him wanted to tell Hawkins all about Ratsey and to plead with him to go another way. But at the same time he was too afraid to speak. It was he, after all, who had informed Ratsey about the traveller only the night before – as he had done many times in the past. Tom had never been a willing part of it but even so he knew that if Ratsey were discovered, he would hang with him.

The forest grew thicker, the silence more profound. Above them, a black crow launched itself out of a tree with a sudden scream. Tom could bear it no more.

"Please, Mr Hawkins!" he exclaimed. "You have to go another way. You're in danger..."

But it was already too late.

Ahead of them, a figure suddenly stepped out, something long and metallic in its hand. The horse reared and tried to find a way round. But there were thick briars on either side. There was no other way.

Gamaliel Ratsey was wearing another, even more

disgusting mask. This one showed the head of a fish, but a fish that was already dead and rotting. Its eyes were white and sightless. Its lips were disfigured as if torn by the fisherman's hook. Where its neck met Ratsey's shoulders, blood and green slime seemed to be oozing out.

But if the mask had been designed to frighten Hawkins, this time it hadn't worked. Quickly, he brought the horse under control, then called out, "What do you want?"

"Your money!" Ratsey replied, his voice muffled behind the mask. "All of it. Your horse also. Your clothes. I like the look of your boots. And I think, while I'm at it, I may also take your life!"

Hawkins said nothing. He jumped down from the horse, leaving Tom feeling very lost and alone. Ratsey glanced up, the blank fish eyes gazing at him. "Tom-Tom!" he exclaimed.

"You know the boy?" Hawkins demanded.

"Know him? Why, he and I are old mates. Drinking friends. And partners in crime."

Hawkins glanced back at Tom, uncertain for the first time. "You knew he would be here?" he asked.

"I tried to warn you," Tom answered, miserably.

"Tried to warn him, Tom-Tom?" Ratsey shook his head. "Tut! Tut! That's not loyal. That's not nice. But enough of this idle chat. Let's kill this fellow, whoever he is, and then we can ride back together..."

But Hawkins had planted his feet firmly on the

ground. He threw back his cloak, revealing his sword. He turned again to Ratsey. "Whatever you may say," he said, "this boy isn't with you. You and he are as different as night and day. I'm taking him with me. And I warn you now to let us pass..."

"Please, Ratsey!" Tom called out, though he knew it was useless. He couldn't even see Ratsey's face but he knew that it would be as emotionless as the dead-fish mask. And he was right.

"Please, Ratsey!" The highwayman echoed the words in a mocking falsetto voice.

Hawkins unsheathed his sword with a great flourish, the metal whispering against the leather scabbard.

Ratsey raised the weapon he was carrying and fired.

It was an arquebus, a type of musket. Tom had never seen such a thing before, never heard anything as loud as the explosion it made. At first he wasn't even sure what had happened. It seemed to him that Hawkins had thrown his own weapon away. Then the traveller turned and to Tom's horror, there was a great hole in the centre of his chest and blood was pouring out, soaking down into his trousers, draining out of him even as Tom watched. Behind him, Ratsey had lowered his gun and was muttering something but Tom, his ears still ringing, couldn't hear him. Smoke curled up from the muzzle of the arquebus. Hawkins staggered towards him.

"To London," he rasped. "Go to Moorfield..." He

lifted a hand and with the last of his strength brought it down hard on the horse's rump. Tom felt the horse leap forward and flailed out, searching for something to hold on to. Somehow his fingers found the horse's mane and he knotted them into it. Out of the corner of his eye he saw William Hawkins collapse, lifeless, to the ground. And there, right in front of him, was Ratsey, the fish mask already off his head and his handsome eyes staring at him with something like disbelief.

"Tom-Tom!" he called out.

Tom couldn't have stopped the horse even if he had wanted to. The next thing he knew, the two of them had left the ground, and soared over Ratsey. Ratsey yelled and dived to one side as the horse just missed him, its hind hooves grazing the side of his face. Tom was yelling too. He seemed to be flying. Then there was a great crash as the horse hit the ground again and if Tom's hands hadn't been buried in the mane he would have been torn loose from the saddle. Even so the breath was punched out of him and it felt as if every bone in his body had been rattled loose. Slipping first one way, then the other, he desperately clung on as the horse thundered through the wood, swerving past the trees, leaving its dead master in the mud behind.

As the sun set that evening, three people sat round a table in the Pig's Head. None of them were speaking. They had not spoken for an hour.

Sebastian Slope was smoking a pipe that smelled of old straw. The reason for this was that it was actually filled with old straw – he had run out of tobacco. Next to him, Henrietta Slope was sipping a tankard of ale, a noisy business lacking, as she did, lips. Opposite them, Gamaliel Ratsey was reading a letter by the light of a candle. He had read it several times already and taken notes but the contents still puzzled him.

"So what does it say?" Henrietta demanded at last. "It's only two pages. It can't be that difficult."

"Actually it's in Latin," Ratsey replied. "It's also in code." He set the pages down. "The letter contains orders," he explained. "The traveller was a knight. Sir William Hawkins. A member of the Gentlemen Pensioners."

"The what?"

Ratsey sighed again. "You really do know nothing about the outside world, do you?" he said. "The Gentlemen Pensioners are the Queen's personal bodyguard. They're closer to the Queen than probably anyone else."

"What? You mean...?" Sebastian had gone completely white. It looked as if he was going to be sick and sure enough a few moments later he was. "Do you mean the Queen sent him?" he continued, when he had recovered.

"The Queen or someone close to her. Yes." Ratsey nodded. "Hawkins was sent to find a boy, the son of Robert the Falconer. Somehow he knew that Tom was the boy. His orders were to carry the boy to London and await further instructions. And that, of course, is where they were heading when Hawkins and I met – so unfortunately for him."

"The Queen!" Sebastian Slope was having trouble breathing. His entire face was like a slice of damp cheese. "If Hawkins was a member of the Mental Intentioners..."

"The Gentlemen Pensioners..."

"If he was working for the Queen, there'll be questions. I mean, when he doesn't show up. They'll send constables. And worse..."

"They'll hang us all," Henrietta whispered. Her fingers fluttered to her throat. "Hanged by the neck!"

"They'll probably draw and quarter us first," Ratsey remarked.

"Oh Gawd!" Henrietta turned round and was as sick as her husband had been a few moments before.

"It wasn't us!" Slope exclaimed. "We didn't kill him!" He jerked his pipe in the direction of Ratsey. "It was you! You shot him in the forest!"

For the first time, Ratsey's eyes grew dark. He was still smiling, but suddenly there was a chill in the room. The candle flame flickered and black shadows slithered across his face. "Whatever happens, let's remember one thing," he said in a low voice. "We're in this together. If one of us goes down, we all do. If they're going to build a scaffold, it'll be a scaffold for three."

"They can't tie us in with him," Henrietta whispered. "Hawkins came here. And he left again. What happened after that nobody knows."

"Nobody except the boy," Ratsey said.

There was a long silence.

"Young Tom saw everything," Ratsey continued after a while. "He knows all about us. And if the Queen or her advisers were ever to get their hands on him, that could be very difficult for us."

"Where is he?" Sebastian snapped. "You had him! You let him go! This is all your fault, Ratsey."

Ratsey sighed again. He closed his eyes. Opened them. Then lashed out with his fist, catching Sebastian right on the nose. "We're all in this together," he went on. "And it seems to me that the one thing we have to do, the only thing we *can* do, is find young Tom."

"How are we going to do that?" Sebastian wailed. Henrietta took out a filthy handkerchief and offered it to him. Both the Slopes looked miserable and terrified.

"We know he's heading for London," Ratsey said in a reasonable tone of voice. "I'll follow him there. I'll find him and I'll kill him."

"You'll never find him in London," Sebastian gasped. "It's a huge place. A vast place. I went there once with my dad to do the Christmas shopping. It was horrible. We'd only been there a few hours and he got murdered. He didn't even have time to get me a present!"

"It is a big place," Ratsey agreed. "But I know people.

And the people know people. If the boy is there, I'll hear of it soon enough." He got to his feet. "I'll see you two love-birds in about a month," he said. "And don't worry about Tom. The boy's as good as dead."

at the red lion

Three days after he had left Framlingham, Tom lost his horse, his food and almost his life.

He had been riding hard and had stopped for the night in a small wood just outside a village. He had been too nervous to go into the village itself. He was travelling outside his parish without a licence and knew that if he was caught he would be flogged. And if they decided he was a beggar or a thief – and how else would a boy like him have his own horse? – they might burn a hole in his ear or slit his nostrils and brand him on the side of his cheek.

And so he was on his own, asleep on a bed of leaves when the three men came. A foot breaking a branch near his head woke him. But he was quick-thinking enough to keep his eyes closed.

"Look at the horse!" a voice whispered.

"It's a beauty!" whispered a second.

"Take it! Take it! And cut the boy's throat!" That was a third voice, slithering out of the night.

"No need to kill him," the first voice replied. "He's asleep..."

"Then take the horse."

"I've got it!"

"Quick..."

And then they were gone.

Tom sat up, shivering. It had been a close escape. If he had so much as opened his eyes, a knife would have been the last thing he would have seen.

It was harder after that. For two whole days he walked. The rain never stopped and soon he felt as if the water were going right through him. He had no food. After twenty-four hours his head was spinning and he could barely see the road ahead. At the start of his journey, he had done his best to avoid people. Now it was the other travellers who avoided him. He was a doomed, half-frozen boy, dying on his feet. Nobody wanted to come near.

On the sixth day, just after the sun had set, Tom came to a town. At least, he assumed it must be a town. He had never seen so many tall and solid buildings so close together.

The first of these was an inn. It was three floors high, its windows ablaze with light and flaming torches in front of the main door. The front of the inn was a brilliant pattern of black beams and white panels with a wooden balcony running all the way along the front. A cobbled pathway led underneath a wide arch and into an inner courtyard and even as Tom watched a great carriage arrived, pulled by four horses, and rattled under and in. Immediately two ostlers appeared, dressed in brown aprons, and ran forward to help the passengers dismount. At the same time, a huge man with a black beard appeared, laughing at nothing in particular and chewing what looked like a leg of lamb. Somehow Tom knew that this was the landlord.

"Welcome, welcome!" the man bellowed. "Everyone is welcome at the Red Lion of Enfield. Come in! Come in!"

Tom watched as the new arrivals went in, laughing and chattering amongst themselves. For a moment he swayed on his feet. He had no more strength left. If this was London, then London would be where he would die. He took a deep breath. His position was hopeless. He had nothing to lose. With the last of his strength, he forced himself across the road. The innkeeper had just seen the last of the guests into the building when he noticed Tom, covered in mud from head to foot and looking more like a broken-down scarecrow than a thirteen-year-old boy.

The innkeeper frowned. "What do you want?" he demanded.

"Please, sir..." Tom had to concentrate to make his lips move. "Can I work for you?"

"Work for me? What the devil makes you think I need a young cozener like you? What work do you want? What work can you do?"

"I can look after the horses, sir. I worked at an inn. In Framlingham..."

"Framlingham?" The innkeeper's eyes narrowed. "That's a long way from here. Run away have you? Do you know what happens to the cursed clapperdudgeons who run away from their masters?"

Tom was too tired to argue. He turned round and was about to leave when the innkeeper grabbed hold of him and yelled out, "Quickly!"

The door opened and a plump, fair-haired woman dressed in an apron and cap came out. She had a narrow face with a pointed chin and such wide eyes that she seemed to be permanently amazed about everything. "Yes?" she demanded.

"See for yourself, Mistress Quickly," the innkeeper replied. "This young apple-squire is asking for work!"

Quickly – for it seemed that was her name – glanced at Tom with distaste. "He's more mud than boy," she remarked. "In fact he's a muddy disgrace."

"Then you deal with him," the innkeeper exclaimed. "The little moon-man wants to work. So give him work. Hard work and plenty of it."

Tom allowed himself to be dragged into the Red Lion, his head spinning. He had never been inside a building quite like it. Pewter plates, piled high with food, flashed in front of his eyes being carried to tables. There were pigeons and pastries, eggs and oysters, lamb, beef, pork, and huge, golden chickens. Hundreds of candles burnt in the inn but they were hardly needed with the glow of not one but three fires, turning everything bright red. And the people! Tom had never seen so many people dressed in the finest clothes, talking and laughing as they ate.

"Through here!"

Tom found himself being pushed through a door and suddenly he was in the kitchen – where, of course, he belonged. But, with a heavy heart, Tom knew that he couldn't work. He could barely stand. And when the woman saw he was good for nothing, he would soon be back out in the rain.

"All right," Mistress Quickly exclaimed. "I want you to sit here, child." She gestured at a seat next to a fire. "Your job is to make sure that the fire doesn't go out. Do you understand?"

"Yes." Tom nodded. "I'm to watch the fire."

"You are also to taste *all* the food you are given. I need to know that it's malicious. I'll ask you to taste a little wine as well, I think. For the same reason. Do you think you can manage all that? Sitting by the fire? Eating and drinking?"

Tom nodded, amazed.

"Good, good, good!" Mistress Quickly beamed. "I'll snatch up with you later." And then she was gone.

Tom couldn't believe his good fortune. He knew of course that these weren't really jobs at all, that the innkeeper and the woman had taken pity on him and had saved him from death by cold and starvation. It was the first time anyone had been kind to him in his entire life and when, a short while later, a smiling girl brought him a plate of meat and bread and a cup of wine, he had to fight to keep the tears from his eyes. After that he slept, half leaning against the wall, the flames from the fire warming his hands and face.

When he awoke something was towering over him. He looked up alarmed, but it was only Mistress Quickly.

"You feeling better?" she asked.

"Yes. Thank you..."

"Please! There's no need to spank me!" She smiled. "Have you ever seen a play?"

"No," Tom replied.

"Then you're in luck. We've got the players in tonight. Come out and see what you think."

The only entertainment Tom had ever seen in Framlingham had been minstrels (usually out of tune) and jugglers. A bear-baiter had once visited the town with an old, half-starved bear. But the sight of the poor animal being stoned and tormented had only made him feel miserable. Another time, a group of players had stayed at The Pig's Head but they hadn't performed – the parish didn't approve of plays. The fact was that Tom had very little idea what a play even was. He doubted he would be able to understand it and thought it would be rather dull.

But when he followed Mistress Quickly into the courtyard, the first thing he heard was roars of laughter from the crowd who now lined the balconies leading round the inside of the inn and who were packed neck-and-neck on the ground below. The players – about a dozen of them – had set themselves up at the far end, using one wall of the inn as the backdrop to a makeshift stage. Torches and candles blazed everywhere turning night into day. And as Tom watched, they acted out their story, turning the Red Lion into another world.

It was a mad story.

The play was about two sets of identical twins, two masters and two servants, who accidentally turned up in the same city. Because they looked exactly the same, the masters kept on confusing the twins and the twins kept on mistaking the masters until everyone was chasing everyone else all around the stage. Tom soon found himself swept up in a way he had never known before. It was as if all his own problems were forgotten. For two hours, William Hawkins, the Slopes and Gamaliel Ratsey simply didn't exist. It was a wonderful feeling, to be so lost in something that nothing else mattered.

If Tom had kept his eyes on the stage like everyone else, he might not have seen what happened next. But he enjoyed watching the audience too – he had never seen so many people having such a good time – and it was while his eyes were on them that he saw the thief at work.

The thief was a boy, a couple of years older than

himself. He was wearing a thick red cloak with a tall hat on his head and brown trousers ballooning out at the knees. The boy had a rather round face, long fair hair and thick lips.

The boy was standing right behind a wealthy-looking merchant and, as Tom watched, he reached forward, his hand disappearing underneath the man's cloak. At the same time, his other hand drew out a short sword and cut through the man's purse. Tom gasped. It had taken less than five seconds and now the purse was in the boy's pocket and he was already moving on to the next person in the crowd.

Mistress Quickly was standing next to Tom. "What is it?" she demanded.

"There! He took that man's purse!" Tom lifted his hand and pointed at the boy. At that very moment, the boy looked up at Tom. And to Tom's astonishment, his face broke into a broad smile.

But Mistress Quickly wasn't amused. "A foist!" she yelled. "There's a pock-picket in the house!"

At once the play was forgotten as the audience exploded. They knew there was a thief among them. The only trouble was, they didn't know who he was.

"There!" Mistress Quickly shouted again.

The thief took one last glance at Tom. Slowly he shook his head as if to reproach Tom for spoiling his fun. Then he pointed at a fat, bald man two rows behind him. "That's him!" the thief cried out.

"What...?" the bald man began, then yelled as

someone punched him full on the nose. The bald man reeled back, blood flying, then crashed into two more members of the audience. This sparked off a second fight and moments later the entire audience was shouting and swearing, exchanging blows and sprawling over the courtyard. On the stage, the actors tried to continue the scene, realized it was hopeless and stopped to watch. Now it was the actors who had become the audience and the audience who provided the entertainment. Just in front of the stage, two men began a sword fight. A very old lady lashed out with a surprisingly strong fist. A merchant had the shirt ripped off his shoulders while two more grappled with each other's beards.

Tom looked down at the battlefield, searching for the boy who had started it all. A moment later he saw him. The boy had reached the archway and was slipping out into the street. The boy looked back and saw Tom. He took out his stolen purse and raised it in a defiant gesture, then drew a quick finger across his nose. His meaning was clear. To hell with you! To hell with you all!

Then the boy turned and a moment later he had gone.

paul's walk

The following morning, Mistress Quickly and the innkeeper said their goodbyes. There was a cart making the short journey from Enfield to London and they had arranged for Tom to be given a ride.

"You look after yourself, young rakehell!" the innkeeper boomed. "And when you get to London, make sure you head for St Paul's."

"Where's that?" Tom asked.

"St Paul's Cathedral. You can't miss it. Ask for Paul's Walk. That's the best place to find work."

"Goodbye!" Mistress Quickly cried. "It was lovely beating you!"

The cart set off and although Tom had slept well the night before, he found his eyes closing once again and soon he had drifted back into sleep.

He was woken by the sound of a bell tolling. He sat up and blinked. The cart was rumbling past a priory with a cluster of neat houses lying in its shadow and at first Tom thought he was still in the countryside. Behind him there were fields and gently sloping hills. But when he twisted round and looked ahead, more and more houses and shops sprang up and a moment later he knew that they had plunged into the city itself.

London!

It was the noise that struck him first. There were people everywhere, shouting and shoving as they tried to reach the market stalls. At the same time, the stall-owners and shopkeepers were shouting back at them, each one of them trying to make themselves heard. "What do you lack? What do you lack?" – this from the shopkeepers, standing in their doorways. "Sweep! Chimney sweep!" "Ripe apples red!" "Fine Seville oranges" – at every street corner there was someone with something to sell. Horses stamped and stumbled in the mud. Cartwheels creaked and rattled. Dogs barked and cows bellowed their protest as they were driven to market. In workshops open to the street, half-naked metalworkers smashed down with their hammers and yelled instructions to their hurrying apprentices. Carpenters in leather aprons sawed and chiselled. A group of sailors wove past, half-drunk already, singing and laughing. So much noise! Tom pressed his hands to his ears and tried to stop his head from spinning.

And then there was the smell. Vegetables and spices in the market. Fruit – fresh and rotting. Great hunks of cheese. Kegs of rich, ruby wine. The smell of people, sweating and dirty. The smell of animals. And, of course, the worst smell of all, coming from an open drain that ran down the centre of the road, a foul-coloured stream that never stopped flowing, carrying all the sewage of London to who could say where!

Tom climbed out of the cart, marvelling at all the people around him. Colourful signs hung in the air, advertising the shops below. A black horse, a white rose, a yellow snake. Higher up, the inhabitants had stretched lines from one side of the street to the other so that they could hang out their clothes which fluttered like misshapen flags against the blue sky. A woman in expensive clothes hurried past, pressing a scent-bottle to her nose and trying not to look at anything. In the distance a group of boys were throwing mud-balls and laughing at a man with dark skin and foreign-looking clothes; presumably a visitor.

"Dirty postcard?" A man with a broken nose, several broken teeth and a badly twisted neck had suddenly stepped in front of Tom. "Want to buy a dirty postcard?" he asked.

"No..."

"Each one's engraved! And you won't find a filthier sonnet!"

"No thank you!"

The innkeeper had advised Tom to go to St Paul's

Cathedral and that at least was easy to find. The driver of the cart pointed the way and Tom followed a narrow, curving lane until it suddenly opened into a great square where a priest, dressed in black and white, was addressing a crowd of a hundred people. The cathedral stood behind them; a mountain of bricks and stone, of soaring windows and towers. Tom wouldn't have believed it was possible to build anything as big as this. The main tower seemed almost to touch the sky – and surely would have if only it hadn't managed to lose its steeple.

He went inside.

It was almost noon and St Paul's was beginning to empty. Tom walked slowly up the central aisle, its great stone pillars standing like some enchanted forest all around him. A door slammed shut and the sound echoed through the chamber. There were a few men lounging against the pillars. Some were talking in low voices. In the shadows, one man was counting coins into the outstretched palm of another. Everyone in the church seemed to be watching someone else and it occurred to Tom that nobody was actually praying.

He reached a tall, wooden door, covered from top to bottom with slips of paper. A handful of men had been examining these as Tom approached but now they dispersed and he found himself alone. The pieces of paper were covered with words. Tom recognized a few of the letters but, of course, he couldn't read.

"What are you looking for, my dear boy?"

The speaker was a small, fat man, almost as round as he was tall. He reminded Tom of a snowman. His eyes were as black as coal. His nose was long and pointed. And his head seemed to balance on his shoulders without the benefit of a neck. He was wearing black trousers and a white shirt, frayed at the elbows. The fur on his collar looked suspiciously like rat.

"What?" Tom wasn't even sure that the man was talking to him.

"You're new in town." The man smiled. His lips were wet and rubbery. "I haven't seen you here before."

"I only got here today." Tom was afraid to give any information away. He had taken an immediate dislike to the man without quite knowing why.

But the man seemed unaware of it. "You've come to the right place," he said. "My name is Grimly. James Grimly at your service!" He tried to bow but his stomach was too round and didn't have anywhere to bend. "So you are looking for work?"

"I might be..."

"How nice." The man ran his eyes over Tom rather as if he were inspecting a horse or a piece of meat. "If you were – that is – looking for work," he went on, "I might be able to help."

"How?"

"I have a large number of people in my employment. Young lads like yourself. James Grimly's boys are well-known on the streets of London."

"What sort of work do they do?" Tom asked, feeling

more uneasy by the minute.

"It's charity work," Grimly explained. He giggled. "Yes. There are people, you see, who need to give to charity. And so it follows that there must be people who *are* charity. That's what I supply. That's my boys."

Tom didn't quite understand this, nor did he like it. "Thank you, Mr Grimly," he said. "But I don't think I'm interested."

"Your choice, my dear fellow. Of course it is! Maybe soon you'll change your mind. But for now I leave you to dine with Duke Humphrey!"

Tom frowned, not knowing what he meant.

Grimly pointed at a large, stone tomb. "Humphrey, Duke of Gloucester!" he explained. "No money? No food? Then you're on your own with him!" The little man laughed and walked away, his boots clattering on the stone floor.

Relieved to see him go, Tom turned and was about to go back the way he had come when he stopped and froze.

The main door must have opened and closed while he was talking to Grimly. A man had come in and was talking to another cluster of men, asking them questions. Even from a distance, Tom recognized his long black hair, his slim, languid body, his penetrating blue eyes. Gamaliel Ratsey had followed him to London. Somehow he had overtaken him on the road. If he so much as raised his head, he would see him. Tom knew he had to hide.

He looked the other way. James Grimly had almost reached the far door and before he knew quite what he was doing, Tom had caught up with him. Grimly's snowball head swivelled on his shoulders. He didn't look surprised to see Tom.

"My dear boy!" he said. "My most likeable fellow! Do I take it that you've changed your mind?"

"Yes," Tom blurted out. "I have." He was almost whispering, afraid that Ratsey would hear him even though he was right on the other side of the cathedral.

"Then let's hurry to my offices before you change your mind again," Grimly said. "We'll have to prepare you for your work. It will mean certain ... changes. The sooner it's done, the sooner you can start."

Tom nodded, although he had heard little of what the man had said.

Leaving Paul's Walk behind them, the two set off together.

Grimly had a yard at the end of a dark, narrow alleyway near the Thames. The city was much quieter here, with fewer people on the streets and a damp, evil-smelling fog in the air. Slimy water and mud rose over Tom's ankles as the two of them hurried towards a pair of mouldering wooden gates.

"My home," Grimly muttered. He opened the gates and ushered Tom inside. The gates led into a rough, partly cobbled courtyard, squeezed between three buildings that seemed to be leaning on each other to stay upright. Tom looked around him. Set in the middle of the courtyard was a single, wooden chair with a high back and solid arms and legs. Tom had no idea what the chair was for. But there was something about it that made him go cold inside.

"Belter!" Grimly called. "Snivel! Get the book! Get out here! We have a new recruit!"

Almost at once a door at the side of the courtyard flew open and two men hurried out. The first of these, the man called Belter, was huge and muscular, completely bald with a face that hadn't quite formed, like an over-sized baby. He was naked to the waist. He had no hair on his chest and his nipples were black. Snivel was older, a crumpled bag of a man, carrying a leather-bound book underneath his withered arm.

"A new recruit?" Snivel rasped. He licked his lip. "From Paul's Walk?" he asked.

"Where else?" Grimly turned to Tom. "We'll prepare you straight away."

"Prepare me?" Tom was getting more nervous by the second. "What do you mean?"

"I thought I told you. It's for charity!"

"Charity!" Snivel agreed.

"What sort of charity?" Tom demanded.

Grimly sighed. "The homeless and the disabled," he explained. "I've got boys all over London. On street corners. Outside churches. They're Grimly's boys."

"You mean they're beggars!"

"Exactly. But they're special beggars. They work

for me and I take half of what they earn. But in return I help them, you see. I *adjust* them." Grimly flicked a finger in Tom's direction. "Take a boy like you. You're a little thin. A little ragged. But how much do you think that's worth? Good people, charitable people, people with money ... they want something more. Oh yes, they might give a penny to a child shivering with cold. But how much do you think they'd give to that same child, *missing a leg*?"

Grimly had barely spoken the last three words before Tom was running for the gate. But Belter had been expecting it. Before Tom had taken two paces he was grabbed from behind and dragged, screaming to the wooden chair. There was nothing he could do as he was forced down, his hands and feet securely fastened with rope. It was over in a matter of seconds. By the time the giant had finished with him Tom was sitting helplessly, unable to move.

"Let me go!" he shouted. "I've changed my mind! I don't want to work for you!"

Grimly touched a finger to his lips. "Don't shout," he said in a soft, soothing voice. "It won't hurt that much."

Belter had produced a dirty canvas bag from somewhere. He dropped it on the cobbled ground and Tom heard it clink.

"Now what shall we do with him?" Grimly asked. "How about one arm and one leg?"

Snivel had opened his book. "We did one of those last week," he said.

"All right then. Just the legs." Grimly smiled at Tom. "He's a handsome fellow. Interesting hair colour. Nice eyes. Let's leave the top half alone."

Belter grabbed hold of him and Tom screamed.

Then the doors of the yard crashed open.

Tom was too far gone to understand fully what was happening but he became dimly aware that Belter had straightened up again and that Grimly was walking forward with a look of annoyance on his face. "You!" he exclaimed. "What are you doing here?"

Tom forced his head to turn so that he could see the new arrival. A boy a couple of years older than himself was standing by the open door, leaning against the wall and smoking a pipe. He was looking at the scene with what could only be described as an amused smile. Tom thought he had seen the boy somewhere before but he knew that was impossible.

"Let the boy go," the new arrival demanded.

"What?" Grimly looked more sad than angry. "But he came here of his own choice," he protested. "I found him at Paul's Walk..."

"Oh yes! And you explained to him all about your little 'adjustments' I'm sure. Just like all the others!"

"Wait a minute! Wait a minute! We can talk about this...!"

Out of the corner of his eye, Tom saw Snivel reaching into a fold in his shirt. While Grimly prattled on, the old man's hand inched out and now it was holding a wicked-looking knife. Tom opened his mouth to call out a warning to the boy but there was no need. In a single movement he swept back his cloak to reveal a short sword which was suddenly out of its scabbard and in his hand, slicing through the air. The blade caught the edge of the knife, tore it out of Snivel's hand and sent it spinning through the air to clatter harmlessly on the ground. Then the point of the boy's sword was at Grimly's throat, pressing against the skin.

"Please!" Grimly's black eyes bulged. A bead of sweat trickled over his neck. "This is just business. It's nothing to do with you. He's my boy. I found him."

The boy shook his head and pressed a little harder with the sword. "Not this one, Grimly. He's a friend of mine. Let him go."

A *friend of mine?* So Tom was right. He had seen the boy somewhere before. But where?

Grimly had one last try. "But look at him!" he moaned. "Nice face. Intelligent eyes. But sad with it. We were just going to take off his legs. He'll earn a fortune."

"Maybe," the boy replied. "But you won't be alive to see it." His hand tightened on the sword. "I've often thought London would be better off without you, Grimly," he said. "All I need is the excuse..."

"No! Take him!" Grimly was on the edge of tears and his voice was a whisper. Belter and Snivel ran forward and a few seconds later the ropes had fallen away and Tom was able to stand up.

"This way..." the boy said. He had lowered his sword but his eyes never left the three men.

Tom staggered over to him and he and the boy left the yard together. It was only when they had reached the end of the alley and emerged into the main street that he realized two things.

The first thing was that he *did* know the boy. He had seen him the night before at the Red Lion, stealing a purse in the middle of the play.

And the second thing was that he wasn't a boy at all. He might be wearing trousers, carrying a sword and smoking a pipe, but Tom had just been rescued by a girl!

moll cutpurse

"My name," she said, "is Moll Cutpurse."

"Cutpurse?" Tom frowned. "Is that your real name?"

"One of them. I've got lots." Moll thought for a moment. "I used to be called Mary but I soon put a stop to that. Much too girlish." She rubbed her chin as if hoping to find stubble there. "You wouldn't want to be a girl," she said. "Not in the sixteenth century!"

"What do you do?" Tom asked.

"What do you think I do?" Moll exclaimed. "I'm a thief. A highly qualified thief. In fact, I came top in my class!"

She and Tom were sitting in a small, square room above a shoe shop. The building was perched on the south bank of the river, so close that Tom could hear the water lapping against the brickwork. The single room contained a bed, two chairs, a table, a cupboard and a small fire that struggled to keep out the damp. However, the windows had glass. The roof didn't leak. And, as Moll was quick to point out, it didn't have rats.

She had warmed up some stew over the fire and served it on two thick slices of bread – she had no plates. Somewhere she had found a bottle of wine. Now the two of them were gazing at each other over the table.

"Do you have parents?" Tom asked.

"My father used to run the shoe shop downstairs," Moll replied. "But he died of the plague. My mother too. I think I had a brother but he disappeared. Anyway, I'm on my own now."

There was a long silence. Moll leant forward and put another log on the fire. The flames reached out tiredly to consume it.

"I suppose you want to know how I found you," Moll said.

"Yes."

"It was just luck, really. I was at Paul's Walk. I go there. Everyone does. I saw you meet up with Grimly and I followed you."

"But why? Why did you save me?"

"Because I wanted to kill you myself."

Tom stared. Moll was still wearing her sword and he waited for her to draw it – but her hands didn't move.

"You cost me plenty at the Red Lion," she went on. "I'd never seen so many purses. I'd have had a dozen of them if it hadn't been for you. And you could have got me hanged!"

"I'm sorry."

"It's a bit late for that now."

Tom gestured at the sword. "So why haven't you?" he asked. "Killed me, I mean."

Moll shrugged. "Because if you were stupid enough to go off with James Grimly you were probably too stupid to know what you were doing at the Red Lion. Anyway, don't ask too many questions or I may change my mind."

There was a brief silence.

"Thank you for rescuing me," Tom said.

"That's all right." Moll took a sip of wine. "The question is – what do I do with you?"

"Can I stay here?"

"No!" Moll sighed. "All right. One night. Maybe two. But I don't like boys. Particularly stupid boys who don't know what they're doing. What *are* you doing? I suppose you're a runaway. Left your master, have you?"

"I didn't run away. It wasn't like that."

"Then what was it like? You might as well tell me. Not that I'm offering to help..."

So Tom told her his story; about his life with the Slopes and Gamaliel Ratsey; the arrival of William Hawkins and the ambush in the forest; Moll's eyes narrowed when she heard Ratsey's name and when Tom told her he had seen Ratsey at Paul's Walk she shook her head doubtfully. "You know him?" Tom asked.

"I've heard of him. Everyone's heard of Ratsey. But it's unlike him to be down here in London. And I think it's bad news for you."

"That's what I thought," Tom agreed.

"He's dangerous. As long as he's here, you're in danger. He'll find you soon enough. And when he does..." Moll drew a finger across her throat.

"That's very encouraging," Tom muttered.

Moll thought for a moment. "Tell me more about Hawkins," she said.

"I've told you everything I know."

"That's the bit of your story that doesn't make sense." Moll took out her pipe and lit it. "He was obviously a gentleman. Maybe even a member of the court. He asks questions about you and about your parents and then he snatches you and brings you back here."

"He said I should go to Moorfield."

"But why? What did he want with you? I mean, you're a nobody. A nothing. A stable boy who barely knows one end of a horse from the other."

"Thanks!"

"And why Moorfield?" Moll sighed and blew out a perfect smoke ring. "I suppose I could take you there."

"You know where it is?"

"Of course I do. It's just outside the city wall. We could walk there in half an hour. But I wouldn't get too excited if I were you. There's nothing there. A few butts. Some windmills. If that's what he brought you all this way to see, he was wasting your time."

"Maybe he lived there."

"Nobody smart lives in Moorfield. How do you think it got its name? It used to be a moor. Now it's a field."

"At least we can look," Tom said, gloomily.

Moll nodded. "All right. We'll look. But it's too late to go there now. The sun will be down in an hour or so. We'll go there tomorrow morning."

"What about tonight?" Tom looked around the room. "You said I could stay here?"

"Yes."

"But there's only one bed."

"No problem. You can have the floor."

From the moment he had walked into Moll's room, Tom had felt that he was being watched. But it was only later that night, as he lay on the floor with a single blanket and the flickering fire to keep him warm, that he realized who by. The room looked out, not just on to the river but also on to London Bridge. The huge bridge with its twenty stone arches and its shops, houses and chapels all crammed together above the water, was one of the great sights of the city.

But as he gazed at it in the moonlight, Tom noticed something else. There *were* three heads turned towards the window, three pairs of eyes fixed on him even now. But they were eyes that saw nothing. The heads they belonged to ended at the neck, cut off and stuck on metal poles.

Traitors. This was the price they had paid.

Tom rolled over and pulled the blanket over his head. But he could still feel the eyes boring into him. And it was a long, long time before he lost himself in the brief escape of sleep.

Moll was right about Moorfield.

She and Tom were standing in a rectangular field, just north of the city wall. Far away to the north, Tom could just make out the shape of three windmills. There were a few cattle grazing here and there. Despite the icy weather – it seemed to be getting colder by the day – a handful of people had come out to practise archery, aiming at two straw-filled targets, the "butts" that Moll had mentioned. It was a sunny day but the sun was white, not yellow, and gave no warmth at all. Somewhere, dogs were barking. Otherwise, Moorfield was empty and silent.

"Seen enough?" Moll asked.

"Yes."

"Maybe you didn't hear him properly. Maybe he didn't want to bring you here."

"He definitely said Moorfield."

Moll shrugged. "Let's go and get a drink," she said. "I'm freezing!"

They turned south and went through Moorgate, back into the city. That was the strange thing about London. It was huge, crowded, the streets and houses jammed into what little space there was between the wall and the river. But walk ten minutes in almost any direction and suddenly you had left it all behind and you were back in the countryside. It was a city surrounded by green.

Moll led Tom into a tavern, took the table nearest the fire and ordered two pints of ale. Neither of them spoke until it came. At last Moll lit her pipe and broke the silence. "So what are you going to do now?" she asked.

Tom was feeling more miserable than ever. In all the time he had been travelling from Framlingham and despite what Moll had said the night before, he had been hoping that Moorfield would mean something, be something. That when he got there everything would make sense. But a field, a handful of cows and three windmills? Why should Hawkins have brought him all the way from Framlingham for that?

"I don't know," he said.

"Maybe you should get out of London. If you've got Ratsey looking for you!"

"But where will I go?" Tom cried. "I haven't got anywhere."

"I'm told Bristol's nice. You could join the navy."

"I'd get sea-sick," Tom said.

"How about the army?"

"That's worse. I'd get shot."

Moll slammed down her tankard. "I knew it was a mistake coming after you," she muttered. "Now I'm stuck with you. A boy! The last thing I need!"

"Maybe I could learn how to be a thief ... like you?"

Tom suggested. But even as he spoke the words, he knew it wouldn't work. Tom lived in a world where there were as many thieves as honest men. He had spent his entire life surrounded by them. He knew that many people had a simple choice. Steal or starve. But even so, there was something inside him that told him that stealing was wrong and that it wouldn't work for him. His heart would never be in it.

Moll must have sensed this because she shook her head. "No."

"Then what?"

"Listen to me." Moll leaned forward. "If you are going to stay in London, you've got to go somewhere where Ratsey won't find you. And that means you can't stay with me, even if I wanted you to. Everyone knows everyone down here. Paul's Walk isn't just a meeting place. It's where everyone finds out about everyone else. That's why he was there yesterday and that's why he'll be there today." Moll looked nervously over her shoulder. "We've been in here half an hour," she went on, "and who knows who's seen us together? Someone could be on their way to Ratsey even now. You stay with me, he'll find you soon enough. Believe me. You won't be safe with me."

Tom nodded, feeling gloomier by the minute.

"We have to find you work. You need money in your pocket and a roof over your head."

"But what sort of work can I do?"

"That's a good question." Moll thought for a minute.

"I could get you into a tavern. You say you've handled horses and there are people I know. No..." She shook her head. "Forget it. Ratsey knows your past and that's the first place he'll look. He's probably checking out every tavern in town even as we sit."

Tom said nothing.

"All right." Moll pointed with her pipe. "We need to get you a job so let's consider your qualifications. Can you cook?"

"No."

"Can you read?"

"No."

"Can you sew?"

"No."

"Can you sing?"

"I've never tried."

Moll sighed. "A typical boy. Completely useless. All right. There's nothing you *can* do. But is there anything you *want* to do? At least that might be worth a try."

Tom thought hard. What did he want to do? Here he was in London, the greatest city in the world. He could be anything he wanted to be. But what did he want to be? Not a thief. Not a beggar. Could he work in the market? No. He would never make himself heard in all that din. How about a shop assistant? No. That would mean handling money and he couldn't count.

And then he remembered. He had only ever been completely happy once in his entire life. For just a few brief hours all his problems had been forgotten and it was as if he had been transported to another world. At that moment, Tom knew that there was only one thing he wanted to be. He wanted to join the people he had seen two nights before, at the Red Lion of Enfield.

"I know what I want to do, Moll," he said. "I want to join the theatre. I want to act."

auditions

"I still think it's a stupid idea," Moll said.

"But you don't like the theatre," Tom replied.

"I love the theatre! I go there all the time."

"Yes. But only to rob the audiences."

It was six o'clock in the morning, two days after their unsuccessful visit to Moorfield. Tom was still lying on the floor, wrapped in a blanket, but Moll was already up and fully dressed – which was hardly surprising as she slept in her clothes.

The day before, she had visited Paul's Walk and come back with exciting news. An advertisement had been posted on the *Si Quis* door (this was the name of the door that Tom had himself noticed). Actors were wanted for a new play that was about to be performed at the Rose Theatre, not far from where Moll lived.

Those interested were to present themselves at the theatre where auditions would be taking place.

And now it was the day of the auditions. Tom had barely slept a wink the night before. It was a strange thing. He had never once in his entire life thought about becoming an actor. But now he had made the decision, there was nothing he wanted more. It was as if it had been in his blood all along but had only now bubbled to the surface.

Moll was holding a package, wrapped in paper. "This is for you."

Tom threw the blanket off and sat up. "What is it?" he asked.

Moll was suddenly uncomfortable. "Don't you even know what it is in four days' time?" she snapped. "It's Christmas Day. So this is your present."

"You went and bought me a present?" Tom was amazed. Nobody had ever bought him anything. Then a nasty thought crossed his mind. "Did you really *buy* it?" he asked.

"I didn't steal it, if that's what you mean. I used my own money."

"But you stole the money..."

"Well ... yes."

Tom unwrapped the package. Inside was a white shirt, a pair of woollen trousers, a waistcoat and, most wonderful of all, a pair of leather boots. Tom held them, marvelling. He had been barefoot for as long as he could remember. This leather, soft and warm in his hands, was something he had only ever dreamed about. He gazed at her, unbelieving.

"It's probably a complete waste of money," Moll said, "but you can't turn up at the audition looking like a vagabond. Get dressed. We ought to be on our way."

They left a few minutes later, Tom wearing his new clothes. Taking off his old clothes had been like shedding his own skin. He had worn the same shirt and trousers for about three years, and they had stayed on him day and night. To walk without feeling the mud or being cut by jagged stones was a completely new experience for him, and he had tripped three times before he had even left the house. As he walked down the street, he wondered how he must look to other people. The clothes Moll had bought weren't new, but they were clean. He felt almost like a genteleman.

The Rose Theatre was a large, round building, part wood, part plaster and part brick. It stood in what had once been a garden – that was how it got its name. It was still early in the morning, but already a lot of actors had come to audition: men in feathered caps and flowing cloaks, preening themselves like pigeons.

Moll stopped opposite the main door. "Well. Good luck," she said.

"Aren't you coming in?" Tom asked.

"No." She shook her head. "There's always a chance I might get recognized. I did this place last month." She took Tom's hand. "You know where to find me if you need me. But I'm sure you'll get a job. You look like an actor. You've got an actor's eyes."

"Thanks, Moll."

"If they do hire you, come back and see me on Christmas Day. I'm going out to dinner. A bit of a reunion. You might enjoy it."

"I'm sure I'll be back tonight," Tom said.

"I hope not," Moll retorted. "My room's only big enough for one. And your feet smell."

Moll turned and walked away. Tom watched her until she'd gone. Then, taking a deep breath, he crossed the road and went into the Rose.

Tom found himself in a circular space with seats rising in three tiers and surrounding him on all sides. In front of him was a raised stage with two pillars holding up a slanting, tiled roof. There were two doors at the back, presumably where the actors made their entrances. The theatre had no roof. If it rained (or snowed – the weather was getting colder and colder) the actors and the audience in front of the stage would get soaked. Only the people in the seats would have any chance of staying dry.

There was a man standing in the middle of the stage, reciting what sounded like a poem in a whiny and monotonous voice. Two other men were watching him, sitting on stools to one side. One of these was tall, with dark, curling hair, a beard and tired eyes. The other was shorter and plumper, more expensively dressed with a silk handkerchief draped over his hand. Both of them looked bored.

The actor had only recited about three lines when the bearded man stood up. "That's enough, thank you," he called out. "Next!"

"But I've only just begun!" the actor whined.

"Don't send a messenger to us. We'll send a messenger to you," the man replied.

The actor left the stage. There was a long line of men snaking round the edge of the theatre. As soon as he had gone, one of them took his place and the line moved forward. Tom walked towards the stage, thrilled and terrified by it at the same time. Could he stand here and perform – perhaps to a hundred or two hundred people?

"Look out!"

With his eyes fixed on the stage, Tom had collided with a young man who had been carrying a sheaf of papers. Now the papers fell out of his hands and cascaded to the floor, some of them carried by the breeze into the very muddiest of puddles. Every page was covered with writing and Tom was horrified to see the words blur and then disappear in a black haze as they came into contact with the water.

"I'm sorry! I'm really sorry..."

Tom did his best to scoop the pages out of the puddle and hand them back to the man.

"Why couldn't you look where you were going?"

"I was looking at the stage. I'm sorry." Tom

straightened up, feeling wretched. Here he was in his brand new clothes and already he had made a complete idiot of himself.

The man glanced at him and softened. "It's all right," he said. "I wasn't looking either. I was thinking about my new play."

Tom looked at the man more carefully. He was in his late twenties, dressed in a black velvet tunic with a high white collar. The man had an unusually intelligent face. His deep brown eyes seemed to look right into you; through you and at you at the same time. His hair, also brown, hung almost down to his neck at the back and sides, but he was already going bald on top.

"A new play?" Tom realized what the man had just said. "Are you a writer?"

"Yes. I suppose I am. As a matter of fact, it's my play they're about to perform here." Tom had picked up the last of the pages and the man wiped it clean using his sleeve and added it to the pile. "My name is Shakespeare," he said. "Bill Shakespeare. Or Will Shakespeare if you like. Or Bill..."

Tom was confused. "Is that with a B or not a B?" he asked.

"B or not a B. B or not a B!" Shakespeare's eyes brightened and he suddenly produced a quill and scribbled something down on one of the pages. "That's rather good," he said. "I might use that."

"What's your play about?" Tom asked, changing the subject. Behind them, the second actor had just been dismissed as brutally as the first. A third actor was taking his place.

"Oh. It's about a Roman general called Titus Andronicus," Shakespeare said. "Actually, it's rather violent. But that's what they want..." He pointed at the two men on the stage. "That's Philip Henslowe. He owns the theatre. The other man is Lord Strange ... and what's really strange is that we work for him at all because between you and me he's a complete idiot. All he ever wants is clowns and acrobats." He sighed, then glanced at Tom. "Are you here to audition?" he asked, suddenly.

"Yes."

"Oh, I see." Shakespeare grimaced. "Actually, I'm awfully sorry, but I don't think they're looking for girls."

"I'm not a girl!" Tom said indignantly.

"No, no, no!" Shakespeare laughed."That's not what I meant. Didn't you know? We don't have girls in the theatre. All the girls' parts are played by boys."

This was something Tom had never known. "Why?" he asked.

"They just are." Shakespeare searched through the pages. "But like I say, there are only two girls in the play and they've both been cast."

"Oh." Tom was disappointed.

"Why do you want to be an actor anyway?" Shakespeare asked. "Have you acted before?"

"No."

"But you've been to a play."

"Only once." Suddenly Tom found himself telling Shakespeare about the play he had seen at the Red Lion. As he started to describe the plot, he saw Shakespeare smile and a moment later the playwright laughed and slapped him on the back. "There's no need to tell me about the play," he said. "It was *The Comedy of Errors*. I wrote it."

Tom gaped. "You're a great writer," he said.

"No, no, no!" Shakespeare blushed. "I'm only just starting out really. But one day ... who knows?"

Despite his meeting with Shakespeare, Tom was feeling lost and dejected as he left the theatre. The visit had been a complete failure. There were no parts for him in the play. He had nowhere to go, no money and no possessions except the clothes he was wearing.

He was so deep in thought that he didn't notice someone slipping out of the theatre behind him. But as he walked down the road the man hurried after him and caught up.

"Excuse me, young sir." The speaker was short and very dark, with narrow, glinting eyes. He was quite bald, apart from two patches of black hair, one above each ear. He also had a moustache, the hairs curling round on each side of his nose. He was dressed exotically in a rich, multi-coloured tunic with a bright red sash across his chest and a matching red plume in his hat. His trousers were mauve, ballooning out above the knee where they were tied tightly with two black ribbons. His stockings were also red. His feet, which were extremely small, were encased in brightly polished black shoes. "I noticed you in the theatre just now," the man went on. There was something foreign about him. Although his English was perfect, there was the trace of an accent, distant and unrecognizable. "You were hoping to perform in a play?"

"Yes." Tom kept on walking.

The man hurried to keep up, almost dancing on his tiny feet. "Then permit me to introduce myself," he said. "My name is Dr Mobius. You've heard of me? No? No matter..." He coughed delicately. "The truth is that I myself have a theatrical company."

That stopped Tom in his tracks. The man smiled at him. He was wearing some sort of perfume and smelled of flowers and musk. "We call ourselves the Garden Players." He waved a set of fingers heavy with rings. "We have a play we wish to perform and I came to the Rose because I'm looking for a boy."

"What sort of play is it?" Tom's mind was reeling and it was the first thing he could think to ask.

Dr Mobius tweaked his moustache. "It's a comedy," he explained. "A very comical comedy in my opinion. But then, I wrote it. It's called *The Devil and his Boy*. You see? I play the devil. But, due to an unfortunate accident, I find myself in need of a boy."

"And you think...?" Tom tried to make sense of his thoughts. "What makes you think I'd be right for the part?" he asked.

Dr Mobius simpered. "I am intuitive," he said. "That is, I am a very sensitive person. I can sense talent in a young man like yourself. The way you carry yourself. The way you speak. Of course..." He whipped out a handkerchief and brushed an imaginary tear from his eye, "...if you are not interested..."

"I'm interested!" Tom exclaimed.

"How interesting! Good!" Suddenly he was businesslike. "It will be three weeks' work. We will pay you six shillings when the job is done. You will live with us, with the Garden Players, and you will receive all food and board." He paused for breath. "What is your name?" he asked.

"Tom. Tom Falconer."

"You are alone in London?"

Tom was about to mention Moll, then thought better of it. She wasn't part of this life. "Yes," he said.

"Then do we have a deal?"

Tom hesitated for a moment. Somewhere, deep inside him, Tom knew something was wrong, that this was simply too good to be true. After all, the last time he had been offered work, it had nearly cost him both his legs. But at the same time, it was a job. A roof over his head. Food. And he would be acting in a play!

"It's a deal," he said.

Dr Mobius stretched out his arm to shake hands and it was then that it happened. He must have lost a button because, for a moment, his sleeve fell away from his arm. Looking down, Tom saw the man's dark skin and there, just above the wrist, a strange mark. It was an eye with a cross in it. And it hadn't been drawn there. It had been burned into his flesh.

The man glanced at Tom, then down to his exposed arm. For a moment his eyes flared and he opened his mouth in what was almost a snarl. But then, he forced the smile back on to his face and pulled the sleeve back down. "My sleeve," he said. "These London tailors don't know what they're doing!" He brought his hand back up in front of Tom. "So, Tom Falconer. I am the devil. Are you going to be my boy? If so, let's shake."

Tom reached out.

They shook.

the garden players

There were eight men in the company known as the Garden Players, but with Tom that figure was brought up to nine.

Tom had followed Dr Mobius back up the south bank of the river. The sun was still shining brightly but Tom couldn't help but notice something rather strange. Mobius preferred the shadows. Whenever the street widened out – when they crossed Long Southwark, for example – his beady eyes searched for darkened alleyways and hidden entrances. If he saw people coming towards him, he chose another way. And so they barely saw anyone as they followed the Thames, heading east, past London Bridge and on to Bermondsey.

They finally arrived at the river itself and Dr Mobius

stopped, blinking in the light. It was snowing now and Tom could see the surface of the Thames beginning to ice over. He wondered how long it would be before he was able to cross it on foot.

"Here we are," Mobius panted, speaking for the first time since they had set off. He waved a hand. "We are here."

"Where...?" Tom began.

The river was lapping at a derelict wooden jetty in front of them. A single ship was moored there, obviously no longer seaworthy. The sails hung in rags from its four masts and there was a gaping hole in its side where the wood seemed to have mouldered away. But there were no buildings close by; no taverns and certainly no theatres.

"The ship, Tom!" Mobius pressed his fingers together. "We hired a ship. A little economy, you understand. We live there. We work – the deck is a perfect stage. We are, if you like, a family afloat. Yes, I like that. The family that floats. And now you are part of our family, Tom. A very welcome part. Please! This way..."

Dr Mobius walked up a half-rotten gangplank and Tom followed.

"This way!" Mobius pointed at a door and a set of steps leading down inside the ship and disappeared. Tom stood for a moment, feeling the deck moving underneath his feet. He had never been on a ship before and had no idea how so much wood and rigging could possibly float when even the smallest stone would sink instantly. But this was no time for such questions. Nervous now, he crossed the deck and went through the door.

There were seven men, sitting in chairs or lying in hammocks around a coal brazier. The room was full of smoke both from the fire and the candles that lit it. Mobius had removed his hat and was helping himself to a glass of sherry from a small wooden cask. "Gentlemen," he said. "Our new boy! Yes! His name is Tom."

The men nodded at Tom and one or two of them smiled. The first thing that Tom noticed was that, like Dr Mobius, they were all rather dark. The oldest of them must have been about forty, the youngest (playing a woman, as it turned out) only a few years older than Tom himself. They were dressed in leather trousers, thick shirts and boots. Sitting there, in the cramped and smoky cabin, they looked more like sailors or soldiers than actors.

Mobius introduced them. "This is Ferdinand. Frederick. Philip. Florian. Francis with an 'i'. Frances with an 'e'. And Fynes." Tom promptly forgot each man's name as he was told it and wondered how he would manage when it came to learning his lines. He was beginning to feel more and more uncomfortable. It wasn't that the men were unfriendly. It was just the way they were looking at him ... soft and secretive. He had thought actors would be more cheerful than this.

"We must start work!" Mobius exclaimed. "Ferdinand – a script for our new friend."

The men swung off their bunks and moved to sit round a low table in the middle of the cabin. They each had a great bundle of paper and one of them produced a copy which he handed to Tom. It was the moment Tom had been dreading. He turned to Mobius, the blood rushing to his face. "I can't read," he said.

But to his surprise, Mobius merely laughed. "It's no problem! We will help you to learn the lines. And when you have learned the lines you won't need to read."

The youngest actor – Florian – a boy with long, fair hair and sad eyes – sat down next to Tom and took his script. "I will read the lines for you," he said. Like Mobius, he spoke with a slightly foreign accent.

For the next ninety minutes, Tom listened as Mobius and the Garden Players read *The Devil and his Boy*.

The play was, as Mobius had said, a comedy. It was about a man called Lucio (played by Dr Mobius) who had just arrived in the city of Venice and who dressed up as the devil in order to win a bet. Very quickly, though, things got out of hand as the people of Venice came to believe that he was the real devil. There was a comical merchant with a beautiful daughter, Isabella, (played by Florian), a comical priest and a comical duke. In fact, everyone in the play was meant to be comical in one way or another. The play ended with the duke and two soldiers, all of them armed with muskets, chasing Lucio and his boy off the stage.

The boy, of course, was Tom's part. He played Antonio, Lucio's servant, but as it turned out this wasn't such a big part after all. Tom appeared in the first three acts and once at the end. His main job was to provide a sort of commentary on the action. "Methinks my master is a scurvy knave" – that sort of thing. But of course he didn't complain. Listening to the actors reading the play, he still found it hard to believe that he was one of them. It did trouble him a little that the play didn't seem to be very good. And it also occurred to him – although of course he couldn't be sure – that not one of these actors could actually act. They all had that strange, very faint foreign accent. And they seemed to be reading their parts with no interest or enthusiasm whatsoever. But it was a start. The Garden Players today. The Rose Theatre tomorrow. At least, that was what Tom told himself.

They reached the end of the fifth act. Florian turned over the last page. There was a moment's pause but nobody applauded or said anything to break the silence.

"So, are there any questions?" Mobius asked.

Tom waited but still nobody spoke. There had been a question he had been meaning to ask from the very start, something that had puzzled him. But for the moment it was out of his mind and he asked instead, "When are we going to perform the play?"

"Soon." Mobius sipped his sherry. "I still have a few little arrangements that have to be, you know, arranged."

"It's a lot to learn." This was Florian who, as Isabella, had one of the largest parts.

"We will work hard." Dr Mobius set down his glass and stared hard at everyone around the table. "From today, none of us leave this ship without my permission. We will rehearse on the deck or – if the snow or the rain of this accursed country makes that impossible – down here. Florian! You will teach Tom his lines. Day and night. We must be ready for our grand opening." He turned to Tom. "From now on, Tom, you are mine. You must remember that. Do as you are told. And take care. We would hate anything accidental to happen to you ... accidentally. You understand?"

Suddenly Tom knew what he had meant to ask before. "The boy who was meant to play my part..." He looked up at Mobius. "What happened to him?"

One of the men shifted uncomfortably on his stool. Next to Tom, Florian cast his eyes down and pretended to study the script.

Dr Mobius sighed and spread his hands, his many rings sparkling in the light of the candles. "Poor Frank," he said. "It's exactly what I mean. Yes. Exactly. You see, he tried to leave the ship one night without asking my permission. Somehow he must have slipped ... in the dark, maybe." Dr Mobius laid a hand on Tom's shoulder. He leant down and gazed straight at him. "He fell into the river and drowned. Make sure the same thing doesn't happen to you!"

* * *

Rehearsals began that afternoon and for the next three days Tom found himself utterly absorbed in the business of producing a play. Fortunately it had stopped snowing and they were able to rehearse on deck. The play demanded lots of running around, sometimes with guns, sometimes with devil's pitchforks, and Tom wondered how they would ever have managed inside.

Because he relied on Florian to read his lines, he found himself closer to the other boy than to anyone else. The rest of the company were as reserved as they had been when he first met them. They rarely spoke to him. But nor did they often speak to each other. They seemed nervous. He wondered if any of them had ever acted before.

It wasn't easy getting Florian to talk either. As the days passed, he learned that the boy was sixteen years old and that Dr Mobius was his uncle.

"When did you start acting?" Tom asked.

"This is my first play."

"Is it something you always wanted to do?"

"No!" Florian fell silent, his sad eyes turning away. "I just do what my uncle tells me to," he said. "Now stop asking questions and let's go through your lines."

Tom was perplexed. But it was only on his second night on the boat that he saw something that actually disturbed him.

All the actors slept in one room – the same room where they had read the play. This was the only room on the ship that was remotely dry or warm enough, although Dr Mobius had a cabin to himself on the other side of the deck. Tom had a hammock next to Florian, with the actor called Ferdinand (who played the merchant) on the other side. However, on that second night, he couldn't sleep. The weather was colder than ever, the river a solid sheet of ice now. He could feel the chill seeping through the woodwork and into his bones.

Next to him, Ferdinand groaned and turned over. The movement pulled back his shirt sleeve and with a start, Tom saw the man's bare arm. There was an eye with a cross burned into the flesh, between the wrist and the elbow. He had seen exactly the same thing on the arm of Dr Mobius.

Tom straightened up. What did it mean? Were *all* the actors carrying the same mark and, if so, why? Why should they have consented to allow themselves to be branded like animals?

Tom lay back down in his hammock and closed his eyes. But that night he didn't sleep a wink.

Another day came and went. Tom had learned all of Act One and Two, and most of Act Three. That only left a short scene in Act Five and he would be ready. But ready for what? Dr Mobius still hadn't said where or when *The Devil and his Boy* was going to be performed. And Tom still hadn't been paid. He had tried asking Florian, but of course without success, and was just summoning up the courage to tackle Dr Mobius himself when the visitor arrived.

It was about four o'clock in the afternoon and already dark, a few flurries of snow gusting against the rotting ship. Tom was watching a scene from Act Four being rehearsed when the man approached the ship. The man was wearing a long brown robe that reached all the way to his feet with a hood drawn over his head. A monk or a friar. The man glanced over his shoulder, then hurried up the gangplank. At that moment, Dr Mobius saw him. "That is, I think, enough for today," he called out, stopping the rehearsal in mid-sentence. "Please return to your cabin. Yes, I think, to the cabin. While I attend to some ... business."

The monk had stood waiting while Mobius spoke. Then Mobius bowed and gestured to his private quarters on the other side of the deck. Still keeping his face hidden underneath the hood, the monk scuttled across the deck and disappeared through the door. Dr Mobius followed him. The door slammed shut behind them.

The other actors were only too pleased to be released from their work in the cold evening air and crowded round the door in their haste to get back to the fire. Florian went with them and suddenly Tom, who had been sitting alone on the deck above, found himself momentarily forgotten.

His first instinct was to follow the others down. It was extremely cold and the last one in would always find himself furthest from the fire. But at the same time he was curious. Why should a monk have suddenly chosen to visit a company of actors and why should Dr Mobius be so eager to see him? He had to know. And suddenly he had an idea. Perhaps there was a way he could find out.

There was a rope lying on the deck. In fact there were ropes all over the ship but this was the only one that hadn't been gnawed at, either by time or by rats. Tom snatched it up and tied it round one of the masts, tossing the other end into the river. Then, taking hold of the rope, he lifted himself over the railing that ran the full length of the deck, and began to lower himself down the side.

Dr Mobius's cabin was directly below him and a little to one side. Hanging in space with his arms outstretched, his feet up against the side of the ship and his head hanging back, Tom was able to manoeuvre himself until he could look in through the window, into the cabin. He was about three metres below the deck and three metres above the frozen water of the Thames. If he let go of the rope he knew that he would fall right through the ice which still wasn't strong enough to support his weight. But it might be strong enough to trap him underneath the surface. Tom imagined himself in the chill, black water. He thought about Frank, the boy whose place he had taken. Would he have frozen before he drowned? Which would have killed him first?

Clinging on even tighter now, Tom looked into the cabin. The first thing he saw was that the monk wasn't a monk at all. He had taken off his robe and underneath he was dressed like a gentleman with a white collar, a black velvet cape, black stockings and black boots. The man had a beard and a moustache, both turning grey. His eyes were narrow and slightly too small for his head. His nose, long and hooked, was slightly too big for it. There was a long, tapering scar on the side of his cheek, shaped like a letter "J". From where Tom was hanging, he could also see a table, a chair, candles and a bed against the wall. But Dr Mobius himself was just out of sight.

"...The money? I haven't come right across London to leave without it."

It was the "monk" talking. With a thrill of excitement, Tom realized that he could hear every word the two men were saying. The cabin window might have had glass once but it had been broken or rotted away long ago. Tom eased himself closer, gently shifting his weight on his feet. He had to be careful. Move too quickly and he might find himself accidentally knocking on their wall.

"Of course I have the money," Mobius replied. A cloth bag appeared, thrown down on the table. It landed with a heavy clink. "But what I want to know, what you must tell me is..." His hand fell on the bag before the other man could take it. "...Do you have what *I* want?"

"It's not easy, damn you," the man muttered. "I'm working on it. I'm sticking my neck out for you. Literally! I could lose my head for this!"

"But you're not doing it for me," Mobius purred. He lifted the bag again. "You're doing it for this. You're going to be very, very rich."

"If anyone finds out, I'm going to be very, very dead."

"They won't."

The man in black stood up and walked over to the window. Outside, Tom twisted away, afraid he was going to be discovered. For a nightmare moment he lost his footing and hung upside down, his neck twisted, and a sky of black ice filling his vision. But the man had turned round. Tom managed to loop the rope over his foot. He was still upside down. But he was safe.

"What about this new boy?" the man asked. "Who is he?"

"He's nobody. Nothing. A creature I picked out of the gutter." Mobius purred quietly and Tom could imagine him stroking his curling moustache.

"He doesn't know?"

"Of course not. He'll play his part and then we'll be rid of him. But we were talking about you, Sir Richard. When will I have a result?"

"Tomorrow. Maybe the day after. They're meeting soon..."

"You can take half the money now. Half later. And don't disappoint me, Sir Richard." There was a brief pause and Dr Mobius moved closer. Tom could just make out the side of his face and part of his body. One eye gleamed in the candlelight. "I have far-reaching friends. You may hide from me but not from them..."

Tom sensed that the interview was coming to an end and quickly pulled himself back up the side of the ship. He thought of the rope, stretching out across the deck. He couldn't risk Dr Mobius or the man he had called Sir Richard finding it.

There was nobody in sight on the deck. Tom climbed over the railing and untied the rope. He was just straightening up when a hand fell on his shoulder. Tom froze, then turned softly.

Florian was standing over him. For a moment neither of them spoke. Tom wondered if the other boy was going to raise the alarm. He must have seen what Tom had been doing. He must know that Tom had been eavesdropping.

But then Florian began to speak, the words tumbling out as a whisper on a frosting cloud of breath. Tom couldn't understand what he was saying. The words made no sense. At last Florian stopped, but then he grabbed hold of Tom's sleeve.

"Tom," he said. "I like you. But you have to go. Don't you see? You're in terrible danger. You must get off this ship. Leave London. Go as far away as you can..."

A door banged open. Mobius was showing the "monk" back to the shore. Florian turned and fled the other way. Tom stepped into the shadows, his mind whirling.

He had barely understood a word of what Florian

had said. And it wasn't just because Tom had been taken by surprise or because all the blood had rushed to his head when he was upside down. No. It was only now that he realized. Florian had spoken to him for a minute, maybe for longer. But whatever language he had been speaking, it certainly wasn't English.

thin ice

There were no rehearsals on Christmas Day. Tom asked if he could leave the ship and was pleasantly surprised when Dr Mobius said yes. In fact, Mobius seemed quite keen for him to take a day's holiday.

Tom was glad to get back on to dry land. He walked for twenty minutes – it was easy to find his way. All he had to do was follow the river back down to London Bridge. Soon he was recognizing familiar landmarks. And it was just before midday when he found himself in front of the shoe shop over which Moll Cutpurse lived.

He was about to call up to her when Moll came out. She stopped and stared at him and, although she did her best to hide it, Tom knew that she was pleased to see him.

"So you decided to come back," she scowled.

"You did say I could look in on Christmas Day," Tom replied.

Moll softened. "Oh yes. Happy Christmas." She ran her eye over him. "Well, you haven't been starving, I can see that," she said. "So does that mean you're an actor now?"

"Yes. I'm in a play!"

"Tried on the dress yet?" She smiled. "You'll look nice in make-up. In fact you'll probably make a much better girl than me." Somewhere in the distance a church clock chimed the hour. It was eleven o'clock. "I was just on my way to a Christmas dinner," Moll continued. "You're not invited, but since everyone there's going to be a crook anyway, I don't suppose they'd mind if you joined in."

It was one of the strangest invitations Tom had ever received, although of course it was also the only invitation he'd ever received. Christmas in Framlingham had only ever meant extra work. "Thank you," he said.

Moll headed back through Southwark and past the great bull-baiting ring at Bankside. The other side of the river was heavily built up but on this side the buildings suddenly stopped, giving way first to gardens and then to open fields. The snow had fallen thicker here. To the south, everything was white with only a few cattle standing out against the landscape. Ahead of them, a single inn stood at the edge of a clump of trees. Moll went up to the door and knocked. The door opened a crack and a pair of dark eyes gazed suspiciously out.

"Moll!" a voice exclaimed.

The door opened fully and Moll and Tom went in.

It was a small inn but it was packed with about twenty or thirty people sitting at a long table, chattering among themselves. As soon as they saw Moll and Tom, they bustled about making a space at the table so that the two new arrivals could sit down.

"Let me introduce you," Moll said to Tom. "That's Black Bob." She pointed at a man who was actually rather pale. "He's a highwayman. And so is One-eyed Jack..." She pointed to a second man. "...Snatcher Sam and old Shagbag, there at the end of the table. Dick the Dealer there is a card sharp." She nodded at a man with a little pointy moustache and the man waved back, a pack of cards suddenly appearing from nowhere in his empty hand. "Over there are the Bird Brothers."

"London's finest burglars," the brothers – two plump men in identical green doublets – chorused in unison.

And then Tom remembered what Moll had said. "They're all crooks..." She had been speaking literally. *Everyone* at the inn was a thief of one sort or another. There were more pickpockets, several confidence tricksters, a passport forger, two hookers, two curbers and two divers. Tom wasn't sure what all these actually did, but they certainly looked very villainous with squinting eyes and wide, toothless smiles. It felt a bit strange to be the only person in the room who hadn't committed some sort of crime but then the food arrived and he soon found himself joining in the party with all his doubts forgotten.

It was a wonderful Christmas feast. There was a peacock pie, a goose and a pair of ducks. A whole boar's head arrived, chewing on an apple and even managing to look fairly cheerful considering it was being served up on a wooden plate. When that was all gone there was a pudding – a model of the Tower of London made entirely out of marzipan – which was carried into the room to cheers and applause. Finally there were hot chestnuts and more mulled ale and then someone brought out a fiddle and everyone began to sing, though, unfortunately, not the same song.

Nobody had minded Tom being there and during the meal the card sharp had shown him how to strip out an ace and one of the confidence tricksters had tried to sell him London Bridge. But he had spent most of the time telling Moll about the Garden Players. He also told her about some of the mysteries of the past few days – the man with the scar who had come to the ship, Florian's warning and the strange marks on the arms of Dr Mobius and the actor called Ferdinand. Moll had made no comment on any of this but her eyes narrowed and as the meal went on she became quiet and thoughtful.

Outside, the sun was beginning to set and Tom considered that it was time to go. He got up and slipped out of the door. Moll came with him and the two of them stood for a minute in the dying light.

"Thank you, Moll," Tom said. He suddenly felt guilty. "I've got no money," he added. "How can I pay for my food?"

"I'll pay your share," Moll said. "You can pay me back when you're a famous actor."

They shook hands. Tom was about to leave but Moll stopped him. "The Garden Players..." she said, suddenly.

"What about them?"

"Nothing about them sounds quite right. A comedy that isn't funny. Dr Mobius. The way they just hired you without even hearing you read." She scowled. "When that boy, Florian, spoke to you, you said he was talking in a foreign language. You don't know what language it was?"

Tom shook his head. "All I know is, it wasn't English."

"Could it have been French? Or Dutch?"

"I don't know, Moll."

"No. You wouldn't." Moll sighed. Inside the tavern, there was a peal of laughter and clapping from the rest of the assembly. "I've got to go back in," Moll said. "But remember, Tom, if you get into any trouble, you only have to ask for me by name. Ask anyone – a beggar, a street-boy, a porter, a water-carrier. Just tell them to fetch Moll Cutpurse. They'll know where to find me."

"I'm not in trouble..." Tom began.

"Not yet. But you might be." Moll shook her head,

then turned round and went back into the inn.

Tom walked away. "I'm not in trouble," he had said. But he hadn't even taken ten paces and he was. Someone stepped out from behind a tree. The blade of a knife flashed in what was left of the fading light. A hand reached out and grabbed him roughly by the shirt, twisting him round.

"Good afternoon, Tom-Tom," Gamaliel Ratsey said in a soft, sing-song voice. "I thought I might find you here."

"Ratsey...!"

"My dear fellow! You don't know how glad I am to see you." Ratsey touched the point of the knife against Tom's neck. "Happy Christmas, by the way."

"How did you find me?"

"Oh, I heard that you and Moll – what's her name? – Cut-throat had teamed up together, so I've been keeping an eye on her. She led me here and I've been waiting ever since." He shivered. "Jolly cold, Tom-Tom. Deadly cold, you might say."

"What do you want with me?"

"I would have thought it was obvious. I must say, you rather let us down running off like that. The Slopes were very disappointed."

"I'm not going back to Framlingham!"

Ratsey smiled and waved the point of his dagger in a circle around Tom's head. "You're not going anywhere," he said.

"You're going to kill me!"

"It does rather look as if I'm going to have to," Ratsey agreed. "The thing is, you see, you know too much about me."

"I won't tell on you, Ratsey," Tom pleaded. "I've got a new life now, in London. I'm an actor. You can forget about me." He took a step back, trying to buy time, desperately searching for the right words. He had always been afraid of Ratsey and knew him for the killer that he was. But he wondered if there wasn't some way he could appeal to him. Surely there had to be some good in the man? "You can't just kill me in cold blood," he went on. "You're not like that..."

"But I am." Ratsey sighed, and for a moment he looked genuinely sad.

"No! You were a soldier. Captain Ratsey! You told me yourself. You fought for the Queen!"

"And what did the Queen ever do for me?" His eyes blazed. "Oh yes, I was once like you, Tom-Tom. A nice boy. A good boy. Fighting for the Queen to save the country. But when the fighting was over and the war was won, what happened? They gave me nothing! No pension. No reward. I was abandoned, left to starve, all on my own..."

"You had parents..."

"I'd run away from home. They didn't want to know me. There was no one to look after poor old Ratsey so I had to learn to look after myself. And that's what I'm doing now, Tom-Tom. I like you. Yes, I do. But, you see, you know too much. And maybe, one day, you'll whisper a few words ... just by accident. Maybe in your sleep! I can't let that happen. I can't take the risk."

It was no good. Tom glanced left and right. They were standing in an open field, underneath a tree. Thick snow lay all around them and in the branches above. There was nobody in sight. Ratsey had led him away from the inn and Tom knew that even if he did call for help, he would be dead long before anyone arrived. Suddenly he felt very cold. Despite his new boots, the snow was reaching up to his ankles, penetrating his bones. The wind blew and a trickle of snow fell out of the tree and on to his neck.

The snow...

"So let's get this over with," Ratsey said. "I'm sorry, Tom. I hope you understand – it's nothing personal."

"Wait a minute, Ratsey!" Tom brought his hands together as if to plead for mercy. He was hoping he *had* learned something about acting in the last few days. "You can't kill me. I'm only a child!"

"It's never stopped me before..."

"But I'm unarmed..." Now Tom turned his palms upwards. "Look! I don't have a weapon..." Slowly, Tom raised his arms.

"Most of the people I kill don't have weapons," Ratsey said, reasonably. "It makes it a lot easier." His fingers tightened on the knife. "Now stop all this nonsense, Tom-Tom. Time's up!"

Tom's hands were now over his head. There was a branch directly above him. His hands closed over it and with all his strength he pulled down.

A great clump of snow fell out of the tree, both on to Tom and on to Ratsey in front of him. Tom had been ready for it. Ratsey hadn't. Ratsey cursed, momentarily blinded. At the same moment, Tom turned and ran.

He was only seconds ahead of Ratsey. The highwayman had recovered fast and scooping the snow out of his eyes had launched himself after Tom. It was a strange, soundless pursuit. They were almost running in slow motion as their feet came down in the thick snow and even the sound of Tom's rasping breath was smothered by the frozen air.

Tom had no idea where he was going but realized – when it was too late – that he had managed to curve away from the inn where he might have found help. As he stumbled through the snow, almost slipping, scrabbling forward, he caught sight of a group of people, weaving slowly down a lane. Should he make for them? No. It was hopeless. They were probably half-drunk and before he could even begin to explain what was happening, Ratsey would have cut his throat.

"Tom...!"

He must have slowed down. Ratsey had almost caught up with him. The knife flashed through the air and Tom cried out as the very tip of it caught him on the shoulders, slicing through his shirt and drawing a line across his skin. The pain and the shock of it propelled him forward. Ratsey stumbled and almost lost his balance. Tom surged ahead.

He reached a row of houses, found an alleyway and ran through it. But it was then that he made his fatal mistake. Even as he ran, he looked back. His legs carried him the next ten metres before he knew what he had done and by the time he saw where he was it was too late.

He was near Bankside. He had entered a long, wooden jetty, stretching out into the River Thames. Unfortunately, the jetty only continued for another twenty metres and stopped. It was a passage to nowhere and before Tom could double back and regain dry land, Ratsey had reached the other end, blocking it.

The man and the boy stopped and stood there, gazing at each other. Ratsey was breathing heavily. His dark hair had flopped across his face and he threw his head back to clear it. His eyes, when they were revealed, were alight with pleasure.

"You're a fast mover, Tom-Tom," he panted.

"Leave me alone, Ratsey..." Tom took two paces back. Two paces closer to the end of the jetty and the River Thames.

Ratsey lifted the knife and took another step. The jetty creaked underneath him.

"Tom, Tom, the piper's son..." Ratsey had begun to sing. "Cannot hide and he cannot run."

Tom had reached the end of the jetty. A wooden ladder led down to the Thames but there were no boats. Ratsey was getting closer. And then, in an instant, Tom knew what he had to do. Without taking his eyes off

Ratsey he grabbed hold of the ladder and lowered himself down.

Not into water. Onto ice.

Ratsey stared for a moment, then darted forward. But he was already too late. Tom had backed away, wobbling uncertainly, but still standing upright on the ice.

"Come back!" Ratsey squealed. His eyes flared and, slipping the knife between his teeth, he turned and launched himself down the ladder. But his feet had barely touched the ice before there was a sharp crack and with a shuddering scream he disappeared into a gaping hole that had suddenly appeared beneath him. If he hadn't been holding on to the ladder he would have been sucked into the black, freezing water. As it was, he barely had the strength to pull himself out and by the time he was back on top of the jetty, his teeth were rattling with cold.

"T-T-T-Tom!" he tried to call out. Tom was standing only a few metres away but now they could have been a world apart. "C-c-come back!" Ratsey grabbed hold of himself as if trying to squeeze out the icy water. He no longer had the knife. He must have dropped it when he plunged into the river. "The ice! It won't hold your weight!"

"No thanks!" Tom slid backwards, not daring to lift his feet off the ice. He could feel it straining under his weight. Nobody else had tried to cross the Thames yet. It had been cold, but not cold enough. The ice was thin. In places it was almost transparent with the water oozing blackly through. But Tom was certain about one thing. He would sooner disappear through the ice and drown than go back to the jetty and face Ratsey again.

He kept walking. He didn't need to look back at Ratsey. He was a boy, small and underweight, and the ice was only just supporting him. Ratsey, as he had already proved, had no chance. Tom turned round and cried out as the ice gave away beneath him. One of his feet shot through into the water which closed around his ankle, instantly sucking out all feeling. Tom twisted sideways. Fortunately the ice was stronger here. With his foot dripping, he fought for balance and found it. For a moment he stood in the middle of the river, wondering which way to go, wondering if he could even find the courage to move.

Hunching his shoulders against the wind whipping up the river from Westminster, Tom continued across. It was much colder than he had thought. Out in the open, with nothing to protect him, his whole body was quickly growing numb. It was also much further than he would have liked. After ten minutes on the ice he wasn't even half way to the other side. A fist of loose snow punched into his face, forcing him to close his eyes. When he looked back, he could no longer see Ratsey. The highwayman must have given him up for lost.

He pressed on. The ice groaned and creaked but gradually the buildings on the other side of the river loomed up ahead of him, almost invisible in the darkness. Another wooden jetty reached out, water lapping at its legs. He took another step. The ice cracked. He yelled out and toppled forward, his arms flying out. Somehow his hands caught hold of wood. One leg disappeared into the water, soaking and freezing him all the way up to the thigh. But then he was out, pulling himself up on to the jetty. Behind him, shards of ice closed over the hole he had just made. More snow fell.

But he'd made it. He was safe.

It was night-time before Tom got back to the ship where the Garden Players were housed. It had taken him two hours to get there, partly because he was cold and exhausted, partly because he had been afraid of bumping into Ratsey. Although it was Christmas Day, the night watchmen were still out. Once he glimpsed a figure carrying a lantern and with a staff resting on his shoulder and he heard the familiar cry:

Eight o'clock, look well to your locks,
your fire and your light. God give you goodnight.

The night still held one final surprise.

Tom had just got back to Bermondsey and was approaching the ship when he saw a man coming down the gangplank. The man came close to him and although he didn't see Tom, Tom recognized him by the monk's hood and robe he was wearing. It was the man with the scar, the one that Dr Mobius had called Sir Richard. The man hurried off into the night. Tom waited until he had gone, then walked over to the gangplank and went up on to the ship.

He had hoped to make it to the cabin without being seen, but he had barely moved before a door opened and Dr Mobius appeared, climbing up from below.

"Tom...?" Dr Mobius had a glass of wine in one hand, a pipe in the other. His cabin was lit by the soft yellow glow of a candle. He stepped out on to the deck.

"I have some good news for you!" Mobius stretched out a hand, his rings glinting in the candlelight. He laid it gently on Tom's head, stroking his hair. "We are going to perform *The Devil and his Boy* in three days' time."

"That's wonderful," Tom said.

"It is better than you think, my dear friend. We have been greatly honoured. Yes, indeed, it is an honour. The performance is to take place in the Palace of Whitehall."

"A palace?" Tom's mind was beginning to spin, but there was more to come.

"Yes, Tom." His lips curled in a slow smile and something brighter than candlelight gleamed in his eyes. "In Whitehall Palace. And we'll be performing in front of the Queen."

first night nerves

The next three days were a whirlwind of activity. There were still lines to be learned, movements to be discussed, fights to be choreographed and costumes to be sewn. And then there were the props and scenery. Like most plays, *The Devil and his Boy* didn't need much scenery – the audience was expected to imagine it. But there were a lot of props and it was one of these that led to a strange and unpleasant incident.

The prop was a pitchfork.

Tom was rehearsing on the deck in the cold morning sunlight. The entire cast was there, some of them acting, the rest sewing or painting. Florian, he noticed, was looking very downcast. In fact, the older boy had barely spoken a word to him since the night of the warning. However, he noticed Florian glance upwards sharply as Dr Mobius appeared from his cabin, carrying two pitchforks.

"This is for you, Tom," Dr Mobius said, handing him one. "When you disguise yourself as a devil, this is what you must carry. Please handle it with great care."

The pitchfork was about two metres long and taking it, Tom was surprised by its weight. Examining it, he soon knew why it was so heavy. The actual prongs themselves were only wood but the length of the pitchfork was a hollow metal tube – if it hadn't been for the prongs, glued to the top, Tom would have been able to look right through it. There was one other slightly strange thing. At the end of the tube, on the inside, some sort of line had been cut. Tom ran his thumb over it, feeling the sharp metal edge pressing into his flesh. Obviously the metal tube had been used for something before it had been turned into a fork. But why hadn't Dr Mobius used a broom handle or even a roll of paper? It would have been lighter and easier to handle.

And it was while they were running around the deck, that Tom dropped his. The pitchfork fell down. The wooden forks snapped off and the metal tube began to roll along the deck.

Everyone froze. The tube was heading towards the very edge of the ship. There were no railings there. There was nothing between it and the river. And then Florian reacted. Acting as if his life depended on it, he threw himself full-length on to the deck. His out-stretched hand caught the tube centimetres away from the edge. He stood up, holding it.

Dr Mobius had watched all this with wide eyes. Tom could see the relief in his eyes as Florian lifted the tube, but in seconds relief had been replaced with fury. His whole face seemed to change. His skin grew darker, the veins standing out on his bald head. His mouth drew back in a snarl and the next thing Tom knew his hand had struck out, crashing into the side of Tom's face and throwing him sprawling on to the deck. With his head spinning, he tried to stand up but Dr Mobius was already there, looming over him.

"You idiot!" Dr Mobius shouted. "You fool! I told you to be careful and you almost lost it!"

"It's only a metal tube!" Tom protested.

"What?" Dr Mobius drew back his foot and Tom was sure he was going to kick him where he lay. But then Florian sprang forward.

"It was an accident," he said. "You don't have to hurt him!"

Dr Mobius stared at his nephew with murder in his eyes. For his part, Florian held his ground, the rod still in his hand. Slowly, Dr Mobius recovered. He looked down. Tom was still on his knees. There was a trickle of blood coming from the side of his mouth. Dr Mobius drew a hand over his eyes as if trying to wipe away the memory of what had just occurred.

"You must forgive me," he said. "That was ... unforgivable of me." He whipped out his handkerchief and offered it to Tom. Tom didn't take it. "You see," he went on, "to play in front of the Queen! It is a considerable honour. And of course ... I am nervous. We are all nervous. And this..." He gestured at the metal tube, then at Tom. "It was first night nerves. I apologize to you. It won't happen again." He took the metal rod from Florian and stepped back. "We shall all take a rest," he exclaimed to the watching actors. "We will start again after lunch."

The actors dispersed. Tom looked for Florian but the other boy had already turned away and gone downstairs. Suddenly resolved, Tom got up and followed him.

He found Florian in the costumes room, at work on the dress that he himself would wear. Tom paused in the doorway. He caught sight of himself in a piece of broken mirror leaning against the wall. There was still a little blood beside his mouth and he wiped it away with his sleeve.

"Thank you," he said.

"That's all right." Florian didn't look up from his work.

"Florian..." Tom moved further into the room. "The other night ... last week. You told me I should get off the ship. You said that I was in danger. What did you mean?"

The other boy turned his head away. The dress he was working on was bunched up in his hands. Tom could almost feel him struggling with himself. But then another of the actors appeared at the door and looked in. "Lunch is ready," he said and went on his way.

Maybe Florian had been about to tell Tom something but the moment had been interrupted and now the spell was broken. "I didn't mean anything," he said. "I shouldn't have said it. Just forget it."

He got up and, brushing past Tom, quickly left the room.

The opening performance of the first night drew closer and closer. They ran through the play once, then again, this time, with costumes as well as props. Florian had been transformed into a girl with a flowing dress, make-up and a wig. Watching him, Tom remembered his meeting with Will Shakespeare and wondered if he could have acted as a girl at the Rose. In his heart, he knew he could. He also knew – although it made him sad – that he would much rather be acting in Shakespeare's new play than in *The Devil and his Boy*.

The last morning came and went. Everyone knew their lines. Francis and Frances, the musicians, knew their tunes. They performed the play one last time, and this time Dr Mobius loaded the muskets so that, as he and Tom were chased off the stage (this was the last scene of the play), there were loud explosions and puffs of smoke behind them.

Dr Mobius was pleased with the effect. "It will give Her Majesty much pleasure. The explosions and the alarms." He rolled his moustache between two fingers.

"Everyone enjoys that in a play. The last act has to be the best!"

That afternoon, they left the boat. A horse and cart had arrived and all the props, costumes, stage furniture and scripts were carried across in trunks and loaded up in the back. Tom was already feeling dry-mouthed and wondered what he would be like when they arrived at Whitehall Palace.

When everything had been loaded, he and Florian climbed into the back. There was room for the two boys and for Dr Mobius at the front of the cart, but everyone else would have to walk. They stood waiting in the cold for a few minutes. Dr Mobius was the last to leave the ship. He looked briefly in the back of the cart.

"Are you ready?" he asked.

"Yes, Dr Mobius."

"Then onward ... to glory!"

Dr Mobius climbed into the front of the cart and a moment later they felt a jolt as it moved off. Tom glanced back. And it was then that he saw something moving on the deck. It was smoke. It was coming up from below, creeping over the deck and curling round the masts. At first he thought he must be mistaken but suddenly a tongue of flame shot out, licked at part of the old rigging and suddenly the whole boat was ablaze.

Tom cried out but Florian leaned over and stopped him. "It's all right, Tom," he said. "We're finished here.

We won't be going back."

The cart rumbled onward. The entire boat was ablaze now, huge flames reaching up to the very top of the masts. As damp as the ship was, the fire seemed to fall on it like a hungry animal, tearing into it, consuming it utterly. The wood cracked and splintered. One of the masts shivered and fell. The flames leapt up. The ice on the river, glowing red now, began to move, pulling away from the doomed vessel. Slowly the old ship folded in on itself.

And then the cart turned a corner and Tom saw no more.

Whitehall Palace was quite unlike anything Tom had dreamed of. He had imagined a single building but as the cart passed the great monument at Charing Cross and trundled underneath the arches of the Holbein Gate, he realized that it was an entire town in its own right. There were soaring chapels and tall, solid towers; elegant stables and neat, compact houses. The entire complex was set in gardens and orchards, spread out on the northern bank of the Thames. Tom found it hard to believe that only a few days before he had been close by, fighting for his life on the fragile ice.

They were stopped by a soldier dressed in a red and black tunic with a sword at his waist and an odd weapon – part spear and part axe – on his shoulder. Sitting at the front of the cart, Dr Mobius produced a letter and handed it to him and the soldier directed them to a large building that was being guarded by two more similarly dressed men. The cart rolled across the last few metres and Tom got down. The two men seemed to take no notice of him. Passing between them, Tom went in – and found himself in the Banqueting Hall where the play was to be performed.

It was a huge space, at least a hundred metres long, held up by slim wooden pillars garlanded with dried flowers and fruit. The walls seemed to be solid stone but looking more closely, Tom was thrilled to realize that the whole building was a trick. The walls were actually made of canvas. What he was standing in was nothing more than a gigantic tent. But what a tent! The ceiling had been painted as if it were the sky – at one end there were silver stars and a moon, at the other a golden sun, shooting out its beams. At least three hundred glass lamps hung inside and wreaths of holly and ivy had been placed everywhere.

A stage had been constructed at one end of the Banqueting Hall. It stood against a screen which the actors could hide behind when they needed to change or were waiting to come on. There were a number of chairs at the other end, one of them larger than the rest and richly padded with velvet and cushions. Tom didn't need to ask who would be sitting here.

Dr Mobius had already started carrying in the costumes and props. Tom wondered if he ought to help but before he could move there was the sound of stamping feet and a dozen soldiers suddenly marched in, forming a line on either side of the entrance. There was a brief pause and then three more men came in, these ones wearing brilliantly coloured slashed doublets and caps, tight stockings and highly polished shoes.

Dr Mobius stopped what he was doing and bowed low. The actors did the same. Tom hesitated for a moment then remembered himself and bowed as well. The man standing in the middle – he also had some sort of chain of office round his neck and carried a white staff – gestured at Dr Mobius, who straightened up.

"My name is Edmund Tilney," he said. "I am Master in the Office of the Revels. You are..." He creased his brow and glanced at the younger man on his left.

"The Garden Players," the man said.

"Quite. And the name of the play you are to perform?"

"*The Devil and his Boy*," Dr Mobius told him.

"Oh yes." The Master of the Revels frowned. "Not an entirely suitable title, I feel," he snapped. "But Sir Richard says he found it most enjoyable."

At the mention of Sir Richard, Tom glanced up. He had barely noticed the third man when he came in but now he realized that it was indeed the same "Sir Richard" who had come – twice – to the boat. There were the narrow eyes and slightly hooked nose. And there – impossible to miss – was the scar, cut on the side of his cheek, shaped like a J.

But even as he stood there uncomfortably with his

back bent and his neck craning up, Tom's mind began to race. As far as he knew, *The Devil and his Boy* had never been performed before. Certainly all the actors had had to learn it from scratch. So how could Sir Richard claim to have seen it?

And why had Sir Richard come to the boat, not only at night but in disguise? He remembered seeing Dr Mobius give him a bag full of coins. What had the money been for?

And, most strangely of all, why were Dr Mobius and Sir Richard pretending they didn't know each other? It wasn't just that they hadn't greeted each other. They weren't even looking each other in the eye.

What exactly was going on?

"All right," Tilney was saying. "The play will begin at eight o'clock, after Her Majesty has finished dinner. There are certain rules which you would be wise to obey." He cast his eyes over the entire company. "None of you are to look at Her Majesty. If she enjoys the play, she may come and speak to you afterwards. If she doesn't, I can assure you that she's the *last* person you'd want to speak to. Don't try to speak to her. You may find it easier just to imagine she isn't here."

He paused for breath. From the way he spoke, Tom imagined that he had done this many times before.

"Now, we have to consider the content of this play. I understand it's a comedy. I hope it's got good jokes."

"The very finest, my lord," Dr Mobius said, bowing again.

"Good. Her Majesty enjoys a laugh. If you don't hear her laughing, I suggest you finish it as quickly as you can. Leave out Acts Three and Four if you have to." He turned to Sir Richard. "There's nothing vulgar in it, is there?" he asked.

"No, my lord," Sir Richard replied.

"Nothing offensive, sacrilegious, unpatriotic or treasonable? I have to remind you that the Bishop of Winchester is in tonight, and you know how touchy he gets. The devil in this play. We're not talking about Satan, I hope?"

"It's not the real devil, my lord," Dr Mobius said.

"Good. Good. Good... Now, let me see." He gestured at Sir Richard. "Sir Richard here is the Clerk Comptroller. If all goes well he'll pay you ten pounds, once the play is finished. If Her Majesty walks out half-way, it'll be five pounds. Do you understand?"

Everyone who had stopped bowing bowed again.

"Now, there's one last thing," Tilney said. "Sir Richard informs me that you fire muskets in the last act."

"They are fake muskets," Dr Mobius exclaimed. "I can assure my lord that Her Majesty will be entertained and not alarmed..."

"Yes! Yes! Yes!" Tilney interrupted. "All your props and luggage will be searched by the Gentlemen Pensioners before she arrives." He gestured at the men in red. "They'll also search every one of you, too. But I think I'd better take a look at these muskets of yours myself."

Dr Mobius nodded and two of the actors carried forward the trunk that contained the two muskets. They opened it and handed the weapons to Tilney who glanced at them briefly. "As you will see, my lord," Mobius explained, "the barrels of the guns are fashioned from wood. They are also solid. No ball could pass through them. The only part of the weapon that is authentic is the firing mechanism. We require this to make the ... small explosions, which, I can assure, my lord, will add a delightful frisson to Her Majesty's evening."

Tilney nodded and set the weapons down. "Very good." He nodded at the Gentlemen Pensioners. "Make sure they're all thoroughly searched."

It took over an hour to search everyone and everything. The Gentlemen Pensioners were the Queen's personal bodyguard and it was their job to ensure that nothing remotely dangerous came anywhere near her. Even a small knife that Mobius used to sharpen his quill was removed. The muskets were examined again and set down on a table along with the pitchforks, the devil horns and all the other bits and pieces from the play. Only when they were completely satisfied did the Gentlemen Pensioners leave and even then two of them remained behind to guard the door and make sure that nobody else tried to enter.

For the next three hours, Tom helped get the stage ready, constructing the scenery, setting out the furniture and ensuring that everything was in its right place. All the props and costumes had to be carried behind the screen and arranged out-of-sight. The instruments had to be tuned. And finally there were hurried consultations with the actors whispering their lines to each other, making sure there was nothing they had forgotten. During all this, Tom noticed, Florian didn't say a word. Once Tom tried to speak to him but the other boy hurriedly broke away as if he were afraid of catching – or giving Tom – the plague.

At last everything was ready. Someone had brought the players some bread, some cold meat and wine, but everyone was too nervous to eat. Dr Mobius, however, poured himself a cup of wine and held it up in a toast.

"Today," he said, "is the day that we make history." All the actors were gathered around listening. They seemed to share the same, strange gleam in their eyes. Only Florian looked sick and kept his head down. "The 28th December 1593," Dr Mobius went on, "It is a day that no one in England will forget. It is a day that will belong to the *Garduna*." He blinked and then turned to Tom with a smile. "I mean, of course, the Garden Players." He lifted his cup. "I drink to you, my friends. To the sacrifice we make for our country. May God bless all of us in this great endeavour. Glory ... and death!"

It seemed a very strange speech to be making just before a play, and a comedy at that. But the actors (apart from Florian) had all whispered a fervent "amen" and Tom joined them, not wishing to be left out. It still puzzled him though and he was about to ask Dr Mobius what he had meant when there was a trumpet fanfare and a sudden murmur of voices on the other side of the screen.

At once the room began to fill up. Tom was forbidden to look round the screen but he heard men and women talking, the clattering of shoes, the scrape of chairs being moved and an occasional burst of laughter. Next to him, Francis and Frances began to give their instruments a final tuning.

And then, as suddenly as it had started, the noise stopped. There was a second fanfare and everyone in the room stood up. Tom still couldn't see anything but he knew what had happened.

The Queen had arrived.

The lights dimmed as most of the candles were blown out.

The audience took their places.

And the play began.

the devil and his boy

The play began with a prologue, delivered by Dr Mobius himself. Tom had heard it twenty or more times but listening to it now from behind the screen, he barely understood a word of it. It was as if there were a wind rushing through his ears. He couldn't hear anything. His mouth was dry. There was no feeling in his arms or legs.

He was, he realized, terrified. He was about to go on the stage in front of Queen Elizabeth and her court. He wondered if his legs would be able to move when his cue came. Not for the first time, he wished he had never left Framlingham. Even life with the Slopes had been better than this.

Act One, Scene One began. Lucio had arrived in Venice. He had no money and nowhere to stay for the night. He called for his servant.

"Antonio! What ho? Antonio...!"

Tom stepped through the screen and onto the stage.

And the strange thing was, he left all his fear behind him. He had never felt such a transformation. It was as if he had stepped out of water onto dry land. Suddenly he was confident. He knew his lines. He knew what to do. It might have been Tom who had stood fearful and quivering behind the screen. But it was Antonio, servant of Lucio who now began to talk, poking fun at his master and finally racing round the stage as he tried to escape a beating.

Tom didn't dare look into the shadows beyond the stage but he could tell that the audience was enjoying the play. They had been silent throughout the prologue and the opening scene but Tom's entrance had cheered them up. They laughed quite a few times and when the scene ended they clapped.

Tom hurried off the stage. He wondered if the Queen herself had clapped with them. The Queen of England, applauding him! But he didn't have time to think about it. The props were laid out on a table behind a fake wall – built for Act Five – and he hurried over and picked up the two pitchforks.

He was halfway back to the stage before he knew something was wrong and even then he wasn't sure what it was. At first he thought he had forgotten something. He had the pitchforks, the rope, the horns. What else was there? On the stage, Dr Mobius was coming to the end of another soliloquoy and Tom knew he had only moments before he had to go back on. He was wearing horns. He had put on his tail.

And then he understood what it was. The pitchforks were much too light. Being careful not to drop them, Tom turned them over in his hands and examined them. He quickly saw what had happened. The forks at the top were the same but the long metal tubes had been replaced with lengths of wood. This made them much lighter to carry and easier to handle too. But Tom was surprised that Dr Mobius should have changed them at this late stage and that he should have done so without telling him.

"Here comes Antonio now!"

Caught up with the pitchforks, Tom had almost missed his cue. He hurried on to the stage, almost dropping them as he went and although Dr Mobius glared at him, this got another laugh from the audience. The rest of the scene was a nightmare. Tom twisted one of his lines so it came out all wrong and completely forgot another. But try as he might, he found it almost impossible to concentrate. Ever since he had joined the Garden Players all sorts of questions had been tapping at the window of his mind. He had tried to ignore them. But now, at the worst possible time, they had returned, louder and more insistent than ever.

Somehow he made it to the end of the scene but when he got backstage a furious Dr Mobius – looking more devilish than ever – marched up to him and grabbed him.

"What are you doing?" he demanded in a hoarse whisper. His eyes were bulging with the effort of not shouting and his make-up had begun to run.

"I'm sorry..." On the other side of the screen, Francis and Frances, the two musicians, were playing a duet.

Dr Mobius closed his eyes, forcing himself to regain control. "Remember what you are doing," he said. "Concentrate!" He glared at Tom, then withdrew into the shadows.

Tom took a deep breath, angry with himself. Dr Mobius was right. Whatever his doubts about the play, the Garden Players and everything to do with them, he couldn't worry about them now. And what was so important about the pitchforks anyway? Once they had been metal. Now they were wood.

The pitchfork rolling across the deck. Florian diving and catching it. Dr Mobius hitting him. "You idiot! You fool! ...You almost lost it!"

Tom shook his head, forcing himself to forget it. Behind the screen, the duet finished. The next scene began.

There were no further mishaps. Tom made no more mistakes, and an hour later he left the stage knowing that he would not be needed now until the very end of Act Five. It was the interval.

With the actors safely hidden behind the screen, the doors were opened and the audience retired for refreshments in another part of the palace. Tom was exhausted. Performing had sucked all the energy out of him. The other actors seemed as tired as he was. They also looked nervous and this was surprising. The play was more than half over. The most difficult scenes were behind them. Why should they seem so nervous now?

Edmund Tilney, the Master of the Revels, had come backstage. The man with the scar came with him. Sir Richard seemed to have caught a cold. He was pale and sweating.

"Her Majesty will be returning for the second half," Tilney said.

"We are honoured." Dr Mobius bowed low.

"Yes. You are." Tilney coughed drily. "The play's too long and it's rather dull. I'd be grateful if you could speed up Acts Four and Five. However, Her Majesty likes the boy – and the one playing the girl. She also likes the music. I take it there is more music?"

"A great deal more," Dr Mobius assured him.

"Good." Tilney glanced at his Clerk Comptroller. "I must say, Sir Richard," he snapped, "this hasn't been one of your best recommendations."

He turned to leave but Dr Mobius stopped him. "Wait until the end of the performance before you pass judgement, my lord," he said. "I think I can promise you that it is a play that Her Majesty will not forget. Nor you either!"

Tilney raised his eyebrows at this but said nothing. He left the room, Sir Richard hurrying after him.

Dr Mobius and the other actors were sitting on benches, some lying on their backs with their eyes closed. Florian was on his own, gnawing at his fingernails and staring into space. It was very dark behind the stage. Tom was glad about that. The darkness helped him think.

Someone had changed the pitchforks. Why? Back on the ship, Dr Mobius had almost killed him when he had dropped one of them. But why had the pitchforks been made of metal in the first place – and why metal tubes?

Metal tubes. For some reason that made Tom think of something. But what? Tom buried his head in his hands and searched through his memory. A metal tube, pointing at him. Of course! He was back in the forest with Hawkins. He was looking at Ratsey's gun.

There were guns in Act Five of *The Devil and his Boy* as well. Tom still hadn't solved the puzzle but suddenly he was filled with dread. The Master of the Revels had checked the muskets himself. Tom remembered what Dr Mobius had said.

"The barrels of the guns are fashioned from wood."

Moving slowly, trying to act as natural as possible, Tom went over to the artificial wall behind which the props were kept. He took one last look to make sure nobody was watching. Then he slipped behind the wall.

The muskets were lying in the right place, waiting for their appearance in Act Five. They looked exactly the same as they had earlier that afternoon when Tilney had examined them, but even as he reached for the nearest one, Tom knew it had changed. Sure enough, it was heavier. He turned it round. The barrel of the gun was no longer made of wood. Nor was it solid.

And in that moment, Tom knew everything.

It was very simple.

Dr Mobius was planning to kill the Queen! He was going to do it at the end of Act Five with muskets that, with the metal rods from the pitchforks screwed into place, were now *real* muskets. One shot for the Queen. One shot for the guard by the door. Maybe Dr Mobius and the Garden Players planned to fight their way out. But Tom had seen the fanatical light in Dr Mobius's eyes. He had a job to do. He wouldn't care what happened to him when it was over.

Gently, Tom lowered the musket back on to the table. What could he do?

He had to save the Queen – but that might be easier said than done. How could he even leave the backstage area without the others seeing? And if he did manage to slip away, where could he go? Who could he tell? Sir Richard was obviously a traitor. What about Edmund Tilney? But if he did speak out, would anyone believe him?

The problem was solved for him.

Tom hadn't heard anyone creeping round behind the wall but the next moment something cold and hard crashed into the back of his neck. His legs buckled under him. The darkness came rushing in. He tried to fight it. But then Dr Mobius hit him again and he was gone.

Tom woke up slowly with a pain in his head and a neck that felt as if it had been tied in a knot. He was lying underneath the table, his face pressed against the floor. He could taste straw and sawdust in his mouth. Even before he opened his eyes, he heard the play being performed in what seemed like the far distance. It took him a minute to make out the words and another minute to recall where they came from. Act Five, Scene Two. Just a few pages until Lucio and Antonio were chased out of Venice by soldiers armed with...

He remembered the muskets and crawled painfully out from under the table. The muskets weren't there. He looked over to the side of the screen and saw Frederick and Philip, two of the actors, dressed as soldiers and carrying the muskets, waiting for their cue. He knew what was going to happen. In about one minute's time, they would walk on to the stage. Nobody would even think of stopping them. They would raise their muskets, loaded and primed. There would be two explosions and the audience probably wouldn't even realize what had taken place. Until they saw the Queen's blood.

Tom had to stop them. But even now he didn't know what to do. Shout out a warning? It wouldn't work. The two actors would fire before the Queen had time to move. Throw himself at Frederick and Philip?

No. Even assuming he could get anywhere near them, he couldn't take on two men at once.

These merry devils must be banished hence.
Go! Call the watch...!

Tom knew the lines. The shooting was about to begin. There was no time to call out a warning. No time to try and explain.

Before he knew what he was doing, he was running – round behind the screen and out onto the stage. All the actors had their backs to him so none of them saw him as he broke into the light and kept on going. Tom just had time to glimpse Florian, turning his head towards him, his eyes widening, and next to him, Dr Mobius himself, his mouth half-open in mid-sentence. He had no real plan. All he knew was that he must put himself in front of the Queen, protect her with his own body if he had to. Only seconds remained before Mobius would fire the first shot. Even now he might be taking aim.

Tom had reached the front of the stage. Everything was a whirl. He tried to position himself, spreading his arms to give the Queen more cover. And it was then that his foot came down on a loose plank. The wood tilted and he lost his balance. With a great cry he pitched forward and, carried by his own momentum, plunged down on to the Queen herself.

Then things didn't so much happen as explode. Tom

fell on top of the Queen, knocking her chair backwards and sending her flying. There was a gasp of disbelief from the surrounding courtiers, screams from the Maids of Honour. Tom just caught sight of the Queen's face, wide-eyed with shock. He was vaguely aware of black teeth and skin with too much make-up. To his horror, the Queen seemed to be wearing a wig which had come loose. He closed his eyes. The very fact that he was touching her was beyond belief. Actually to be lying on top of her, his body on hers, his hands around her throat ... it was enough to give an Archbishop a heart attack. He couldn't look. He didn't dare.

But even though it had all gone horribly wrong, he knew that he had succeeded in what he set out to do. His attack had taken Dr Mobius by surprise. Already the audience had closed in on the Queen. The Gentlemen Pensioners were running in from all sides to pull him off.

Tom didn't know if Dr Mobius had a musket now or not. But it didn't matter.

He had no clear aim.

Dr Mobius did have a musket. He had snatched it from Frederick even as Tom ran past. Standing at the front of the stage, he waved it at the writhing, panicking mass that had been a courtly audience only seconds before. He caught sight of a stockinged leg, a jewelled foot and fired.

The sound of the explosion seemed huge and suddenly the hall was filled with smoke and the smell of gunpowder. But the shot had missed. One of the courtiers had been shot in the back of his leg. With blood spurting from the wound, he cried out and fell to the ground.

The gunshot only added to the panic in the hall. Nobody quite knew where it had come from. All they knew was that one of the actors, the boy, had gone mad and thrown himself at the Queen and now somebody else had decided to join him. At least a dozen pairs of hands had grabbed Tom and he felt himself being ripped apart while, still underneath him, the Queen had brought up her fists and was vigorously punching him on the nose and the stomach.

But at least some of the courtiers had kept their heads. The boy on top of the Queen was an outrage. But now there was a musket somewhere in the room – and that was a deadly danger. Acting out of instinct, the courtiers had moved to surround the Queen, forming a human wall for her protection. At the same time, the Gentlemen Pensioners had formed a front line, making for the stage.

Dr Mobius knew he was finished. He grabbed the second musket and once again stared into the commotion. But now there was no sign of the Queen at all. With a loud oath, he fired again, as if he could aim through so much writhing flesh and blood and still, miraculously find his target. The second shot did get some way through. It hit Tom in the shoulder. He felt it slamming into his body, white hot and furious. It was like the sting of some terrible insect. Tom screamed. At the same time he felt himself being plucked away. He opened his eyes and caught one last sight of the Queen. It was as if she were being sucked into a tunnel in front of him. A fist hit him on the side of the face. Another hand tore at his hair. He was flung to the floor, his bones crashing into wood, and when he tried to move he found that he was pinned there, held down by at least five men.

Up on the stage, the actors were trying to fight their way out. But the two muskets, with their single shots gone, were useless now and they had no other weapons. It was all over very quickly. Only two of the actors – the two who had also played musical instruments – were killed. Later on it would be agreed that they had run on to the swords held up to stop them leaving, preferring to kill themselves rather than face imprisonment, torture and a more protracted death.

The Queen had been helped to her feet and disappeared with a swirl of silk. She was followed by bishops and courtiers, secret agents and councillors, already arguing amongst themselves, and by ladies-in-waiting who had turned into ladies-in-wailing as they sobbed in both terror and relief.

Someone rapped out an order and Tom was scraped off the floor and lifted out of a puddle of his own blood. He stood, swaying on his feet. A couple of men supported him. He could never have stood on his own. Somehow he managed to bring his eyes into focus and saw Sir Richard, standing at the edge of the crowd. The Clerk Comptroller's face had gone completely white – all of it except for the scar which stood out, dark red and throbbing. His eyes were filled with terror.

But then another man, someone Tom had never seen before pushed his way forward. This man was dressed in black and grey with a chain of office around his neck and a sword in his belt. The man had soft, green eyes. His face was long and thin. "Who are you?" he asked.

Tom tried to answer. He opened his mouth but nothing came out.

The man with green eyes looked at him more in puzzlement than in anger. "Why did you do it?" he asked.

"I didn't..." It took all Tom's strength to whisper the two words and even as he spoke them he knew it would be no good. Everyone in the room had seen what had happened. Nobody would believe him.

"Take him away!" the man said. "The others to the Tower for interrogation. This boy to Newgate. He has lain a hand on the most glorious person of Her Majesty. He has ... *attacked* her! Such sacrilege is unheard of and we must ensure that no one does hear of it. Hang him tomorrow at first light. We'll learn from the others the reason for what happened here."

"Wait..." Tom began.

But already he was being dragged backwards out of the Banqueting Hall. He felt the cold night air rushing over his shoulders and its touch brought fresh pain from the wound in his back. There was a cart and a horse already waiting and brutally, like a sack of potatoes, he was thrown into the back. Two guards climbed in with him. The horse was whipped forward.

Tom thought he was going to faint with the shock, the pain, the knowledge of what was to come. The night began to spin but before he let it take him, he forced his eyes open and looked out. They had just passed through the Holbein Gate. There were a few late-night revellers on the other side, making their way home with a servant – a link boy – lighting their way. Tom lifted himself in the cart and before his two guards could stop him, called out, "Find Moll Cutpurse! Tell her it wasn't me! Tell her that Tom—!"

Then the guards reached him, grabbed him and pulled him down and Tom could say no more. Had the link boy even heard him? Tom didn't know and he was too exhausted to care. He closed his eyes and drifted into sleep as the cart rattled on through the night.

on the scaffold

It was seven o'clock in the morning and Gamaliel Ratsey was enjoying a healthy breakfast of hot porridge, bread, honey and milk in the tavern where he had been staying since his arrival in London. The owners of the tavern had let him have his bed and breakfast at a special rate. In return, Ratsey had promised not to kill them.

He looked up. Someone was standing over him, watching him with soft, attentive eyes. Automatically, Ratsey's hand twitched for the hilt of his sword. Then he relaxed. It wasn't a man but a boy, and not a boy but a girl. He knew at once who it was.

"Moll Cut-throat!" he exclaimed. "This is a surprise."

"It's Cutpurse," Moll replied. "May I join you?"

"It looks like you already have." Ratsey scooped up

a mouthful of porridge. "Have you come to bring me the boy?"

"Not exactly." Moll gazed curiously at Ratsey as if trying to make him out. "I have something to tell you," she said.

"Go on." Ratsey gave her his best, choirboy smile

"Tom Falconer is in Newgate. He's going to be hanged at eleven o'clock this morning."

Ratsey chuckled. "Is he, indeed? How do you know?"

"I heard last night."

Quickly, Moll told Ratsey how she had been woken by the link boy and how, at first light she had gone to Newgate Prison to find out what had taken place. Nobody had wanted to tell her anything but she had bribed one of the guards with sixpence and heard the complete story from him.

"Tom is accused of trying to kill the Queen," she told Ratsey now.

"That's ridiculous!"

"Of course it is. Tom would never try to kill anyone. All he wanted to do was act in a play. But these people he got involved with ... they called themselves the Garden Players, but I've been asking around and nobody has heard of them – and from what Tom told me they weren't English."

"Maybe they were French."

"Or Dutch. Or Spanish. It doesn't matter. All that matters is that Tom can't have had anything to do with it. But he's going to hang in less than four hours if you and I don't do something."

"You and I?" Ratsey choked on his porridge. "You're mad! Why should I care if they hang the boy? They'll be doing me a favour."

"Is that your answer?"

"Yes. I always liked Tom. To be honest with you, I was never looking forward to murdering him. But what on earth makes you think I'd want to help him?"

This was the moment Moll had been dreading. She knew she'd taken a huge chance coming here. But she needed Ratsey's help and this was the only way. "I know who you are, Ratsey," she said. "But I also know who you used to be."

Ratsey's eyes narrowed. The smile faded from his lips. "What the devil are you talking about?" he asked.

"I'm talking about Captain Ratsey. The famous soldier who fought in the Irish campaigns and single-handedly captured the fort at Smerwick." She nodded gravely. "Oh yes, I've heard all the stories about you," she went on. "People talk about Sir Francis Drake and Sir Walter Raleigh. But you could have been a bigger hero than either of them."

"Could have been! Could have been! But that was then!" Ratsey threw down his spoon. "That was a long time ago. Now I'm Ratsey the robber. Ratsey the killer. It's too late for me now."

"That's what I'm trying to tell you. This could be your last chance!" Moll reached out to take his arm but Ratsey pulled it away. "People like us, Ratsey – pickpockets and highwaymen. What sort of life do we have? Always afraid. Always on the run. Until one day they catch up with us and then..." Moll drew her hands to her throat. "But this is a chance to do one good thing. To be remembered as heroes. To make something of ourselves."

Ratsey fell silent. "So what are you suggesting, Moll Cut-price?" he demanded at length. "We just walk into Newgate and pull Tom out?"

"No. We go to Whitehall – to the Queen."

"What? Old Queeny!"

"Yes. We'll tell her she's made a mistake. We'll make her listen to us..."

"You think they'll even allow us in?"

"I know how to get us in, Ratsey. But I can't do it alone." Moll gripped his arm and this time he let her. "Doesn't Tom deserve a chance?" she said. "You said you liked him. Save his life and maybe you'll be saving your own. Think of what you were. Think of what you still can be."

Ratsey sighed. "My father always said I'd come to no good," he said. "He said I'd end up on the wrong end of a rope."

"So prove him wrong."

Ratsey thought for a long minute. He stuck a finger in his porridge and stirred it, then licked the finger. The porridge was cold. He sighed again. Then, finally, he saluted. "All right. All right. Captain Ratsey reporting for duty," he muttered. "Now tell me. What's the plan?"

There were fourteen prisons in London but Newgate was the most feared. It was reserved for the very worst criminals and all of them arrived in the knowledge that they would not be staying long. Nine steps led to the way out. A rope and a trapdoor. Tom, however, was about to set the record for the shortest stay of all. And although the guards argued about this, they were fairly sure that he would be the youngest person they had ever hanged.

Tom awoke in a small, square cell, lying on a thin layer of straw with a tattered blanket over his legs. A small, barred window – another square – looked out on to grey sky and little else. He was not alone. A short, round man was lying on a bench, his knees tucked into his ample stomach, snoring loudly. Tom sat up. His shoulder, where he had been shot, still hurt dreadfully and there was no movement at all in his right arm. He was filthy and his head ached.

The man on the bench grunted, sat up and rubbed his eyes. Tom barely glanced at him but the man gazed at Tom, shook his head, then... "My dear fellow!" he exclaimed. "It's John, is it not? No, it's not. It's Tim! No, it's not. It's Tom!" He smiled. "There have been so many boys. So many charming boys. I'm afraid I get a little hazy with names."

Now Tom recognized his cell-mate. The last time

they had met, he had been interested in removing Tom's legs. The man was James Grimly. "What are you doing here?" Tom was so astonished that the words just tumbled out.

"A most serious misunderstanding with the authorities. They take a dim view, it would seem, of my ... adjustments. Quite why, I cannot say. I feel London will be a much less cheerful place without Grimly's boys. But there you are." He sighed. "One or two of my boys became rather ill," he admitted. "In fact, not to put too fine a point on it, they died. So now they've decided to adjust *me*." He ran a finger across his throat. "Permanently."

"They're going to hang me too," Tom said.

"My poor fellow! What did you do?"

Tom half-smiled. "I tried to kill the Queen."

"Good lord!" Grimly blinked rapidly. "I have to say, Tom, I'm quite shocked. The Queen!" He coughed, glanced at Tom, then looked away. "Mr Bull should be in any time now," he said.

"Mr Bull?"

"The hangman." Grimly smiled. "I'm sure he'll be delighted to meet up with you! Delighted, I'm absolutely sure."

The cart was old and piled high with loaves. As it rolled into Whitehall Palace a couple of guards wandered over and glanced at the driver, a small, plump man who was also completely white – being covered from head to toe in flour.

"You're late!" one of the guards said.

"The oven went out," the driver – who was also the baker – replied. "The fool of a boy fell asleep in the night." The second guard was meanwhile searching underneath the cart. "What's going on?" the driver exclaimed. "You know me well enough. What do you think I'm hiding?"

"We had some trouble here last night," the first guard explained. His partner straightened up. "All right! Move on..."

The cart continued round to the kitchen entrance. The driver looked left and right, then whistled softly. A moment later, all the loaves heaved and separated as two figures, now as flour-covered as the driver, pulled themselves from under the pile.

"Thanks, Walter," Moll said.

"You owe me one for this, Moll," the baker muttered. He took a tray off the back. "Give me one minute."

Moll Cutpurse and Gamaliel Ratsey looked a bizarre sight as they crept over to the kitchen of Whitehall Palace; a girl in boy's clothes and a man in a mask, both of them bristling with weapons and covered in flour. Ratsey's mask was a small one and suited his name for it was in the shape of a rat. Moll had tried to stop him from wearing it but Ratsey had insisted. It was either with the mask or not at all.

The kitchen was heaving with cooks, under-cooks, waiters and boys already hard at work on the midday meal. Half a deer was rotating slowly on a metal spit turned by a fat boy who was sweating as much as the meat he was cooking. Ratsey and Moll waited at the door as the baker went past them, calling out "Fresh bread!" He walked to the far side of the kitchen. Just as he reached the counter, the tray tipped and the rolls went everywhere. The baker cried out and crashed to the ground. At that moment, with all eyes on the accident, Moll and Ratsey slipped through the kitchen and out the other side.

They found themselves in a larder, filled with cured hams, salted fish and pickled vegetables. For a moment Moll thought they had walked into a cupboard but there was a second door leading out and, taking it, they found themselves in a long passage.

"Which way?" Ratsey whispered.

"Up!"

There was a staircase straight ahead of them, but before they could reach it a yeoman suddenly appeared, walking directly towards them. Moll acted at once, grabbing him by the arm and swinging him around so that his back was to Ratsey. At the same time Ratsey lashed out, his fist catching the man in his neck. Moll caught him as he fell.

They reached the stairs and hurried up them. A second corridor led directly above the first, but this one was much more smartly decorated, with tapestries, curving wooden tables and oil paintings.

"We've got to find the Presence Chamber," Ratsey said.

"Will the Queen be there?"

"She might be. If she's not there, we can try the Watching Chamber and if she's not there she might be in the Great Hall."

"If she's not there, we're in trouble," Moll said.

And that was when the Gentlemen Pensioners appeared. Not just two or three but an entire platoon on a routine patrol. They had stepped out of an archway at the end of the corridor and now they were gazing at Moll and Ratsey with a mixture of astonishment and outrage.

"What was that about trouble?" Ratsey said.

"Back!" Moll shouted.

They turned and ran the way they came, aware of the thunder of feet and the clatter of weapons behind them.

"In here!" Ratsey had reached another door and, grabbing hold of Moll, dragged her in.

They found themselves in a library, a room filled from floor to ceiling with precious books, many of them bound in gold and silver, some of them also decorated with pearls and precious stones. Two windows looked out on to gardens and a tennis court but there was no way to climb down. The room had only one door and even as Ratsey slid a heavy chair across to block it, they heard the sound of the guards and the hammering of fists on wood. There was no way out. They were trapped.

Ratsey threw himself into the chair, adding his

weight to the barrier while Moll checked the windows, quickly returning with a shake of her head. Outside, the hammering stopped. The guards knew where they were. All they had to do now was wait.

"Well, so much for that," Ratsey muttered. It was impossible to see his face behind the rat mask but he sounded only a little bit depressed. "It looks like we're stuck."

"Maybe we can explain..." Moll began.

"I wonder if we'll be hanged, drawn and quartered?" Ratsey mused. "I always wondered what it would be like..."

Outside the door, the hammering started again but this time with some solid metal tool. A panel of wood splintered. An axe-head jutted through. Ratsey drew his sword. Moll drew hers. And then one of the bookshelves swung open and a man stepped into the room.

He was an old man, dressed in a black robe, with a beard reaching down to his chest. Curiously, he was smiling. Even more curiously, he was holding a cat.

"Moll Cutpurse and Gamaliel Ratsey, I believe," he said. He spoke with a Welsh accent. "You'd better come this way. The guards will be breaking in any minute."

A second axe slammed into the door. Another panel of wood cracked open.

"Who are you?" Moll demanded.

"And where did you come from?" Ratsey asked.

"I'm not sure we have time for introductions," the old man said.

The door was struck twice more. One of its hinges shattered. Now they could hear the guards, shouting in triumph.

"This way!" The old man gestured at the secret passage behind the bookshelf. Moll and Ratsey exchanged a glance, then ran in. The old man and the cat followed them. The shelf of books swung shut behind them.

"Follow me," the old man said.

They were in a narrow passage lined with bricks on both sides and lit by a series of oil lamps. It seemed to run the entire length of the palace with other passages and even staircases leading off. It was almost like a secret palace within the palace, a hidden network connecting every room in the building. The old man knew exactly where they were going. Humming softly to himself, and still carrying the cat, he hurried on ahead, not even pausing to check that the other two were behind. At last he stopped beside a large panel of wood.

"This will lead you into the Presence Chamber," he said. "I can't promise that the Queen will be there. You may have scared her away with all the fuss. But you may still find what you want."

"Who are you?" Moll asked.

"My name is John Dee."

Ratsey was suspicious. "How did you know who we were? And why are you helping us?"

"Either we can spend all day talking or you can go in there and save the boy," Dee replied. He paused for a reply but there was none. "I'll wish you a good day," he said.

"Good luck!"

Dr Dee turned and walked away from Moll and Ratsey, heading back down the passage. For a moment neither of them spoke. Either they were going mad or the last words had just been spoken by the cat.

At length, Moll laid a hand on the wooden panel and turned to Ratsey. "Are you ready?" she whispered.

"Yes."

"Then let's go."

She pushed.

The Presence Chamber was full that morning: Privy Councillors and Clerks, Gentlemen Ushers and Grooms, Bishops and Ambassadors. But even as Moll stumbled through a curtain and into the centre of the darkly panelled room, she realized that she had failed. The throne was empty. There was no Queen.

For a moment, everyone froze. To the assembled courtiers it was as if two nightmare creatures – one with the face of a rat – had suddenly been conjured out of thin air. As Moll and Ratsey stood there, taking everything in, the spell was suddenly broken. Swords and knives were drawn. Doors crashed open and soldiers appeared, running and shouting. Ratsey had a knife in one hand and a sword in another. Moll also held a dagger. But it was useless. They were completely surrounded. And they were outnumbered by at least fifty to one.

"Put down your weapons!" someone exclaimed.

"This is the Queen's Presence Chamber!"

"Traitors!"

Ratsey twisted round, his knife raised. "I'm not a traitor!" he said.

"We came to see the Queen!" Moll cried, knowing it was useless. The guards were already moving in. She and Ratsey could kill one, two, three of them. But it wouldn't do any good. They would be cut down where they stood.

"Where did you come from?" A man who looked as if he was in charge had forced his way to the front of the circle. It was the man with green eyes who had spoken to Tom only the night before. "What do you want with Her Majesty?"

"To tell her she was wrong about Tom!"

"Who?"

"The boy! The boy who attacked her!"

"You know him? You're part of his company?"

"Yes – we know him. No – we're not with him."

The man with green eyes became alert, his face suddenly grave. "Take them!" he snapped.

Before Ratsey and Moll could do anything, they were seized from behind. Their arms were wrenched back, their weapons falling uselessly to the ground. Ratsey's mask was torn off along with Moll's hat. In seconds, they were completely pinned down, unable to move.

"You're making a mistake!" Moll shouted. "You've

got this all wrong."

"Take them to prison for interrogation," the man with the green eyes said. "And I want to know how they got in here!"

"Yes, Lord Moorfield." One of the guards bowed and signalled with his head. Moll and Ratsey were pulled backwards out of the room.

They had almost reached the door before Moll's brain began to buzz.

Sir William Hawkins. His last cry: "Go to Moorfield." Not a place! A person!

"Moorfield!" she cried out. "Tom is the boy you're looking for. The boy from Framlingham! He's the boy you sent Hawkins to find!"

But Moll was already out of the room.

The heavy door slammed shut as she and Ratsey were dragged away.

They knew when a hanging was going to take place. Just after eleven a hush descended on Newgate. The shouting of the prisoners, the mad laughter, the booming of doors and the rattling of chains suddenly stopped and the corridors seemed empty, haunted. Then there was a groan as one door opened. And everyone knew. They had come for Tom Falconer.

Tom stood up as the door crashed open and Mr Bull, the hangman, came in. He glanced first at James Grimly, who was cowering on the bunk with his head in his hands, then at Tom. "Good morning," he said. "I believe you and I have an appointment."

Tom nodded. The hangman wasn't at all what he had expected. Mr Bull was a small, neat man dressed in a blue, velvet tunic. Now he gestured with one hand and four guards marched in to surround Tom. "This won't take a minute," he said.

One of the guards grabbed Tom's arms and, ignoring his wound, tied his hands behind his back. Then, with Mr Bull at the front, and the guards on all four sides, Tom was led down a corridor, past a series of barred doors. The corridor was arched, the brickwork ancient and blood red. The straw under his feet was filthy but Tom couldn't smell it. He couldn't hear anything. All his senses seemed to be failing him ... even his sight. The darkness seemed to be rushing in.

They walked to the end of the corridor and down a staircase carved out of stone. Tom had thought they would be going outside the prison but the stairs led to another corridor and then to a final archway. The scaffold stood in a room at the far end.

The strange thing was, Tom wasn't afraid. He was amazed. The scaffold was just how he had always imagined it. It was exactly the same as the drawings he had seen schoolboys make in Framlingham: three pieces of wood, a trapdoor with a lever and, hanging over it, a noose. As simple as that.

The scaffold had been erected in a great chamber, closed to the outside world apart from a series of small windows set too high up to see through. The chamber was shaped like the dome of a cathedral, the walls made of bare brick. The size of the place made the scaffold seem small and insignificant.

Mr Bull coughed discreetly and the party moved forward. Nine steps – Tom would count them now. He reached the first and stumbled. With his hands tied behind him and unable to balance himself, he might have fallen but one of the guards reached out and steadied him. He began to climb.

As he took the first step, a figure appeared from underneath the scaffold. This was a huge man, bare-chested, with a black hood over his face. Tom glanced enquiringly at Mr Bull who shook his head. Tom understood. Mr Bull organized the business. He was, if you like, the artist. But the actual work itself, that had to be left to a hired hand.

Tom reached the top of the scaffold and stood in the middle of the platform. He could just make out the cracks of the trapdoor that would open when the lever was pulled. The wooden planks creaked slightly underneath him. He tried to swallow but his mouth was too dry. The hooded man had followed him up and leaned forward to pull the noose around his head. For a moment his arms, and the huge muscles of his chest, were close to Tom's face. Tom caught the slightly bitter smell of the man's sweat. He jerked away and felt the touch of the rope around his neck. It was hairy and tickled.

Tom hadn't seen any drummers, but suddenly the

chamber was filled with a steady drumming, starting low but rising in volume as the beat got faster. He had expected a blindfold but none had been offered. What should he look at? What would be the last thing he ever saw? He tried to concentrate his sight on the daylight streaming in through the upper windows but out of the corner of his eye he could see the hooded man reach for the lever.

Tom closed his eyes.

Mr Bull nodded. The hooded man's hand tightened.

"Stop!"

It was a woman's voice, loud and authoritative, the sort of voice that had to be obeyed. The single word had come from the door but it seemed to explode in the chamber, echoing off the walls. The drumming stopped instantly. The hooded man, Mr Bull and the four guards fell to their knees. Tom slowly turned his head, the noose rubbing against his neck.

Queen Elizabeth swept into the room and she had never looked more awesome or more majestic. She was wearing a billowing dress of black satin decorated with gold buckles rising all the way up the front to her neck. Her face was surrounded by a collar of dazzling white with a great band of white pearls hanging from her neck. She had come to a halt in a circle of light lancing down from one of the windows and in the dark interior she seemed to burn gold and white and every colour of the spectrum. Her eyes burned brightest of all. And they were staring at Tom.

"Bring the boy down," she said.

For a moment nobody moved. Then everyone ran for the steps, fighting to be the first to reach the boy who was now dangling from the rope, having fainted where he stood.

five heads

The Queen came to see Tom a few days later.

He had been taken to the Tower, not to one of the prisons but to a comfortable room overlooking the Thames. As soon as he had been strong enough to walk, he had tried the door and had been pleased to discover that it wasn't locked. There had been other surprises. The room had a bed with sheets of pure linen. And Tom had been brought clothes that were finer and more expensive than anything he had ever seen. He had been given wonderful food. The wine had come in a real glass.

And now, here was the Queen of England, standing in his room. Just the two of them. Alone.

Impossible!

Tom bowed low, fixing his eyes on the floor. He

heard the Queen sweep into the room and sit down on a chair. After a long silence, wondering if he dared, Tom looked up.

"They call you Tom Falconer," the Queen said.

"Yes, Your Majesty."

"Tom..." The Queen was staring at him with a whole range of contrary emotions in her eyes. She seemed happy and sad, angry and pleased, aloof but uncertain, royal and yet somehow afraid. It was late in the afternoon. The sun was beginning to set. The Thames was flowing from silver to a burning red. "Sit down, Tom," the Queen said.

There was only one chair in the room. Tom sat down on the bed.

"How is your wound, child?"

"Much better, thank you, Your Majesty." His wound had been cleaned and bandaged. It was hurting now – a sure sign that it was beginning to heal.

The Queen bowed her head.

"I have done you great wrong," she said.

"It's all right, Your Majesty. You weren't to know..."

The Queen waved a hand to silence him and fell silent. Sitting on the chair, just a few centimetres away, she looked much more like the old woman she undoubtedly was. Her skin was heavily made-up, but Tom could still see the wrinkles. He already knew (although it shamed him to remember) that her bright red hair was a wig. Her teeth were entirely black. And yet her pale skin and bright blue eyes reminded him of someone. He wondered who.

"I have to talk to you about ... other matters, Tom," the Queen said. "But I shall begin with Dr Mobius and the Garden Players." She paused. "As I am sure you've guessed, they weren't an acting company at all. In fact they were Spanish, members of a secret organization called the *Garduna*. They were going to kill me, even though they knew they would all die themselves. And they would have succeeded, if it hadn't been for you."

She smiled. "I know now – at least, I believe I have guessed – exactly what you were doing that night. You were trying to protect me. Am I right?"

"Yes, Your Majesty." Tom hung his head in shame. "I didn't mean to embarrass you."

"I have done much, much worse to you, child. But I will come to that soon. As you probably know, the man who calls himself Dr Mobius had bribed one of my officers. Sir Richard Brooke..."

"The man with the scar!"

"A man who will have more than a scar by the time I've finished with him! He worked for my Lord Chamberlain. Between them, they choose which plays I see. Sir Richard was paid well to introduce the Garden Players. But soon it's going to be his turn to pay..."

"How did you find out, Your Majesty?" Tom asked. He was slowly getting used to the fact that he was having a quiet chat with the richest and most powerful woman in the world. He was even beginning to enjoy it. "How did you find out that I wasn't on their side?"

"You have your two friends to thank for that."

"Two...?"

"Moll Cutpurse and Gamaliel Ratsey."

"What?" Ratsey had *helped* him? The very thought made Tom's head spin.

"They broke into my Presence Chamber and although I had already retired, they had the good fortune to come upon one of my spies. A man by the name of Henry Moorfield."

"Moorfield?" Tom gasped. "I thought it was a place!"

"You were told to go to Moorfield by Sir William Hawkins. I know. And this is where it gets difficult, Tom. This is where it finishes and where it starts."

There was a long silence. Then, to Tom's astonishment, the Queen rose from the chair, came over and sat down next to him on the bed. Gently, she laid her hands on his face, one underneath his chin and one on the side of his cheek and turned him so that she could look into his eyes. At the same time, Tom looked into her eyes – he couldn't avoid it – and saw how sad they had become.

"Listen to me," she said, and her voice was a whisper. "You must never tell anyone else what I am going to tell you. Believe me, Tom. It's a secret that could destroy us both – and the entire country with us."

She hesitated. Then...

"More than forty years ago, when I was just sixteen years old, I made a dreadful mistake. My father had died and the king – Edward – was only a boy, younger than you.

"He was too young to reign on his own, so the Council elected a man to look after him – a Protector. That man was called Edward Seymour. And the mistake I made was to fall in love with his brother.

"Thomas Seymour – yes, he had the same name as you – was a rogue and a ruffian and a fool. But he was also handsome, brave, and he made me laugh. He was much older than me and he was married but ... well, one thing led to another and he..." She found it difficult to frame the words. "He left me with a child!

"Those were dangerous times, Tom. The day I learned I was pregnant, Thomas Seymour was arrested – for treason." She sighed. "He was no more a traitor than I was but, as I told you, he was a fool, and two months later, he lost his head. And there was I, left behind, carrying his baby! If anyone had found out, Tom, believe me, my head would have gone too. As it was, I was sent here, to the Tower and interrogated. Luckily, I kept my head. And my secret. But it was close.

"I left the Tower and went to Hatfield and it was there, in complete secrecy, that I gave birth to a child, a boy. I called him Thomas, after his father, but I saw him for only one day. It was too dangerous to keep him close. It hurt me, Tom, but I knew I had no choice. A servant of mine had the baby passed to a wet-nurse and smuggled away. He was taken to a family in Suffolk who agreed to adopt him. They also changed his name. They called him Robert."

Tom stared. He couldn't believe what he was hearing. And he was already beginning to see what was about to come.

"After I lost the child, I thought about him every hour of every day," the Queen went on. "But then a time came when I had to force myself to forget him, to pretend that he didn't exist." She sighed. "It was difficult becoming queen. It was difficult staying queen. And it's *still* murderously difficult being queen. And admitting to having an illegitimate child by a man executed for treason forty-four years ago would only make it all the more difficult. I've had no choice. I've had to forget my own child."

"What happened to him?" Tom asked. But he already knew.

"Something went wrong. The family that was supposed to be looking after him failed me. Thomas – or Robert as he now was – grew up to become the falcon keeper at Framlingham Castle. But then there was an accident. He fell off a horse..."

"You're talking about my father," Tom said.

"Yes."

There was a long silence.

"You're my grandmother," Tom said.

"Yes." The Queen took Tom's hand in her own, holding it as if it were a precious object rather than flesh and blood. "I never knew your father had died.

And I never knew that you had been born," she said. "Not until recently."

"And so you sent Sir William Hawkins to find me?"

"Yes. He didn't know who you really were, although he may have guessed. He was a spy. He was clever."

"You know how he died?"

"Yes. We managed to get the truth out of that scoundrel, Ratsey, and believe me, Tom, he should lose his head for his part in all this. But, well, we can discuss that later."

The Queen stood up. "I'll come back this evening," she said. "Then we can talk again."

"Wait a minute!" It suddenly occurred to Tom that he had completely dropped the "Your Majesties". And he had just told the Queen what to do! "There is one thing," he said. "You told me that nobody must know. So what you're saying is, I'm your grandson. But I'm not going to be king."

"The question of who'll be king is something the whole country has been asking," the Queen replied. "And I wish Parliament would stop bothering me about it. I could introduce you, if you wanted, Tom. And perhaps the people might accept you. On the other hand, it could lead to a bloody civil war." She shrugged. "Do you want to be king?"

"I don't think so," Tom said.

"Well, I can see you've inherited a little common sense," the Queen said. She paused, suddenly serious. "But think about this, Tom. I can help you become whatever you want. Think about it. We'll meet again this evening."

That evening, Tom and the Queen met for the last time.

"I want to ask you a favour," Tom said.

"Go on."

"I've been thinking about Florian. He was one of the Garden Players. Have you...?" Tom hesitated to say it.

"He hasn't been executed, Tom. Not yet."

"Will you spare him, Your Majesty?" Tom blushed without quite knowing why. "I know he was part of it, but I don't think he wanted to be. Dr Mobius was his uncle. He just did what he was told. The same as me when I was at The Pig's Head."

The Queen didn't look pleased. "It's not a good idea to spare your enemies," she said, "because it gives all your other enemies ideas." She softened. "But if you really think he was forced into it, I could just have him tortured..."

"Couldn't you just let him go?"

"If you insist. Is there anything else?"

Tom smiled. "I was wondering about Moll and Ratsey..."

"Two vagabonds! A pickpocket and a highwayman. I have to say, Tom, for someone with royal blood in you, you've been keeping some pretty low company. But you're alive and I have them to thank for it. What do you want me to do with them? Don't tell me you want me to knight them!"

"Will you let them go?"

"I already have. Mistress Cutpurse left with a bag of gold for her pains."

"What about Ratsey?"

"He was lucky to escape with his life." Suddenly the Queen was stern. "Maybe he wasn't entirely to blame for what he became, Tom. And every man deserves a second chance. But I tell you this. If he ever ends up on one of my scaffolds – and I'm certain he will – I won't be there to help."

"I understand."

The Queen sat next to Tom once again and held him in her arms. "But what of you, Tom? Have you thought what you're going to do? I can give you a house and land. I can make you a lord..."

"I don't want to be a lord, Your Majesty." Tom smiled. "I want to be an actor!"

"What?"

"There's a man I met. His name is William Shakespeare..."

The Queen nodded. "Yes. I've heard of him. I'm told he's rather good."

"I met him when I was trying to get into the Rose Theatre. We got on quite well and I'm sure he'd help me if..."

"I'm not sure I approve of players," the Queen said. "They're a rowdy lot at the best of times. But if you're sure that's what you really want..."

"It is. More than anything in the world."

"I'll have a word with Master Shakespeare." She stood up and once again she was sad. "I think it would be easier for both of us if we kept apart," she said. "But if you ever need my help, Tom, I'm very easy to find."

"I'm sure, Your Majesty."

"And if you can't be my grandson, you can still be my friend. After all, you did save my life."

"I'll always be your servant." Tom bowed.

The Queen turned and left the room.

A few weeks later, rehearsals began for a new play that was to be performed at the Rose Theatre in the early spring. The play was called *Romeo and Juliet*. It was a love story.

Tom had only a small part in the play. He had been cast as a servant and he had only a few lines. But it was a start. And what mattered to him was that he was an actor, an official member of the Company of the Admiral's Men.

He had seen Moll only once since winter had ended. She had come to the theatre to wish him luck and had stayed just long enough to pick-pocket a couple of spectators before heading off to a thieves' dinner-and-dance in Shoreditch. Gamaliel Ratsey had gone straight back to Suffolk without bothering to say goodbye. Tom had to admit he was rather glad. The trouble with Ratsey was you never knew if he was going to shake your hand or cut your throat.

"Tom!" Shakespeare was calling him now, a great pile of papers in one hand, a feather quill in the other. The two of them spent much of their time together. Tom loved giving Shakespeare ideas for new plays. In return, Shakespeare was teaching Tom how to read.

Tom hurried to join his friend.

At the same time, a short way up the Thames, four men and one woman were gazing in Tom's direction, as if trying to see what he was doing. Dr Mobius was the first of them. Then came James Grimly, Sir Richard Brooke and finally Sebastian and Henrietta Slope. They were almost unrecognizable by now, as they'd been there for several weeks. Five heads on five spikes high above London Bridge.

Beneath them, the river flowed gently past, the water glistening in the dying light.

Goodnight, goodnight!
Parting is such sweet sorrow
That I shall say goodnight
till it be morrow...

afterword

This is the chapter you don't have to read.

But for those of you who want to know, a lot of *The Devil and his Boy* is based on truth. Many of the characters, for example, were alive in 1593. Elizabeth I and Shakespeare, of course, but also Gamaliel Ratsey, Moll Cutpurse, Philip Henslowe, Lord Strange, Edmund Tilney (Master of the Revels), Dr John Dee and even Mr Bull, the hangman.

I have tried to describe London as it was in the sixteenth century. Paul's Walk really was at the heart of the City – it was the place where people went to find work – and there was an open area called Moorfield, just north of Moorgate. The Rose Theatre, Newgate Prison and Whitehall were all much as I've described and the Banqueting Hall at Whitehall really was made of cloth (it was replaced with a solid structure in the reign of King James). Framlingham is also a real town. You can still visit the castle with its peculiar twisted chimneys. Even now, nobody knows why they were built.

As to the events described in this book... It is certainly true that the young Elizabeth had a close relationship with Thomas Seymour, brother of the Protector. It was also rumoured that she carried his child. Elizabeth herself wrote, "...that there goeth rumours abroad which be greatly both against my honour and honesty (which above all things I esteem) which be these: that I am in the Tower and with child by my lord Admiral..."

There were also many people who hated the Queen and wanted her dead – mainly the Spanish. The *Garduna* was a secret organization, closely linked with the Inquisition. Its members were also known as the Holy Warriors of Spain.

Moll Cutpurse was a famous thief of the sixteenth century. She is even the subject of a play – *The Roaring Girl*. Moll did dress up in boys' clothes. She was involved with a "school for crime". And she was the daughter of a shoemaker. It's nice to know that she lived until she was seventy, a remarkable age, before she died of dropsy.

Gamaliel Ratsey was less fortunate. The most famous highwayman of his time, Ratsey did have noble parents and had served in Ireland before he took to crime (many thieves were unemployed soldiers). He was also well-known for his horrible masks. Eight years after this book ends, Ratsey was betrayed by a friend and taken prisoner. He was hanged.

John Dee is an interesting character. He was Queen Elizabeth's personal magician, a Welshman who spent much of his life searching for the secret of how to turn base metal into gold. Dee also owned a "stone of vision" – I didn't make it up. There's no record, however, of his owning a talking cat!

Wherever possible, in *The Devil and his Boy*, I have tried to use accurate details from the sixteenth century. For example, dinner at The Pig's Head would have cost you "sixpence downstairs and eightpence up". London boys did enjoy throwing mud balls at strangers. And so on.

That said, however, it is quite possible that teachers will find some mistakes in this book. These mistakes are entirely deliberate. I put them in to keep the teachers happy.

Anthony Horowitz

READ OTHER GREAT BOOKS BY ANTHONY HOROWITZ...

THE ALEX RIDER SERIES

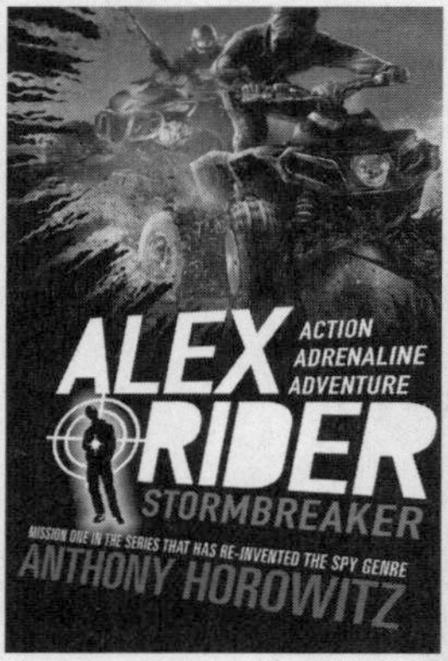

Alex Rider – you're never too young to die...

High in the Alps, death waits for Alex Rider...

Sharks. Assassins. Nuclear bombs. Alex Rider's in deep water.

Alex Rider has 90 minutes to save the world.

Once stung, twice as deadly. Alex Rider wants revenge.

He's back – and this time there are no limits.

Alex Rider bites back…

Alex Rider – in the jaws of death…

One bullet.
One life.
The end starts here.

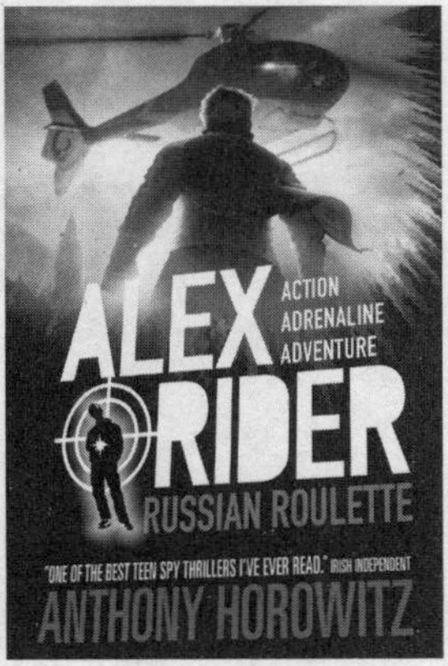

Get your hands on the deadly prequel

ALEX RIDER
ACTION ADRENALINE ADVENTURE

THE MISSION CONTINUES AT
alexrider.com

ACTION. ADRENALINE. ADVENTURE.

alexrider.com /alexrideruk

WELCOME TO THE DARK SIDE OF ANTHONY HOROWITZ

THE POWER OF FIVE

BOOK ONE
He always knew he was different.
First there were the dreams.
Then the deaths began.

BOOK TWO
It began with Raven's Gate.
But it's not over yet. Once
again the enemy is stirring.

BOOK THREE
Darkness covers the earth.
The Old Ones have returned.
The battle must begin.

BOOK FOUR
An ancient evil is unleashed.
Five have the power to defeat it.
But one of them has been taken.

BOOK FIVE
Five Gatekeepers.
One chance to save mankind.
Chaos beckons. Oblivion awaits.

LOOKING BACK, Henry Parker could honestly say that he had never wanted to hurt anyone. Certainly, it had never occurred to him that he would one day plan and then execute the perfect murder of an internationally well-known children's author ... even if that was what actually happened. To begin with, all Henry wanted to do was write...

Anthony Horowitz is the author of the number one bestselling Alex Rider books and The Power of Five series. He has enjoyed huge success as a writer for both children and adults, most recently with the latest adventure in the Alex Rider series, *Russian Roulette*, and the highly acclaimed Sherlock Holmes novel, *The House of Silk*. His latest novel, *Moriarty*, is also set in the world of Sherlock Holmes and was published in October 2014. Anthony was also chosen by the Ian Fleming estate to write the new James Bond novel which will be published this year. Anthony has won numerous awards, including the Bookseller Association/Nielsen Author of the Year Award, the Children's Book of the Year Award at the British Book Awards, and the Red House Children's Book Award. In 2014 Anthony was awarded an OBE for Services to Literature. He has also created and written many major television series, including *Injustice*, *Collision* and the award-winning *Foyle's War*.

You can find out more about Anthony and his work at:
www.alexrider.com
@AnthonyHorowitz

Return to GROOSHAM GRANGE

More wickedly funny books

by Anthony Horowitz

The Devil and His Boy

Groosham Grange

Return to Groosham Grange

The Switch

More Bloody Horowitz

The Diamond Brothers books:

The Falcon's Malteser

Public Enemy Number Two

South by South East

The Blurred Man

The French Confection

I Know What You Did Last Wednesday

The Greek who Stole Christmas

Return to GROOSHAM GRANGE

ANTHONY
HOROWITZ

WALKER
BOOKS

For Cassian

This is a work of fiction. Names, characters, places and incidents are either the product of the author's imagination or, if real, are used fictitiously. All statements, activities, stunts, descriptions, information and material of any other kind contained herein are included for entertainment purposes only and should not be relied on for accuracy or replicated as they may result in injury.

First published 1999 by Walker Books Ltd
87 Vauxhall Walk, London SE11 5HJ
as *The Unholy Grail*

This edition published 2015

2 4 6 8 10 9 7 5 3 1

This book has been typeset in Sabon

Printed in Germany by GGP Media GmbH

British Library Cataloguing in Publication Data:
a catalogue record for this book is available from the British Library

ISBN 978-1-4063-6473-6

www.walker.co.uk

CONTENTS

TOP SECRET

To The Right Reverend Morris Grope
Bishop of Bletchley

Dear Bishop,

I have now been at Groosham Grange for three months. I've had a terrible time. The teachers here are all monsters. The children are evil … and worse still, they enjoy being evil. They even get prizes for it! I hate having to pretend that I like it here, but of course it's the only way to be sure that nobody finds out who I really am.

But all the time I'm thinking about my mission, the reason you sent me here. You wanted me to find a way to destroy the school and the island on which it stands. And the good news is that I think it can be done. At last I have found a way.

It seems that all the power of Groosham

Grange is concentrated in a silver cup. They call this cup the Unholy Grail. It's kept hidden in a cave – nobody can get close to it. But once a year it's taken out and given as a prize to the boy or girl who has come top in the school exams. This will happen just a few weeks from now.

I've also been doing some research. Looking in the school library, I found an old book of sorcery and spells. In the very back there was a poem. This is what it said:

BEWARE THE SHADOW THAT IS FOUND
STRETCHING OUT ACROSS THE GROUND
WHERE ST AUGUSTINE ONCE BEGAN
AND FOUR KNIGHTS SLEW A HOLY MAN
FOR IF THE GRAIL IS CARRIED HERE
THEN GROOSHAM GRANGE WILL DISAPPEAR

And now the good news, your Holiness! I've worked out what the poem means. And if I can get my hands on the Grail, then I will have accomplished my mission and Groosham Grange will be no more.

With best wishes to you and to Mrs Grope,

Your obedient servant,

X

Secret agent at Groosham Grange

SPORTS DAY

It was Sports Day at Groosham Grange – the egg and spoon race – and the egg was winning. It was running on long, elegant legs while the spoon struggled to keep up. In another corner of the field, the three-legged race had just been won, for the second year running, by a boy with three legs, while the parents' race had been cancelled when someone remembered that none of the parents had actually been invited.

There had been one unfortunate incident during the afternoon. Gregor, the school porter, had been disqualified from javelin-throwing. He had strolled across the pitch without looking and although he hadn't actually entered the competition, one of the javelins had unfortunately entered him. Mrs Windergast, the school matron, had taken him to the sick-bay with two metres of aluminium jutting out of his shoulder, but it was only when he got there that she had discovered that he couldn't actually get through the door.

Otherwise everything had gone smoothly. The teachers' race had been won, for the third year running, by Mr Kilgraw (dressed in protective black clothing) and Mr Creer. As one was a vampire and the other a ghost it was hardly surprising that the race always ended in a dead heat. At four o'clock, the high jump was followed by a high tea: traditionally it was served on the school battlements.

If anyone had happened to see the sixty-five boys and girls gathered together along with their seven teachers around the sandwiches and strawberries and cream they would have thought this was an ordinary sports day at an ordinary school ... even if the building itself did look a little like Frankenstein's castle. Looking closer, they might have been puzzled by the fact that everyone in the school was wearing, as well as their sports kit, an identical black ring. But it would only be if they happened to catch sight of Mr Fitch and Mr Teagle, the two heads of Groosham Grange, that they might begin to guess the truth.

For the heads of the school were just that. Two heads on one body: the result of an experiment that had gone horribly wrong. Mr Teagle, bearded and wearing a boater, was eating a cucumber with a pinch of salt. Mr Fitch, bald and hatless, was chewing a triangle of bread with a little butter. And the two men were both enjoying what would be a perfect sandwich by the time it disappeared down the same, single throat.

Of course, Groosham Grange was anything but ordinary. As well as the ghost, the vampire and the head with two heads, the other teachers included a werewolf, a witch and a three-thousand-year-old woman. All the children there were the seventh sons of seventh sons and the seventh daughters of seventh daughters. They had been born with magical powers and the school's real purpose was to teach them how to use those powers in the outside world.

"So what's the last race?" Mr Teagle asked, helping himself to a cocktail sausage. The wrinkled sausage at the end of its long wooden stick somehow reminded him of Gregor after his recent accident.

"The obstacle race," Mr Fitch replied.

"Ah yes! Good, good. And who are the finalists?"

Mr Fitch took a sip of plain, black tea. "William Rufus. Jill Green. Jeffrey Joseph. Vincent King. And David Eliot."

Mr Teagle popped two sugar-lumps and a

spoonful of milk into his mouth. "David Eliot. That should be interesting."

Ten minutes later, David stood on the starting line, surveying the course ahead. The obstacle race would be, he was certain, like no other obstacle race in the world. And he was equally certain that he would win it.

He had been at Groosham Grange for almost a year. In that time he had grown six inches, filled out a bit so he looked less like a street urchin, more like a sprinter. He wore his brown hair long now, thrown back off a face that had become paler and more serious. His blue-green eyes had become guarded, almost secretive.

But the real changes had been happening inside him. He had hated the school when he had first arrived ... but that had been before he had discovered why he was there. Now he accepted it. He was the seventh son of a seventh son. That was how he had been born and there was nothing he could do about it. It seemed incredible to him that once he had fought against the school and tried to escape from it. Today, a year later, he knew that there was nowhere else he would rather be. He belonged here. And in just two weeks' time he knew he would walk away with the school's top prize: the Unholy Grail.

There was a movement beside him and he

turned to see a tall, fair-haired boy with square shoulders and a smiling, handsome face, walking up to the starting line. Vincent King was the newest arrival at Groosham Grange. He had only come to the school three months before, but in that time he had made astonishing progress. From the moment the school's secrets had been revealed to him and he had been awarded his black ring, he had surged ahead and, although David was well ahead in the school exams, there were some who said that Vincent could still catch up.

Maybe this was one of the reasons why David didn't like the other boy. The two of them had been in competition from the very start, but recently the sense of competitiveness had bubbled over into something else. David mistrusted Vincent. He wasn't sure why. And he was determined to beat him.

David watched as Vincent stretched himself, preparing for the race. Neither of them spoke to each other. It had been a while since they had been on talking terms. At the same time, Jill Green strolled over to them. Jill was David's best friend – the two of them had arrived at the school on the same day – and he was annoyed to see her smile at Vincent.

"Good luck," she said.

"Thanks." Vincent smiled back.

David opened his mouth to say something but then Jeffrey and William arrived and he realized it was time to take his place on the starting line. Mr Kilgraw – who taught Latin – appeared, carrying a starting pistol in his black-gloved hand. The rest of the school were standing a short distance away, watching.

"Take your places," the Latin teacher said.

He raised the gun.

*"Sistite! Surgite! Currite…!"**

He fired. Two hundred metres above him, a crow squawked and plunged to the ground. The race had begun.

The five runners set off along the course, racing down the green to the first obstacle – a net hanging thirty metres high from a wooden frame. Jeffrey had taken an early lead, but David was amused to see him make his first mistake and start climbing the net. For his part, he muttered a quick spell and levitated himself over it. William and Jill turned themselves into dragonflies and flew through it. Vincent had dematerialized and reappeared on the other side. The four of them were neck and neck.

The second obstacle in the race was a shallow pit filled with burning coals. All the children had studied Hawaiian fire-walking and David didn't even hesitate. He took the pit in eight strides, noticing out of the corner of his

*Ready, steady, go!

eye that William had forgotten to tie one of his shoelaces and had set light to his Nike trainer. That left three.

With the cheers of the rest of the school urging them on, David, Jill and Vincent twisted round the oak-tree at the end of the course and disappeared completely. How typical of Mr Creer to sneak a dimensional warp into the race! One second David was running past the tree with the cliffs ahead of him and the grass swaying gently in the breeze, the next he was battling through a cyclonic storm of wind and poisonous gases on a planet somewhere on the other side of the universe. It had to be Jupiter from the look of it. Sixteen moons hung in the night sky over him and the gravity was so intense that he could barely lift his feet. The smell of ammonium hydrosulphide made his eyes water and he was glad that he had reacted quickly enough to remember to hold his breath.

He could hear Jill catching up with him, her feet scrunching on the orange and grey rubble of the planet's surface. Glancing quickly over his shoulder, he also saw Vincent, rapidly gaining ground. He staggered past the remains of a NASA space probe, heading for a flag that had been planted about a hundred metres away. His teeth were already chattering – the planet was freezing cold – and he cried out as he was hit by a primordial gas cloud that completely blinded him. But then he was aware that there was grass under his feet once again and, opening his eyes, he saw that he was back on Skrull Island. He had passed the third obstacle. The finishing line was ahead. But there were still three more challenges before he got there.

He looked back. Jeffrey and William were far behind. Vincent had overtaken Jill and was only about twenty metres away. With his attention on the other boy, David almost ran straight into the giant spider's web that was the next obstacle. It had been spun between two trees, almost invisible until you were in it and David had to twist desperately to avoid the threads. Even so, a single strand – thick and sticky – caught his arm and he had to waste precious seconds tearing it free. Somehow, though, he managed to get through. He tumbled to the ground, somersaulted forward, then got up and ran.

"Come on, Vincent! You can do it!"

David knew that there were as many people cheering him as there were Vincent. But it still irritated him to hear Vincent's name being called out by his friends. His anger spurred him on and he easily cleared the six hurdles ahead of him without even thinking about the ten thousand volts of electricity to which they were connected. That just left the bottomless pit with two narrow planks to carry the runners on to the end.

His foot hit the left plank. It was less than six centimetres wide and bent slightly as it took his weight. David swayed as he fought to regain his balance and that was when he made his second mistake. He looked down. The pit ran all the way through the centre of the earth and out the other side. One slip and he would find himself in New Zealand. David had never been fond of heights and right now he was suspended over what looked like an impossible lift shaft, though without the advantage of a lift. Again he had to waste time fighting off the rush of dizziness and nausea. And that was when Vincent overtook him.

David didn't even see the other boy. He was aware only of a shape rushing past him on the other plank. Biting his lip, he forced himself forward. Ten steps, the wooden surface bouncing and bending underneath him, and then he had reached the other side with Vincent between him and the finishing line. Meanwhile, Jill had caught up. She had taken the same plank as him and she was so close that he could almost feel her breath on the back of his neck.

With one last effort, David pushed ahead. The red tape that would end the race was fifty metres ahead. Vincent was just in front of him. The cheering spectators were on both sides, Mr

Kilgraw holding a stopwatch, Mr Fitch and Mr Teagle applauding and Mrs Windergast giving mouth-to-mouth to the injured crow.

David didn't know what he was going to do until he did it. He was still holding the strand of spider's web and with a flick of his hand he threw it in front of him. Even if anyone had been close enough to see what he had done, it might have looked like an accident, as if he had just been trying to get rid of it. The piece of web twisted round Vincent's left ankle and hooked itself over his right foot. It wasn't enough to stop him but it made him stumble and at that exact moment David overtook him and with a final gasp felt the tape of the finishing line break over his chest.

It was over. He had won.

The entire school went crazy. Everyone was yelling now. David collapsed on to the soft grass and rolled on to his back, while the clouds, the people and the fluttering tape spun around him. Vincent thudded to a halt, his hands on his thighs, panting. Jill had come in third, William fourth. Jeffrey had managed to get himself stuck in the web and was still hanging in the air some distance behind.

"Well done, David!" Mr Creer was standing by the finishing line with a ghost of a smile on his lips. But all his smiles were quite naturally ghostly. "Well run!"

David had beaten Vincent, but he felt no pleasure. As he got to his feet, he was ashamed of himself. He had cheated in front of the entire school, he knew it, and it only made him feel worse when Vincent came over to him with an outstretched hand.

"Good race," Vincent said.

"Thanks." David took the hand, wishing he could undo what he had just done but knowing that it was too late.

He turned to find Jill looking at him strangely. Of course, she had been closest to him when it happened. If anyone could have seen what he'd done, it would have been her. But what would she do? Would she tell?

"Jill..." he began.

But she had already turned her back on him and now she walked away.

ON THE ROCKS

David was sitting on a long, rocky outcrop, with the cliffs rising up behind him and the sea lapping at his feet. It was one of his favourite places on Skrull Island. He loved the sound of the waves, the emptiness of the horizon, with the great bulk of the Norfolk coastline a grey haze somewhere beyond. He would sit here with the wind rushing at his cheeks and the taste of sea-spray on his lips. This was where he came to think.

Twenty-four hours had passed since Sports Day and the excitement of the obstacle race, and in all that time his mood hadn't changed. He was depressed, disappointed with himself. There had been no need to win the race. There were no prizes or cups given out on Sports Day. So what reason did he have to cheat?

"Vincent King…" he muttered to himself.

"What about him?"

He looked round and saw Jill Green walking towards him. She had changed as much as he had in the year she had been at Groosham Grange. She was quieter, more relaxed ... and prettier. With her long dark hair and pale skin, she looked rather like a young witch, which was, of course, exactly what she was.

She sat down next to him. "I can't believe what you did yesterday," she said.

"You saw..."

"Yes."

"I was stupid." David was glad she had brought up the subject even though he was almost too ashamed to talk about it. "I didn't mean to do it." He sighed. "But I couldn't let him win. I just couldn't. I don't know why."

"You don't like him."

"No."

"But why not? Vincent's bright. He's popular. And he's very good-looking."

"That's why I don't like him," David said. He thought for a minute. "He's too perfect altogether. If you ask me, there's something funny about him."

"And if you ask me," Jill said, "you're just jealous."

"Jealous?" David picked up a loose stone and threw it into the sea. He waited until it had disappeared, then reached out with one hand.

The stone rocketed out of the water and slapped itself back into his palm. He handed it to Jill.

"Very clever," she muttered, sourly.

"Why should I be jealous of Vincent?" David said. "If you're talking about the Unholy Grail, he hasn't got a chance."

"He's only thirty points behind you. He could still catch up."

There were just two weeks until 31 October – Hallowe'en – the most important day in the school's calendar. For this was when the Unholy Grail would be presented to the new Student Master. Throughout the year, all the marks from all the exams had been added up and published on a league table which hung on a wall outside the heads' study. David had been top of the league from the start.

But Vincent had risen so fast that his name was now only one below David's and, although everyone agreed the distance between them was too great, nothing was ever certain, particularly in a school like Groosham Grange. There was, after all, one exam still to go – Advanced Cursing. And David had to remember, it was also possible to lose marks. You could have them deducted for bad behaviour, for being late ... and for being caught cheating in a sports day race.

"Do you like him?" David asked.

"Yes."

"Do you fancy him?"

"That's none of your business." Jill sighed. "Why are you so bothered about him?"

"I don't know." David shivered. The waves were whispering to him, he was sure of it. But he couldn't understand what they were saying. His hand felt cold where it had touched the stone. "There's something wrong about him," he said. "Something phoney. I can feel it."

In the distance, a bell rang. It was a quarter to four, almost time for the last two lessons of the day: French with Monsieur Leloup, then general witchcraft with Mrs Windergast. David wasn't looking forward to the French. He was almost fluent in Latin and spoke passable Ancient Egyptian, but he couldn't understand the point of learning modern languages. "After all," he often said, "I can summon up fourteen demons and two demi-gods in Egyptian, but what can I ask for in French? A plate of cheese!" Nonetheless, Groosham Grange insisted on teaching the full range of GCSE and A level subjects as well as its own more specialized ones. And there were serious punishments if you travelled forward in time just to miss the next lesson.

"We'd better move," he said.

Jill took hold of his arm. "David," she said. "Promise me you won't cheat again. I mean, it's not like you..."

David looked straight into her eyes. "I promise."

Ahead of them, Groosham Grange rose into sight. Even after a year on the island, David still found the school building rather grim. Sometimes it looked like a castle, sometimes more like a haunted house. At night, with the moon sinking behind its great towers to the east and west, it could have been an asylum for the criminally insane. The windows were barred, the doors so thick that when they slammed you could hear them a mile away. And yet David liked it – that was the strange thing. Once it had been new and strange and frightening. Now it was his home.

"Are your parents coming?" Jill asked.

"What?"

"In two weeks' time. For prize-giving."

David had hardly seen Edward and Eileen Eliot since the day he had started at Groosham Grange. Parents very rarely came to the school. But as it happened, he had received a letter from his father just a few days before:

Dear David,

This is to inform you that your mother and I will be visiting Groosham Grange for prize-giving on 31 October. We will also be bringing my sister, your Aunt Mildred, and will then drive her home to Margate. This means that I will be spending only half the day at the school. To save time, I am also sending you only half a letter.

And that was where it ended. The page had been torn neatly in two.

"Yes. They're coming," David said. "How about yours?"

"No." Jill shook her head. Her father was a diplomat and her mother an actress, so she hardly ever saw either of them. "Dad's in Argentina and Mum's acting in *The Cherry Orchard*."

"Has she got a good part?"

"She's playing one of the cherries."

They had reached the school now. Jill glanced at her watch. "It's two minutes to four," she said. "We're going to be late."

"You go ahead," David muttered.

"Cheer up, David." Jill started forward, then turned her head. "You're probably right. You'll win the Grail. There's nothing to worry about."

David watched her go, then turned off, making his way round the East Tower and on through the school's own private cemetery. It was a short cut he often used. But now, just as he reached the first grave, he stopped. Before he knew what he was doing he had crouched down behind a gravestone, all other thoughts having emptied out of his head.

Slowly, he peered over the top. A door had opened at the side of the school. There was nothing strange about that except that the door was always locked. It led into a small antechamber in the East Tower. From there a stone staircase spiralled two hundred metres up to a completely circular room at the top. Nobody ever went into the East Tower. There was nothing downstairs and the old, crumbling stairway was supposedly too dangerous to climb. The whole place was out of bounds. But somebody was about to come out. Who?

A few seconds later the question was answered as a boy stepped out, looking cautiously about him. David recognized him at once: his blond hair thrown back in a fancy wave across his forehead and his piercing blue eyes, which were now narrow and guarded. Vincent King had been up to something in the East Tower and he didn't want anyone to know about it. Without turning back, he pulled the door shut behind him, then hurried away in the direction of the school.

David waited a few moments before rising from behind the gravestone. He was going to be late for his French lesson and he knew it would get him into trouble but his curiosity had got the better of him. What had Vincent been doing inside? He started forward. The tower rose up in front of him, half strangled by the ivy that twisted around it. He could just make out the slit of a window beneath the battlements. Was it just a trick of the light or was something moving behind it? Had Vincent been meeting someone high up in the circular room?

He reached out for the door.

But then a hand clamped down on his shoulder, spinning him round as somebody lurched at him, appearing from nowhere. David caught his breath. Then he relaxed. It was only Gregor, the school porter.

Even so, anyone else being stopped by such a creature on the edge of a cemetery would probably have had a heart attack. Gregor was like something out of a horror film, his neck broken and his skin like mouldy cheese. At least the javelin had been removed from his back, although he evidently hadn't changed his shirt. David could still see the hole where the javelin had gone in.

"Vareyoo goink, young master?" Gregor asked in his strange, gurgling voice. Gregor chewed on his words like raw meat. He also chewed raw meat. His table manners were so disgusting that he was usually made to eat under the table.

"I was just..." David wasn't sure what to say.

"Butzee lessons, young master. Yoom issink zee lovely lessons. You shoot be hurryink in."

Gregor moved so that he stood between David and the door to the tower.

"Hold on, Gregor," David began. "I just need a few minutes…"

"No minutes." Gregor lurched from one foot to the other, his hands hanging down to his knees. "Is bad marks for missink lessons. And too many bad marks and there izno Unnerly Grail for the young master. Yes! Gregor knows…"

"What do you know, Gregor?" Suddenly David was suspicious. It was almost as if Gregor had been waiting for him at the tower. Had he seen Vincent coming out? And why had he suddenly mentioned the Grail? There was certainly more to this than met the eye … which, in Gregor's case, was about three centimetres below his other eye.

"Hurry, young master," Gregor insisted.

"All right," David said. "I'm going." He turned his back on the porter and walked quickly towards his classroom. But now he was certain. He had been listening to the voice of his sixth sense when he was down on the rocks – and hadn't Groosham Grange taught him that the sixth sense was much more important than the other five?

Something was going on at the school. In some way it was connected to the Unholy Grail. And whatever it was, David was going to find out.

FLYING LESSON

David opened the classroom door nervously. He was ten minutes late, which was bad enough, but this was French with Monsieur Leloup, which was worse. Monsieur Leloup had a bad temper – hardly surprising considering he was a werewolf. Even on a good day he had been known to rip a French dictionary to pieces with his teeth. On a bad day, when there was going to be a full moon, he had to be chained to his desk in case he did the same to his class.

Fortunately, the full moon had been and gone but even so, David walked gingerly into the room. His empty desk stared accusingly at him in the middle of all the others. Just as he reached it, Monsieur Leloup turned from the blackboard.

"You are late, Monsieur Eliot," he snapped.

"I'm sorry, sir…" David said.

“Ten minutes late. Can you tell me where you have been?”

David opened his mouth to speak, then thought better of it. He could see Vincent out of the corner of his eye. Vincent had the desk behind his. He was pretending to read his book but there was a half smile on his lips, as if he knew what was going to happen. “I was just out walking,” David said.

“Walking?” Monsieur Leloup sniffed. “I shall deduct three marks from the league table. Now will you please take your seat. We are discussing the future perfect…”

David sat down and opened his book. He had got off lightly and he knew it. Three marks deducted still left him twenty-seven ahead. There was no way Vincent could catch up, no matter what happened in the last exam. He was fine.

Even so, David concentrated more than usual for the next fifty minutes just in case he was asked something, and he was relieved when the bell rang at five o'clock and the lesson was over.

He joined the general stream out of the class and down the corridor to the last lesson of the day. He found this one a lot more interesting: general witchcraft, taught by Mrs Windergast. Even after a year at the school, David still hadn't quite got used to the matron's methods. Only a week before he had gone to her with a headache and she had given him not an aspirin but an asp. She had fished the small, slithering snake out of a glass jar and held it against his head … an example of what she called sympathetic magic. David had found it a rather unnerving experience – although he'd been forced to admit that it worked.

Today she was discussing the power of flight. And she wasn't talking about aeroplanes.

"The broomstick was always the favoured vehicle of the sisterhood," she was saying. "Can anyone tell me what it was made of?"

A girl in the front row put up her hand. "Hazel wood?"

"Quite right, Linda. Hazel wood is the correct answer. Now, who can tell me why some people believe that witches used to keep cats?"

The same girl put up her hand. "Because 'cat' was the old word for broomstick," she volunteered.

"Right again, Linda." Mrs Windergast muttered a few words. There was a flash of light and, with a little shriek, Linda exploded. All that was left of her was a puddle of slime and a few strands of hair. "It is never wise to know all the answers," Mrs Windergast remarked, acidly. "To answer once is fine. To answer twice is showing off. I hope Linda will have learned that now."

Mrs Windergast smiled. She was a small, round woman who looked like the perfect grandmother. But in fact she was lethal. She had been burned at the stake in 1214 (during the reign of King John) and again in 1336. Not surprisingly, she now tended to keep herself to herself and she never went to barbecues.

"Linda was, however, quite right," she continued. She pulled a broomstick out from behind the blackboard. "Witches never had cats. It was just a misunderstanding. This is my own 'cat' and today I want to show you how difficult it is to control. Would anyone like to try it?"

Nobody moved. All eyes were on Linda's empty desk and the green smoke still curling above it.

Mrs Windergast pointed. "Vincent King..."

Vincent stood up and moved to the front of the classroom. David's eyes narrowed. Mrs Windergast was obviously in a bad mood today. Maybe Vincent would say something to annoy her and go the same way as Linda. Or was that too much to hope?

"My broomstick is very precious to me," Mrs Windergast was saying. "I normally keep it very close to me – as do all witches. So this is very much an honour, young man. Do you think you could ride it?"

"Yeah – I think so."

"Then try."

Vincent took hold of the broomstick and muttered some words of power. At once the stick sprang to attention and hovered in the air, a few metres above the ground. Gracefully, he climbed on to it, swinging one leg over it as if it were a horse. David watched, annoyed and showing it. It seemed there was nothing Vincent couldn't do well. He had both feet off the ground now, hovering in space as if he had been born to it.

"Try moving," Mrs Windergast suggested.

Vincent concentrated and slowly rose into the air, perfectly balanced on the broomstick. Gently he curved round and headed over the blackboard, the handle ahead of him, the twigs trailing behind. He was smiling, growing in confidence, and David was half tempted to whisper the spell that would summon up a minor wind-demon and knock him off balance.

But in the end there was no need. When things went wrong they all went wrong at once. The broomstick wobbled, the end pitched up, Vincent cried out and the next moment he fell off and crashed to the floor with the broom on top of him.

"As you can see," Mrs Windergast trilled, "it's not as easy as it looks. Is there any damage,

Vincent dear?"

Vincent got stiffly to his feet, rubbing his shoulder. "I'm all right," he said.

"I meant the broomstick." Mrs Windergast picked it up and cast a fond eye over it. "I never let anyone ride it as a rule," she went on. "But it seems undamaged. Well done, Vincent. You may return to your seat. And now..." She turned to the blackboard, "...let me try to explain the curious mixture of magic and basic aerodynamics that makes flight possible."

For the next forty-five minutes, Mrs Windergast explained her technique. David was sorry when the final bell went. He had enjoyed the lesson – Vincent's fall in particular – and he was still smiling as he left the classroom. Linda followed him out. She had been reconstituted by Mrs Windergast but she was looking very pale and sickly. David doubted if she would ever make a decent black magician. She'd probably end up as nothing worse than a traffic warden.

There was a knot of people outside in the corridor. As David came out he saw that one of them was Vincent.

"That was bad luck," Vincent said.

"What?" Maybe it was just an innocent remark but already David felt his hackles rise.

"Losing three marks in French. That narrows the gap."

"You're still a long way behind." It was Jill who had spoken. David hadn't seen her arrive but he was glad that she seemed to have taken his side.

"The exams haven't finished yet." Vincent shrugged and once again David was irritated without knowing why. Did he dislike Vincent just because he was his closest rival or was there something more? Looking at his easy smile, the way Vincent slouched against the wall – always so superior – he felt something snap inside.

"You looked pretty stupid just now," he said.

"When?"

"Falling off the broomstick."

"You think you could have done better?"

"Sure." David wasn't thinking. All he knew was that he wanted to goad the other boy, just to get a reaction. "You're going to have to get used to coming second," he went on. "Just like in the race..."

Vincent's eyes narrowed. He took a step forward. "There was only one reason I came second..." he began.

He knew what David had done. He had felt the web slipping over his foot. And he was going to say it, now, in front of everyone. David couldn't let that happen. He had to stop him. And before he knew what he was doing, he suddenly reached out and pushed Vincent hard with the heel of his hand. Vincent was taken off balance and cried out as his bruised shoulder hit the wall behind him.

"David!" Jill cried out.

She was too late. Without hesitating, Vincent bounced back, throwing himself on to David. David's books and papers were torn out of his hands and scattered across the floor. Vincent was taller, heavier and stronger than him. But even as he felt the other boy's hand on his throat he couldn't help feeling pleased with himself. He had wanted to get past Vincent's defences and he'd done it. He'd taken the upper hand.

Right now, though, Vincent's upper hand was slowly strangling him. David brought up his knee, felt it sink into Vincent's stomach. Vincent grunted and twisted hard. David's head cracked against the panelling.

"What's going on here? Stop it at once!"

David's heart sank. Of all the people who could have happened along the corridor just then, Mr Helliwell was unquestionably the worst. He was a huge man with wide shoulders and a round, bald head. He had only recently joined the school, teaching arts and crafts by day and voodoo by night. He came from Haiti where he was apparently so feared as a magician that people actually fainted if he said "Good morning" to them and for six months the postman had been too scared to deliver the mail – which didn't matter too much as nobody on the island was brave enough to write. David had somehow found himself on the wrong side of Mr Helliwell from the very start and this was only going to make things worse.

"David? Vincent?" The teacher looked from one to the other. "Who started this?"

David hesitated. He was blushing and it was only now that he realized how stupid he had been. He had behaved like an ordinary boy at an ordinary school. At Groosham Grange, there was no worse crime. "It was me," he admitted.

Vincent looked at him but said nothing. Jill and the other onlookers seemed to have vanished. There were just the three of them left in the corridor. Mr Helliwell glanced down at the floor. He leant forward, picked up a sheet of paper and quickly read it. He handed it to David. "This is yours."

David took it. It was the letter from his father.

"You started the fight?" Mr Helliwell asked.

"Yes," David said.

Mr Helliwell considered. His grey eyes gave nothing away. "Very well," he said. "This is going to cost you nine marks. And if I see you behaving like this again, I'll send you to the heads."

Mr Helliwell turned and walked away. David watched him go, then leant down and picked up the rest of his books and papers. He could feel Vincent watching him. He glanced up.

Vincent shrugged. "Don't blame me," he said.

And then he was on his own. In one afternoon he had lost an incredible twelve marks! His lead had gone down by almost half – from thirty to eighteen. At lunch-time he had been right at the top of the league table, secure, unassailable. But now...

David gritted his teeth. There was only one more exam to go. It was his best subject. And he was still a long way ahead of Vincent. The Unholy Grail would be his.

Scooping up the last of his books, David set off down the empty corridor, the sound of his own footsteps echoing around him.

FRAMED

That night David had a bad dream.

Vincent King was part of it, of course. Vincent laughing at him. Vincent holding the Unholy Grail. Vincent slipping out of the East Tower and disappearing like a wisp of smoke into one of the graves.

But there were other, more frightening things woven into the night canvas. First there were his parents – only they weren't his parents. They were changing, transforming into something horrible. And then there was a face that he knew, looming over him. He would have been able to recognize it but he was lying on his back, in pain, blinded by a fiery sun. And finally he saw the school, Groosham Grange, standing stark against a darkening sky. As he watched, a bolt of lightning streaked down and smashed into it. A great crack appeared in the stonework. Dust and rubble exploded out.

And that was when he woke up.

There were nine dormitories at Groosham Grange. The one that David slept in was completely circular with the beds arranged like numbers on a clock-face. Vincent had been put in the same room as him, his bed opposite David's, underneath a window. Propping himself up on one elbow, David could see the other boy's bed, clearly illuminated by a shaft of moonlight flooding in from above. It was empty.

Where could Vincent be? David glanced at the chair beside Vincent's bed. Wherever he had gone, he had taken his clothes with him. Outside, a clock struck four. At almost exactly the same moment, David heard a door creak open somewhere below and then swing shut. It had to be Vincent. Nobody else would be up and about in the middle of the night. David threw back the covers and got out of bed. He would find out what was going on.

He got dressed quickly and crept out of the room. There had been a time when he would have been afraid to wander through the empty school in the darkness, but the night no longer held any fear for him. And he knew the building with its twisting corridors and sudden, plunging staircases so well that he didn't even need to carry a torch.

With the wooden stairs creaking beneath his feet, he made his way to the ground floor. Which door had he heard open and close? Ahead of him, the main entrance to the school rose up about ten metres, a great wall of oak studded with iron. The door was bolted securely from inside so Vincent couldn't have passed through there. Behind him, going back underneath the staircase, a second door led into the Great Hall, where meals were served.

This door was open but the room behind it was shrouded in darkness and silent but for the flutter of the bats that lived high up in the rafters.

David reached the bottom of the staircase and stood silently on the cold, marble floor. He was surrounded by oil paintings, portraits of former heads and teachers; a true collection of old masters. All of them seemed to be looking at him, and as he moved forward the eyes swivelled to follow him and he heard a strange, musty whispering as the pictures muttered to one another.

"Where's he going? What's he doing?"

"He's making a mistake!"

"Don't do it, David."

"Go back to bed, David."

David ignored them. To one side a passage stretched out into the darkness, blocked at the end by a door he knew led into the library.

There were two more doors facing each other halfway along the passage. The one on the left led into the office of Mr Kilgraw, the assistant headmaster. As usual it was closed and no light showed through the crack. But on the other side of the passageway ... David felt the hairs on the back of his neck tingle. A square of light stretched out underneath the door. This one was marked HEADS. The room behind it belonged of course to Mr Fitch and Mr Teagle.

David was certain they weren't in their study. Only that afternoon they had complained of the very worst thing they could possibly get – a headache – and had announced they were going to bed early. Mr Fitch and Mr Teagle had no choice but to sleep in the same bed (though with two pillows) and rather curiously both men talked in their sleep, often having animated conversations right through the night.

But if Vincent was behind the door, what was he doing there? Going as quietly as he could – even the slightest movement seemed to echo throughout the school – David tiptoed along the corridor. Slowly, he reached out for the handle, his hand throwing an elongated shadow across the door. He hadn't even worked out what he would do when he discovered Vincent. But that didn't matter. He just wanted to see him.

He opened the door and blinked. The room was empty.

Closing the door behind him, David entered the heads' inner sanctum. The room was more like a chapel than a study, with its black marble floor and stained-glass windows. The furniture was solid and heavy, the desk a great block of wood that could have been an altar. Leather-bound books lined the walls, the shelves sagging under their weight. David knew he would be in serious trouble if he was found here. Nobody was allowed in this room unless summoned. But it was too late to turn back now.

The light that he had seen came from a lamp on a chest of drawers that stretched the whole length of the room. David ran his eyes along the surface, past a tangle of test-tubes and pipes, a stuffed rat, a human skull, a laptop, a pair of thumbscrews and a German helmet from the First World War. He was puzzled. What, he wondered, was the laptop for?

But this was no time to ask questions. Vincent wasn't in the room. That was all that mattered. *He* shouldn't be here either. He had to go.

It was as he turned to leave that he saw it. There was a small table in the far corner with a circular hole in the wall just above it. A picture lay face up on the carpet nearby. A safe! Somebody had taken down the picture and opened the safe. Like a moth to a flame he moved towards the table. There were four sheets of paper lying on the top. David knew what they were even before he reached out and picked them up. He looked down at the front cover.

GROOSHAM GRANGE EXAMINING BOARD
General Certificate of Secondary Education
ADVANCED CURSING

He was standing beside the open safe, holding the exam papers when the door crashed open behind him. With a dreadful lurching feeling in his stomach he looked round, knowing that he had been set up, knowing that it was too late to do anything about it. Mr Fitch and Mr Teagle were there, wearing dressing-gown and pyjamas. With them (and this was the only surprise) was Mr Helliwell. He was fully dressed. All three men – or all two and a half – were gazing at him in disbelief.

"David...!" Mr Fitch exclaimed. His long, hooked nose curved towards David accusingly.

"What are you doing here?" Mr Teagle demanded. He was wearing a nightcap with a pompom dangling just next to his chin. He shook his head disapprovingly and the pompom swung back and forth as if in agreement.

"I never thought it would be you, David,"

Mr Helliwell said. The voodoo teacher looked genuinely astonished – and sad. He turned to the heads. "I heard someone go into your office," he explained. "But I never dreamed..."

"You were quite right to come to us, Mr Helliwell," Mr Fitch said.

"Quite right," Mr Teagle agreed.

"You can leave us now," Mr Fitch continued. "We'll take care of this."

Mr Helliwell paused as if he was about to say something. He glanced at David and shook his head. Then, with a quiet "Good night", he turned and left the room.

Mr Fitch and Mr Teagle remained where they were.

"Do you have anything to say for yourself, David?" Mr Teagle asked.

David thought for a moment. The bitterness of his defeat was in his mouth and he wanted to spit it out. But he knew when he was beaten. Somehow he had been lured into a trap. The portraits had tried to warn him but he hadn't listened and now it was too late to talk himself out of it. What could he say? The safe was open. The exam papers were in his hand. There was nobody else in the room. Trying to explain would only make matters worse.

He shook his head.

"Really, I am very disappointed in you," Mr Fitch said.

"And I am disappointed too," Mr Teagle stroked his beard. "It's not just that you were cheating. That would be bad enough."

"But you were *caught* cheating," Mr Fitch continued. "That's even worse. How could you be so clumsy? So amateurish?"

"And why did you even bother?" Mr Teagle asked. "You would easily have come first in Advanced Cursing without stealing the papers. Now we'll have to change all the questions. Completely rewrite the exam..."

"The exam is on Wednesday," Mr Fitch sighed. "That only gives us two days."

"We have no choice," Mr Teagle said. "We'll have to start again." He turned to David. "You won't believe this," he went on, "but writing exams is almost as boring as doing them! It's all most annoying."

Both men nodded at the same time, narrowly missing banging their heads together. Still David said nothing. He was furious with himself. He had walked into this. How could he have been so stupid?

"Are you aware of the seriousness of this offence?" Mr Teagle asked.

David was blushing darkly. He couldn't keep silent any longer. "It's not the way it looks," he said. "It's not what you think..."

"Oh no," Mr Fitch interrupted. "I suppose you're going to tell us that you were framed."

"Maybe you didn't mean to come in here and look at the exams," Mr Teagle suggested, sarcastically.

David hung his head low. "No," he whispered.

"Do you realize the gravity of this offence?" Mr Fitch asked.

"Very grave," Mr Teagle agreed. "Very grave indeed."

Mr Fitch sighed. "Sometimes I wonder, David, if you're suited to Groosham Grange. When you first came here, you fought against us. In a way you're still fighting. Do you really think you belong here?"

Did he belong at Groosham Grange? It was something that, in his darker moments, he had often wondered.

When he had first come to the school, he had indeed fought against it. As soon as he had learned about the secret lessons in black magic he had done everything he could to escape, to tell the authorities what he knew, to get the place closed down. It had only been when he had found himself trapped and helpless that he had changed his mind. If you can't beat them...

But here he was, a year later, determined to become the number one student, to win the

Unholy Grail. He remembered the fear he had once felt, the sense of horror. Classes in black magic! Ghosts and vampires! Now he was one of them – so what exactly did that make him? What had he become in the year he had been here?

He became aware of the heads, waiting for an answer.

"I do belong here," he said. "I know that now. But..." He hesitated. "I'm not evil."

"Evil?" Mr Teagle smiled for the first time. "What is good and what is evil?" he asked. "Sometimes it's not as easy as you think to tell them apart. That's still something you have to learn."

David nodded. "Maybe that's true," he said. "But all I know is ... this is my home. And I do want to stay."

"That's good. I'm glad to hear it." Mr Fitch was suddenly business-like. "But tonight's performance is going to cost you ten marks..."

"Fifteen," Mr Teagle cut in.

"...fifteen marks. Do you have anything to say?"

David shook his head. He was feeling sick to the stomach. Fifteen marks! Add that to the twelve marks he had lost earlier in the day and that left...

"David?"

...just three marks. Three marks between

Vincent and him. How had it happened? How had Vincent managed to lure him here?

"No, sir." His voice was hoarse, a whisper.

"Then I suggest you go back to bed."

"Yes..."

David was still holding the exam papers. Clenching his teeth, feeling the bitterness rising inside him, he jerked his fingers open, dropping them back on to the table. He hadn't read a single question.

He left the study and walked back along the passage and past the portraits, trying to ignore them tut-tutting at him as he went. With his mind still spinning, he climbed the stairs and found his way back to the dormitory. He stopped by his bed. Vincent was back. His clothes were on the chair, his body curled up under the blankets as if he had never been away. But was he really asleep? David gazed through the darkness at the half smile on the other boy's face and doubted it.

Silently, David undressed again and got back into bed. Three marks. That was all there was between them. Over and over again he muttered the figure to himself until at last he fell into an angry, restless sleep.

THE EXAM

Wednesday quickly came and with it the last examination of the year: Advanced Cursing.

There was a tradition at Groosham Grange that all the ordinary exams were taken upstairs, in the Great Hall. But for the more secretive ones, the exams relating to witchcraft and black magic, the pupils went downstairs through the network of tunnels and secret passages that lay beneath the school and into an underground chamber where sixty-five desks and sixty-five chairs had been set up, far away from the prying sun. This, then, was to be the final testing ground: a hidden cavern amongst the stalactites and stalagmites with a great waterfall of crystallized rock guarding the way out.

The exam was to start at eleven o'clock. At a quarter to, David made his way downstairs. His mouth was dry and he had an unpleasant feeling in the pit of his stomach. It was crazy. When it came to Advanced Cursing, everyone agreed he was untouchable. At the same time, he knew that it was one of Vincent's weakest subjects. That morning he had checked the league table one last time. He was still in first place. Vincent was three marks behind. After that there was a gap of seventeen marks to Jill, who was in third place. Looking at the notice-board had told him what he wanted to know. This exam was between him and Vincent. And Vincent didn't have a chance.

So why was he feeling so nervous? David opened the door of the library and went in. Ahead of him there was a full-length mirror and he glanced at his reflection while he walked towards it. He was tired and it showed. He hadn't slept well since his encounter in the heads' study. He was still having the dreams: his parents, the school breaking up and the face that he was sure he recognized.

He was right up against his reflection now. He scowled at himself briefly, then walked into the glass. The mirror rippled around him like water and then he had passed through it and into the first of the underground passages. His breath steamed slightly in the cold air as he followed the path down and he could feel the moisture clinging to his clothes. The examination room lay straight ahead, but on an impulse David took a fork, following a second passageway to the right. This was no more than a fissure in the rock, so narrow in places that he had to hold his breath to squeeze through. But then it widened out again and David found himself face to face with what he had come to see.

The Unholy Grail was kept in a miniature grotto, separated from the passageway by six iron bars. The bars were embedded in the rock, and there was no visible way through to the chamber behind. The Grail stood on a rock pedestal, bathed in an unnatural silver light. It was about fifteen centimetres high, a metallic grey in colour, encrusted with dark red stones that were either rubies or carbuncles. There was nothing very extraordinary about it to look at. But David found that his breath had caught in his throat. He was hypnotized by it. He could sense the power that the Grail contained and he would have given anything to reach through the bars and hold it in his hand.

This was what he was fighting for. He would take the exam and he would come first. Nobody would stop him.

"David...?"

Hearing his name, David swung round guiltily. He had been so absorbed in the Grail that he hadn't heard anyone approach. He turned and saw the arts, crafts and voodoo master, Mr Helliwell, standing at the entrance. He was wearing a dark, three-piece suit. It was the old-fashioned sort and made him look like a funeral director. "What are you doing here?" he asked.

"I was just looking..." David was being defensive. After their meeting two nights before, he had nothing more to say. But to his surprise Mr Helliwell moved closer and there was a frown of puzzlement on his face. "David," he began. "I want to talk to you about the other night."

"What about it?" David knew he was being deliberately rude but he was still angry about what had happened.

Mr Helliwell sighed. The light was reflecting off the huge dome of his head and his round, grey eyes seemed troubled. "I know you're upset," he said. "But there's something I have to tell you. I don't believe it was you who opened the safe."

"What?" David felt a surge of excitement.

"I was as surprised as anyone to find you in that room," the teacher went on. "Let me explain. I was doing my rounds when I saw someone come down the stairs. It was dark, so I didn't see who it was. But I could have sworn they had fair hair, lighter than yours."

Fair hair. That was Vincent. It had to be.

"I saw them go into the heads' study, and that was when I went to fetch Mr Fitch and Mr Teagle." Mr Helliwell paused. "Whoever was inside the study had left the door half open. I'd swear to that. Only, when we got back the door was closed. And *you* were inside."

"I didn't open the safe," David said. Now that he had started he couldn't stop. "Someone set me up. They wanted me to be found there. They knew you'd gone for the heads. And they must have slipped out just before I arrived."

"Someone...?" Mr Helliwell frowned. "Do you have any idea who?"

For a moment David was tempted to name Vincent King. But that wasn't the way he did things. He shook his head. "Why didn't you tell the heads what you'd seen?" he asked.

Mr Helliwell shrugged. "At the time it seemed an open and shut case. It was only afterwards..." He stroked his chin. "Even now I'm not sure. I suppose I believe you. But it's your word against..."

...against Vincent's. David nodded. The trap had been too well prepared.

Mr Helliwell pulled a fob-watch from his waistcoat pocket and looked at it. "It's almost eleven o'clock," he said. He reached out and put a firm, heavy hand on David's shoulder. "But if you have any more problems, you come to me. Maybe I can help."

"Thank you." David turned and hurried back down the passageway. He was feeling ten times more confident than an hour before. He had let Vincent beat him once. There wouldn't be a second time.

He would take the exam and he would come first. And the Unholy Grail would be his.

* * *

GROOSHAM GRANGE EXAMINING BOARD
General Certificate of Secondary Education

ADVANCED CURSING

Wednesday 24 October 11.00 a.m.

TIME: 2 hours

Write your name and candidate number in ink (not in blood) on each side of the paper. Write on one side of the paper only, preferably not the thin side.

Answer *all* the questions. Each question is to be answered on a separate sheet.

The number of marks available is shown in brackets at the end of each question or part question. The total for this paper is 100 marks.

Candidates are warned not to attempt to curse the person who set this exam.

1. Write out in full the words of power that would cause the following curses (30):
   a) Baldness (5)
   b) Acne (5)
   c) Bad breath (5)
   d) Amnesia (5)
   e) Death (10)

CAUTION: Do not mutter the words of power as you write them. If anyone near you loses their hair, breaks out in spots, smells like an onion, forgets why they're here and/or dies, you will be disqualified.

2. Your aunt announces that she has come to stay for Christmas and New Year.

   She is seventy years old and leaves a lipstick mark on your cheek when she kisses you. Although you are fifteen, she still insists that you are nine. She criticizes your clothes, your hair and your taste in music. As usual, she has brought you a book token.

   Describe in two hundred words a suitable curse that would ensure she spends next Christmas in (10):

a) The intensive care unit of your local hospital OR
b) A rice field in China OR
c) A crater on the dark side of the moon

3. What is thanatomania? Define it, giving two historical examples. Then describe how you would survive it. (35)

4. Write down a suitable curse for THREE of the following people (15):
   a) Elephant poachers (5)
   b) People who talk in cinemas (5)
   c) Litter bugs (5)
   d) Cigarette manufacturers (5)
   e) Bullies (5)

5. Describe how you would re-create the Great Plague using ingredients found in your local supermarket. (10)

It was as easy as that.

As soon as David had run his eyes over the questions, he knew he was going to be all right. He had even revised the Great Plague a few nights before and the rest of the exam was just as straightforward.

So he was smiling when the clock struck one and Mr Helliwell called time. While everyone else remained in their seats, Vincent and another boy who had been sitting in the front row got up and started collecting the papers. It was Vincent who came over to David's desk. As he handed his answers over, David lifted his head and allowed his eyes to lock with Vincent's. He didn't say anything but he wanted the other boy to know. I got every question right. Nothing can stop me now.

Mr Helliwell dropped the papers into his leather bag and everyone was allowed to leave. Once they were back out in the open air, David caught up with Jill. It was a beautiful afternoon. The sun felt warm on his neck after the chill of the cave.

"How did it go?" he asked.

Jill grimaced. "Awful. What on earth is thinatomania?"

"Thanatomania. It's a sort of multiple curse," David explained. "It was when a witch wanted to hurt a whole town or village instead of just one person." He shuddered. "I don't know why they teach us about things like that. It's not as if we'd ever want to curse anyone."

"No," Jill agreed. "But most of the stuff you learn at school you never actually use. You just have to know about it, that's all." She took his arm. "So how did you do?"

David smiled. "It was easy."

"I'm glad you think so." Jill looked away. In

the distance, Vincent was walking off on his own towards the East Tower. He was smiling and there was a spring in his step. "I wouldn't count your chickens too soon," she said. "There goes Vincent. And he looks pretty confident too."

David remembered her words over the next few days. There were more lessons but with the final exam over, the league table was officially closed. Everything now hinged on Advanced Cursing and although David was sure of himself, although he pretended he wasn't thinking about it, he still found himself hanging around the notice-board near the heads' study where the results would eventually be posted.

And he was there one evening when Mr Kilgraw, the assistant headmaster, appeared, a sheet of paper in one hand and a drawing pin in the other. David felt his heartbeat quicken. There was a lump in his throat and a tingling in the palms of his hands. Nobody else was around. He would be the first to know the result.

Forcing himself not to run, he went over to the notice-board. Mr Kilgraw gave him a deathly smile. "Good evening, David."

"Good evening, sir." Why didn't Mr Kilgraw say anything? Why didn't he congratulate David on coming first, on winning the Unholy Grail?

With difficulty, he forced his eyes up to take in the notice-board. And there it was:

ADVANCED CURSING – RESULTS

But the name on the top was not his own.

Linda James, the girl who had been disintegrated by Mrs Windergast, was first.

David blinked. What about the name underneath her?

William Rufus had come second.

Then Jeffrey Joseph.

It wasn't possible.

"A very disappointing result for you, David." Mr Kilgraw was talking, but David hardly heard him. He was panicking now. The typed letters on the list were blurring into each other as he searched through them for his name. There was Vincent, in ninth place with sixty-eight points. And there he was, two places below … eleventh! He had scored only sixty-five. It was impossible!

"Very disappointing," Mr Kilgraw said, but there was something strange in his voice. It was as soft and as menacing as ever, but there was something else. Was he pleased?

Eleventh… David felt numb. He tried to work out where it left him on the league table. Linda had scored seventy-six points. He was eleven behind her, three behind Vincent. He had lost the Grail. He must have.

"I was quite surprised," Mr Kilgraw went on. "I would have thought you would have known the meaning of thanatomania."

"Thanato...?" David's voice seemed to be coming from a long way away. He turned to Mr Kilgraw. He could hear footsteps approaching. News had got out that the results were there. Soon there would be a crowd. "But I *do* know," David said. "I wrote it down..."

Mr Kilgraw shook his head with a sad smile. "I marked the papers myself," he said. "You didn't even tackle the question."

"But ... I did! I got it right!"

"No, David. It was Question Three. I must say, you got everything else right. But I'm afraid you lost thirty-five points on that one. You didn't hand in an answer."

Hand in an answer...

And then David remembered. Vincent had collected the papers. He had handed them to Vincent. And following the instructions at the top of the exam, each question had been answered on a separate sheet. It would have been simple for Vincent to slip one of the pages out. David had been so confident, so sure of himself, that he hadn't even thought of it. But that must have been what had happened. That was the only possibility.

There were about twenty or thirty people milling around the notice-board now, struggling to get closer, calling out names and numbers. David heard his own name called out. Eleventh with sixty-five points.

"That means he's first equal," somebody shouted. "He and Vincent King have tied in first place."

"So who gets the Unholy Grail?"

Everybody was chattering around him. Feeling sick and confused, David pushed his way through the crowd and ran off, ignoring Jill and the others who were calling after him.

There was no moon that night. As if to add to the darkness, a mist had rolled in from the sea, slithering over the damp earth and curling up against the walls of Groosham Grange. Everything was silent. Even Gregor – sound asleep on one of the tombstones in the cemetery – was actually making no sound. Normally he snored. Tonight he was still.

Nobody heard the door creak open to one side of the school. Nobody saw a figure step out into the night and make its way over the moss and the soil towards the East Tower. A second door opened and closed. Inside the tower, a light flickered on.

But nobody saw the lantern as it turned

round and round on itself, being carried ever higher up the spiral staircase that led to the battlements. A bloated spider scuttled out of the way, just managing to avoid the heel of a black leather shoe that pounded down on the concrete step. A rat arched its back in a corner, fearful of the unaccustomed light. But no human eye was open. No human ear heard the thud, thud, thud of footsteps climbing the stairs.

The secret agent reached a circular room at the top of the tower, its eight narrow windows open to the night. To one side there was a table, some paper and what looked like a collection of boxes. From inside the boxes came the sound of flapping and a strange, high-pitched squeak. The agent sat down and drew one of the sheets of paper forward. And began to write:

TOP SECRET

To the Bishop of Bletchley

All is going according to plan. Nobody suspects. Very soon the Unholy Grail will be ours. Expect further news soon.

Once again there was no signature at the bottom of the page. The agent scrawled a single X, then folded the letter carefully and reached into one of the boxes. It wasn't actually a box but a cage. His hand came out again holding something that looked like a scrap of torn leather except that it was alive, jerking and squealing. The agent attached the message to the creature's leg, then carried it over to the window.

"Off you go." The words were a soft whisper in the darkness.

A brief flurry. A last cry. And then the message was gone, carried off into the swirling night.

NEEDLE IN A HAYSTACK

"It's a very unusual situation," Mr Fitch said. "We have a tie."

"David Eliot and Vincent King," Mr Teagle agreed. "Both have six hundred and sixty-six points."

"It's a bit of a beast," Mr Fitch remarked, tetchily. "What are we going to do?"

Both men – or rather, both heads – looked round the table. The two of them were in the staff room, sitting in a single, high-backed chair. It was midday. Arranged around the table in front of them were Mr Kilgraw, Mr Helliwell, Mr Creer, Mrs Windergast, Monsieur Leloup and the oldest teacher in the school (by several centuries), Miss Pedicure. Miss Pedicure taught English and history, although at the start of her career there hadn't been any history to teach (as nothing had happened) and English hadn't been invented.

People either spoke Norse or simply grunted. She was now so frail and wrinkled that everyone would stop and stare whenever she sneezed, afraid that the effort might cause her to disintegrate.

Mr Kilgraw grimaced, for a moment revealing two razor-sharp vampire teeth. There was a glass of red liquid on the table in front of him which might have been wine, but probably wasn't. "Is it not a tradition," he enquired, "in this circumstance to set some sort of trial? A tie-breaker?"

"What sort of trial do you have in mind?" Mrs Windergast asked.

Mr Kilgraw waved a languid hand. Because it was the middle of the day, the curtains in the room had been drawn for him but enough of the light was filtering through to make him even paler than usual. "It will have to take place off the island," he said. "I would suggest London."

"Why London?" Miss Pedicure demanded.

"London is the capital," Mr Kilgraw replied. "It is polluted, over-crowded and dangerous. A perfect arena..."

"Here, here!" Mrs Windergast muttered.

"You agree?" Mr Kilgraw asked.

"No. I was saying that the trial ought to take place here, here ... on the island."

"No," Mr Fitch rapped his knuckles on the table. "It's better if we send them out. More challenging."

"I have an idea," Mr Kilgraw said.

"Do tell us," Mr Fitch gurgled.

"Over the last year we have tested these boys in every aspect of the magical arts," Mr Kilgraw began. "Cursing, levitation, shape-changing, thanatomania..."

"What's thanatomania?" Mr Creer demanded.

Mr Kilgraw ignored him. "I suggest we set them a puzzle," he went on. "It will be a trial of skill and of the imagination. A meeting of two minds. It will take me a day or two to work out the details. But at least it will be final. Whoever wins the contest comes top of the league and takes the Unholy Grail."

Everyone around the table murmured their assent. Mr Fitch glanced at Mr Helliwell. "Does it seem fair to you, Mr Helliwell?" he asked.

The voodoo master nodded gravely. "I think that David Eliot deserves the Grail," he said. "If you ask me, there's something funny about the way he's lost so many marks in such a short time. But this will give him a chance to prove himself. I'm sure he'll win. So I agree."

"Then it's decided," Mr Teagle concluded. "Mr Kilgraw will work on the tie-breaker. And perhaps you'll let me know when you've sorted something out."

Two days later, David and Vincent stood

in one of the underground caverns of Skrull Island. They were both dressed casually in jeans and black, open-neck shirts. Mr Kilgraw, Mr Helliwell and Miss Pedicure were standing opposite them. At the back of the cave were two glass boxes that could have been shower cubicles except that they were empty. The boxes looked slightly ridiculous in the gloomy setting of the cave – like two theatrical props that had wandered off stage. But David knew what they were. One was for Vincent. The other was for him.

"You are to look for a needle in a haystack," Mr Kilgraw was saying. "Some needles are bigger than others – and that may point you in the right direction. But the needle in question is a small statue of Miss Pedicure. I will tell you only that it is blue in colour and six centimetres high."

"It was taken from my mummy some years ago," Miss Pedicure sniffed. "I've always wanted to have it back."

"As for the haystack," Mr Kilgraw went on, "that is the British Museum in London. All I will tell you is that the statue is somewhere inside. You have until midnight to find it. And there is one rule..." He nodded at Mr Helliwell.

"You are not to use any magical powers," the voodoo teacher said. "We want this to be a test of stealth and cunning. We have helped you boys a little. We have arranged for the alarm system at the museum to turn itself off tonight and we have opened one door. But there will still be guards on duty. If you're caught, that's your own problem."

"It's seven o'clock now," Mr Kilgraw said. "You have just five hours. Do you both understand what you have to do?"

David and Vincent nodded.

"Then let us begin. Whichever of you finds the statuette first and brings it back to this room will be declared the winner and will be awarded the Unholy Grail."

David glanced at Vincent. The two of them hadn't spoken to each other since the results of the exam had been announced. The tension between them almost crackled like static electricity. Vincent swept a blond lock of hair off his face. "I'll be waiting for you when you get back," he said.

"I'll be back here first," David replied.

They stepped into the boxes.

"Let the tie-breaker begin," Mr Kilgraw commanded.

David felt the air inside the box go suddenly cold. He had been standing with his hands pressed against the glass, looking at Mr Kilgraw. Then, slowly at first but accelerating quickly, the glass box began to turn. It was like a fairground ride except that there was no music, no sound at all, and he didn't feel sick or giddy. Mr Kilgraw spun past him, a blur of colour that had lost all sense of shape, blending in with the walls of the cave as the box turned faster and faster. Now the whole world had dissolved into a wheel of silver and grey. Then the lights went out.

David closed his eyes. When he opened them a moment later, he found he was looking at a street and a hedge. Swallowing, he pulled his hands away from the glass, leaving two damp palm prints behind. The box was illuminated from above by a single, yellow bulb. A car drove past along the street, its headlights on. David twisted round. Something bumped against his shoulder.

He was in a telephone box. Not a modern kiosk but one of the old, red telephone boxes with a swinging door that stood in the middle of Regent's Park, London. It took him a moment to open it but then he was standing on the pavement, breathing the night air. There was no sign of Vincent. He looked at his watch. Seven o'clock. He had travelled two hundred kilometres in less than a second.

But he was still a long way from the museum. Vincent would already be on his way. And this was his last chance...

David crossed the road and broke into a run.

In fact he took a taxi to the museum. He caught one in Baker Street and ordered the driver to go as fast as possible.

"The British Museum? You must be joking, mate! There's no point going there now. It's closed for the night. Anyway, aren't you a bit young to be out on your own? You got any money?"

David had no money. Neither of the boys had been given any – it was part of the test. Quickly, he hypnotized the driver. He knew he wasn't allowed to use magic, but Mr Kilgraw had often told him that hypnosis was a science and not a magical power, so he decided it wouldn't count.

"The British Museum," he insisted. "And put your foot down."

"Foot down? All right, guv'nor. Whatever you say. You're the boss." The driver shot through a red light, zigzagged across a busy intersection with cars hooting at him on all sides and accelerated the wrong way down a one-way street. The journey took them about ten minutes and David was relieved to get out.

He paid the driver with a leaf and two pebbles he had picked up in the park. "Keep the change," he said.

"Cor! Thanks, guv'nor." The cab driver's

eyes were still spinning. David watched him as he drove off across a pavement and into a shop window, then slipped through the open gates of the British Museum.

But why were the gates open?

Had Mr Helliwell arranged it for him? Or had Vincent got there first?

Feeling very small and vulnerable, David crossed the open space in front of the museum. The building itself was huge, bigger than he remembered. He had once heard that there were four kilometres of galleries inside and looking at it now, its classical pillars arranged in two wings around a vast, central chamber, he could well believe it. His feet clattered faintly across the concrete as he ran forward. A well-cut lawn, grey in the moonlight, stretched out as flat as paper on either side of him. There was a guard-hut next to the gate but it was deserted. His shadow raced ahead of him, snaking up the steps as if trying to get into the building before him.

The main entrance to the museum was locked. For a moment David was tempted. A single spell would open the door. He could simply move the tumblers inside the lock with the power of thought or else he could turn himself into smoke and creep in through the crack underneath. But Mr Helliwell had said:

no magic. And this time David was determined not to cheat. He would play by the rules.

It took him ten minutes to locate the side door that Mr Kilgraw had opened. He slipped through and found himself standing on a stone floor beneath a ceiling that was so far above him that, in the half light, he could barely see it. Doors led off to the left and right. Straight ahead there was an information desk and what looked like a souvenir shop. A grand staircase guarded by two stone lions swept up to one side. Which way should he go?

It was only now that he was here that David grasped the enormity of the task that faced him. Miss Pedicure had lived for three thousand years. And she had lived in just about every part of the world. So this statue of her – which had once belonged to her mother – could come from anywhere and any time. It was six centimetres high and it was blue. That was all he knew.

So much for the needle. But what of the haystack?

The British Museum was enormous. How many exhibits did it hold? Ten thousand? A hundred thousand? Some of them were the size of small buildings. Some of them, in fact, *were* small buildings. Others were no bigger than a pin. The museum held collections from Ancient Greece, Ancient Egypt, Babylon, Persia, China; from the

Iron Age, the Bronze Age, the Middle Ages, every age. There were tools and pottery, clocks and jewellery, masks and ivory… He could spend a year in the place and still get nowhere close.

David heard the rattle of a chain and pressed himself back against the wall, well into the shadows. A guard appeared, walking down the stairs and into the main hall. He was dressed in blue trousers and a white shirt, with a bunch of keys dangling from his waist. He paused in the middle of the entrance hall, yawned and stretched his arms, then disappeared behind the information desk.

Crouching in the dark, David considered. As far as he could see, he had two choices. One: search the museum as quickly as he could and hope he would strike lucky. Two: look for some sort of catalogue and try to find the statuette listed there. But even if a catalogue existed, how would he know what to look for? It was hardly likely that Miss Pedicure's name would turn up in the index and there were probably statuettes in just about every room in the building.

That only left the first option. Straightening up again, David crossed the hall and climbed the staircase that the guard had just come down. He would have to hope for a little luck.

Three and a half hours later he was back where he'd started.

His head was pounding and his eyes were sore with fatigue. The stairs had led him up past a Roman mosaic and on into Medieval Britain. He had back-tracked into the Early Bronze Age (dodging a second guard) and had somehow found his way into Ancient Syria … which was indeed seriously ancient. He must have looked at about ten thousand objects all neatly laid out in their glass cases. He felt like a window-shopper in some sort of insane supermarket and he hadn't found anything remotely like Miss Pedicure's statuette. After a while, he barely knew what he was looking at. Whether it was a Late Babylonian jug or an Early Sumerian mug no longer made any difference to him. David had never been very fond of museums. But this was torture.

Standing once again in the entrance hall, he looked at his watch. It was a quarter to eleven. Less than two hours of the challenge remained … assuming that Vincent hadn't found the statuette and left with it long ago.

Another guard crossed the entrance hall. "Who's there?" he called out.

David froze. He couldn't be found, not now. But then a second guard, a woman, appeared from the door on the right. "It's only me."

"Wendy? I thought I heard someone…"

"Yeah. This place gives me the shivers. I've

been hearing things all night. Footsteps…"

"Me too. Fancy a cup of tea?"

"Yeah. I'll put the kettle on…"

The two guards walked off together and David ducked back through another open door just opposite the main entrance. It led into the most amazing room he had ever seen.

It was vast, stretching the entire length of the museum. It was filled with a bizarre collection of animals, people, and creatures that were both. Everything looked Egyptian. Huge Pharaohs carved in black stone sat with their hands on their knees, frozen solid as they had been for thousands of years. On one side, two bearded men with lions' feet and dragons' wings crouched, staring at each other in grim silence. On the other, a gigantic tiger stood poised as if about to leap into the darkness. Further down the gallery there were animals of all shapes and sizes, facing in different directions like guests at a nightmare cocktail party.

David froze. He had seen Vincent before he had heard him. The other boy was moving incredibly quietly and would himself have seen David had he not been looking the other way. David noticed that Vincent had taken his shoes off and was holding them in his hand. It was a good idea and one that David should have thought of himself.

Vincent was looking as lost and as tired as David. Crouching down behind a brass baboon, David watched him pass. As he went, Vincent rubbed his forehead with the back of one hand and David almost felt sorry for him. He had never liked Vincent and he didn't trust him. But he knew what he was going through now.

A minute later Vincent had gone. David stood up. Which way now? Vincent hadn't found the statue yet, and that was good, but it didn't help him. He looked once more at his watch. There was little over an hour left.

Left or right? Up or down?

At the far end of the gallery he could see a collection of sarcophagi and several obelisks – some carved with hieroglyphics like Cleopatra's Needle – plus four gods with the heads of cats.

And that was when he knew.

In fact he should have known from the start. This challenge was all about skill, not chance. Mr Helliwell had said it himself: *a test of stealth and cunning*. What he and Mr Kilgraw had said, what Miss Pedicure had said, and what he had just seen ... put them all together and the answer was obvious.

David knew where he was going now. He should have known hours ago. He looked around him for a sign, then ran off down the gallery.

He just hoped he wasn't already too late.

WAX

Between them, Mr Kilgraw, Mr Helliwell and Miss Pedicure had given him all the clues he could have asked for. David played back what they had said.

Some needles are bigger than others ... that may point you in the right direction.

Well, David had just seen the biggest needle of all – a stone pillar that had made him think of Cleopatra's Needle on the Thames. And what direction had that come from? Egypt!

And then Miss Pedicure: *It was taken from my mummy...*

She wasn't talking about her mother, of course. The statuette had been buried with her, part of an Egyptian mummy.

That was where he was going now. The head of a giant ram watched him without interest as he plunged into the Egyptian rooms of the museum. The statuette would be somewhere here – he was certain. How could he have wasted so much time? If only he'd stopped and thought first…

The first room he entered was filled with more sarcophagi – the stone coffins that contained the mummies. There were about a dozen of them on display, brightly coloured and strangely cheerful. It was as if the Ancient Egyptians had chosen to gift-wrap their dead. Some of the cases were open and, glancing inside, David saw hunched, shrivelled-up figures in dirty grey bandages. Strange to think that Miss Pedicure had once looked like that – although when it was raining and she was in a bad mood, she sometimes still did.

David hurried into the next room. What he was looking for would be displayed separately, in one of the side cases. How much time did he have left? There were still hundreds of objects on display all around him. His eyes raced past dolls, toys, mummified cats and snakes, jugs, cups, jewellery … and then he had found it! It was right in front of him, a blue figure about the size of his hand, lying on its back as if sunbathing. David rested his hand on the glass and stared at the little doll, at its black hair, thin face and tapered waist. He recognized Miss Pedicure at once. The statue was labelled:

Glazed Companion doll. XVIIIth Dynasty. 1450 BC.

It was incredible. The English and history teacher had hardly changed in three thousand years. She was even carrying the same handbag.

Somebody coughed at the end of the gallery and David froze. But it was only another guard, making for a side room and an early-twenty-first century cup of tea. He tilted his watch. It was just after eleven. He had more time than he thought. He lifted the cover of the glass case and took out the statuette.

The Unholy Grail was his.

At half past eleven, David climbed the escalator at Baker Street tube station and emerged into the street. He had preferred to take the train back to Regent's Park, losing himself in the crowds underground. It was only a ten-minute walk back to the telephone box. The statuette was safely in his pocket. He had plenty of time.

It was a cool evening with a touch of drizzle in the breeze. David wondered where Vincent might be now. The other boy was probably still in the British Museum, desperately searching for the statue. Even if he did work out the puzzle and find the display case, he was too late. It was too bad. But the best man had won.

A motorcyclist accelerated through a puddle,

sending the water in a spray that just missed David. On the other side of the road, a bus without passengers rumbled through a yellow light and turned towards the West End. David continued on past Madame Tussaud's. His father had taken him to the famous waxworks museum once but it hadn't been a successful trip. "Not enough bankers!" Mr Eliot had exclaimed and had left without even visiting the Chamber of Horrors. The long, windowless building was silent. The pavement outside, crowded with tourists and ice-cream sellers by day, was empty, glistening under the street lights.

David felt a gust of cold air tug at the collar of his shirt. Behind him he heard the sound of splintering wood. He thought nothing of it. But unconsciously he quickened his pace.

The road continued up to a set of traffic lights. This was where Regent's Park began – David could see it in the distance, a seemingly endless black space. He glanced behind him. Although the pavement had been empty before, there was now a single figure, staggering about as if drunk. It was a man, wearing some sort of uniform and boots. He was weaving small circles on the pavement, his arms outstretched, his feet jerking into the air. It was as if he had never walked before, as if he were trying to find his balance.

David turned the corner, leaving the drunk – if that was what he was – behind. He was beginning to feel uneasy but he still didn't know why.

The path he was following crossed a main road and then continued over a humpback bridge. Suddenly he was out of the hubbub of London. The darkness and emptiness of Regent's Park was all around him, enclosing him in its ancient arms. Somewhere a dog barked in the night.

"Just slow down..."

He muttered the words to himself, somehow relieved to hear the sound of his own voice. Once again he looked at his watch. A quarter to twelve. Plenty of time. How had he allowed one crazy drunk to spook him like this? Smiling, he looked back over his shoulder.

The smile died on his lips.

The man had followed him into the park. He was standing on the bridge now, lit by a lamp directly above him. In the last few minutes he had learnt how to walk properly and he was standing to attention, his eyes glittering in the light. He was much closer and David could see him clearly – the brown boots, the belt, the strap running across his chest. He wasn't wearing a uniform but a sort of brown suit, the trousers ballooning out at the thighs. David recognized him instantly. He would have known even without the black swastika in the red and white armband on the man's right arm. How could he fail to recognize the thin black hair sweeping down over the pale face and, of course, the famous moustache?

Adolf Hitler!

Or at least, Adolf Hitler's waxwork.

David remembered the gust of cold air he had felt. There was always a touch of coldness in the air when black magic was being performed and the blacker the spell the more intense the coldness. He had felt it but he had ignored it. And the splintering sound! The creature must have broken the door to get out. Who could have animated it? Vincent? David stared at the Hitler waxwork, feeling sick. And even as he backed away, a horrible thought occurred to him. Hitler had been first out of Madame Tussaud's. But was he alone?

The question was answered a second later. The Hitler waxwork jerked forward, his legs jackknifing in the air. Behind him, two more figures appeared, rising like zombies over the top of the humpback bridge. David didn't wait to see who they might be. Three words were echoing in his mind.

Chamber of Horrors.

He tried to remember who was exhibited in that part of Madame Tussaud's. He had a nasty feeling he might be meeting them at any moment.

David turned and ran. But it was only now that he saw how carefully the trap had been laid. Three more waxworks had made their way into the park and were approaching him from the other direction. One was dressed only in a dirty white night-gown and black clogs. It was carrying something in its hands. David stared. It was a victim of the French Revolution. It was carrying its head! Behind it came two short men in prison uniform. David didn't recognize either of them – but they had recognized him. Their eyes seemed to light up as they shuffled forward, arms outstretched. David saw a gate in the fence, half open. He ran through it and into the inner heart of the park.

He found himself on a patch of lawn with a set of tennis courts to one side and an unpleasant, stagnant pool on the other. The field was dotted with trees and he made for the nearest one, grateful at least that it was a dark night. But even as he ran, the clouds parted and a huge moon broke through like a searchlight. Was that part of the magic too? Was Vincent even controlling the weather?

In the white, ghostly light, the whole park had changed. It was like something out of a bad dream. Everything was black, white and grey.

The Hitler waxwork had already reached the gate and passed through with the two prisoners. The French Revolution victim had been left behind. This waxwork had tripped over a tree root and lost its head and although the head was shouting "Over here!" the rest of the body hadn't found it yet.

But that was the only good news.

Another half dozen waxworks had somehow found their way to the park and were spreading out, searching through the trees. There was a man dressed entirely in black with a doctor's bag in one hand and a huge, curving knife in the other. Jack the Ripper! And right behind him came a lady in Victorian dress, horribly stabbed, blood (wax blood, David had to remind himself) pouring out of a gaping wound in her chest. She had to be one of the women he had killed. Behind him, David heard a dreadful gurgling sound and turned just in time to see a third, white-faced waxwork rising through the scummy surface of the pool. The models were everywhere. David crouched behind a tree, trying to lose himself in it. He was surrounded and knew that it was only a matter of time before he was found.

"There he is, Adolf!" somebody shouted.

A short, dark-haired man in a double-breasted suit had climbed out of a ditch, an ugly scar twisting down his wax cheek. It was a face that David recognized from old black and white films: the American gangster, Al Capone. He walked quickly across the grass, then brought his hands up in front of his chest. There was a metallic click. Capone was holding a machine-gun. He had just loaded it.

With his breath rasping in his throat, David left the cover of the tree and broke into a run. The wax models were all around him, some like sleepwalkers, others more like clockwork toys as they scuttled forward. He felt horribly exposed out in the moonlight but he had no choice. He had to find the telephone box, but where was it? He made a quick calculation and started forward, then dived to the ground as a spray of machine-gun bullets sliced through the air, a centimetre above his head. Al Capone had fired at him. And somehow David knew that the bullets were the one thing there that weren't made of wax.

Someone stepped out in front of him, blocking his way. It was a small man in an old-fashioned wing-collar shirt and a smart grey suit. He had wispy, ginger hair and a small moustache. His eyes twinkled behind round, wire-framed glasses. The man held up the palms of his hands. "It's all right," he said. "I'm a doctor."

"A doctor?" David panted.

"Yes. Doctor Crippen!"

The man had pulled out a vicious-looking hypodermic syringe. David yelled and lashed out with his fist, catching the little man straight on the nose. He felt his fist sink into the soft wax and when he jerked it back he had left a round imprint inside the figure's head. David ran. Behind him he could hear Hitler shouting out orders in manic German. Jack the Ripper was lumbering up behind him with the hideous knife raised above his head.

Meanwhile, another man, this one in gleaming silver armour, had just come in through the open gate. He had long black hair, tied behind his neck, and two of the cruellest eyes David had ever seen. Swords and daggers, at least a dozen of them, protruded from him in every direction. It was Attila the Hun, one of the most bloodthirsty warriors in history, and David had no doubt whose blood he was thirsting for now.

The grass curved round behind the tennis courts, bordered on the edge by a thicket of trees and shrubs. David plunged into the shadows, glad to be out of the glare of the moon. The darkness seemed to confuse the waxworks because they hung back, one or two of them bumping into each other, almost as if they were afraid to cross the line from light into dark. There was an iron fence straight ahead of him.

David ran over to it, grabbing it with both hands.

His heart was thudding madly in his chest and he stopped to catch his breath and give himself time to think. They hadn't got him yet! There was still time to reach the telephone box and make his way back to Groosham Grange. David jerked one hand down to his trouser pocket. The statuette was still there.

Vincent! He breathed the name through clenched teeth. This had to be Vincent's work. He must somehow have followed David from the museum and conjured up the spell as he walked past Madame Tussaud's. Of course, he had cheated. Vincent had broken the single rule of the contest – not to use magic – and the worst of it was that there was nothing David could do. What spell could he use to destroy the waxworks? And if he used magic, wouldn't he be disqualifying himself?

David was gripping the fence so hard that the metal bit into his hands. He looked over the top, into the next enclosure and for the first time since he had reached the park he felt a surge of hope. The telephone box was in sight – and it was unguarded. It was only ten to twelve. All he had to do was climb the fence and he would be home and dry!

He took one last look back. With Hitler at

the head of them, just about all the waxworks were congregating on the fence, a semicircle that had already begun to close in. Only two of the waxworks had stayed behind: the drowned man and the Victorian woman. They had found the Frenchman's lost head and, despite his protests, were playing tennis with it on one of the courts. Jack the Ripper was edging forward with a diabolical smile, his wax lips parted to reveal two jagged lines of wax teeth. Dr Crippen had two more syringes and a surgical knife. Al Capone was behind him, trying to elbow his way past. David wasn't sure if their glass eyes could make him out in the shadows. But slowly they were heading towards him.

It was time to go. He swung round, preparing to heave himself over the fence. Too late. He saw a movement out of the corner of his eye. Something hit him full in the face and he was thrown back, off his feet. For a moment the world spun and then his shoulders hit the earth and all his breath was punched out of him.

"It's all right, everyone! I've got him! Do come quickly!"

The voice was shrill and excited. There was a rustle of leaves and a snapping of twigs and a large woman dressed in blue stepped forward. David tried to stand but all his strength had left him. The woman was wearing a billowing velvet and silk dress that made her look enormous. Her head was crowned by a silver and diamond tiara that sparkled even out of the moonlight and there was a Weight Watchers badge pinned to her lapel. She hadn't come out of the Chamber of Horrors. Lying, dazed, on a bed of leaves, David instantly recognized the ginger hair and perfect smile of the Duchess of York. She had hit him with her handbag.

"Good work, Your Highness," Dr Crippen muttered. His wax nose was bent out of shape where David had hit him and one of his eyes had fallen out.

"Ja. Sehr gut, Fräulein Fergie," Hitler agreed.

David wrenched the statuette out of his pocket and tried to stand up. The park was spinning round him, moving faster and faster. He tried to speak, to utter a few words of some spell that might yet save him. But his mouth was dry and the words would not come. He looked up into the leering, lifeless faces that surrounded him and raised a hand. Then the Duchess hit him again and he was out cold.

THE EAST TOWER

"He's lying," David said. "I found the statuette. He stole it. And he used magic to do it."

David was standing in Mr Kilgraw's study with Vincent only a few paces away. His clothes were dishevelled and there was a large bruise above his cheek where the handbag had hit him. Mr Helliwell stood in one corner of the room, resting his chin on one hand, watching the two boys quietly. Mr Kilgraw sat behind his desk with the statuette in front of him. David felt like snapping it in half. And he felt much the same about Vincent.

"I admit he found it first," Vincent said. He took his hands out of his pockets. "I've told you. I worked out the puzzle and found the cabinet, but I was too late. I guessed David had taken it so I went back to the telephone box. That was when I saw him with the statuette lying next to him. I figured he must have tripped over or something so I took the statuette. I didn't see any waxworks though," he added.

"Didn't see them?" David curled his fists. "You sent them!"

"I had nothing to do with it."

"Then who did?"

"That's enough of this!" Mr Kilgraw said, fluttering his hand for silence. His voice was little more than a whisper, but then the assistant headmaster rarely spoke loudly. He leaned back in his chair. "The trial is over," he said. "And Vincent has won."

"But sir..." David began.

"No!" Mr Kilgraw pointed a finger. "David, you talk about cheating, but it seems to me that it was only a few days ago that you were discovered trying to steal the papers for the last exam."

"That was Vincent too," David replied. "He set me up."

"And then there's the question of Sports Day. The obstacle race..."

David fell silent. He was blushing and he knew it. The obstacle race! Mr Kilgraw had known about it all the time. There was nothing David could say now. He had cheated once in his life and because of that nobody would ever trust him again.

"We don't need to prolong this discussion," Mr Kilgraw said. "Whatever happened tonight, Vincent won. He was the first back and he brought the statue with him. Mr Helliwell...?"

In the corner, the voodoo teacher shrugged. "I'm sorry, David," he said. "But I have to agree."

"Then that's that. Vincent King takes first place on the league. At prize-giving it will be he who is presented with the Unholy Grail."

"Thank you, sir." Vincent glanced again at David. "I mean it, David," he said. "I didn't want it to happen this way."

"Like hell..."

"Don't ever compare anything to hell until you've been there!" Mr Kilgraw snapped, and now he was really angry. "I have to say you've been a complete disappointment, David. And not just tonight. Fighting in the corridor. Trying to steal the exam paper and then whining and complaining when you failed to answer all the questions. You used to be our most promising pupil. But now I even wonder if it's worth your staying here at Groosham Grange."

"So do I," David growled. He regretted the words as soon as they were out but it was too late. Mr Kilgraw had heard.

"That's a decision you have to make," he

said. "If you want to leave, nobody will stop you. But remember, once you've gone, you can't come back. We'll never see you again..."

David opened his mouth to speak but there was nothing to say. He took one last look at Vincent who was doing his best to avoid his eyes. Mr Helliwell sighed and shook his head. Mr Kilgraw's hand closed round the statue. "And now if you'll excuse me," he said, "this has to go back to the museum. It'll be daylight soon and we wouldn't want it to be missed."

Jill Green was waiting for David outside the study. She was about to ask him what had happened, but one look at his face told her all she needed to know.

"So he won then," she said.

David nodded.

"Does it really matter, David? I mean, what's so important about the Unholy Grail anyway?" She took his arm. "You're still the best magician in the school. You don't need a cup to prove it."

"I told Mr Kilgraw I wanted to leave Groosham Grange," David said.

"What?" Jill stiffened beside him, genuinely shocked.

David sighed. "I didn't know what I was saying but ... you remember when we first came here? We didn't want to be witches or magicians. We hated it here!"

"That was before we knew about our powers."

"Yes. And now we're happy here. But that means we've changed, Jill. Maybe we've changed for the worse. Maybe we've become..."

"What?

"It doesn't matter."

But lying in bed, two hours later, David couldn't get the thought out of his mind. Had he become evil? It was true that he had cheated in the race and despite what Jill had said, he would have done anything to get his hands on the Unholy Grail. Even the name worried him. Unholy. Did it also describe him?

What is good and what is evil? Sometimes it's not as easy as you think to tell them apart...

He remembered what Mr Fitch (or was it Mr Teagle?) had said to him but he still wasn't sure what the head had meant. Good or evil? Stay or go? Why did everything have to be so complicated?

On the other side of the dormitory, Vincent turned in his sleep and pulled the sheets over him. David thought back to their first meeting. Vincent had arrived one July morning, carried over on the ferry that connected Skrull Island with the mainland. Handsome, athletic and quiet, Vincent seemed to fit in much faster than David had. In just a few weeks he had found his way through the mirror in the library and been given his own black ring. Maybe that was part of the trouble. The two of them had been in competition almost from the start and David had never bothered to find out anything about him; his home life, his parents, where he had come from.

How had he come to mistrust Vincent? Because of the East Tower. He had spotted Vincent coming out of the forbidden tower, next to the school's graveyard, and that had been the start of it. There was some sort of mystery connected with the place. Gregor knew. The school porter had stopped David going in.

David pushed his covers back and got out of bed. It was three o'clock in the morning; a cold, foggy night. He was probably mad. But he couldn't sleep anyway and he had nothing else to do. Whatever Vincent was really up to, he would find the answer in the East Tower. And he would go there now.

The night was bitterly cold. As David tiptoed through the school's graveyard his breath frosted and hung in the air around his head. Somewhere an owl hooted. A fat spider clambered down one of the gravestones and disappeared into the soil.

Something moved at the edge of the graveyard. David froze. But it was only a ghost, leaving its grave for a few hours' haunting. It hadn't seen him. Slowly, he moved on.

And there was the East Tower, looming out of the darkness ahead of him. David gazed at the crooked brickwork, the tangle of dark green ivy that surrounded it, the empty windows and, far above him, the broken battlements. He checked one last time. There was nobody around. He moved towards the entrance.

The only way into the East Tower was through a curved oak door, at least one metre thick. David was sure it would be locked but no sooner had he touched it than it swung inward, its iron hinges creaking horribly. There was something very creepy about the sound. For a moment he was tempted to go back to bed. But it was too late now. He had to settle this. He stepped inside.

The inner chamber of the tower was pitch black. A few tiny shafts of moonlight penetrated the cracks in the brickwork but the central area was a gaping hole. David didn't have a torch or even a box of matches with him. But he didn't need them. He closed his eyes and whispered a few words set down by the Elizabethan magician called John Dee. When he opened them again, the interior glowed with a strange green light. It was still gloomy but he could see.

The lower floor was empty, the ground strewn with rubble, a few nettles and poisonous herbs poking through. David sniffed the air. Although it was faint, there was something that he recognized, a smell that was at once familiar and yet strange. There was a sound somewhere high above, a sort of fluttering and a high-pitched whine. Ahead of him, a stone staircase climbed upwards, spiralling around on itself. David knew that the whole building was condemned, that any one of the stone slabs could crumble and send him crashing to certain death. But there was no other way. He had no choice.

He began to climb the stairs. The East Tower was fifty metres high. The staircase, pinned precariously to the outer wall, seemed to go on for ever and David was beginning to get dizzy when at last he found himself at the top. There was a coin in his trouser pocket and on an impulse he flicked it over his shoulder, into the hole at the centre of the stairs.

"One … two … three … four … five…"

It was a long time before the coin reached the bottom and tinkled on the concrete floor below.

Something moved. David heard a thin clatter like two pieces of cardboard being ruffled against each other. One step at a time, he moved across the concrete flagstones of the upper chamber. He had forgotten to put on any socks and he could feel the frozen air writhing around his ankles. For a second time he heard the strange, high-pitched whining. It was some sort of animal. What animal? What was this place?

He was in a completely circular room. Two of the narrow windows, quite close to each other, had mouldered, and now there was only a large, irregular gap. Opposite this, right up against the wall, there was a long wooden table with what looked like two or three baskets on top. Also on the table were an open book, a pile of paper, two candles, a quill pen and a leather-bound book.

David whispered three words. The candles ignited.

It was easier after that. David crossed over to the table and picked up one of the baskets. He felt something flutter between his hands. The front of the basket was a barred door, closed with a twist of wire. David looked inside and now saw what the animal was. A bat. Blind and frightened, it tried to fly, ricocheting off the sides of the cage.

What was Vincent doing with a collection of bats? David put down the cage and went over to the book. He scooped it up and examined it.

It was an old exercise book, each page packed with writing so cramped and tiny that it was unreadable. David flicked through the pages. At last he arrived at a section he could read in the light of the candles. A poem:

Beware the shadow that is found
Stretching out across the ground
Where St Augustine once began
And four knights slew a holy man
For if the Grail is carried here
Then Groosham Grange will disappear

The Grail! Groosham Grange… What did it all mean?

David concentrated on the text. Saint Augustine. He was the man who had brought Christianity to England in the first century. But where had he begun? David racked his brain, trying to remember his history lessons with Miss Pedicure. Augustine had first landed in Thanet, Kent. But that wasn't right. Of course … it was Canterbury! Canterbury Cathedral where four knights had slain Thomas à Becket in the reign of Henry II. Suddenly it was all crystal clear.

Carry the Unholy Grail into the shadow of Canterbury Cathedral and the school would disappear!

So that was what Vincent was planning. He wanted to destroy the school and had learned that the only way to do it was to get his hands on the Grail. But first he had to get rid of David – and he had done that brilliantly, baiting him to start with, then framing him and finally cheating him. In just three days' time, Vincent would be presented with his prize. And what then? Somehow he would smuggle it off the island. He would carry it to Canterbury. And then…

But what about the bats?

David put down the book and went over to the pile of paper. Paper, candles and bats. They were right next to each other. And when you added them together, what did you get? Candles to see by. Paper to write on. Bats to…

"Homing bats," he muttered. Why not? Homing bats were more reliable than homing pigeons. And they were perfect for carrying secret messages. They preferred the dark.

David felt in his trouser pocket and pulled out a pencil. It was such an old trick that he was almost ashamed to be trying it. Softly, he scribbled the pencil along the top sheet on the pile of paper, shading it grey. When he had pencilled over the entire sheet, he picked it up and held it against the candle flame.

It had worked. David could read five faint lines written in the same tight hand as the notebook:

EVEN MORE TOP SECRET THAN USUAL

To the Bishop of Bletchley

David Eliot is out of the running. The Grail will be delivered on Prize-giving Day. Departure from the island will proceed as planned. Am confident that a few days from now, Groosham Grange will no longer exist.

The note was signed with a cross.

Smiling to himself, David wandered over to the broken window and gazed out into the night. Just a few hours before, he had been considering packing his bags and leaving the school. Everything was different now. The sheet of paper and the notebook were all he needed. Once he showed them to the heads, the truth would come out.

What happened next took him completely by surprise. One moment he was standing on the edge of the tower. The next he was toppling forward as something – someone – crashed into the small of his back. He hadn't seen them. He hadn't heard them. For a second or two his hands flailed at the empty air. He tried to regain his balance but then whoever it was pushed him again and he fell out of the window, away from the tower, into the night.

He was dead. A fall of fifty metres on to the cold earth below would kill him for sure. The wind rushed into his face and the whole world twisted upside down. There was no time to utter a spell, no time to do anything.

With a last, despairing cry, he thrust his hand out, grabbing at the darkness, not expecting to find anything. But there was something. His fingers closed. Somehow his arm had caught a branch of ivy. He gripped tighter. He was still falling, pulling the ivy away with him as he went. But the further he fell, the thicker the ivy became. He was tangled up in it and it was slowing him down. More branches wrapped themselves around his chest and his waist. He came to a halt. With the ground only thirty metres away, the ivy reclaimed him, springing him back, crashing him into the brickwork. David shouted with pain. His arm had almost been torn out of its socket. But a few moments later he found himself dangling in mid-air. He was no longer falling. He was alive.

It took him thirty minutes to disentangle himself and climb the rest of the way down, and when he finally found himself on the ground once again he felt dizzy and sick. He took a deep breath, then looked back up. The window where he had been pushed was almost out of sight, terribly high up. It was a miracle that he was alive at all.

Even so, he knew what he had to do. As much as the idea appalled him, he had to be certain and so, forcing himself on, he went back into the East Tower and all the way back up the stairs. The top chamber was empty this time. And his worst fears had been realized. The pile of papers, the bats and the notebook were gone.

PRIZE-GIVING

The orange Rolls Royce was tearing up the motorway at a hundred miles an hour. All around it, cars were hooting, swerving and crashing into the hard shoulder as they tried to get out of the way.

"Shouldn't you be driving on the *left* side of the road, dear?" Mrs Eliot demanded.

"Nonsense," Mr Eliot replied, poking her with the cigarette lighter. "We're part of Europe now. I drive on the right in France and Switzerland. I don't see why I shouldn't do the same here."

Mrs Eliot's false eyelashes fluttered as an articulated lorry jackknifed out of their path, its horn blaring. "I think I'm going to be sick," she muttered.

"Well put your head out of the window," Mr Eliot snapped. "And this time remember to open the window first."

Edward and Eileen Eliot were on their way to Norfolk in their specially converted Rolls Royce. Mr Eliot was unable to walk, which would have been sad except that he had never really liked walking in the first place and much preferred his wheelchair. He was a short, round man with more hair in his nostrils than on his head. His wife, Eileen, was much taller than him with so many false parts – hair, teeth, nails, eyelashes – that it was hard to be sure what she looked like at all.

They were not alone in the car. Wedged into the very corner of the back seat was a small, shrivelled woman in a drab cotton dress. She had pale cheeks, crooked teeth and hair that could have fallen off a horse. This was Mildred, Edward's sister. After eleven years of marriage, her husband had recently died of boredom. Mildred had talked all the way through the funeral and had only stopped when one of the undertakers had finally hit her with a spade.

"What's that funny rattling noise, Edward?" she asked now as the car turned off the motorway, went the wrong way round a roundabout and raced through a set of red lights.

"What rattling noise?" Mr Eliot demanded.

"I think it must be the engine," Mildred sniffed. "Personally I don't trust these English cars," she went on in her thin, whiny voice. "They're so unreliable. Why didn't you buy a nice Japanese car, Edward? The Japanese know how to build cars. Why didn't you...?"

"Unreliable!" Mr Eliot screamed, interrupting her. He wrenched the steering wheel, sending the car off the road and on to the pavement. "This is a Rolls Royce you're talking about! Do you know how much a Rolls Royce costs? It costs thousands! I didn't eat for a month after I bought my Rolls Royce. I couldn't afford petrol for three years!"

"They're very reliable," Eileen Eliot agreed, sticking her finger into the cigarette lighter to demonstrate. There was a flash as the dashboard short-circuited and she electrocuted herself.

"The Japanese couldn't build a Rolls Royce in a thousand years," Mr Eliot continued, unplugging his wife. "In fact they couldn't even pronounce it!" He jammed his foot down on the accelerator but he must have taken a wrong turning as he was now shooting through a playground with mothers and children hurling themselves into the flower-beds to get out of the way. "What sort of road is this?" he demanded, angrily.

"The Japanese have marvellous roads," Mildred remarked. "And bullet trains..."

"I'll bullet you..." Mr Eliot growled. He stamped down and the Rolls Royce smashed through a fence, leapt over the pavement and headed on towards the Norfolk coast.

Two hours later, they arrived.

Because it was on an island, Groosham Grange was unreachable by car – even by Rolls Royce – and the last part of the journey had to be undertaken by boat. Mr Eliot had parked right beside the sea and now he wheeled himself down to a twisting wooden jetty that jutted out precariously over the water. There was a boat waiting for them – an old fisherman's trawler. The old fisherman was sitting inside.

Seeing Mr Eliot, he stood up. "More parents?" he demanded.

Mr Eliot examined the man with distaste. He looked like something out of a pirate film, what with his black beard and single gold earring. "Yes," he said. "Will you ferry us over?"

"I will. I'll ferry you there. I'll ferry you back. I been doing it all day." The man spat. "Parents! Who needs 'em!"

"What's your name?" Mr Eliot demanded.

"Bloodbath. Captain Bloodbath." The captain squinted. "And I take it that's your lovely wife?"

Mr Eliot glanced at Mildred, who was standing beside him. She had a large, bulging handbag on her arm. "She's not my wife and she's not lovely," he replied. "My wife is under the car."

“I’ve fixed it!” Eileen Eliot called out and sat up, catching her head on the exhaust with a dull clang. There was oil on her dress and more on her face. She had a spanner in one hand and another one between her teeth. “I think you must have cracked a cylinder when you ran over that cyclist,” she said, joining the others on the jetty.

“Typical English workmanship,” Mildred muttered.

Mr Eliot took one of the spanners and hit her with it. “Let’s get on the boat,” he said.

A few minutes later, Captain Bloodbath cast off and, belching black smoke and rumbling, the boat began the crossing. The Captain sat at the front, steering, and Mr Eliot was surprised to see that his hands seemed to be made of steel.

“They’re ally-minium!” Bloodbath exclaimed, noticing the banker staring at him. He clapped his hands together with a loud ping. “My own hands was pulled off last spring. Lost at sea. The boys made these ones for me in metalwork class. Very handy they are too!”

“Delightful,” Mrs Eliot agreed with a weak smile.

There was a slight mist on the water but as they chugged forward, it suddenly parted. And there were the soaring cliffs of Skrull Island with the waves crashing and frothing on the jagged black rocks below. The boat pulled into a second jetty and then there was a five-minute drive up the steep road to the school with Gregor, who was simpering and sniggering at the wheel.

"I'm not sure I think too much of the staff," Mrs Eliot whispered. "I mean, that man with no hands! And unless I'm mistaken, this driver is completely deformed!"

The car stopped. Mildred uttered a little scream and leapt out.

"What's happened?" Mr Eliot exclaimed. "Has she been stung by a wasp?"

"It's David!" Mildred threw her hands up above her head. "Oh David! I hardly recognized you!" she warbled. She slapped her hands limply against her cheeks. "You've grown so tall! And you've put on weight! And your hair's so long. You've completely changed!"

"That's because I'm not David," the boy she was talking to said. "That's David over there..."

"Oh..."

By this time, Mr Eliot had been helped out of the car and he and Eileen Eliot were looking uncertainly at the school. The sun was shining and the whole building had been decked out for the day with a few strips of bunting and flags. A refreshment tent had been set up in the grounds.

But even so it still looked rather grim.

David walked over to them. “Hello, Mother,” he said. “Hello, Father. Hello, Aunt Mildred.”

Mr Eliot eyed his son critically. “How many prizes have you won?” he asked.

David sighed. “I’m afraid I haven’t won any.”

“Not any!” Mr Eliot exploded. “That’s it then! Back in the car! We’re going home.”

“But we’ve only just got here,” his wife protested.

Mr Eliot wheeled over her foot. “Well we’re off again,” he yelled. “I won a prize every year I was at Beton College. I won prizes for history, geometry and French. I even won prizes for winning prizes! If I hadn’t won a prize, my father would have sliced me open with a surgical knife and confiscated one of my kidneys!”

By now Mr Eliot had gone bright red. He seemed to be having difficulty breathing and his whole face was contorted with pain. Mrs Eliot took out a bottle of pills and forced several of them into his mouth. “You shouldn’t upset your father, David,” she said. “You know he has trouble with his blood pressure. Sometimes his blood doesn’t have any pressure at all!”

“I’m sorry,” David muttered.

By the time Mr Eliot had recovered, Gregor had taken the car back to the jetty to fetch another batch of parents and so he was forced to stay. Fortunately for David, Mr Helliwell chose that moment to come over and introduce himself. The voodoo teacher was dressed in his smartest clothes for prize-giving: black suit and tails, wing collar and, perched on his head, a crooked, black hat. He had also painted his face white with black rings around his eyes. Both Mildred and Mrs Eliot trembled as he approached, but Mr Helliwell couldn't have been more friendly. "You should be very proud of David," he said.

"Why?" Mr Eliot asked.

"He's coming on very well." Mr Helliwell smiled, showing a line of teeth like tombstones. "He may have been unlucky, not getting the prize, but otherwise he's had a good year. I'm sure he'll get a good report."

David was grateful to the teacher despite himself. But he still couldn't meet Mr Helliwell's eyes. The memory of the trial and what had happened afterwards was still too raw.

"Perhaps you would like me to show you round the school," Mr Helliwell said.

"Round it?" Mrs Eliot asked. "Why can't we go in it?"

"He means in it, you idiotic woman," Mr Eliot snapped.

"This way..." Mr Helliwell winked at David and set off behind the electric wheelchair. Eileen

Eliot and Mildred followed.

"They have much more modern schools in Tokyo," Mildred said. She pulled her handbag further up her arm. "The Japanese have a wonderful education system..."

And then they were gone, entering the building through one of the open doors. They had quite forgotten David. But that suited him fine. The day was moving too fast. He needed time to think.

There were about thirty-five sets of parents on the island, more than eighty people in all, what with various aunts, uncles and friends. All of them were milling about in their best clothes, the women with hats and handbags, the men smug and smiling. Of course, they weren't going to be allowed to see everything. A lot of the school's equipment – the skulls, five-fingered candle-holders, wands, magic circles and the rest of it – had been hidden away. For the next ten minutes they would wander around the grounds and then they would all assemble in the marquee where Mr Kilgraw would make a speech and Vincent King would be awarded the Unholy Grail.

David knew that this would be the critical moment. It would be the only time when Vincent would have the Grail in his hands. If he was going to get it off the island, he would have to do it today.

And that was the one thing he still didn't know. How did Vincent plan to remove the Grail?

It seemed to him that there was only one way – in Captain Bloodbath's boat. But that had been kept well secured ever since David himself had stolen it a while back. So what was Vincent going to do? David had been surprised to discover that Vincent's parents weren't coming to prize-giving – so they couldn't take it for him. But perhaps he had someone in the crowd: a fake uncle or aunt. Perhaps the Bishop of Bletchley himself was here, in disguise. Even now he could be waiting to seize it. And with so many people coming and going, it would be easy to smuggle it away.

But David had no idea what the Bishop looked like – in disguise or out of it. There were plenty of parents with white hair and saintly faces. He could be any one of them. David glanced at the marquee. Vincent was standing in the sunlight with Monsieur Leloup, looking very dashing in a blazer and white trousers. The French teacher was introducing him to a group of parents, obviously flattering him. David felt a surge of jealousy. That should have been him.

"Seen anything?"

Jill had come up behind him and caught hold of his arm. David had told her everything that had happened the morning after his fall from the East Tower. Only Jill, his closest friend on the island, would have believed him – and even she had taken a lot of persuading. But in the end she had agreed to help.

David shook his head. "No. Everything's so ordinary. But I know it's going to happen, Jill. And soon..."

"Maybe you should go to the heads, David."

"And tell them what?" David sighed. "They'd never listen to me."

"Look out!" Jill gestured in the direction of the school. "I think your parents are coming back."

"Do you want to meet them?"

"No thanks." Jill hurried off. She stopped a few paces away and turned round. "Don't worry, David," she said. "I'll keep an eye on Vincent."

Over by the marquee, Vincent glanced suddenly towards them. Had he overheard what she had just said?

But then Mr Helliwell reached David, still following his father in the wheelchair.

"An excellent school," Mr Eliot was saying. "I am most impressed. Of course, it is a little unnatural for boys and girls to be here together. At Beton College, where I went, there were only boys. In fact, even the headmaster's wife was a boy. But I suppose that's progress..."

"Absolutely," Mr Helliwell smiled politely. "Now if you'll excuse me..." The teacher hurried off towards the marquee.

Mr Eliot turned to his son. "Well, David," he said. "I can see it was a good decision to send you here."

"Your father does make wonderful decisions," Mrs Eliot agreed.

"I have suggested to Mr Helliwell a little more use of the cane," Mr Eliot went on. He nodded to himself. "What I always say is that a good beating never hurt anyone."

Mrs Eliot frowned. "But darling, if it didn't hurt, how could it be a good beating?"

"No, my love. What I mean is..."

But before Mr Eliot could either explain or demonstrate what he meant, a bell rang. The prize-giving was about to begin.

Mr and Mrs Eliot, Mildred and David joined the other parents. What with the narrow entrance and the number of people trying to get in, it was another quarter of an hour before they finally took their places. David looked around him, at the rows of seats stretched out underneath the canvas and the platform raised at the far end with the staff of Groosham Grange taking their places along it. He saw Vincent, sitting on his own. Then Mr Kilgraw stood up and everyone hushed.

But already there was something wrong. David looked one way, then another. Something had caught his eye. What was it? And then he saw, right at the back, near the entrance, an empty seat.

Mr Kilgraw had begun to speak but David didn't hear a word. He was scanning the audience, searching through the faces, the boys and the girls, the teachers and the parents…

But she wasn't there. The empty seat.

Jill had promised to keep an eye on Vincent. Vincent had overheard her. And now Jill had disappeared.

CRACKS

"Good afternoon, ladies and gentlemen," Mr Kilgraw began. The flaps had been drawn across the marquee to protect him from the sun, but just to be safe he was also wearing a slightly incongruous straw hat. "Welcome to Groosham Grange on this, our annual Prize-giving Day. May I begin by apologizing on behalf of the heads, Mr Fitch and Mr Teagle, who are unable to attend today. Mr Fitch has yellow fever. Mr Teagle has scarlet fever. If they get too close to each other, they go a nasty shade of orange.

"This has been a very successful year for Groosham Grange. Some might even say a magical year. I am pleased to tell you that our new biology laboratory has been built by workmen who were actually created in our old biology laboratory. Well done Lower Fifth! Our Ecology Group has been busy and we now have our own Tropical Rain Forest on the south side of the island. Congratulations also to the Drama Group. They really brought *Frankenstein* to life. So, for that matter, did our physics class.

"It's not all work at Groosham Grange, of course. Our French class visited France. Our Ancient Greek class visited Ancient Greece. A school inspector visited us. And if you happen to pass through the cemetery, I hope you'll visit him. As usual, our staff has made many sacrifices. I would like to thank them and I ought also to thank the sacrifices..."

David found it hard to concentrate on what Mr Kilgraw was saying. He was sitting between his mother and father. Aunt Mildred, who was next to Edward Eliot, had already fallen asleep and was whistling softly through her nose. David was in the middle of the marquee, completely surrounded by parents: bald parents, fat parents, parents with red veins in their noses and wax in their ears, parents in expensive jewellery and expensive suits. He felt as if he was drowning in parents. Was this what he would be like one day? It was a horrible thought.

And it didn't make it any easier to think. David knew that the next few minutes would be critical. Once Vincent had the Unholy Grail, anything could happen. How would Vincent get the Grail off the island? Would he carry it himself, slipping away with the crowd? Or would he pass it to someone in the crowd – and if so, who? And what about Jill? David wanted to get up and look for her now but he knew that he couldn't. He was too close to Vincent. He was trapped.

"At Groosham Grange there is only one winner," Mr Kilgraw was saying. "And there is only one prize..."

David turned his attention back to the platform and saw that the assistant headmaster was holding something in his hands. Even from this distance he knew what it was. For the parents – bored and beginning to fidget – it was no more than a silver chalice decorated with red stones. But for David, the Unholy Grail seemed to glow with a light of its own. He could feel it reaching out to him. He had never wanted anything so much in his entire life.

"It is the school's most valued trophy," Mr Kilgraw went on. "In fact you could say that without it there would be no Groosham Grange. Every year it is presented to the student whose work, whose general behaviour and whose overall contribution to school life has put him or her at the top of the league. This year, the contest was particularly close..."

Was David imagining it or did Mr Kilgraw search him out, his eyes glittering as they locked into David's? It was almost a challenge. For the space of a heartbeat the two of them were alone beneath the canvas. The parents had gone. Vincent had gone. And David's hands twitched, reaching out to take what was rightfully his.

Then it was over.

"...but it gives me great pleasure to announce that the winner, our most distinguished pupil, is – Vincent King!"

David reluctantly joined in the general applause, at the same time trying to smile. Vincent stood up and went on to the stage. He shook hands with Mr Kilgraw. Mr Kilgraw muttered a few words. Vincent took the Grail and sat down again. The applause died away. And that was it. The Unholy Grail was his.

Mr Kilgraw spoke for another five minutes and David counted every one of them. The prize-giving might be over but he knew that his work was only beginning. Whatever happened, he intended to stick close to Vincent – and to the Grail. He would just have to worry about Jill later.

But it wasn't as easy as David had hoped. As soon as Mr Kilgraw had finished his speech, everyone stood up at once in a rush for the sherry and sausage rolls that Gregor and Mrs Windergast were serving at the back of the marquee. At the same time, Vincent was surrounded by people, examining the Grail and congratulating him, and it was as much as David could do to keep sight of him at all.

Worse than that, he still had his parents to deal with. Mr Eliot was in a bad mood. "I am disappointed," he was saying as he tore a sausage roll into shreds. "I wish I wasn't your father, to be frank. In fact I wish I was Frank's father. He won three prizes at Beton College."

"I just hope the neighbours don't find out," Mrs Eliot wept, gnawing at her fingers. "My own son! I can't bear it! We'll have to move. I'll change my name. I'll have plastic surgery..."

Aunt Mildred nodded in agreement. "My neighbour's children won *lots* of prizes," she announced. "But then, of course, they have a Japanese au pair..."

David craned his neck, searching for a gap between the three of them. The crowd that had formed around Vincent had separated again and suddenly Vincent had gone. David wasn't sure how he'd done it. But he had left the marquee.

Then Gregor limped over to them with a tray of food. "Sumfink tweet?" he gurgled.

"What?" Aunt Mildred asked.

"He's asking if you want something to eat," David translated. He glanced at the tray. "It's toad-in-the-hole," he said. "And I think Gregor's used real toads."

"I think it's time we went," Mildred whispered, going rather green.

Ten minutes later, David saw his parents into the car that would take them back down to the jetty and the boat.

"Goodbye, David," his father said. "I'm afraid I have not enjoyed seeing you. I can see now that your mother and I have always spoiled you."

"We ruined you," Mrs Eliot wept. Her make-up was flowing in rivers down her cheeks.

"I blame myself," Mr Eliot went on. "I should have beaten you more. My father beat me every day of my life. He used to buy cane furniture so that he could beat me with the chairs when he wasn't sitting on them. He knew a thing or two about discipline. Whack! Whack! Whack! That's all boys understand. Start at the bottom, that's what I say..."

"Don't excite yourself, dear," Mrs Eliot murmured.

Just then Aunt Mildred came running up to the car. "Sorry I'm late," she whined in her thin, nasal voice. "I couldn't find my handbag. Bye-bye, dear." She pecked David on the cheek. "Do come and visit me in Margate soon." She got into the car, heaving her handbag on to her lap. "I'm sure it wasn't as heavy as this when I set out this morning," she prattled on. "I can't think how I lost it. That nice teacher found it for me. Honestly, I'd forget my own head if it wasn't..."

She was still talking when Gregor started the car and they rattled off down the hill. David watched them until they were out of sight. Then he set off in the direction of the school.

Where could Vincent have gone?

David's first thought was the jetty but he decided not to go down there yet. He didn't want to follow his parents and the more he thought about it the less likely it was that Vincent would try to stow away on the boat. Captain Bloodbath was too careful – and anyway, it would be far easier to give the Grail to someone else and let them carry it for him. Vincent had to be somewhere in the school. David would find him and confront him with what he knew. But he had to move fast.

First he checked the marquee. The parents were starting to thin out, a few clusters of them still chatting with the staff, the rest walking with their sons and daughters towards the jetty. Mr Kilgraw had left. He would have gone inside to escape the sunlight. Mrs Windergast was still there, clearing away the food, and David went over to her.

"Excuse me," he said. "Have you seen Vincent?"

The matron smiled at him. "Not for a while, my dear. I suppose you want to congratulate him."

"Not exactly." David left the marquee.

In the next half hour he tried the library, the dormitory, the dining room, the hallways and the classrooms. He looked into the heads' study and Mr Kilgraw's study. Both rooms were empty. Then he tried the cemetery at the edge of the wood. There was no sign of Vincent.

David walked back to the school, feeling increasingly uncomfortable. Everything felt wrong. It was about two o'clock and the sun was shining but there was no warmth in the air, and no breeze, not even the faintest whisper of one. The light hitting the school was hard, unsparing. It was as if he had stepped out of real life and into a photograph, as if he were the only living thing.

He heard a sound high up, a faint rattling. He looked up, then blinked as something hit him on the side of the cheek. He rubbed the skin with the tips of his fingers. He had been hit by a pebble and a scattering of dust but he was unhurt. He squinted up in the direction of the sound. One wall of Groosham Grange loomed high above him, a grey gargoyle jutting out at the corner. There was a crack in the brickwork. It was only a small crack, zigzagging horizontally under the gargoyle, but David was sure it hadn't been there before. It looked too fresh, the edges pink against the grey surface of the bricks. It was no more than ten centimetres long. It was a crack, that was all.

But even as David lowered his head there was another soft rattle and a second shower of dust. He looked up again and saw that the crack had lengthened, curving up around the gargoyle. At the same time, a second crack had formed a few centimetres below. Even as he watched, a few pieces of mortar detached themselves from the wall and tumbled down to the earth below. And now there were three cracks, the longest about two metres and perhaps a centimetre wide. The gargoyle was surrounded by them. Its bulging eyes and twisted mouth almost looked afraid.

Suddenly David knew. He remembered the verse:

For if the Grail is carried here
Then Groosham Grange will disappear

The disappearance of Groosham Grange had begun.

The Unholy Grail had already left the island.

The question was, had Vincent gone with it? David knew that he had to find the other boy fast. How far away was Canterbury? He had no doubt that the Grail was already on its way there. Perhaps it was already too late.

But with the onrush of panic came another thought. He had forgotten to look in the one place where he was most likely to find Vincent, the one place that had been tied in with the mystery from the start: the East Tower. Even if the Grail had gone, Vincent might be hiding out there and if he could just find Vincent he might yet be able to recapture the Grail. David broke into a run. As he went, a fourth, larger crack opened up in the wall just beside his head.

He reached the door of the tower and without stopping to think, kicked it open and ran in. After the brightness of the afternoon light, the darkness inside the building was total. For about five seconds David was completely blind and in that time he realized three things.

First, that Vincent had been there recently. There was a smell in the air, the same smell that David had noticed the night he had nearly been killed.

Second, that he should have gone in more cautiously and allowed his eyes time to get used to the darkness.

And third, that he was not alone.

The hand that reached out and grabbed him by the throat was invisible. Before he could utter a sound a second hand clamped itself over his mouth. This hand was holding a pad of material soaked in something that smelled of rotting fruit and alcohol. And as David choked and struggled and slipped into unconsciousness, he thought to himself that the hand was very big, surely far too big to belong to Vincent.

But if it wasn't Vincent, who on earth could it be?

VINCENT

David's arms, wrists and shoulders were hurting. It was the pain that woke him – that and someone calling his name. He opened his eyes and found himself hunched up on the floor with his back against the wall of a room that he recognized. He was in the upper chamber of the East Tower. Somebody had knocked him out, carried him upstairs, tied him up and left him there.

But who?

All along he had been certain that Vincent King was his secret enemy and that it had been Vincent who was plotting to steal the Grail. Now, at last, he knew that he had been wrong. For there was Vincent right opposite him, also tied up, his hair for once in disarray and an ugly bruise on the side of his face. Jill was sitting next to him, in a similar state. She was the one calling to him.

David straightened himself. "It's all right," he said. "I'm awake."

He tried to separate his wrists but it was impossible. They were tied securely behind his back with some sort of rough rope. He could feel it cutting into his flesh and it was as much as he could do to wiggle his fingers. He pushed himself further up against the wall, using the heel of his shoe against the rough flagstones. "Just give me a few seconds," he said. He shut his eyes again and whispered the first few words of a spell that would bring a minor Persian demon to his assistance.

"Forget it," Vincent cut in and David stopped in surprise. The other boy had hardly ever talked to him. Usually they did their best to avoid each other. But now it seemed that they were on the same side. Even so, Vincent sounded tired and defeated. "If you're trying some magic, it won't work," he said. "I've already tried."

"Look at the door," Jill said.

David twisted his head round uncomfortably. There was a shape painted on the closed door. It looked like an eye with a wavy line through it.

"It's the eye of Horus," Vincent said. "It creates a magical barrier. It means…"

"…it means we can't use our powers," David

concluded. He nodded. "I know."

Gritting his teeth, he see-sawed his wrists together, trying to loosen the rope. It cost him a few inches of skin and gave him little in return. His hands had rotated and his palms could meet. He might have been able to pick up something if there was anything in the tower to pick up. But that was all.

He gave up. "Who did this?" he asked.

Vincent shook his head. "I don't know. I never saw them."

"Nor me," Jill added. "I was following Vincent like you said. But just before the prize-giving started, I decided to take a quick look in here. Someone must have been waiting. I didn't see anything."

"Nor did I," David muttered, gloomily.

"Why *were* you following me?" Vincent asked.

Jill jerked her head in David's direction. She was unable to keep a sour tone out of her voice. "He thought you were going to steal the Grail."

Vincent nodded briefly. "That figures," he muttered.

"I knew *someone* was going to steal the Grail," David said. He was blushing again. He had been wrong from the start, horribly wrong, and his mistake could end up killing all of them. He thought back now, remembering everything that had happened. And the words poured out.

"I was set up that night in the heads' study. I was never trying to steal the exam. And I did know what thanatomania means. Somebody stole part of my answer. And what about the waxworks? OK – maybe it wasn't you who sent them after me, but I wasn't making it up. Somebody stole the statuette so that you could win." David realized he wasn't making much sense. He slumped back into silence.

"Is that why you were against me from the start?" Vincent asked.

"I wasn't..."

"You never gave me a chance."

David knew it was true. He wasn't blushing because he had been wrong but because he had been cruel and stupid. He had thought the worst of Vincent for the simple reason that he didn't like him, and he didn't like him because the two of them had been in competition. Vincent was right. David had never given him a chance. They had been enemies from the start.

"How was I to know?" David muttered. "I didn't know you..."

"You never asked," Vincent said. There was a pause and he went on. "I didn't want to come here," he said. "I didn't have any parents. My dad left when I was a kid and my mother didn't want to know. They put me in an institution ... St Elizabeth's in Sourbridge. It was horrible.

Then I got moved here." He took a deep breath. "I thought I'd be happy at Groosham Grange, especially when I found out what was really going on. All I wanted was to be one of you, to be accepted. I didn't even care about the Unholy Grail."

"I'm sorry..." David had never felt more ashamed.

"I did try to be friends with you, but everything I did just made it worse." He sighed. "Why did you think it was me? Why me?"

"I don't know." David thought back. "I saw you coming out of the tower," he said, knowing how lame it sounded. "And that night, when I was caught looking at the exam papers ... did you come here then?"

Vincent nodded. "Yes."

"Why?"

Vincent thought for a moment, then answered. "I smoke," he said. "I started smoking cigarettes when I was at Sourbridge and I've never given up."

"Smoking!" David remembered the smell. He had come across it twice but he hadn't recognized it: stale tobacco smoke. "I don't believe it!" he said. "Smoking is mad. It kills you. How can you be so stupid?"

"You've been pretty stupid too," Jill muttered.

David fell silent. "Yes," he agreed.

Vincent struggled with his ropes. "I suppose it's a bit late now to think about giving up."

The words were no sooner spoken than there was a distant rumble, soft and low at first but building up to a sudden crash. David looked out of the window. The sky was grey, but it wasn't the colour of nightfall. It was an ugly, electric grey, somehow unnatural. There was a storm closing in on Skrull Island and sitting high up in the tower, right in the middle of it, he felt very uncomfortable indeed.

"I think..." he began.

He got no further. The whole tower suddenly trembled as if hit by a shockwave and at the same moment Jill cried out. A great chunk of wall right next to her simply fell away leaving a gap above her head. Outside, the air swirled round in a dark vortex and rushed into the room. There was a second crash of thunder. The chamber shook again and a crack appeared in the floor between David and Vincent, the heavy flagstones ripping apart as if they were made of paper.

"What's happening?" Jill cried.

"The Grail's left the island," David shouted. "It's the end..."

"What are we going to do?" Vincent said.

David glanced at the door, at the symbol painted in white on the woodwork. Even if he could have reached the eye of Horus, he would have been unable to rub it out. But while it was there, there was no chance of any magic. If they were going to escape, they would have to use their own resources. He searched the floor, trying not to look at the crack. There were no broken bottles, no rusty nails, nothing that would cut through the rope. Opposite him, Vincent was struggling feverishly. He had worked his hands loose but his wrists were still securely tied.

A third crash of thunder. This time it was the roof that was hit. As Jill screamed and rolled on her side to protect herself, two wooden rafters crashed down, followed by what felt like a tonne of dust and rubble. Vincent completely disappeared from sight and for a moment David thought he had been crushed. But then Vincent coughed and staggered on to his knees, still fighting with his ropes.

"The whole place is falling apart!" Jill shouted. "How high up are we?"

"Too high up," David shouted back. The crack in the floor had widened again. Quite soon the entire thing would give way and all three of them would fall into a tunnel of broken stone and brickwork with certain death fifty metres below.

Then he had a thought. "Vincent!" he called out. "After the prize-giving you came in here to have a cigarette."

"Yes," Vincent admitted. "But don't tell me it's bad for my health. Not now!"

"You've got cigarettes on you?"

"David, this is no time to take it up," Jill wailed.

"Yes," Vincent said.

"What were you going to light them with?"

Vincent understood at once. For the first time, David found himself admiring the other boy and knew that if only they'd been working together from the start, none of this would have happened. Contorting his body, Vincent spilled the contents of his pockets on to the floor: a handful of coins, a pen, a cigarette lighter.

Moving with his hands tied behind his back wasn't easy. First he had to turn himself round, then grope behind him to pick up the lighter. At the same time, David shuffled across the floor, pushing himself with his feet. He stopped at the crack, feeling the floor move. Jill cried out a warning. David threw himself forward. The thunder reverberated all around – closer this time – and a whole section of the floor, the section where David had just been sitting, fell away leaving a jagged black hole. David crashed down, almost dislocating his shoulder. Far below, he heard the flagstones shatter at the bottom of the tower and breathed a sigh of relief that he hadn't fallen with them.

"Hurry!" Vincent urged him.

Bruised and aching, David manoeuvred himself so that he was back to back with the other boy. For her part, Jill had edged closer to them. The whole chamber was breaking up. Nowhere was safe. But if one went, all would go. There was some sort of comfort in that.

"This is going to hurt," Vincent said.

"Do it," David said.

Fumbling with his fingers, afraid he would drop it, Vincent flicked the lighter on. He had to work blind, sitting with his back to David, and there was no time to be careful. David felt the flame of the lighter sear the inside of his wrist and shouted out in pain.

"I'm sorry..." Vincent began.

"It's not your fault. Just keep going."

Vincent flicked the lighter back on, trying to direct the flame to where he thought the ropes must be. The wind was rushing into the chamber through the holes in the wall and ceiling. David could hear it racing round the tower. He winced as the lighter burnt him once again but this time he didn't cry out. He was grateful the flame hadn't blown out.

More brickwork fell. Jill had gone white and David thought she was going to faint, but then he saw that falling plaster had covered her from head to toe. Jill wasn't the fainting sort. "I can smell burning," she said. "It must be the rope."

"Unless it's me," David muttered.

He was straining his arms, trying to avoid the flame. It felt as if he had been sitting there for ever. But then there was a jerk and his hands parted. Another few seconds and he was standing up, free, the two ends of the singed rope hanging from his wrists. Next, he released Vincent. The cigarette lighter had badly burned the other boy's thumb and the side of his hand. David could see the red marks. But Vincent hadn't complained.

Then it was Jill's turn. With Vincent's help, the ropes came away quickly and then the three of them were racing across the floor even as it fell away beneath them. Soon there would be nothing left of the tower. It was as if there were some invisible creature inside the storm, devouring the stone and mortar.

David reached the door first. It was unlocked. Whoever had tied them up had been confident about their knots. Clinging on to Jill, with Vincent right behind him, David made his way down the spiral staircase. About halfway down, two more flagstones fell past, narrowly missing them before shattering with an explosive crash. But the lower parts of the tower were holding up. The further they went, the safer they became. They reached the bottom unharmed.

But when they emerged into the open air, everything had changed.

Skrull Island was black, lashed by a stinging acid rain. The clouds writhed and boiled like something in a witch's cauldron. The wind stabbed at them, hurling torn plants and grass into their faces. There was nobody in sight. To one side, the cemetery looked wild and derelict with several of its gravestones on their sides. Groosham Grange itself looked dark and dismal, like some abandoned factory. A lattice-work of cracks had spread across it. Many of its windows had been smashed. The ivy had been torn away and hung down, a tangled mess. There was a flash of lightning and one of the gargoyles separated from the wall, launching itself into the blackness of the sky with an explosion of broken plaster.

"The Grail..." Vincent began.

"It's begun its journey south," David shouted. "If it reaches Canterbury, that'll be it...!"

"But who took it?" Jill demanded. "If it wasn't Vincent, who was it?"

"And what can we do?" Vincent held up a hand to protect his eyes from the hurtling wind. "We've got to get it back...!"

"I don't know!" David cried.

But suddenly he did know. Suddenly a whole lot of things had fallen into place. He knew who had the Grail. He knew how it had been smuggled off the island. The only thing he didn't know was how he could possibly reach it.

Then Vincent grabbed his arm. "I've got an idea," he yelled.

"What?"

"We can get off the island. One of us..."

"Show me!" David said.

The thunder crashed again. The three of them turned and ran into the school.

PURSUIT

It was getting very hot inside the Rolls Royce.

Mr Eliot ran a finger round his collar and flicked on the on-board computer showing the engine temperature. The engine's heat was normal but he was sweating. His wife was sweating. Even the leather upholstery was sweating. In the back seat, all Aunt Mildred's make-up had run and she now looked like a Sioux Indian in a rainstorm. It was very odd. The sun was shining but it was already late in the day. How could it be so warm?

"I think I'm going to faint," Mrs Eliot muttered and promptly did, her head crashing into the dashboard.

"Oh no!" Mr Eliot wailed.

"Is she hurt?" Mildred asked, clutching her handbag tightly to her chest and peering over the seat.

"I don't know," Mr Eliot replied. "But she's cracked the walnut panelling. Do you know how much that panelling cost me? It cost me a fortune! It's made out of South American walnuts!"

"I think she's dead," Mildred whispered.

Mr Eliot poked his wife affectionately in the ear. "No. She's still breathing," he said.

By now all the windows in the Rolls Royce had steamed up which, as they were still driving at ninety miles per hour down the motorway, made things rather difficult. But Mr Eliot still clung grimly to the steering wheel, overtaking on the inside and swerving on the outside. At least he was driving on the correct side of the road.

"Why don't you turn on the air conditioning?" Aunt Mildred suggested.

"Good thinking!" Mr Eliot snarled. "Pure mountain air. That's what you get in a Rolls Royce. In fact I could have bought a mountain for the amount it cost me."

"Just do it, dear," Mildred panted as her lipstick trickled over her chin.

Mr Eliot pressed a button. There was a roar and before either of them could react they were engulfed in a snow-storm that rushed at them through the air-conditioning vents, filling the interior of the car. In seconds their sweat had frozen. Long icicles hung off Mr Eliot's nose and chin. His moustache had frozen solid. The intense cold had the effect of waking Mrs Eliot up but by now her face had stuck to the surface of the dashboard. On the back seat, Aunt Mildred had virtually disappeared beneath a huge snow drift that rose over her like a white blanket. The Rolls Royce swerved left and right, sending a Fiat and a Rover hurtling into the crash barrier. Mr Eliot's hands were now firmly glued to the steering wheel.

"What's going on?" he screamed, his breath coming out in white clouds. "I had the car serviced before I left. It was a Rolls Royce service man. And all Rolls Royce service men are regularly serviced themselves. What's happening? This is motorway madness!"

"There's a service station," Aunt Mildred whimpered. "Why don't we stop for a few minutes?"

"Good idea!" Mr Eliot agreed and wrenched the car over to the left.

It took them ten minutes to extract themselves from the frozen Rolls Royce, which they left to thaw slowly in the sun. Eileen Eliot had to be chiselled off the dashboard and then had to use a blowtorch to separate Edward Eliot from the steering wheel, but eventually the three of them were able to make their way up the concrete ramp that led to the Snappy Eater café.

The Snappy Eater was a typical English motorway restaurant. The tables were plastic. The chairs were plastic. And the food tasted of plastic. A few motorists were sitting in the brightly coloured room, surrounded by artificial flowers, listening to the piped music and miserably nibbling their luke-warm snacks. Outside, the traffic roared past and the smell of burning tyres and petrol hung heavy in the air.

Mildred looked round her and sniffed. "They have wonderful service stations in Japan," she muttered. "You can get marvellous sushi..."

"What's sushi?" Eileen asked. She was feeling rather car-sick.

"It's raw fish!" Mildred explained enthusiastically. "Lovely strips of raw fish, all wet and jelly-like. All the Japanese motorway restaurants have them."

"Oh God!" Mrs Eliot gurgled and ran off in the direction of the toilet.

"I love Japanese food," Mildred continued, sitting down at a table and heaving her handbag in front of her.

"Why don't you shut up about Japan, you interfering old goat?" Mr Eliot asked as he wheeled himself next to her. He snatched the menu. "Here. They've got battered cod and chips. You can have that raw. Better still, you can have it battered. I'll batter you myself..."

A few minutes later, Eileen Eliot returned and they ordered two plates of vegetarian spaghetti and one portion of cod. But things had already begun to change inside the Snappy Eater.

Nobody noticed anything at first. The roar of the traffic drowned out the screams of the children who had been playing outside on a slide shaped like a plastic dragon. But the dragon was no longer plastic. It had already swallowed two of the children and was chasing a third with very real claws and fiery breath. About fifty metres away, at the garage, motorists dived for cover as several of the pumps fired high-velocity bullets in all directions. Instead of serving unleaded petrol, it seemed the pumps had decided to give out unpetrolled lead.

Inside the restaurant, the piped music was still oozing out of the speakers – but now it really was oozing out. It was dripping down like honey, only bright pink and much stickier. The plastic flowers were being attacked by plastic wasps. All the waiters and waitresses had broken out in spots. The one who was serving the Eliots had lost all his hair as well.

"Oh goodness!" Mildred exclaimed as her meal was set in front of her. "This cod is swimming in grease!"

And it was. It appeared that the chef had

neglected to kill it and the silvery fish was happily swimming in a large bowl of cold grease.

"I'm not sure about this spaghetti..." Eileen Eliot began. But the spaghetti was also not sure about her. It had come alive. Like an army of long, white worms, it slithered and jumped out of the bowl and, giggling to itself, raced across the table top.

The same thing had happened to Mr Eliot's. "Get back on my plate!" he demanded, jabbing at the table with a fork. But the spaghetti ignored him, hurrying away to join two naked and headless chickens that had just escaped from the kitchen, running out on their drumsticks.

"This place is a madhouse!" Mr Eliot said. "Let's get out of here!"

Eileen and Mildred agreed, but even leaving the restaurant wasn't easy. The revolving doors were revolving so fast that walking into them was like walking into a food processor, and two policemen and a lorry driver had already been shredded. But eventually they found a fire exit and made their way round to the carpark where their car was waiting.

"This would never happen in Japan," Mildred exclaimed.

"I'll put her in the boot!" Mr Eliot muttered

as he started the engine. "I wish I'd never brought her..."

"What is going on?" Eileen Eliot moaned.

The Rolls Royce reversed over somebody's picnic and into a wastepaper basket. "Margate, here we come!" Mr Eliot cried.

Mildred Eliot sat miserably on the back seat with her handbag beside her. Although she hadn't noticed it and probably wouldn't have mentioned it if she had, the handbag had begun to glow with a strange green light. And there was something inside it, humming softly and vibrating.

The Rolls Royce swerved back on to the motorway and continued its journey south.

David clung on for dear life, suspended between the ocean bubbling below and the storm clouds swirling above. Every gust of wind threatened to knock him off his perch and the wind never stopped. There wasn't a muscle in his body that wasn't aching and yet he couldn't relax, not for an instant. He had to concentrate. With his hands clamped in front of him, his arms rigid, his face lashed by the rain, he urged the broomstick on.

It had been Vincent's idea.

Mrs Windergast's broomstick was the only way off the island. Even if they had been able to take Captain Bloodbath's boat, the sea was far too rough for sailing. Mrs Windergast had taught them the basic theory of broomstick flying. True, they had never tried it before and certainly not in a full-blown storm. But as soon as Vincent had suggested it, David knew it was the only way.

They had taken the broomstick from Mrs Windergast's room. Normally the door would have been locked and the room would certainly have been protected by a magic spell. But everything had changed in the storm. The staff and pupils had vanished, taking shelter in the caverns below while the elements – the sea, the wind, the lightning and the rain – joined forces to destroy the island. Mrs Windergast's room was empty but one of the windows had been shattered and pools of water and broken glass covered the carpet. There were papers everywhere. The curtains flapped madly against the wall. The broomstick lay on its side, half hidden by a chair.

"You know where you're going?" Jill called out. She had to raise her voice to make herself heard above the storm.

David nodded. A half-remembered line here and a few spoken words there had come together and everything had clicked. He had worked it out.

His parents. After they left Groosham Grange

they were taking Mildred back to her home in Margate. Edward Eliot had told him as much in the letter he had written a few weeks before. And where was Margate? Just a few miles north of Canterbury.

And what had Aunt Mildred said as she got into the car? *I'm sure it wasn't as heavy as this when I set out...* She had lost her handbag. It had been handed back to her – but heavier than before. David was certain. Somebody had hidden the Grail inside the handbag. And she had unwittingly carried it off the island.

Clutching the broomstick in Mrs Windergast's room, David knew that he had to fly south, somehow find the orange Rolls Royce and intercept it before it reached Margate. Someone would be waiting for it at the other end. But who? That was still a mystery.

"Be careful," Vincent said. "It's not as easy as it looks."

"And hurry, David," Jill added. "The school's powers are failing. If the Grail gets too close to Canterbury, the broomstick won't fly. You'll fall. You'll be killed."

Feeling slightly ridiculous, David pushed the broomstick between his legs with the twigs poking out behind. How had Mrs Windergast done it? He concentrated and almost at once felt the stick pushing upwards. His feet left the floor and then he wasn't exactly flying but wobbling above the carpet, trying to keep his balance.

"Good luck," Vincent said.

David turned round in mid-air. "Thanks," he said. Then he and the broomstick lurched out of the window and into the storm.

The first few minutes were the worst. The wind seemed to be coming at him from all directions, invisible fists that punched at him again and again. The rain blinded him. He knew he was climbing higher but in what direction, north or south, he couldn't say. The broomstick worked through some sort of telepathy. He only had to think "right" to go that way. But if he thought too hard, the broomstick would spin round like a fairground ride and it was as much as he could do to hang on. He glimpsed Groosham Grange, rising at a crazy angle in the corner of his eye. Then it was upside-down! He had to get his bearings. He felt sick and exhausted and the journey hadn't even begun. He forced the broomstick up the right way. With his body tensed, he resisted the force of the storm. He was about a hundred metres up. And at last he had control.

And so he flew. The broomstick had no speed limit and seemed to have left the island behind in only seconds. The Norfolk coastline was already visible ahead. He relaxed, then yelled out as he collided with a flock of seagulls. Again he was blinded, aware only of grey feathers and indignant cries all around him. The control was broken and the broomstick plunged down, pulling David after it, his stomach lurching. The sea rushed up to swallow him.

"Up!" David shouted and thought it too, clamping his mind on it. Despite everything, he didn't panic. Already he understood that panic would freeze his mind and without a clear mind he couldn't fly. He relaxed everything, even his hands. And at once the broomstick responded. It had swooped down but now it curved gently up. The sea had gone. As the broomstick rose higher, David saw dry land below, the sandy beaches of the Norfolk coast. He had left the storm behind him. The sun was shining.

Swallowing hard, he turned the broomstick south and set off in pursuit of the Unholy Grail.

After David had gone, Vincent and Jill left Mrs Windergast's room and made their way downstairs, heading for the network of underground caves beneath the school. The wind was still howling outside and as they reached the main staircase a huge stained-glass window suddenly exploded inwards, showering them with multicoloured fragments of glass. They ran into the library, intending to pass through the mirror that concealed the passage down – but the windows in the room had been shattered by the storm and the mirror had broken too. A single crack ran down its face, effectively sealing it. Jill knew that if they tried to pass through a cracked mirror, they would be cut in half.

"Outside!" Vincent shouted. Jill nodded and followed him.

It was even worse outside than they had imagined. The entire island was in the grip of something like a volcanic eruption. Whole trees had been torn up, the gravestones in the cemetery blown apart, the larger tombs thrown open. The sky was midnight black, crossed and re-crossed by streaks of lightning that were like razor blades slashing at the air. The whole of the East Tower had collapsed in on itself. The rest of the school looked as if it was about to do the same.

"Look!" Jill pointed and Vincent followed her finger to the gargoyles that surrounded Groosham Grange. Their eyes were shining, bright red in the darkness, like warning lights before a nuclear explosion. At the same time, something huge and terrifying was rising up in the far distance behind the school. Jill had only just seen what it was before Vincent had grabbed her, throwing her into the safety of one of the tombs.

It was a tidal wave. The whole world disappeared in a silver-grey nightmare as the wave pounded down on the school, completely engulfing the cemetery, the wood, everything. A second later, the ground was shaken by some awful convulsion below and Jill found herself thrown into Vincent's arms.

"How much longer?" she cried. "How much more can the school take?"

Vincent had gone quite pale. He was cold and soaking wet, drenched by the water that had found its way into the tomb. "I don't know," he said. "The Grail must be getting closer to Canterbury." He looked up into the pitch-black sky. "Come on, David," he whispered. "We're running out of time."

The power of the Unholy Grail was growing steadily. And it was becoming more unpredictable and more out of control the further it was taken from Groosham Grange.

"I feel very peculiar," Mildred was saying. "It must be something I ate. I'm blowing up all over."

Eileen Eliot turned round and looked into the back of the car. The small, shrivelled woman was expanding as if someone had connected her to an air hose. Her handbag lay next to her, humming and glowing brilliantly. Mildred's shoulders and chest had torn through her clothes and she had lost a great deal of her hair. There was also something rather odd about her eyes. "It's true, Edward," Eileen squeaked. "I think we'd better take her to a doctor."

But Edward Eliot ignored her. He himself had changed during the last few minutes. His skin had become thicker, pinker. His hands and face were covered unevenly with bristles and his ears and nose had changed shape.

"Edward...?" Eileen quavered.

Mr Eliot snorted and stamped his foot down on the accelerator. Except he no longer had a foot. His shoe had come off to reveal what looked remarkably like a pig's trotter.

Eileen Eliot slumped in her seat and began to cry. All around her, the entire world was bending and twisting out of shape as the familiar turned into the insane.

One moment they were approaching a zebra crossing. Then the air seemed to shimmer and a moment later a whole herd of zebras had emerged in a stampede from a post office. Cat's eyes set in the tarmac disappeared as the cats – panthers, jaguars and tigers – leapt out to terrorize the unfortunate people of Margate. Pelican lights sprouted wings and flew off. A humpback bridge spouted a great spray of water before being harpooned by a party of Icelandic tourists.

Inside the handbag, the Unholy Grail hummed and glimmered.

Mildred's dress tore in half. She was enormous now and when she spoke again, it was not English that came out of her lips. It was Japanese. Her cheeks bulged and her great, fat legs stuck out like tree stumps.

Eileen Eliot realized what had happened. Aunt Mildred had always loved the Japanese. Now she had become one. A sumo wrestler.

"Edward..." she wept.

Mr Eliot snorted again. He was no longer able to speak. His mouth and nose had moulded themselves together and jutted forward over what was left of his chin. His teeth had also doubled in size. The sleeves of his jacket and shirt had torn open to reveal two pink, knotted arms, covered in the same spiky hair that bristled out of his neck and face.

Edward Eliot had always been a road-hog. And so the Unholy Grail had turned him into one.

Eileen Eliot took one look at him and screamed. "This can't be happening!" she whimpered. "It's horrible. Horrible! I wish I was ten thousand miles from here."

The Unholy Grail heard her. There was a sudden *whoosh!* and she felt herself being sucked out of the car in a tunnel of green light, her clothes being torn off as she went. For a few seconds the whole world disappeared. Then she was falling, screaming all the way. The ground rushed up at her and the next thing she knew she was standing in a pool of cold and muddy water that reached up to her waist.

Mrs Eliot had travelled thousands of kilometres. She was standing in a paddy field in China, surrounded by some very surprised Chinese rice farmers. Mrs Eliot smiled and fainted.

Mr Eliot had seen his wife disappear. He turned and stared at the empty seat ... not a good idea at seventy miles per hour. The next thing he knew, the car had left the road and crashed into a lamppost. Of course he hadn't bothered with a seat-belt and he was hurled, snorting and squealing, through the very expensive smoked-glass front window, out on to the pavement. Wedged in the back, her huge stomach trapped by the front seat, Aunt Mildred was unable to move. But at least her flesh had cushioned her from the impact.

The back door of the Rolls Royce had been torn open in the collision and Mildred's handbag had rolled out. It lay on the pavement, glowing more powerfully than ever. Awkwardly, Mildred poked an arm out and tried to reach it. But before her podgy fingers could close on the bag, someone appeared, leaning down to snatch it away.

Mildred gazed at the figure in astonishment. "You!" she said.

But then the person had gone. And the handbag had gone too.

Far below him, David could see the chaos that was the centre of Margate and knew with a surge of excitement that he was getting closer. He was flying at two hundred metres – high enough, he hoped, not to be seen from the ground but low enough to avoid any passing planes. He had had one nasty fright as he had crossed the Thames Estuary at Sheerness and a DC10 taking off from City Airport had cut right in front of him. There had also been some unpleasant air currents to negotiate over the flat Suffolk countryside. But he was almost there. He had done it.

But the worst surprise was still to come.

David had flown inland, leaving Margate behind him. He was actually beginning to enjoy the journey, the rush of the wind in his hair, the complete silence, the sense of freedom as he soared through the late afternoon sunlight. The broomstick was responding instantly to the slightest suggestion. Up, down, left, right – he only had to think it and he was away.

Then suddenly it stopped.

David's stomach lurched as the broomstick plummeted down and it was only by forcing his thoughts through his clenched hands and into the wooden shaft that he was able to regain control. The broomstick continued forward but more hesitantly. Then it shuddered and dipped again. David knew his worst fear had been realized. Just as Jill had warned, the Grail was approaching Canterbury. And the closer it got, the less powerful he became. Groosham Grange with all its magic was falling apart – and that included the broomstick. It was like a car running out of petrol. He could actually feel it coughing and stammering beneath him. How much further could he go?

And then he saw the cathedral. It stood at the far end of a sprawling modern town, separated from it by a cluster of houses and a swathe of perfectly mown grass. The cathedral stretched from east to west, a glinting pile of soaring towers, arched windows and silver-white roofs that looked, from this height, like some absurdly expensive Hornby model. It was there, only a few kilometres away. David urged the broomstick on. It surged obediently forward but then dropped another fifty metres. David could feel its power running out.

The broomstick reached the High Street of

Canterbury and followed it up and over the elegant Christ Church Gate and past the cathedral itself. David found himself high above the central tower. Looking down, he could see right into the cloisters. He could hear organ music drifting through the stone walls. Leaning to one side, he tilted round, looking for somewhere to land.

And that was when the broom's power failed. There was nothing he could do. Like a wounded bird he fell out of the sky, spinning round and round, still clinging to the useless broomstick that was now above his head. The cathedral had disappeared, whipped out of his field of vision. He could see the grass rushing up at him, a solid green wall.

David turned once in the air, cried out, then hit the ground and lay still.

CANTERBURY CATHEDRAL

He was still alive. He knew because of the pain. David wasn't sure how many bones there were in the human body but it felt as if he had broken every one of them. He was surprised he could even move.

He was lying on the grass like one of those chalk drawings you get after a murder. His arms and legs were sticking out at strange angles. His head was pounding and he could taste blood where he had bitten his tongue. But he was still breathing. He guessed that at the last minute the broomstick must have slowed his fall. Otherwise he wouldn't have been on the grass – he would have been underneath it.

He opened his eyes and looked around him. He had landed in the very middle of the cathedral close. On one side of him there was a wooden building – the Cathedral Welcome

Centre – and a couple of trees. Behind there was a row of houses that included the Cathedral Shop. The cathedral itself was in front of him, above him, looming over him.

It began with two towers that at some time had become home to a family of black, ragged birds. Ravens or crows perhaps. They were swooping in and out of the pointed windows, launching themselves into the sky. Then there were two lines of smaller towers, so intricately carved that they looked like something that might have grown at the bottom of the sea. At the far end there was a taller tower. It stood poised like a medieval rocket about to be launched. The sun was trapped behind it, low in the sky.

The sun…

With an effort, David sat up and saw that this third tower was casting a shadow that stretched out across the lawn, stopping only a few metres from where he lay. At the same time, he saw somebody moving towards him.

The solitary figure walked steadily forward. David squinted, raising himself on his arm. The pain made him cry out but he still couldn't see who it was. He was blinded by the light shafting into his eyes and he was still dizzy and disorientated after his fall.

"Hello, David," Mr Helliwell said.

Mr Helliwell.

He should have known all along.

David had suspected Vincent because Vincent was new. But so was Mr Helliwell. He had joined the staff at Groosham Grange at about the same time. Again, he had believed it was Vincent who had stolen one of his exam papers because Vincent had collected them. But who had he handed them to? Mr Helliwell. With his voodoo powers, it would have been easy for the teacher to animate the waxworks and, of course, he had been part of the contest in London from the start. Always Mr Helliwell. He had befriended David's parents at the prize-giving and it had been he who had found Aunt Mildred's lost handbag.

"Are you surprised to see me?" Mr Helliwell asked and smiled. In his ragged black suit, top hat and tails, he looked like some sort of mad scarecrow or perhaps a circus entertainer down on his luck.

"No," David said.

"I never thought you'd escape from the East Tower," the voodoo teacher said. He glanced at the fallen broomstick. "I presume that's Mrs Windergast's," he went on. "You really have been very resourceful, David. Very brave. I'm sorry it's all been for nothing."

He brought his hand up and now David saw

the Unholy Grail nestling in his huge palm. David tried to move but there was nothing he could do. It was just the two of them and the Unholy Grail. The cathedral had shut for the evening and the close itself was empty. The sun was creeping down towards the horizon and the whole building was shining with a soft, golden light. But the shadows were still sharp. The shadow from the third, single spire was as clear as ever, edging closer towards him as the sun set. All Mr Helliwell had to do was hold out his arm. The Unholy Grail would pass into the shadow of Canterbury Cathedral. Groosham Grange would fall.

"It's the end, David," Mr Helliwell said, his voice low and almost sad. "In a way, I'm glad you're here to see it. Of course, once I pass the Grail into the shadow, you'll crumble into dust. But I always liked you. I want you to know that."

"Thanks," David muttered through gritted teeth.

"Well. I suppose we'd better get it over with." The hand holding the Grail moved slowly. The Grail passed through the last of the sunlight.

"Wait!" David shouted. "There's one thing I want to know!"

Mr Helliwell hesitated. The Grail glittered in his hand only centimetres from the shadow of the cathedral.

"You've got to tell me," David said. He tried to stand but his legs were still too weak. "Why did you do it?"

Mr Helliwell considered. He looked up at the sky. "There's still thirty minutes' sunlight," he said. "If you think you can trick me, boy..."

"No, no." David shook his head. Even that hurt him. "You're far too clever for me, Mr Helliwell. I admit it. But I've a right to know. Why did you set me up? Why did Vincent have to win the Unholy Grail?"

"All right." Mr Helliwell relaxed, lowering the Grail. But the shadow stayed there, hungry, inching ever closer.

"When I started making my plans, I didn't care who won the Unholy Grail," Mr Helliwell began. "But then I happened to see that letter from your father." David remembered. He had dropped it in the corridor, after the fight with Vincent. Mr Helliwell had picked it up. "When I saw that your parents were coming to the prize-giving and then going on to Margate, it was too good an opportunity to miss. Somehow I'd slip it into their luggage and they'd carry it off for me. Nobody would suspect.

"But then I realized that I couldn't let you win it, David. If you had the Grail and then it disappeared, your parents would have been stopped before they got anywhere near the jetty.

People would assume you'd given it to them. But Vincent was perfect. He had no parents, no relatives. While everyone was looking for him, nobody would be looking for you or for anyone connected with you."

"So you sent the waxworks."

"Yes. I followed you to London. I was always there."

"But there's still one thing you haven't told me." The pain in David's shoulder and leg was getting worse. He wondered if he could stop himself from passing out. At the same time, his mind was racing. Was he completely helpless? Did he have any power left? "Why did you do it, Mr Helliwell?" he asked. "Why?"

The teacher laughed, a booming hollow laugh tinged with malice. "I know what you're thinking," he said. "You really believe you can catch me off guard?" Mr Helliwell reached out with his foot and pushed David back down on to the grass. David cried out and the world swam in front of his eyes but still he forced himself to stay conscious. "You are searching for magic, boy. But you have none. We've talked enough. It's time for you to join the dust of the earth..."

The Grail came up again.

"Why did you do it?" David shouted. "You were the best. One of the great voodoo magicians.

You couldn't have faked that. You were famous..."

"I was converted!" Mr Helliwell snapped out the three words and even as he spoke them a strange light came into his eyes. "An English missionary – the Bishop of Bletchley – came to Haiti and I met him. My first thought was to turn him into a toad or a snake or a water-melon. But then we got talking. We talked for hours. And he showed me the error of my ways."

"What do you mean?"

"All my life I had been evil, child. Like you. Like everyone at Groosham Grange. He persuaded me that it was time to do good. To crush the school and to kill everybody in it."

"That doesn't sound very good to me," David remarked. "Crushing and killing! What had we ever done to you?"

"You were evil!"

"That's nonsense!" And even as David began to speak he at last understood what Mr Fitch and Mr Teagle had been trying to tell him. The difference between good and evil.

"Groosham Grange isn't evil," he went on. "It's just different – that's all. Monsieur Leloup may be a werewolf and Mr Kilgraw may be a vampire but that's not their fault. They were born that way. And what about Mr Creer? Just because he's a ghost, it doesn't mean he hasn't got a right to be left in peace!"

"Evil!" Mr Helliwell insisted.

"Look who's talking!" David replied. "You're the one who's been lying and cheating. You're the one who pushed me out of the tower – and when that didn't work, you tied me up and left me to die. You stole the Unholy Grail – my parents have probably been disintegrated by now – and you've also destroyed half of Margate. You may think you're some sort of saint, Mr Helliwell, but the truth is you probably did less damage when you were a fully-fledged black magician back on Haiti!"

"You don't know what you're saying, boy..." Mr Helliwell's face had grown pale and there was a dull red flicker in his eyes. "I did what I did for the good of mankind."

"It doesn't matter why you did it or who you did it for," David insisted. "It's easy enough to say that, isn't it? But when you stop and think about what you're doing ... that's different. You're crushing and killing. You said it yourself. And I don't think that makes you a saint, Mr Helliwell. I think it makes you a monster and a fanatic."

"I ... I ... I..." Mr Helliwell was beside himself with rage. His eyes were bulging and one corner of his mouth twitched. He tried to speak but only saliva flecked over his lips. "Enough!"

he hissed. "I've listened to enough!"

Mr Helliwell raised the Unholy Grail. For a moment it caught the sun, magnifying it and splintering it into a dazzling ball of red light. The shadow cast by the one, solitary spire reached out for the Grail.

And David pushed.

In the last few seconds he had formed a plan and had stored up all his remaining strength to make it work. He had argued with the teacher to keep him busy, to divert his attention from what was about to happen. *Because as long as the Unholy Grail was out of the shadow, some power remained.* David used that power now. Guided by him, Mrs Windergast's broomstick suddenly leapt off the grass and hurtled, faster than a bullet, towards Mr Helliwell's head.

The teacher ducked. The broomstick whipped over his shoulder and continued its journey up.

"Missed!" Mr Helliwell threw back his head and laughed. "So that was what you were trying? Well, it didn't work, David. And so ... goodbye!"

With a malevolent smile, he jerked his arm out, thrusting the Unholy Grail into the shadow of Canterbury Cathedral.

But the shadow was no longer there.

Mr Helliwell frowned and looked down at

the grass. The sun was shining, uninterrupted by the spire.

"What...?" he began.

He looked up.

When David had sent the broomstick on its final journey, he hadn't been aiming at the voodoo teacher. Its flight had continued, over the man's head and up into the air, towards the cathedral. It had found its target in the church spire and, strengthened by David's magic, the wooden handle had passed clean through the stone, slicing it in half. The top of the spire had been cut off. The sun had been allowed through. The Unholy Grail was still protected by its light.

"You...!" Mr Helliwell growled.

He never finished the sentence. The broomstick had sliced through a tonne of stone. The top of the spire, a massive chunk that tapered to a point, crashed down.

It landed on Mr Helliwell.

David couldn't look. He heard a single, high-pitched scream, then a sickening thud. Something fell on to the grass, next to his hand. He reached out and took it. It was the Unholy Grail.

Moving slowly, David forced himself up on to his feet and staggered away from the rubble, taking the Grail with him. Every movement hurt him. After every step he had to stop and catch his breath. But soon he was away from the shadow of Canterbury Cathedral and, pressing the Grail against his chest, he continued on through the safety of the dying evening light.

DEPARTURE

The waves rolled in towards Skrull Island, glittering in the morning sun, then broke – silver – on the slanting rocks. A gentle breeze wafted over the shoreline, tracing patterns in the sand. Everything was peaceful. Butterflies danced in the warm sunshine and the air was filled with the scent of flowers.

It was actually the first week of December and the rest of England was covered by snow, with biting winds and cloudy skies. But the magic had returned to Groosham Grange along with the Unholy Grail. And after all the excitement, Mr Fitch and Mr Teagle had decided to give everyone three weeks' extra summer sun as a reward.

The school had been quickly restored. The moment the Grail had been put back in its right place, Groosham Grange had risen out of the rubble as proud and as strong as it had been before. Indeed, there were even a few improvements. Several of the classrooms had repainted themselves in the process and a new computer wing had mysteriously risen out of the swampland that lay to the west of the cemetery.

The staff had also been busy. It had taken a long and complicated spell to repair all the damage that had been done to both Margate and to Canterbury Cathedral, but they had managed it. Then they had made everyone involved – from the waiters and waitresses at the Snappy Eater to the police and ordinary citizens – forget everything that had happened. The Eliots and Aunt Mildred had been restored and returned home. It was small wonder that the entire school was in need of a holiday.

Two months had passed since David's flight to Canterbury. He was sitting now in Mr Kilgraw's darkened study, one leg in plaster, his face still bruised and pale. The assistant headmaster was sitting opposite him. "So have you come to a decision?" he asked.

"Yes, sir," David said. "I've decided I want to leave the school."

Mr Kilgraw nodded but said nothing. A chink of sunlight spilled through a crack in the curtain and he glanced at it distastefully. "May I ask why?" he said.

David thought for a moment. It seemed to him that he had been thinking about what he was going to say for weeks. But now that it was time to put it into words, he wasn't so sure. "I do like it here," he said. "I've been very happy. But…" He drew a breath. "I just think I've had enough magic. I feel I've learned everything I want to learn and now it's time to go back into the real world."

"To learn about life."

"Yes. I suppose so. And anyway…" This was the difficult part. "When I look back at what happened with Vincent and everything, I still think I was to blame. The truth is, I really wanted the Unholy Grail. I wanted it more than anything I've ever wanted in my life and that made me behave … badly." He broke off. The words sounded so feeble somehow. "I'm worried about how I behaved," he concluded. "And so I think it's time to go."

"Maybe you want to learn more about yourself," Mr Kilgraw said.

"I suppose so."

The assistant headmaster stood up and to David's surprise he was smiling. "You're a very remarkable young man," he said. "Our top student. The rightful winner of the Unholy Grail. And you're right. We've taught you everything you need to know. We already knew that. Why do you think we allowed all this to happen?"

It took David a few seconds to play back what Mr Kilgraw had just said and understand the meaning. "You knew about Mr Helliwell!" he stammered.

"We knew more than perhaps we pretended. But, you see, we had to be sure that you were ready. Think of it as one final test. Before your departure."

"But..." David's mind was reeling. "The Grail! Canterbury Cathedral! He came so close..."

The smile on Mr Kilgraw's face broadened. "We had complete faith in you, David. We knew you wouldn't let us down."

He went over to the door and opened it. David stood up, supporting himself on a stick. "Where do you think you'll go?" Mr Kilgraw asked.

"Well, I'm not going home, if that's what you mean," David said. "I thought I'd see a bit of the world. Mrs Windergast says that Tibet is very interesting at this time of the year..."

"You'll fly?"

"Yes." Now it was David's turn to smile. "But not on a plane."

Mr Kilgraw held out a hand. "Good luck," he said. "And remember, we'll always be here if you need us. Make sure you keep in touch."

They shook hands. David left the study and went back outside. One of the junior classes was out on the lawn – or rather, as they were practising levitation, just above it. Gregor, who had been trying to get a suntan, was sitting in a deckchair, his body gently smoking. The sun was still high in the sky. David followed the path over to the top of the cliffs. His favourite place on the island.

Vincent and Jill were waiting for him, sitting together, looking at the waves.

"Did you tell him?" Jill asked, as he arrived.

"Yes."

"What did he say?"

"He wished me luck."

"You'll probably need it," Vincent said. "I'm sorry you're going, David. I'll really miss you."

"I'll miss you too, Vincent. And you, Jill. In fact I'll even miss Gregor. But I expect we'll meet again. Somehow I don't think I've heard the last of Groosham Grange."

Vincent nodded and stood up. Jill took David's arm. And together the three friends walked down towards the sea.

Photograph © Jon Cartwright

Anthony Horowitz is the author of the number one bestselling Alex Rider books and The Power of Five series. He has enjoyed huge success as a writer for both children and adults, most recently with the latest adventure in the Alex Rider series, *Russian Roulette*, and the highly acclaimed Sherlock Holmes novel, *The House of Silk*. His latest novel, *Moriarty*, is also set in the world of Sherlock Holmes and was published in October 2014. Anthony was also chosen by the Ian Fleming estate to write the new James Bond novel which will be published this year. Anthony has won numerous awards, including the Bookseller Association/Nielsen Author of the Year Award, the Children's Book of the Year Award at the British Book Awards, and the Red House Children's Book Award. In 2014 Anthony was awarded an OBE for Services to Literature. He has also created and written many major television series, including *Injustice*, *Collision* and the award-winning *Foyle's War*.

You can find out more about Anthony and his work at:
www.alexrider.com
@AnthonyHorowitz

GROOSHAM GRANGE

More wickedly funny books

by Anthony Horowitz

The Devil and His Boy

Groosham Grange

Return to Groosham Grange

The Switch

More Bloody Horowitz

The Diamond Brothers books:

The Falcon's Malteser

Public Enemy Number Two

South by South East

The Blurred Man

The French Confection

I Know What You Did Last Wednesday

The Greek who Stole Christmas

Groosham Grange

Anthony Horowitz

WALKER BOOKS

For Nicholas

First published 1995 by Walker Books Ltd
87 Vauxhall Walk, London SE11 5HJ

This edition published 2015

2 4 6 8 10 9 7 5 3 1

This book has been typeset in Sabon

Printed in Germany by GGP Media GmbH

British Library Cataloguing in Publication Data:
a catalogue record for this book is available from the British Library

ISBN 978-1-4063-6474-3

www.walker.co.uk

CONTENTS

EXPELLED

It was dinner time at 3, Wiernotta Mews.

Mr and Mrs Eliot were sitting at the dinner table with their only son, David. The meal that night had begun with a large plate of raw cabbage with cheese sauce because Mr and Mrs Eliot never ate meat. The atmosphere in the room was distinctly chilly. That afternoon, the last day of the Christmas term, David had brought home his school report. It had not made pleasant reading.

"Eliot has not made progress," the maths teacher had written. "He can't divide or multiply and will, I fear, add up to very little."

"Woodwork?" the carpentry teacher had written. "I wish he would work!"

"If he stayed awake in class it would be a miracle," the religion teacher had complained.

"Very poor form," the form master had concluded.

"He'll never get ahead," the headmaster had agreed.

Mr Eliot had read all these comments with growing anger. First his face had gone red. Then his fingers had gone white. The veins in his neck had gone blue and his tongue had gone black. Mrs Eliot had been unsure whether to call a doctor or take a colour photograph, but in the end, and after several glasses of whisky, he had calmed down.

"When I was a boy," he moaned, "if my reports weren't first class, my father would lock me in a cupboard for a week without food. Once he chained me behind the car and drove up the M1 and that was only because I came second equal in Latin."

"Where did we go wrong?" Mrs Eliot sobbed, pulling at her mauve-tinted hair. "What will the neighbours say if they find out? They'll laugh at me! I'm ruined!"

"My father would have killed me if I'd had a report like this," Mr Eliot continued. "He'd have tied me down to the railway line and waited for the 11.05 from Charing Cross..."

"We could always pretend we haven't got a son," Mrs Eliot wailed. "We could say he's got a rare disease. We could say he fell off a cliff."

As you will have gathered from all this,

Mr and Mrs Eliot were not the best sort of parents you could hope to have. Edward Eliot was a small, fat, bald man with a bristling moustache and a wart on his neck. He was the head of a bank in the City of London. Eileen Eliot was about a foot taller than him, very thin with porcelain teeth and false eyelashes. The Eliots had been married for twenty-nine years and had seven children. David's six elder sisters had all left home. Three of them had married. Three of them had emigrated to New Zealand.

David had been sitting at the far end of the polished walnut table, eating a polished walnut, which was all he had been given. He was short for his age and also rather thin – this was probably the result of being brought up on a vegetarian diet without really liking vegetables. He had brown hair, green-blue eyes and freckles. David would have described himself as small and ugly. Girls found him cute, which in his mind was even worse.

For the last half-hour his parents had been talking as if he wasn't there. But as his mother served up the main course – leek and asparagus pie with grated carrot gravy – his father turned and stared at him with a twitching eye.

"David," he said. "Your mother and I have discussed your report and we are not pleased."

"We are not!" Mrs Eliot agreed, bursting into tears.

"And I have decided that something must be done. I tell you now, if your grandfather were still alive he'd have hung you upside down by your feet in the refrigerator. That's what he used to do to me if I so much as sneezed without asking permission! But I have decided to be a little less severe."

"That's right! Your father's an angel!" Mrs Eliot sniffed into her lace handkerchief.

"I have decided, as far as you are concerned, to cancel Christmas this year. There will be no stocking, no presents, no turkey and no snow."

"No snow?" Mrs Eliot queried.

"Not in our garden. If any falls, I shall have it removed. I have already torn December 25 out of my diary. This family will go from December 24 to December 26. However, we shall have two December 27s to make up for it."

"I don't understand," Mrs Eliot said.

"Don't interrupt, my precious," Mr Eliot said, hitting her with a spoon. "If it weren't for your mother," he went on, "I would also give you a sound beating. If you ask me, there's not enough caning in this house. I was caned every day when I was a child and it never did me any harm."

"It did do you a bit of harm," Mrs Eliot muttered in a low voice.

"Nonsense!" Mr Eliot pushed himself away from the table in his electric wheelchair. "It made me the man I am!"

"But, darling. You can't walk..."

"A small price to pay for perfect manners!"

He turned the motor on and rolled towards David with a soft, wheezy noise. "Well...?" he demanded. "What have you got to say?"

David took a deep breath. This was the moment he had been dreading all evening. "I can't go back," he said.

"Can't? Or won't?"

"Can't." David pulled a crumpled letter out of his pocket and handed it to his father. "I was going to tell you," he said. "I've been expelled."

"Expelled? Expelled!"

Edward Eliot sank into his wheelchair. His hand accidentally struck the controls and he shot backwards into the roaring flames in the fireplace. Meanwhile Eileen Eliot, who had been about to take a sip of wine, uttered a strangled shriek and spilt the whole glass down her dress.

"I didn't like it there anyway," David said. He wouldn't normally have dared mention it. But he was in so much trouble already that a little more could hardly hurt.

"Didn't like it?" his father screamed, pouring a jug of water over himself to put out the fire.

"Beton College is the best public school in the country! All the best people go to Beton. Your grandfather went to Beton. Your great-grandfather went to Beton twice he liked it so much. And you can sit there and tell me...!"

His hand found the carving knife and he might have thrown it at his only son had Mrs Eliot not thrown herself on to him first, taking six inches of stainless steel into her chest. "Why didn't you like it?" he rasped as she slid in a heap on to the carpet.

David swallowed. He'd already marked the door out of the corner of his eye. If things got really bad he might have to make a dash for the bedroom. "I thought it was silly," he said. "I didn't like having to say good morning to the teachers in Latin. I didn't like cleaning other boys' boots and wearing a top hat and tails and having to eat standing on one leg just because I was under thirteen. I didn't like not having any girls there. I thought that was weird. And I didn't like all the stupid rules. When I was expelled they cut my tie in half and painted my jacket yellow in front of the whole school..."

"But that's tradition!" Mr Eliot screeched. "That's what public schools are all about. I loved it at Beton. It didn't bother me that there were no girls. When I married your mother I didn't even know she was a girl. It took me ten years to find out!"

He reached down and plucked the carving knife out of Mrs Eliot, then used it to tear open the letter. He read:

Dear Mr Eliot,

I very much regret to have to tell you that I have been forced to expel your son, David, for constant and wilful socialism.

Quid te exempta iuvat spinis de pluribus una?

Yours sincerely,

The Headmaster,
Beton College

"What does it say?" Mrs Eliot moaned as she slowly picked herself up from the floor.

"Socialism!" In two trembling hands Mr Eliot was holding the letter which suddenly separated as he tore it in half, his elbow catching his wife in the eye.

"I don't want to go to public school," David said miserably. "I want to go to an ordinary school with ordinary people and—"

It was as far as he got. His father had pushed the controls of the wheelchair to fast forward and was even now hurtling towards him with the carving knife while his mother screamed in pain. It seemed that he had just driven over her. David made a bolt for the door, reached it and slammed it shut behind him.

"If I'd talked to my father like that he'd have made me drink a gallon of petrol and then..."

That was all he heard. He reached his bedroom and threw himself on to his bed. Downstairs he could just make out the clatter of breaking dinner plates and the muffled shouts of his parents as they blamed each other for what had happened.

It was over. It hadn't even been as bad as he had expected. But lying alone in the gloom of his bedroom, David couldn't help wondering if there wasn't going to be worse to come.

THE PROSPECTUS

By the following morning a little sanity had returned to the Eliot household and although David had not dared leave the safety of his bedroom yet, his parents were sitting down at the breakfast table almost as if nothing had happened.

"Are you feeling better today, my little bowl of nuts, oats, dried fruit and whole wheat flakes?" Mrs Eliot enquired tenderly.

"We are not a muesli," Mr Eliot replied, helping himself to some. "How is the stab wound, my dear?"

"Not too painful, thank you, my love."

They ate their cereal in silence. As usual Mr Eliot read the *Financial Times* from cover to cover, clicking his teeth, sniffing and occasionally giggling as he found out which of his clients had gone bankrupt that day. On the other side of the table, Mrs Eliot, in a bright pink dressing-gown with matching hair curlers, hid behind the *Daily Mail* and slipped a little vodka into her cereal bowl. She liked a breakfast with schnapps, crackle and pop.

It was only when they had begun their boiled eggs that they remembered David. Mr Eliot had just bashed his egg with a teaspoon when his eyes glazed over and his moustache quivered.

"David..." he snarled.

"Do you want me to call him?" Mrs Eliot asked.

"What are we going to do with him?" Mr Eliot hammered at the egg again – too hard this time. The egg exploded, showering his wife with shell. With a loud sigh he threw down the spoon and tapped the *Financial Times*. "I had always hoped he would follow me into banking," he said. "That's why I bought him a pocket calculator when he was seven and a briefcase when he was eight. Every Christmas now for ten years I've been taking him to the Stock Market as a special treat. And what thanks have I got for it, eh? Expelled!" Mr Eliot grabbed hold of the *Financial Times* and tore it into a dozen pieces. "Washed up! Finished!"

Just then there was a clatter from the hallway as the post arrived. Mrs Eliot got up and went to see what had arrived but her husband went on talking anyway.

"If only I could find a school that could lick him into shape," he muttered. "Not one of these namby-pamby modern places but somewhere that still believes in discipline. When I was young, I knew what discipline meant! These days, most children can't even spell it. Whip, whip, whip! That's what they need! A good bit of bamboo on their bums!"

Mrs Eliot walked back into the breakfast room holding the usual bundle of bills and also a large brown envelope.

"Groosham Grange..." she said in a puzzled voice.

"What?"

"That's what it says on here." She held out the brown envelope. "It's postmarked Norfolk."

Mr Eliot snatched up a knife and Mrs Eliot dived behind the table, believing he was going to use it on her again. Instead he slit open the envelope before pulling out the contents.

"Strange..." he muttered.

"What is it, my dearest?" Mrs Eliot asked nervously over the edge of the table.

"It's a prospectus ... for a boy's school." Mr Eliot wheeled himself closer to the window where the sun was streaming in. "But how could anyone have known that we'd be looking for a new school for David?"

"Perhaps Beton College told them?" his wife suggested.

"I suppose so."

Mr Eliot opened the prospectus and a letter slid out. He unfolded it and read out loud.

> Dear Mr Eliot,
>
> Have you ever wondered where you could find a school that could lick your son into shape? Not one of those namby-pamby modern places but somewhere that still believes in discipline? And has it ever worried you that these days most children can't even spell discipline?

Mr Eliot lowered the letter. "Good heavens!" he said. "That's remarkable!"

"What is?" Mrs Eliot asked.

"I was saying exactly the same thing only a moment ago! Almost word for word!"

"Go on."

Mr Eliot picked up the letter.

> Then allow us to introduce you to Groosham Grange. As you will see from the enclosed prospectus, we are a full boarding school and provide a unique environment for children aged twelve to sixteen who have proved themselves unsuited to

modern teaching methods.

Groosham Grange is situated on its own island off the coast of Norfolk. There is no regular ferry service to the island so there are no regular holidays. In fact pupils are permitted only one day's holiday a year. Parents are never invited to the school except in special circumstances – and only if they can swim.

I feel confident that your son will benefit from the excellent facilities and high teaching standards of Groosham Grange. I look forward to hearing from you in the next half-hour.

Yours sincerely,

John Kilgraw
Assistant Headmaster

"Half-hour?" Mrs Eliot said. "That doesn't give us very long to make up our minds!"

"Mine's already made up!" Mr Eliot snapped. "Only one day's holiday a year! That's a sound idea if ever I heard one." He flicked through the prospectus which, curiously, contained no photographs and was written in red ink on some sort of parchment. "Listen to this! They teach everything ... with a special emphasis on chemistry, ancient history and religious studies.

They have two language laboratories, a computer room, a fully equipped gymnasium and they're the only private school in the country with their own cemetery!" He tapped the page excitedly. "They have classes in drama, music, cookery, model-making ... and they've even got a class in astronomy."

"What would they want to have a class in a monastery for?" Mrs Eliot asked.

"I said astronomy – the study of the stars you ridiculous woman!" Mr Eliot rolled up the prospectus and hit her with it. "This is the best thing that's happened all week," he went on. "Get me a telephone."

There was a number at the bottom of the letter and Mr Eliot dialled it. There was a hiss, then a series of clicks. Mrs Eliot sighed. Her husband always hissed and clicked when he was excited. When he was in a really good mood he also whistled through his nose.

"Hello?" he said, once the connection had been made. "Can I speak to John Kilgraw?"

"This is Mr Kilgraw speaking." The voice was soft, almost a whisper. "I take it this is Mr Eliot?"

"Yes. Yes, it is. You're absolutely right!" Mr Eliot was amazed. "I got your prospectus this morning."

"And have you come to a decision?"

"Absolutely. I wish to enrol my son as soon as possible. Between you and me, Mr Kilgraw, David is a great disappointment to me. A massive disappointment. For many years I hoped he would follow in my footsteps – or at least in my wheelchair tracks, as I can't walk – but although he's almost thirteen he seems totally uninterested in merchant banking."

"Don't worry, Mr Eliot." The voice at the other end seemed to be devoid of emotion. "After a few terms at Groosham Grange I'm sure you'll find he's ... quite a different person."

"When can he start?" Mr Eliot asked.

"How about today?"

"Today?" Mrs Eliot was craning her neck to listen to the receiver. Mr Eliot swung it at her, catching her behind the ear. "I'm sorry, Mr Kilgraw," he said as she went flying. "That was just my wife's head. Did you say today?"

"Yes. There's a train leaving Liverpool Street for King's Lynn at one o'clock this afternoon. There will be two other pupils on it. David could travel with them."

"That's wonderful! Do you want me to come too?"

"Oh no, Mr Eliot." The assistant headmaster chuckled. "We don't encourage parents here at Groosham Grange. We find our pupils respond more quickly if they are completely removed from home and family. Of course, if you really want to make the long and tedious journey..."

"No! No! I'll just put him in a taxi to the station. On second thoughts, make that a bus."

"Then we'll look forward to seeing him this evening. Goodbye, Mr Eliot."

The phone went dead.

"They've accepted him!" Mr Eliot crowed. Mrs Eliot held the telephone out and he slammed the receiver down, accidentally crushing three of her fingers.

Just then the door opened and David came in, now wearing a T-shirt and jeans. Nervously he took his place at the table and reached out for the cereal packet. At the same time his father rocketed towards him and snatched it away, sending muesli in a shower over his shoulder. Mrs Eliot had meanwhile plunged her swollen fingers into the milk. David sighed. It looked as if he was going to have to give breakfast a miss.

"You don't have time to eat," Mr Eliot declared. "You've got to go upstairs and pack."

"Where am I going?" David asked.

"You're going to a wonderful school that I've found for you. A perfect school. A glorious school."

"But it's the end of term..." David began.

"The terms never end," his father replied. "That's what's so glorious about it. Pack your mother and kiss your clothes goodbye. No!" He banged his head against the table. "Kiss your mother and pack your clothes. Your train leaves at one."

David stared at his mother, who had begun to cry once again – though whether it was because he was leaving, because of the pain in her fingers or because she had somehow managed to get her hand jammed in the milk jug he could not say. There was obviously no point in arguing. The last time he'd tried arguing, his father had locked him in his bedroom and nailed up the door. It had taken two carpenters and the fire brigade a week to get it open again. Silently, he got up and walked out of the room.

It didn't take him long to pack. He had no uniform for the new school and no idea what books to take. He was neither happy nor particularly sad. After all, his father had already cancelled Christmas and whatever the school was like it could hardly be worse than Wiernotta Mews. But as he was folding his clothes he felt something strange. He was being watched. He was sure of it.

Closing his case, he walked over to the window and looked out. His bedroom had a view over the garden which was made entirely of plastic, as his mother was allergic to flowers. And there, standing in the middle of the plastic lawn, he saw it. It was a crow, or perhaps a raven. Whatever it was, it was the biggest bird he had ever seen. It was pitch-black, its feathers hanging off it like a tattered cloak. And it was staring up at the bedroom, its glistening eyes fixed on him.

David reached down to open the window. At the same moment, the bird uttered a ghastly, gurgling croak and launched itself into the air. David watched it fly away over the rooftops. Then he turned back and got ready to leave.

TRAVELLING COMPANIONS

David arrived at Liverpool Street Station at twelve o'clock. True to his word, his father had sent him on the bus. His mother hadn't come either. She had gone into hysterics on the doorstep and Mr Eliot had been forced to break a milk bottle over her head to calm her down. So David was quite alone as he dragged his suitcase across the forecourt and joined the queue to pick up his ticket.

It was a long queue – longer, in fact, than the trains everyone was waiting to get on. David had to wait more than twenty minutes before he reached a window and it was almost one o'clock before he was able to run for his train. A seat had been reserved for him – the school had arranged that – and he just had time to heave his case on to the luggage rack and sit down before the whistle went and the train began to move. Pressing his face against the glass, he stared out. Slowly the train picked up speed and London shuddered and rattled away. It had begun to rain. The scene could hardly have been more gloomy if he had been sitting in a hearse on the way to his own funeral.

Half an hour later they had travelled through the suburbs and the train was speeding past a number of dreary fields – all fields look much the same when they're seen through a train window, especially when the window is covered with half an inch of dust. David hadn't time to buy himself a book or a comic, and anyway his parents hadn't given him any money. Dejectedly, he slumped back in his seat and prepared to sit out the three hour journey to King's Lynn.

For the first time he noticed that there were two other people in the compartment, both the same age as him, both looking as fed up as he felt. One was a boy, plump, with circular wire-framed glasses. His trousers might have been the bottom of a school uniform. On top he was wearing a thick jersey made of so much wool that it looked as if the sheep might still be somewhere inside. He had long black hair that had been blown all over the place, as if he had just taken his head out of the washing machine. He was holding a half-eaten Mars bar, the toffee trailing over his fingers.

The other traveller was a girl. She had a round, rather boyish face with short brown hair and blue eyes. She was quite pretty in a way, David thought, or would have been if her clothes weren't quite so peculiar. The cardigan she was wearing could have belonged to her grandmother. Her trousers could have come from her brother. And wherever her coat had come from it should have gone back immediately, as it was several sizes too big for her. She was reading a magazine. David glanced at the cover and was surprised to see that it was *Cosmopolitan*. His mother wouldn't even allow *Cosmopolitan* in the house. She said she didn't approve of "these modern women", but then, of course, his mother was virtually prehistoric.

It was the girl who broke the silence. "I'm Jill," she said.

"I'm David."

"I'm J-J-Jeffrey." It was somehow not surprising that the fat boy had a stutter.

"I suppose you're off to this Ghastly Grange?" Jill asked, folding up the magazine.

"I think it's Groosham," David told her.

"I'm sure it will be gruesome," Jill agreed. "It's my fourth school in three years and it's the only one that doesn't have any holidays."

"W-w-one day a year," Jeffrey stammered.

"W-w-one day's going to be enough for me," Jill said. "The moment I arrive I'm heading out again."

"You'll swim away?" David asked. "It's on an island, remember."

"I'll swim all the way back to London if I have to," Jill declared.

Now that the ice had been broken, the three of them began to talk, each telling their own story to explain how they had ended up on a train bound for the Norfolk coast. David was first. He told them about Beton College, how he had been expelled and how his parents had received the news.

"I was also at p-p-public school," Jeffrey said. "And I was expelled too. I was c-c-caught smoking behind the cricket pavilion."

"Smoking is stupid," Jill said.

"It wasn't m-m-my fault. The school bully had just set fire to me." Jeffrey took off his glasses and wiped them on his sleeve. "I was always being b-b-bullied because I'm fat and I wear glasses and I've got a s-s-stutter."

Jeffrey's public school was called Godlesston. It was in the north of Scotland and his parents had sent him there in the hope of toughening him up. It had certainly been tough. Cold showers, twenty mile runs, porridge fourteen times a week – and that was just for the staff.

At Godlesston, the pupils had been expected to do fifty press-ups before morning chapel and twenty-one more during it. The headmaster had come to classes wearing a leopard skin and the gym teacher had bicycled to the school every day, which was all the more remarkable as he lived in the Midlands.

Poor Jeffrey had been completely unable to keep up and for him the last day of term really had been the last. The morning after he had been expelled, his father had received a prospectus from Groosham Grange. The letter that went with it had been rather different from David's. It had made the school sound like a sports complex, a massage parlour and an army training camp all rolled into one.

"My dad also got a letter from them," Jill said. "But they told him that Groosham Grange was a really classy place. They said I'd learn table manners, and embroidery and all that sort of stuff."

Jill's father was a diplomat, working in South America. Her mother was an actress. Neither of them were ever at home and the only time she spoke to them was on the telephone. Once her mother had bumped into her in the street and had been unable to remember who she was. But like David's parents, they were determined to give her a good education and had sent her to no less than three private schools.

"I ran away from the first two," she explained. "The third was a sort of finishing school in Switzerland. I had to learn flower arranging and cookery, but I was hopeless. My flowers died before I could arrange them and I gave the cookery teacher food poisoning."

"What happened then?" David asked.

"The finishing school said they were finished with me. They sent me back home. That was when the letter arrived."

Jill's father had jumped at the opportunity. Actually, he had jumped on an aeroplane and gone back to South America. Her mother hadn't even come home. She'd just been given two parts in a Christmas pantomime – playing both halves of the horse – and she was too busy to care. Her German nanny had made all the arrangements without really understanding any of them. And that was that.

By the time they had finished telling their stories, David realized that they all had one thing in common. One way or another they were "difficult" children. But even so, they had no idea what to expect at Groosham Grange. In his parents' letter it had been described as old-fashioned, and for boys only. Jeffrey's parents had been told it was some sort of educational assault course. And

Jill's parents thought they were sending their daughter to a posh ladies' college.

"They could be three completely different places," David said. "But it's the same school."

"And there's something else p-p-peculiar," Jeffrey added. "It's meant to be on an island next to N-N-Norfolk. But I looked on the map and there are no islands. Not one."

They thought about this for a while without speaking. The train had stopped at a station and there was a bustle in the corridor as people got on and off. Then David spoke.

"Listen," he said. "However bad this Groosham Grange is, at least we're all going there together. So we ought to make a pact. We'll stick together ... us against them."

"Like the Three M-M-Musketeers?" Jeffrey asked.

"Sort of. We won't tell anybody. It'll be like a secret society. And whatever happens, we'll always have two people we can trust."

"I'm still going to run away," Jill muttered.

"Maybe we'll go with you. At least we'll be able to help you."

"I'll lend you my swimming trunks," Jeffrey said.

Jill glanced at his bulging waist, thinking they would probably be more helpful if she used them in a parachute jump. But she kept the thought to herself. "All right," she agreed. "Us against them."

"Us against th-th-them."

"Us against them." David held out his hand and the three of them shook.

Then the door of the compartment slid open and a young man looked in. The first thing David noticed was his dog-collar – he was a vicar. The second thing was that he was holding a guitar.

"Is that free?" he asked, nodding at one of the empty seats.

"Yes." David would have preferred to have lied. The last thing he needed right now was a singing vicar. But it was obvious that they were alone.

The young man came into the compartment, beaming at them in that horrible way that very religious people sometimes do. He didn't put his guitar up on the luggage rack but leant it against the opposite seat. He was in his thirties, with pink, rosy cheeks, fair hair, a beard and unusually bright teeth. As well as the dog-collar he was wearing a silver crucifix, a St Christopher medallion and a BAN THE BOMB sign.

"I'm Father Percival," he announced, as if anybody was slightly interested in who he was. "But you can call me Jimbo." David glanced at his watch and groaned silently. There were still at least two hours to King's Lynn and already the priest was working himself up as if any moment he was going to burst into song.

"So where are you kids off to?" he demanded. "Going on hols together? Or having a day out?"

"We're going to s-s-school," Jeffrey told him.

"School? Fab! Triffic!" The priest looked at them and suddenly realized that none of them thought it was at all fab or triffic. "Hey – cheer up!" he exclaimed. "Life's a great journey and it's first-class all the way when you're travelling with Jesus."

"I thought you said your name was Jimbo," Jill muttered.

"I'll tell you what," the vicar went on, ignoring her. "I know how to cheer you youngsters up." He picked up his guitar and twanged at the strings. They were horribly out of tune. "How about a few hymns? I made this one up myself. I call it 'Jesus, You're My Buddy' and it goes like this..."

In the hour that followed, Jimbo played six of his own compositions, followed by 'Onward Christian Soldiers', 'All Things Bright and Beautiful' and, because Christmas was approaching, a dozen carols. At last he stopped and rested his guitar on his knees. David held his breath, praying that the vicar wouldn't finish off with a sermon or, worse still, pass the collection plate around the carriage. But he seemed to have exhausted himself as well as them.

"So what are your names?" he asked.

Jill told him.

"Great! That's really super. Now tell me – Dave, Jeff and Jilly – you say you're off to school. What school's that?"

"Groosham Grange," David told him.

"Groosham Grange?" The vicar's mouth dropped open. In one second all the colour had drained out of his face. His eyes bulged and one of his cheeks, no longer rosy, twitched. "Groosham Grange?" he whispered. His whole body had begun to tremble. Slowly his fair hair rippled and then stood on end.

David stared at him. The man was terrified. David had never seen anyone quite so afraid. What had he said? He had only mentioned the school's name, but now the vicar was looking at him as if he were the devil himself.

"Grrooosss..." The vicar tried to say the words for a third time but they seemed to get caught on his lips and he hissed like a punctured balloon. His eyeballs were standing out like ping-pong balls now. His throat had gone dark mauve and it was evident from the way his body shuddered that he was no longer able to breathe.

"...ssss." The hiss died away. The vicar's hands, suddenly claws, jerked upwards, clutching at his heart. Then he collapsed, falling to the ground with a crash, a clatter and a twang.

"Oh dear," Jill said. "I think he's dead."

SKRULL ISLAND

The vicar had suffered a massive heart attack but he wasn't actually dead. The guard telephoned ahead, and at King's Lynn station a British Rail porter was standing by to whisk him away on a trolley to a waiting ambulance. David, Jill and Jeffrey were also met. One glance at the man who was looking out for them and they would have quite happily taken the ambulance.

He was horribly deformed. If he had been involved in a dreadful car crash and then fallen into an industrial mangle it could only have improved him. He was about five foot tall – or five foot short rather, for his head was closer to the ground than to his shoulders. This was partly due to the fact that his neck seemed to be broken, partly due to his hunched back. One of his eyes was several centimetres lower than the other and he had swollen cheeks and thin, straggly hair. He was dressed in a loose leather jacket and baggy trousers. People walking along the station were trying so hard not to look at him that one unfortunate woman accidentally fell off the platform. In truth it was hard to look at anything else. He was holding a placard that read GROOSHAM GRANGE. With a sinking heart, David approached him, Jeffrey and Jill following behind.

"My name is Gregor," he said. His voice came out as a throaty gurgle. "Did you have a good journey?"

David had to wait for him to say this again because it sounded like, "Dit yurgh av aghoot churnik?" When he understood, he nodded, lost for words. "Bring your bags then, young masters," Gregor gurgled. "The car is outside."

The car was a hearse.

It had been repainted with the name of the school on the side, but there could be no disguising the shape, the long, flat area in the back where its grisly contents should have lain. The people in the street weren't fooled either. They stopped in respectful silence, taking off their hats as the three children were whisked away towards their new school. David wondered if he wasn't in the middle of some terrible nightmare, if he wouldn't wake up at any moment to find himself in bed at Wiernotta Mews. Cautiously, he pinched himself. It had no effect. The hunchback hooted at a van and cursed. The hearse swept through a red light.

Gregor was a most peculiar chauffeur. Because of his height and the shape of his body, he could barely see over the steering wheel. To anyone out in the street it must have looked as if the car were driving itself. It was a miracle they didn't hit anybody. David, sitting in the front seat, found himself staring at the man and blushed when Gregor turned and grinned at him.

"You're wondering how I came to look like this, young master?" he declared. "I was born like it, born all revolting. I gave my mother the heebie-jeebies, I did. Poor mother! Poor Gregor!" He wrenched at the steering wheel and they swerved to avoid a traffic island. "When I was your age, I tried to get a job in a freak show," he went on. "But they said I was overqualified. So I became the porter at Groosham Grange. I love Groosham Grange. You'll love Groosham Grange, young master. All the young masters love Groosham Grange."

They had left the city behind them now, following the coastal road up to the north. After that, David must have dozed off because the next thing he knew the sky had darkened and they seemed to be driving across the sea, the car pushing through the dark green waves. He rubbed his eyes and looked out of the window.

It wasn't the sea but a wide, flat field. The waves were grass, rippling in the wind. The field was empty but in the distance a great windmill rose up, the white panelled wood catching the last reflections of the evening sun. He shivered. Gregor had turned the heater on in the car but he could feel the desolation of the scene creeping in beneath the cushion of hot air.

Then he saw the sea itself. The road they were following – it was barely more than a track – led down to a twisted wooden jetty. A boat was waiting for them, half-hidden by the grass. It was an old fishing boat, held together by rust and lichen. Black smoke bubbled in the water beneath it. A pile of crates stood on the deck underneath a dirty net. A seagull circled in the air above it, sobbing quietly to itself. David hardly felt much better.

Gregor stopped the car. "We're here, young masters," he announced.

Taking their suitcases, they got out of the car and stood shivering in the breeze. David looked back at the way they had come but after a few twists and turns the road disappeared and he realized that they could have come from anywhere. He was in a field somewhere in Norfolk with the North Sea ahead of him. But for the windmill he could have been in China for all the difference it would have made.

"Cheerful, isn't it," Jill said.

"Where are we?" David asked.

"God knows. The last town I saw was called Hunstanton, but that was half an hour ago." She pulled her cardigan round her shoulders. "I just hope we get there soon," she said.

"Why?"

"Because the sooner we arrive, the sooner I can run away."

A man had appeared, jumping down off the boat. He was wearing thigh-length boots and a fisherman's jersey. His face was almost completely hidden by a black beard, as black as the eyes which shone at them beneath a knotted mass of hair. A gold ring hung from his left ear. Give him a sword and an eye-patch and he could have walked straight out of *Treasure Island*.

"You're late, Gregor," he announced.

"The traffic was bad, Captain Bloodbath."

"Well, the tide is worse. These are treacherous waters, Gregor. Treacherous tides and treacherous winds." He spat in the direction of the sea. "And I've got a treacherous wife waiting for me to get home, so let's get moving." He untied a rope at the end of the jetty. "All aboard!" he shouted. "You ... boy! Weigh the anchor."

David did as he was told although the anchor weighed so much that he could hardly lift it. A moment later they were away, the engine coughing, spluttering and smoking – as indeed was Captain Bloodbath. Gregor stood beside him. The three children huddled together at the back of the boat. Jeffrey had gone an unpleasant shade of green.

"I'm not m-m-much of a sailor," he whispered.

The captain had overheard him. "Don't worry!" he chortled. "This ain't much of a boat!"

A mist had crept over the water. Now its ghostly white fingers stretched out for the boat, drawing it in. In an instant the sky had disappeared and every sound – the seagull, the engine, the chopping of the waves – seemed damp and distant. Then, as suddenly as it had come, it parted. And Skrull Island lay before them.

It was about two miles long and a mile wide with thick forest to the east. At the southern end, a cliff rose sharply out of the frothing water, chalk-white at the top but a sort of muddy orange below. A twist of land jutted out of the island, curving in front of the cliff, and it was to this point that Captain Bloodbath steered the boat. Another jetty had been built here and there was an open-top Jeep standing nearby. But there was no welcoming committee, no sign of the school.

"Stand by with the anchor!" the captain called out. Assuming he meant him, David took it. Bloodbath spun the wheel, slammed the engine into reverse and shouted. David dropped the anchor. Jeffrey was sick over the side.

They had arrived.

"This way, young masters. Not far now. Just a little more driving." Gregor was the first on land, capering ahead. Jeffrey followed, weakly dragging his suitcase. David paused, waiting for Jill. She was watching Captain Bloodbath, who was already raising the anchor, backing the boat out.

"What are you waiting for?" he asked.

"We may need that boat one day," Jill muttered. "I wonder if he ever leaves it."

"Captain Bloodbath..." David shivered. "That's a funny name."

"Yes. So how come I'm not laughing?" Jill turned round and trudged along the jetty to the Jeep.

It took them five minutes to reach the school. The track curved steeply upwards, rising to the level of the cliffs, then followed the edge of the wood. Jeffrey had grabbed the seat in the driving compartment next to Gregor. David and Jill were sitting in the back, clinging on for dear life. Every time the Jeep drove over a stone or a pot-hole – and there were plenty of both – they were thrown about a foot in the air, landing with a heavy bump. By the time they arrived, David knew what it must feel like to be a salad. But he quickly forgot his discomfort as he took in his first sight of Groosham Grange.

It was a huge building, taller than it was wide; a crazy mixture of battlements, barred windows, soaring towers, slanting grey slate roofs, grinning gargoyles and ugly brick chimneys. It was as if the architects of Westminster Abbey, Victoria Station and the Brixton gasworks had jumbled all their plans together and accidentally built the result. As the Jeep pulled up outside the front door (solid wood, studded with nails and sixteen inches thick) there was a rumble overhead and a fork of lightning crackled across the sky.

Somewhere a wolf howled.

Then the door creaked slowly open.

MR KILGRAW

A woman stood in the doorway. For a moment her face was a livid blue as the lightning flashed. Then she smiled and David saw that she was, after all, human. In fact, after the peculiar horrors of Gregor and Captain Bloodbath, she seemed reassuringly normal. She was small and plump, with round cheeks and grey hair tied in a bun. Her clothes were Victorian, her high collar fastened at the neck with a silver brooch. She was about sixty years old, her skin wrinkled, her eyes twinkling behind gold half-glasses. For a moment she reminded David of his grandmother. Then he noticed the slight moustache bristling on her upper lip and decided that she reminded him of his grandfather too.

"Hello! Hello!" she trilled as the three of them climbed down from the Jeep. "You must be David. And you're Jill and Jeffrey. Welcome to Groosham Grange!" She stood back to allow them to enter, then closed the door after them. "I'm Mrs Windergast," she went on. "The school matron. I hope the journey hasn't been too tiring?"

"I'm tired," Gregor said.

"I wasn't asking you, you disgusting creature," the matron snapped. "I was talking to these dear, dear children." She beamed at them. "Our new arrivals!"

David looked past her, taking in his surroundings. He was in a cavernous entrance hall, all wood panels and musty oil paintings. A wider staircase swept upwards, leading to a gloomy corridor. The hall was lit by a chandelier. But there were no lightbulbs. Instead, about a hundred candles spluttered and burned in brass holders, thick black smoke strangling what little light they gave.

"The others are already eating their evening meal," Mrs Windergast said. "I do hope you like blood pudding." She beamed at them for a second time, not giving them a chance to answer. "Now – leave your cases here, Jeffrey and Jill. You follow me, David. Mr Kilgraw wants to see you. It's the first door on the left."

"Why does he want to see me?" David asked.

"To welcome you, of course!" The matron seemed astonished by the question. "Mr Kilgraw is the assistant headmaster," she went on. "He likes to welcome all his new pupils personally. But one at a time. I expect he'll see the others tomorrow."

Jill glanced at David and shrugged. He understood what she was trying to tell him. Mrs Windergast might seem friendly enough but there was an edge to her voice that suggested it would be better not to argue. He watched as Jill and Jeffrey were led away across the hall and through an archway, then went over to the door that the matron had indicated. His mouth had gone dry and he wondered why.

"I expect it's because I'm terrified," he muttered to himself.

Then he knocked on the door.

A voice called out from inside and, taking a deep breath, David opened the door and went in. He found himself in a study lined with books on one side and pictures on the other with a full-length mirror in the middle. There was something very strange about the mirror. David noticed at once but he couldn't say exactly what it was. The glass had been cracked in one corner and the gilt frame was slightly warped. But it wasn't that. It was something else, something that made the hairs on the back of his neck stand up as if they wanted to climb out of his skin and get out of the room as fast as they could.

With an effort, he turned his eyes away. The furniture in the study was old and shabby. There was nothing strange about that. Teachers always seemed to surround themselves with old, shabby furniture – although the dust and the cobwebs were surely taking things a bit too far. Opposite the door, in front of a red velvet curtain, a man was sitting at a desk, reading a book. As David entered, he looked up, his face expressionless.

"Please sit down," he said.

It was impossible to say how old the man was. His skin was pale and somehow ageless, like a wax model. He was dressed in a plain black suit, with a white shirt and a black tie. As David sat down in front of the desk, the man closed the book with long, bony fingers. He was incredibly thin. His movements were slow and careful. It was as if one gust of wind, one cough, or one sneeze would shatter him into a hundred pieces.

"My name is Kilgraw," he continued. "I am very happy to see you at last, David. We are all happy that you have come to Groosham Grange."

David wasn't at all happy about it, but he said nothing.

"I congratulate you," Mr Kilgraw went on. "The school may seem unusual to you at first glance. It may even seem ... abnormal. But let me assure you, David, what we can teach you, what we can offer you is beyond your wildest dreams. Are you with me?"

"Yes, sir."

Mr Kilgraw smiled – if you could call a twitching lip and a glint of white teeth a smile. "Don't fight us, David," he said. "Try and understand us. We are different. But so are you. That is why you have been chosen. The seventh son of the seventh son. It makes you special, David. Just how special you will soon find out."

David nodded, searching for the door out of the corner of his eye. He hadn't understood anything Mr Kilgraw had said but it was obvious that the man was a complete nutcase. It was true that he had six elder sisters and six gruesome aunts (his father's sisters) who bought him unsuitable presents every Christmas and poked and prodded him as if he were made of Plasticine. But how did that make him special? And in what way had he been chosen? He would never have heard of Groosham Grange if he hadn't been expelled from Beton.

"Things will become clearer to you in due course," Mr Kilgraw said as if reading his mind. And in all probability he had read his mind. David would hardly have been surprised if the assistant headmaster had pulled off a mask and revealed that he came from the planet Venus. "But all that matters now is that you are here. You have arrived. You are where you were meant to be."

Mr Kilgraw stood up and moved round the desk. There was a second, black-covered book resting at the edge and next to it an old-fashioned quill pen. Licking his fingers, he opened it, then leafed through the pages. David glanced over the top of the desk. From what he could see, the book seemed to be a list of names, written in some sort of brown ink. Mr Kilgraw reached a blank page and picked up the quill.

"We have an old custom at Groosham Grange," he explained. "We ask our new pupils to sign their names in the school register. You and your two friends will bring the total up to sixty-five who are with us at present. That is five times thirteen, David. A very good number."

David had no idea why sixty-five should be any better than sixty-six or sixty-four, but he decided not to argue. Instead, he reached out for the quill. And it was then that it happened.

As David reached out, Mr Kilgraw jerked forward. The sharp nib of the quill jabbed into David's thumb, cutting him. He cried out and shoved his thumb into his mouth.

"I'm so sorry," Mr Kilgraw said. He didn't sound sorry at all. "Are you hurt? I can ask Mrs

Windergast to have a look at it, if you like."

"I'm all right." David was angry now. He didn't mind if Mr Kilgraw wanted to play some sort of game with him. But he hated being treated like a baby.

"In that case, perhaps you'd be so good as to sign your name." Mr Kilgraw held out his pen but now it was stained bright red with David's blood. "We won't need any ink," he remarked.

David took it. He looked for ink on the desk but there wasn't any. The assistant headmaster was leaning over him, breathing into his ear. Now all David wanted was to get out of there, to get something to eat and to go to bed. He signed his name, the nib scratching red lines across the coarse white paper.

"Excellent!" Mr Kilgraw took the pen and slid the book round. "You can go now, David. Mrs Windergast will be waiting for you outside."

David moved towards the door, but Mr Kilgraw stopped him. "I do want you to be happy here, David," he said. "We at Groosham Grange have your best interests at heart. We're here to help you. And once you accept that, I promise you, you'll never look back. Believe me."

David didn't believe him but he had no intention of arguing about it now. He went to the door as quickly as he could, forcing himself not to run. Because he had seen what was wrong with the mirror. He had seen it the moment after he had signed his name in blood, the moment he had turned away from the desk.

The mirror had reflected everything in the room. It had reflected the desk, the books, the curtains, the furniture, the carpet and David himself.

But it hadn't reflected Mr Kilgraw.

THE FIRST DAY

7.00 a.m.

Woke up with a bell jangling in my ear. The dormitory is high up in one of the school's towers. It is completely circular with the beds arranged like the numbers on the clock face. I'm at seven o'clock (which is also the time as I sit here writing this). Jeffrey is next to me at six o'clock. His pillow is on the floor, his sheets are all crumpled and he has somehow managed to tie his blanket in a knot. No sign of Jill. The girls all sleep in another wing.

7.30 a.m.

I am now washed and dressed. One of the boys showed me the way to the bathroom. He told me his name was William Rufus, which was a bit puzzling as I saw the name-tape on his pyjamas and it said James Stephens. I asked him why he was wearing somebody else's pyjamas but he just smiled as if he knew something that I didn't. I think he does know something I don't!

I don't think I like the boys at Groosham Grange. They're not stuck up like everyone at Beton College, but they are ... different. There was no talking after lights out. There was no pillow fight. Nothing. At Beton College every new boy was given an apple-pie bed – and they used real apple pies. Here, nobody seems at all interested in me. It's as if I weren't here at all (and I wish I weren't).

7.45 a.m.

Breakfast. Eggs and bacon. But the bacon was raw and the eggs certainly didn't come out of a chicken! I have lost my appetite.

9.30 a.m.

William Rufus – if that really is his name – took me to my first lesson. He is short and scrawny with a turned-up nose and baby-blue eyes. He was just the sort who would always have been bullied at Beton, but I don't think there is any bullying at Groosham Grange. Everyone is too polite. I don't believe I just wrote that! Whoever heard of a polite schoolboy?

William and I had a weird discussion on the

way to the classroom.

"It's double Latin," he said.

"I hate Latin," I remarked.

I thought we'd have at least one thing in common, but I was wrong. "You'll like it here," he told me. "It's taught by Mr Kilgraw and he's very good."

He looked at his watch. "We'd better hurry or we'll be late."

"What's the punishment for being late?" I asked.

"There are no punishments at Groosham Grange."

Good Latin teachers? A school with no punishments? Have I gone mad?

But double Latin wasn't as bad as it sounded. At Beton College it was taught as a "dead" language. And the teacher wasn't much healthier. But Mr Kilgraw spoke it fluently! So did everyone else! By the end of the lesson they were chatting like old friends and nobody even mentioned Caesar or the invasion of Gaul.

Another odd thing. It was a bright day, but Mr Kilgraw taught with the shutters closed and with a candle on his desk. I asked William Rufus about this.

"He doesn't like the sun," William said. At least, I think that's what he said. He was still talking in Latin.

11.00 a.m.
Saw Jill briefly in the break. Told her about this diary. She told me about her day so far. For some reason she's in a different class to Jeffrey and me.

"I had Mr Creer for modelling," she said.

"Pots?" I asked.

"Completely pots. We had to make figures out of wax. Men and women. And he used real hair."

Jill showed me her thumb. It was cut just like mine. She had seen Mr Kilgraw immediately after breakfast.

"I'm seeing him after lunch," Jeffrey said.

"Bring your own ink," Jill suggested.

12.30 p.m.
English with Miss Pedicure.

Miss Pedicure must be at least a hundred years old. She is half blind and completely bald. I think she's only held together by bandages. She seems to be wrapped up in them from head to toe. I could see them poking out of her sleeves and above her collar. It took her fifteen minutes to reach her chair and when she sat down she almost disappeared in a cloud of dust.

Miss Pedicure does have perfect teeth. The only trouble is, she keeps them in a glass on the corner of her desk.

She taught Shakespeare. From the way she talks, you'd think she knew him personally!

1.15 p.m.
Lunch. Mince. But what was the animal before it was minced? I think I am going to starve to death.

3.00 p.m.
I was meant to have French this afternoon but the teacher didn't show up. I asked William Rufus why.

WILLIAM: It must be a full moon tonight. Monsieur Leloup never teaches when there's going to be a full moon.

ME: Is he ill?

WILLIAM: Well, he isn't quite himself...

We all had books to read but I couldn't make head nor tail of them. I spent most of the lesson writing this, then examined the other kids in the class. I know most of their names now. Marion Grant – red-headed with freckles and big teeth. Bessie Dunlop – thin and pretty if you don't look too close. Roger Bacon – Hong Kong Chinese. Since when was Roger Bacon a Chinese name?

In fact all these names sound wrong. Bessie just doesn't look like a Bessie. Why is it that I think everyone is sharing some sort of horrible secret? And that Jeffrey, Jill and me are the only ones on the outside?

4.30 p.m.
Football. We played with an inflated pig's bladder. I scored a goal, but I didn't feel too good about it. You should try heading an inflated pig's bladder...

6.00 p.m.
We ate the rest of the pig for tea. It was turning on a spit with an apple in its mouth. At least I managed to grab the apple!

6.30 p.m.
I am back in Monsieur Leloup's classroom doing prep. That's what I'm supposed to be doing anyway. Instead I'm writing this. And I've just noticed something. I suppose I noticed it from the very start. But it's only just now that I've realized what it is.

Everyone in the class is wearing a ring. The same ring. It is a band of plain gold with a single black stone set in the top. What on earth does it mean? I've heard of school caps and school badges, but school rings?

I have re-read my first day's diary. It doesn't make a lot of sense. It's as if I've been seeing everything on a video recorder that's been fast forwarded. I get the pieces but not the whole picture.

But if I wrote down everything I'd end up

with a whole book. And something tells me I ought to leave time for my will.

7.30 p.m.
An hour's free time before bed. No sign of Jeffrey or Jill. Went for a walk in the fresh air.

The football field is at the back of the school. Next to it there's a forest – the thickest I've ever seen. It can't be very big but the trees look like a solid wall. There's a chapel at the back and also a small cemetery.

Saw Gregor sitting on a gravestone, smoking a cigarette. "Too many of those, Gregor," I said, "and you'll be under it!" This was a joke. Gregor did not laugh.

8.15 p.m.
Happened to see Jeffrey chatting to William Rufus. The two looked like the best of friends. Is this worrying?

8.40 p.m.
In bed. The lights go out in five minutes.

I had a bath this evening. The bathroom is antique. When you turn on the tap the water rushes out like the Niagara Falls, only muddier. Got out of the bath dirtier than when I went in. Next time I'll shower.

After I'd finished writing the last entry in this diary, I put it away in the cupboard beside the bed with a pencil to mark the place. When I got back, the diary was in exactly the same position, but the pencil had rolled out.

SOMEBODY READ THIS WHILE I WAS OUT OF THE ROOM!

So I won't be writing any more so long as I'm at Groosham Grange. I have a feeling it would be better to keep my thoughts to myself.

Questions:

Are all the names false? If so, why?

What is the meaning of the black rings?

What's really going on at Groosham Grange?

And don't worry, whoever's reading this. Somehow I'm going to find the answers.

IN THE DARK

Despite his resolution, David had learnt nothing by the end of the next day. The school routine had ticked on as normal – breakfast, Latin, history, break, maths, lunch, geography, football – except that none of it was remotely normal. It was as if everything, the lessons and the books, was just an elaborate charade, and that only when it was sure that nobody was looking the school would reveal itself in its true colours.

It was half past seven in the evening. David was working on an essay in the school library – a room that was unusual in itself in that it didn't have any books. Instead of bookshelves, the walls were lined with the heads of stuffed animals gazing out of wooden mounts with empty glass eyes. Not surprisingly, David hadn't found it very easy to concentrate on Elizabethan history with two moles, an armadillo and a wart-hog staring over his shoulder.

After twenty minutes, he gave up. He had no interest in the Spanish Armada and he suspected he could say the same for Miss Pedicure (who also taught history). He examined the page he had just finished. It was more ink-blots and crossing out than anything else. With a sigh he crumpled it in a ball and threw it at the dust-bin. It missed and hit the large mirror behind it. David sighed again and went over to retrieve it. But it had gone. He searched behind the dust-bin, under the chairs and all over the carpet in front of the mirror. But the ball of paper had vanished without trace. Suddenly, and for no good reason, David felt nervous. He glanced over his shoulder. The wart-hog seemed to be grinning at him. He hurried out of the library, slamming the door behind him.

A narrow, arched passageway led out from the library and back into the main hall. This was the passage he had come down on his first evening at Groosham Grange. It went past the door of Mr Kilgraw's study and now he paused outside it, remembering. That was when he heard the voices.

They were coming from the room opposite Mr Kilgraw's, a room with a dark panelled door and the single word HEADS painted in gold letters. So Groosham Grange had not one but two headmasters! David filed the knowledge away, puzzled that he hadn't yet seen either of them. He quickly looked about him. The other pupils had already left the library ahead of him. He was alone in the passage. Pretending to tie up his shoelace, he knelt beside the door.

"...settled in very well, I think." David recognized the voice at once. There could be no mistaking the dusty syllables of Mr Kilgraw. "The girl was a touch difficult in her modelling class, but I suppose that's only to be expected."

"But they all signed?" This was a high-pitched, half-strangled voice. David could imagine someone inside the room, struggling with a tie that was tied too tight.

"There was no problem, Mr Teagle." Mr Kilgraw laughed, a curiously melancholy sound. "Jeffrey – the boy with the stutter – came in last. He brought his own pencil. And two bottles of ink! In the end I had to hypnotize him, I'm afraid. After that, it was easy."

"You think this Jeffrey is going to be difficult?" This voice was the softest of the three. The second headmaster didn't speak so much as whisper.

"No, Mr Fitch," Mr Kilgraw replied. "If anything, he'll be the easiest. No. The one I'm worried about is Eliot."

"What's wrong with him?"

"I don't know for sure, Mr Teagle. But he has a certain strength, an independence..."

"That's just what we need."

"Of course. But even so..."

David was desperate to hear more of the conversation but just then Mrs Windergast appeared, walking towards the library. Seeing him, she stopped and blinked, her eyes flickering behind the half-glasses.

"Is there anything the matter, David?" she asked.

"No." David pointed feebly at his shoes. "I was just tying my lace."

"Very wise of you, my dear." She smiled at him. "We don't want you tripping over and breaking something, do we? But perhaps this isn't the place to do it – right outside the headmasters' study. Because somebody might think you were eavesdropping and that wouldn't be a very good impression to give in your first week, would it?"

"No," David agreed. He straightened up. "I'm sorry, Mrs Windergast."

He moved away as quickly as he could. The matron brushed past him and went into the headmasters' study. David would have given his right arm to have heard what they were saying now. But if he was found outside the door a second time, they would probably take it.

Instead he went in search of Jeffrey and Jill. He found them outside the staff room. Jill was examining the pigeon holes, each one labelled with the name of one of the teachers.

"Have you seen Monsieur Leloup's pigeon hole?" she asked, seeing him.

"What about it?"

"It's got a pigeon in it." She pointed at it, grimacing. The bird was obviously dead. "It looks like some wild animal got it."

"What's it doing there?" David asked.

"You'll have to ask Monsieur Leloup," Jill said.

"If he ever sh-sh-shows up," Jeffrey added.

Together they walked back down the corridor. One side was lined with lockers. The other opened into classrooms. A couple of boys passed them, making their way up to the dormitories. There was almost an hour until the bell went, but it seemed that most of the pupils of Groosham Grange had already gone to bed. As ever, the silence in the school would have been better suited to a museum or a monastery. In the entire day, David hadn't heard a door slam or a desk bang. What was going on at Groosham Grange?

They found an empty classroom and went into it. David hadn't been in this room yet and looked around him curiously. The walls were covered with posters showing various animals – inside and out. Instead of a desk, the teacher had a long marble slab which was covered with scientific apparatus: a burner, a small metal cauldron and various bottles of chemicals. At the far end, a white rat cowered in a cage and two toads stared unhappily out of a glass tank. The skeleton of some sort of animal stood in one corner.

"This must be the biology lab," David whispered.

"I wish it was," Jill shook her head. "All this stuff has been left out since my first class this afternoon."

"What c-c-class was that?" Jeffrey asked.

"Cookery."

David swallowed, remembering the mince.

Jill sat down behind one of the desks. "So let's compare notes," she said.

"Our first two days at Groosham Grange," David agreed.

"Jeffrey – you go first."

Jeffrey had little to say. He was the most miserable of the three of them, still confused after his meeting with Mr Kilgraw. He hadn't done any work at all and had spent the whole of the last lesson writing a letter to his mother, begging her to take him away. The only trouble was, of course, that there was nowhere to post it.

"I hate it here," he said. "It isn't t-t-tough like I thought it would be. But it isn't anything like I th-th-thought it would be. All the t-t-teachers are mad. And nobody's t-t-teased me about my stammer."

"I thought you didn't like being teased," David said.

"I d-d-don't. But it would be more n-n-normal if they did."

"Nothing's normal here," Jill broke in. "First of all they make us sign our names in blood. The lessons are like no lessons I've ever sat through. And then there's the business of the rings."

"I saw them too," David said.

"They're all wearing the same ring. Like some sort of bond."

"And I've found out more." David went on to describe his discoveries of the day, starting with the mystery of the pyjamas. "I may be wrong," he said, "but I get the feeling that everyone here is using false names."

"There's a boy in my class called Gideon Penman," Jill muttered.

"Exactly. What sort of a name is that?"

"B-b-but why would they have false names?" Jeffrey asked.

"And why do they want our real names in blood?" Jill added.

"I found out something about that too," David said and went on to describe the conversation outside the headmasters' study. He left out the bit about Jeffrey being the weakest of them mainly because he thought it would be cruel to mention it. But also because it was probably true. "All I can say is that the sooner we're out of here the better," he concluded. "There's something nasty going on at Groosham Grange. And if we stay here much longer I think it's going to happen to us."

Jeffrey looked accusingly at Jill. "I thought you were going to r-r-run away."

"I will." Jill glanced out of the window. "But not tonight. I think there's going to be another storm."

The storm broke a few minutes later. This time there was no lightning, but the cloudburst was spectacular nonetheless. It was as if the sea had risen up in a great tidal wave only to come crashing down on the school. At the same time, the wind whipped through it, tearing up the earth, punching into the brickwork. Loose shutters were ripped out of their frames. A gravestone exploded. A huge oak tree was snapped in half, its bare branches crashing into the soil.

It was the sound of the falling tree that woke David for the second time that day. Scrabbling in his bedside cabinet, he found his torch and flicked it on, directing the beam at his watch. It was just after midnight. He lay back against the pillow, gazing out of the window. There was a full moon; he could just make out its shape behind the curtain of rain. When he was a child, David had never been frightened by storms. So he was surprised to find that he was trembling now.

But it wasn't the weather. In the brief moment that the torch had been on, he had noticed something out of the corner of his eye, something that hadn't been fully registered in his mind. Sitting up again, he turned it back on, then swung the beam across the dormitory. Then he knew what it was.

Jeffrey was asleep in the bed next to him, his head buried underneath the covers. But otherwise the two of them were alone. When the lights had gone out at nine-thirty, the other boys in the dormitory had already been asleep. Now their beds were empty, the covers pulled back. He directed the torch on to their chairs. Their clothes had gone too.

Quietly, he slipped out of bed and put on his dressing-gown and slippers. Then he went to the door and opened it. There were no lights on in the school. And the silence was more profound, more frightening than ever.

He tried a second dormitory, then a third. In each one the story was the same. The beds were empty, the clothes were gone. Outside, the rain was still falling. He could hear it pattering against the windows. He looked at his watch again, certain that he was making some sort of crazy mistake. It was twenty past twelve. So where was everybody?

He could feel his heart tugging against his chest as if it were urging him to go back to bed and forget all about it. But David was wide awake now. He would get to the bottom of this even if it killed him. And, he thought to himself, in all probability it would.

He tiptoed down the corridor, wincing every time he stepped on a creaking floorboard. Eventually he reached a fourth dormitory. He shone the torch on the handle of the door.

Behind him, a hand reached out of the gloom.

It settled on his shoulder.

David felt his stomach shrink to the size of a pea. He opened his mouth to scream and only managed to stop himself by shoving the torch between his teeth. It was a miracle he didn't swallow it. Slowly he turned round, the back of his neck glowing bright red with the beam of the torch shining through his throat.

Jill stood opposite him. Like him, she was wearing a dressing-gown and slippers. She looked even more frightened than he did.

"Where are they?" she whispered. "Where have they gone?"

"Nggg..." David remembered the torch in his mouth and pulled it out. "I don't know," he said. "I was trying to find out."

"I saw them go." Jill sighed, relieved to have found David awake and out of bed. "It was about twenty minutes ago. One of them woke me up as she left the dormitory. I waited a bit and then followed them."

"So where did they go?" David asked, repeating Jill's own question.

"I saw them go into the library," Jill replied. "All of them. The whole school. I listened at the door for a bit but I couldn't hear anything, so then I went in myself. But they weren't there, David." Jill took a deep breath. David could see that she was close to tears. "They'd all vanished."

David thought back. He had been in the library after tea, surrounded by the stuffed animal heads. It was a small room, barely big enough for sixty-three people. Apart from a table, a mirror, a dozen chairs and the animals, there was nothing in it. And that included doors. There was only one way in. Only one way back out again.

"Maybe they've all gone outside?" he

suggested. "Through a window."

Jill scowled at him. "In this weather? Anyway, the windows in the library are too high. I know. I tried..."

"Then they must be somewhere in the school."

"No." Jill slumped against the wall, then slithered down to sit on the floor. She was exhausted – and not just through lack of sleep. "I've looked everywhere. In the classrooms, in the dining hall, in the staff room ... everywhere. They're not here."

"They've got to be here somewhere!" David insisted. "They can't just have disappeared."

Jill made no answer. David sat down next to her and put an arm around her shoulders. Neither of them spoke. David's last words echoed in his thoughts. "They've got to be here somewhere! They can't just have disappeared."

But sitting in the dark and silent passage he knew that he was wrong.

Impossible though it seemed, they were alone in Groosham Grange.

CHRISTMAS

Three days before Christmas it began to snow.

By Christmas Day the whole island had been blanketed out. The ground was white. The sea was white. It was difficult to tell where one ended and the other began, and standing in the fields you felt like a single letter on a blank page in an envelope waiting to be posted.

There was no central heating at Groosham Grange. Instead, huge logs burned in open fireplaces, crackling and hissing as if they were angry at having to share their warmth. All the windows had steamed up and the plumbing shuddered, groaned and gurgled as the water forced its way through half-frozen pipes. A colony of bats that inhabited one of the northern towers migrated downstairs for warmth and ended up in the dining-room. Nobody complained. But David found mealtimes something of a struggle with about a hundred eyes examining his rhubarb crumble upside down from the rafters.

Apart from the bats and the weather, nothing else had changed at the school. At first David had been surprised that nobody seemed to care about Christmas. Later on he had glumly accepted it. Captain Bloodbath came to the school once a week, on Tuesdays, but he never brought any letters or took any so there were no Christmas cards. There were no Christmas decorations either. David had seen Mrs Windergast with an armful of holly and that had raised his spirits – at least until lunchtime, when he had had his first taste of holly soup. There was no Christmas tree and, of course, no Christmas presents. Despite the snow, nobody threw any snowballs and the only snowman turned out to be Gregor, who had dozed off on his gravestone just before the heaviest fall and had to be thawed out the next day.

Only one teacher even mentioned Christmas, and this was Mr Creer in religious studies. Mr Creer was the only normal-looking teacher in the whole school. He was the youngest too, about thirty, short with curly hair and a neat moustache. His full name was Ronald Edward Creer. David had been a little unsettled to see the same name on a tombstone in the school cemetery – "Drowned off Skrull Island: 1955-1985" – but he had assumed it was a relative. Nonetheless, Mr Creer did smell very strongly of seaweed.

"Christmas, of course, has very little to do with Christianity." Mr Creer gave the class a ghostly smile. All his smiles were rather ghostly. "There were festivals at the end of December long before Christianity appeared; the Roman 'Saturnalia' and the Persian 'Birth of the Sun', for example. In the north it is a festival of the dark spirits, for it is at Christmas that the dead return from their graves."

This was all news to David. But he had to admit that living in London and being surrounded by tinsel, department-store Santas, last-minute shopping, mince pies, puddings and too many old films on TV, Christmas had never had much to do with Christianity there either.

Christmas Day began like any other day: baths, breakfast, three lessons, then lunch. For some reason, however, the lessons in the afternoon had been cancelled and David and Jill found themselves free to wander as they pleased. As usual, all the other pupils went to bed. That was what they did whenever they had any free time. Then, late at night, they would go to the library. And then they would disappear.

David and Jill had tried to follow them several times, determined to get to the bottom of the mystery, but without success. The trouble was that there was no way they could follow the others into the library without being seen, and by the time they opened the door everyone had gone. One afternoon they searched the room thoroughly, certain that there must be a secret passage. But if there was a secret passage, it must have had a spectacularly secret entrance. All the walls seemed to be made of solid brick. A fireplace with a stone mantelpiece dominated one of them, and there was a full-length mirror in a frame decorated with bronze flowers on the other. But though David pressed and prodded all the animals while Jill fiddled with the mirror and even tried to climb up the chimney, they didn't find anything.

And where was Jeffrey during all this?

In the weeks that they had been at Groosham Grange, Jeffrey had changed and this worried David more than anything. He still remembered Mr Kilgraw's words. "If anything, he'll be the easiest..." It was certainly true that Jeffrey had taken to spending more and more time by himself and less and less time with David and Jill. Quite a few times now, David had seen him in deep conversation with William Rufus and although he had questioned him about it, Jeffrey had refused to be drawn. Although there were no books in the library, he seemed to be reading a lot; old, dusty books with yellowing pages bound in cracked leather.

It was Jill, with her short temper, who had finally started an argument. She had rounded on him one evening in an empty classroom as they talked about their progress – or lack of it.

"What's wrong with you?" she demanded. "You're beginning to act as if you actually like it here!"

"Perhaps I d-d-do," Jeffrey replied.

"But the whole school is mad!"

"All p-p-public schools are mad. But it's a lot b-b-better than Godlesston."

"But what about our promise?" David reminded him. "Us against them."

"We may be ag-g-gainst them," Jeffrey said. "But I'm not so sure that they're ag-g-gainst us."

"Then why don't you just go off and join them?" Jill snapped.

It looked as if Jeffrey had.

David and Jill were alone as they trudged across the playing fields, up to their ankles in snow. They knew every inch of the island by now. Groosham Grange was in the north. A forest sprawled all the way down to the eastern side. Its trees could have been sculpted out of stone and looked at least a thousand years old. The point, where the jetty stood, was at the southernmost end. This was a long, flat area below the multicoloured cliffs which soared up behind. David was sure that he could see the entrance to a cave at the bottom of the cliffs and would have liked to explore it, but there was no way they could reach it. The cliffs themselves were too sheer to climb down and the point was separated from the cave by an inlet, the waves pounding at the rocks and sharpening them into needlepoints.

There was also a river on the island – although it was more of a wide stream – running from the north into a lake beside the forest. This was where they went to now. The water had frozen over and they had thought it would be fun to go skating. But they didn't have any skates. And anyway, they didn't feel much like having fun ... even if it was Christmas Day.

"Have you learnt anything since you got here?" Jill asked.

David considered. "Not really," he admitted. "But then there are never any tests or exams or anything so it doesn't really seem to matter."

"Well, I've learnt one thing." Jill picked up a stone and threw it across the lake. It hit the ice and slithered into a tangle of weeds. "The boat comes every Tuesday. Captain Bloodbath unloads all the supplies and then he and Gregor drive up to the school. So for about one hour there's nobody on the boat."

"What of it?" David asked, suddenly interested.

"The day after Boxing Day is a Tuesday. And when they're up at the school there is going to be somebody on the boat. Me."

"But there's nowhere to hide." David had been with Jill when she had examined the boat a week before. "We looked."

"There isn't room for two," Jill admitted. "But I reckon one of us can squeeze inside the cabin. There's a heap of old rags on the floor. I think I can hide underneath."

"So you're really going." David couldn't help feeling sad as he spoke the words. Jill was his only true friend in the school. With her gone, he would be more alone than ever.

"I've got to go, David," Jill said. "If I stay here much longer I'm going to go crazy ... like Jeffrey. But once I'm away, I'll send a letter to the authorities. They'll send someone over. And I bet you anything you like, the school will be closed down a week later."

"Where will you go?" David asked.

"I've got four brothers and two sisters to choose from," Jill said. She smiled. "We were a big family. I was number seven!"

"Did your mother have brothers and sisters?" David asked.

Jill looked at him curiously. "What on earth has that got to do with anything?"

"I just wondered..."

"As a matter of fact she was a number seven, too. I've got six uncles. Why do you want to know?"

"Seventh daughter of a seventh daughter," David muttered and said no more. It meant something. It had to mean something. But what?

He was still pondering over it later that evening as he sat by himself in the library. Christmas dinner – if you could call it that – had been ham and chips, the chips only slightly warmer than the ham. David was feeling really depressed for the first time since he had arrived. Jill had gone to bed early and there wasn't even any television to cheer him up. There was one television in the school but it was a black and white model held together by Sellotape. The volume switch had fallen off and the reception was so bad that the screen always resembled a miniature snowstorm. It was fine if you were watching a programme about deaf and dumb coal workers in Siberia. Otherwise it was useless.

The door opened and he looked up. It was Jeffrey.

"Hello," he said.

"Hello, D-D-David." The fat boy stood hovering beside the door as if he was embarrassed to have been caught there.

"I haven't seen you around for a while," David said, trying to sound friendly.

"I know. I've been b-b-busy." Jeffrey looked round the room, his eyes darting behind his wire-frame spectacles. "Actually, I w-w-was looking for W-W-William."

"Your new friend?" Now David sounded scornful. "Well, he's not here. Unless of course he's under the c-c-carpet or in the f-f-fireplace or wherever it is they all go at night! And all I can say is, if you want to join them, they're welcome to you."

"I d-d-didn't..." Jeffrey stammered to a halt, blushing, and David felt angry with himself for having lost his temper. He opened his mouth to speak again but at the same time Jeffrey backed out of the room, shutting the door behind him.

David got up. *He'll be the easiest.* Once again Mr Kilgraw's words echoed in his mind. Of course Jeffrey would be the easiest of the three of them – whatever it was that Groosham Grange had planned. He was fat. He wore glasses and he had a stutter. He was one of life's victims, always the one to be bullied. And by rejecting him, David had just played right into their hands. It had been three against the rest when they began. But his own thoughtlessness had left Jeffrey out there on his own.

Quickly, he left the library. Jeffrey had already disappeared down the corridor but David didn't mind. If he could find out what was really going on at Groosham Grange – behind the façade of the lessons and everyday school life – then perhaps he might be able to put a stop to it, saving Jeffrey and himself at the same time. And he was in the perfect place to start looking. The answer had to be in one of two rooms.

He began with the door marked HEADS. In all the time he had been at the school he had never once seen the two headmasters, Mr Fitch and Mr Teagle. But for the fact that he had heard their voices, he wouldn't have believed they even existed. Now he knocked gently on the door. As he had expected, there was no reply. Glancing over his shoulder, he reached for the handle and turned it. The door opened.

David had never been in the headmasters' study before. At first sight it reminded him more of a chapel than a study. The windows were made of stained glass showing scenes from what looked like the Last Judgement, with devils prodding naked men and women into the flames. The floor was made of black marble, and there was no carpet. The bookcases, filled with ancient books like the one Jeffrey had been reading, reminded him of pews and there was even a pulpit in one corner, a carved eagle supporting a Bible on its outstretched wings.

The room had one riddle of its own. There were two headmasters at Groosham Grange. So why was there only one desk, only one chair, only one gown on the clothes-stand behind the door? David could find no answer to that – and no answers to anything else. The desk drawers were locked and there were no papers lying around. He spent five fruitless minutes in the study. Then he left as quietly as he had gone in.

It took more courage to sneak into Mr Kilgraw's study opposite. David remembered the last time he had been there – he still had a mark on his thumb to show for it. Eventually he opened the door. "He can't eat you," he muttered to himself, and wished that he believed it.

There was no sign of the assistant headmaster but as he crossed the carpet, he felt he was being watched. He stopped, scarcely daring to breathe. He was quite alone in the room. He moved again. The eyes followed him. He stopped again. Then he realized what it was. The pictures...! They were portraits of grim old men, painted, it would seem, some years after they had died. But as David moved, their eyes moved with him so that wherever he was in the room they were always looking at him.

He paused beside what looked like a chest

of drawers and rested his hand against it. The wood vibrated underneath his fingertips. He pulled his hand away and stared at it. Had he imagined it? No – standing there alone in the study, he could hear a faint humming sound. And it was coming from the chest.

Squatting down, he reached for one of the drawers and pulled it. That was when he made his first discovery. The whole chest was a fake. All three drawers were no more than a front and swung open like a door. The chest was actually a modern refrigerator.

David peered inside and swallowed hard. The chest might be a fridge but it certainly didn't contain milk, butter and half a dozen eggs. Instead, about thirty plastic bags hung from hooks, each one filled with a dark red liquid. "It's wine," he whispered. "It's got to be wine. Of course it's wine. It can't be anything else. I mean, it can't be..."

Blood!

But even as he slammed the door and straightened up, he knew that it was. Wine didn't come in bags. Wine was never labelled AB POSITIVE. He didn't even want to ask what thirty pints of it were doing in Mr Kilgraw's study. He didn't want to know. He just wanted to get out of the study before he ended up in another eight bags on a lower shelf.

But before he had reached the door, he managed to stop himself. It was too late to back out now. This might be the last chance he had to search the study. And time was running out for Jeffrey. He took a deep breath. There was nobody around. Nobody knew he was there. He had to go on.

He walked over to the desk. The book that he had signed on his first evening at the school was still in its place and with a shaking hand he opened it. He tried to lick his thumb but his mouth was as dry as sandpaper. His eye fell at once on the last three names: DAVID ELIOT, JILL GREEN, JEFFREY JOSEPH. Although they had faded from red to brown, they were still fresher than the names on the other pages. Leaning over the desk, he began to read.

It took him about thirty seconds to realize that there wasn't one single name in the book that he recognized. There was no William Rufus, no Bessie Duncan or Roger Bacon. So he had been right. The other pupils had taken false names some time after their arrival. The only question was – why?

He closed the book. Something else had attracted his attention, lying at the far corner of the desk. It hadn't been there that first night. In fact David had never seen one before, at least not off someone's hand. It was a ring, a special ring with a black stone set in plain gold. David reached out for it ... and yelled. The ring was white-hot. It was as if it had just come out of the forge. It was impossible, of course. The ring had been lying there on the wooden surface ever since he had come into the room. It had to be some sort of illusion. But illusion or not, his fingers were still burnt, the skin blistering.

"What are you doing here?"

David twisted round, the pain momentarily forgotten. Mr Kilgraw was standing in the room – but that was impossible too. The door hadn't opened. David had heard nothing. The assistant headmaster was dressed as usual in black and white as if he was on his way to a funeral. His voice had sounded curious rather than hostile but there could be no mistaking the menace in his eyes. Clutching his hand, David desperately grappled for an excuse. *Ah well*, he thought to himself. *Refrigerator, here I come.*

"What are you doing here, David?" Mr Kilgraw asked for a second time.

"I ... I ... I was looking for you, sir."

"Why?"

"Um..." David had a flash of inspiration. "To wish you a happy Christmas, sir."

Mr Kilgraw's lips twitched in a faintly upwardly direction. "That's a very charming thought," he muttered in a tone of voice that actually said, "A likely story!" He gestured at David's hand. "You seem to have burnt yourself."

"Yes, sir." David blushed guiltily. "I saw the ring and..."

Mr Kilgraw moved forward into the room. David was careful to avoid glancing in the mirror. He knew what he would see – or rather, what he wouldn't see. He waited in silence as the assistant headmaster sat down behind the desk, wondering what would happen next.

"Sometimes it's not wise to look at things we're not meant to, David," Mr Kilgraw said. "Especially when they're things that we don't understand." He reached out and picked up the ring. David winced, but it lay there quite coolly in the palm of his hand. "I have to say that I am very disappointed in you," Mr Kilgraw went on. "Despite the little talk we had, it seems that you aren't making any progress at all."

"Then why don't you expel me?" David asked, surprising himself with his sudden defiance. But then there was nothing he would have liked more.

"Oh no! Nobody is ever expelled from Groosham Grange." Mr Kilgraw chuckled to himself. "We have had difficult children in the past, but they come to accept us ... as you will one day."

"But what do you want with me?" David couldn't contain himself any longer. "What's going on here? I know this isn't a real school. There's something horrible going on. Why won't you let me leave? I never asked to come here. Why won't you let me go and forget I ever existed? I hate it here. I hate all of you. And I'm never going to accept you, not so long as I live."

"And how long will that be?" Suddenly Mr Kilgraw's voice was ice. Each syllable had come out as a deadly whisper. David froze, feeling the tears welling up behind his eyes. But he was certain about one thing. He wouldn't cry. Not while he was in front of Mr Kilgraw.

But then it was as if Mr Kilgraw relented. He threw down the ring and sat back in his chair. When he spoke again, his voice was softer.

"There is so much that you don't understand, David," he said. "But one day things will be different. Right now you'd better get that hand looked at by Mrs Windergast."

He raised a skeletal finger to the side of his mouth, thinking for a moment in silence. "Tell her that I suggest her special ointment," he went on. "I'm sure you'll find it will give you a most ... refreshing night's sleep."

David turned round and left the study.

It was quite late by now and as usual there was nobody around in the corridors. David made his way upstairs, deep in thought. One thing was sure. He had no intention of visiting

Mrs Windergast. If Mr Kilgraw was keeping fresh blood in his refrigerator, who knows what he might find in her medicine cupboard? His hand was hurting him badly. But any pain was preferable to another session with the staff of Groosham Grange.

He was therefore annoyed to find the matron waiting for him outside her surgery. There must have been some sort of internal telephone system in the school because she already knew what had happened to him.

"Let me have a look at your poor little hand," she trilled. "Come inside and sit down while I get a plaster. We don't want it going septic, do we? My husband went septic – God rest his soul. All of him! It was a horrible sight at the end, I can tell you. And it only began with the teeniest scratch..." She ushered David into the surgery even as she spoke, giving him no chance to argue. "Now you sit down," she commanded, "while I open my medicine box."

David sat down. The surgery was small and cosy with a gas fire, a colourful rug and home-made cushions on the chairs. Embroideries hung on the wall and there were comics scattered on a low coffee table. David took all this in while the matron busied herself at the far end, rummaging in a mirror-fronted cabinet.

As she opened it, David caught the reflection of a bird on a perch. For a moment he thought he had imagined it, but then he turned round and saw the real thing, next to the window. The bird was a black crow. At first David assumed it to be stuffed, like the animals in the library. But then it croaked and shook its wings. David shivered, remembering the crow he had seen in his garden the day he had left home.

"That's Wilfred," Mrs Windergast explained as she sat down next to him. "Some people have goldfish. Some people have hamsters. But I've always preferred crows. My husband never liked him very much. In fact it was Wilfred who scratched him. Sometimes he can be very naughty! Now – let's have a look at that hand."

David held out his burnt hand and for the next few minutes Mrs Windergast busied herself with antiseptic creams and plasters. "There!" she exclaimed when she had finished. "That's better!"

David made to stand up, but the matron motioned at him to stay where he was.

"And tell me, my dear," she said. "How are you finding Groosham Grange?"

David was tired. He was fed up playing games. So he told her the truth. "All the kids are weird," he said. "The staff are crazy. The island is horrible. And the school is like something out of a horror film and I wish I was back at home."

Mrs Windergast beamed at him. "But otherwise you're perfectly happy?" she asked.

"Mrs Windergast—"

The matron held up her hand, stopping him. "Of course I understand, my dear," she said. "It's always difficult at first. That's why I've decided to let you have a bit of my special ointment."

"What does it do?" David asked suspiciously.

"It just helps you get a good night's sleep." She had produced a tub of ointment out of her apron pocket, and before David could stop her she unscrewed the lid and held it out to him. The ointment was thick and charcoal grey but surprisingly it smelt rather pleasant. It was a bitter smell, some sort of wild herb. But even the scent of it somehow relaxed him and made him feel warm inside. "Just rub it into your forehead," Mrs Windergast coaxed him, and now her voice was soft and far away. "It'll do wonders for you, just you wait and see."

David did as he was told. He couldn't refuse. He didn't *want* to refuse. The ointment felt warm against his skin. And the moment it was on, it seemed to sink through, spreading into the flesh and all the way through to his bones.

"Now you just pop into bed, David." Was it still Mrs Windergast talking? He could have sworn it was a different voice. "And have lots of lovely dreams."

David did dream that night.

He remembered undressing and getting into bed and then he must have been asleep except that his eyes were open and he was aware of things happening around him. The other boys in his dormitory were getting out of bed. Of course, that was no surprise. David rolled over and closed his eyes.

At least, that was what he meant to do. But the next thing he remembered, he was fully dressed and following them, walking downstairs towards the library. He stumbled at the top of the stairs and felt a hand steady him. It was William Rufus. David smiled. The other boy smiled back.

And then they were in the library. What happened next was confusing. He was looking at himself in a mirror – the mirror that hung opposite the fireplace. But then he walked into the mirror, right into the glass. He expected it to break. But it didn't break. And then he was on the other side. He looked behind him. William Rufus tugged at his arm. He went on.

Walls of solid rock. A twisting path going

deeper and deeper into the ground. The smell of salt water in the air. The dream had become fragmented now. It was as if the mirror had broken after all and he was seeing only the reflections in the shattered pieces. Now he was in some huge chamber, far underground. He could see the stalagmites, a glistening silver, soaring out of the ground, reaching up to the stalactites that hung down from above. Or was it the other way round...?

A great bonfire burnt in the cave, throwing fantastic shadows against the wall. The whole school had congregated there, waiting in silence for something ... or someone. Then a man stepped out from behind a slab of natural stone. And that was one thing David could not bring himself to look at, for it was more horrible than anything he had yet seen at Groosham Grange. But later on he would remember...

Two headmasters, but only one desk, only one chair.

The dream disconnected in the way that dreams do. Words were spoken. Then there was a banquet, a Christmas dinner like no other he had ever had before. Meat sizzled on the open fire. Wine flowed from silver jugs. There were puddings and pastries and pies and for the first time the pupils at Groosham Grange laughed and shouted and acted like they were actually alive. Music welled out of the ground and David looked for Jill. To his surprise he found her and they danced together for what seemed like hours, although he knew (because it was a dream) that it might have been only minutes.

And then finally there was a hush and everybody stood still as a single figure pressed through the crowds towards the stone slab. David wanted to call out but he had no voice. It was Jeffrey. Mr Kilgraw was waiting for him and he had the ring. Jeffrey was smiling, happier than David had ever seen him. He took the ring and put it on. And then, as one, the whole school began to cheer, the voices echoing against the walls, and it was with the clamour in his ears that...

David woke up.

He had a headache and there was an unpleasant taste in his mouth. He rubbed his eyes, wondering where he was. It was morning. The cold winter sun was streaming in through the windows. Slowly, he propped himself up in bed and looked around.

And he was in bed, in his usual place in the dormitory. His clothes were just as he had left them the night before. He looked at his hand. The plaster was still neatly in place. All around him, the other boys were dressing, their faces as blank as ever. David threw back the covers. It really had been no more than a dream. He half-smiled to himself. Walking through mirrors? Dancing with Jill in some underground cavern? Of course it had been a dream. How could it have been anything else?

He got out of bed and stretched. He was unusually stiff this morning, as if he had just completed a twenty mile run. He glanced to one side. Jeffrey was sitting on the bed next to him, already half-dressed. David thought back to their parting in the library and sighed. He had some making up to do.

"Good morning, Jeffrey," he said.

"Good morning, David." Jeffrey sounded almost hostile.

"Look – I just wanted to say I'm sorry about yesterday. All right?"

"There's no need to apologize, David." Jeffrey pulled his shirt on. "Just forget it."

In that brief moment David noticed a lot of things. But they all rushed in on him so quickly that he would never be quite sure which came first.

Jeffrey had changed.

He didn't just sound hostile. He was hostile. His voice had become as bleak and distant as all the others.

He wasn't stuttering any more.

And the hand that was buttoning up his shirt was different too.

It was wearing a black ring.

A LETTER

On Boxing Day, David sat down and wrote a letter to his father.

Groosham Grange,
Skrull Island,
Norfolk

26th December

Dear Father,

This is a very difficult letter to write.

It was so difficult, in fact, that he tore up the first sentence three times before he was satisfied and even then he wasn't sure that he had spelled "difficult" correctly.

I know that I have always been a disappointment

to you. I have never been interested in merchant banking and I was expelled from Beton College. But I now see that I was wrong.

I have decided to get a job as a teller in the Bank of England. If the Bank of England won't have me I'll try the Bank of Germany. I'm sure you'd be proud of me if I were A Teller the Hun.

He crossed out the last sentence too. Then the bell for lunch went and it was another hour before he could sit down and begin the next paragraph.

But there is something I have to ask you.

PLEASE TAKE ME AWAY FROM GROOSHAM GRANGE. It's not that I don't like it here (although I don't like it at all). But it's not at all what you were expecting. If you knew what it was really like here, you'd never have sent me in the first place.

I think they are involved in black magic. Mr Kilgraw, the assistant headmaster, is a vampire. Mr Creer, who teaches pottery, religious studies and maths, is dead, and Miss Pedicure, who teaches English and history, ought to be, as she is at least six hundred years old! You'll think I'm mad when you read this ...

David read it back and decided that he quite possibly was. Could all this really be happening to him?

... but I promise you, I'm telling the truth. I think they want to turn me into some sort of zombie like they did to my friend Jeffrey. He won't talk to me any more. He won't even stutter to me. And I know that if I stay here much longer, I'll be next.

David took a deep breath. His hand was aching and he realized that he was clutching the pen so hard that it was a miracle the ink was reaching the nib. Forcing himself to relax, he pulled the page towards him and began again.

I can't describe all the things that have happened to me since I got here. But I've been stabbed, drugged, threatened and half-scared to death. I know Grandpa used to do all this to you when you were young, but I don't think it's fair when I haven't done anything wrong and I don't want to be a zombie. Please at least visit the school. Then you'll see what I mean.

I can't post this letter to you because there's no post-box on the island and if you've written to me, I haven't got it. I'm going to give this to a friend of mine, Jill Green.

She's planning to escape tomorrow and has promised to send it to you. I've also given her your telephone number and she'll call you (reversing the charges). She'll be able to tell you everything that's happened and I just hope you believe her.

I must stop now as it's time for the afternoon lesson - chemistry. We're being taught the secret of life.

Help!

Your son,

David

At least nobody had come into the library while he was writing. David had been scribbling the words with one eye on the door and the other on the mirror with the result that the lines had gone all over the place and reading them again made him feel seasick. But it would have to do. He folded the page in half and then in half again. He didn't have an envelope but Jill had promised to buy one – along with a stamp – as soon as she reached the mainland.

If all went according to plan, Captain Bloodbath would arrive at ten o'clock the following morning. Jill would skip the second lesson and hide near the jetty. As soon as Gregor had unloaded the supplies and driven the captain up to the school, she would slip on to the boat and underneath the rags. The boat would leave at eleven. And by midday Jill would be well on her way, hitchhiking south. She had to get away. She was his only hope. But that wasn't the only worry in David's mind as he hurried along to the chemistry laboratory. She might send the letter. His father might read it. But would he believe it? Would anyone believe it?

David still wasn't sure if he believed it himself.

THE INSPECTOR

Jill didn't even get off the island.

She was discovered by Captain Bloodbath huddling under the rags and was jerked, trembling and miserable, back on to dry land.

"So you thought you could fool me, my pretty?" he exclaimed with a leering grin. "Thought I didn't know the waterline of my own boat? I'd know if there was an extra sprat on board. Hitch a free ride to the mainland – is that what you had in mind? Well, you'd have to sail a few high seas before you could bamboozle a Bloodbath!"

For a whole week after that, Jill waited in trepidation for something to happen to her. As David had somewhat unhelpfully told her, if you were caught trying to run away from Beton College, your head was shaved and you had to spend a month walking round with your shoelaces tied together. But in fact nothing happened. There really were no punishments at Groosham Grange. If Captain Bloodbath had even bothered to mention the incident to any of the staff, they didn't take the slightest bit of notice.

And so the two of them were still there as the snow melted and the winter dripped and trickled its way towards spring. They had been on the island now for seven weeks. Nothing about the school had changed – they were still both outsiders. But David knew that he had changed. And that frightened him.

He was beginning to enjoy his life on the island. Almost despite himself he was doing well in class. French, history, maths ... even Latin came easily to him now. He had got a place in the first eleven football team and although no other school came to the island he still enjoyed the games – even with the pig-bladder balls. And then there was Jill. David depended on her as much as she did on him. They spent all their free time together, walking and talking. And she had become the closest friend he had ever had.

So he was almost grateful that her escape had failed – and it was that that worried him. Despite the sunshine and the first scent of spring, something evil was going on at Groosham Grange. And slowly, surely, it was drawing him in. If he liked it there now, how long would it be before he became a part of it too?

Jill kept him sane. Operation Bottle was her idea. Every day for a week they stole whatever bottles they could get their hands on and then threw them into the sea with messages asking for help. They sent bottles to their parents, to the police, to the Department of Education and even, in one desperate moment, to the Queen. David was fairly certain that the bottles would sink long before they reached the coast of Norfolk or at least get washed back up on the island. But he was wrong. One of the bottles arrived.

It was Mr Leloup who announced the news.

The French teacher was a small, bald, timid-looking man. At least, he was small, bald and timid-looking at the start of the month. But as the full moon approached, he would gradually change. His body would swell out like the Incredible Hulk, his face would become increasingly ferocious and he would develop a full head of hair. Then, when the full moon came, he would disappear altogether, only to appear the next day back to square one. All his clothes had been torn and stitched together so many times that he must have been surrounded by at least a mile of thread. When he got angry in class – and he did have a very short temper – he didn't shout. He barked.

He was angry that morning, the first day in February.

"It would appear zat the school 'as a leetle prob-lame," he announced in his exaggerated French accent. "The busybodies een the Department of Education 'av decide-dead to pay us a viseet. So tomorrow we must albee on our best be-evure." He glanced meaningfully at Jill and David. "And no-buddy is to speak to zis man unless 'ee speaks to them."

That evening, Jill was hardly able to contain her excitement.

"He must have got one of our messages," Jill said. "If the Department of Education find out the truth about Groosham Grange, they'll close it down and that will be the end of it. We'll be free!"

"I know," David muttered gloomily. "But they won't let us anywhere near him. And if they see us talking to him, they'll probably do something terrible to him. And to us."

Jill looked at him scornfully. "Have you lost your bottle?" she demanded.

"Of course I haven't," David said. "How else do you think he got the message?"

Mr Netherby arrived on the island the next

morning. A thin, neat man in a grey suit with spectacles and a leather briefcase, he was ferried over by Captain Bloodbath and met by Mr Kilgraw. He gave them a small, official smile and a brief, official handshake and then began his official visit. He was very much the official. Wherever he went he took notes, occasionally asking questions and jotting down the answers in a neat, official hand.

To David and Jill's disgust, the whole school had put on a show for him. It was like a royal visit to a hospital when the floors are all scrubbed and the really sick patients are taken off their life support machines and hidden away in cupboards. Everything that Mr Netherby saw was designed to impress. The staff were all in their best suits and the pupils seemed lively, interested and – above all – normal. He was formally introduced to a few of them and they answered his questions with just the right amount of enthusiasm. Yes, they were very happy at Groosham Grange. Yes, they were working hard. No, they had never thought of running away.

Mr Netherby was delighted by what he saw. He couldn't fail to be. As the day wore on he gradually unwound and even the sight of Gregor, humping a sack of potatoes down to the kitchen, only delighted him all the more.

"The Council is very keen on the employment of disabled people," he was heard to remark. "He wouldn't by any chance be gay as well?"

"He's certainly very queer," Mr Kilgraw concurred.

"Excellent! Excellent! First class!" Mr Netherby nodded and ticked off a page in his notebook.

By the end of the day, the inspector was in a thoroughly good mood. Although he had been sorry not to meet the heads – Mr Kilgraw had told him that they were away at a conference – he seemed entirely satisfied by everything he had seen. David and Jill watched him in dismay. Their only chance seemed to be slipping away and there was nothing they could do about it. Mr Kilgraw had managed things so that they had never been allowed near him. He hadn't visited any of their classes. And whenever they had drawn near him, he had been quickly steered in the opposite direction.

"It's now or never," Jill whispered as Mr Kilgraw led his visitor towards the front door. They had just finished prep and had half an hour's free time before bed. Jill was clutching a note. She and David had written it the evening before and then carefully folded it into a square. The note read: THINGS ARE NOT WHAT THEY SEEM AT GROOSHAM GRANGE. YOU ARE IN

GREAT DANGER. MEET US ON THE CLIFFS AT 7.45 P.M. DO NOT LET ANYONE ELSE SEE THIS NOTE.

Mr Kilgraw and the inspector were walking down the corridor towards them.

"A most enjoyable day," Mr Netherby was saying. "However, I have to tell you, Mr Kilgraw, that my department is rather concerned that we have no record of Groosham Grange. You don't even appear to have a licence."

"Is that a problem?" Mr Kilgraw asked.

"I fear so. There'll have to be an enquiry. But I can assure you that I'll be filing a most favourable report..."

Jill and David knew what they had to do.

They moved at the same time, walking swiftly into the corridors as if they were hurrying to get somewhere. Halfway down they bumped into the two men who had stood aside to let them pass. At that moment, David pretended to lose his balance, knocking Mr Kilgraw back into the lockers. At the same time, Jill pressed the square of paper into Mr Netherby's hand.

"Sorry, sir," David muttered.

It had taken less than three seconds. Then they were moving away again as if nothing had happened. But the assistant headmaster hadn't seen anything. Mr Netherby had the note. The only question was, would he turn up at the cliffs?

As soon as the two men had turned the corner, Jill and David doubled back, then left the school through a side exit that led into the cemetery. Nobody saw them go.

"What's the time?" David asked.

"Quarter past seven."

"Then we've got half an hour..."

They ran across the playing fields, past the lake and into the forest. It was a warm, cloudless night. The moon lit their path as they raced for the cover of the trees but neither of them looked up, neither of them saw.

It was a full moon.

They stopped, panting, at the edge of the forest.

"Are you sure this is a good idea?" David asked.

"We've got to come this way," Jill said. "If we take the road, somebody may see us."

"But this forest gives me the creeps."

"The whole island gives me the creeps."

They pressed on through the forest. Here, with the moon shut out by a ceiling of leaves, everything was very dark and very still. It was like no forest David had ever seen. The trees seemed to be tied together in knots, thorns and briars snaking round the ancient trunks. Fantastic mushrooms bulged out of the ground only to ooze a horrible yellow when they trod on them. Nothing stirred: not a bird, not an owl, not a breath of wind.

Then the wolf howled.

Jill seized hold of David so suddenly that she nearly tore off his shirt. "What is it?" she whispered.

"I think it was a dog," David whispered back.

"I've never heard a dog like that."

"It sounded like a dog."

"You're sure?"

"Of course I'm sure."

The wolf howled again.

They ran.

They ran whichever way they could, dodging under the low-lying branches and leaping over the undergrowth. Soon they were hopelessly lost. The forest had swallowed them up, an impossible maze that seemed to grow even as they fought their way through it. And the animal, whatever it was, was getting closer. David couldn't see it. He almost wished he could. Instead he sensed it and that was much, much worse. His imagination screamed at him. The wolf, hooking its claws into the flesh at the back of his neck. The wolf, snarling ferociously as its drooling jaws lunged at his throat. The wolf...

"We can't go on!" Jill almost sobbed the words, sliding to a halt.

David stopped beside her, breathless, his shirt soaked with sweat. Why had they ever decided to come this way? He had stumbled and fallen into a bed of thistles and his right hand was on fire. And their twisting path had led them into a dead end of branch and bramble. David looked around him. A heavy stick lay on the ground, blown down in one of the storms. Clutching it with both hands, he dragged it free of the nettles and picked it up.

"David...!"

He turned round. And now he could see something. It was too dark to tell what it was. A wolf, a man ... or something between the two? It was just a shape, a mass of black fur with two red eyes glowing in the centre. He could hear it too. A soft, snuffling sound that made his skin crawl.

There was no way back. The creature was blocking the path.

But there was no way forward.

The creature leapt.

David swung the stick.

He had shut his eyes at the last second, but he felt the heavy piece of wood make contact. His arm shuddered. The creature screamed. Then there was a sound of the undergrowth crashing and breaking and when he opened his eyes again it had gone.

Jill stepped forward and laid a hand on his shoulder.

"That was no dog," she said.

"Then what was it?"

"I don't know." Jill looked thoughtfully back up the path. "But it howled with a French accent."

They had reached the southern end of the island where the land sloped steeply down, curving round to the point. Climbing through the last tangles of the forest, they crossed the road and ran to the end of the cliffs, where they had arranged to meet Mr Netherby. Jill glanced at her watch. They had made it with ten minutes to spare.

They waited there, high up above the sea.

The top of the cliff was flat and peaceful with a soft carpet of grass. Twenty metres below, the waves glittered in the moonlight, splashing against the rocks that jutted out, looking as if they had torn through the very fabric of the sea.

"Do you think he'll come?" David asked.

"I think he's already here," Jill said.

There was somebody walking across the grass towards them, a black silhouette against the pale sky. He was still about two hundred yards away but as he drew closer they saw that he was clutching an attaché case. Seeing them, he stopped and glanced over his shoulder. The man was afraid. They could tell simply from the way he walked.

He had covered about fifty yards, following the edge of the cliff, when it happened. At first David thought he had been stung by a wasp. But then he remembered that it was only March and there were no wasps. The man jerked, his head snapping back. One hand reached for the side of his neck. Then it happened a second time, only this time it was his shoulder. He clutched it, spinning round as if he had been shot. But there had been no gunshot. There was nobody in sight.

The man – and it was Mr Netherby – screamed as one of his knees gave way beneath him, his voice thin and high-pitched. Then it was his back. Falling to the ground he arched up and screamed again, both hands clawing at the air.

"What's wrong with him?" Jill whispered, her eyes wide and staring.

David shook his head, unable to speak.

It was a dreadful sight made more dreadful by the stillness of the night and the soft witness of the moon. Mr Netherby was jerking about like an out-of-control puppet as first one part of his body, then the next, was attacked. Jill and David could only stand and watch. When it seemed that Mr Netherby must be dead, he reached out and grabbed his attaché case, then somehow staggered to his feet. For a moment he stood there, swaying on the very edge of the cliff.

"I shall have to report this!" he called out.

Then something struck him in the heart and he toppled backwards into the darkness, plummeting down to the rocks.

David and Jill said nothing for a very long time. Then David gently put his hand round her shoulders. "We'd better go back," he said.

But for David the night was not yet over.

They had slipped into the school unnoticed and whispered a trembling "good night" in the corridor. The other boys had already gone to bed and were sleeping as David undressed and slipped between the sheets. But he couldn't fall asleep. For what seemed like hours he lay there, thinking about what had happened and wondering what would happen next. Then he heard it.

"David..."

It was his own name, whispered in the darkness by someone who was not there. He turned over and buried his head in the pillow, certain that he must have imagined it.

"David..."

There it was again, soft, insistent, not just in his ear but inside his very head. He sat upright and looked around him. Nobody stirred.

"David, come to us..."

He had to obey. Almost in a trance he got out of bed, put on his dressing-gown and crept noiselessly out of the dormitory. The school was swathed in darkness but downstairs in the main hall he could see an open doorway with a solid rectangle of light stretching out on to the carpet. That was where the voice wanted him to go ... into the staff room. He hesitated, afraid of what he would find inside, but the voice urged him on. He had to obey.

He walked down the staircase and, without knocking, entered the room. There, in the harsh light, the trance ended as David found himself face to face with the entire staff of Groosham Grange.

Mrs Windergast was sitting in an armchair closest to the door, knitting. Next to her sat Mr Creer, his eyes closed, scarcely breathing.

Gregor crouched beside the fireplace, muttering to himself. Opposite the fireplace, Mr Leloup was also seated, one side of his face purple and swollen. David remembered the creature in the wood, how he had beaten it off, and he was not surprised when the French teacher glanced at him with venom in his eyes. But it was Miss Pedicure who drew his attention. She was sitting at a table in the middle of the room and as David came in she giggled and threw something down. It was a wax model, thin, with spectacles, clutching a tiny wax attaché case. Pins had been stuck into its neck, its arms, its legs and its chest with one pin – the thirteenth – buried in its heart.

"Please come in, David."

Mr Kilgraw was standing in front of the window with his back to the room. Now he turned round and walked back into the room, pausing at the end of the table. His eyes flickered from David to the wax doll. "Did you really think that you could fool us?" he said. There was no menace in his voice. His tone was almost matter-of-fact. But the menace was still there in the room, swirling through the air like cigarette smoke. "When you wrote that letter, you signed Mr Netherby's death warrant. Regrettable, but you gave us no choice."

He raised his head and now his eyes settled on David.

"What are we going to do with you, David? You are doing well in class. You are, I think, beginning to enjoy yourself on the island. But still you resist us. We have your body. We have your mind. But you still refuse to give us your spirit."

David opened his mouth to speak but Mr Kilgraw silenced him with one gesture of his hand.

"We are running out of time," he said. "In fact we have only a few days remaining. I would be sad to lose you, David. We all would. And that is why I have decided on desperate measures."

Mr Kilgraw picked up the doll and plucked the pin out of its heart. A single drop of bright red blood dripped onto the table.

"You will report to the study at one o'clock tomorrow," he said. "I think it's time you saw the heads."

THE HEADS

I think it's time you saw the heads.

David had overheard the heads talking. He had been inside their study. But in all his time on the island he had never once seen Mr Fitch or Mr Teagle.

He hardly got a wink of sleep that night. Somewhere in the back of his mind he was angry. It wasn't fair. The bottles had been Jill's idea, so why had he been singled out? And what would the heads do with him when they got him? At Beton College any visit to the headmaster invariably meant six strokes of the cane. Even at the end-of-term sherry party he would generally cane several of the boys and even, on one memorable occasion, a couple of the parents. And there were two headmasters at Groosham Grange. Did that mean he could expect twelve?

He finally fell asleep at about two o'clock.

It was a troubled sleep with dreams of wolves and black rings and mirrors with no reflections. At one point in the dream he was standing on the cliffs watching Mr Netherby fall. Only it was he who was holding the wax doll, he who was jabbing the pins into it. Then his father wheelchaired himself across the grass, waving a packet of muesli, and David pointed at him and muttered something he didn't understand and his father exploded in flames and...

He woke up.

The day dragged on like a sack of bricks. Maths, then history, then English literature... David didn't see Jill all morning which, in his present mood, was probably just as well. He hardly took in a word that was said to him. He could only think of his appointment and his eyes were drawn to the clocks on the classroom walls. The minute hands seemed to be moving slower than they should have been. And the other pupils knew. Every now and then he caught them glancing at him. Then they would whisper among themselves. The teachers did their best to ignore him.

At last the time came. David was tempted to run away and hide – but he knew it would do him no good. The staff would find him and drag him out and whatever they might think of him, he didn't want to act like a coward. At one o'clock exactly he stood outside the headmasters' study. He took a deep breath. He raised his hand. He knocked. "Come ..."

"... in."

Both of them had spoken, Mr Fitch taking the first word, Mr Teagle the second. David went in.

The sun must have passed behind a cloud for it was dark in the room, the light barely penetrating the stained glass windows. The black marble floor, too, made the study seem darker than it had any right to be in the middle of the day. David closed the door behind him and moved slowly towards the desk. There were two men sitting behind it, waiting for him.

No. One man.

But...

And then David saw with a spidery surge of horror that brushed against the bottom of his spine and scuttled all the way up to his neck. There was only one headmaster at Groosham Grange – but two heads. Or to put it another way, the heads really were heads. Mr Fitch was quite bald with a hooked nose and vulture eyes. Mr Teagle had thin grey hair, a tiny beard and glasses. But the two heads were joined to one body, sitting in a dark suit and bright green tie behind the single desk in the single chair. The two heads had a neck in the shape of a letter Y.

Even as David fainted he found himself wondering which of them had chosen the tie.

He woke up back in the dormitory, lying on his own bed.

"Are you feeling better, my dear?"

Mrs Windergast was sitting on the bed next to him, holding a sponge and a basin and watching him anxiously. She had loosened his collar and mopped his face with cold water.

"You obviously weren't quite ready to see the heads," the matron crooned on. "It can be a very upsetting experience. Poor Mr Fitch and Mr Teagle were both so distinguished and good-looking until their little accident."

If that was a "little" accident, David thought to himself, what would you call a major calamity?

"We're all very worried about you, David." Mrs Windergast leaned forward with the sponge but David reared away. It might only be water in the basin, but at Groosham Grange you never knew. One quick slosh and you might wake up with three extra eyes and a passion for fresh blood.

The matron sighed and dropped the sponge.

"The trouble is," she said, "we've got to you rather late, and now we don't have much time left. How long now? Two days only! It would be such a shame to lose you, really it would. I think you're a nice boy, David. I really wish...!"

"Just leave me alone!" David turned his eyes away from her. He couldn't bear looking at her. Mrs Windergast might be just like somebody's grandmother. But the somebody was probably Jack the Ripper.

"All right, dear. I can see you're still upset..."

Mrs Windergast stood up and bustled out of the dormitory.

David stayed where he was, glad to be alone. He needed time to think, time to work things out. Already the memory of the headmasters had faded, as if his brain were unwilling to hold on to the image. Instead he thought about what Mrs Windergast had just told him. "Two days only." Why only two days?

And then it clicked. He should have realized at once. Today was March 2. Without any holidays and with no post arriving on the island, it was all too easy to forget the date. But March 4 – in two days' time – was one day he could never forget. It was his birthday, his thirteenth birthday.

And then he remembered something else. Once, when he was chatting to Jeffrey – that was when he was still able to chat to Jeffrey – the fat boy had mentioned that he was unlucky enough to have a birthday that fell on Christmas Day. In the rush of events he had managed to forget all about it, but now he remembered. It had been on Christmas Day that Jeffrey had changed. That was when he had been given his black ring. On his thirteenth birthday.

In just two days' time, David's own turn would come. Either he would accept the ring and all that came with it or...

But he couldn't even consider the alternative.

David swung himself off the bed and got to his feet. He couldn't wait any longer. He had no more time. He knew he had to escape from Groosham Grange. He knew when he had to go.

And suddenly he knew how.

ESCAPE!

The next day, one day before David's thirteenth birthday, Captain Bloodbath returned to the island. It was a Tuesday and he had brought with him three crates of supplies. There was to be a big party the following night – and David had no doubt that he was supposed to be the guest of honour. But he had no intention of being there. If things worked out the way he hoped, the guest of honour would be on a train to London before anyone guessed!

The sun was already setting as he and Jill crouched behind a sand dune, watching Gregor and the captain unload the last of the crates. The boat had arrived late that day. But it was there – David's last chance. He had hardly uttered a word since his encounter with the heads, and Jill, too, had been strangely silent as if she was upset about something. But it was she who finally broke the silence.

"It's not going to work," she said. "I told you, David. There's nowhere you can hide on the boat. Not without him noticing."

"We're not going to hide on the boat," David replied.

"Well, what *are* we going to do then? Steal it?"

"Exactly."

Jill stared at him, wondering if he was joking. But David's face was pale and serious.

"Steal the boat?" she whispered.

"When we first came to the island, he left his keys in the ignition. I noticed then." David ran a dry tongue over dry lips. "It's the last thing anybody would expect. And it's our only hope."

"But do you know how to steer a boat?"

"No. But it can't be very different from a car."

"You can't drown in a car!"

David took one last quick glance back up the cliffs. Gregor and the captain had disappeared and there was no sound of the Jeep. He tapped Jill on the shoulder and they ran forward together, the shingle crunching under their feet. The boat was bobbing up and down beside the jetty. Captain Bloodbath hadn't dropped anchor but he had tied the boat to a bollard with a knot that looked like six snakes in a washing machine.

Ignoring it for the moment, David climbed on board and went over to the steering wheel, searching for the keys. The deck swayed underneath him and for a horrible moment he thought that he'd been wrong from the start – that the captain had taken the keys with him. But then the boat swayed the other way and he saw the key-ring, an emerald skull, swaying at the end of a chain. The key was jutting out of the ignition. He let out a deep breath. In just a few minutes they would be away.

"How does it work?"

Jill had got on to the boat and was standing beside him, her voice challenging him to explain. David ran his eyes over the controls. There was a steering wheel – that was easy enough – and a lever that presumably sent the boat either backwards or forwards. But as for the rest of the buttons and switches, the dials and the compass, they could have been designed to send the boat on a one-way journey to the moon and David wouldn't have been any the wiser.

"So how does it work?" Jill asked again.

"It isn't difficult." David glanced at her irritably. "You just turn the key..."

"Then why don't you?"

"I'm going to."

He did.

Nothing happened.

David turned it again, twisting it so hard that he almost bent it in half. But still the engine refused to cough or even whimper.

"We could always swim..." Jill began.

At the same moment, David reached out and hit a large red button above the key. At once the engine chugged noisily to life, the water bubbling and smoking at the stern.

"I'll see to the knot..." David began, moving away from the wheel.

"No." Jill leant down and snatched up a fish gutting knife that had been lying on the deck. "You stay with the controls. I'll see to the knot."

The boat was tied at the very front and to reach the rope Jill had to climb back over the edge and on to the jetty. She stopped beside the bollard and set to work. It was a sharp knife but it was also a thick rope and although she sawed back and forth with all her strength she didn't seem to be getting anywhere. David waited for her on the boat, the wooden planks of the deck humming and vibrating beneath him. The engine seemed to be noisier than ever. Would they hear it back at the school? He looked up.

And froze.

Captain Bloodbath was coming back. The sound of the engine must have been carried up and over the cliff by the wind. Or perhaps he and Jill had been missed from tea? Either way, the result was the same. They had been discovered and Captain Bloodbath and Gregor were speeding down the road in the Jeep, heading in their direction.

"Jill!" David called out.

But she had seen them already. "Stay where you are!" she shouted back and doubled her efforts, sawing at the rope like a berserk violinist. By now she had cut halfway through, but Gregor and the captain were getting closer with every second that passed. Already they were approaching the bottom of the cliffs. It would take them only another twenty seconds to reach the jetty.

Jill glanced up, took a quick breath, then bent over the rope again, hacking, stabbing and slicing with the knife. The rope was fraying now, the strands separating. But still it refused to part completely.

"Hurry!" David shouted.

There was nothing he could do. His legs had turned to stone. The jeep reached the end of the jetty and screeched to a halt. Captain Bloodbath and Gregor leapt out. Jill's face twisted with fear, her hair blowing in the wind. But she still sawed. The knife bit into the rope. Another strand broke free.

Gregor was slightly ahead of the captain, his

feet clambering down the jetty towards her. Jill cried out and sliced down the knife.

The rope broke in half.

"Jill!" David called out.

But it was too late. Gregor had leapt forward like a human toad and now he was on her. Before Jill could move, his arms and legs were around her, dragging her to the ground.

"Go, David! Go!" she screamed.

David's hand slammed down on the lever. He felt the boat lurch underneath him as the propeller boiled the water. The boat slid out backwards into the open sea, trailing the broken rope across the jetty.

Then Captain Bloodbath dived forward. With a yell of triumph his hands found the rope and clamped shut on it.

The boat was several feet out now. Jill was watching it with despairing eyes, pinned down on the jetty by the dwarf. Gregor was cackling horribly, his single eye bulging. The engine screamed. The propeller churned up white water and mud. But the boat was going nowhere. Captain Bloodbath was holding on to it, digging his heels into the wood, like a cowboy with a wild stallion. His mouth was set in a grimace. His face had gone crimson. David couldn't believe what he was seeing. The captain had to let go! He couldn't possibly stand the strain – not with the engine at full strength.

But he hadn't pushed the reverse lever all the way down. An inch remained. With a cry of despair, David threw himself on to it, forcing it the rest of the way.

Captain Bloodbath still held on! It was an impossible tug-of-war, a man against a boat. The boat was rearing away, almost out of the water. But the man refused to let go, his hands fixed like vices on the rope...

"Aaaaaaargh!"

Captain Bloodbath screamed. At the same moment the boat shot backwards as if catapulted.

David stared in disbelief.

The captain's hands were still clutching the rope, but they were no longer attached to his arms. The force of the engine had pulled them clean off and as the boat rocketed away they fell off, dropping into the sea with a faint splash like two pale crabs.

David twisted the wheel, feeling sick. The boat spun round. He jammed the lever forward. The water erupted. And then he was away, leaving Groosham Grange, Skrull Island, Jill and a now handless Captain Bloodbath far behind him.

THE GHOST TRAIN

David ran through the field, the grass reaching up to his armpits. Behind him the boat stood, not moored to the jetty, but buried in it. The crossing had been far from smooth.

And now it was the morning of the next day. What with the mist, the currents and the unfamiliar controls, it had taken David longer than he had thought to make the crossing and it had been dark when he had crashed into the coast of Norfolk. He had been forced to spend the night in the wrecked cabin and it was only when daylight had come that he had realized he had ended up exactly where he had begun weeks ago.

The field climbed gently upwards towards the brilliant white windmill that David had first noticed from the hearse. On closer sight, the windmill turned out to be broken-down and deserted, battered by the wind and the rain. The sails themselves were no more than frameworks of twisted wood, like skeleton insect wings. If David had been hoping to find a telephone there, he was disappointed. The windmill had died a hundred years ago and the telephone lines had passed it by.

But on the other side he found a main road and stood there swaying, cold and exhausted. A car sped past and he blinked. It was almost as if he had forgotten what an ordinary car looked like. He glanced nervously over his shoulder. There was no way that anybody could follow him from the school. But with Groosham Grange you never knew, and he felt lost and vulnerable out in the great silence of the plain.

He had to get to the nearest town and civilization. He had no money. That meant hitchhiking. David stretched out a hand and flicked up a thumb. Surely someone would stop. Someone had to stop.

Seventy-seven cars went by. David counted them all. Not only did they refuse to stop but some of them actually accelerated as if anxious to avoid him. What was wrong with him? He was just an ordinary, crumpled, tired thirteen-year-old out in the middle of nowhere trying to get a lift! Thirteen! "Happy birthday!" he muttered to himself. Grimly, he stuck his thumb out and tried again.

The seventy-eighth car stopped. It was a bright red Ford Cortina driven by a jolly, fat man called Horace Tobago. Mr Tobago, it turned out, was a travelling salesman. As he explained, he sold practical jokes and magic tricks. Not that he needed to explain. As David sat down, his seat let out a rude noise. The sweet he was offered was made of soap. And there were two doves, a rabbit and a string of rubber sausages in the glove compartment.

"So where have you come from?" Horace asked, lifting his chin to allow his bow tie to revolve.

"From school," David muttered.

"Running away?" Horace lifted his eyebrows one at a time and wiggled his nose.

"Yes." David took a deep breath. "I have to get to a police station."

"Why?"

"I'm in danger, Mr Tobago. The school is mad. It's on an island – and they're all vampires and witches and ghosts ... and they want to turn me into one of them. I've got to stop them!"

"Ha ha ha haaargh!" Horace Tobago had a laugh like a cow being strangled. His face went bright red and the flower in his buttonhole squirted water over the dashboard. "So you're a bit of a practical joker yourself, are you, David?" he exclaimed at last. "Like a bit of a giggle? Maybe I can sell you a stink bomb or a piece of plastic sick..."

"I'm telling the truth!" David protested.

"Course you are! Course you are! And my name is Count Dracula!" The joke salesman laughed again. "Vampires and witches. What a wheeze, old boy! What a wheeze!"

David got out of the car at the first town, Hunstanton. Mr Tobago had laughed so much during the journey that there were tears streaming down his cheeks and a fake wart had fallen off his chin. He was still shrieking with laughter as he drove away waving, playing-cards tumbling out of his sleeves. David waited until the car had gone. Then he set off.

Hunstanton was a resort town. In the summer it might have been full of colour and life but out of season it was something of a last resort, a tired jumble of grey slate roofs and towers, shops and pavilions sloping down a hillside to the edge of a cold and choppy sea. There was a quay with a cluster of fishing boats half-wrapped in their own nets and looking for all the world like the fish they were meant to catch. In the distance a number of grey tents and wooden boards surrounded what might, in the summer, be a fun fair. In these sunless days of spring, there was precious little fun to be seen anywhere.

He had to find a police station. But even as he began to search for one, he was struck by a nasty thought. Horace Tobago hadn't believed a word he had said. Why should the police? If he went in there spouting on about black magic and witchcraft, they would probably call the local asylum. Worse still, they might hold him there and call the school. He was thirteen years old now. And it was a fact of life that adults never believed thirteen-year-olds.

He paused and looked around him. He was standing outside a library and on an impulse he turned and went in. At least there was something he could do – find out more. The more he knew, the more he could argue his case. And books seemed the best place to start.

Unfortunately, Hunstanton Library did not have a large section on Witchcraft. In fact there were only three books on the shelf and two of them had accidentally strayed out of Handicrafts, which were on the shelf next door. But the third looked promising. It was called *Black Magic in Britain* by one Winny H. Zoothroat. David flicked through it, then carried it over to the table to read in more detail.

> COVENS A gathering of witches, usually numbering thirteen or a multiple of thirteen. The

main reason for this is that twelve is often considered a perfect number – so the figure thirteen comes to mean death. Thirteen is also the age at which a novice will be introduced.

INITIATION A new witch is often required to sign his or her name in a black book which is kept by the master of the coven. It is customary for the name to be signed in the novice's own blood. Once the novice has signed, he or she will be given a new name. This is the name of power and might be taken from a past witch as a mark of respect.

WITCHES Well-known witches in Britain include Roger Bacon, who was famed for walking between two Oxford spires; Bessie Dunlop, who was burned to death in Ayrshire and William Rufus, a 13th-century Master-Devil.

SABBAT The witches' sabbath – it takes place at midnight. Before setting out for the sabbat, the witches rub an ointment of hemlock and aconite into their skin. This ointment causes a dream-like state and, they believe, helps with the release of magical powers.

MAGIC The best-known magic used by witches is called "the law of similarity". In this, a wax model stands in for the victim of the witch's anger. Whatever is done to the model, the human victim will feel.

The witch's most powerful magical tool is the familiar, a creature who acts as a sort of demonic servant. The cat is the most common sort of familiar but other animals have been used, such as pigs and even crows.

David lost track of time as he sat there reading the book. But by late afternoon, he had learnt just about everything he wanted to know about Groosham Grange, as well as quite a bit that he didn't. The book had one last surprise. David was about to pick it up and return it to the shelf when it fell open on another page and his eyes alighted on an entry that leapt off the page.

GROOSHAM GRANGE *See publisher's note.*

Curiously, David turned to the end of the book. There was a brief note on the last page, written by the publisher.

When she was writing this book, Winny H. Zoothroat set out for the county of

Norfolk to research Groosham Grange, the legendary "Academy of Witchcraft", where young novices were once taught the art of Black Magic.

Unfortunately, Miss Zoothroat failed to return from her journey. Her typewriter was washed ashore a few months later. Out of respect to her memory, the publishers have decided to leave this section blank.

An academy of witchcraft! The words were still buzzing in David's head as he left the library. But what else could Groosham Grange have been? Fluent Latin, wax model-making, weird cookery and very un-Christian religious studies ... it all added up. But David had never wanted to be a witch. So why had they chosen him?

He was walking down the High Street now, past the shops which were preparing to close for the day. A movement somewhere in the corner of his eye made him stop and glance back the way he had come. For a moment he thought he had imagined it. Then the same misshapen, limping figure darted out from behind a parked car.

Gregor.

Somehow the dwarf had reached Hunstanton and David knew at once that he must be looking for him. Without even thinking, he broke into a run, down the hill and out towards the sea. If he was found, he knew what would happen to him. The school would kill him rather than let him tell his story. They had already killed twice for sure. How many other people had ended up in the cemetery at Skrull Island earlier than they had expected?

It was only when he had reached the sea front that he stopped to take a breath and forced himself to calm down. It was a coincidence. It had to be. Nobody at the school could possibly know that he was still in Hunstanton.

A few feet away from him, Gregor giggled. The hunchback was sitting on a low brick wall, watching him with one beady eye. He pulled something out of his belt. It was a knife, at least seven inches long, glinting wickedly. Still giggling, he licked the blade. David turned and ran again.

He had no idea where he was going. The whole world was swaying and shuddering each time his foot thudded against the cold concrete pavement. All he could hear was his own tortured breathing. When he looked back again, the dwarf was gone. Hunstanton lay in the distance behind him. He had reached the end of the promenade.

Sagging tents and warped wooden kiosks surrounded him. The funfair! He had wandered right into the middle of it.

"Fancy a ride, sonny?"

The speaker was an old man in a shabby coat, a cigarette dangling out of the corner of his mouth. He was standing beside the ghost train. Three carriages – blue, green and yellow – stood on the curving track in front of the swing doors.

"A ride?" David glanced from the ghost train to the sea front. There was no sign of Gregor.

"A test run." The old man squeezed his cigarette and coughed. "Bit of luck you turning up. You can have a free ride."

"No thanks..." Even as David uttered the words, Gregor appeared again, shuffling into the fairground area. He hadn't seen David yet, but he was searching. The knife was still in his hand, held low, slanting upwards.

David leapt into the carriage. He had to get out of sight. A couple of minutes on a ghost train might be enough. At least Gregor couldn't follow him in there.

"Hang on tight." The old man pressed a switch.

The carriage jerked forward.

A second later it hit the doors. They broke open, then swung shut behind it. David found himself swallowed up by the darkness. He felt as if he were suffocating. Then a light glowed red behind a plastic skull and he breathed again.

If the skull was meant to frighten him, it had had the opposite effect. It reminded him that this was just an entertainment, a cheap funfair ride with plastic masks and coloured light bulbs. A loudspeaker crackled into life with a tape-recorded "Awooo!" and David even managed a smile. A green light flicked on. A rubber spider bounced up and down on an all-too-visible wire. David smiled again.

Then the carriage plunged into a chasm.

It fell through the darkness for so long that the air rushed through David's hair and he was forced back into the seat. At the last moment, when he was sure he would be dashed to pieces at the bottom of the track, it slowed down as if hitting a cushion of air.

"Some ride..." he whispered to himself. It was a relief to hear the sound of his own voice.

Another light flashed on – a light that was somehow less electric than the ones that had gone before. A soft bubbling sound was coming out of the loudspeakers, only suddenly David wondered if there were any loudspeakers. It sounded too real. He could smell something too; a damp, swamp-like smell. Before the fall, he had been able to feel the tracks underneath the carriage. Now it seemed to be floating.

A figure loomed out of the darkness – a plastic model in a black cloak. But then it raised its head and David saw that it was not a model at all but a man, and a man that David knew well.

"Did you really think you could escape from us?" Mr Kilgraw asked.

The ghost train swept forward. Mrs Windergast stepped out in front of it. "I never thought you'd be so silly, my dear," she twittered.

David flinched as the carriage hurtled towards her, but at the last moment it was pulled aside by some invisible force and he found himself staring at Mr Fitch and Mr Teagle, both of them illuminated by a soft blue glow.

"A disappointment, Mr Fitch."

"A disaster, Mr Teagle."

The ghost train lurched backwards, carrying David away. Miss Pedicure waved a finger at him and tut-tutted. Monsieur Leloup, half-man, half-wolf, howled. Mr Creer, pale and semi-transparent, opened his mouth to speak but sea water flowed over his lips.

He could only sit where he was, gripping the edge of his seat, scarcely breathing as, one after another, the entire staff of Groosham Grange appeared before him. Black smoke was writhing round his feet now and he could make out a red glow in the distance, becoming brighter as he was carried towards it. Then suddenly something clanged against the back of the carriage, just above his head. He looked up. Two hands had clamped themselves against the metal, the fingers writhing. But the hands weren't attached to arms.

David yelled out.

The ghost train thundered through a second set of doors. The red glow exploded to fill his vision, a huge setting sun. A cool breeze whispered through his hair. Far below, the waves crashed against the rocks.

The ghost train had carried him back to Skrull Island. The yellow carriage was perched on the grass at the top of the cliff. There were no tracks, no models, no funfair.

It was the evening of his thirteenth birthday and the darkness of the night was closing in.

THROUGH THE MIRROR

The school was deserted.

David had gone to bed, too depressed to do anything else. His escape had come to nothing. He had been unable to find Jill. He had just had the worst birthday of his life. And if things went the way he was expecting, it would probably also be the last.

But he couldn't sleep. Where was everybody? It had been about six o'clock when he had got back to the school. In four hours, lying in the dark, he had neither seen nor heard a soul. Not that there were any souls at Groosham Grange. They had all been sold long ago – and David knew who to.

A footfall on the bare wooden planks of the dormitory alerted him and he sat up, relaxing a moment later as Jill walked in.

"Jill!" He was relieved to see her.

"Hello, David." She sounded as depressed as he felt. "So you didn't make it?"

"I did. But ... well, it's a long story." David swung himself off the bed. He was still fully dressed. "Where is everybody?" he asked.

Jill shrugged. It was difficult to see her face. A veil of shadow had fallen over her eyes.

"What happened to you after I took the boat?" David asked.

"We can talk about that later," Jill replied. "Right now there's something I think I ought to show you. Come on!"

David followed her out of the dormitory, slightly puzzled by her. She looked well enough and he assumed that nobody had punished her for her part in the escape. But she seemed cold and distant. Perhaps she blamed him for leaving her behind. David could understand that. In a way, he still blamed himself.

"I've found out a lot of things about Groosham Grange, David," she went on as they walked down the stairs. "And a lot about the staff."

"Jill..." David reached out to stop her. "I'm sorry I had to go without you."

"That's all right, David. It all worked out for the best." She smiled at him, but her face was pale in the gloomy half-light of the hall. Breaking away, she pressed forward, moving towards the library. "All the staff here are ... well, they're not quite human. Mr Kilgraw is a vampire, Mrs Windergast is a witch. Mr Fitch and Mr Teagle are black magicians. They used to be two people until one of their experiments went wrong. Mr Creer is a ghost and Miss Pedicure has lived for ever."

"But what do they want with us?" David said.

"They want to teach us." Jill had reached the library door. She turned the handle and went in. "You're a seventh son of a seventh son. I'm a seventh daughter of a seventh daughter."

"What about it?"

"It means we're witches. We were born witches. It's not our fault. It's not anybody's fault, really. But like all the kids here we have powers. The teachers just want to show us how to use them."

"Powers?" David grabbed hold of Jill and swung her round so that she faced him. She didn't resist, but her eyes seemed to look through rather than at him. "I don't have any powers. Nor do you."

"We've got them. We just don't know how to use them." Jill was standing in front of the mirror. She reached out and rapped her knuckles against the glass. Then she turned to David. "Use your power," she challenged him.

"Go through the mirror."

"Through the glass?" David looked from the mirror to Jill and back again. He remembered his dream, how he had walked through the glass and into the underground cavern. But that had been just a dream. Now he was awake. The glass was solid. Only Jill, it seemed, had cracked.

"You can do it, David," she insisted. "You've got the power. All you have to do is use it!"

"But..."

"Try!"

Angry, confused, on the edge of fear, he wrenched himself away from her, hurling his shoulder at the glass. He would smash the mirror. That would show her. Then he would find out what was wrong with her.

His shoulder sank into the glass.

Taken by surprise, thrown off balance, David almost stumbled. His head and his raised palms made contact with the mirror – made contact with nothing – passed through the barrier as if there were no barrier at all. It was like falling into a television set. One moment he was in the library, the next he was breathing in the cold air of the tunnel, leaning against the damp and glistening rock.

He looked back the way he had come. The tunnel seemed to end with a sheet of steel. That was what the mirror looked like from the other side. Then Jill stepped through it as if it were a sheet of water and stopped, her hands on her hips.

"You see," she said. "I told you you could do it."

"But how did you know about it?" David asked.

"I know a lot more..."

She brushed past him and continued down the tunnel. David followed, wondering if he was still asleep after all. But everything felt too real. He shivered in the breeze, tasted the salt water on his lips, felt the weight of the rocks hemming him in. The passage dipped down and his ears popped as the pressure increased.

"Where does this lead to?" he asked.

"You'll see."

When it seemed that they had walked half a mile, David became aware of a strange, silver glow. There had been no light bulbs or torches to light the way and he realized now that the tunnel had been filled with the same silvery glow as if it were a mist rising from a subterranean lake. Jill stopped, waiting for him to catch up. He hurried forward, out of the tunnel and into...

It was a huge cavern, the cavern of his dream. Stalactites and stalagmites hung down, soared up, as if carved from the dreams of Nature itself. One entire wall was covered by a petrified waterfall, brilliant white, a frozen eternity. In the middle of it all stood the sacrificial block, solid granite, horribly final. Mr Kilgraw was standing behind it. He had been waiting for them. Jill had led him to them.

David spun round, searching for something he knew he would find, something he should have seen from the start. And there it was, on her third finger. A black ring.

"Jill...!" He shook his head, unable to speak. "When were you thirteen?" he demanded at last.

"Yesterday," Jill said. She looked at him reproachfully. "You never wished me a happy birthday. But I don't mind, David." She smiled. "You see, we were wrong. We were fighting them. But all the time they were really on our side."

The despair was like quicksand, sucking him in. There was no more fight in him. He had failed – failed to escape, failed to do anything. Jill had been taken. She was one of them. At last he was finally alone.

And now it was his turn.

They had come for him.

As one, the pupils of Groosham Grange moved out of the shadows at the edge of the cavern, forming a circle around him. The rest of the staff appeared behind Mr Kilgraw. David walked slowly to the granite block. He didn't want to walk there. But his legs would no longer obey his commands.

He stopped in front of Mr Kilgraw. The other pupils had closed the circle, locking him in. Everyone was looking at him.

"You have fought us long and hard, David," Mr Kilgraw said. "I congratulate you on your courage. But the time for fighting is over. Today is your thirteenth birthday. Midnight is approaching. You must make your choice.

"Listen to me, David. You are the seventh son of a seventh son. That is why you were brought to Groosham Grange. You have powers. We want to teach you how to use them."

"I'm not a witch!" David cried. The words echoed around the cavern. "I never will be!"

"Why not?" Mr Kilgraw had not raised his voice but he was speaking with an intensity and a passion that David had never heard before. "Why not, David? Why do you refuse to see things our way? You think ghosts and witches and vampires and ghosts and two-headed monsters are bad. Why? Do you know what that is, David? It's prejudice. Racial prejudice!"

Mr Fitch and Mr Teagle nodded appreciatively. Mrs Windergast muttered a brief "Hear! Hear!"

"There's nothing bad about us. Have we hurt

you? True, we had to see to Mr Netherby, but that was no fault of ours. You brought him here. We were only protecting ourselves.

"The trouble is, you've seen too many horror films. We vampires have never had a fair deal on the screen. And look at werewolves! Just because my good friend Monsieur Leloup likes the occasional pigeon salad when there's a full moon, everyone thinks they've a right to hunt him down and shoot silver bullets in him. And what about Mr Creer? All right, so he's dead. But he's still a very good teacher – in fact, he's a lot more lively than quite a few living teachers I could mention."

"But I'm not like you," David insisted. "I don't want to be like you."

"You have power," Mr Kilgraw replied. "That is all that matters. And the real question you should be asking yourself, David, is, do you really want to stay with your parents and follow your singularly unpleasant father into merchant banking? Or do you want to be free?

"Join us, and you'll be rich. We can teach you how to make gold out of lead, how to destroy your enemies just by snapping your fingers. We can show you how to see into the future and use it for yourself. Think of it, David! You can have everything you want ... and more. Look at Miss Pedicure! She's lived for ever. So can you...

"All right, I admit it. We are, frankly, evil. My friends Mr Fitch and Mr Teagle are more evil than any of us. They've won awards for being evil. But what's so bad about being evil? *We've* never dropped an atom bomb on anyone. *We've* never polluted the environment or experimented on animals or cut back on National Health spending. Our evil is rather agreeable. Why do you think there have been so many books and films about us? It's because people like us. We are actually rather pleasantly evil."

While Mr Kilgraw had spoken, the sixty-four pupils of Groosham Grange, novice witches and young adepts all, had tightened the circle. Now they were moving closer to David, their eyes bearing down on him. Jill was next to Jeffrey. William Rufus was on the other side. Sixty-four black rings glowed in the underground light.

Mr Kilgraw held the sixty-fifth.

"I have enjoyed the fight, David," he said. "I didn't want it to be easy. I admire courage. But now it is midnight." He reached out with his other hand. Gregor scurried forward and gave him his knife.

"Here is your choice," he went on. "The ring or the knife? You can reject us one final time. In that instance, I regret that I will be forced to plunge the blade into your heart. I can assure you that it will hurt me more than it will hurt you. And we'll give you a decent burial in the school cemetery.

"Alternatively, you can accept us, take a new name and begin your education in earnest. But there can be no going back, David. If you join us, you join us for ever."

David felt himself being forced down on to the granite block. The circle of faces spun round him. There was the ring. And there was the knife.

"Now, David," Mr Kilgraw asked. "What do you say?"

SEVENTH SON

"When I was a boy," Mr Eliot said, "I had to work in my holidays. My father made me work so hard I'd have to spend three weeks in hospital before I could go back to school."

"But David's only got one day's holiday," Mrs Eliot reminded him, pouring herself a glass of gin.

"I am aware of that, my dear." Mr Eliot snatched the glass out of her hand and drank it himself. "And if you ask me, one day is much too long. If I'd been expelled from Beton College my father would never have spoken to me again. In fact he'd have cut off my ears so I wouldn't hear him if he spoke to me accidentally."

The two parents were sitting in the living-room of their house in Wiernotta Mews. Edward Eliot was smoking a cigar. Eileen Eliot was stroking Beefeater, her favourite Siamese cat. They had just eaten lunch – ham salad served in true vegetarian style, without the ham.

"Maybe we should take him to a film or something?" Mrs Eliot suggested nervously.

"A film?"

"Well ... or a concert..."

"Are you mad?" Mr Eliot snapped. He leant forward angrily and stubbed his cigar out on the cat. The cat screeched and leapt off Mrs Eliot, its back claws ripping off most of her stockings and part of her leg. "Why should we take him anywhere?" Mr Eliot demanded.

"Perhaps you are right, my love," Mrs Eliot whimpered, pouring the rest of the gin on to her leg to stop the bleeding.

Just then the door opened and David walked in.

He had changed since his departure for Groosham Grange. He was thinner, older, somehow wiser. He had always been quiet. But now there was something strange about his silence. It was like a wall between him and his parents. And when he looked at them, it was with soft, almost merciless, eyes.

Mr Eliot glanced at his watch. "Well, David," he said. "You've got seven hours and twenty-two minutes before your holiday's over. So why don't you go and mow the lawn?"

"But it's a plastic lawn!" Mrs Eliot protested.

"Then he can go and wash it!"

"Of course, dear!" Mrs Eliot beamed at her husband, then fainted from loss of blood.

David sighed. Seven hours and twenty-two minutes. He hadn't realized there was still so much time.

He lifted his right hand.

"What's that you're wearing?" his father demanded.

David muttered a few words under his breath.

There was no puff of smoke, no flash of light. But it was as if his parents had been photographed and at the same time turned into those photographs. Mrs Eliot was halfway out of her chair, slumping towards the carpet. Mr Eliot was about to speak, his mouth open, his tongue hovering over his teeth.

It was a simple spell. But they would remain that way for the next three weeks.

David rubbed his black ring thoughtfully. He had spoken the words of power with perfect pronunciation. Mrs Windergast would have said that three weeks was overdoing it when a few hours would have been enough, but then she was a perfectionist and all David's spells tended to be on the strong side. Maybe he was just a little enthusiastic.

He went upstairs and lay down on his bed.

A chocolate milk shake materialized in thin air and began to float towards him. He was looking forward to the next term at Groosham Grange. He and Jill would both be taking their first GCSEs in the summer: Telepathy, Weather Control, Wax Modelling and (the trickiest of the four) Advanced Blood Sacrifice.

And what then? He sipped the milk shake and smiled. He'd got it exactly right – thick with plenty of chocolate. He still blushed when he remembered his first attempt. In cookery class he'd conjured up a perfect milk shake: banana flavour with two scoops of ice-cream. But he'd forgotten to include a glass. It was only recently that he'd got used to his powers, begun to enjoy them.

So what would he do with them? Black magic or white magic? Good or evil?

He would leave that decision until later – at least until he'd passed his exams. And David was certain that he would pass. He was the seventh son of a seventh son. And he had never felt better in his life.

THE ALEX RIDER SERIES

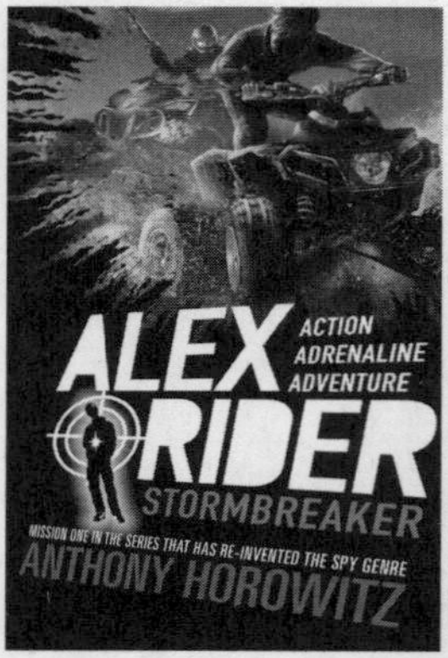

Alex Rider – you're never too young to die…

High in the Alps, death waits for Alex Rider…

Sharks. Assassins. Nuclear bombs. Alex Rider's in deep water.

Alex Rider has 90 minutes to save the world.

Once stung, twice as deadly. Alex Rider wants revenge.

He's back – and this time there are no limits.

THE ALEX RIDER SERIES

Alex Rider bites back…

Alex Rider – in the jaws of death…

One bullet.

One life.

The end starts here.

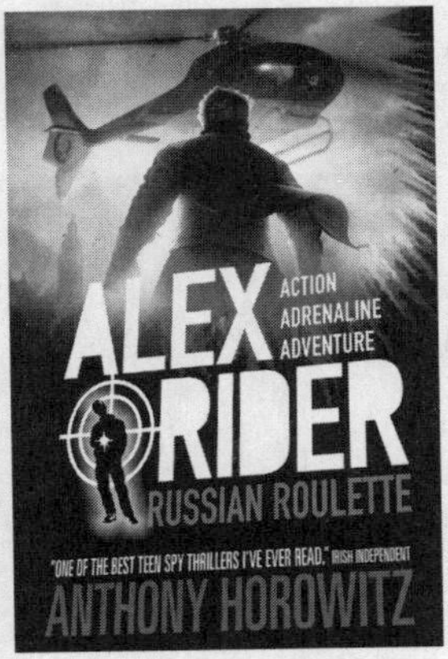

Get your hands on the deadly prequel

ALEX RIDER

ACTION ADRENALINE ADVENTURE

THE MISSION CONTINUES AT alexrider.com

ACTION. ADRENALINE. ADVENTURE.

alexrider.com /alexrideruk

WELCOME TO THE DARK SIDE OF ANTHONY HOROWITZ

THE POWER OF FIVE

BOOK ONE

He always knew he was different.
First there were the dreams.
Then the deaths began.

BOOK TWO

It began with Raven's Gate.
But it's not over yet. Once
again the enemy is stirring.

BOOK THREE

Darkness covers the earth.
The Old Ones have returned.
The battle must begin.

BOOK FOUR

An ancient evil is unleashed.
Five have the power to defeat it.
But one of them has been taken.

BOOK FIVE

Five Gatekeepers.
One chance to save mankind.
Chaos beckons. Oblivion awaits.

Anthony Horowitz is the author of the number one bestselling Alex Rider books and The Power of Five series. He has enjoyed huge success as a writer for both children and adults, most recently with the latest adventure in the Alex Rider series, *Russian Roulette*, and the highly acclaimed Sherlock Holmes novel, *The House of Silk*. His latest novel, *Moriarty*, is also set in the world of Sherlock Holmes and was published in October 2014. Anthony was also chosen by the Ian Fleming estate to write the new James Bond novel which will be published this year. Anthony has won numerous awards, including the Bookseller Association/Nielsen Author of the Year Award, the Children's Book of the Year Award at the British Book Awards, and the Red House Children's Book Award. In 2014 Anthony was awarded an OBE for Services to Literature. He has also created and written many major television series, including *Injustice*, *Collision* and the award-winning *Foyle's War*.

You can find out more about Anthony and his work at:

www.alexrider.com

@AnthonyHorowitz

THE DIAMOND BROTHERS IN...

South by South East

"Anthony Horowitz is the lion of children's literature." Michael Morpurgo

"Horowitz has become a writer who converts boys to reading."
The Times

"A first-class children's novelist."
TES

More wickedly funny books

by Anthony Horowitz

The Devil and His Boy

Groosham Grange

Return to Groosham Grange

The Switch

More Bloody Horowitz

The Diamond Brothers books:

The Falcon's Malteser

Public Enemy Number Two

South by South East

The Blurred Man

The French Confection

I Know What You Did Last Wednesday

The Greek who Stole Christmas

THE DIAMOND BROTHERS IN...

South by South East

ANTHONY HOROWITZ

WALKER
BOOKS

This is a work of fiction. Names, characters, places and incidents either are the product of the author's imagination or, if real, are used fictitiously. All statements, activities, stunts, descriptions, information and material of any other kind contained herein are included for entertainment purposes only and should not be relied on for accuracy or replicated as they may result in injury.

First published 1997 by Walker Books Ltd
87 Vauxhall Walk, London SE11 5HJ

This edition published 2015

2 4 6 8 10 9 7 5 3 1

This book has been typeset in Sabon

Printed in Germany by GGP Media GmbH

British Library Cataloguing in Publication Data:
a catalogue record for this book is available from the British Library

ISBN 978-1-4063-5705-9

www.walker.co.uk

CONTENTS

TIM DIAMOND INC.
23 THE CUTTING, CAMDEN TOWN, NW1

Dear Reader,

This is the third book in the Diamond Brothers series, and if you enjoyed the other two, maybe you need help. My name is Tim Diamond and I'm in the books. I also get 1.5 per cent of every copy sold ... otherwise I wouldn't touch them with a barge pole. And if I did touch them with a barge pole, it would only be to push them into a canal.

Let me tell you why.

First of all, the books make me look like an idiot. People seem to forget that I was the one who solved the mystery of the missing chocolate Maltesers and the dead gangster in *The Falcon's Malteser* and that I also uncovered the identity of the master criminal known as The Fence in *Public Enemy Number Two*. OK, maybe I did get a bit of help from my thirteen-year-old brother, Nick, but it's my name on the door. And I should know. I paid for the paint.

You might like to know that I had a very successful year as a police officer before I became a private detective. I caught three cat burglars and even managed to return the cats. I arrested a female impersonator (although admittedly it was on our third date). Not bad for one of the "boys in blue", you might think ... and in my case I even had the matching underwear. I've never mentioned this before, but I was actually recommended for a medal for bravery. I went all the way to Buckingham Palace to collect it but at the last minute I was too scared to go in.

But anyway, you'll notice when you read the books that Nick takes all the credit. He's my kid brother and he's got to be kidding!

I mean, take the time we were chased by an aeroplane with machine guns through a cornfield in Holland ... you'll get to that bit in Chapter Ten, and at the time I didn't think there was going to be a Chapter Eleven. We were being shot at by a serial killer, and it looked like the two of us were going to be shredded wheat. Nick claims that he was the one who worked out our brilliant escape, but that's not how I remember it. I think I was the man with the plan. But while he's the one telling the story, who's going to listen to me?

I even telephoned my new editor at Walker Books to complain. Her name is Kris Croat and she was recently asked to work on the Diamond Brothers books – which is strange, because she's a woman of few words and most of them don't make any sense. She learned English as a second language and unfortunately she still prefers Hungarian. When she gets over-excited, we have to hire a translator. Most of her books have never sold a copy outside of Budapest.

"I want to write the next book," I told her.

"Hello?" she replied. I could imagine her reaching for an English dictionary. She's a big woman with muscular arms that are covered in tattoos. *Where's Wally?* Maisy the mouse. Some of Walker's biggest successes began life on her biceps.

"This is Tim Diamond!" I said.

"Hello, Tim!" She has a strange sing-song voice. What's also really strange is that it's hopelessly out of tune. "To hear from you, it is a pressure."

"I think you mean ... a pleasure."

"No I don't."

"Well, I've just read *South by South East*..."

"That's great, Tim. Because nobody else has."

"The reason why I'm ringing is because I don't think it's fair. Half of it isn't true!"

"It makes you look like a very stupid person. Yes?"

"Exactly!"

"And you say the other half of it is not true?"

"Listen to me, Miss Croat." I had to remind myself that this wasn't a sensitive woman on the other end of the line. She'd spent six years working in a Hungarian slaughterhouse before she went into children's publishing. She was one of the very few editors who could strangle a horse with her bare hands. "I want another author," I snarled.

"It's time to get rowling," she agreed.

"JK Rowling?" I exclaimed.

"No. It says here in my phrase book 'time to get rolling'. Goodbye!" She rang off.

There are times when my life seems completely hopeless. Then I call Walker Books and I know it is.

If you've seen my books before you may have noticed that this one has a completely different cover. It was actually designed for a completely different book, but they didn't want it so it was given to me. But it's the same old author. Anthony Horowitz has achieved a new level of success this year ... unfortunately it's several levels below the one he achieved last year. I wouldn't like to say that his career's in trouble, but I notice he's been getting less shelf space in Waterstone's. And they've put him in a section marked HISTORY.

Anyway, that's the end of this introduction. I know it's a bit short, but right now I'm in the middle of another investigation. I'm investigating why nobody has paid me to write it. And to make matters worse, I've been having trouble with my new computer. It's also Hungarian and when you press the spell check it self-destructs.

But I like to remember what my grandmother told me: reading is the most important thing in life, and books will always make you happy. She said that to me on the way to the mobile library. Unfortunately, it ran her over.

Tim Diamond

McGUFFIN

What can I tell you about Camden Town? It's a place in north London with a market and a canal. What you can't find in the market you'll find floating in the canal – only cheaper.

And that's why we'd moved to Camden Town. Because it was cheap. Our new offices were small and sleazy but that was OK because so were most of our clients. We hadn't taken much with us. Just some old furniture and some bad memories. And the door. It was cheaper to bring the door with us than get another one painted.

TIM DIAMOND INC.
PRIVATE DETECTIVE

That's what it said on the glass.

They were the last words Jake McGuffin ever read. But when you're being chased by two Dutch killers with a knife and a gun and your name on both of them, you don't have time to start a paperback book.

It was a long, hot summer. Although I didn't know it then, it was going to be longer and hotter for me than for anyone else. The day it all started, it was my turn to make lunch – but I'd just discovered there was no lunch left to make. I'd done my best. I'd got a tray ready with plates, knives, forks, napkins and even a flower I'd found growing on the bathroom wall. All that was missing was the food.

"Is that it?" Tim asked as I carried it in. He was sitting behind his desk, making paper boats out of pages from the phone book. "A carton of milk?"

"Half a carton," I replied. "We had the other half for breakfast." It was true. Half a carton of long-life milk was all that stood between us and starvation. "I'll get some glasses," I said.

"Don't bother." Tim reached for a cardboard box on the corner of his desk. He turned it upside down. A single straw fell out. "That's the last straw," he announced.

I'd been living with my big brother, Herbert Timothy Simple, ever since my parents decided to emigrate to Australia. Herbert called himself Tim Diamond. He also called himself a private detective. Neither was true. He wouldn't have been able to find a fingerprint on the end of his own finger. Dead bodies made him feel queasy. When it came to pursuing an investigation, he was so hopeless that the investigation usually ended up pursuing him.

I gazed sadly at the milk. "You need a job, Tim," I said.

"I've applied for jobs, Nick," Tim protested. He slid open a drawer in his desk. It was bulging with letters. "Look! I've applied for hundreds of jobs."

"How many rejections have you had?" I asked.

He scowled. "These *are* the rejections." He fumbled in the pile for a minute and pulled one out, his face brightening. "Here's one I haven't heard from yet," he said.

"Maybe your application got lost in the post."

Tim opened the letter and spread it out in front of him. "Head of Security at the Canadian Bank in Pall Mall," he read out. "Forty thousand quid a year plus luncheon vouchers and car. In other words, meals and wheels."

"When will you hear?" I asked.

"Don't worry. The phone'll ring..."

"We don't have a phone," I reminded him. "We got cut off."

Tim's face fell. He folded the letter and put it back in the drawer.

"Things aren't so bad," he muttered. "I'll get a case sooner or later. I bet you any day now somebody's going to knock on the door."

Somebody knocked on the door.

Tim gulped like he'd just swallowed a chicken bone. He looked around him. What with the lunch tray on the desk, the paper boats and everything else, the office hardly looked like the headquarters of a successful private eye. And here was a potential client knocking at the door! For a moment he froze. Then we both went into action.

The paper boats went into the bin. Tim opened another drawer and threw the knives, forks and napkins inside. At the same time, I grabbed the milk carton and slipped it into a vase on a shelf. That just left the tray. Tim handed it to me. I looked for somewhere to put it. I couldn't see anywhere so I put it on a chair and sat on it.

"Come in!" Tim called out. He was bent over the desk, scribbling away at a blank sheet of paper. It would have looked more impressive if he'd been using the right end of the pen.

The door opened.

Our visitor was carrying a gun – and it was the gun that I looked at first. It was small, snubnosed, a dull, metallic grey. So was the visitor. He was only a little taller than me and he was so pale he could have just stepped out of one of those old black and white films they show on TV. He had a square chin, close-cropped hair and small eyes that seemed to be hiding behind the thick lenses of his spectacles. Either he was extremely short-sighted or his optician was. Or maybe it was just that he felt safer behind bulletproof glasses.

He shut the door behind him. It must have been raining outside because there were big drops clinging to his forehead and dripping off the hem of his coat. Or maybe he was sweating. "You Tim Diamond?" he asked.

"Yeah, I'm Tim Diamond," Tim agreed.

The man moved further into the room and saw me. For a moment the gun pointed my way and my hands flickered automatically towards a position somewhere above my head. "Who are you?" he demanded.

"I'm Nick Diamond," I said. "His brother."

His eyes travelled down. "Why are you sitting on a tray?" he demanded.

"Because I feel like a cup of tea." It was the first thing to come into my head but the answer must have satisfied him because a moment later, walking over to the window, he'd forgotten me.

"I didn't catch your name," Tim said.

"Jake McGuffin." The man peered out of the window, his eyes as narrow as the venetian blind we'd sold the week before. He glanced back over his shoulder at the door. "Is that the only way in?"

Tim nodded. "Are you in some sort of trouble?" he asked.

"Somebody's trying to kill me," McGuffin said.

He turned away from the window just as a

high-velocity bullet fired from the street drilled a neat hole through the pane, flashed across the room a bare millimetre from his face, smashed the vase on the shelf opposite and exposed the carton of milk I had hidden there earlier. Milk fountained out.

"What makes you think that, Mr McStuffing?" Tim enquired.

I was staggered. Even McGuffin had gone pale. But evidently Tim just hadn't noticed there was anything wrong. The truth was he was so wrapped up in his own performance that he probably wouldn't have noticed if his visitor had been hit then and there. I edged closer to the filing cabinet, ready to hurl myself behind it if any more bullets blasted into the room.

McGuffin slipped the gun into a shoulder holster and moved across the carpet, keeping clear of the window. "I need to use a phone," he said. The words came out fast, urgent.

"Why?" Tim asked.

McGuffin hesitated. I think he still hadn't worked Tim out. But then he had other things on his mind.

"You can tell me, Mr McMuffin," Tim went on. He tapped his nose. "I'm a private nose with an eye for trouble. Trouble is my middle name."

McGuffin looked around the room. If he could have seen a telephone I reckon he would have used the flex to strangle Tim and then made his call uninterrupted. But whoever was waiting for him outside had him cornered. Time was running out. He had no choice. "OK," he said. "I'll tell you."

He sat down opposite Tim and took out a cigarette. "You got a light?" he asked.

Tim switched on his desk light. McGuffin scrunched his cigarette on the desktop. He seemed to have got a lot older in the last few minutes. "Listen," he said. "I'm an agent. It doesn't matter who I work for."

"Who *do* you work for?" Tim asked.

"It doesn't matter. I'm on the track of a man called Charon. He's a killer, an assassin, the head of a murder organization that's bigger than Esso."

Tim was puzzled. "Charon?" he asked. "What sort of name is that?"

"It's a code name," McGuffin explained. "It comes out of the Greek myths. You ever hear of Hades, the Greek underworld? In the old legends, it's where people went when they died. Charon was the person who took them there. He was the ferryman of the dead."

The sun must have gone behind a cloud. For the first time that summer I felt cold. Maybe it was the breeze coming in through the bullet hole.

"Nobody knows who Charon really is," McGuffin went on. "He can disguise himself at the drop of a hat. They say he's got so many faces his own mother wouldn't recognize him."

"Do you know his mother?" Tim asked.

"No." McGuffin took a deep breath. "There's only one way to recognize Charon," he said. "He's lost a finger."

"Whose finger?" Tim asked.

"His own. He only has nine fingers."

Tim smiled. "So that'll help you finger him!"

McGuffin closed his eyes for a few seconds. He must have hoped he was dreaming and that when he opened them he'd be somewhere else. "Right," he said at last. "But I've got no time. Charon is about to kill a Russian diplomat called Boris Kusenov."

"I've heard of him," I muttered. And it was true. I'd seen the name in the last newspaper I'd read. It had been underneath my chips.

"If Kusenov dies, that's it," McGuffin went on. "The Iron Curtain goes back up. There'll be another arms race. Maybe even war..."

"As bad as that?" Tim asked.

"I'm the only man who can stop him. I know when Charon plans to kill him. And I know how. I've got to make that call."

Tim shrugged. "That's too bad, McNothing. We don't have a phone."

"No phone..." For a moment I thought he was going to murder Tim. He'd told us everything. And he'd got nothing for it. His hands writhed briefly. Maybe he was imagining them round Tim's throat.

"There's a phone box round the corner, in Skin Lane," I suggested.

McGuffin had forgotten I was even in the room. He looked at me, then at the bullet hole. The bullet hole was like a single eye and that seemed to be looking at me too. "It's an alley," I added.

"Outside." McGuffin licked his lips. I could see his problem. If he waited here much longer, Charon would come in and get him. And next time it might not be a single bullet. One grenade and we'd all be permanently disconnected, like the telephone. On the other hand, if he stepped out into the street he'd be a walking target. And I doubted if Charon would miss a second time.

But McGuffin was obviously used to thinking on his feet. Suddenly he was out of the chair and over the other side of the room where Tim's raincoat was hanging on a hook. "I'll give you fifty pounds for the coat," McGuffin said.

"But you've already got a coat," Tim observed.

"I've got to get out of here without being seen."

McGuffin pulled off his own coat. Underneath he was wearing an off-white suit that had probably been white when he put it on.

It didn't quite hide the gun, jutting out of a shoulder holster where most people carry a wallet. He put on the raincoat, folding the collar up so that it hid most of his face. Finally he produced fifty pounds out of nowhere and threw them down on the desk, five ten pound notes which were the best thing I'd seen all day. Tim wasn't going to complain either. The coat had only cost him ten pounds in the Oxfam shop and even they had probably made enough profit out of it to buy another ox.

McGuffin took a deep breath. He hesitated for one last moment. And then he was gone. The door clicked shut behind him.

I got off the tray. "What do you think?" I asked.

Tim opened his eyes. The money was sitting right in front of him. "Fifty quid!" he exclaimed.

"I wonder who he was working for?"

"Forget it, Nick," Tim pocketed the money. "It's none of our business. I'm just glad we're not involved."

I picked up McGuffin's coat, meaning to hang it back on the hook. As I lifted it, something fell out of one of the pockets. It was a key. There was a plastic tag attached to it and in bright red letters: *Room 605, London International Hotel.*

I looked at the key. Tim looked at me. We were involved, all right.

SOUTH BY SOUTH EAST

Maybe I should have emigrated to Australia.

My parents had left the country three years before, when I was eleven, and of course they'd meant to take me with them. I'd got as far as Heathrow. But while my parents had got jammed up in one door of the aircraft, I'd slipped out another. Then I'd legged it across the main runway, leaving the screams of the engines – and of my mother – behind me. I remember stopping at the perimeter fence and turning round. And there they were, my mum and dad, flying off to Australia without me. As the plane soared away into the setting sun there was a big lump in my throat and I realized I'd laughed so much I'd swallowed my chewing-gum.

Ever since then I'd been living with Tim. Twice I'd almost been killed with him. I should have remembered that as we set off together in search of McGuffin. Perhaps this was going to be third time unlucky.

"Are you sure about this?" Tim asked as we walked together.

I jiggled the key in my hand. "We're just going to give it back," I said.

As we approached Skin Lane, a street cleaner limped round the corner, stabbing at the pavement with a broken, worn-out brush. The cleaner wasn't looking much better himself. Maybe it was the heat. There was a dustcart parked in the alley and that puzzled me. Why hadn't the cleaner taken the cart with him? Meanwhile Tim had walked on and, looking past him, I saw Jake McGuffin standing in the telephone box with the receiver propped under his chin.

"He's still there," I said.

"Yes." Tim sniffed. "But look at that. He's only had my coat five minutes and he's already spilled something all down the front."

"What?" Suddenly I wasn't feeling so good. The hairs on the back of my neck were standing up, which was strange, because I didn't know I had any hairs on the back of my neck. Leaving the cart, I moved quickly past Tim. McGuffin watched me approach but his eyes didn't focus. I reached out to open the door.

"Wait a minute, Nick," Tim said. "He hasn't finished talking."

I opened the door.

McGuffin had finished talking. The telephone was dead and any minute now he'd be joining it. The stuff he had spilled down the coat was blood, his own blood, and it was Charon who had done the spilling. Even as I opened the door I saw the shattered pane of glass where the bullet had passed through on its way to McGuffin's heart. And at the same time, I knew that the man with the broom – Charon – had just made a clean getaway.

I was holding the door. For a moment I was trapped behind it. Tim was standing in front of me, his mouth open, his eyes wide. Then McGuffin pitched forward, landing in Tim's arms. He was still alive. He began to talk. I would have heard what he said but it was exactly then that a train decided to pass overhead, and for the next few seconds the air was filled with the noise of grinding, creaking metal. The brick walls of the alley caught the sound and batted it back and forth like a ping-pong ball. I saw McGuffin's lips move. I saw Tim nod. But I didn't hear a word. I tried to move round but the glass door was still between me and them. By the time I managed to close it and get over to them, the train was gone.

So was McGuffin.

Tim let him go and he sprawled out on the tarmac. I tried to talk but my lips were too dry. I took a deep breath and tried again. "What did he say?" I asked.

"Suth," Tim said.

"Suth? You mean – south?"

"Yes."

"Was that all?"

"No. He said 'bee'."

"A bumblebee?"

"No." Tim shook his head. "Just 'bee'."

"South. Bee..."

"Suff-iss."

"Suff-iss?"

Tim looked at me sadly. "I couldn't hear," he wailed. "The train was too loud..."

"I know!" I forced myself not to shout at him. "But you were closest to him, Tim. You must have heard what he said."

"I've told you. Suff. Bee. Suff-iss."

"Suff. Bee. Suff-iss?" I played it over in my head a few times. "You mean south by south east? Was that what he said?"

Tim brightened. "Yes! That was it, Nick! I mean, that's what it must have been. South by south east! That's exactly what he said."

"South by south east." I made a quick calculation, then turned round so that I faced the corner of Skin Lane, away from the High Street.

"A dead end," Tim said. He looked down at the body, his face going the colour of mouldy cheese. If we stayed here much longer he was going to pass out on me.

"You're not going to faint, are you?" I asked.

"No!" Tim was indignant.

"You usually faint when there's a dead body."

"No I don't."

"You even fainted when your goldfish died."

"That was grief!"

"We'd better call the police," I said.

Tim glanced at the phone box but I shook my head. "We can't use that one. Fingerprints..."

We half walked, half ran. The police station was a half-mile away. It seemed we were doing everything by halves. It even took us half an hour to get there. The trouble was that Tim was seeing Charon all over the place now. A woman with a pram, a traffic warden, a man waiting for a bus ... they all had him paralysed with terror and he would only speak to the desk sergeant in the station when he had counted his ten fingers.

The desk sergeant listened to our story with a cold smile, then showed us into a back room while he went to find a senior officer. I was beginning to wonder if we hadn't made a mistake going there.

Then the door opened and I *knew* we'd made a mistake.

The senior police officer was Chief Inspector Snape.

Snape was a tough, round-shouldered bull of a man. Wave a red flag at him and he'd probably flatten you. He had the sort of flesh you'd expect to see hanging upside down in a butcher's shop. Snape hardly ever smiled. It was as if nobody had taught him how. When his lips did twitch upwards, his eyes stayed small and cold.

But without any doubt, the worst thing about Snape was his sidekick, Boyle. And with Boyle, kick was exactly the word. Boyle loved violence. I once saw a photograph of him in full riot gear – shield, truncheon, tear gas, grenade, helmet – and that had been taken on his day off. He was shorter than Snape, with dark, curly hair that probably went all the way down to his feet.

"Well, well, well," Snape muttered. "If it isn't Tim Diamond!"

"But it is!" Tim replied, brilliantly.

"I know it is!"

Snape's eyes glazed over. Perhaps he was remembering the time when Tim had put together an Identikit picture and the entire police force of Great Britain had spent two months looking for a man with three eyes and an upside-down mouth. "There never was another police constable like you," he rasped.

"Thank you, Chief." Tim grinned.

"I'm not flattering you! I fired you!" Snape had gone bright red. He pulled out a chair and threw himself into it, breathing heavily.

Boyle edged forward. "Are you all right, sir?"

"Yes. I'm all right, Boyle."

"You want me to..." Boyle winked and nodded his head in Tim's direction.

"No. I'm all right." Snape seemed to have collected himself. He glanced at a typed sheet of paper. "So what is all this nonsense?" he demanded. "Spies and killers and bodies in telephone boxes."

"It's the truth," I said.

That brought a dark look from Boyle. "I'll get the truth," he growled.

"No, Boyle." Snape shook his head tiredly.

"I can use the lie detector, sir."

"No, Boyle. You short-circuited it – remember?"

"Look, Chief Inspector," I said. "If you don't believe us, why don't you come back with us? We can show you the body."

Snape considered. "All right," he said. "We'll come with you and take a look. But I warn you, laddie. If you're wasting our time..."

I've been in a police car quite a few times and normally it's fun. But Snape was a slow driver. He didn't put on the siren and the only flashing light was his petrol gauge. By the time we got back to Skin Lane, events had overtaken us. So had half the traffic in London.

He parked the car. We got out. Tim and I had shared the back seat and we were a few paces behind Snape as he turned the corner into the alley. Boyle went between us. We all stopped at the same moment.

"Well?" Snape demanded.

Tim's mouth dropped open. "It's gone," he said.

I looked past him. He was right. McGuffin's body had vanished. But that wasn't the strange part.

So had the telephone box.

ROOM SERVICE

"I don't think Snape believed my story," Tim said.

"Whatever makes you think that, Tim?" I asked.

We'd just been thrown into prison for wasting police time. We were sitting on two bunk beds in a small square cell lit by a single bulb.

Snape hadn't believed a word we'd said – but for once I couldn't blame him. I mean, how often do secret agents drop in on you, swap coats, get shot and then vanish in a puff of smoke, taking the nearest telephone box with them? Even Tim was having trouble working it out.

"Maybe somebody stole the telephone box," he muttered.

"What about the body?" I asked.

"No. It couldn't have been the body, Nick. The body was dead."

Something hard was jabbing into my pocket. At first I thought it was the mattress but as I shifted my weight I realized it was the hotel key. In the excitement I'd forgotten all about it. I suppose I could have shown it to Snape, but I don't think it would have helped. By the time he got to the London International Hotel the whole place would probably have vanished too.

I took the key out and held it up. It took Tim a moment or two to remember what it was. Then he groaned.

"We've got to go there," I said. "Room 605—"

"Why?" Tim cut in.

"You heard what McGuffin said. If this Russian of his gets killed, he was talking about nuclear war ... the end of the world!"

"Maybe he was exaggerating."

"Well, *somebody* believed him, Tim."

"How do you know?"

"They shot him."

Snape let us out the next morning with another warning about wasting police time. I noticed that he hadn't wasted a police breakfast on us, and the first thing we did was get a McBreakfast at the nearest McDonald's. We left the place feeling slightly McSick and hopped on a bus that took us across town to the London International Hotel.

The hotel was one of those great piles on twenty-seven storeys with hot and cold running tourists in every room. This was the middle of the summer season, and the building was packed with Japanese and Germans and Scandinavians all milling round searching for someone who could speak their language and knew where Harrods was.

Nobody stopped us as we made our way across to the lift and took it up to the sixth floor, and there was nobody around in the corridor either. We walked on and arrived at room 605. It was a door just like all the others. So why did it seem so solid, so threatening? I handed Tim the key.

"You want me to open it?" he asked.

"Yeah," I said.

"But we don't know what's on the other side."

"That's why we've got to open it."

I knocked on the door first, just to be sure.

Then I stood back while Tim opened it with the key. We slipped in quickly and shut the door behind us. And there we were, inside Jake McGuffin's room. I wondered how long it would be before the hotel realized he'd checked out. Permanently.

There was nobody there. I don't know what I'd been expecting but it was just an ordinary hotel room: twin beds, bathroom and colour TV. It had a nice view of Hyde Park and windows that didn't open so you couldn't throw yourself out when the bill arrived. The beds hadn't been slept in, of course, but there was still some of McGuffin's stuff spread about – a couple of ties on the back of a chair, a pen on the table, a suitcase on the stand by the door.

"There's no one here," Tim said.

"OK. Let's move."

I started with the suitcase but there was nothing interesting inside it, just some shirts and socks and a couple of handkerchiefs. Meanwhile Tim had thrown open the bedside cupboard and was rummaging about inside.

"Nick?" he demanded suddenly.

"Yes?"

"What are we searching for?"

It was a good question, only maybe he should have asked it five minutes before. I shut the suitcase. "We've got to find out who McGuffin was working for and where he'd been," I said. "Anything that can lead us to Charon. Names, addresses, telephone numbers..."

"Sure." Tim snatched up a book of matches lying in an ashtray beside the bed.

"London International," he muttered. "I've heard that name somewhere before."

"Yes, Tim," I said. "It's the name of this hotel."

"Right." He put the matches down and

looked underneath the pillows. I didn't know what he hoped to find there. I thought it better not to ask.

In the meantime, I'd crossed over to the low table that ran underneath a mirror along the far wall – and that was where I found it. It was a ticket: seat number 86 to something called the Amstel Ijsbaan. Whatever the something was, it had to be foreign. The only word in the English language that I know with a double "a" in it is "Aagh". The ticket had a little illustration in one corner: a pair of skating boots.

"Come and look at this!" I called Tim over and handed him the ticket.

He examined it. "Do you think he was an ice-skater?" he asked.

"McGuffin?" I shook my head. "He didn't look like one."

"You're right," Tim agreed. "He wasn't wearing shiny tights."

I took the ticket back. "Maybe he was going to meet somebody there," I said.

"Amstel Ix-barn." Tim turned the words over in his mouth. "Do you think it's a play?"

"Not a very catchy title," I muttered.

There was a sudden rattle at the door. Both of us froze. Somebody was trying a key in the lock and somehow I got the feeling it wasn't room service. "Quick!" I whispered. I gestured at the bathroom. As the main door opened we disappeared inside. I took the ticket with me.

Two men came into the bedroom. I had swung the bathroom door shut behind me but left a crack so I could see them. The first man was thin and pale, about thirty-five years old, dressed in a dark suit with hair cut so close that when he spoke you could see the skin move on his skull. The second man was exactly the same. Maybe they hadn't been born twins but whatever work they did had turned them into mirror reflections of each other. They even wore the same sunglasses. You couldn't see their eyes.

"OK, Ed," the first one said. "This is the room."

"Right, Ted."

The second one – Ed – moved forward and grabbed McGuffin's suitcase. Then he started throwing things into it … the ties, the pen, everything McGuffin had left behind. Meanwhile Ted had pulled a mobile phone out of his jacket pocket and was talking quietly to someone somewhere outside.

"Red? This is Ted. I'm here with Ed. You wait with Ned. We'll be five minutes." He switched it off. "Come on! Let's move it," he muttered. His accent was faintly American but I got the feeling he was English.

"I'll clear the bathroom," Ed announced.

Ed was already moving towards the door. I just had time to grab hold of Tim and jerk him backwards into the bath. As Ed opened the bathroom door, I swept the shower curtain across but it was still a close thing. As he busied himself at the sink, scooping up McGuffin's toothbrush and razor, he was only separated from us by a thin sheet of plastic. Next to me, Tim seemed to be crying. I wondered what had upset him. Then I looked up and realized that the shower was dripping on his nose.

Ed moved out. We got out of the bath and went to the door. Tim had snatched up a lavatory brush in self-defence.

The two men had cleared the room. All McGuffin's things were in his suitcase and the suitcase was in Ted's hand. And that might have been it. They might have walked out of there and been none the wiser. But it had been Tim who had opened the door to McGuffin's room. He had had the key in his hand. And he had left it on the bed. I saw it about half a second before Ted. Then Ted saw it.

"Ed!" he said.

"Ted?"

"The bed!"

Ed looked at the bed and saw the key lying on top of the duvet. As one, the two men's heads turned towards the bathroom. Ted reached into his jacket and pulled out a gun. Then he started moving towards the bathroom. Things looked bad. I was trapped in the bathroom with a quivering brother and a lavatory brush. There was no other way out.

And then, suddenly, the bedroom door opened. Ted spun round. The gun vanished so fast that if he'd missed the holster he'd have stabbed himself with it. A housemaid had chosen that moment to walk into the room. She stood there now with a pile of fresh towels in her hands. She seemed a little surprised to see the two men.

"Excuse me," she said. "I have new towels."

I realized it was time to move. Grabbing a towel off the handrail I walked straight out of the bathroom with Tim close behind. I didn't even look at Ed and Ted. I knew I had to move quickly. The way Ted had concealed the gun told me that he didn't want to start any shooting with witnesses about. Before he had time to change his mind I had walked up to Ed and Ted as if I worked for the hotel too.

"Hi," I said. "These are the old towels."

"Yes," Tim added. "They're very old."

I threw the towels at the two men and ran.

We sprinted out of the room and back down the corridor. I knew that Ed and Ted were close behind us. I'd heard them curse and now their feet were thudding down on the soft-pile carpet. The corridor seemed to stretch on for ever and I couldn't remember the way to the lift. I thought of turning and somehow fighting it out but I knew it was a bad idea. Find people. Instinct told me. You'll be safe in a crowd.

Luck must have been on my side because we found the lift just as it reached the sixth floor and the door slid open. I dived in and stabbed at a button. I didn't even notice which one. I just wanted the door to close before Ed and Ted arrived. The door seemed to be taking for ever. Then I realized Tim was leaning on it. I yanked him out of the way. The door slid shut and there was a soft hum as we began to go down. It wasn't the lift that was humming, by the way. It was Tim. I think it must have been the relief.

The lift carried us all the way down to the ground floor and the moment the doors opened we were out. We crossed the lobby and went through the revolving doors. No sooner were we in the sunlight than a taxi drew up in front of us. Even then I thought it was a little odd. There was a taxi rank to one side with several cabs waiting. But this one had come from nowhere, jumping the queue.

"Where to?" the driver asked.

I threw open the door and got in. "Camden Town," Tim said. I looked through the back window. There was no sign of Ed or Ted.

But as we set off, there was a nasty feeling in my stomach and I knew it wasn't car sickness. The driver took a left turn, then a right. Which was funny, because if I'd been going to Camden Town, I'd have taken a right turn, then a left.

"We're going the wrong way," I said.

"What…?" Tim began.

The driver pressed a button and there was a loud click as the cab doors locked themselves automatically. Then he put his foot down on the accelerator and Tim and I were thrown back into our seats as the cab rocketed round a corner.

The driver wasn't going anywhere near Camden Town. We were prisoners on a one-way journey to who-could-say where. Well, one thing was certain. We wouldn't be leaving a tip.

NUMBER SEVENTEEN

The taxi took us into the centre of London, down Oxford Street and into the shabby end of Clerkenwell. We turned into Kelly Street, a road that went from nowhere to nowhere with nothing worth visiting on the way and stopped at Number Seventeen. It was a broken-down red-brick building on four floors. You entered through a set of glass doors. Immediately behind them was a wide empty space that might once have been a shop. Now all it was selling was dust.

"Out!"

The driver was a man of few words, but then "thank you" and "goodbye" would have been enough words for me. Now that I'd taken a closer look at him, I saw that he'd come off the same assembly line that had produced Ed and Ted and I guessed they must have telephoned him from the hotel. He had the same sort of gun too. And he was pointing it at us in just the same way.

He'd unlocked the doors and we got out of the taxi and walked towards the glass doors. There was nobody in sight in Kelly Street. Otherwise we might have tried to make a break for it. I hesitated, but only for a moment.

"Kidnap *and* murder," I said. "You think you can get away with it?"

"Yeah," Tim added. He nodded at the cab. "And you've parked on a yellow line."

"Just keep moving," the driver said, waving.

He led us down a corridor and through a door that opened on to a bare, uncarpeted staircase. The concrete felt cold underneath my feet as we climbed up and I wondered who or what would be waiting for us at the top. There was a rusting fire extinguisher attached to the wall. The driver reached out and turned the tap. It looked as if he'd gone crazy. There was no fire that I could see and anyway no water was coming out. A moment later I understood. Part of the wall swung open – a secret door, and the extinguisher was the handle.

"That's very neat," I said. "But what do you do if the place catches fire?"

We stepped through the wall. And suddenly we were surrounded.

There were people everywhere. In front of the entrance there was a pretty receptionist taking calls on an even prettier telephone system. I hadn't seen so many flashing lights since Christmas. There were five or six offices on either side and the central area was being criss-crossed by suits with men inside. You could hear the jangle of telephones from every direction and voices talking softly like they were frightened of being overheard or even, for that matter, heard.

"Tim...!"

I nudged Tim and pointed. Another door had opened and I could see into what looked like a fully working laboratory with its own collection of technicians in white coats. But you didn't need a microscope to see what they were working on. They had the telephone box from the alley. And they were taking it apart piece by piece. I watched as one man sprayed the glass with some sort of powder while another unscrewed the telephone receiver. But then the taxi driver prodded me with his gun and gestured at the door nearest the receptionist. "In there," he said.

We went in. It was an office like any other with a desk, a computer screen, a few leather chairs and lighting as soft as the executive carpet. Sitting behind the desk was an elderly man with grey hair that had probably come with the job. He was a black man, dressed in a three-piece suit and an old school tie. His movements were slow, but his narrow, grey eyes seemed to move fast.

"Please sit down," he said. "I'll be with you in a minute." He punched a few letters on his keyboard but the screen was turned towards him so I couldn't see what he was writing. Meanwhile, Tim had shifted onto the edge of his seat and was craning to look over the top of the desk. The man noticed him and stopped typing. "Is there something wrong?" he enquired.

Tim coughed. "You're only using two fingers," he said.

"Yes." The man smiled and held up his hands. "But I do have a complete set." He pushed the keyboard away. "So you know about Charon?"

"Maybe..."

"Of course you do, Mr Diamond. You are Tim Diamond, I presume?"

Tim stared. "How do you know that?"

"I was guessing. We found a name tag in the coat that McGuffin was wearing when he ... left the company." I couldn't help smiling at that. "I presume he exchanged coats with you in an attempt to escape from Charon. That was the sort of thing McGuffin would have tried. And you must have found the hotel key in his coat. Am I correct?"

"Keep talking," Tim muttered.

"I have your details here on the computer," the old man went on. He glanced at the screen. "Tim Diamond Inc. Detective Agency. Camden Town." He turned to me. "You're not on my file."

"I'm his brother," I said.

"Ah." He typed a few words onto the screen.

"Nick Diamond. Want me to spell it?"

"I think I can manage."

"And what exactly is it that you do manage, Mr..." Tim began.

"My name is Mr Waverly." He smiled. "I am the chief executive of this organization."

"And what organization is that?"

Waverly lowered his voice. "I take it you've heard of MI6."

"I've driven up it," Tim said.

"No," Waverly corrected him. "You're thinking of the M6 motorway to Birmingham. I'm talking about intelligence."

Tim's face brightened. "Then you're talking to the right person!" he announced.

"Military intelligence!" Waverly explained.

"Spies," I added.

"McGuffin was an agent working for me," Waverly went on. "He was pursuing a killer known only as Charon. I don't know how much he had told you, but Charon has a contract on a Russian diplomat by the name of Boris Kusenov."

"How do you know that?" I asked. I didn't

think it was an important question when I asked it. It was just something I wanted to know. But it seemed I'd touched on a sore point because suddenly he looked less like the head of the British Secret Service and more like a used car salesman with a second-hand secret.

"It doesn't matter how," he said and I realized that it did matter a lot. "All that matters is that he doesn't kill Kusenov on British soil."

"Suppose he stays on the pavement?" Tim asked.

Mr Waverly swallowed hard. "I mean, we have to ensure that Kusenov is not killed while he is anywhere in Britain," he explained, choosing his words carefully. "It would have huge international repercussions. That is why it is essential that you tell me everything McGuffin told you."

"But he didn't tell us anything," I said.

"That's right," Tim agreed. "He wanted to use a telephone but we haven't got one. So he went out to use the one in the alley." He jerked a thumb in the direction of the laboratory. "He was lucky you hadn't taken it before he got there."

"We took the call box *after* he was killed, Mr Diamond," Waverly said. "McGuffin got through to this office. He told us where he was. Then he was shot. So we took the telephone box to search it for clues."

"Did you find any?" I asked.

"Not yet. But he must have left something. McGuffin was a resourceful operative. He was secretive. A loner. But he'll have done everything he can to get a message to us."

There was a pause.

Tim and I glanced at each other. Waverly may have been hiding something, but we had to tell him everything we knew. After all, he was the head of MI6. And that meant he was on our side.

"How about 'south by south east'?" I said.

"What?"

"They were his last words," Tim explained.

"Just that? South by south east?" Waverly tapped the words into the computer then pressed the button that would send them hurtling into the data bank. The screen bleeped a few times. He pressed another button. "Nothing," he muttered.

Tim got to his feet. "Well, there's nothing more we can do for you..." he began.

"Please sit down, Mr Diamond!"

There was a silence of about thirty seconds as he sat there, calculating. He had plans for us. I could see them forming – faster than the computer signals – in those soft, grey eyes. At last he stretched out a hand and pressed a button on his intercom.

"Miss Jones," he said. "Could you get a drink for our guests?" Then he turned back to us. "I have a proposition for you," he said.

"I want you to work for me. We have to find Charon and you can help."

"Now wait a minute..." Tim began.

Waverly ignored him. "We're running out of time, Mr Diamond. Boris Kusenov arrives in England in just a few days' time. But we no longer have any leads. We have no connection with Charon." He took a deep breath. "Except you."

"Me?" Tim squeaked.

"Charon knows that McGuffin spoke to you before he died. When he discovers that you're working for MI6, maybe he'll get worried."

"How will he discover that?" I asked.

"We'll make sure he finds out."

I couldn't believe it. I played back the sentence in my head and realized that was just what it was. A death sentence. We were going to be the bait in a trap for Charon. And if we got wiped out along the way, I don't think Waverly would even send flowers to the funeral.

Even Tim seemed to have come to the same conclusion. "You can't do it!" he exclaimed. "I'm not a secret agent..."

"You are now," Waverly replied.

The door opened and Miss Jones came in, carrying a tray. She was a short, dumpy woman with hair tied up in a bun – but I hardly noticed her. She had two glasses on the tray. They were filled with a green liquid that was almost luminous. Somehow I didn't think it was apple juice.

"I thought you might be thirsty," Waverly said.

"I was until she came in," I replied.

"Please drink..."

It was a command, not an invitation, and I got the feeling that something nasty would happen to us if we refused. Mind you, I knew something nasty was going to happen to us anyway. We didn't have much choice. I held up the glass.

"Down the hatch," Tim said.

"Yeah. And into the coal cellar," I added.

We drank.

The juice tasted sweet and minty – like mouthwash. I think I began to feel its effects even before it had reached my throat.

"I can give you one piece of guidance in your task," Waverly went on, but already his voice was in the next room. He seemed to be shrinking behind the desk, like we were looking at him through the wrong end of a telescope. "McGuffin wasn't working alone. He'd been in touch with the Dutch Secret Service..."

"I didn't know the Dutch had a secret service," I said. The words came out thick and heavy.

"That's how secret they are," Mr Waverly explained. "We don't even know the name of the agent he was working with. But he had a number. 86. Can you remember that?"

"68," Tim said.

"89," I corrected him.

"86," Mr Waverly corrected me.

The room was spinning round and round. Now I knew what a CD felt like. Only instead of music, all I could hear was Waverly's voice, the words slurring together, echoing around me. "You're on your own, Diamond," he was saying. "On your own ... on your own."

"Where's Nick?" Tim asked.

"On the floor," I replied.

A moment later the carpet rushed up at me, and I was.

BIRDS

"Waverly was hiding something," I said.

Tim and I were sitting back in the Camden Town office, which was where we'd woken up. Whatever it was in the drink we had been given, it was powerful stuff. My head was still hurting. My tongue felt like someone had used it to dry the dishes.

"What was he hiding?" Tim asked. He wasn't looking much better than me. It was four o'clock in the afternoon. We'd been unconscious for about six hours.

"I don't know. It was something to do with Boris Kusenov. How did Mr Waverly find out that Charon was planning to kill him? And why is it so important that it doesn't happen in Britain?"

"Maybe it would be bad for the tourist trade."

Tim poured himself a cup of tea. "He

offered me a job!" he exclaimed. "A spy! Working for MI6!"

I shook my head. I didn't want to disillusion him but he had to know. "You're not a spy, Tim," I told him. "You're a sitting target."

Tim stood up. "What do you mean?"

"I mean – when Charon hears you're working for MI6, he'll come gunning for you. Or knifing. Or harpooning. That's what Mr Waverly wants."

"Why? Didn't he like me?"

"If Charon comes after you, he'll be too busy to go after Kusenov. And of course, it gives Waverly another chance to catch him."

"You mean – he's using me?"

"Yes."

"Over my dead body!"

"Exactly..."

Tim sat down again behind his desk. Then he stood up. Then he sat down again. I was beginning to get a crick in my neck watching him, but at last he swung round and I realized that he was actually furious. "How dare he!" he squeaked. "Well, I'm going to show him!"

"What are you going to do?"

"He kidnapped me. He drugged me. And now he's trying to get me killed. What do you think I'm going to do? I'm going to the police!"

"Snape?" I grimaced. "Are you sure that's such a good idea?"

But Tim wouldn't let me talk him out of it. And that was how – the very same day that we'd been released from jail for wasting police time – we found ourselves knocking on the door, asking to be let back in again. The desk sergeant wasn't pleased to see us. We left him chewing the desk while a constable went to fetch Chief Inspector Snape.

Then Snape himself arrived, with Boyle, as ever, just a few steps behind. "I do not believe it!" he exclaimed in a cracked voice.

"But Chief ... I haven't told you yet," Tim replied.

So Tim told him: the hotel room, the two MI6 agents, the taxi ride, Kelly Street, Mr Waverly ... everything. Snape listened without interrupting, but I got the idea that he wasn't taking Tim seriously. Maybe it was the way he rapped his fingernails on the table and stared out of the window. Maybe it was his occasional sniff of silent laughter. Meanwhile Boyle stood with his back against the wall, smirking quietly to himself.

"So that's it?" Snape enquired when Tim had finished. "You really expect me to swallow that?"

"But it's the truth!" Tim insisted. He turned to me. "Tell him!" he exclaimed.

"It's the truth," I agreed. What else could I say?

Snape considered. "Very well," he muttered

at length. "Let's take a look at Number Seventeen. But I'm warning you, Diamond..."

He drove us back to Kelly Street and stopped at the bottom. We walked the last fifty metres – with Snape's driving that had to be the fastest part of the journey. Eleven, thirteen, fifteen ... I counted off the numbers of the buildings as we went past. It was all just like I remembered it. Then we reached Number Seventeen.

It wasn't there any more.

At least, there was something there only it wasn't what had been there the last time we were there. It was as confusing as that. The empty window, the dust and the bare floorboards had been replaced by a pretty shop that looked as if it had been there for years. There was a wooden sign above the door that read: *Bodega Birds*. But these weren't the oven-ready variety. You could hear them squawking even out in the street: budgies and canaries and just about every other species of feathered friend. "Hello!" someone shouted. I think it was a parrot.

Tim had seen all this too. "Wait a minute!" he cried in a high-pitched voice. For a moment he sounded remarkably like a parrot himself. "The birds. They weren't there!"

"So how did they get here then?" Snape asked. "I suppose they just flew in?"

"I don't know!"

We went in. I looked for the door that led to the staircase. At least that was still in place, only now you had to step past a row of canaries to reach it. But then there were birds everywhere, twittering in their cages or rocking backwards and forwards on their perches. The back of the shop was lined with shelves stacked high with bird-food, bird-toys, bird-baths and everything else you might need if you happened to be a bird. And none of it was new. As far as we could tell, it had all been there for years.

"This is the wrong place!" Tim said.

"It's Number Seventeen," Snape growled.

"Can I help you?" The speaker was an elderly woman in a bright pink cardigan, white blouse and beads. She had small, black eyes and a pointed nose like a beak. Give her a few feathers and you'd have had difficulty finding her among the birds. She had shuffled round from behind the counter and, with fingers that were thin and bent, began to stroke a big blue parrot.

"Are you the manager here?" Snape asked.

"Yes. I'm Mrs Bodega." Her voice was thin and high-pitched.

"How long has this shop been here?"

Mrs Bodega worked it out on her fingers. "Let me see," she trilled. "I opened the shop two years before my husband died – and that was nine years ago. My husband was pecked to death, you know. The birds did love him! But they didn't know when to stop. So ... eight years plus two years. That's ten years in all."

She tickled one of the parrots. The parrot swayed on its perch and preened itself against her. "This is Hercule," she went on. "He was my husband's favourite. We called him Hercule after that nice detective, Hercule Parrot."

At least that amused Boyle. "Hercule Parrot," he muttered and stuck out a finger. The parrot squawked and bit it.

"Are you looking for anything in particular?" Mrs Bodega asked.

Snape turned to Tim. "Well?"

"She's lying!" Tim exclaimed. "This shop wasn't here." He nudged me. "Tell him!"

I had a feeling I was wasting my time but I tried anyway. "It's true," I said. "This is all a fake. And this woman..." I pointed at Mrs Bodega. "She must be some sort of actress."

"I'm no such thing. Who are you? What do you want?"

Boyle pulled his swollen finger out of his mouth and went over to Snape. "Give me five minutes, sir," he pleaded. "Just five minutes. Alone with them."

"No, Boyle," Snape sighed.

"Five minutes with the parrot?"

"No." Snape closed his eyes.

Tim was utterly confused. Mrs Bodega was watching us with a mixture of innocence and indignation. "All right," Snape said. "Just tell me where these agents of yours took you."

"They took us upstairs," Tim said. He pointed. "There's a staircase behind that door."

"There's no such thing!" Mrs Bodega muttered.

"I'll show you!"

Tim marched forward and threw open the door. He'd taken two more steps before he realized what I'd seen at once. The staircase was no longer there. He'd walked into a broom cupboard. There was a crash as he collided with an assortment of buckets and brooms. A shelf gave way and clattered down bringing with it about five years' supply of bird-seed. Tim simply disappeared in a gold-and-white shower of the stuff. It poured down on him, forcing him to his knees, burying him.

And then it was all over. There was a small mountain of bird seed on the floor with two legs jutting out of it. The mountain shifted and broke open. Tim stuck his head out and coughed. Bird seed trickled out of his ear.

Snape had seen enough. "So they took you into a broom cupboard, did they?" he snarled. He caught one of the brooms. "I suppose this was your brush with MI6?"

"Chief Inspector! Listen..."

It was too late for that. Snape dropped the broom and grabbed hold of Tim, and, at the same time, I winced as Boyle's hand clamped itself onto my shoulder. A moment later my feet had left the floor. All around me, the birds were screeching and whistling and fluttering. It was as if they were laughing at us. But then maybe they knew. They weren't the only ones who were going to be spending the night behind bars.

HIGH SECURITY

This time Snape locked us up for two days. Boyle wanted to throw the book at us but fortunately he didn't have a book. I'm not even sure Boyle knew how to read.

As soon as we were released, we headed back to the office. Tim wasn't talking very much. He didn't say anything on the bus, not even when I took the window seat. And he only muttered a few words of surprise when he found a letter waiting for him on our doormat. Not many people ever wrote to Tim. There were the electricity and the gas bills, of course, but they weren't exactly chatty. Mum and Dad sometimes dropped us cards: Australia's hot, England's not, we love you a lot … that sort of thing. But usually the only letters on the doormat read: *Please wipe your feet.*

This letter came in a smart white envelope, postmarked London. Tim finally opened it in the office while I poured the tea. To celebrate our release, I'd used new teabags. It was a short letter but he took a long time to read it. Maybe it was good news.

"So what is it?" I asked at last.

"It's a job." Tim smiled for the first time since we'd been locked up and passed the letter across to me. It came from the Canadian Bank in Pall Mall and was signed by a woman called Louise Meyer. Briefly, it invited Tim to an interview to discuss the position of Head of Security.

"What is this...?" I began.

"Don't you remember?" Tim said. "I told you. I applied for the job a couple of months ago." He snatched the letter back. "They need a new Head of Security."

"But you don't know anything about security," I said.

"Yes I do!" Tim looked at me indignantly. "I put burglar alarms in the office," he reminded me.

"And burglars stole them," I reminded him.

Tim ignored me.

"Aren't you forgetting something?" I went on. "What about Charon? What about MI6?"

"What about them?"

"You can't just ignore them! You heard what McGuffin said. And you still don't know what south by south east means..."

"I don't think it means anything." Tim

sniffed. "Anyway, it's none of my business. Banking is my business."

I gave up. "When's the interview?" I asked.

Tim quickly re-read the letter. "This Meyer woman wants to see me at two o'clock this afternoon," he said. He sprang out of his chair. "This afternoon! That's today!"

It was already half past twelve. The next twenty minutes were spent in a frantic attempt to prepare himself. He put on a suit, a tie and a shirt while I polished his shoes. I didn't do a great job but then I was using furniture polish. Finally he dragged a leather attaché case out of a cupboard. Actually, it wasn't leather – it was kangaroo skin; an unwanted Christmas present. Mum had given it to Tim. Tim had given it to me. I'd given it to Oxfam. They'd given it back. You can't get much more unwanted than that. But now he took it because he thought it made him look good. The clock struck one. He was ready.

"I'll come with you," I said.

"Sure." Tim nodded. "You can wait outside."

We got another bus back into town and this time Tim was in a better mood. He was rehearsing his answers all the way there, whispering to himself and nodding. The other passengers must have thought he was mad. I wasn't even sure myself. But he'd completely forgotten about McGuffin and Charon. That much was obvious. And that was his big mistake.

It happened just as we got off at Pall Mall. There had been about a dozen people on the top deck with us and I hadn't really noticed any of them. But one of them had followed us down and just as we stepped off the bus, he reached out and tapped Tim on the shoulder.

"Excuse me," he said. "You've forgotten this." And he gave Tim back his kangaroo-skin attaché case. That was all there was to it. I got a flash of a dark face and a beard. Then the bus had moved off and we were standing on the pavement. That was all there was to it. But I was uneasy. I didn't know why.

"Tim..." I called out.

But Tim had already arrived outside the Canadian bank. I could tell it was Canadian because of the flag on the roof and the bronze moose on the door. It was a small, square building, one floor only. In fact it looked more like a high-class jeweller's than a High Street bank. Everything about it was quiet and discreet. Even the alarms were muffled so they wouldn't disturb the neighbours. I caught up with Tim just before he went in.

"I think we ought to talk," I said.

"I know what to say," he replied. "You wait here."

He went in. I looked at the clock above the door. There wasn't one. And that was strange because when I'd been standing next to Tim, I'd definitely heard the sound of ticking. I thought about the attaché case again. And suddenly the skin on my neck was prickling and my mouth had gone dry. Either Tim was in serious trouble or I was going down with the flu.

It wasn't the flu. I'd never felt better in my life. And now I had to act quickly. I'd hardly glimpsed the man on the bus but I knew now why he had taken the case and what he had put inside it.

I also knew that if I'd stopped to count his fingers, I wouldn't have reached ten.

Tim had disappeared into the bank. I plunged in after him, off the street and into the white marble banking hall. It was cool inside, out of the summer heat. The marble was like ice and even the potted plants seemed to be shivering in the air-conditioning. My eyes swept past the cashiers, the plush leather furniture, the tinkling chandeliers. I saw Tim just as he walked through a door at the far left corner. That had to be Mrs Meyer's office. Gritting my teeth, I prepared to follow him. Somehow I had to get him out of there. Already it might be too late.

I'd taken just one step before a hand clamped down on my shoulder and I was twisted round to face the biggest security guard I'd ever seen.

"What do you want then?" he demanded.

"I want to open an account," I said. It was the first thing to come into my head. He smiled mirthlessly. "Oh yes? I suppose you think this is some sort of piggy-bank?"

"Well they certainly seem to employ a few piggies."

Five seconds later I found myself back out on the street with a neck that felt as though it had been through a mangle. I wondered if the Canadian security guard had ever worked as a lumberjack. He would have only had to smile at a tree to knock it down.

Maybe it was the sun, but the sweat was beginning to trickle down my neck as I walked round behind the bank. It was on a corner, separated from the pavement by a narrow line of flower-beds. Slowly, I tiptoed through the tulips peering in through the ground floor windows. Fortunately, they were fairly low down and because of the hot weather some of them were partly open. I heard snippets of conversation, the jangle of coins, telephones ringing. At the sixth window I heard Tim's voice. He was already being interviewed by Louise Meyer.

"Tell me, Mr Diamond," the manager asked. "Do you have any experience of security?"

"Not exactly security, Lucy," Tim replied. He paused. "Do you mind if I call you Lucy?"

"I prefer to be more formal."

"That's OK, Lucy. You can call me Mr Diamond."

Another tulip snapped underneath my feet as I shifted closer to the window. I reached up to the window-sill, then pulled myself up and looked through the glass.

I could see Tim sitting right in front of me, facing the window. Louise Meyer was opposite him, behind her desk. She was a tough, no-nonsense businesswoman. She was wearing a dark blue suit cut so sharply she could have opened a letter with her sleeve.

"I don't have much experience of security, Lucy," Tim went on. "But I do have the security of experience."

I looked round the office. It was a big room, dominated by the desk, with a few chairs, a cocktail cabinet, a map of Canada and a heavy filing cabinet. There was a sort of alcove just outside the office, a miniature reception area, and I could make out an old-fashioned iron safe jutting out from the wall. Tim had forgotten to bring his case into the office. He had left it on top of the safe.

"So you've never worked in a bank," Louise Meyer said.

"You could say that," Tim replied.

"Well – have you?"

"No."

I waved. Tim was staring right at me but he

was so wrapped up in himself that he didn't notice anything. I thought of tapping on the glass but I didn't want Meyer to hear. I just wanted Tim out of there and the attaché case with him.

"But let's talk about your bank, Lou," Tim went on. "Frankly, I'd feel safer leaving my money in a paper bag at a public swimming pool."

"You would?" Mrs Meyer was astonished.

"You've got more holes here than a fishing net. If you ask me, a robber could crack this place in about fifteen seconds flat."

"You think so?"

"I know it." Tim slumped into his chair. He was obviously enjoying himself.

I waved harder, jumped up and down and whistled. Tim ignored me. "Have you checked who I am, Lulu?" he asked the manager. "I could be a crook myself."

"Well..." I saw Mrs Meyer's hand reaching out for the alarm button under her desk.

"I could have a gun on me right now."

"Wait a minute, Mr Diamond." Mrs Meyer was getting nervous and anyone except Tim would have seen it.

"I could have a partner waiting outside..."

"Could you?" Louise Meyer turned in her seat to look out of the window. That was when she saw me. I was frozen with one hand in the air like I was about to punch my way through the glass. I opened my mouth to explain.

"And I could have a bomb," Tim added.

And that, of course, was when the bomb went off.

I didn't even realize what had happened at first. There was a flash of red light and the window seemed to curve out towards me. I must have been off-balance from the start because my legs jackknifed under me and I was thrown back onto the flower-bed. This was just as well. A torrent of burning air and jagged glass missed my head by a fraction as half the office was blown out into the street.

Somehow I managed to get back to my feet. I was glad they were still at the end of my legs. I gave myself a quick examination. There was blood on my shirt and it looked like my colour but otherwise I seemed to be in one piece. It was raining. I blinked. The rain was made of paper. I looked closer and realized what was happening. It was raining money, Canadian dollars and English pounds blown out of the manager's personal safe. As I staggered round to the front door, I snatched a few notes and put them in my pocket. I had a feeling I was going to need them.

Inside, the calm of the bank had been shattered. So had the marble floor. The cashiers were in hysterics, the alarm-bells jangling, the air thick with dust. I couldn't see the security guard, which was probably just as well.

Then I saw Tim. He had walked back into the main banking hall as if he were in a daze, which, in fact, he probably was. His clothes were in rags, his face was black, and he seemed half-stunned. But like me, he was still in one piece.

Then the security guard staggered towards him. At the same time Louise Meyer appeared in the shattered doorway. Her two-piece suit was now a four-piece suit. Her make-up had been blown off. And she was completely covered in dust. Now, with the security guard only millimetres away from Tim, she shouted out, "Don't go near him! He's got a gun!"

"No I haven't," Tim protested.

Suddenly I knew there was only one way out of this. "Yes you have!" I shouted.

"Have I?" Tim saw me. And he understood. "Yes I have!" he exclaimed. "I've got a gun!"

It worked. The cashiers began screaming again and the security guard backed away. For a moment the way out was clear but already I could hear the first police sirens slicing their way through the London traffic. It was time to go.

"Tim!" I shouted. He saw me and ambled over to the door. "Let's get out of here!"

We went. Nobody tried to stop us. As far as they were concerned, we were dangerous criminals. I didn't know where we were going or what we were going to do. I was just glad to be out of there. But as we passed through the front door, Tim stopped and turned round.

"Wait a minute, Nick," he said. "I still haven't heard if I've got the job."

A police car turned the corner. I grabbed Tim and ran.

CHAIN REACTION

One hour after the bank blast, Tim was a wanted man. Suddenly his picture was in the papers and on TV. Identikit pictures had appeared so fast you'd think the police had had them printed in advance just in case they needed them. Once again we were Public Enemies – but all we'd managed to take from the bank was two hundred dollars and some travellers' cheques. I changed the dollars and used some of the money to buy Tim a new shirt. That hardly left enough to get us a room for the night.

We couldn't go back to the office. That was the first place they'd come looking for us. We needed a cheap hotel somewhere quiet, where they didn't look at their guests too closely. Somewhere that needed guests so badly they wouldn't look at all.

We found the hotel on the wrong side of

Paddington. In fact it wasn't a hotel but a guest house; a narrow, grimy building with no name on the door, but a "Vacancies" sign in the window. It was halfway down a cul-de-sac so there would be no passing traffic. And you couldn't reach it from the back either. The Paddington railway tracks cut right through the garden. Try mowing the lawn and you'd be run over by a train.

"What do you think?" Tim asked.

"It's fine," I said. I rang the bell.

The door was opened by a thin, elderly woman in a grey cardigan that she had knitted herself. About halfway through she must have lost the pattern. Underneath it there was a shabby dress hanging over a hideous pair of slippers with pink pom-poms.

"Yes?" she said.

"You got a room?" Tim asked.

"Oh yes! Come in! I've got lots of rooms."

The lady led us through a dark, depressing hallway and into a reception room that wasn't much better.

This room had six lumpy chairs and a coffee-table stained with coffee. Two elderly men were sitting at a table playing chess. A third man was in an armchair with his back to us.

"My name is Mrs Jackson," the lady told us. She spoke like a duchess, rolling each word between her lips. "Let me introduce you to my guests." She gestured at the plump, fair-haired man in the armchair. "Mr Blondini is in the theatre!" she announced. The man in the armchair grinned and tried to stand up. But he couldn't, as he was wearing a straitjacket and there were about a dozen chains snaking round his arms, legs and chest. "Mr Blondini is an escapologist," Mrs Jackson explained.

"Just practising!" Mr Blondini added, heaving frantically with his shoulders.

Mrs Jackson went over to the two men playing chess. The first of them was short with close-cropped hair and a monocle. "This is Mr Webber," she said. "Mr Webber is from Germany. But otherwise he's perfectly nice."

"Check!" Mr Webber snapped, moving his bishop with such force that it snapped too.

"And this is Mr Ferguson." The other player was tall and thin, a timid-looking man with curly hair. Mrs Jackson drew Tim aside. "Do try not to mention mountains or tall buildings to him," she whispered. "Mr Ferguson suffers terribly from vertigo."

Tim waved at Mr Ferguson. "Hi!" he said.

Mr Ferguson rolled his eyes and fainted.

Mrs Jackson frowned. "I have a room on the first floor," she said. "How many nights will it be?"

"We'll be here until the end of the week," I lied.

"It's thirty pounds a night. Cash in advance."

I nodded and Tim counted out three ten pound notes.

Mrs Jackson snatched them hungrily. “Room twelve on the first floor at the end of the corridor,” she said. She stopped and looked more closely at Tim. “Do I know you?” she said. “Your face is very familiar. What did you say your name was?”

“It’s ... it’s...” Tim stared blankly at me.

I glanced at the ten pound notes in Mrs Jackson’s hands. “It’s Queen,” I said. “We’re the Queen brothers.”

“Oh yes?”

“Good night, Mrs Jackson.”

I grabbed Tim and we made our way upstairs. At the top, I turned and looked back. The landlady was still there, watching us, her eyes glinting in the half-light. I nodded at her and she spun on her heel, disappearing the way she had come.

“She knows who we are!”

“No, Tim. Maybe she saw you on the news. But I don’t think she recognized you...”

We were sitting in room twelve a few minutes later. The room was about as inspiring as the rest of the hotel. It had one ancient bed, a couch and a swirly carpet that had lost most of its swirls. Tim was lying on the bed. I was sitting next to him, thinking. We couldn’t stay long at this guest house. Not at thirty pounds a night. We had to go somewhere. But where?

It seemed to me we had only one choice. Tim was now a wanted bank robber. Snape would never believe our story about the bomb, not after the telephone box and the pet shop. No, Mr Waverly – the real Mr Waverly – had us right where he wanted us. We had to help him find Charon. It was our only chance.

But where could we start? Sitting on the bed, I thought about what he had told us. One of his agents, Jake McGuffin, had been following Charon's trail but he hadn't been working alone. Waverly had mentioned a Dutch secret agent. A man with no name – but a number. Seventy-six or eighty-six...

Eighty-six! It meant something to me. I was sure of it. I had seen or heard the number somewhere before. And sitting there on the lumpy mattress, I suddenly remembered where.

"Tim!" I exclaimed. I stood up and pulled the ticket out of my pocket. This was the ticket to the ice-rink that I had found in McGuffin's hotel room. And I was right! There was a number printed in the left-hand corner.

The number was eighty-six.

I showed it to Tim. "Don't you see?" I said. "I think this is a ticket to an ice-rink in Amsterdam. McGuffin and the Dutch agent must use it as a meeting place." I pointed at the two words at the top of the ticket. "Amstel Ijsbaan.

Do you think that sounds Dutch?"

"It's all Greek to me," Tim said.

"Amstel..." Just for once I wished I'd concentrated more in geography lessons. "Isn't that a river," I said. "In Amsterdam?" It was all beginning to make sense. "We have to go there."

"To Amsterdam?"

"We'll find the ice-rink. We'll find 86. And he'll help us find Charon."

"And then what?"

"I don't know, Tim. I'm completely in the dark..."

That was when the lights went out.

Suddenly it was pitch black in the room. At the same time there was a click and a rush of cool air as the door was opened and even as I stood up to take my bearings, I felt myself grabbed and thrown back on the bed. I heard Tim cry out. Then someone grabbed my hand and I felt a circle of cold metal closing around my wrist. There was a second click, closer this time and more distinct. I tried to move my hand and found that I couldn't.

And then the lights went back on and I found myself staring at Mrs Jackson and two of her lodgers – Mr Webber and Mr Ferguson. But that wasn't the worst of it. Tim was lying next to me and now I saw that they had managed to handcuff us together. And, most bizarre of all, Mrs Jackson was holding a gun.

A moment later, Mr Blondini came into the room. He had obviously been the one controlling the main fuse. "Did you get them?" he asked.

"Oh yes!" Mrs Jackson pursed her lips. "Who'd have thought it?" she went on. "A dangerous criminal sleeping in my house!"

"It's not true!" I said.

"That's right!" Tim agreed. "I hadn't gone to bed yet."

"He's not a dangerous criminal!" I explained. "He hasn't done anything!"

"Then why is his face here?" Mr Ferguson asked. He produced a copy of that day's *Evening Standard* with Tim's face on the front page. So that was how they had recognized us.

"We'd better call the police." Mrs Jackson was still aiming the gun at us. She turned to Mr Webber. "Do you know the number?"

"Nine, nine, nine," the German said.

"All right," she muttered. "I'll look it up in the phone book."

"I've already called them," Mr Blondini said. "They're on the way."

"Good!"

I looked around me, trying to find some way out of this situation, but there was nothing I could do, not while Mrs Jackson had the gun. The gun ... I'd been held up at gunpoint quite a few times in my life. The Fat Man, Johnny Powers, Big Ed – they'd all tried it at one time or another. But now I looked at her, I saw there was something wrong about Mrs Jackson. It wasn't just her. It was the way she was holding the gun. Or perhaps it was the gun itself…

And suddenly I knew. "Have you got a cigarette, Mrs Jackson?" I asked.

"You're too young to smoke," she scowled.

"Then why are you offering me a light?" I pointed at the gun. My hand was chained to Tim's and he pointed at it too.

"What…?" Tim began.

The front doorbell rang. The police had arrived.

"Move!" I shouted.

We leapt off the bed and pushed past Mrs Jackson and her friends, making for the door. They were too surprised to do anything and a moment later we were out of the room. I could feel the chain straining at my wrist as Tim hesitated. I suppose he was afraid that we were about to get shot. But I knew better. It hadn't been a real gun at all but a fancy cigarette-lighter. And how had I guessed? Maybe it was just intuition. But the single word "Dunhill" printed on the barrel had probably helped.

Down below, the police were hammering at the door. That meant we could only go up. We found a second staircase and clambered up it, arriving on the second floor. This was also the top floor. We had nowhere else to go. Behind me I heard Mrs Jackson hurrying down to let the police in. We had maybe ten seconds before we were taken.

There was a window at the end of the corridor. Pulling Tim with me, I went over to it. The window was at the back of the house. There was a narrow alley – about two metres across – and then a lower building. The roof of the other building was a few metres below us. It was flat, covered in black asphalt.

"We can jump," I said.

"We can't," Tim quavered.

"We've got to." I opened the window and Tim and I crawled out onto the sill. The handcuffs didn't make it easy. We hovered there for a few seconds. Behind us, I could hear the police racing up the stairs.

"Jump!"

I launched myself into space. Tim did the same. Like some sort of clumsy, prehistoric bird we soared out of the house. For a horrible moment I thought I wasn't going to make it. And if I didn't make it, nor would Tim. The chain would drag him back and we'd both end up as so many broken bones on the pavement below. But then the asphalt roof rushed up and hit me in the chest. My legs still hung in space but enough of me had reached the building to save me. I twisted to the right. Tim was lying beside me.

"Close..." he rasped and wiped his brow. He used the chained hand and I had to wipe his brow too.

The building was some sort of office block. We found a skylight in, a flight of stairs down and a glass door out. Nobody saw us go. There were about a dozen police cars parked in the street at the front but everybody was concentrating on Mrs Jackson's guest house so we simply walked away. We held hands until we were round the corner. But then, of course, we were still very much attached.

TRAIN REACTION

Getting across London again wasn't easy – but we had no choice. If we really were heading for Amsterdam, that meant a ferry from Dover. If we wanted to get to Dover we had to start at Victoria. And that meant holding hands through Hyde Park and on through Knightsbridge to the other side of London.

The chances of our reaching Victoria without being seen must have been a thousand to one against, but somehow we managed it. We emerged in front of the main forecourt where the taxis and buses were locked into what had become a frozen mosaic of black and red. All we had to do now was to find the right train.

"Where's the ticket-office?" I muttered the question more to myself than to Tim, but unfortunately he heard me.

"I'll ask," he said. He turned to someone standing nearby. "Excuse me," he went on.

"Can you tell me where the ticket-office is?"

"Certainly, sir. It's through the main entrance and on the left."

It was the "sir" that alerted me. I looked round and nearly died on my feet. Tim had just asked a policeman.

Even then we might have slipped away. But Tim had realized what he had done. He went bright red. He squeaked. He hid his head behind his arm. If the policeman hadn't noticed him before, he couldn't help but look twice then. I hurried Tim away. But it was already too late. Looking back over my shoulder, I saw the policeman staring after us. He was talking into his radio at the same time.

We didn't buy a ticket. I knew that the police would soon be after us and that would be the first place they'd look. Our only chance was to get out of Victoria as quickly as possible on a train. I dragged Tim across the main concourse. There was a train to Dover leaving in nine minutes. Would it pull out before the police pulled in? I decided to take a gamble. We took the train.

As we climbed on, Tim stopped me. "Look!"

I followed his eyes. "Network South East!" he explained.

It was true. We were travelling Network South East. The words were written on the side of the carriage. "So what?" I asked.

"We're going south by South East!" Tim said.

I had to admit that he had a point. South by south east. Was that what McGuffin had meant by his final words? "Let's get on," I said.

We walked down the train, looking for the quietest carriage. We were still chained together of course and I was frightened that somebody might notice. But the other passengers were too busy getting out their sandwiches and newspapers. We had just reached First Class when the train jolted and began to move forward. We were on the way.

The second-class carriages had been almost full. First Class was almost empty. But as I began to move forward again, I noticed a young woman, sitting on her own, reading a book. At least, she *had* been reading the book. Now she was staring at us.

She was a few years older than Tim, dressed in a smart shirt and suit with a silk scarf and grey, suede gloves. I thought she might be an actress or maybe the head of a fashion firm. She had long fair hair, a little make-up and soft, suntanned skin. Her eyes were a shade of green that made me think of cats and Egyptian princesses and witchcraft.

She knew who we were. There could be no doubt of it. "Sit down!" she said.

I hesitated. But I could see we had no choice.

I sat down, pulling Tim with me.

"Tim Diamond!" She smiled as she said the words. As far as she knew, Tim was a wanted criminal, a dangerous bank robber. But she was treating the whole thing like a joke.

"Hello!" Tim's voice sounded peculiar.

I glanced at him. He had gone bright red and his lips were wobbling. For a minute I thought he was train sick. Then I realized it was something much, much worse. Tim had fallen in love.

"I'm Tim," he said. "This is another brick."

"I'm sorry?"

"My brother, Nick," he corrected himself.

The woman glanced at our handcuffs. "Is that chain the one you pull in emergencies or do you always travel like that?" she asked. Her voice had an accent. She wasn't English, that was for sure. But what was she? Who was she? And why hadn't she sounded the alarm?

"I can explain..." I began.

"There's no need to." She smiled again and I had to admit it was a pretty smile. "My name is Charlotte Van Dam," she went on. "I'm Dutch and I'm a writer. Crime stories. I'm on my way home from a convention in London."

"How unconventional," Tim gurgled.

"If you know who he is, how come you aren't calling the cops?" I asked.

She leaned forward and put a hand on Tim's knee. Tim squirmed in his seat and blushed.

"I know an innocent man when I see one," she said. "And your brother has got the most lovely big, wide, innocent eyes."

Yeah. They match his lovely big, wide, innocent brain, I thought. But I decided to say nothing. If Charlotte Van Dam was crazy enough to fancy Tim, that might just help us. And right now we needed all the help we could get.

"So tell me, Timothy," she said. "What takes you to Dover?"

"Well ... the train does," Tim replied. As brilliant as ever.

"You're on the run from the police!" she whispered. And now I understood. She'd been writing crime fiction all her life but now she'd just met the real thing. No wonder she was excited. "Are you going to leave the country?" she asked.

In the end we told her the whole story, just as we had told Snape a few days before. The only difference was that she believed us. And not only did she believe us – she was enthralled.

"I want to help!" she gasped, when we had finished. "I can find this man you're seeking."

"86?" I said.

"Yes. The secret agent. I can go to the Amstel Ijsbaan for you. I live in Amsterdam. I speak the language. Please, you must let me go!"

Tim shook his head. "But Charlotte, it could be dangerous."

"Charon could be there," I agreed.

"Yes. And you might slip on the ice," Tim added.

Charlotte moved closer to Tim and looked at him adoringly. I could almost hear the violins playing in the background. She was in love with Tim! It was incredible. "You're just like every character I've ever written about," she murmured.

"You do horror stories too?" I said.

Her lips moved closer to his. "Tim..."

"Charlotte..."

"The train's slowing down!" She broke free – and it was true. The train had slowed down while we were talking and now it had stopped completely. But we weren't in a station. We were in the middle of a field.

"I wonder..." she began. She got out of her seat and went over to the section between our carriage and the next. This was the only part of the train where there was a window you could open. I watched as she opened it and stuck her head out.

At the same time, the train started up again and quickly picked up speed.

When Charlotte came back, she looked worried. "It was a police block," she said. "Five of them just got on the train."

Sure enough, as the train continued, we

passed a police car parked next to the track. We were sitting right in the middle of the train. The policemen had got on at the front. I guessed it would take them less than a minute to reach us.

"How did they know you were on the train?" Charlotte asked.

"I don't know," Tim replied.

But I did. He had asked a policeman for directions at Victoria Station. The policeman must have followed us and seen us get onto the train.

"You're going to have to jump!" Charlotte said.

"Jump...?" I looked out of the window. We were already doing twenty miles per hour and moving faster by the second.

"Quickly!"

"Can we pull the communications cord first?" Tim asked.

"No." Charlotte shook her head. She'd already got it all worked out. A typical writer. "If you pull the cord, it will tell the police you were here."

"And there's a fifty pound fine," I added.

"Move!"

Still chained together, Tim and I got out of our seats and moved to the nearest door. Charlotte followed. Fortunately there were only a couple of other passengers near us and they were so buried in their papers that they didn't see us go.

We reached the nearest exit door. Tim pulled it open and stood there with the wind buffeting his face. The train was moving very fast now and I could see he had changed his mind about the plan. To be honest, I wasn't too wild about it either.

"Good luck," Charlotte said.

"Actually..." Tim began.

"Goodbye!" Charlotte said.

Tim fell out of the train and in that split second I realized two things: one – that Charlotte had given him a helpful push; and two – that I was still chained to him. With a yell I launched myself after him.

I felt the wind grab me. For a moment everything was a blur. Then long grass rushed up at me from all sides. I heard Tim yell, the sound blending in with the roar of the train. I could feel his weight at the end of the chain, still pulling me forward. There was a sickening thud as my shoulder came into contact with the earth. And then everything was blue, green, blue, green as I rolled down a hill between the grass and the sky. I couldn't see Tim any more and wondered if he'd managed to pull off my arm.

Then I must have blacked out for a moment. The next thing I knew, I was lying on my back, winded and only half-conscious. A pair of eyes that I thought I knew well loomed over me.

"Tim?" I muttered.

"Moo," came the reply. It was a cow. And it seemed as astonished as I was that I was still alive.

I raised my hand and was grateful to see it was still there. It seemed that I hadn't broken any bones in the fall – but I had broken the handcuffs. A length of chain trailed away from my wrist.

There was a loud groan a short distance away and Tim popped up behind a small bush. It had been a big bush until he had rolled through it. Tim had been less fortunate than me. As soon as we were separated, he had rolled through six nettles, a clump of thistles, a cowpat and the bush.

"Next time, we take a bus!" he muttered as I tried to tidy him up. The cow ambled over and tried to eat his sleeve. "Shoo!" Tim cried out. The cow put its head down to the ground and took a bite out of one of his shoes.

We chased the cow away and found Tim's other shoe. A few minutes later we crossed the field leaving the railway line behind us. There was a gap in the hedge and a lane on the other side. We turned left, following our noses. Actually, Tim's nose had been stung so badly, it now pointed both ways.

But he didn't complain. He was limping along beside me, deep in thought. For a long time neither of us spoke. Then, at last, he sighed. "Charlotte!" I'd had a feeling he was thinking about her. "You know, I really think she likes me."

I shrugged. "Well, she was certainly smiling when she pushed you off the train."

We reached a crossroads. This time there was a sign. Dover straight ahead. But it didn't say how far.

"How far do you think it is?" Tim asked.

"It can't be more than a couple of kilometres," I said. Tim grimaced. "I'm not sure I can make it, kid. I think I've twisted both my ankles."

I looked down. "No you haven't," I said. "You've got your shoes on the wrong feet."

"Oh."

We walked a little further and suddenly there we were. We were high up with the sea – a brilliant blue – below us. The port of Dover was a knotted fist with a ferry and a hovercraft slipping through its concrete fingers even as we watched. And to our left and to our right, as far as we could see, a ribbon of white stretched out beneath the sun. The White Cliffs of Dover. We had made it to the edge of England. But now we had to go further, over the water and away from home.

We slipped into the crowded port without being noticed. Maybe the police were still waiting for us at the station. Maybe they had given up on us and gone. There was a ferry leaving for Ostend in ten minutes. We took it. Despite what I'd been able to save from the bank robbery, we were getting low on cash so we only bought one-way tickets.

But as I said to Tim, if we didn't find Charon in Amsterdam, it was unlikely that we would be coming back.

THE SECRET AGENT

To be honest, I'm not crazy about Amsterdam. It's got too many canals, too many tourists and most of its buildings look like they've been built with a Lego set that's missing half its pieces. Also, the Dutch put mayonnaise on their chips. But if you like bicycles and cobbled streets, flower stalls and churches, I suppose there are worse places you can go.

We arrived the next morning after hitch-hiking up from Ostend. That was one good thing about Amsterdam. After three hours with a lorry driver, a cheese salesman and a professional juggler (who dropped us in the middle of the city) we realized that just about everyone in the place spoke English. This was just as well. Ten minutes after we'd set off in search of the Amstel Ijsbaan, we were hopelessly lost. It wasn't just that we couldn't understand the street signs. We couldn't even pronounce them. We found our way by asking people. Not that that was much help.

Me: "Excuse me. We're looking for the Amstel Ijsbaan."

Friendly local: "Go along the canal. Turn left at the canal. Continue until you see a canal. And it's on a canal."

There were hundreds of canals and they all looked exactly the same. In fact if you went on holiday in Amsterdam you'd only need to take one photograph. Then you could develop it a few dozen times. We must have walked for an hour and a half before we finally found what we were looking for: a low, square building on the very edge of the city, stretching out into the only open space we'd seen. Like the rest of the place, the sign was old and needed repair. It read: AMS EL IJSBAAN.

"There's no 'T'," I said.

"That's all right," Tim muttered. "I'm not thirsty."

We went in. An old crone was sitting behind the glass window of the ticket office. Either she had a bad skin disease or the window needed cleaning. As Tim went over to her she put down the grubby paperback she had been reading and looked up at him with suspicious eyes.

"*Kan ik u misschien helpen?*" she said. It sounded like she was gargling, but that's the Dutch language for you. Tim stared at her.

"Hoeveel kaartjes wilt u?" she demanded more angrily.

You didn't have to be Einstein to work out what she was saying. After all, she was a tick-etseller and we needed tickets. But Tim just stood there, rooted to the spot, mumbling in what sounded like GCSE French. I stepped forward.

"Twee kaarties alstublieft," I said and slid some money under the window. The old woman grunted, gave us two tickets and went back to her book.

"What did you say?" Tim demanded.

"I asked for two tickets."

"But when did you learn to speak Dutch?"

"On the ferry. I looked in a phrase book."

Tim's face lit up. "You're brilliant, Nick!"

"Not really." I shrugged. "It's just a phrase I'm going through."

We passed through a set of double doors. We could hear the ice rink in the distance now, or at least the music booming out over the speakers.

I noticed that Tim had picked up a pair of skates.

"We're here to look for 86," I reminded him. "We're not going skating."

"86 could be on the ice," he said.

"But Tim ... can you skate?"

"Can I skate?" He grinned at me. "*Can* I skate!"

Tim couldn't skate. I watched him fall over three times – and that was before he even reached the ice. Then I left him and began to search for the secret agent who called himself 86. How would I recognize him? He was hardly likely to have a badge with the number on it. A tattoo, perhaps? I decided to look out for anyone who seemed strange or out-of-place. The trouble was, in a run-down Dutch skating rink in the middle of the summer, *everyone* seemed out of place.

The ice rink was enormous. It was like being inside an aircraft hangar. It was rectangular in shape, surrounded by five rows of plastic seats rising in steps over the ice. There was an observation box at one end and the terrace café at the other. Everything was slightly shabby, old-fashioned ... and cold. The ice was actually steaming as it caught the warm air from outside and chilled it. There were only about half a dozen skaters out there and, as they glided along the surface of the rink, they seemed to disappear into the fog like bizarre, dancing ghosts.

There was also a handful of spectators. An old lady sat knitting. She might have been aged eighty-six but I somehow doubted that she was the agent. An ice-cream seller was sitting on his own, looking depressed because nobody was buying his ice creams. The nearest he got to eighty-six was the 99-flakes he was advertising.

I glanced back at Tim. He had fallen over again. Either that, or he was trying to ice-skate on his nose.

But there was one good skater on the ice, a real professional in a black tracksuit. If you've ever watched ice-skaters, you'll know that they seem to move without even trying. It's almost as though they're flying standing up. Well, this man was like that. I watched him as he sped round in a huge figure of eight. Then I turned back and began to thread my way through the remaining spectators.

That was when I saw them. They were sitting down in the middle of the highest row of seats with their legs spread out on the seats below them. One was tall and thin, dressed in a grey suit with a bow tie. At some time in his life he'd had a nasty argument with someone ... and I mean nasty. The someone had left a scar that started just to the side of his left eye and ran all the way down to his neck. I'd never seen a scar quite like it. It looked like you could post a letter in it. His companion was shorter, dressed in jeans, white T-shirt and black leather jacket. He had hair like an oil-slick and a face that seemed to have been moulded by somebody with large thumbs. He didn't need a scar. He was ugly enough already.

Why had I noticed them? It was simple.

They weren't watching the ice. I got the feeling they were watching me – and as I walked past them, following a line of seats a few rows below, I felt their four eyes swivelling round and sticking to me like leeches in a swamp. Even as I went, I wondered if one of them could be Agent 86. But I didn't ask. I didn't want to know.

The music changed from classical to jazz.

Tim fell over more jazzily this time. The professional swung round him in another smooth circle. Scarface and Ugly were still sitting where I'd seen them, only now they were looking away. I decided to ignore them.

But where was 86?

I walked up to the top row, passing seat eighty-six as I went. It was empty. I turned back and took one last look at the rink. Tim was sitting on the ice, shaking his head, and suddenly I wanted to laugh. The man in the black tracksuit had skated two figures round him. I could see the figures cut by the blades in the surface of the ice. An eight and a six.

I ran back down to the edge of the rink and called to Tim. That was a mistake. I'd allowed myself to get excited and I'd shown it. And although I only half-noticed it then, I had good reason to remember it later.

Scarface and Ugly were watching me again.

* * *

We found the tracksuit in the changing room but the skater was no longer in it. He was taking a shower. We waited until he came out, a white towel wrapped round his waist. He was a tough, broad-shouldered man. The water was still glistening off muscles that would have looked good on a horse. He had pale skin and grey, watchful eyes that reminded me of my old friend Inspector Snape. He sat down between Tim and me without seeming to notice either of us.

"86?" I said.

He just sat there as if he hadn't even heard me. Then slowly he turned his head and looked at me with an expressionless face. "I don't know you," he said.

Tim took over. "I liked the skating," he said. "You always practise figures?"

The skater shrugged. "What of it?" His English was almost perfect, but with a slight American accent.

"I'm a friend of a friend of yours," Tim explained. "A guy called McMuffin."

"McGuffin," I corrected him.

The skater shook his head. Water dripped out of his hair. "I don't know this name..."

Tim smiled. He was playing the private detective now – cooler than the ice on the rink. "Well, here's something else you don't know," he drawled. "McGuffin is in his McCoffin."

The skater seemed uninterested. "Who are

you?" he demanded.

"The name's Tim Diamond. Private eye."

"How about you?" I asked.

"My name is Rushmore. Hugo Rushmore. I'm sorry to hear about your friend but I can't help you. I'm just a skater. That's all."

For a moment I almost believed him – but the figures cut in the ice couldn't have been just a coincidence. And without Agent 86, we were nowhere.

I decided to have one last try. "Please, Mr Rushmore," I said. "You've got to help us."

Still he looked blank. And then I remembered the ticket that I had found in McGuffin's hotel room, the ticket that had brought us all this way. I still had it in my pocket. I fished it out and handed it to him.

"McGuffin gave us this," I said. "Before he died."

Rushmore took the ticket. It was as if I'd said the right password or turned on some sort of switch. A light came on in his eyes. "All right," he said. "Let's get a drink."

We went up to the café terrace I'd seen before. It had a view over the rink, but either the day had got warmer or the ice had got colder, because there was so much mist you could hardly see it.

I could just make out two figures standing at the far end and thought of Scarface and

Ugly but they were too far away and the mist washed them out. Rushmore was drinking a Coke and had bought us both milk shakes, which would have been nicer if someone had remembered to shake the milk.

"There's not a lot I can tell you," he began. "I do a little work for the Dutch Secret Service..."

"What sort of work?" Tim asked.

"That's a secret. But I'll tell you this much. I was ordered to look after Jake McGuffin while he was over here. His boss – Mr Waverly – was desperate to find Charon." Rushmore paused and considered. "There was something odd going on," he added. "Something Waverly hadn't told Jake."

"You mean, Waverly was keeping something back?" I said.

"That's right. There was a connection between Mr Waverly and Charon. It was as if they knew each other in some way. Jake said the whole thing stank. But he never found out what it was..."

A connection between Waverly and Charon. It seemed impossible. After all, Waverly was the one who wanted to find Charon. It was all getting confusing. "What was McGuffin doing here in Holland?" I asked.

"He'd followed Charon over here." Rushmore finished his Coke. "The last time I saw him he was planning to check out some old house just outside the city."

"You know the name?" Tim asked.

Rushmore nodded. "Yes. It's called the Winter House. The *Villa de Winter*, in Dutch. It's about twenty kilometres from Amsterdam."

"Twenty kilometres..." Tim tried to work it out on his fingers. He didn't have enough fingers.

"Twelve miles," I said. I turned to Rushmore. "Could you take us there?"

His eyes narrowed. "It could be dangerous."

"That's all right," Tim chimed in. "You can go in first."

Rushmore looked from Tim back to me. "All right," he said. "The rink closes at six today. Come back at five past. I'll drive you out this evening."

We stood up.

"See you later, Mr Skater," I muttered.

"Yeah. Watch how you go, Hugo," Tim added. I looked down at the ice, searching for the figures that I'd glimpsed behind the mist. But the ice was empty. The two of them had gone.

We got back to the ice rink at six o'clock after an afternoon in Amsterdam. It was still light outside, but once we'd passed through the swing doors into the old building it was as if we'd entered some sort of artificial Arctic night. The ticket-seller had gone home. The lights had been turned off and the windows with their frosted glass and wire grills kept most of the sunlight out. The rink itself stretched out silent and empty, with the mist still curling gently on the surface. The music was switched off, too. But the machine that made the ice was still active. I could hear it humming and hissing like some sort of mythical creature, its pipes spreading out like tentacles, chilling everything they touched.

"Where is he?" I whispered. My words were taken by the cold air and sent scurrying up towards the rafters. *Where is he? Where is he?*

I could almost hear the echo.

The mist on the ice folded over itself, rolling towards us.

"What…?" Tim began.

There was something on the ice. It was in the very middle, a grey bundle that could have been somebody's old clothes.

"Wait here," I said.

I walked through the barrier and onto the ice. I could feel it, cold underneath my shoes. As I walked forward, my feet slid away from under me and I had to struggle to stay upright. The ice-making pipes rumbled softly below. The mist swirled round my ankles, clinging to my skin. I wanted to hurry but I was forced to be slow.

At last I reached the bundle.

It was Rushmore. The Dutch secret agent must have been on his way to meet us, crossing the ice when he was stopped. Somebody had found out who he was and had known about his connection with McGuffin. And they had made sure that he wouldn't help us.

He had been stabbed twice. The blades were still in his back, one between his shoulders, the other just above his waist. There was a pool of blood around his outstretched hand. It had already frozen solid.

I took one last look at the body and at the blades, long and silver and horribly appropriate. Because whoever had killed Hugo Rushmore, professional ice-skater and spy, hadn't used knives.

They'd used a pair of ice-skating boots.

SHREDDED WHEAT

We spent the night at a cheap motel on the edge of Amsterdam. Our money was low and so were we. Rushmore had been our only link in a chain that might lead us to Charon and now he was dead. Worse still, it seemed that Charon knew we were in Amsterdam. How else could he have got to the ice-rink before us?

It was raining when we got to the Van Bates Motel. We were shown to our room by a thin, twitchy manager who didn't speak a word of English. In the end we had to get his mother down to translate.

All I wanted was a shower and a bed, but the shower wasn't working and as usual Tim took the bed. There was a TV in one corner of the room. It was tuned to the BBC – the ten o'clock news. I didn't want to hear the news but I was somehow glad to hear another English voice. I listened. And suddenly I was glad I'd turned it on.

There was a reporter on the screen. He was standing outside Sotheby's, the auction house in New Bond Street, London.

"Boris Kusenov—" They were the first two words I'd heard. That was what had caught my attention— "is considered to be the key figure in the struggle for power at the Kremlin."

The picture changed. Now the reporter was inside the auction house, standing in front of a large canvas. For a moment I thought the TV had broken. Then I realized. This was modern art.

"Kusenov is in England to bid for a canvas by the surrealist painter, Salvador Dali," the reporter's voice went on. "Titled 'The Tsar's Feast', it depicts Tsar Nicholas II offering stale bread to his dissatisfied serfs..."

Well, that may have been what it looked like to him. To me the picture looked like a bent watch beside a pink lake being examined by two oversized amoebas. Had Kusenov come all the way from Russia just to buy this? The TV screen cut to a picture of the reporter. He answered the question for me.

"Kusenov came to Britain unexpectedly because of his belief that the painting should hang in Russia. Although it is expected to reach almost a million pounds, he will be bidding for it when it is auctioned at Sotheby's in two days' time."

The reporter smirked at the camera and the programme cut back to the studio and the next news item.

"Police have completely lost the track of the dangerous criminal, Tim Diamond, who..."

I turned the set off. I'd heard quite enough about *him*.

"Kusenov," I muttered. Tim was sitting upright on the bed. The sound of his own name had evidently woken him up. "He's already in England."

"Is that bad?" Tim asked.

I sighed. It wasn't bad. It was terrible. "It means we're running out of time. Charon could move at any moment." I thought for a minute. "We've got to find this Winter House," I said. "We need help."

Tim's eyes lit up. "Charlotte!"

"You'd better call her."

Tim called her. The phone rang about six times before we were connected. Charlotte answered in Dutch.

"Charlotte?" Tim interrupted. "It's me ... Tim."

"Tim?" There was a pause and I wondered if she'd forgotten who he was. But then she continued breathlessly. "Thank goodness you rang. I have to see you. I think I've found something."

"What?" Tim asked.

"I can't tell you. Not over the telephone. Let's meet somewhere safe." Another pause. I could hear heavy breathing. It took me a few seconds to realize it was Tim's. Then Charlotte cut in again. "Just outside Amsterdam, in the Flavoland. There's a crossroads and a bus stop. Can you meet me there tomorrow morning? At nine."

"Tomorrow?" Tim crooned. "But that's a whole day away!"

"I know."

"I'll be there."

Tim hung up. "Tomorrow," he said. "Just off the Flavobahn. In Autoland."

"I heard," I said.

And I had heard. Charlotte was frightened and Rushmore was dead. Charon, it seemed, was everywhere. How long would it be before he moved in on us?

Take a bus north out of Amsterdam and after a while you'll come to the Flavoland. When you look for a view and find you haven't got one, that's when you'll know you're there. The Flavoland used to be the bottom of the sea until someone had the bright idea of taking the water away. What was left was a great, flat, wide, empty nothing. Dutch farmers use it to grow their crops in, and that's all there is: fields of corn, wheat, barley and maize stretching out to a horizon as regular as a plate. There isn't one hill in the Flavoland. There are no trees. And the birds are too bored to whistle.

There was only one bus stop in the area and it was right next to the crossroads that Charlotte had described. The bus-driver tried to stop us getting out – he must have thought we were crazy – but we insisted.

"When does the next bus arrive?" I asked.

"Tomorrow," he replied.

And then it was gone, kicking up a cloud of dust, and we were alone with the wind and the wheat.

Really alone.

I looked behind me. Nothing. I looked ahead. Nothing. The road was just two lines that ran together and the bus was already a speck at the far end. The wheat rippled gently in the breeze. It was a hot day. The sun was beating down and with no hills and no trees there were no shadows. We were in the middle of a giant frying pan. And there was no sign of Charlotte.

Tim looked at his watch. "She's late."

I could hear a faint droning. At first I thought it was a wasp. Out of the corner of my eye I saw something small passing in front of the sun. But it wasn't an insect. It was a plane, spraying the crops about two or three kilometres to the south. I watched as it flew in a straight line, parallel to the horizon. I could see it more clearly now, an old wooden propeller plane with two sets of wings on each side, like something out of the First World War. It was leaving a silvery cloud behind it, thin drops of pesticide or something drifting down onto...

"That's funny," I said.

"What's that?" Tim asked.

"That plane's dusting crops where there ain't no crops."

The plane turned sharply and began to fly towards us. I could hear the propeller chopping at the air. The engine sounded angry. For a long time I just stood there watching it. Maybe it was the heat. Maybe I was tired. I didn't realize I was watching my own death.

But then the plane swooped down and before my brain had time to tell me what was going on my legs were hurling me out of the way as the whole thing sliced through the air millimetres above where my head had just been. Tim shrieked and threw himself in the other direction. For a moment everything went dark as the plane blotted out the sun. The propeller whipped up the surface of the road, stinging my eyes. And then it was gone, climbing upwards and at the same time turning for the next attack.

Tim got to his knees, coughing and blinking. I don't think he'd quite understood what was happening. "Low flying..." he muttered.

I nodded. "Any lower and it wouldn't need wings."

"Do you think...?"

But even Tim had worked out what I was thinking. It was Charon. Somehow he had found out about our meeting with Charlotte.

I remembered now how scared she'd been on the telephone. Maybe she'd been followed. Maybe she was already dead.

Charon was up there. And we had nowhere to run, nowhere to hide. Because that was exactly where we were. Nowhere.

I was still wondering which way to run when the plane swept down again. And this time there was an even more unpleasant surprise. Two of its wings were fitted with machine-guns. I saw the sparks of red and heard the chatter of the bullets. A section of the road leaped up at me, the tarmac shattering. Tim dived to one side and I tried to follow him but then something punched me hard on the shoulder and I was thrown on my back. The plane rushed past, the wind battering and blinding me. I knew I had been hit but I didn't know how badly. I was hurting all over.

But then the plane had gone and somehow I had got to my feet. I looked round for Tim. His face was white but it could have been dust. The plane was banking steeply, preparing for the next attack. Third time lucky...?

We only had one chance. "Come on!" I shouted. "The wheat!"

"I can't!" Tim was frozen. The plane had almost completed its turn.

"Why not?"

"My hay fever…!"

"Tim!" It was incredible. Charon had us right in his sights and Tim was worrying about his hay fever. Any minute now he'd have more holes in him than a Swiss cheese and the next time he sneezed, he'd do it in fourteen directions at once. But this was no time to argue. Ignoring the pain in my shoulder, I grabbed hold of him and pushed him off the road.

The plane dived again, invisible this time, and a great patch of wheat tore itself apart spectacularly around me. Tim sneezed. At least he hadn't been hit. But this was hopeless. We could stumble through the field until the whole thing looked like a plate of cornflakes but we'd end up as the free gifts in the middle. Eventually Charon would pick us off. We had to do something. Now.

And then I saw them. They'd been left in the middle of the wheat and they had both fallen over into a sad and useless heap. They were made of wire and old broomstick handles with punctured footballs for heads. Scarecrows. Even the most cowardly of crows wouldn't have been scared by them but they'd given me an idea.

I searched for the plane. It was at its furthest point, turning again. Then I yelled at Tim. "Take off your jacket!"

"Why?"

"Just do it!"

I pulled off my own jacket. It hurt me and as my sleeve came free I saw that it was soaked in blood. But it would just have to wait. I grabbed hold of one of the scarecrows and threw it towards Tim. Miraculously he'd got the idea without my having to explain it. We had no time. The plane had almost completed its turn, a shimmering dot in the face of the sun. I hoped that Charon would be blinded by the glare, that he wouldn't see what we were doing. I'd managed to get my jacket onto the smaller scarecrow. It hung off the wooden framework clumsily and the football face – black and white and half deflated – looked nothing like mine. At least, I hope it didn't. I glanced back. The plane had completed its turn. It was coming at us, out of the sun.

"Tim…?"

He'd hung his own jacket onto the other scarecrow. Carefully, we leaned them against each other, shoulder to shoulder. They swayed but stood upright like two drunken friends. The noise of the plane reached me and I almost felt the wheat shiver behind me.

"Duck!" I shouted.

We threw ourselves into the wheat at the

same moment as the bullets erupted again. I looked up and saw the two scarecrows only a metre or two away cut in half by the scythe of gunfire. The plane roared overhead. And then it was all over. The plane continued the way it had come, disappearing in the distance. The scarecrows lay in tatters on a bed of shredded wheat. The wind stroked the rest of the crop as if trying to soothe it after what had happened.

We stood up. We wouldn't be wearing our jackets again. The bullets had turned them into so many handkerchiefs. Tim gazed up at the sky, "You think it was Charon?" he said.

"Who else could it have been?" I replied.

"A farmer..."

"What? Using machine-gun bullets to spray the crops?"

Tim considered. "Maybe it was an organic farmer."

I shook my head. "I don't think so."

There was a long silence. I found I was unconsciously gripping my arm. I could feel the blood seeping through my fingers.

Tim was deep in thought. At last he spoke. "If it was Charon," he muttered, "he'll think we're dead now. And if he thinks we're dead, he won't try and kill us."

"Right," I agreed.

Tim brightened. "Well, I suppose that's a shot in the arm." Then he saw the blood.

"Nick!"
"What?"
"You've been shot in the arm."
"I know."

Tim took a step forward. His face had gone a cheesy-white and I knew what was about to happen. And a moment later it did. With a little moan, he crumpled and joined the two scarecrows, stretched out in the heat. He never had been able to stand the sight of blood.

I just stood where I was, clutching my arm. It was hurting more now, but that was good. It reminded me that I was still alive.

CHARON

"Now, this won't hurt..."

Why do doctors always say that before they hurt you?

Dr Monika Bloem wasn't even a doctor. She was a vet. We'd found her farmhouse just outside the Flavoland as we'd walked back towards the city. I wasn't too happy about being treated by someone who was more comfortable with dogs and rabbits, but I didn't have much choice. I'd left about half a litre of my blood in a dotted line along the road and although it may have looked pretty, I didn't have enough to continue it all the way to Amsterdam.

Dr Bloem (it rhymed with "room") was a short, serious woman in a white coat. She had a neat clinic lined with cages of various sizes, and it was easy to see that she was married to her work. Her best man had probably been a goat.

There were pictures of animals everywhere – even in the frames on her desk. She had only agreed reluctantly to treat a human being. And she had fed me two lumps of sugar first.

Sure enough there was a moment of excruciating pain as she probed my wound with a pair of tweezers but then she was backing away with a red, glistening bullet firmly trapped between the prongs.

"You are feeling all right?" she asked. Her English was accented, not as good as her surgical skills.

"Well, I'm still a bit faint..." Tim began.

She glared at him. "I mean your brother."

I flexed my arm. "I'm OK, Dr Bloem," I said.

"You are lucky, I think." The doctor dropped the bullet into a kidney tray. It hit the bottom with a dull clang. "A centimetre to the left and it would have hit an artery."

"Yeah," Tim agreed. "And it could have been worse. A centimetre to the right and it would have hit me!"

Dr Bloem unwrapped a packet of bandages. "You know, I think you are not telling me the truth," she said as she did it. "How did the bullet get into the arm?"

"Well..." I began. This was tricky. We hadn't had time to make up a sensible explanation and our story – like my arm – was full of holes.

"Your brother said you were hurt in a car accident," Dr Bloem went on.

"It's true!" Tim explained. "It was the driver of the car."

"Yes," I added. "He accidentally shot me."

Dr Bloem didn't believe us but she wrapped the bandage round my arm and tied a knot. "It is finished," she said. "You should be OK now."

"Thanks, Doc." I tried the arm again. It was throbbing but most of the pain had gone.

"So how will the two of you get back to town?" Dr Bloem asked. "I would take you but I have another patient. He's a little horse."

"Has he tried gargling?" Tim said.

Dr Bloem ignored him. "You can walk – but it's a long way. So maybe you should ask for a ride. There's a big house just one kilometre up the road. Near a windmill."

"What's it called?" I asked.

Dr Bloem smiled at me. "It's called the *Villa de Winter*," she said. "The Winter House."

I'd never seen a house quite like the Winter House. It was built out of red and white bricks but not with any pattern. The colours seemed to zigzag across the walls, colliding with each other, then bouncing away again. The whole building could have been put together by a thief. The towers had been stolen from a castle, the windows from a church, the grey slate roof from a railway station.

The house was set back from the road. Tim and I had climbed over a fence to get in and we were squatting some distance from the building itself, spying on it through a bush.

"Do you think this is where Charon lives?" Tim asked.

I nodded. "This is where McGuffin came before he was killed."

"Right." Tim gazed at the house. "If only we could see through the wall."

"We can!" I said.

"How?"

"The window..."

We broke cover and sprinted across the lawn to the side of the house. Our shadows reached it first. There was nobody in sight, but now I could hear the sound of a piano drifting out of one of the windows. I recognized the music – but only just. It was Beethoven's "Moonlight Sonata", but played very badly. It occurred to me that the pianist might be missing a finger.

"Listen!" I nudged Tim.

"Is it a record?" Tim asked.

"Yes. Nobody's ever played it that badly."

Tim's mouth dropped open. "Charon!"

"It figures. He killed McGuffin. And now he's murdering Beethoven."

We had both been crouching down but now

I straightened up and tried to lever myself onto the window sill above me. Tim was horrified. "What are you doing?"

"It could be our only chance to see what Charon looks like," I said.

And it could have been. But just as my fingers grabbed hold of the woodwork I heard a car. It was coming up the drive, heading for the main entrance. I dropped down again and squatted next to Tim. At the same time the piano playing stopped and I heard a door close. There were two dustbins just beside us. I edged closer to them, using them to hide behind.

The car had stopped. Two men got out. I recognized them, although I had only seen them once before. They had faces you were unlikely to forget. Scarface and Ugly – the two men from the skating-rink. The gravel crunched under their feet as they walked towards the door. The noise made me think of the skates in Rushmore's back, and I swallowed hard.

Tim was staring after them. I tugged at his sleeve. "Let's go in," I whispered.

He opened his mouth to argue but I didn't give him time. There was a door just on the other side of the window and, for once, luck was on our side – it was open. Making sure that Tim was still following me, I went in, up a short flight of steps and into a corridor paved with black and white tiles – like in one of those old Dutch paintings. The corridor must have led into a hall. I could hear voices in the distance, the two guests being welcomed. There was another door on our left. It opened into a large room with a desk, four or five antique chairs and a grand piano. It had to be Charon's room. I slid across the polished floor and found my feet on a Chinese rug.

"What are we doing?" Tim hissed.

What *were* we doing? Already I could hear the rap of footsteps making their way back along the corridor. Charon was about to come in with his two friends. If they found us there, I doubted they'd invite us to stay for tea...

"Quick!" There was an alcove to one side, half-covered by a heavy, ornamental curtain. We ran behind it and pulled it the whole way across. A second later, Charon and the two new arrivals walked in.

I heard them close the door and come into the room. Someone was talking in rapid Dutch. I couldn't understand a word of it, nor did I recognize the voice. A second person spoke. I didn't recognize his voice either. But this time I did understand one word of it. The name Waverly. Why were they talking about the head of MI6? Rushmore had told us that there was some sort of secret connection between them. Was that what they were discussing now?

It was infuriating. I was stuck behind the curtain with Tim. I couldn't understand a word that was being spoken. And I couldn't see anything either. Why had we even bothered to come in? I glanced at Tim. There was a tiny chink of light on one side of his cheek. I followed it back to the curtain. The curtain was torn! I hadn't noticed it before but there was a small hole, right in the middle. I leaned forward and put my eye against it, trying not to move the material. I could feel my heart pounding against my chest. At last I was going to see Charon!

But it wasn't to be. Charon had chosen the antique chair that had its back to the curtain. Looking through the hole I could see Scarface, smoking a cigarette in the chair opposite him, and Ugly, standing to one side. But Charon was concealed.

And then he spoke. It was a single word and I didn't understand it, but at least I had heard his voice. It was a chesty sort of voice, not deep. Had I heard it somewhere before?

His hand stretched out and I saw the four fingers open in a palm-up gesture. At the same time, Ugly hurried forward with a small white hammer. It was another antique, probably made of ivory. What were they doing with it? Ugly jabbered away for about one minute and I got the sense that they were wrapping things up. If only Charon would stand up ... every nerve in my body was screaming at him to get out of the chair.

It was Scarface who got to his feet. He walked across towards the curtain and I was forced to retreat from the eyehole, away into the shadow. There were more mutterings behind him. The door opened and I knew even without looking that Charon was on his way out. Sure enough, when the door closed, the room was silent. I had been that close to unravelling the biggest mystery of all. But not quite close enough.

"Have they gone?" Tim whispered.

"They've gone..." I pushed back the curtain and went out into the room. Charon might have left but his desk was still there. I just hoped he didn't lock his drawer.

"Did you see his face?" Tim asked.

"No. But I heard a bit of what they said. They were talking about Mr Waverly."

I pulled open the top drawer. I'm not sure what I was looking for. Would Charon have a driving licence, a photograph of himself, a credit card?

Surely there would be something to tell me who he was? But the drawer was empty apart from three paperclips, a comb, a small mirror covered in some sort of powder and a half-smoked packet of cigarettes.

It told me nothing. I wasn't thinking. It should have told me who Charon was.

I tried the second drawer. And that was where I found it. It was an ordinary cheque, made out for the sum of four hundred thousand guilders. Payable to "Charon Enterprises". And signed by…

I showed it to Tim. "Four hundred thousand guilders!" he exclaimed. "That's…" But as usual his mathematics wouldn't stretch that far.

"It's about £120,000," I said. "But look at the signature."

Tim read it. His eyes bulged. "Mr Waverly!"

"That's right," I said. "Mr Waverly is the one who's paying Charon to kill Kusenov."

"But why?" Tim demanded. "He was the one who wanted to *stop* Charon."

"I know." I pocketed the cheque. None of it made any sense – but at least I had some sort of evidence against Waverly. "Come on." I moved towards the door. "Let's get out of here."

"Let's take the window," Tim said, moving the other way.

"And keep it quiet. OK?"

He opened the window. Alarm bells exploded throughout the house.

It was too late to argue now. We dived head first through the window together, hit the grass in a somersault and staggered to our feet. A door crashed open behind us and I glimpsed Scarface hurtling towards us. But I was already halfway across the lawn, running with all my strength towards the undergrowth that might offer somewhere to hide. There was a bang and something whizzed past my head. My arm was suddenly hurting again. Hadn't I been shot at enough for one day?

We jumped over the first shrubs and sprinted on through the rough woodland at the edge of the house. Ugly had joined Scarface. I heard him shout something in Dutch. There was a second shot. Tim screamed. I wheeled round.

"Are you hit?" I demanded.

"No. I stepped on a stinging nettle."

"We've got to find the road."

We found the road about thirty seconds before Scarface and Ugly found us. Even as we climbed over the fence and dropped down on to the tarmac, the wood was torn to splinters by another burst of gunfire. But there were no cars on the road. No buses. Nothing. We still hadn't got away.

"Where now?" Tim panted.

"There!"

Dr Bloem had said the Winter House was near a windmill and there it was, a few hundred metres away, its huge sails turning slowly in the wind.

It was our only hope. We had nowhere else to hide and I knew that Scarface and Ugly would be over the fence – or perhaps through it – in seconds. With Tim close behind me I crossed the road. There was only one door and it was open.

One way in. One way out. It was only when I was inside that I realized we were trapped. Worse still, Scarface and Ugly had seen us go in. I saw them now, guns in their hands, slowly crossing the road towards us. Scarface was smiling. It made his scar bend in the middle so that it was like the point of an arrow. And the arrow was pointing at me.

"They're coming after us!" Tim was close to panic. "What are we going to do?"

"Hide!"

Tim went one way. I went another.

The inside of the windmill was like nothing I'd imagined. In fact it seemed bigger inside than out, with a mass of slowly turning wooden beams, wheels and great stones all meshing together like the workings of some fantastic clock. Four separate staircases ran up in different directions. One led to a door that opened on to an outer gallery, and this was the one I chose. I felt trapped inside the mill. If anybody was going to shoot me, I'd prefer it to be in the open.

I scrabbled up the staircase – it was more like a ladder – wondering which way Tim would go. But I didn't have time to worry about him. Even as I reached the top and the sunlight, I saw Scarface grab the bottom of the ladder and start up. Maybe fifteen seconds separated us. I had to find somewhere to hide.

But where? I was on a narrow wooden platform that circled all the way round the windmill about four metres above the ground … too high to jump. There were no other doors. I could run round and round in circles. But there was no other way up and the way back was blocked. A great shadow swept over me as one of the sails sliced down, cutting diagonally across the platform.

The sail…

I knew it was a crazy idea even as I started moving towards it. If you think a windmill's sails are slow and gentle, think again. Even when the wind is down they move at speed and they're strong enough to stun an ox. I was just lucky this wasn't a windy day.

As the next section of the sail swung round I leaped forward and grabbed it. Somehow my hands found the rough wooden framework behind the canvas. My arms were almost pulled out of their sockets. But an instant later, without any effort at all, I had been jerked off my feet and into the air, spinning round with the sail in an enormous, sickening, heart-stopping circle.

I clung on desperately. At the same time I kicked out with my feet and managed to find a grip between the wood and the canvas. I was left pinned to the sail – like a fly on flypaper as it spun me silently round and round, the green grass whirling away, the blue sky streaking in. It was as if the whole world were being stirred in a gigantic pot.

I shut my eyes. I couldn't watch.

But would Scarface see me? I could imagine him standing on the platform, circling it once, searching for me. Would he look up? I was behind the sail so unless he was standing at the back of the windmill I had to be hidden from him.

The windmill must have turned thirty times. I'd lost count after the fifteenth revolution. Everything I'd eaten in the last two days was threatening to leave my stomach. My arms and legs were groaning, feeling the weight of every turn. The wind dropped again. The sail slowed down. I'd had enough. As the platform veered up at me, I let go and fell in an untidy heap onto the hard wooden surface. If Scarface was still there, if he shot me now, it would only come as a relief.

But Scarface had already gone. I was too giddy to get to my feet but as I lay there, exhausted, I saw the assassins running across the fields below. They must have assumed I'd jumped down and got away. Then the nasty thought struck me.

Had they found Tim?

It was another five minutes before I found

the strength and the balance to get up. Even then the ladder down was a nightmare. I could still feel the motion of the sail inside my head and the ladder twisted away from me like a snake. It was ominously silent below. The only sound was the grinding of the massive stone as it turned in endless circles, crushing whatever got in the way into dust.

There was no sign of Tim.

Using my hands to keep myself upright, I staggered round the lower level. There were great sacks of flour to one side and, at the back, a loose heap of the stuff, stretching half-way up the wall. The platform above my head was empty. The door leading out was closed.

"Tim!" I shouted. "Where are you?"

Silence. I was starting to worry.

"Tim! It's all right! They've gone!"

Then something moved. I turned round. The loose flour, piled two metres high against the wall, was shifting. It was like watching a miniature avalanche.

A hand reached out, clawing at the air. The whole pile broke open and I was just able to make out a figure, fighting its way free. Flour was everywhere, billowing out into the air. Somehow Tim had managed to bury himself in it. Now he was free.

He stood there, completely white from head to foot. Maybe Ugly *had* shot him and this was his ghost.

"Hab day gob?" he asked.

There was flour in his nose and mouth. He sneezed. Flour cascaded out of his hair and a little pink circle appeared around his nose and mouth.

"Have they gone?" he tried again.

"Yeah. Are you all right?"

"I'm all white," Tim mumbled. At least, that's what it sounded like.

"Let's move."

We stalked out of the windmill, Tim leaving white footprints behind him. The sails were still turning slowly behind us.

In the last twelve hours we'd been machine-gunned through a cornfield and stitched up by a vet. We'd found Charon's headquarters and we'd come infuriatingly close to seeing Charon. We'd stolen Mr Waverly's cheque and we'd almost been shot getting away with it.

And now we were dead on our feet. We needed a bath and a long, long sleep. Because you had to admit – both of us had been through the mill.

STAGE FRIGHT

Twenty-four hours later we found ourselves on the platform of Central Station in Amsterdam. We'd paid our bill at the Van Bates Motel and bought two tickets to England. That was the end of our money. And here we were at the end of the line.

"I don't get it," Tim said. He'd managed to get rid of most of the flour but I noticed his hair was still a bit white at the sides. Maybe that was permanent. After the experiences of the last few days I wouldn't have been surprised. "I thought we weren't going back to England," he went on.

"We have to," I explained. "We've got to warn the Russian – Boris Kusenov. He can't trust Mr Waverly. Because it looks like Waverly is the one who is paying to get him killed."

"Right." Tim thought about it. "And he

can't trust anyone with hammers."

"Yeah. You tell him that."

But that was still a puzzle. We had seen Charon handling an antique white hammer. But what was he going to do with it? Bludgeon Kusenov to death?

And there was something else. South by south east. McGuffin's dying words. In all the excitement I had almost forgotten all about them. But we still hadn't found out what they meant.

"Nick!" Tim pointed.

It was the last person I'd expected to see. Charlotte Van Dam was walking along the platform, dressed in a light suit, carrying a handbag. I thought she was going to see us but at the last minute she forked off to the left and went into a smart café to one side.

"What's she doing here?" I muttered.

"She must be taking a train," Tim suggested.

"I know that," I said. "But where to? And why didn't she meet us in the wheatfield?"

Tim considered. "I don't know. Let's ask her."

"Yes. Let's ask."

The café at platform 2b resembled something out of an Agatha Christie novel, all wood panelling and marble bars with waiters in white aprons and tea that came in bone china, not plastic cups. Charlotte was sitting by a window that looked back out over the platform towards the trains. A waiter was serving her with a cup of hot chocolate and a croissant that could have been a late lunch. It was two o'clock. Our train to Ostend left at twenty past.

We went over to her. She saw us and for a moment there was something in her eyes that wasn't exactly pleasure. It was there and then it was gone. She smiled and stood up.

"Tim!" she exclaimed. "I've been so worried about you!" She kissed him lightly on the cheek.

Tim blushed. "You have?"

"Of course I have. Ever since I read about that ice-skater getting killed..."

"Rushmore," I muttered.

"The late 86," Tim added.

"Yeah," I said. "They finally got his number."

Charlotte sat down and waved us both to a seat. "So tell me what's been happening to you," she said.

Tim shifted uncomfortably. "Charlotte," he began. "We went to the Flavoland like you said. But you never turned up."

She shook her head, guiltily. "I know. I couldn't."

"Why not?" I asked.

She looked up. "Oh Tim – Nick ... I've lied to you."

"I don't believe you!" Tim said.

"I have. You see ... I'm not really a mystery writer."

Tim frowned. "What *do* you write then, Charlotte?"

"I don't write at all!" She took a deep breath.

"I'm a spy," she said. "I work for the Dutch Secret Service – like 86. I couldn't tell you before because I'm working undercover. You see, I'm on the track of Charon too."

"That still doesn't explain why you didn't meet us," I said.

"I was going to. But at the last minute I found I was being followed. There were two men. One of them had a scar."

"Short and ugly," Tim muttered.

"Yes. It was a short and ugly scar. I had to get away from them. But by the time I'd shaken them off, it was too late to come."

Tim turned to me. "You see," he said. "I told you there would be an explanation."

"How did the two of them get on to you?" I asked.

"I don't know. It's Charon. He seems to know everything I do before I do it. I can't move without..." She broke off. Her eyes were staring out of the window. "Oh my God!"

I twisted round. And suddenly I felt tired.

They hadn't seen us yet but Scarface and

Ugly were on the platform outside. And they were about to come in.

"It's them!" Charlotte whispered. She had stood up and the colour was draining from her face. "We've got to split up."

"Right." Tim turned to Charlotte. "I'll go with you."

"Thanks, Tim," I said.

But Charlotte was already moving away, making for the kitchens at the back. "No. You go your way. I'll go mine."

Tim opened his mouth to call after her. But she'd already gone.

She'd left her gloves on the table. I picked them up. They'd make a nice souvenir for Tim.

Then Scarface and Ugly arrived.

There were two exits from the restaurant. As they came in one, we went out the other. A staircase led down, away from the platform, right next to the restaurant. We took it. It looked like we'd just have to give the two-twenty Ostend train a miss.

The staircase took us down and out of the station. I didn't need to look to know that Scarface and Ugly were after us. I could hear the grunts and protests of innocent bystanders as they were brutally shoved out of the way.

"In here!" I shouted.

Tim didn't hear me. As I dived into a building on the other side of the road, I saw him disappear round the corner. We had split up again, but maybe that was for the best. At least one of us might get away.

I skidded to a halt and looked around me. As I'd run in, I'd thought the building was a library or perhaps a museum. But now I saw that it was in fact a small, old-fashioned theatre. There was a ticket-office beside the door and a poster showing an old man in an evening suit. There were cards tumbling out of his hands and the name, Mr Marvano, written underneath. A magician – just what I needed. Maybe he could help me disappear.

The show had already begun. The ticket-seller was reading a newspaper and there were no ushers on the door. I tiptoed through the foyer and into the darkness of the auditorium. I just hoped Scarface and Ugly hadn't seen me go in.

Mr Marvano was standing on the stage, an old man with a round, pink face and silver hair, looking rather sad in his tails and white bow tie. As I came in he had just finished some sort of trick with a cane and a silk scarf. He had turned one of them into the other. There was a thin pattering of applause. Mr Marvano picked up a pack of playing-cards and began to explain the next trick in Dutch. I took a seat in the back row. There were plenty of empty seats.

It was cool inside the theatre. I could feel the perspiration beading on my face. I wondered how much of the show I would have to watch before it was safe to go out. It didn't make any sense. How had Scarface and Ugly managed to turn up at the station? Charlotte had said that Charon seemed to know everything she did – before she did it. How? In London, at the ice-rink and now in Amsterdam, Charon always seemed to be one step ahead.

There was more applause and I glanced at the stage. A Queen of Spades was rising, seemingly on its own, out of Mr Marvano's top pocket.

"Was this the card you picked?" the magician asked. He said it in Dutch but I understood anyway. I'd seen it, and heard it all, before.

Somebody appeared, walking down the aisle, and stopped at the end of my row. I looked round and froze. It was Scarface.

I half rose, planning to slide out the other way. But another shape loomed out of the darkness, blocking that way, too. Ugly had come round the other side. I was trapped between them.

The magician was calling something out from the stage. Ugly produced what looked like a folding comb and pressed a button on the side. It was a flick-knife. About twenty centimetres of steel sprang out of his fist, slanting towards me. Scarface began to move closer. Ten seats and he would be on to me.

I had a wall behind me and people in front. I had nowhere to go.

Mr Marvano had finished what he was saying. There was a long pause. Ugly was closing in from his side, too. The flick-knife flashed momentarily in one of the lights trained on the stage. I looked back the other way. Scarface carried no weapon but his fingers, long and skeletal, stretched out towards my throat.

"And now, please, I require a volunteer from the audience." Mr Marvano had tried it in Dutch and found no takers so now he tried English. Only three seats separated me from Scarface on one side and Ugly on the other.

My hand shot up. "I volunteer!" I shouted.

Every eye in the theatre turned to look at me. A spotlight swivelled round and everything went white as it hit me in the eyes. Scarface and Ugly froze where they were, just outside the beam. Somehow Ugly had managed to spirit away the knife. Ignoring them, I clambered over a seat, almost landing in the owner's lap. But a moment later I was away, moving towards the stage while the audience urged me on with another round of applause. For the time being, anyway, I was safe.

Mr Marvano had wheeled a big, multi-coloured box onto the stage. It was about the size of a washing-machine with a round hole in the top and about a dozen slots around the sides. I didn't much like the look of it but it was too late to back out now. Mr Marvano grabbed my hand and beamed at me through teeth that looked even older than him.

"And what's your name?" he asked, again in English.

"Nick."

"Nick. Thank you. And now, Nick, I am telling you the trick."

He wheeled the box towards me and opened it. It was empty inside. But now I saw that if I knelt down inside it and if he closed it, I would be neatly trapped with my head protruding from the round hole at the top. I didn't much care for the idea. For a moment I thought of making a break for it and trying to find a way out of the theatre. But I had lost sight of Scarface and Ugly. And while they were around I was safer here, on the stage, in the light.

"I am calling this the Mexican dagger box," Mr Marvano said. He repeated the words in Dutch. "Now I am asking you please to step inside." I hesitated, then stepped in. The audience watched in silence but I could barely see them behind the glare of the spotlights.

I knelt down. Mr Marvano closed the box shut and pressed four studs, locking it. I tried to move. But the box must have been smaller than I had thought. I was completely trapped, with the wooden sides pressing against my back, my shoulders and my arms. From the outside it must have looked like I was taking a Turkish bath. I wasn't too happy about being on the inside. What was it he had said about Mexican daggers...?

"The box is locked – here, here and here," the magician explained. "And now I will get the Mexican daggers." He waved a finger at me. "Don't go away!"

There was no chance of that. Painfully, I swivelled my head round and watched him as he ambled off the stage. The audience laughed and I realized I probably looked even more stupid than I felt. There was a rack of silver knives hanging in the wings, but no sign of any technicians or stage hands. Mr Marvano reached out to take the knives.

But then Ugly appeared, suddenly looming up behind him. He lashed out with a fist, catching Mr Marvano on the side of the jaw. The magician crumpled. Ugly half-caught him but then let him fall, at the same time dragging off his tailcoat. It was a neat trick, but I was the only person who had seen it. A moment later, Scarface stepped out from behind the curtain. Quickly, he put on Mr Marvano's jacket. Then, pushing the rack of Mexican daggers, he walked onto the stage. The audience stirred, puzzled. I smashed an elbow against the side of the box. My old wound from the wheatfield flared up again. The box didn't even creak.

"Good evening, ladies and gentlemen," Scarface said. He spoke in English, perhaps for my benefit. "I'm afraid Mr Marvano has been taken ill. So he asked me to finish the trick."

He snatched up one of the daggers. It was even more lethal than Ugly's switchblade, about twenty-five centimetres longer with a wide, curving blade. The handle was decorated with some sort of fake Aztec design. Maybe the dagger was fake, too. But from where I was sitting, it certainly looked real.

Slowly he advanced towards me. I had never felt more helpless. I couldn't move. I couldn't breathe. All I could do was watch. And Scarface was enjoying every second of it.

He smiled at me, a smile that was full of hatred.

"Wait a minute..." I began.

"The first knife, ladies and gentlemen," Scarface said.

He slammed it in. I shut my eyes and winced. Was I dead? Was I even wounded? I opened my eyes. Scarface looked as surprised as I did. The knife had certainly gone in the box one side. It had come out the other. But it didn't seem to have gone through me.

The audience was surprised, too. They seemed to have woken up now. Perhaps they could tell that this new magician had a quality that the last one had lacked. Complete insanity, for example. They broke into louder, more enthusiastic applause.

Scarface picked up two more knives. Snarling, he plunged them into the box. Both of them passed right through without even scratching me. The audience clapped again.

Snarling and muttering to himself in Dutch, Scarface picked up the rest of the knives. There were twelve in all. One after the other he stabbed them into the box, each time waiting for me to cry out and then exit into a better world. But none came close. I was untouchable.

By now I was doing a good impersonation of a pin-cushion. The audience was delighted. There were no more knives left and, for that matter, no slots in which to stick them. But Scarface hadn't finished. His hand went into his pocket and when it came out he was holding Ugly's switchblade. He pressed the button and the blade shot out.

The audience fell silent. He bent down over me. I could see the veins throbbing under his skin and one of his eyes had developed a twitch. "There are no more holes, Diamond," he hissed. "This one is for you."

"Thirteenth time lucky?" I asked.

He snarled. "You were a fool to meddle in our affairs."

"I was only doing it for the medals, Scarface," I said.

"Goodbye..."

He took careful aim. This time he wasn't going to bother with the box. His eyes were on my throat, right underneath my chin. Slowly, deliberately, he lifted the switchblade in his hand.

The audience waited. In the wings, Ugly leered at me over the unconscious body of Mr Marvano. The switchblade stopped, high above me.

I shut my eyes and waited. There was nothing else I could do.

THE WRONG MAN

The whole scene was frozen in the glare of the spotlights: Scarface, the knife, the waiting audience. Then everything happened at once.

The knife flashed down. There was a gunshot. Scarface screamed and reeled back, clutching his hand. The knife hit the stage and stuck there, quivering, in the wood. Ugly twisted round, trying to see what was happening. Scarface bent over his cradled hand and groaned. Blood seeped out between his fingers and dripped onto his legs.

"Good shot, Ted."

"Thanks, Ed."

"Lower the curtain, Red."

The men from M16 had sprung out of nowhere. Now they swarmed over the stage while the audience – evidently in a good mood – gave them a cheerful round of applause. Ugly had put up a token resistance. One of the agents had given him a token punch on the nose and now he was out cold. Two more of them dragged Mr Marvano off while Ed and Ted grabbed hold of Scarface himself. His hand was bleeding very badly now. Ted's bullet had smashed right through it, and I can't say I was sorry.

Red lowered the curtain. Ted came over to me. He was wearing the same dark suit he'd had on at the London International the first time we'd met, and the same sunglasses. But now he took off the shades and looked me straight in the eyes.

"Are you OK, kid?" he asked.

"Yes," I said. I was fine – except that I still couldn't move.

Ted opened the box. "That was some trick," he said.

"They probably do it with mirrors," I agreed.

Then Tim came in between two more agents. Ned and Zed, perhaps.

"We found him outside," one of them said. "He was hiding in a dustbin."

"Rubbish!" Tim exclaimed.

"Yes. He was hiding in the rubbish."

Tim shook himself free and came over to me. "Are you OK?" he asked.

"I'm fine," I said. But it wasn't true. I'd been chased enough. I felt as if I hadn't stopped running for weeks. I turned to Ted. Or maybe it was Ed. "Please. I want to go home," I said.

* * *

"I'm very glad to see you," Mr Waverly said. "As soon as I got a report that you were in Amsterdam, I realized that you'd gone after Charon. So I sent my agents over to look after you. They spotted you just in time. Luckily for you..."

Tim and I had been flown over to London and now we were back more or less where we'd begun; at Number Seventeen, Kelly Street. Only this time there was no Bodega Birds. The headquarters of MI6 was just how it had been the first time, with Mr Waverly examining us with his hooded grey eyes over the polished leather surface of his desk. Ted and Ed stood guard by the door.

"You may have rescued us," I said. "But it was you who got us into this mess to start with."

Mr Waverly shrugged. "That was really your own fault," he said. "How were we to know that Charon would try to kill you?"

He sounded innocent but I knew better. Mr Waverly had somehow let Charon know that we were working for MI6. He had drugged us and dumped us. We were his sitting targets. And when he had sent his men across to Amsterdam, it hadn't been to rescue us. It had been to find Charon.

"I expect you have a lot of questions," Mr Waverly said.

"I've got one," Tim cut in. "What happened to the birds?"

"The birds?" It took the head of MI6 a moment to work out what he was talking about. "Oh – you mean Bodega Birds. That was just a front. We had to do that. You see, we couldn't allow you to get the police involved."

"Sure," I agreed. "They might have found out that it was you who paid Charon to kill Boris Kusenov."

That got him. For one second his eyes were unguarded and I saw the panic that was hiding behind those small, faded pupils. Behind him, Ted and Ed shifted uneasily. All three of them were like guilty schoolboys who had just been caught smoking behind the gym. "How did you find out?" Waverly asked.

I reached into my pocket and pulled out the cheque that I had found in Charon's drawer. "I found this," I said.

Mr Waverly hardly needed to look at it. He knew what it was. He coughed and ran a hand through his hair. "I have to congratulate you," he said. "You've been very resourceful."

"So why did you do it?" I demanded. "If you wanted to stop Charon, why did you pay him in the first place?"

Waverly sighed. I think he was actually relieved to get the confession off his chest. "It was an operation that went horribly wrong," he began.

"I'm sorry," Tim chimed in. "I didn't know you'd been ill."

"I haven't been ill, Mr Diamond!" Waverly paused. This was going to be more difficult than he'd thought. "We had to find Charon," he went on at last. "Too many people had died. Not just in England. America. France. Even Russia. It was always Charon. So we decided to mount an operation to bring him in. To unmask him. And we came up with an idea. The simplest way to find him was to become his client."

"How did you do that?" I asked.

"It was easy. He had a number of agents working for him. The man who knocked out the magician, for example. We got a message to them. They passed it to Charon."

"So you hired him to kill Kusenov."

"Yes. We chose Kusenov because we knew he had no intention of coming to England. He doesn't like England. In fact he never leaves Moscow. In other words, in order to kill him, Charon would have to go to Russia. And so of course, there was something he would need..."

"An aeroplane?" Tim suggested.

"A visa. You can't enter Russia without a visa. Don't you see? It was brilliant. All we had to do was monitor all the people applying for a visa to Russia and one of them would *have* to be Charon. And of course if anyone who applied for a visa had only nine fingers..."

"So you never really wanted Kusenov dead."

"Oh no. That was just the point. We were certain that Charon would be unable to kill him. He was meant to be an impossible target."

Suddenly I understood. Waverly was right. It had been a brilliant plan until it had gone terribly wrong. "But Kusenov decided to come to England after all!" I said.

"Exactly. That wretched painting, 'The Tsar's Feast', came up for auction at Sotheby's. Kusenov was a collector, and he had this fixation about the artist, Salvador Dali. He believed the painting had to hang in Russia – so he came over to bid for it. It was the last thing we'd expected."

"I get it..." I said.

"I don't," Tim muttered.

I turned to him. "If Charon had killed Kusenov on British soil and the Russians had then found out he'd been paid by MI6—"

"It's too horrible to contemplate." Waverly finished the sentence. He had sunk into his chair as if he were deflating.

"You still haven't found Charon," I said. "Kusenov still isn't safe."

"My dear boy." Mr Waverly recovered quickly. "The man with the scar! He *was* Charon."

"Scarface...?"

"Yes. He's in a prison cell now. It has to be him. He has only four fingers on his right hand."

I thought back to the theatre in Amsterdam. I couldn't believe what I was hearing. "Of course he's only got four fingers on his right hand!" I exclaimed. "Ted shot the other one off!"

That sent a ripple of alarm through the three agents. Quickly they conferred. Then Ted spoke. "It's true I shot him in the hand," he admitted. "But I didn't see him lose a finger."

"He must have lost it!" I insisted. "He certainly had all his fingers when we first met."

Ted shook his head smugly. "Relax, kid. Your Mr Scarface is Charon, all right."

"Has he admitted it?" I asked.

"No. But we'll crack him."

Personally, I doubted Ted could even crack a walnut without help from a friend but I didn't say that. I turned back to Mr Waverly. He was my only hope. "Mr Waverly," I said. "I know that Scarface is not Charon. Please believe me. You've got the wrong man."

But Mr Waverly wasn't having any of it. Suddenly he was all suit and old school tie. "I think I can be the best judge of this," he said.

"Why?"

"Because I'm the head of MI6 and you're just a fourteen-year-old boy!"

Tim shrugged. "He has a point."

I started to speak, then bit my tongue. There was no point arguing with them. I'd be better off working it out on my own. "What about us?" I asked.

Mr Waverly smiled. "You can go," he said. "I've had a word with the police. That business with the bank. Everything's been explained. You're no longer wanted."

We weren't wanted. Not in any sense of the word.

Tim stood up. "So that's it," he said.

"That's it."

"Right." Tim thought for a moment. "I don't suppose you could lend us the bus fare home?"

We walked home. Every step of the way the same thought went through my mind. They've got the wrong man. They've got the wrong man. I knew Charon wasn't Scarface. He had been in the room at the Winter House with Ugly and a third man. It was the third man who was Charon.

I thought back to the desk, the drawer with the cigarettes, the mirror and ... something else. I couldn't remember any more. I was tired. I needed to rest. But I couldn't – not yet. They'd got the wrong man.

Tim picked up a newspaper on the way back. Someone had left it on a bench and now that the adventure was over he was keen to cut out any photographs of himself. But there wasn't even a mention of him. He was yesterday's news, already forgotten.

We climbed the stairs into the office and while Tim went through the paper again I put on the kettle and made us some tea. By the time I'd carried it into the office and sat down opposite Tim, my mind had begun to click into action. Carefully, I set out the pieces of the puzzle and tried to make sense of them.

Charon.

A white hammer.

A mirror in a drawer.

South by south east.

We still didn't know what McGuffin had been trying to tell us. Had he really wanted us to travel south on the South East rail network? Was that all it boiled down to? I still couldn't believe it could have been as unimportant as that. I thought back to the moment he had died, struggling to speak in Tim's arms, with the train thundering past overhead.

"They're auctioning that painting today," Tim said. He folded the paper in half and tapped one of the articles.

South by south east.

"There's a story about it here."

"A story about what?"

"The painting." He read out the headline. "Sotheby's. 'Tsar's Feast'."

South by...

I sat up. "What?"

Tim sighed. "I was just telling you—"

"I know. What did you say? The headline..."

Tim waved the paper in my direction. "'The Tsar's Feast'! It's the first lot to come under the hammer this afternoon."

I snatched the paper. "Of course!" I shouted. "You've done it, Tim! You're brilliant!"

Tim smiled. "Yeah. Sure I am." The smile faded. "Why? What have I done?"

"You've just said it. The hammer...!"

"Where?"

"At Sotheby's!" I turned the paper round and showed him the headline. "That's what McGuffin was trying to tell you. But what with the train and everything you didn't hear him properly."

"What?"

"He didn't say south by south east. He said Sotheby's ... 'Tsar's Feast'."

I grabbed Tim's wrist and twisted it round so that I could look at his watch. It was half past one. "When does the auction start?" I yelled.

"Two o'clock."

"Half an hour. Maybe we can still get there in time..."

I was already moving for the stairs but Tim stayed where he was, his eyes darting from the newspaper to me then back to the paper.

"The auction?" he muttered. "Why do you want to go there?"

I stopped with my hand on the door. "Don't you see?" I said. "We've got to stop it."

"Stop the auction?"

"Stop Charon. He's planning to blow up Kusenov."

UNDER THE HAMMER

We managed to catch a bus outside the office – but were we going to make it? The traffic was heavy and the bus was slow. I looked at Tim's watch. It was already twenty to two. We weren't going to make it.

Tim must have read my thoughts. "Why don't we telephone them?" he said.

"They'd never believe me."

Tim shifted uncomfortably in his seat. I stared at him. "You don't believe me either!" I exclaimed.

"Well, it does seem a bit—"

"Listen." I knew I was right. I'd worked it out. I *had* to be right. "You remember the hammer we saw at the Winter House? An antique white hammer…?"

"Yes."

"It was an *auctioneer's* hammer. The painting is going under the hammer. That means, when it's sold, the auctioneer will hit down with the hammer."

"Yes!"

"Well, Charon's going to swap the real hammer with the one we saw. That must have been what they were talking about. The fake hammer will make some sort of electrical contact..."

Tim's eyes lit up. "You mean ... Charon's going to electrocute the auctioneer?"

"No. It must be a bomb. The hammer will detonate it. That's how he plans to kill Kusenov. The moment the painting is sold, the whole place will be blown sky high!"

The bus slowed down again. This time it was another bus-stop and the oldest woman in the world was waiting to get on. Worse still, she had about fourteen shopping bags with her. It would take all day. Quarter to two. If the bus moved off at once and didn't stop again we might just make it. But the traffic was as thick as ever. I made a decision.

"We'll run," I said.

"What – all the way?" Tim cried.

But I was already moving. We had fifteen minutes, and a bus that was going nowhere. This was clearly not the time for a chat.

Sotheby's main auction house is in New Bond Street, right in the middle of Mayfair. If you ever find yourself in the area, don't try to go window-shopping. You won't even be able to afford the window. It's at number thirty-five, just one more smart door among all the others.

As we spun round the corner from Oxford Street and staggered down the last hundred metres, I could hear the chimes of clocks striking two. There was no security in sight on the door. Kusenov had to be there. The auction had begun. But Mr Waverly must have thought he was safe.

I reached the door, but even as my hand stretched out to push it open I was struck by a nasty thought. If there was a bomb – and I was pretty sure there was – it could go off at any time. The moment the auctioneer struck his hammer, that would be it. Did I really want to go inside? I glanced at Tim who must have had much the same thought. He was standing on the pavement, kicking with his heels as if they'd somehow got glued to the surface.

"We have to go in," I said.

"Nick..."

I left him out there. I'd made up my mind. I had to stop the auction. He could do as he pleased.

The auction house was busy that day. There were people moving up and down the stairs and along the corridor which must have led to a secondary auction room. Somebody pushed past carrying an antique doll, a label still attached to its leg.

Someone else went the other way with a bronze-framed mirror. For a moment I caught sight of my own reflection. I looked tired and bedraggled.

And young. Would they even allow a fourteen-year-old into the auction?

"Good afternoon, ladies and gentlemen..."

The voice crackled over an intercom system that had been installed above the reception desk. It was a plummy voice – the sort that belongs to someone who'd been born with a silver spoon in his mouth. Maybe Sotheby's were auctioning that, too. "Lot number one is by a painter who made an explosive impact on surrealism in Europe," it went on. "Salvador Dali. It is entitled 'The Tsar's Feast' and is painted in oils on canvas. I shall open the bidding at £100,000."

I turned to Tim who had decided to come in after all. He was standing next to me. "It's begun..." I said.

"Where?" he asked.

I looked around. "Upstairs."

But Mr Waverly hadn't completely relaxed his guard on Boris Kusenov. MI6 might not be involved any more, but he had handed the case over to the police and before we'd even reached the first step two uniformed officers had moved out of an alcove to block our way.

"Now where do you think you're going?" one of them asked.

"£200,000..." The first bid had been made. I heard it over the intercom.

I tried to push forward. "I want to go to the auction..." I explained.

"Bit young for that, aren't you?" The second policeman laughed. "Run along, sonny. It's adults only."

"You don't understand." I was speaking through gritted teeth. "You've got to let me pass..."

"£300,000 to the gentleman from Moscow."

"You heard what I said." The second policeman wasn't laughing any more. He was blinking at me with small, unintelligent eyes. I knew the sort. If he was reincarnated as an ape, it would be a step up.

"Please..." Tim muttered. "We want to see Mr Grooshamov."

"Boris Kusenov," I corrected him. "He's in danger."

"What danger?" the first policeman asked.

The intercom crackled into life. "£400,000 to the lady in the front row." Then immediately, "Back to the gentleman from Moscow. £500,000. Thank you, sir."

"You've got to get up there," I insisted. "Kusenov is in danger. We're all in danger. The whole place is going to go up."

"I think you'd better come with us," the first policeman said.

"£600,000 to the gentleman at the back."

"Go with you where?" I asked.

"Down to the station."

"£700,000 to Mr Kusenov."

"This is hopeless!" I wanted to tear my hair out. There were maybe only seconds left. And I'd had to come up against PC Plod and his best friend, Big Ears. There was only one thing left to do. It was the oldest trick in the book – but I just hoped they hadn't read the book. I pointed up. "Look!" I shouted.

The two policemen looked up. So did Tim.

I pushed my way through and on to the first stair. One of the policemen grabbed me. I broke free, then pushed him hard. He lost his balance and fell on to the second policeman. Tim was *still* looking up, wondering what I'd pointed out. But then both policemen collided with him and all three of them fell down in a tangle. The staircase was free. I bounded up.

"£750,000 to the young lady..."

The top of the stairs was blocked by two attendants who were coming down with an antique sofa. I skidded down onto my back and slithered underneath it. One of the attendants called out to me but I ignored him. I just hoped they would block the staircase enough to delay the two policemen below.

"£850,000 to Mr Kusenov. £900,000. Back to you, Mr Kusenov..."

I could hear the bidding but I couldn't see

the auction room. There was a large, square room hung with faded watercolours and prints but it was empty. Then I noticed an archway on the other side. I ran through, my feet pounding on the frayed carpets. At last I had arrived.

"£950,000 to Mr Kusenov. Do I have any advance on £950,000?"

I burst into the auction room and took everything in with one glance.

"Going once..."

There was the canvas itself, "The Tsar's Feast", that had started all the trouble by bringing Kusenov to England in the first place. It was bigger than I had imagined it, standing in a gold frame on an easel right at the front of a raised platform. An assistant stood next to it.

Then there was the auctioneer, a tall thin man in a three-piece suit. He was standing behind an ornate wooden desk. He was holding the white antique hammer in his hands.

There were about two hundred people in the gallery, all crammed together in narrow rows running across its width. Kusenov was sitting in the middle of them. He was everything I'd imagined he would be: grey hair, granite face, small, serious eyes, suit. That's the thing about the Russians. They always look so ... Russian.

Kusenov had been given a police guard – and

if I hadn't recognized him I'd have known him from the company he kept. Chief Inspector Snape was sitting on one side of him. A bored-looking Boyle was on the other. Why, I wondered, had they been chosen? The long arm of the law? Or the longer arm of coincidence? Either way it was bad news for me. Somehow I had to cross the full length of the auction hall – fifty or more metres – to get the hammer. I had two policemen who'd be arriving behind me any time now. And I had Snape and Boyle ahead.

"*Going twice...*"

The auctioneer lifted his hammer. I'd been standing there for only one second but already I'd run out of time. The hammer was about to come down on "The Tsar's Feast". There weren't any more bids. As far as this auction went there would never be any more bids.

Unless...

There was only one thing I could do. I lifted a hand. "One million pounds!" I called out.

The auctioneer had been about to strike down with the hammer. But now he stopped. There was an astonished murmur from the audience and everyone turned to look at me. I took a few steps into the gallery. The auctioneer stared at me. Then he turned to his assistant and whispered a few words.

"Who are you?" he demanded at last.

I could see he wasn't sure what to say. "I'm

a bidder," I said. "And I bid a million pounds."

All the time I was talking I was moving further into the gallery, getting closer to the hammer. I was aware of everybody watching me.

Out of the corner of my eye I saw Snape and Boyle stand up and start moving round to cut me off. But I had to keep going.

"You're just a boy!" the auctioneer exclaimed. The hammer turned in his hand.

"I know," I said. "But I get a lot of pocket-money."

There was another murmur from the audience. Kusenov was staring at me. Then Snape broke out of the end of his row and moved to the front of the room.

"Wait a minute," he called out. "I know that boy!"

"So do I," Boyle snarled, catching up with him.

The auctioneer gazed at the two men unhappily. "Who are you?" he quavered.

"We're the police," Snape snapped. "And the boy has got no money at all!"

The auctioneer looked as if he was about to burst into tears. Clearly he had never dealt with a situation like this. "Well ... please..." he stammered. "The last bid stands at £950,000."

"A million and a half!" I called out.

"What?" the auctioneer groaned.

"Boyle!" Snape shouted. "Arrest him!"

Boyle grimaced. "Right."

The auctioneer tried to ignore us all.

"£950,000," he announced. "*Going...*"

I took another step forward. "I'll buy the hammer!" I exclaimed.

"*Going...*" The auctioneer was determined to go through with it. I couldn't stop him.

Boyle was moving faster now, heading towards me. And then, at the last moment, Tim appeared in the archway at the back of the gallery. Somehow he had shaken off the two policemen.

"Where's the bomb?" he asked.

"Bomb?" Snape cried.

Everybody froze.

I lunged forward and grabbed the hammer from the auctioneer's hands. "Tim!" I shouted.

I turned round and threw it. The hammer flew high above the audience, twisting in the air. Tim reached up and caught it.

Boyle lurched towards me.

I stepped to one side.

Boyle missed and toppled forward. His outstretched hands went over my head and through the canvas of "The Tsar's Feast". There was a loud ripping sound as the rest of Boyle followed them, his head and shoulders disappearing through the frame.

In the audience, Kusenov fainted.

The auctioneer gazed sadly at the ruined painting. He shook his head.

"*Gone,*" he muttered. What else could he say?

SPECIAL DELIVERY

"Do you know," I said, "there was enough dynamite under Kusenov's seat to blow up half of London.

"Which half?" Tim asked.

It was three days later and I was reading the newspaper reports of the attempted killing at Sotheby's. I'd been right about the hammer. The auctioneer's dais had been rigged up with a wire connected to a detonator and nineteen sticks of dynamite under the floor. If the hammer had come down, Kusenov would have been blown to pieces. It made me sweat just to think that I'd been there.

Of course, not everything had got into the press. My name, for example. According to the newspapers, it was Chief Inspector Snape of Scotland Yard who had raised the alarm and saved the life of the visitor from Moscow. I was merely an "unknown teenager" in the last paragraph who had disrupted the auction shortly before the bomb was discovered.

We'd heard nothing from Mr Waverly. I suppose he'd wanted to keep himself and MI6 well out of it. Since we'd saved his neck for him you'd have thought he might have dropped us a line or something, but that's the secret service for you. Happy enough to be secret. But not so keen on doing you a service.

And so at the end of it all we were more or less back to square one. It was five o'clock in the afternoon and a carton of milk sat on the table between us. I'm not sure if it was tea or supper. It would probably have to do for both.

"There were nineteen sticks of dynamite, Tim," I said, reading from the paper. "Charon really wanted Kusenov dead."

"Right," Tim said.

"It's a shame we never found out who he was."

Tim poured the milk. "He was a Russian diplomat, Nick."

"Not Kusenov. Charon. The police never found him."

"He was probably the last person you'd have expected, Nick." Tim raised his glass. "Mind you, I'd have worked it out in the end. I've got a sixth sense."

"Well," I muttered, "you missed out on the other five..."

There was a knock at the door. The last

time we'd had a knock on the door, it had cost us a week of our lives. We'd been chased, kidnapped, gassed, blown up, pushed off a train, shot at and generally manhandled and we hadn't actually earned a penny out of it. This time neither of us moved.

But a moment later the door opened and a motorbike messenger came in. He was dressed in black leather from head to foot, his face hidden by his visor. Almost subconsciously I found myself counting his fingers. They were all there. Five of them were holding a long, narrow cardboard box.

"Tim Diamond?" he asked.

"That's me," Tim said.

"Special delivery..."

The messenger put down the package. I signed for it and showed him out. By the time I had shut the door, Tim had opened the box and pulled out a single, red rose.

"Don't tell me," I said. "It's from Mr Waverly."

"No." Tim blushed. "It's from Charlotte."

"Charlotte?" The last time we had seen her had been at the station in Amsterdam. I had almost forgotten her. "What does she want?"

"She wants to see me." There was a white card enclosed with the box. "This evening."

"Where?"

Tim crumpled the card in his hand. "She wants to see me alone."

"How do you know?"

"She's written it. And she's underlined it. In red ink."

"You can still tell me where she wants to meet you."

Tim blushed and I realized he was still as much in love with Charlotte as he had ever been. It was incredible. I'd never once imagined Tim going out with a girl, mainly because it was impossible to imagine a girl who would want to go out with Tim. I mean, he wasn't bad-looking or anything like that. But if you were an attractive, sophisticated woman, would you want to spend your time with someone who still cried when he saw *The Railway Children*? Tim had no sex-appeal. He wore Dennis the Menace boxer shorts in bed.

And yet Charlotte Van Dam was after him. She had said so herself. And she'd underlined it. In red ink...

"It doesn't matter where we're meeting," Tim said. He had gone as red as the rose by now. What had she written on the card? "It's just me and her..." He went into the kitchen for a shower. I heard the rattle of the water hitting the curtain. Then there was the slapping of wet feet on floorboards as he went into his bedroom. He sneezed. The water must have been cold. There was the slam of a door. Then silence.

Twenty minutes later he reappeared in a

crumpled linen suit with a pale blue handkerchief in his top pocket. He had washed and combed his hair. He had shaving foam in one ear and a little talcum powder in the other.

"I'll be back later" he said.

"Have fun," I muttered.

"Don't wait up."

I finished the milk and threw the carton in the direction of the bin. It hit the edge and bounced onto the floor. What would I do if Tim moved in with a girlfriend? What if she was crazy enough to marry him? Maybe the two of them would go and live together in Holland – and where would that leave me?

I had nothing to do, so I started to clean up. I plumped up the cushions and rearranged the dust on the mantelpiece. There was a shirt lying on the carpet so I put it in the filing cabinet – under "S". That was when I found the gloves. They were on the floor, under the shirt. They belonged to Charlotte. She had left them behind when she'd run from Amsterdam station.

I picked them up, meaning to put them in the top drawer of the desk. But as I held them, they dangled down and I found myself staring at them. There was something wrong about them, something that didn't quite add up. I spread them out on the palm of my hand. It was obvious, but I couldn't see it. And thirty seconds must have passed before I finally did.

The left-hand glove had only four fingers.

It was as if someone had grabbed hold of my throat with a hand made of ice. I felt all my breath being sucked up into my chest. A little sound came out of my nose. Automatically, I scrunched the glove up in my hand as if I was trying to wring water out of it.

Charlotte's glove. Charon's glove.

And of course it had been obvious from the start. Only Charlotte had known that we were going to meet 86. We had given her the name of the ice-rink on the train. The moment she had arrived in Amsterdam, she had sent her two agents, Scarface and Ugly, to take care of the secret agent, to stop him from leading us to her. They must have arrived just after we did.

Her very names should have told me. Both of them began with the same four letters – Charon and Charlotte. So why hadn't I seen it? Maybe I was more of a sexist than I thought, but I'd never imagined an international killer being a woman. Everyone – McGuffin, Mr Waverly, Rushmore – had spoken of Charon as a man. Maybe that had been her most effective weapon. She had played on other people's preconceptions, hidden behind them. She had known. Nobody would ever suspect a woman.

But I should have guessed that, too. When I had searched Charon's desk at the Winter House, I'd discovered a small mirror covered in some sort of powder. If I'd thought about it, I'd have known what it was: the mirror from a powder compact. With a sprinkling of face powder. It should have told me. It was a woman's desk, not a man's. And if I'd only seen that, everything else would have fallen into place.

I made a mental note to read more feminist literature – but not right now. Tim had gone to an appointment with a killer. If Charlotte blamed him for saving Kusenov ... I had to find him before he reached her.

I ran into his bedroom. There were clothes everywhere – except in the wardrobe. He must have tried on everything before he'd chosen the linen suit. I started heaping up the trousers and shirts. I had to find the little white card that had come with the rose.

There was no sign of it. When I'd thrown out all the clothes, I started on his *Beano* collection, his bills, and six years' subscription to *True Detective*. There must have been nine layers between me and the carpet. If you wanted to hoover this room it would probably take you a week to find the Hoover. And I was looking for one small card. What if he had taken it with him?

What if ...?

I forced myself to think. Tim hadn't gone straight into his bedroom. He'd taken a shower first. The shower...

The flat was so small, we didn't have room for a bathroom. The shower was at the back of the kitchen in a sort of alcove. I dashed in there, skidding on the floor, which was covered in water. Tim's shower-cap was perched on the kettle. There were three bars of soap in the fridge.

But the card was nowhere to be seen.

I emptied every drawer in the place. Knives and forks clattered to the ground. Tea towels and tablecloths flew into the corners. I searched in the dustbins, the ovens, the cupboards ... and finally I found it, pinned to the wall behind the door. It read:

Hampstead Heath funfair
7.00 p.m. today
The Tunnel of Love
Charlotte

The Tunnel of Love! No wonder Tim had blushed so much when he read it. I looked at my watch. It was half past six. Hampstead was only a couple of kilometres up the road. I could still get there in time.

I was out of the office and running before I'd even started to think. Tim had an appointment with a killer. He was in love. I was going to save him. But I was unarmed.

As I hit the High Street and started up the hill, the night was drawing in. And somehow I knew that the Tunnel of Love was going to be longer and darker than it had ever been before.

Whirling lights. Crowds. The smell of hot dogs and the jangle of different tunes fighting with each other in the warm evening air. The fair had come to Hampstead Heath and lay sprawled out across the grass for as far as I could see. It was five to seven. I had run all the way in the heat of the evening and for a moment I stood where I was, swaying on my feet. On one side of me came the wail of the ghost train; on the other, a rattle and a scream as a painted carriage whirred round a metal track. I can't say I'm a big fan of funfairs. I can't afford the fares so I never have much fun. But that evening the Hampstead Heath fair was looking its best. There must have been a thousand people there. Maybe more. Tim was one of them. I had five minutes to find him.

I pressed forward, past the coconut shies, the Hall of Mirrors, the helter-skelter and the big wheel. There was a blast of organ pipes and a huge merry-go-round started up, its multicoloured horses leaping and plunging at the end of their twisted golden poles. The Tunnel of Love was on the other side. I saw it and I saw Tim at the same time. He was sitting in a boat with Charlotte; number eleven. Before I could reach them, the boat had drifted off into the mouth of the tunnel. A short, fat man pocketed the one pound fare and looked around for any other customers. But it must have been too hot for love. There was no one else around.

The Tunnel of Love was a big, wooden structure with plastic walls that were meant to look like stone but still looked like plastic. You went through it all in a little boat which was carried along on a shallow river. I almost smiled at that. Charon was the ferryman of the dead in Greek mythology. Well, it looked like Tim had just bought himself a ticket.

I couldn't go into the tunnel. I didn't have the money for a ticket and anyway I doubted if the man would let me ride alone. But if the entrance was blocked, the exit wasn't. I ran past the merry-go-round. For a moment the horses galloped beside my shoulder. Then I had left them behind me as I reached the end of the tunnel where the water gushed out before looping round to start all over again. Without stopping to think, I went into the tunnel.

There was only one way in and that was along the artificial river. The water lapped over my ankles as I splashed through the soft glow of this plastic lovers' world. If you've ever been into a Tunnel of Love, you'll know what I'm talking about. The river looped and zigzagged, going nowhere – slowly. There were a few plastic cupids – dressed-up shop dummies floating under the roof. I went past what must have been the high point of the ride, a couple of dummies done up as Romeo and Juliet.

The only sound in the place was the echo of the fairground music outside and the trickle of the water. Add a plastic skeleton or two and the place could have just as easily doubled as another ghost train.

A ferry bobbed round the corner and I stepped up onto one of the banks to let it sail past me. I watched it go with an unpleasant feeling in my stomach. It was number eleven. But it was empty.

"You ruined everything. You and your interfering brother..."

The voice was a malevolent hiss. I stepped forward softly. A thick black wire snaked in front of my foot. It was plugged into a second wire that trailed along to a socket in the wall. I realized that I had found the power source for the entire tunnel and at once half an idea came to mind. I leaned down and picked up the wire, cradling the connector in my two hands. Now, if I pulled the two wires apart, I would plunge the tunnel into darkness. The only trouble was, I'd probably electrocute myself at the same time.

"Charlotte..." Tim protested.

Still holding the wire, I tiptoed forward and

looked round the next corner. Charlotte was standing on a triangular piece of dry land in front of a mock-up of Snow White and Prince Charming. But there was nothing very charming about her. She was holding a gun. And she was aiming it at Tim.

"I should have killed you when I had the chance," Charlotte rasped, and now I recognized the voice I had heard at the Winter House outside Amsterdam.

"But I thought you loved me!"

"Loved you? I can't stand you...!"

"Oh..." I had never seen Tim look sadder.

Charlotte raised her gun. "I'll enjoy killing you," she said. "And then I shall kill your brother. I enjoy killing people, you see. It's my business. But it's also my pleasure and so I'll build up an even bigger network of assassins. Everyone in the world wants someone else dead. I will provide the service. I will be the head of a multinational murder organization. I'll float shares on the stock market! I'll be number one."

She was insane. I could see it now. She was Charon. Pure murder.

Her finger tightened on the trigger.

I took another step forward – into sight.

"Tim!" I shouted. "Duck!"

I pulled the two wires apart.

There was a flash and the whole tunnel went pitch black. But even in that second, Charon had wheeled round and fired; not at Tim but at me. I felt the bullet whip past my face. I fell back and dropped the wires.

"I'll kill you!" Charon screamed. Her voice was a thin, inhuman wail in the darkness. "I'll kill both of you."

I heard her step towards me. I couldn't see anything.

"No!" That was Tim.

"What…?" That was Charon.

There was a splash and – perhaps half a second later a terrible blue flash like nothing I had ever seen before. I was lying on my back, but in that flash I saw everything. Tim had realized Charon was coming for me.

He had pushed her into the river. But what he hadn't known was that the live cable I had dropped was also in the water. And when Charon had hit the surface, the circuit had been completed.

There was nothing we could do. There was another blue flash. Charon floated, rigid, in the water. Then the entire system short-circuited and the blackness returned.

We watched as the ambulance men carried Charon away. The electrical charge hadn't been strong enough to kill her, but it would be a while before she could stand up again and when she did the first thing she'd need would be a new hairdresser. The top of her head looked like a giant toilet-brush.

The police had been called and we were sipping cups of hot, sweet tea while we answered their inevitable questions. I suppose they thought we were in shock. But Charon was the one who'd got the biggest shock of all.

I didn't say very much. The fairground was still spinning and echoing all around us and I felt lost in all the noise and the bright lights. I had to face it: I had come to save Tim's life, but in the end it was he who had saved mine. I looked at him, sipping his tea from a plastic cup and suddenly I felt almost affectionate. Maybe I was in shock after all.

"Thanks, Tim," I said.

"It wasn't me who got the tea," Tim replied. "It was one of the policemen."

Behind me, the merry-go-round had started up again for the thousandth time, and that made me think. People got killed. Bad things happened. But at the end of the day, life was only another ride and, like it or not, I'd been given a ticket, so what else could I do but hang on and enjoy it and save the tears for when it was time to get off?

Anthony Horowitz is the author of the number one bestselling Alex Rider books and The Power of Five series. He has enjoyed huge success as a writer for both children and adults, most recently with the latest adventure in the Alex Rider series, *Russian Roulette*, and the highly acclaimed Sherlock Holmes novel, *The House of Silk*. His latest novel, *Moriarty*, is also set in the world of Sherlock Holmes and was published in October 2014. Anthony was also chosen by the Ian Fleming estate to write the new James Bond novel which will be published this year. Anthony has won numerous awards, including the Bookseller Association/Nielsen Author of the Year Award, the Children's Book of the Year Award at the British Book Awards, and the Red House Children's Book Award. In 2014 Anthony was awarded an OBE for Services to Literature. He has also created and written many major television series, including *Injustice*, *Collision* and the award-winning *Foyle's War*.

You can find out more about Anthony and his work at:

www.alexrider.com

@AnthonyHorowitz

THE DIAMOND BROTHERS IN...

The Falcon's Malteser

"Anthony Horowitz is the lion of children's literature." Michael Morpurgo

"Horowitz has become a writer who converts boys to reading."
The Times

"A first-class children's novelist."
TES

More wickedly funny books

by Anthony Horowitz

The Devil and His Boy

Groosham Grange

Return to Groosham Grange

The Switch

More Bloody Horowitz

The Diamond Brothers books:

The Falcon's Malteser

Public Enemy Number Two

South by South East

The Blurred Man

The French Confection

I Know What You Did Last Wednesday

The Greek who Stole Christmas

THE DIAMOND BROTHERS IN...

The Falcon's Malteser

ANTHONY HOROWITZ

WALKER BOOKS

For Dursley McLinden
29.5.65 – 7.8.95
who played Tim Diamond in the film and in the TV series

First published 1995 by Walker Books Ltd
87 Vauxhall Walk, London SE11 5HJ

This edition published 2015

2 4 6 8 10 9 7 5 3 1

This book has been typeset in Sabon

Printed in Germany by GGP Media GmbH

British Library Cataloguing in Publication Data:
a catalogue record for this book is available from the British Library

ISBN 978-1-4063-5706-6
www.walker.co.uk

CONTENTS

TIM DIAMOND INC.
23 THE CUTTING, CAMDEN TOWN, NW1

Dear Reader,

My name is Tim Diamond, but I don't know why I'm telling you that because the one thing I don't need right now is an introduction. The last time I introduced myself, I took two bullets in the chest. It's lucky I was hiding behind the chest at the time or I could have got hurt. Getting shot at is all in a day's work for me and I'm glad I don't do overtime. The streets where I live are pretty mean. And I mean mean. And not at all pretty. You'd be surprised how many people knock on my door, come into my office and try to kill me. Some of them don't even knock. But that's the sort of business I'm in. I'm a private eye and a lot of the people I meet like to keep their finger on the trigger – even the ones who can't afford the whole gun.

My guess is that you'll have heard of me. At the very least, you'll have seen my advertisement in the Yellow Pages. TIM DIAMOND, PRIVATE DETECTIVE: THE BEST IN THE   . I'd have liked to say more but they were charging by the word. Anyway, this book will tell you just about everything you need to know about me except my shoe size – and in case you're wondering, it's ten and a half. Eleven in wet weather.

So why am I writing this?

Well, the publishers – Walker Books – are relaunching "The Falcon's Malteser" with a new cover and, of course, a new price-tag. You see that picture on the front? It took their team of designers sixteen weeks working night and day to come up with it. Maybe it would have been easier if they'd read the book first. But that's the thing about publishers. I've met livelier people in a cemetery. They're paid almost nothing and they're worth every penny of it.

In case you're wondering (and I can't imagine why you would be), Walker Books is based in south London, right next to the River Thames ... and if something goes splash in the night, it's probably the managing director. He never used to be suicidal – not until he looked at his sales figures.

They work in a building which is old and crumbling and desperately in need of a face-lift ... a bit like my editor. Actually, she's had so much plastic surgery they've run out of plastic, and the last time she sneezed she turned into someone else. It's scary what people will do to keep themselves looking good – and she wasn't great when she started. Anyway, Walker Books needs your pocket money. They're so desperate, they'll even take your pocket. Remember that book token you got for Christmas that's been in your bottom drawer ever since? They want it. To you it may be another crummy paperback but to them it's lunch.

And that's why they asked me to write this introduction. I got a call from my editor at the start of the month. Her name is Jane Winterton and on top of all the cosmetic surgery she has a voice that sounds like fingers being scratched down a blackboard, or maybe an animal in pain.

Talk to her for too long and you want to throw yourself onto the nearest train. Or under it.

"Tim," she said. "We need your help."

"Who's been killed?" I asked. "And it had better not be the accountant."

"Oh, no," she simpered. "Mr Lloyd is fit and bouncing."

"Yeah. Like his cheques."

"What we need is one thousand, five hundred words for the new edition of "The Falcon's Malteser". We'll pay you fifty pounds."

"Fifty pounds?" I tried to work out the rate per word but I quickly gave up. I didn't have a pocket calculator small enough. "What's the idea?" I demanded.

"Well, obviously your brother Nick is the one who actually writes the books. But we thought it might be fun to hear something from you. Straight from the horse's mouth, so to speak."

She was the one calling me the horse. What a laugh! You should have seen her teeth.

"What if I'm busy?" I growled.

"Are you?"

I glanced around the empty office. It was true that right now I was between cases. My last client had asked me to find out who was stealing supplies from his glue factory, but he'd disappeared and I was beginning to think he must have come to a sticky end.

"OK," I said. "I'll think about it."

"We'd like something by the end of the week."

"I'm not sure about that. How about Friday?"

"See what you can do..." She rang off.

So that's the introduction to the introduction.

Here's the introduction. If you keep reading you might even get to the book.

I never dreamed when I set up as a private detective that I'd end up living with my kid brother, Nick – and if I'd thought I was going to dream it, I wouldn't have bothered going to sleep. Look at it from my point of view. I was twenty-eight. He was eleven. The day he walked through the door, his voice hadn't even broken – which is more than you could say for the door. The whole office was falling apart. The trouble was that business had been a bit slow … in fact it could have been overtaken by a one-legged tortoise with a twenty-a-day cigarette habit. I had no money. No clients. And suddenly there was an extra mouth to feed. Worse still, that mouth was connected to an extra stomach.

The thing is, Nick was meant to have moved to Australia with our parents. I thought I'd seen the last of him when I waved goodbye at Heathrow Airport, but it turned out he had other ideas because by the time I got back to the flat he was already there.

The strange thing is that in a way I'm glad he never did make it to Australia. "The Falcon's Malteser" was our first case together and there were moments now and then when it was good to have someone around. I mean, from the moment Johnny Naples walked into my office, I knew this was no ordinary case. What was he doing with a box of Maltesers? Why did he need me to look after it? And why was the Fat Man so desperate to get his hands on it? The fact of the matter was that I needed someone to talk to.

"Two brains are better than one," I said to Nick.

"Sure, Tim," he replied. "But I guess we'll just have to manage with one between us."

I'm not sure what he meant by that. Nick has a strange sense of humour.

You might like to know that there are other books written about me: "Public Enemy Number Two", "South by South East", and "The French Confection", "I Know What You Did Last Wednesday", "The Greek Who Stole Christmas" and "The Blurred Man". Personally I haven't read them, because I was too busy being in them. Oh – and you may be wondering, who's this guy Anthony Horowitz whose name appears on the covers? He also works for Walker Books: they pay him to knock the books into shape after Nick has finished. I've never met him and they tell me I haven't missed much. Apparently he writes his own stuff too, and a lot of people have compared him to JK Rowling – but without the money or the good looks. What that man doesn't know about writing would fill a book ... and nobody would read that one either.

So here it is. "The Falcon's Malteser." Teachers say that reading books is good for you, so get stuck into this one and prove them wrong.

Tim Diamond

THE PACKAGE

There's not much call for private detectives in Fulham.

The day it all started was a bad one. Business was so slack it was falling down all around us. The gas had been disconnected that morning, one of the coldest mornings for twenty years, and it could only be a matter of time before the electricity followed. We'd run out of food and the people in the supermarket downstairs had all fallen about laughing when I suggested credit. We had just £2.37 and about three teaspoons of instant coffee to last us the weekend. The wallpaper was peeling, the carpets were fraying and the curtains ... well, whichever way you looked at it, it was curtains for us. Even the cockroaches were walking out.

I was just wondering whether the time hadn't finally come to do something constructive –

like packing my bags and going back to Mum – when the door opened and the dwarf walked in.

OK – maybe you're not supposed to call them dwarves these days. Vertically challenged ... that's what it says in the book. But not this book. The truth is, this guy was as challenged as they come. I was only thirteen but already I had six inches on him and the way he looked at me with cold, unforgiving eyes – he knew it and wasn't going to forget it.

He was in his mid forties, I guessed. It was hard to say with someone that size. A short, dark stranger with brown eyes and a snub nose. He was wearing a three-piece suit, only the pieces all belonged to different suits like he'd got dressed in a hurry. His socks didn't match either. A neat moustache crowned his upper lip and his black hair was slicked back with enough oil to interest an Arab. A spotted bow tie and a flashy gold ring completed the picture. It was a weird picture.

"Do come in, Mr..." my brother began.

"Naples," the dwarf, who already was in, said. His name might have come out of Italy but he spoke with a South American accent. "Johnny Naples. You are Tim Diamond?"

"That's me," my brother lied. His real name was Herbert Timothy Simple, but he called himself Tim Diamond. He thought it suited his image. "And what can I do for you, Mr Venice?"

"Naples," the dwarf corrected him. He climbed on to a chair and sat down opposite my brother. His nose just reached the level of the desk. Herbert slid a paper-weight out of the way to give his new client a clear view. The dwarf was about to speak but then he paused. The nose was turned on me. "Who is he?" he demanded, the two h's scratching at the back of his throat.

"Him?" Tim smiled. "He's just my kid brother. Don't worry about him, Mr Navels. Just tell me how I can help you."

Naples laid a carefully manicured hand on the desk. His initials – JN – were cut into the ring. There was so much gold around that third finger he could have added his name and address too. "I want to deposit something with you," he said.

"Deposit?" Herbert repeated quite unnecessarily. The dwarf might have had a thick accent, but it certainly wasn't as thick as my brother. "You mean ... like in a bank?" he continued, brilliantly.

The dwarf raised his eyes to the ceiling, took in the crack in the plaster and then, with a sigh, lowered them on to Herbert. "I want to leave a package with you," he said, briskly. "It's much important you look after it. But you must not open it. Just keep it here and keep it safe."

"For how long?"

Now the dwarf's eyes darted across to the window. He swallowed hard and loosened his bow tie. I could see that he was scared of something or somebody in the street outside. Either that or he had a thing about double glazing.

"I don't know," he replied. "About a week maybe. I'll come back and collect it … when I can. You give it to nobody else except for me. You understand?"

Naples pulled out a packet of Turkish cigarettes and lit one. The smoke curled upwards, a lurid blue in the chill morning air. My brother flicked a piece of chewing-gum towards his mouth. It missed and disappeared over his shoulder.

"What's in the package?" he asked. "That's my business," the dwarf said.

"OK. Let's talk about my business then." Herbert treated his client to one of his "Don't mess with me" smiles. It made him look about as menacing as a cow with stomachache. "I'm not cheap," he went on. "If you want a cheap private click, try looking in the cemetery. You want me to look after your package? It'll cost you."

The dwarf reached into his jacket pocket and pulled out the first good thing I'd seen that week: twenty portraits of Her Majesty the Queen, each one printed in brown. In other words, a bundle of ten-pound notes, brand new and crisp. "There's two hundred pounds here," he said.

"Two hundred?" Herbert squeaked.

"There will be another hundred when I return and pick up the package. I take it that is sufficient?"

My brother nodded his head, an insane grin on his face. Put him in the back of a car and who'd need a plastic dog?

"Good." The dwarf stubbed out his half-smoked cigarette and slid off the chair. Then he removed a plain brown envelope from another pocket. It was quite thick with some thing vaguely rectangular bulging in the centre. It rattled faintly as he put it on the desk. "Here is the package," he said. "Once again, look after it, Mr Diamond. With your life. And whatever you do, don't open it."

"You can trust me, Mr Nipples," my brother muttered. "Your package is in safe hands." He waved one of the safe hands to illustrate the point, sending a mug of coffee flying. "What happens if I need to get in touch with you?" he asked as an afterthought.

"You don't," Naples snapped. "I get in touch with you."

"Well there's no need to be touchy," Her bert said.

It was then that a car in the street backfired. The dwarf seemed to evaporate. One moment he was standing beside the desk. The next he was crouching beneath it, one hand inside his jacket. And somehow I knew that his finger wasn't wrapped round another bundle of money. For about thirty seconds nobody moved. Then Naples slid across to the window, standing to one side so that he could look out without being seen. He had to stand on tip-toe to do it, his hands perched on the sill, the side of his face pressed against the glass. When he turned round, he left a damp circle on the window. Hair oil and sweat.

"I'll see you again in a week," he said. He made for the door as fast as his legs could carry him. With his legs, that wasn't too fast. "Look after that package with your life, Mr Diamond," he repeated. "And I mean ... your life."

And then he was gone.

My brother was jubilant. "Two hundred pounds just for looking after an envelope," he crowed. "This is my lucky day. This is the best thing that's happened to me this year." He glanced at the package. "I wonder what's in it?" he murmured. "Still, that needn't worry us. As far as we're concerned, there's no problem."

That's what Herbert thought. But right from the start I wasn't so sure. I mean, two hundred pounds is two hundred pounds, and when you're throwing that sort of money around there's got to be a good reason. And I remembered the dwarf's face when the car backfired. He may have been a small guy, but he seemed to be expecting big trouble.

Just how big I was to find out soon enough.

TIM DIAMOND INC

The two hundred pounds lasted about half a day. But it was a good half-day.

It began with a blow-out at a café round the corner. Double eggs, double sausage, double chips and fried bread but no beans. We'd been living on beans for the best part of a week. It had got so bad I'd been having nightmares about them with giant Heinz cans chasing me down the High Street.

After that, Herbert put an ad in the local newsagent for a cleaning lady. That was crazy, really. There was no way we could afford a cleaner – but on the other hand, if you'd seen the state of our place, maybe you'd have understood. Dust everywhere, dirty plates piled high in the sink and old socks sprawled across the carpet from the bedroom to the front door as if they were trying to get to the launderette under their own steam. Then we took a bus into the West End. Herbert bought me a new jacket for the next term at school and bought himself some new thermal underwear and a hot-water bottle. That left just about enough money to get two tickets for a film. We went to see *101 Dalmatians*. Herbert cried all the way through. He even cried in the commercials. That's what sort of guy he is.

I suppose it was pretty strange, the two of us living together the way we did. It had all happened about two years back when my parents suddenly decided to emigrate to Australia. Herbert was twenty-eight then. I'd just turned eleven.

We were living in a comfortable house in a nice part of London. I still remember the address: 1, Wiernotta Mews. My dad worked as a door-to-door salesman. Doors was what he sold; fancy French sliding doors and traditional English doors, pure mahogany, made in Korea. He really loved doors. Ours was the only house in the street with seventeen ways in. As for my mum, she had a part-time job in a pet shop. It was after she got bitten by a rabid parrot that they decided to emigrate. I wasn't exactly wild about the idea but of course nobody asked me. You know how some parents think they own their kids? Well, I couldn't even sneeze without written permission signed in duplicate.

Neither Herbert nor I really got on with

our parents. That was one thing we had in common. Oh yeah ... and we didn't get on with each other. That was the second thing. He'd just joined the police force (this was one week before the Hendon Police Training Centre burnt down) and could more or less look after himself, but of course I had as much independence as the coffee table.

"You'll love Australia," my dad said. "It's got kangaroos."

"And boomerangs," my mum added.

"And wonderful, maple-wood doors..."

"And koalas."

"I'm not coming!" I said.

"You are!" they screamed.

So much for reasoned argument.

I got as far as Heathrow. But just as the plane to Sydney was about to take off, I slipped out the back door and managed to find my way out of the airport. Then I high-tailed it back to Fulham. I'm told my mum had hysterics about 35,000 feet above Bangkok. But by then it was too late.

Now, by this time, Herbert had finished with the police force or to put it more accurately, the police force had finished with Herbert. He'd finally got the sack for giving someone directions to the bank. I suppose it wasn't his fault that the someone had robbed it, but he really shouldn't have held the door for the guy as he came out. But in the mean-time, he'd managed to save up some money and had rented this run-down flat in the Fulham Road, above a supermarket, planning to set himself up as a private detective. That's what it said on the door:

TIM DIAMOND INC
PRIVATE DETECTIVE

Inside, you went up a staircase to a glass-fronted door which in turn led into his office, a long, narrow room with four windows looking out into the street. A second door led off from here into the kitchen. The staircase continued up to a second floor where we both had a bedroom and shared a bathroom. The flat had been made available to Herbert at a bargain basement price, probably because the whole place was so rickety it was threatening to collapse into the basement at any time. The stairs wobbled when you went up and the bath wobbled when you turned on the taps. We never saw the landlord. I think he was afraid to come near the place.

Dark-haired and blue-eyed, Herbert was quite handsome – at least from the opposite side of the street on a foggy day. But what God had given him in looks, He had taken away in brains. There may have been worse private detectives than Tim Diamond (the only inc in the building was the stuff he put in his pen). But somehow I doubt it.

I'll give you an example. His first job was to find some rich lady's pedigree Siamese cat. He managed to run it over on the way to see her. The second job was a divorce case – which you may think is run-of-the-mill until I tell you that the clients were perfectly happily married until he came along.

There hadn't been a third case.

Anyway, Herbert was not overjoyed to see me that day when I turned up from Heathrow carrying a hold-all that held exactly nothing, but where else could I go? We argued. I told him it was a *fait accompli*. We argued some more. I told him what a *fait accompli* was. In the end he let me stay.

Mind you, I often wondered if I'd made the right decision. For a start, when I say I like a square meal a day I don't mean a sawn-off Weetabix, and it's no fun starting the winter term in clothes you grew out of the summer before, with more holes in your socks than a Swiss cheese. We could never afford anything. Her Majesty's Government helped Herbert out a little, which is a fancy way of saying that he got the dole, and my parents sent the occasional cheque for my upkeep, but even so Herbert never managed to make ends meet. I tried to persuade him to get himself a sensible job anything other than private detection – but it was hopeless. As hopeless as Herbert himself.

Anyway, we got back to the flat around eleven and were making our way up the stairs past the office when Herbert stopped. "Wait a minute, Nick," he said. "Did you leave the door open?"

"No," I said. "That's strange..."

He was right. The door of the office was open, the moonlight pouring out of the crack like someone had spilt a can of silver paint. We made our way back downstairs and went in. I turned on the light.

"Oh dear," my brother said. "I think we've had visitors."

That was the understatement of the year. A stampede of wild bulls would have left the place in better order. The desk had been torn open, the carpets torn up, the bookshelves torn apart and the curtains torn down. The old filing cabinet would have fitted into so many matchboxes. Even the telephone had been demolished, its various parts scattered around the room. Whoever had been there, they'd done a thorough job. If we'd been invited to a wedding, we could have taken the office along for confetti.

"Oh dear," Herbert repeated. He stepped into the rubble and picked up what was now a very dead cactus. A moment later, he dropped it, his lower jaw falling at about the same speed. "My God!" he shrieked. "The envelope!"

He stumbled over to the remains of his desk and searched in the remains of the top drawer. "I put it here," he said. He fumbled about on the floor. "It's gone!" he moaned at last. He got back to his feet, clenching and unclenching his fists. "The first job I've had in six months and now I've gone and lost it. You know what this means, don't you? It means we won't get the other hundred pounds. I'll probably have to pay back the two hundred we've already spent. What a disaster! What a catastrophe! I don't know why I bother, really I don't. It's just not fair!" He gave the desk a great thump with his boot. It groaned and collapsed in a small heap.

Then he looked at me. "Well, don't just stand there," he snapped.

"What am I meant to do?" I asked.

"Well … say something."

"All right," I said. "I didn't think it was a very good idea to leave the package in your desk…"

"It's a fat lot of use telling me now," Herbert whined. It looked as though he was going to cry.

"I didn't think it was a good idea," I continued, "so I took it with me." I pulled the envelope out of my jacket pocket where it had been resting all evening.

My brother seized it and gave it a big, wet kiss. He didn't even thank me.

THE FAT MAN

We didn't get much sleep that night. First we had to make our beds – and I'm not just talking sheets and blankets. Whoever had wrecked our office had done the same for the rest of the flat. It took about forty nails and two tubes of superglue before the beds were even recognizable, and then I found that Herbert had managed to stick himself to the door handle and had to spend another hour prising him free with a kitchen-knife. By then it was morning and I was too tired to sleep. Herbert sent me out for a loaf of bread while he put on the kettle. At least they hadn't dismantled the kettle.

There were three letters on the doormat and I brought them up with the bread. One was a bill. One was postmarked Sydney, Australia. And the third had been delivered by hand. Herbert filed the bill under "W" for waste-paper basket while I opened the Australian letter.

Darling Herbert and Nicky (it read),

Just a quick note as Daddy and me are about to go to a barbecue. They have lots of barbecues in Australia. The weather's lovely. The sun never stops shining – even when it's raining. You really ought to come out here.

I hope you are well. We miss you both very, very much. Have you solved any crimes yet? It must be very cold in England so make sure you wrap up well with a vest. I know they tickle, but pneumonia is no laughing matter. I'm enclosing a little cheque so you can go to Marks & Spencer.

Must go now. Daddy's at the door. He's just bought a new one.

I'll write again soon.

Love, Mumsy

It was written on the back of a postcard showing a picture of Sydney Opera House. There was a cheque attached with a paper-clip: seventy-five pounds. It wasn't a fortune, but at least it would pay for a few more tubes of superglue. Herbert pocketed the cheque. I kept the card.

The third letter was the most interesting. It was typed on a single sheet of paper with no address at the top. It was a big sheet of paper, but it was a short letter.

DIAMOND –

TRAFALGAR SQUARE. 1.00 P.M. BE THERE.

The Fat Man.

"Who the hell is the Fat Man," I asked.

"The Fat Man..." Herbert muttered. His face had gone a sort of cheesey white and his mouth was hanging open. The last time I had seen him look like that had been when he found a spider in the bath.

"Who is he?"

Herbert was tugging at the letter. It tore in half. "The Fat Man is about the biggest criminal there is in England," he croaked.

"You mean ... the fattest?"

"No. The biggest. He's involved in everything. Burglary, armed robbery, fraud, arson, armed burglary ... You name it, he's behind it."

"How do you know?" I asked.

"From when I was a policeman," Herbert explained. "Every crook has a file at New Scotland Yard. But the Fat Man has a whole library. He's clever. Nobody's ever been able to arrest him. Not once. A traffic warden once gave him a parking ticket. They found her a week later, embedded in concrete, part of the M6 motorway. Nobody tangles with the Fat Man. He's death."

Herbert pressed the two halves of the letter together as if he could magically restore them. Personally, I was more puzzled than afraid. OK – so there was this master-criminal called the Fat Man. But what could he want with a no-hoper like Herbert? Obviously it had to be something to do with the dwarf's mysterious package. Had the Fat Man been responsible for the destruction of the flat? It seemed likely and yet at the same time I doubted it. You don't tear someone's place apart and then casually invite them to meet you in Trafalgar Square. One or the other – but not both. On the other hand, if he hadn't done it, who had?

"What are we going to do?" I asked.

"Do?" Herbert looked at me as though I were mad. "We're going! When the Fat Man invites you to jump in front of a tube train, you don't argue. You just do it. And you're grateful he wasn't in a bad mood!"

So later that morning we took the number 14 bus into the West End. This time I left the package – carefully hidden – back at the flat.

It had been ransacked once and I figured that nobody would think of looking for it there a second time.

"How will we recognize the Fat Man?" I asked.

"I've seen mugshots," Herbert said.

"You mean – you even had pictures of him on your mugs?"

Herbert didn't laugh. You could have tickled the soles of his feet with an ostrich feather and he wouldn't have laughed. He was so scared, he could barely talk. *And* he ate the bus tickets.

The bus dropped us in Piccadilly Circus and we walked across to Trafalgar Square. It was another cold day with a bite in the air that bit all the way through. The tourist season had ended weeks before but there were still a few of them around, taking photographs of each other against the grey December sky. The Christmas decorations had gone up in Regent Street – it seemed that they'd been up since July – and the stores were wrapped in tinsel and holly. Somewhere, a Salvation Army band was playing "Away in a Manger". I felt a funeral march would have been more appropriate.

Trafalgar Square is a big place and the Fat Man hadn't been too specific about the meeting-point so we positioned ourselves right in the middle, under Nelson's Column. There were a few tourists feeding the pigeons. I felt sorry for them. Who'd be a pigeon in London … or for that matter a tourist? I had a Picnic bar so I pulled out a couple of peanuts and fed them myself. I ate the rest of it. It was ten to one and in all the excitement I'd missed out on breakfast. Taxis, buses, cars and lorries rumbled all around us, streaming down to the Houses of Parliament and across to Buckingham Palace. I leant against a lion, looking out for anyone with a hundred centimetre waist. A pigeon landed on my shoulder and I gave it another peanut.

Big Ben struck one. According to my watch, it was five minutes fast.

"There he is," Herbert said.

I didn't see him at first. At least, I saw him but I didn't see him. A pink Rolls Royce had pulled up at the kerb, ignoring the blasts of the cars trapped behind it. A chauffeur got out, strolled round to the back and opened the door for one of the thinnest men I had ever seen. He was so thin that, as he moved towards us, he was like a living skeleton. His clothes – an expensive Italian suit and fur-lined coat – hung off him like they were trying to get away. Even his rings were too big for his pencil fingers. As he walked, he kept adjusting them to stop them sliding off.

I looked from him to Herbert and back again. "That's the Fat Man?" I asked.

Herbert nodded. "He's lost weight."

He reached us and stopped, swaying slightly as if the wind was going to blow him away. Close to, he was even more peculiar than far away. Hollow cheeks, hollow eyes, hollow gut. The man was a drum with the skin. stretched tight over bones that you could probably see when the light was behind him.

"Mr Diamond?" he said.

"Yes," Herbert admitted.

"I'm the Fat Man."

There was a long silence. Herbert was too afraid to talk, but I don't like long silences. They make me nervous. "You don't look fat to me," I said.

The Fat Man chuckled unpleasantly. Even his laughter was hollow. "Who are you?" he demanded.

"Nick Diamond," I told him, adopting my brother's name. "I'm his kid brother."

"Well, my dear boy, might I suggest that you keep your young mouth closed? I have business with your brother."

I kept my young mouth closed. The Fat Man didn't bother me, but I was interested to know what his business was. Meanwhile, the chauffeur had followed him from the Rolls, carrying a folding chair and a tub of corn. The chauffeur was wearing glasses that were so dark they didn't show his eyes but two reflections of yourself. He unfolded the chair and handed his master the corn.

"Thank you, Lawrence," the Fat Man said. "You can wait in the car."

The chauffeur grunted and walked away.

The Fat Man sat down, then dug a hand into the tub and threw a spray of pods across the concrete. The pigeons came at us in a rush. He smiled briefly.

"You look well," Herbert muttered.

"Thank you ... Timothy, if I may so call you." The Fat Man was genuinely pleased. "My doctor advised me to lose weight." He shrugged. "One must bow to the voice of reason – although some might say I have taken it a touch far. For the past year I have eaten nothing but yogurt and have shed a hundred and thirty-five kilograms. I have, however, retained my old nickname for professional purposes." The hand dug again, scattering more corn for the pigeons. "On the subject of which," the Fat Man continued, "I will be brief. You were visited yesterday by an old friend of mine. A small friend. I am led to understand that he might have entrusted you with something, something that I want. Something that I'm willing to pay for."

Herbert said nothing so I chipped in. "How much?"

The Fat Man smiled at me a second time. He had dreadful teeth. In fact he was pretty dreadful all over.

"You seem a bright lad," he said. "I'm sure the nurses will just adore you in the casualty ward."

I shrugged. "We don't have it," I said.

"You don't?" His eyebrows lifted themselves towards his bald head. At the same time, he fed the pigeons.

"Our place was turned over last night," I explained. "Perhaps you know about that already. Whoever did it, took what you're looking for."

"That's right!" Herbert agreed. "That's what happened."

The Fat Man looked at us suspiciously. He was pretty sure that we were lying. But he couldn't be certain. A pigeon landed on his head with a flutter of grey feathers. He punched it off, then threw corn at it. At last he spoke. "Taken?" he murmured.

"Absolutely," Herbert said. "When we got back from the cinema, it wasn't there. Otherwise we'd love to give it to you. Really we would."

I groaned silently. We'd have been all right if only Herbert had kept his mouth shut. But he couldn't have convinced a six-year-old and I could tell that the Fat Man had seen right through him. I glanced nervously at the chauffeur, who was watching us from the front seat of the Rolls. Was he armed? Almost certainly. But would he try anything in the middle of Trafalgar Square?

"Very well," the Fat Man said, and suddenly his voice was colder than the winter wind. "We shall play the game your way, my friends. If you want to find out what the bottom of the Thames looks like on a December night, that's your affair." He stood up and now his face was ugly. Actually, it had been ugly before he had even started but now it was even worse. "I want the key," he growled. "Perhaps, soon, you will find it again. Should such a happy event take place, I'm confident you won't be foolish enough to keep it from me." He dipped two fingers into his top pocket. When he pulled them out again, he was holding a card which he gave to Herbert.

"My number," he went on. "I am a patient man, Timothy. I can wait all of forty-eight hours. But if I haven't heard from you in two days, I think you may wake up to find that something very unpleasant has happened to you. Like you no longer have any feet."

"Why do you want this ... key so badly?" I demanded.

The Fat Man didn't answer me. We'd hit it off – him and me. The way he was looking at my head, I figured he'd like to hit that off too. But then his eyes wandered. He jerked his hand, sending the rest of the corn flying. The pigeons were all around him, bowing their heads at his feet.

"I hate pigeons," he said in a faraway voice. "Flying rats! London is infested with them. I hate the noise they make, day and night, the filth that they leave behind them. The government ought to make them illegal. And yet they're encouraged! It makes me sick to think of them scuttling across the pavements, infesting the trees, carrying their germs and diseases..."

"So why do you feed them?" I shouldn't have asked, but I had to know.

The Fat Man laughed briefly, mirthlessly. Then he spun the empty carton in my direction. "Poisoned corn," he said.

He walked back to the car and got in. A few feet away, a pigeon suddenly gurgled and keeled over on its side. A moment later, two more joined it, their feet sticking up in the air. By the time the Rolls Royce had reached the corner of Trafalgar Square and turned off towards Hyde Park, we were surrounded by corpses.

"Do you think he's trying to tell us some thing?" I said.

Herbert didn't answer. He wasn't looking much better than the pigeons.

OPENING TIME

Before the bus had even arrived to take us back to Fulham, we both knew that we were going to have to open the dwarf's package. We hadn't had it twenty-four hours but already our flat had been ransacked and we'd attracted the poisonous attention of the biggest crook in the country. OK – so Johnny Naples had paid us two hundred pounds. He made us promise not to open the envelope. But promises are easily broken. So are necks. I knew which I wanted to see get broken first.

There was a woman waiting at the door when the bus dropped us off. What with the dwarf and the Fat Man, I figured I'd already seen enough weird people for one day, but it seemed that today, like buses and musketeers, they were coming in threes.

She was an old woman with grey, curling hair that stuck out like someone had just electrocuted her. Her lipstick, a vivid shade of crimson, was pretty electrifying too. Her skin was a mass of wrinkles, hanging on her like an old coat. An old coat hung on her too, a sort of seaweed green with artificial fur trimmings. She had a hat like a tea cosy on her head and a bulging carpetbag in her hand. Although this was a high street in the middle of Fulham, her feet were lost in blue fluffy slippers.

We assumed that she had drifted out of the local lunatic asylum and let ourselves into the flat, ignoring her. It was only when we got into the office and found her still behind us that we realized that she had been waiting to see us. Now she took one look at the wreckage and whistled, smacking her lips together afterwards as if she'd just swallowed a toffee.

"Cor blimey!" she exclaimed. "Luv-a-duck! What a blooming mess!"

"Who are you?" Herbert demanded.

"Charlady," she replied. She gave us a big, crimson smile. "I saw your ad in the newsagent."

With everything that had happened, we'd quite forgotten about our advertisement for a cleaner. But here a cleaner was.

"Oh yes," Herbert muttered. "What's your name?"

"Charlady."

"Yes. I know." He frowned. I shrugged. Maybe she didn't understand English. Maybe somebody had dropped her when she was a baby. Herbert tried again, more slowly. "What – is – your – name?"

"Charlady!" she said for a third time. "Betty Charlady. That's my name. But you can call me Betty."

Without waiting for an invitation, she stepped further into the room, waving a feather duster which she had produced out of nowhere like a demented magician. Herbert and I looked at each other as she brushed it lightly across the remains of a shelf. The shelf fell off the wall. The cleaning lady scowled. "Crikey!" she said. "Wot a disaster. You don't need a blooming cleaner 'ere, luv. You need a master carpenter!"

"Wait a minute..." Herbert began.

"Don't you worry!" she interrupted. The duster had vanished and now she was holding a hammer. "It won't take me a minute. I'll soon 'ave this place looking like new."

I didn't doubt her. The carpetbag was so bulky it could have had a box of nails, a screwdriver and even a stepladder concealed in it too. But Herbert had managed to hold her down long enough to get her attention.

"I ... we ... well..." He'd got her attention, but he didn't know what to do with it.

"How much do you charge?" I asked.

"Twenny a day," she chirped, then, seeing the look of dismay on our faces, "Well ... a tenner for you. You look nice enough lads to me. And a private detective too! I love detective stories. Ten quid a day and I'll bring me own tea bags. What do you say?"

I could see Herbert was about to send her on her way so I moved quickly. We'd spent the two hundred pounds but we still had the cheque that Mum had sent us that morning. If Betty Charlady could re-build the flat and then clean it too – and all for ten pounds a day – it seemed too good a bargain to miss.

"You can start on Monday," I said.

"Nick..." Herbert protested.

"Do you really want to live in this?" I asked, pointing at the room.

"E's right," Betty chipped in. "E's a lovely boy, ineee! Wot is 'e? Your bruvver?" Herbert nodded. "E's a real knock-out." She curtsied at me. "A proper little gentleman. Monday, you say? Well, I'd still like to start now if it's all the same with you. Strike while the iron is 'ot, as I always say."

"The iron's in about a hundred pieces," I said. "Along with the ironing-board."

It wasn't that funny, but she threw back her head and laughed like a drain. You know the sort of gurgling sound that water makes when you take the plug out of the bath? Well, that was the sort of drain she laughed like.

"We're rather busy now," Herbert said. I could see he was itching to get at that package.

"Can you come back on Monday?"

"I'll be 'ere," Betty promised. "Nine o'clock on the dot."

"Make it ten."

"Ten o'clock, then." She curtsied again. "Wot a little darling – eh?" She winked. "Ten o'clock. Blimey!" Then she went.

We waited until we heard the outer door close before we retrieved the package. There was a loose floorboard in the office – in fact there were more loose floorboards than sound ones – and I'd hidden it underneath, covering it with a layer of dust. Herbert took the envelope and I shook it. Once again it rattled. He was about to open it, but then he froze.

"It could be a bomb," he whispered.

"A bomb?" I repeated. "Why should Naples have left us a bomb?"

"Well..."

"And who would search the place for a bomb?"

Herbert nodded. "That's right," he said. "You're right, Nick. Of course it isn't a bomb. I mean, there's no way it could be a bomb." He laughed. "I mean, who could possibly think..." He thrust it into my hands. "You open it."

With a little smile, he retreated into the far corner of the room, leaving the package with me. I shook it again. The Fat Man had said he wanted "the key". Whatever the package contained, it certainly wasn't a key. It sounded more like marbles – a lot of marbles in a cardboard container. I could feel the lid bending under my fingers. Herbert was watching me like a hawk. No. He was more like a rabbit. I tossed the package into the air and caught it. He blinked and shivered.

A bomb? Of course not.

But it could still be booby-trapped.

I stuck my thumb under the flap and slid it slowly sideways, trying to feel for a concealed wire or thread. Johnny Naples hadn't used a lot of spit when he stuck it down. Perhaps his tongue had been as dry as mine was now. The flap came loose without tearing. I caught a flash of red inside. There was a box of some sort. I tilted the package.

The box slid out on to the floor. Herbert dived for cover. But there was no bang.

And then we were both looking down, wondering if we'd gone crazy. Or perhaps we were about to go crazy. Certainly someone, somewhere had to be crazy.

There was only one thing in the dwarf's package.

It was a box of Maltesers.

D FOR DWARF

I don't know if you're into sweets. Personally, I can do without them. With the sort of pocket money I get, I have to do without them. I mean, with my pocket money, I can't even afford pockets. Anyway, Maltesers are those chocolate balls that crunch when you eat them. In America they have something similar called Malted Milk-balls. I expect you can buy them just about anywhere in the world.

The question was, Why had Johnny Naples paid out two hundred pounds to have us look after a box of sweets? Why had someone gone to so much trouble – wrecking the flat – to get their hands on them? And how had the Fat Man got mixed up in all this? Chocolates were the last things he needed – he was on a diet. It just didn't make sense.

We'd opened the box up. In for a penny, in for a pound (or 146g, to be exact). The contents certainly looked like ordinary Maltesers. They smelled ordinary. And they tasted ordinary. Herbert had some sort of idea that they might be chocolate-covered diamonds or something. It was only after I'd eaten half a dozen of them that he changed his mind and suggested that they might contain some sort of new-fangled poison. If looks could kill, I'd bury my brother.

"What we've got to do," Herbert said, "is find Naples."

For Herbert that was a pretty brilliant piece of deduction. The Fat Man had given us two days to get back to him. Johnny Naples had said he'd return in about a week. That left five days in which all sorts of unpleasant things could happen. The only trouble was, Naples hadn't told us where we could reach him. We had no address, no telephone number.

Herbert echoed my thoughts. "I wonder how we could get hold of him?" he asked.

"We could try Yellow Pages," I suggested. "V for vertically challenged?"

"Yes!"

I groaned as he reached for the telephone book. "I was only joking," I said.

"Were you? Of course you were!" Herbert dropped the book and gazed out of the window.

Meanwhile, I was fingering the envelope.

The Maltesers hadn't told us anything, but

looking underneath the flap I found a small, white label. The dwarf, in a hurry to seal the package, must have missed it. "Look at this," I said.

Herbert took the envelope. "It's an envelope," he said.

"Yes. But look at the label."

Herbert found it and held it up to the light. "Hammett's," he read. "18p." He frowned. "That's cheap for a box of Maltesers."

I shook my head. "That's the price of the envelope, not the sweets," I explained. "Look – the price is handwritten, but the name is printed. Hammett's ... that must be the stationer's or newsagent where he bought the envelope to put the Maltesers in."

"That's terrific!" Herbert exclaimed. "That's great, Nick." He paused. "But how does it help us?"

"If the dwarf wanted to buy an envelope, he probably bought it fairly near wherever he's staying," I said. "So all we have to do is find out how many Hammett's shops there are in London, visit them all and ask them if they remember selling an envelope to Naples."

Herbert sighed. "They probably sell hundreds of envelopes," he said. "And they must have thousands of customers."

"Yeah. But how many of their customers are dwarfs?"

"That's true." He considered. "So how do

we find Hammett's?"

"We look in the Yellow Pages."

Herbert snatched up the book again. Then he turned and looked at me disdainfully. "That was my idea in the first place," he said.

I didn't argue. Arguing with someone like Herbert is a bit like hitting yourself with a brick.

As it turned out there were six Hammett's in London.

We found them under the section headed "Newsagents and news vendors." There were three south of the river, one in Notting Hill Gate, one in Kensington and one in Hammersmith. By now it was too late to visit them all, so we decided to take the three in the south first and pick up some second-hand furniture from a friend with a shop near Clapham Common at the same time. It took us a couple of hours and a lot of wasted shoe leather but at least that evening we were able to sit down again.

The next day was a Saturday. We left the flat for a second time but struck out in Kensington and Hammersmith. That just left Notting Hill Gate. The last Hammett's was a run-down place on the Portobello Road in the middle of the famous antiques and bric-a-brac market. The sun was shining and the market was busy with young couples splashing out on Victorian brass towel-holders and Edwardian stripped pine blanket boxes. The air was thick with the smell of chips and over-cooked kebabs. Outside the shop there was an old boy selling genuine antique number plates. Doubtless they had fallen off a genuine antique lorry.

The shop was small and dark. That seemed to be the trademark of the entire Hammett chain. You probably know the sort of place: sweets and chocolates on one side, newspapers and magazines on the other with the dirty stuff on the top shelf. Herbert made straight for it, thumbing through a copy of *Playboy*, "looking for clues" as he put it. Meanwhile, I took a quick look at the stationery and odds-and sods section. This was the first branch we'd visited that actually stocked the right-sized envelopes. I examined a price label. The handwriting was the same.

There was only one man behind the counter. He was about forty, a cigarette dangling out of the corner of his mouth, his skin the unhealthy shade of white that comes from sitting in a dingy newsagent's all day smoking. While Herbert continued his own private investigation, I took the envelope and went over to him.

"Excuse me," I said. "I know this is going to sound crazy, but do you remember selling one of these envelopes to a dwarf?"

The man looked past me at Herbert. "Are you going to buy that?" he barked. Herbert pushed the magazme away from him and blushed. Then he came over and joined us. "Now, what do you want, son?" the newsagent asked.

"My brother's a private detective," I explained. "We're trying to find a dwarf … greasy hair, suntan. We think he bought an envelope here a couple of days ago."

"Yeah … I remember that." The newsagent nodded. "A short guy…"

"Most dwarfs are," I muttered.

"Came in here … last Thursday."

It had been Thursday when Johnny Naples came to see us. I was beginning to get excited, but then Herbert had to pipe up. "Diamond's the name," he said. "Tim Diamond."

"He didn't tell me his name," the newsagent said.

"No. I'm telling you my name."

The newsagent frowned at me. "Is he all right?" he asked.

"Sure." I scowled at Herbert. "Look – this is important. Did the dwarf buy anything else here? Like some Maltesers, for example."

I could see that the man was beginning to have second thoughts about the state of my own sanity, but he knew I was serious. He considered for a minute. "He didn't buy any sweets," he said. "But … now I remember. He had a box of Maltesers with him when he came in. I saw him put them in the envelope. What else did he buy? There was something…" He snapped his fingers. “It was a pair of scissors.” Now it all came back. “He was in a hurry. Nervous sort. Kept on looking out into the street. Like he was being followed or something. He bought an envelope and a pair of scissors. Then he went.”

“We need to find him,” I said.

“Is he in some sort of trouble?” the newsagent asked.

“He might be if we don’t find him,” I replied.

“But he won’t necessarily be if we do,” Herbert added unnecessarily.

The newsagent hesitated. He didn’t trust us. If I had been him, I wouldn’t have trusted us either. Just then the door opened and some body else came in – to buy a packet of cigarettes or something. “Look, I don’t have time to waste with you two jokers,” the newsagent said. “You want to speak to the dwarf, you’ll find him at the Hotel Splendide at the bottom of the Portobello Road.”

“How do you know?” I said.

“I know the owner. He told me he had a dwarf staying there.”

“And what’s the owner’s name?” Herbert asked.

“Jack Splendide.”

The further you go down the Portobello Road, the crummier it gets. It’s just about OK until you reach the Electric Cinema, but after that it's downhill all the way. You come to a flyover at the bottom by which time you're in a different world. You've left the antique shops and the bustling stalls behind you. Now you're in a flat wasteland, up to your ankles in litter. It's amazing how quickly a short walk can take you from one side of London to the other.

The Hotel Splendide was the sort of place that would be hard to find unless you knew it was there – perhaps the sort of place you might choose if you didn't want to be found. It was right at the far end of the Portobello Road, halfway down a narrow cul-de-sac, nestling in the armpit of the flyover which swept round the building as if holding it in a clammy, concrete embrace. You wouldn't get much sleep at the Hotel Splendide, not with the traffic roaring past only a couple of metres from your bedroom window. For the top floor of the building, beneath the flat roof, was level with the raised highway. Roll over in bed and you risked being run over by a lorry. That is, if the bedbugs and cockroaches hadn't got you first.

It was a square, ugly building, the colour of mouldy cheese. A red neon sign with the name glowed behind a first-floor window, only the glass was so dirty you could hardly read it. A row of dustbins stood outside the entrance, their overflowing garbage adding to the delightful atmosphere. You know how some guides award knives and forks to hotels in recognition of their quality? Well, the Hotel Splendide wouldn't even have merited a toothpick.

There was a drunk lying half-asleep next to the dustbins, the top of a wine bottle poking out of the brown paper bag that he clutched in one hand. A dog – an Alsatian – lay sprawled beside him. It was drunk too. We stepped past them and went into the hotel. The door was hanging off its hinges. The interior smelt of sweat and disinfectant.

We found ourselves in what passed for a reception area. Some hotels advertize theatres and restaurants. In this one the posters advertized soup kitchens and delousing clinics. There was a counter opposite the door and behind it an unshaven man reading a cheap paperback.

The paperback was even cheaper than this one and it didn't have as many pages which was just as well because the guy who was reading it didn't look as if he was up to *War and Peace*. He was wearing a grimy shirt and jeans with one of those stomachs that have managed to force their way over the top of the belt and sag down to the thighs. He was sucking a cigar that had gone out perhaps a week ago. He didn't look up as we approached. He flicked a page in his book, grunted and went on reading.

"You Jack Splendide?" Herbert asked.

"Who wants to know?" He talked without moving his lips. But the cigar waggled between his teeth.

"The name's Diamond," Herbert said. "I'm a private eye."

"Ya don't say!" Splendide yawned and went back to the book.

"We're looking for someone who's staying here," I explained. "A dwarf. His name's Johnny Naples. He owes a client of ours a lot of bread."

"That's right," Herbert said. "And if we find him, we'll cut you in for a slice."

We were making it all up, of course, but it was the only way to get past the hotel manager. He jerked a thumb in the direction of the stairs. "Room 39," he said.

We climbed five flights of stairs, trying to stop them creaking beneath our feet. The carpet was threadbare, the walls damp and discoloured. We could hear TV sets blaring away in the distance and a baby crying. I reckon I'd have cried if I'd had to stay there. Room 39 was at the back of the hotel, at the bottom of a corridor. We guessed it was 39 because it came after 37 and 38. But the number had fallen off. The door was closed.

"Do you think this is a good idea?" Herbert whispered.

"Have you got a better one?" I asked.

"We could go home..."

"Come on, Tim," I said. "We've found him now. It can't hurt to—"

That was as far as I got. The gunshot wasn't loud, but it was close enough to make me jump the way you do when a car backfires or somebody drops a plate. It had come from the other side of the door. Herbert froze, then tried to lurch away, but fortunately I managed to grab hold of his jacket. I didn't want to go into the room by myself. I didn't want to go into the room at all. But if I'd run away then, I'd never have forgiven myself.

Still clutching Herbert, I opened the door. It wasn't locked. In the Hotel Splendide, the rooms didn't have locks. Some of them didn't even have doors.

The first thing I saw was a flapping curtain and a shadowy figure disappearing outside. I couldn't even tell if it was a man or a woman. There was just the flash of a leg hanging over the edge of the sill and then it was gone.

It was a small room, just big enough for a bed, a table, a chest of drawers and a corpse. I closed the door behind me. Johnny Naples was lying on the bed. He wasn't dead yet but the big red splodge on his shirt told me that his time was running out about as quickly as his blood. I went over to the window and looked outside. But I was too late. Whoever had climbed out had jumped the short distance to the flyover and run for it. Maybe they'd had a car waiting for them. Anyway, they were gone.

The dwarf groaned and I looked back again. The room was probably in a mess to begin with but I guessed there had been a fight. There was a chair upturned on the floor and a lamp had been knocked over on the table. My eyes fell on a packet of book-matches. I don't know why I picked them up and put them in my pocket. I knew we didn't have a lot of time and that any clue – no matter how small – might help. Maybe it was just that I didn't want to look at the dwarf. Anyway, that's what I did.

Johnny Naples opened his mouth and tried to speak.

"The falcon..." he said. Then a nasty, bubbling sound.

Then... "The sun..." That was it. His eyes closed. The mouth stayed open.

D for Dwarf. D for dead.

Herbert had picked something up off the carpet.

"Nick..." he began.

It was a gun. And it was still smoking.

And he was still standing there, holding it, when the door crashed open again. The man who had been drunk outside the Hotel Splendide was standing there and he had a gun too. The Alsatian was with him, growling softly.

There were two more people behind him.

"Police!" he shouted.

Herbert fainted.

The man swung round to cover him. "You're under arrest," he said.

THE FALCON

Johnny Naples was taken to the morgue. We were taken to the Ladbroke Grove police station. I don't know which of us got the better treatment. While he was carried out on his back, covered with a nice clean sheet, we were dragged out, handcuffed together and thrown into the back of a van. It had turned out, of course, that the drunk in the street had been a plain-clothes policeman. The Alsatian was a plain-clothes police dog. The Hotel Splendide had been the subject of a major police stake-out and we'd more or less had our chips the moment we'd walked in.

We were left to stew in a bare-bricked interrogation room. Or to freeze, rather. That place couldn't have been much warmer than the morgue. There was one metal table, three metal chairs and five metal bars on a window that would have been too small to climb out of anyway. A blackboard lined one wall and there was a poster on the other reading "Crime doesn't pay", underneath which somebody had scrawled "nor does policework". The room smelt of stale cigarette smoke. I wondered how many hardened criminals had grown harder waiting there.

Herbert had said little since he woke up. But after about twenty minutes he suddenly looked around as if he had only just realized where he was. "Nick..." he said.

"Yes?"

"Do you think ... you don't think the police think I had anything to do with what happened to the dwarf, do you?" he asked.

"No," I replied soothingly. "You went up to see him. There was a gunshot. You were found holding a smoking gun. The dwarf was dead. I'm sure the police won't think you're involved."

At that moment there was a rattle as a key was turned in the lock and the door swung open. Herbert groaned. The man who had just come in didn't look too happy either.

"Herbert Simple," he said.

"Inspector Snape," Herbert muttered in a strangled voice.

"Chief Inspector Snape," the man growled. "No thanks to you."

The Chief Inspector was blond-haired and built like a rugby player, with those slightly squashed shoulders that come from too many scrums. His skin was the colour of raw bacon and he spoke with a northern accent. He was wearing an off-white shirt that had probably been pure white when he put it on and a tie that had slipped over his collar in its struggle to get away from his bulging neck. He was followed by a smaller, squatter version of himself with black, permed hair, an open-neck shirt and a gold medallion glittering in the forest of his chest. The assistant – if that's what he was – stood there, pounding one fist into the palm of his hand, looking at us with unfriendly, muddy-brown eyes. Well, if these are the cops, I thought, hate to meet the robbers.

"Herbert Simple," Snape repeated, drawing up a chair.

"Can I hit him?" the other policeman asked.

"No, Boyle." The Chief Inspector smiled unpleasantly. "Herbert Simple." He said the name a third time, chewing on the words like they were stuck in his teeth. "The worst police constable that ever served in my station. In two months you did more damage than the Kray brothers managed in twenty years. The day you left, I cried like a baby. Tears of pleasure. I never thought … I hoped, I prayed that I would never see you again." His pig-like eyes were turned on me. "And who are you, laddy?" he asked.

"His brother," I said.

"Bad luck, son. Bad luck."

"Can I hit *him*?" Boyle asked.

"Relax, Boyle." The Chief Inspector took out a cigarette and lit it. "Now, the question I'm asking myself is, Why should a luckless, hopeless, brainless ex-policeman like Herbert Simple be mixed up with a man like Johnny Naples?"

"I didn't shoot him!" Herbert cried.

"I believe you." Snape's nostrils quivered as they blew out two streams of smoke. "If you'd wanted to shoot the dwarf, you'd have probably missed and shot yourself in the foot. After all, when we sent you for weapons training, you managed to shoot the instructor. But the fact still remains that your fingerprints are on the gun – and nobody else's. So perhaps you'd better tell me what you were doing there."

"Naples was my client," Herbert squeaked.

"Your client?"

"He's a private detective," I explained.

"A private detective?" Chief Inspector Snape began to laugh. He laughed until the tears trickled down his cheeks. At last he managed to calm himself down, wiping his eyes with the back of his hand. Boyle handed him a handkerchief and he blew his nose noisily. "Now I've heard everything!" he said. "A private detective. And your client's dead. That makes sense. The moment he came to you he was a marked man. But what private detection did Naples want?"

"It's private," I said.

That wiped the smile off Snape's face. At the same time, Boyle grunted and lumbered towards me. I'd seen prettier sights in London Zoo. Fortunately for me, Snape held up a hand. "Forget it, Boyle," he snapped.

"But Chief..."

"He's under-age."

Boyle grunted again and punched the air. But he hung back.

"You should watch yourself, son," Snape said. "Boyle here is very into police brutality. He watches too much TV. The last suspect we had in here ended up in intensive care and he was just in for double parking."

"It's still private," I said.

"All right," Snape grumbled. "If you want to see your big brother arrested for murder..."

"Nick...!" Herbert whimpered.

"Wait a minute," I said. "We don't have to break a client's confidence."

"He's dead," Snape said.

"I noticed. But he's still our client." I gave him my friendliest smile. "Look, Chief Inspector," I said. "You tell us what you know and we'll tell you what we know. That seems fair to me."

Snape looked at me thoughtfully. "How old are you?" he asked.

"Thirteen."

"You're smart for your age. If you go on as smart as this, maybe you won't reach fourteen."

"Just tell us."

"Why should I? How do I know you know anything at all."

"We know about the key," I said. "And about the falcon."

I admit that was two shots in the dark. The Fat Man had mentioned a key and with his dying breath Johnny Naples had muttered something about a falcon. Neither of them made any sense to me, but I had gambled that they would mean something to this Snape character. And I was right. He had raised an eyebrow at the mention of the key. The other one joined it when I followed with the falcon.

He finished the cigarette, dropped the butt and ground it out with his heel. "OK," he said. "But you'd better be on the level, Nick. Otherwise I'll let Boyle spend a little time alone with you."

Boyle looked at me like he was trying to work out a new pattern for my face.

"Johnny Naples flew in here from South

America a month ago," Snape began. "We picked him up when he came through passport control, then we lost him, then – just a few days ago – we found him again at the Hotel Splendide. We've had him under observation ever since. You and your brother were the first people to see him as far as we know. He never went out – not while we were watching."

"Why were you watching him?" Herbert asked.

"That's what I'm trying to tell you," Snape snapped. He lit himself another cigarette. He didn't look like a chain-smoker, but that's the sort of effect my big brother has on people. "Johnny Naples was a nobody," Snape went on. "A quack doctor with a run-down practice in the back streets of La Paz, Bolivia. But with his last patient he struck lucky. You already know about the Falcon, but I wonder how much you know? His full name, for example – Henry von Falkenberg. I reckon he was out of your league. To be fair, von Falkenberg was in a league of his own.

"Look – every country has its big crooks. In England the Fat Man is probably number one. America has the godfathers. In Italy there are the Fettucine brothers. But the Falcon was an internationalist. He was half-English, half-German, loyal to neither country and living, when we last heard of him, in Bolivia. There wasn't a single criminal organization in the world that he wasn't doing business with. You steal a lorry-load of mink coats in Moscow? You sell it to the Falcon. You want to buy a kilo of cocaine in Canada? Just have a word with the Falcon. He was the number one, the top man, the king of crime. If there was a country in the world where the police didn't want him, he'd have taken it as a personal insult.

"Now, like any big businessman, the Falcon needed funds – a financial platform on which to build his deals. But unlike most businessmen, he couldn't just open an account at your local building society. He didn't trust the Swiss banks. He didn't trust his own mother-which is probably why he had her rubbed out back in 1965. The only currency the Falcon would deal in was diamonds: uncut diamonds. The franc might fall, the rouble might rise – but diamonds held their own. In every major city he had his own little stash of diamonds: in Paris, Amsterdam, New York ... and London. In fact, London was the centre of his operations, so that's where he had the biggest stash. We can't be sure, but we believe that perhaps only a mile from here, he'd managed to conceal diamonds to the value of three and a half million pounds."

He paused for effect and he got it. I licked my lips. Herbert shook his head and whistled.

"The Falcon was a great criminal," Snape continued. "But a month ago his luck ran out. He could have been arrested. He could have been machine-gunned by a rival gang. But in the end he was run over by a bus. It was a crazy end to a crazy life. It happened just outside La Paz airport as he crossed the road to catch a plane to England. We believe he was carrying the key to the diamonds with him. And the man who just happened to be on the scene, who travelled with him in the ambulance on the way to the hospital, was Johnny Naples.

"So the Falcon is lying on his back with the life running out of him and he – and only he – knows where a fortune in diamonds is hidden. Now, we can't be certain, but people who are dying tend to blurt out secrets that they would otherwise keep to themselves and we believe the Falcon told Johnny Naples where he could find those diamonds. Look at it this way. A few days later, Naples junks in his job and takes a first-class flight to London. There's no reason why he should have come here unless you put two and two together and make..."

"Three and a half million," I said.

"Right." Snape stood up and walked over to the blackboard. He had produced a piece of chalk from his pocket. "So Johnny Naples flies to the end of the rainbow; in this case, England. But he's not alone. Because all sorts of people are interested in the diamonds now that the Falcon is dead." He turned round and scrawled a name on the blackboard.

The Fat Man

"He's number one. The Fat Man had often done business with the Falcon. If anybody knew about the secret stash it would be him. And he could use the money. Give the Fat Man three and a half million pounds and maybe he could go international himself. He could become the next Falcon. He probably knew where the dwarf was staying before we did. Did he kill Johnny Naples? If so, he'll be on his way to the diamonds … and that's bad news for all of us."

Snape wrote a second name beneath it.

Beatrice von Falkenberg

"She's the dark horse," Snape continued. "The Falcon's wife – his widow – once Holland's greatest actress. He fell in love with her when he saw her in *Othello*. She played the title role. From all accounts it wasn't a happy marriage. She spent six months of the year in London and six months in La Paz. Did he ever tell her where the diamonds were hidden? If he didn't, she'll want to know..."

Two more names followed.

William Gott
and Eric Himmell

"They were the Falcon's right-hand men, his two lieutenants. If they could get their hands on the diamonds, they'd have enough money and enough power to take over the Falcon's empire. Gott and Himmell are killers. Although they were born in Germany, they were both educated at Eton. During that time, the vicar and the PE instructor went missing and the assistant headmaster was found hanged with his own old school tie. They arrived in London the day after Johnny Naples. They're here now, and they're deadly."

The Professor

"He's another mystery. But if anybody knows where the diamonds are, it's likely to be him. He was the Falcon's technical adviser, his tame egg-head. He was brilliant but crooked. For example, he invented computer fraud five years before someone invented the computer. If the diamonds are in some sort of safe, he'll have probably built it. But about a year ago he went missing. He could be dead. Nobody's heard of him since then."

Snape turned to the blackboard and wrote a final name.

Herbert Simp

That was as far as he got. The chalk broke in his hand.

"And at last we come to you," he said.

"Hopeless, horrible Herbert Simple. You say Johnny Naples was your client. I want to know why. I want to know what he wanted. I want to know what he said. I want to know what you two are doing mixed up in all this and I want to know now!"

He paused.

Things were beginning to make some sort of sense. Not a lot of sense, mind you, but at least we knew what stakes we were playing for. Johnny Naples had come to London in search of three and a half million pounds and he had left us a box of Maltesers. It wasn't a lot to go on, but it was all we had. The trouble was, if we told Snape what Naples had given us, we'd lose that too. The way I saw it was like this. A lot of people were interested in what had taken place in our office that Thursday morning. The Fat Man was one of them. And perhaps it had been Gott and Himmell who had ransacked the place that same night. Sooner or later they'd come gunning for us and if the worst came to the worst, we'd have to give them the Maltesers. Which meant we had to keep them from Snape.

And – OK – I'll be honest. If we were really sitting on the key to a fortune, I wanted to be the one to turn it. There were plenty of things I could do with three million pounds. I reckoned I'd let Herbert keep the other half.

"Come on," Snape growled. "It's your turn.

What did Naples want?"

There was another long silence. Boyle shuffled forward and I noticed that this time Snape made no move to stop him.

"Naples came here looking for the money," I said. "You were right there. But he was followed. He was afraid. That's why he came to see us. He thought we'd be able to give him some sort of protection."

"Nick!" Herbert muttered.

"He didn't tell us anything more than that..."

Boyle's hand clamped down on the back of my neck. He half-dragged me to my feet. Now I knew how a piece of scrap iron feels when it's picked up by a mechanical grabber. Iwaited for him to crush me. "You're lying," he hissed.

"Scouts honour!" I pleaded.

"You knew about the key," Snape reminded me.

"Only because Naples mentioned it. But we haven't got it. You can search the office if you like."

"We already have," Boyle said.

"Then you'll know that somebody tore it apart. Look – if we knew anything, why do you think we went to the Hotel Splendide? The place was searched and we got scared. We went to see Naples to ask him what was going on, but by the time we got there, he was dead. Honest!"

For a moment the only sound in the room was a vague creaking as my neck splintered in Boyle's grip. But then he must have got some sort of signal from Snape. He released me and I collapsed in my chair. My legs had turned to jelly. I could hardly move my head.

"OK. We'll play it your way, son," Snape said humourlessly. "We'll let you go. I don't believe you and nor will the Fat Man or any of the other nasties waiting for you out there. It'll be interesting to see which one of them gets to you first."

"And I suppose you'll stand by and watch," I muttered, rubbing my neck.

"Don't worry," Snape said. "We'll be round to pick up the pieces."

GRANNIES

It's funny how the smell of police stations sticks on you long after you've gone. Snape was decent enough to get a police car to take us home and we carried the smell with us, down past the Albert Hall and through Earl's Court. They say that good detectives have a "nose" for crime. They "sniff" out clues and when things are going well, they're on the right "scent". After a couple of hours in the Ladbroke Grove interrogation room, I could see what they mean. The strong arm of the law could do with a strong under-arm deodorant.

We had a bath when we got in and changed into fresh clothes. Then Herbert suggested we should go out and get something to eat. I didn't argue. He'd been very quiet since we'd walked in on the dead dwarf and I could tell something was brewing. Perhaps he was finally going to pack in the private detective business and send me packing too. All the same, I dug the Maltesers up from beneath the floorboard and took them with me. That was funny too. Before, when I hadn't known what they were worth, I'd slung them about like you would any packet of sweets. Now that I knew they carried a three and a half million pound pricetag, I could feel them burning a hole in my pocket.

We walked down the Fulham Road towards Kensington Station. Herbert was still quiet. And he was jumpy. When a guy stopped us to ask us the time, he jumped, disappearing behind a parked car. I found him there a minute later, crouching down, pretending to tie up his shoes. It would have been a bit more convincing if his shoes had had laces. The truth was, Herbert was afraid, certain we were being watched. The taxi-driver on the other side of the road, the old man walking his dog, the couple kissing at the bus stop ... as far as Herbert was concerned, any one of them could have been working for the Fat Man, for Beatrice von Falkenberg, for the police ... whoever.

We stopped at a fast-food restaurant called Grannies. It got the name because all the hamburgers were served in granary bread buns. As a sort of publicity stunt, someone had also had the bright idea of only employing grannies – little old ladies with grey hair and glasses. The only trouble with all this was that for a fast-food restaurant, it was actually pretty slow. The chef must have been about a hundred and two. One of the waitresses used a walking-frame. But the food's OK and we were in no hurry. We took a table by the window. Herbert chose the chair that looked out. There was no way he was going to sit with his back to the street.

We ordered Grannyburgers and chips with chocolate milkshakes on the side and hardly said anything until it arrived. I picked up the tomato ketchup holder and squeezed it. The stuff spat out, missing the plate and splattering on to the white table. It looked like blood.

Herbert put his knife and fork down. "Nick..." he began.

"Herbert?" I said expectantly. Actually, I knew what to expect now. I should have seen it coming.

"This case is getting out of hand," he said. "I mean ... it's getting dangerous. The way things are going, I reckon somebody could soon get hurt."

"You mean – like Johnny Naples?" I reminded him.

"Right." Herbert stared at the tomato sauce, his lip curling. "And he wasn't just hurt," he went on. "I mean, he probably was hurt. But he was also killed."

"You can't get more hurt than that," I agreed.

He nodded. "So what I'm saying is, maybe it's time you split. You're a good kid, Nick. But you're only thirteen. This is a case for Tim Diamond."

It was incredible. Maybe it was the shock of what had happened that day or maybe it was the milkshake, but Herbert was trying to get rid of me. "This is a case for Tim Diamond" – it was a line out of a bad movie, but Herbert really believed it. I could see him switching into his private detective role even as he sat there, shoulders slumped, eyes hard. He'd have had a cigarette dangling out of the corner of his mouth if cigarettes didn't make him throw up.

"I figured I'd send you to Aunty Maureen in Slough," he went on. I shuddered. Aunty Maureen, my mother's sister, had a semi-detached house and a semi-detached false hip. She was only fifty years old but in need of round-the-clock nursing. Whenever I stayed with her, I ended up as her round-the-clock nurse. "Or you could always go to Australia," Herbert added.

I took a deep breath and pronged a forkful of french fries. Whenever Herbert got into these moods, I had to tread carefully. If I ever suggested that the great Tim Diamond needed any help from his thirteen-year-old brother, I'd have been on the next plane to Sydney faster than you could whistle "Waltzing Malteser".

"It's nice of you to think of me, Tim," I said. "And I don't want to get in your way. But I reckon I'd be safer with you."

"Safer?" He took a bite out of his burger.

"Sure. I mean, the Fat Man could come for me in Slough. I might get kidnapped, or brutally beaten with Aunty Maureen's false hip."

"That's true."

"But I feel safe with you," I continued. "Back in the Hotel Splendide, for example. I don't know what I'd have done without you."

Herbert smiled modestly.

"The way you fainted. It was ... heroic."

Now he scowled. "You're not taking the mickey, are you?"

"Me? No way."

I felt it was time to bring the conversation to a close so I took out the box of Maltesers and put them on the table.

"That's what we should be worrying about," I said. "Three and a half million pounds, Herbert. And it's our only clue."

"I don't get it," Herbert said. Herbert never did.

"Look..." I spoke slowly, trying to make it easy for him. "Johnny Naples comes to England with the key to a fortune. That's what the Fat Man asked us for – remember? A key. Now, all he's got is this box of Maltesers, but maybe he doesn't know what it means either."

"How do you know that?" Herbert asked.

"Because Snape told us that the dwarf had been in England for a whole month before he was killed. Maybe the Falcon didn't have time to tell him everything before he died. Naples had a rough idea and came over here to look."

"Go on."

"All right. So Naples comes to England. He checks into the Hotel Splendide. And he starts looking. But unfortunately for him, there are lots of people interested in him. The same people who are now interested in us. But Johnny Naples still manages to find out what the Maltesers mean. He takes them with him – like you'd take a treasure map. So that nobody will see what he's carrying, he buys an envelope to put them in. He goes from the hotel to Fulham. But then he sees that he's followed. So what does he do?"

"I don't know," Herbert said, breathlessly. "What does he do?"

"He comes to us. He's in the street and he happens to see your name on the door. You're a private detective. That's perfect. And maybe your name rings a bell."

"No, Nick," Herbert interrupted. "It's the little button by the door that rings the bell..."

"No," I groaned. "I mean Tim *Diamond*. Diamonds are what this is all about."

"Oh – I see."

"Johnny Naples comes in and gives us the envelope. You remember how scared he was?

He knew that he was being followed. So he gives us the package – which is what everybody wants – and promises to come back when the heat is off."

"But he didn't come back," Herbert said.

"No. Because he got killed."

"Oh yes!"

"And now we've got the Maltesers. And if we can work out where he was going and what he was going to do with them when he got there, we'll be rich."

"That's terrific!" Herbert exclaimed. As I had hoped, all thoughts of Slough and Aunty Maureen had left his head. Quickly, he finished his meal. Then he picked up the box. "Perhaps the diamonds are inside," he suggested. "Covered in chocolate."

"No," I said. "I doubt if you could fit three and a half million's worth inside and anyway, I've already eaten six of them and they certainly didn't taste like diamonds."

"Then what…?"

It was a good question. You can go and buy a box of Maltesers in any sweetshop, but to save you the money, let me just describe the box we had. It had the name written in white letters on a red background, surrounded by pictures of the chocolate balls themselves. This was on the top and on all four sides. On one side it also carried the inspiring message – "The lighter way to enjoy chocolates" and on the other, the weight: 146g 5.15 oz.

There was more on the bottom. It read "Chocolates with crisp, light honeycombed centres" and then there was the usual blurb about the milk solids and the vegetable fat that had achieved this miracle. In addition there was a guarantee: "This confectionary should reach you in perfect condition... " and a line asking you to keep your country tidy.

After that, there was a red code number: MLB 493 and, in a red panel, "Best before 28-12-96". In the left-hand corner, painted in blue, was the bar-code, the series of thick and thin lines that you get on all products these days. There was a number beneath that too: 3521 201 000000. And that is about as complete a description of a box of Maltesers as you are ever going to find in a library or bookshop.

It was not very helpful.

The waitress hobbled over and we ordered two Grannypies. We sat in silence, waiting for them to arrive. The question was, how could you hide the location of a fortune in diamonds on a box of sweets – and for that matter, why choose a box of sweets in the first place? The answer was in our hands and even then I might have been able to guess, for the truth is, I had forgotten one important detail. One thing that Johnny Naples had done had slipped my mind. I was still trying to work it out when Herbert spoke.

"Any luck?" he asked.

"No."

We finished our puddings and ordered the bill.

"How about the little dots?" Herbert asked.

"Little dots?"

"Under the letters." He pointed at the Maltesers. "They could spell out another message."

"But there aren't any little dots," I said.

"They could be written in invisible ink."

"I can't see it."

"That's because it's invisible." He smiled triumphantly.

"Listen," I said. "If Johnny Naples didn't know what the Maltesers meant, he'd have had to find out – right?"

"Right," Herbert agreed.

"So if we can work out where he went while he was in England, maybe we'll find out, too."

"Right." Herbert frowned. "But he's dead. So where do we start?"

"Maybe here," I said.

I took out the book of matches that I had found in the hotel and gave it to him. They belonged to a place called the Casablanca Club with an address in the West End. There was a map on the inside of the cover and three matches left.

"Where did you get this?" Herbert asked.

"I picked it up in the dwarf's room at the

hotel," I said. "I thought it might be useful."

"Yes." Herbert considered. "We'll go there tomorrow," he said. "If we can work out where Johnny Naples went while he was in England, maybe we can find out what the Maltesers mean."

I nearly choked on my milkshake. "That's brilliant!" I exclaimed.

"Sure thing, kid," Herbert said.

I didn't remind him that I'd said exactly the same thing only a few moments before. But nor did he remind me about Slough. This might be a case for Tim Diamond, but so long as I played my cards right, it seemed there was still room for his little brother Nick.

THE CASABLANCA CLUB

We were woken up at nine the next morning by the engineer who'd come to mend the phone and we just had time to fall asleep again before we were woken up by Betty Charlady who'd come to mend the flat. She had brought with her a sack of tools and was soon assembling Herbert's desk, hammering away at the wood with a mouth full of nails. It seemed incredible that she should do all this for a lousy ten pounds a day, but I assumed I brought out the motherly instinct in her. Strange how I could never do the same for my mother.

While Herbert got dressed and shaved, I nipped out for eggs, milk and bread. We hadn't had time to cash the cheque and money was running low so I had to squeeze more credit out of the supermarket owner. The owner – Mr Patel – is a decent old stick.

He also owns a decent old stick which he tried to hit me with as I ran out without paying, but at least I was able to rustle up a decent breakfast for Herbert and me, and a cup of tea for Mrs Charlady.

After breakfast, Herbert rang the Casablanca Club and I discovered that it would be open that night – although to members only. Betty Charlady was screwing a chair back together in the office at the time and she must have overheard the call for when she came into the kitchen she was scowling.

"Wassis Casablanca Club?" she asked.

"It's in Charing Cross," I said. "We're going there tonight."

"You shouldn't do it, Master Nicholas," Betty muttered. "At your age."

I handed her a cup of tea. She took it and sat down, her eyes searching across the table for a biscuit. "It's part of our investigation," I explained. "A client of ours may have gone there so we have to go there, too."

But Mrs Charlady wasn't impressed. "These London clubs," she said. "They're just dens of innik-witty." She shook her head and the grey curls of her hair tumbled like lemmings off a cliff. "You go if you have to. But I'm sure no good will come of it..."

Nonetheless, Herbert and I made our way to the Casablanca Club that same night, arriving just after twelve. There's a corner of Charing

Cross, just behind the station, that comes straight out of the nineteenth century. As the road slopes down towards the river, you leave the traffic and the bright lights behind you and suddenly the night seems to creep up on you and grab you by the collar. Listen carefully and you'll hear the Thames water gurgling in the distance and as you squint into the shadows you'll see figures shuffling slowly past like zombies. For this is down-and-out territory. Old tramps and winos wander down and pass out underneath the arches at the bottom, wrapped in filthy raincoats and the day's headlines.

The Casablanca Club was in the middle of all this. A flight of steps led down underneath a dimmed green bulb and if you didn't know what you were looking for, there was no way you'd find it. There was no name, no fancy sign. Only the tinkle of piano music that seemed to seep out of the cracks in the pavement hinted that in the dirt and the dust and the darkness of Charing Cross, somebody might be having a good time.

We climbed down to a plain wooden door about five metres below the level of the pavement. Somebody must have been watching through the spyhole for it opened before we had time to knock.

"Yes?" a voice said.

Friendly place, I thought.

"Can we come in?" Herbert asked.

"You members?"

"No."

"Then beat it!"

The door swung shut. At the last moment, Herbert managed to get his foot in the crack. There was a nasty crunching sound as his shoe, and possibly his foot too, got chewed up in the woodwork, but then the door swung open again and I managed to push my way through and into the hall. A bald man in a dinner jacket gave me an ugly look. If he ever wanted to give anyone a pretty look, he'd need major plastic surgery.

"We're friends of Johnny Naples," I said. The man shrugged. "Why didn't you say so before?" he asked.

"You didn't ask," I said.

He opened the door again. Herbert was writhing on the concrete outside, clutching his mangled foot. "Instant membership – ten quid," the bald man said. He glanced at me. "You're under-age," he muttered.

"You don't look too good yourself," I replied.

"How old are you?" he asked.

"Twenty-five."

"Twenty-five?" He sneered. "You got a driving licence?"

"No. I got a chauffeur."

I walked on, leaving Herbert to find the

money and pay. In the dim light I could have been any age. Anyway, I was taller than Johnny Naples had ever been and they'd allowed him in.

Funnily enough, the first waiter who saw me mistook me for the dwarf in the half-light. "Mr Naples!" The words were two drops of oil squeezed into my ear and I was led to a table at the front of a large room. There was so much smoke in the air that my eyes had more water in them than the house whisky. I loosened my tie and sat down. It felt like there was more smoke in the air than there was air in the smoke. Another waiter passed. "Good evening, Mr Naples."

He put a silver bucket and two glasses on the table. I leant forward. There was a bottle of champagne in the bucket, surrounded by ice-cubes, already uncorked. "With the compliments of the house," the waiter said. I scratched my head. The dwarf must have been quite a regular here. Came regular, drank regular… I wondered what else he did regular at the Casablanca Club.

I looked around me. There were perhaps a hundred people there, sitting at tables or crowding round the bar where three black-tied waiters shook cocktails behind a curving marble counter. The air was filled with the hubbub of conversation, as thick and as indistinct as the cigarette smoke. There was a dance floor at one end but tonight there was no band, just a black pianist stroking the ivories with fingers that looked too stubby to sound so good. Right in front of my table there was a stage about the size you'd expect a stage to be in a run-down drinking club. The place had no windows and no ventilation. The smoke had smothered the light, strangled the plants and it wasn't doing a lot for me either.

I drank some champagne. I'd never drunk the stuff before and I can't say I really liked it. But I was thirsty and it was free. Herbert joined me, muttering about the ten pounds and a moment later a spotlight cut through the clouds and the crowd fell silent. A figure moved on to the stage, a woman in her fifties, who dressed like she was in her thirties, with jewellery flashing here and there to keep your eyes off the wrinkles. She was attractive if you didn't look too closely. At one time she might even have been beautiful. But the years hadn't been good to her. They'd taken the colour out of her hair, put a husk in her voice, hollowed out her throat and slapped her around a bit for good measure.

I drank some more champagne. The bubbles were going right up my nose and dancing behind my eyes. The pianist had come to the end of a tune but as the woman moved forward he began another and she sang almost as if she didn't care what she was doing. She sang two or three songs. When she finished, she got a scattering of applause and as the talk started up again, she moved down to our table and sat opposite me. Only when she was close enough to see the pinks of my eyes (the whites had gone that colour in all the smoke) did she see who I was.

"You're not Johnny," she said.

"We're friends of his..." I said. I let the sentence hang in the air. I needed her name to complete it.

"Lauren Bacardi," she said. "Where's Johnny?"

I looked at Herbert. From the way she was talking, the little guy had obviously meant something to her and I didn't know how she would take the news. I hoped he'd think of a gentle way to tell her. You know, with a bit of tact.

"He's dead," Herbert said.

"Dead?"

"Yup." He nodded. "Dead."

She took out a cigarette and lit it. I guessed she needed something to do with her hands. After all, to smoke in the unique atmosphere of the Casablanca Club, you didn't actually need to light another cigarette. "Was he ... killed?" she asked.

"Yeah," I said. I drank some more champagne. The more I drank, the better I liked it. "You knew him?"

She smiled sadly. "We were friends." Her eyes were far away. They seemed further away than her nose. Maybe it was the champagne. I thought she was going to get up and walk out of our lives. The way things turned out, it would have been better if she had. But the pianist had slid into a bluesy number and she needed to talk. "Johnny and I knew each other for ten years," she said. "But we never met. Not until a month ago.

"We were pen-pals. He was in South America. I was over here. Maybe you'll laugh at me, but we kind of fell in love by post." She flicked ash on to the carpet. "We wrote letters to each other for ten years and he never even mentioned that he was a dwarf. I only found out a month ago when he came over and by then I'd more or less agreed to marry him. The little rat..."

She puffed at her cigarette. I knocked back the champagne. Herbert was watching both of us anxiously.

"He came over," she went on. "He just turned up one day on my doormat. No. He was standing on a chair on the doormat – to reach the bell. He had these plans. We were going to be rich. We'd buy this little house in the South of France with low ceilings. Johnny didn't like high ceilings. He told me that he knew where he could lay his hands on three and a half million pounds – enough money to take me away from all this…"

She raised her hands, taking in the whole of the Casablanca Club with ten chipped and nicotine-stained fingernails.

"Did he have anything with him?" I asked. "A box, for example?"

"You mean the Maltesers?" Lauren Bacardi smiled. "Sure. He never went anywhere without them. He seemed to think they were important, but he didn't know why. It nearly drove him mad … if he wasn't mad already. I mean, how could a box of sweets be worth all that dough?"

I poured myself some more champagne. Herbert whisked it away before I could drink it. I wanted to argue but suddenly there were two of him and I wasn't feeling so good.

"But maybe he was on the level," Lauren went on. "Why else would anyone want to wipe him out? I mean, Johnny never hurt anyone in his life. He was too small.

"And he was afraid – all the time he was in England. He wouldn't stay at my place. He hid himself away in some flea-pit hotel and whenever we went out together he always made like he was being followed. I thought he was imagining things." A single tear trickled down her cheek, turning a muddy brown as it picked up her make-up. "Just my luck," she whispered. "Johnny getting himself killed just one day after he'd found the answer."

"He found the diamonds?" Herbert cried.

"No." She shook her head. "Just the answer. We were out together one day and he saw something; something that made everything make sense."

"What was it?" Herbert and I asked more or less together.

"Miss Bacardi?" the waiter interrupted. "There's someone at the door with some flowers for you."

"For me?" She got to her feet, swaymg slightly in front of us. "Just give me one minute."

She moved away in the direction of the front entrance, followed by the waiter. I reached for the bottle but Herbert stopped me. "Do you know how much that stuff costs?" he hissed.

"It was free," I told him.

"Well … you're only thirteen. What would Mum say?"

"Mum..." I muttered and for a fraction of a second actually missed her. That was when I knew that I'd had more than enough to drink.

Neither of us said anything for a while, and in that silence I became aware of a little voice whispering in my ear. It was my common sense. It was trying to tell me something that I'd have known at once ifi hadn't had so much to drink. Something was wrong. I played back what had just happened and suddenly I knew what it was. The flowers. Why had the waiter made Lauren Bacardi walk all the way to the entrance instead of bringing them to her? And there was something else. Maybe it was just a coincidence. Maybe it didn't mean anything. But now I remembered. The waiter had spoken with a German accent. I was on my feet making for the door before I knew what I was doing. Herbert ran after me, calling my name. But I wasn't going to stop and explain what was going on. I pushed my way through the crowd, ignoring the shouts of protest and the crash of breaking glass. That was one time I was glad I wasn't fully grown. Before anyone could see me to grab hold of me I was gone.

I reached the door and the cold night hit me like an angry woman, slapping my face and tearing at my hair. The first thing I saw was the remains of what had been a bouquet of flowers. But now the cellophane was torn and the flowers were scattered over the steps, the stalks broken. At the same time, I heard someone calling out. It was Lauren Bacardi. I took the steps three at a time and as I reached the street, I just had time to catch sight of her being bundled into the back of a dark blue van. A shadowy figure slammed the door and ran round to the front. The engine was already running. A moment later, so was I.

I ran across to the van, meaning ... I don't know. I guess I thought I'd be able to pull the door open and get Lauren out, but of course it was locked. So instead I jumped on to it, slamming into the metal like a hamburger hitting a griddle and hung on for dear life as the van roared away. I'd managed to get a foothold of sorts on the licence plate and I had one hand on the door handle, one hand curled round the rim at the edge. I was half spread-eagled and travelling at about thirty miles an hour when the van turned a corner. Whoever was driving put their foot down then. Perhaps they'd heard they had an unwelcome passenger. I reckon the van was doing sixty when I was thrown off. It was hard to tell. After all, I was sort of somersaulting through the air and if I'm going to be honest I might as well add my eyes were tightly closed like I was praying – which, in fact, I was.

All I knew was that me and the van had parted company. It roared off to the left, its tyres screaming. I flew off to the right. I should have been killed. I could have been killed. But if you go down that part of London at night, you'll find that the offices put a lot of junk out on the pavements, to be cleared up by the refuse trucks the next day. My fall was broken by a mountain of cardboard boxes and plastic bags. Better still, the bags were full of paper that had been put through the shredder; computer print-outs and that sort of thing. It was like hitting a pile of cushions. I was bruised. But nothing broke.

A minute later Herbert reached me. He must have been convinced that I was finished because when I got to my feet and walked towards him, brushing paper cuttings off my sleeves, he almost fainted with surprise.

"Did you get the van's number?" I asked. He opened and closed his mouth again with out speaking. It was a brilliant impersonation of a goldfish. But I wasn't in the mood to be entertained.

"The licence plate..." I said.

"No."

"Why not?"

"You were standing on it..." He still couldn't believe what he'd just seen.

I looked back down the empty road. Lauren Bacardi had been about to tell us something important and now she was gone. Our only chance of finding the secret of the Maltesers might have gone with her.

"Let's get a taxi home," I said.

“NICE DAY FOR A FUNERAL”

I wasn’t feeling too good the next day. I woke up wishing I hadn’t, tried to close my eyes and groaned into the pillow. There was something unpleasant in my mouth. I tried to spit it out but I couldn’t. It was my tongue. Outside, it was raining. I could hear the water pitter-pattering against the windows and dripping through the leak in the bathroom ceiling. I looked out. It was another grey London day with little yellow spots dancing in the air. I figured a couple of Alka-Seltzer would see to the spots but it looked like we were going to be stuck with the weather.

It took me about twenty minutes to get out of bed. The tumble I had taken the night before must have been harder than I had thought. My right shoulder had gone an interesting shade of black and blue and it hurt when I moved my fingers. Actually it hurt when I moved anything.

Somehow I managed to wiggle out of my quilt and, bit by bit, I forced the life back into my battered frame. But it was an hour before I'd made my way downstairs and into the kitchen. It was still raining.

Herbert was sitting there reading a newspaper. When he saw me, he flicked on the kettle and smiled brightly.

"Nice day for a funeral," he said.

"Very funny," I groaned, reaching for the medicine chest.

"I'm being serious." Herbert slid the news paper in front of me.

I opened the medicine chest – a red plastic box with a white cross on it. It contained two plasters and a tin of cough sweets. Clearly Herbert wasn't expecting an outbreak of bubonic plague. I groaned for a second time and pulled the newspaper before me. With an effort, I managed to get the print to unblur itself.

Herbert was right. There was going to be a funeral later in the day – just a few minutes down the road as luck would have it. Or was it luck? I wasn't thinking straight, that was my trouble. The guy being buried was one Henry von Falkenberg. It appeared that the Falcon had flown home.

There was nothing about the Falcon's three and a half million pounds in the paper. They didn't even mention he'd been a crook. In fact it was just one of those fill-in stories, the sort of thing they print between the crossword and the gardening report when they haven't got enough news. This was a story about a wealthy businessman living in Bolivia who had once lived in England and had decided that he wanted to be buried there. The only trouble was, the week he'd died, there'd been a baggage handler's strike in La Paz and – now that he was dead – "baggage", included him. He'd spent the last four weeks sharing an airport deep-freeze with a load of corned beef from Argentina.

But now the strike was over and von Falken berg could be buried in his family plot just down the road from our flat. It was too good an opportunity to miss, hungover or not. How many of the names on Snape's blackboard would turn up to pay their last respects to the Falcon?

We had to be there.

Herbert reached for the telephone book. "3521201," he said.

"What's that?" I asked.

"Brompton Cemetery."

I'd written the number down for him and he rang them. He spoke briefly before he put the phone down.

"The funeral's at twelve," he said. "Recommended dress: black tie and wellington boots."

Perhaps you know Brompton Cemetery – a stretch of ground between Fulham Road and the Brompton Road – a stone's throw away from the football ground. I sometimes walked there on Sundays which isn't as creepy as it sounds. After all, there's not much grass in Fulham and with the sun shining it isn't such a bad place to be. Anyway, the best thing about walking in a cemetery is walking out again. Don't forget, not everyone can.

From the Fulham Road you pass between a pair of tall, black iron gates and follow the path. You don't even know you're in a cemetery until you're a short way up and pass the first graves. It's pretty at first. This is the old part of the cemetery, the romantic bit with the grass waist high and the stones poking out at odd angles like they've grown there too. Then you turn a corner and there's a cluster of buildings curving round an open space like some sort of weird Victorian summer house. Now everything is flat and you can see all the way up to the Brompton Road, a green stretch with the crosses sticking up like the masts of a frozen armada.

We got there at five to twelve, squelching through the rain and the mud, our raincoats pulled up tight around the neck. About a dozen people had braved the weather to make their farewells to the Falcon … and the Argentinian Corned Beef Company had sent a wreath, which was a nice gesture. The first person we met was a less pleasant surprise:

Chief Inspector Snape, looking about as cheerful as the cemetery's residents. Boyle was behind him, dressed in a crumpled black suit with a mourning band on his arm.

"Simple and Simple," Snape cried, seeing us. "I was planning to visit you as soon as this little shindig was over."

"Why?" Herbert asked.

"We've been receiving reports of an incident in Charing Cross. I thought you might be able to help us with our enquiries into the disappearance of a certain singer. One Lauren Bacardi. It looks like a kidnap. And guess which kid is our prime suspect?"

"Search me," I said.

"I probably will one of these days," Snape assured me. He smiled at his little joke and I have to admit that jokes don't come much more little than that. "I've got you for murder, for kidnap, for under-age drinking, failing to pay for one bottle of champagne and causing a disturbance," he went on. "I could lock you up right now."

"You're dead," Boyle whispered.

Snape sighed. "Thank you, Boyle."

"Why don't you arrest us?" I asked.

"Because you're more useful to me outside. I mean, you'd be nice and safe in a cosy police cell, wouldn't you?" He gestured at the other mourners now grouping themselves around the grave. "I'm still waiting to see what happens to you. Come on, Boyle!"

Snape and Boyle went over to the grave. We followed them. It turned out that the Falcon was to be buried in the old part of the cemetery where the grass was at its highest, the gravestones half buried themselves. There was a vicar standing in the rain beside what looked like some sort of antique telephone box. It was a stone memorial, about two metres high, mounted by a stone falcon, its beak slightly open, its wings raised. There was a stone tablet set in the memorial below, with a quotation from the Bible cut into it.

THE PATH OF THE JUST IS AS SHINING LIGHT,
THAT SHINETH MORE AND MORE
UNTO THE PERFECT DAY.

Proverbs iv 18

The names of the dead von Falkenbergs were written beneath it: a mother, a father, two grandparents, a cousin .. . there were seven of them in all. A rectangular hole had been cut into the earth to make room for an eighth. As we approached, the coffin was being lowered. Henry von Falkenberg had come to join his ancestors.

It was raining harder than ever. The vicar had begun the funeral service, but you could hardly hear him for all the splashing. I took the opportunity to examine the other mourners. It was a pity about the weather. What with the umbrellas, the turned up collars and the hunched shoulders it was impossible to see half of them. If the sun had been shining I'd have got a better look.

But I did recognize Beatrice von Falkenberg. It had to be her – a tall, elegant woman in black mink with a servant holding an umbrella over her from behind. Her eyes and nose were hidden by a widow's veil but I could see a pair of thin lips set in an expression of profound boredom. She was dabbing at her eyes with a tiny white handkerchief but she didn't look too grieved to me. Snape had said that she had been Holland's greatest actress. She wouldn't have won any Oscar for this particular performance.

There was a man standing a short way from her and he caught my attention because he alone carried neither raincoat nor umbrella. He was short and pudgy with silver hair, round glasses in a steel frame and a face like an owl. As the vicar droned on, he shuffled about on his feet, occasionally steadying himself against a gravestone. Like the widow, he didn't look exactly heartbroken. His eyes were fixed on the von Falkenberg memorial but it was easy to see that his mind was miles away.

Who else was there? I recognized a journalist who worked on the local newspaper and who had done a piece on Herbert and me when we'd set up the business. But apart from Snape, Boyle and the widow, the rest of the crowd were strangers to me. The vicar was hurrying through the service now, tripping over the words to get to the end and out of the rain. His surplice was splashed with mud and pages of his Bible were straggling out of the spine. When he scooped holy dirt into the grave, the wind caught it and threw it back in his eyes. He blinked, spat out an amen and ran. Beatrice von Falkenberg turned and went after him. Snape and Boyle hung back. Owl-face jammed his hands into his pockets and sauntered off in the other direction, towards the Brompton Road.

"Very moving. Very touching."

It was a familiar voice and it came from beneath a multicoloured golfing umbrella held by a man who had crept up to stand beside me. I looked round. It was the Fat Man. I should have known that he would be there. "How nice to see you again," he said in a voice that said exactly the opposite.

"Come on," I said to Herbert. I wanted to get back to the flat, out of the rain.

But the Fat Man blocked my way. "Do you like funerals?" he asked. "I'm thinking of arranging one. Yours."

"I'm too young to die," I said. "What brings you here, Fat Man?"

"Von Falkenberg and I were old friends … very dear friends," he explained. "There was something about him that I very much admired..."

"Yeah – his money," I said. "Well, we still haven't found your key. Perhaps you ought to ask Gott or Himmell."

He obviously knew the names. His eyes narrowed and his mouth twitched as if he had just swallowed one of his poisoned corn pellets.

"We are looking for it, Mr Fat Man," Herbert said.

"And we'll let you know as soon as we've found it."

"I gave you two days." The Fat Man plucked the carnation out of his button-hole and threw it into the grave. "You've run out of time." Then he turned his back on us and walked away.

I'd had enough. Coming to the funeral had been a mistake – a dead end in every sense of the word. We hadn't picked up anything apart, perhaps, from double pneumonia. And if it had been a chance to meet a few old friends, they were all old friends I'd have preferred to avoid. Herbert sneezed. "I need a shot of Scotch," he said for the benefit of the undertaker or anyone else who might be listening. I knew that once we got back to the flat, he'd actually fix himself with a shot of cod-liver oil.

But I was wrong there. Things didn't turn out quite the way I expected.

We made a couple of stops on the way back. Herbert had cashed the cheque and we had enough money to lash out on a packet of Alka Seltzer and another box of Maltesers.

"What do you want them for?" Herbert asked.

"I've got a headache," I said.

"No ... the Maltesers."

So I explained. Whoever had snatched Lauren Bacardi might know by now that Johnny Naples had spent the last month of his life traipsing around London with a box of Maltesers. And they might come looking for them. The dwarf's box was still safely hidden underneath the floor. I'd bought the second box as a sort of insurance. I'd leave it somewhere nice and easy to find, just in case anyone else broke in.

We got back to the flat and let ourselves in, dripping on the doormat. Maybe I noticed that the street door was unlocked when it wasn't supposed to be. Maybe I didn't. I don't remember. What with the rain, I was just glad to be in. We went upstairs. Herbert sneezed again. The office door was open and this time I did notice.

"Herbert," I said.

We went into the office. Herbert's eyes must have gone straight to the desk because he went and picked something up. "What's this doing here?" I heard him say.

But I didn't look at him. My eyes were on the corpse stretched out beside the window. It took me a minute before I remembered where I'd seen him before, but I should have known from the moment I saw the chauffeur's uniform. It was Lawrence, the Fat Man's driver.

He was still wearing his one-way glasses, but one of the lenses had become a spider's web of cracks, shattered by the bullet that had gone one-way through it.

"Nick..." Herbert whimpered in a voice of pure jelly.

I looked up. And I saw it all.

"What's this doing here?" Herbert had asked. I replayed the words in my head. "This" was a gun. It had been lying on the carpet beside the desk. Now he was holding it. At that moment, the door opened. Snape and Boyle had followed us in. And there was me kneeling beside another dead man. There was Herbert, again, holding the gun that had just killed him. And there were the two policemen looking at us in open-mouthed astonishment.

"You're..." Snape began.

"No..." Herbert moaned.

"I don't believe it," I said.

CROCODILE TEARS

Herbert and I spent the night back at the Ladbroke Grove police station. I'd never slept behind bars before not that I got a lot of sleep that night either. There was a double bunk in our cell and I took the top level, with Herbert underneath. He'd caught a nasty cold in the cemetery and every time I was about to drift away he'd let loose with a deafening sneeze and I'd be awake again. The bunk wasn't too comfortable either: just a narrow board with an inch-thick mattress, a sheet and two blankets you could have struck a match on. I dropped off around midnight. Then I climbed back on and tried to get some sleep.

"Nick…" It could have been any time when Herbert's disembodied voice floated up out of the darkness.

"Yes?" I said.

"Are you awake?"

"No. I'm sleeptalking."

"Nick, I've been thinking." Herbert paused, sneezed, continued. "Maybe I'm not cut out to be a private detective after all."

"Whatever makes you think that, Herbert?" I asked.

"Well ... I'm wanted for two murders, kidnap and disturbing the peace. The Fat Man wants to kill me. My flat has been torn apart. And I haven't actually been able to detect anything."

"You may have a point," I agreed.

He sighed. "In the morning I'll tell Snape everything. He can have the Maltesers. I wish I'd given them to him in the first place."

That woke me up like a bucket of iced water. Three and a half million pounds in diamonds and he wanted to give them away! I leant over the side of the bunk. It was so dark that I couldn't see a thing but I hoped that I was addressing Herbert's ear rather than his feet. "Herbert," I said. "If you whisper one word about those Maltesers, I will personally kill you."

"But Nick..."

"No, Herbert. Those Maltesers are the only hope you've got."

"But ... uh ... uh..." He sneezed again. "But I might get sent to prison!" he protested.

"Don't worry," I said. "I'll visit you every Friday."

They woke us up at seven in the morning. We were allowed to wash and then a guard brought us each a mug of tea. I asked for a bacon sandwich but all I got was a nasty look. Then it was back into the interrogation room – for Herbert but not for me. Snape stopped me at the door. Boyle was with him, growling softly. That was one guy I wanted to steer clear of. I wouldn't even have trusted Boyle to take my fingerprints. Not if I wanted to keep my fingers.

"You can go, laddy," Snape said. "It's only big brother we want."

"How long are you going to keep him for?" I asked. "It's only five days to Christmas."

"So?"

"He hasn't had time to buy my present yet."

Snape was unimpressed. "We'll keep him as long as it takes," he said. "I'll tell a social worker to visit you – to make sure you're all right."

"I'll visit him!" Boyle grunted.

"No you won't, Boyle!" Snape hissed.

I jerked a thumb at the police assistant. "He needs a social worker more than me," I said.

Boyle lumbered a few steps towards me but then Snape grabbed hold of him. For a minute it was as if I wasn't there.

"You're being ridiculous, Boyle." Snape muttered. "I've told you about those violent videos..."

"I just want to..." Boyle began.

"No! No! No! How many times do I have to tell you. This isn't the right sort of image for a modern metropolitan police force."

"It used to be," Boyle growled.

"In Transylvania," Snape replied. He turned back to me. "Go on, son. Out of here." he said. I glanced at Herbert who sneezed miserably. The door slammed. And suddenly I was alone.

I didn't do much that morning. There wasn't much I could do. As I sat in Herbert's office with my feet up on his desk I tried to work out who might have pulled the plug on the Fat Man's chauffeur and why. By mid-morning I had it more or less figured. It went like this: The Fat Man has given us two days to come up with the goods and we've run out of time so he decides to have a rummage round our flat for himself. He sees us arriving at the Falcon's funeral and that gives him the chance he wants. While he holds us up in the cemetery – there was no other reason for the little chat we had – his faithful chauffeur and housebreaker, Lawrence, is turning the place over. At least, that's what he thinks.

But whoever kidnapped Lauren Bacardi (and my money's still on Gott and Himmell) has been asking her questions. She tells them about the box of Maltesers. So they nip back to pick them up and that's when they find

Lawrence. Maybe there's a fight. Maybe they just didn't like him. Either way, they shoot him just before Herbert and I get back from the funeral. They make a hasty exit through the bathroom window and over the roof. We get left with the body.

Simple as that.

I opened the drawer of Herbert's desk. The box of Maltesers was still there – the fake box that I'd bought myself. The real box was still under the floorboard, covered in dust. I was just about to pull it out and have another look at it when the telephone rang.

"Hello?" It was a woman's voice. Soft, hesitant, perhaps foreign. I figured she must have a wrong number. I didn't know any soft, hesitant, perhaps foreign women. But then she asked, "Tim Diamond?"

"He's not here," I told her. "I'm his partner."

"His partner?"

"Yeah – but right now I'm working solo. How can I help you?"

There was a pause at the other end of the line. Then the lady made up her mind. "Can you come out ... to Hampstead? I need to see you."

"Who is this?"

"Beatrice von Falkenberg."

That made me think. So the black widow had finally come crawling out of the wood-work – or to be more accurate, the telephone exchange. What did she want me for?

"Suppose I'm busy ..." I said.

"I'll make it worth your while."

"You'll pay for the tube fare?"

"Take a taxi."

I agreed so she gave me an address on the West Heath Road and told me to be there by twelve. I wondered if this was another decoy if the moment I was gone somebody else would be elbowing their way into the flat. But so long as the fake Maltesers were in the desk, I reckoned I was covered. I changed my shirt and ran a comb through my hair. When I left, I was still a wreck, but at least I was a slightly tidier wreck. Once the widow discovered I was only thirteen years old, I didn't think she'd really care how I dressed.

I'd charge her for a taxi but I took the tube to Hampstead and then walked. Hampstead, in case you don't know it, is in the north of London in the green belt. For "green", read "money". You don't have to be rich to live in Hampstead. You have to be loaded. It seemed to me that every other car I passed was a Rolls Royce and even the dustbins had burglar alarms. I got directions from a traffic warden and walked round the back of the village. A quarter of an hour later I arrived at the Falcon's lair.

It was a huge place, standing on a hill over

looking the Heath. Whoever said crime doesn't pay should have dropped by for an eyeful. It was the sort of house I'd have dreamed about – only I'd have had to take a mortgage out just to pay for the dream. Ten bedrooms? Eleven? It could have slept fifteen or more under those gabled roofs and with the price of property in that part of town I reckoned forty winks would probably cost you ten quid a wink. And that was just the top floor. Through the windows on the ground floor I could glimpse a kitchen as big as a dining room and a dining room as big as a swimming pool. There was a swimming pool too, running along four windows to the right of the front door. Mind you, the way things were around here, that could have just been the bath.

I reached out and pressed the front door bell. It went *bing-bong*, which was a bit of an anti-climax. After all that had gone before, I'd been expecting a massed choir. The door opened and there was another anti-climax. Beatrice von Falkenberg opened it herself. So what had happened to the butler? She looked at me with disinterest and mild distaste. I could see we were going to get along fine.

"Yes?" she asked.

"I'm Nick," I said. "Nick Diamond. You asked me to come here."

"Did I?" She shrugged. "I was expecting someone older."

"Well... I can come back in twenty years, if you like."

"No, no ... come in."

I followed her in, suddenly feeling like a scruffy kid in bob-a-job week. She was young for a widow; maybe about forty, with black hair clinging to her head like a bathing cap. Her skin was pale, her lips a kiss of dark red. She was wearing some sort of houserobe with a slit all the way up to her waist and she moved like she had never left the stage – not walking but flowing. Everything about her spelt class. The slim, crystal champagne glass in one hand. Even the tin plate with the lumps of raw meat in the other.

"I was about to feed my pet," she explained.

"Dog?" I asked.

She glanced at the plate. "No. I think it's beef."

We'd gone into the room with the swimming-pool. It had been designed so that you could sit around it in bamboo chairs sipping cocktails from the bar at the far end, watching the guests swim. Only there were no bamboo chairs, the bar was empty and I was the only guest. I looked around and suddenly realized that although I was in a millionaire's house, the millions had long gone. There was no furniture. Faded patches on the walls showed where the pictures had once been. The curtain-rails had lost their curtains. Even the potted plants were dead. The house was a shell. All it contained was a widow in a houserobe with a glass of champagne and a tin of raw meat.

"Fido!" she called out. "Come on, darling!"

Something splashed in the water. I swallowed. Apart from the widow in the houserobe with the champagne and the tin of raw meat it seemed that the house also contained an alligator. The last time I saw an alligator it was hanging on some rich woman's arm with lipsticks and purses inside. But this one was no handbag. It was very alive, waddling out of the pool, its ugly black eyes fixed on the plate of meat.

"Don't worry," the widow said. "He's very fond of strangers."

"Yeah – cooked or raw?" I asked.

She smiled and tossed Fido a piece of meat. Its great jaws snapped shut and it made a horrid gulping sound as its throat bulged, sucking the meat down. She held up a second piece. "I want the Maltesers," she said.

"Maltesers?"

She threw the piece of meat but this time she made sure that it fell short so the creature had to stalk forward to get it. It stalked forward towards me. "They belonged to my husband," she went on. "The dwarf stole them, I want them back."

I pointed at the alligator. It was getting too close for comfort. As far as I was concerned, a hundred miles would have been too close for comfort. "Do you have a licence for that thing?" I asked.

"I don't know," she said. "It was a present from my late husband."

"Have you ever thought about pussy cats?"

"Fido ate the pussy cats."

I thought of turning and running but I couldn't be sure I'd make it to the door. The alligator had short, wrinkled legs but at the moment I can't say mine felt much better. It was only a metre or so away. Its black eyes were fixed on me, almost daring me to make a move. The whole thing was crazy. I'd never been threatened with an alligator before.

"I don't have the Maltesers," I said. "Tim has them."

"And where is he?"

"In prison ... Ladbroke Grove police station."

She paused for a long minute and looked at me with cold eyes. The eyes burrowed into me, trying to work out if I was telling the truth. In the end they must have believed me because she laughed and threw the rest of the meat into the swimming-pool. The alligator corkscrewed round and dived after it.

"I like you," she said. "You're not afraid." She walked over to me and put an arm round my shoulders. She hadn't managed to frighten me so now she was trying to charm me. She wouldn't manage that either. Given a choice, I'd have preferred to go out with the alligator.

"When Henry von Falkenberg died," she said, "all his money went with him. This house isn't mine, Nick. I've had to sell the contents just to pay the rent. Even Fido is going to the zoo. It breaks my heart but I can't afford to keep him. And now I don't have a friend in the world." There were tears in her eyes. Crocodile tears, I thought. Or alligator. "There is only one hope for me, Nicholas. The Maltesers. Henry wanted me to have them. They belong to me."

"What's so special about them?" I asked.

"To you – nothing," she replied. "But to me ... They're worth five hundred pounds if you'll get them back for me. That's how much I'll pay you."

"I thought you had no money."

"I'll find it. Maybe Fido will end up as suitcases after all."

She walked me back to the door and opened it.

"Talk to Herbert," she said. "When the police release him, bring the Maltesers here. I will have the money, I swear it. And to you they are useless. You must see that."

"What about my taxi fare home?" I asked.

"When you come with the Maltesers..." She shut the door.

"See you later, alligator," I muttered.

So that was Beatrice von Falkenberg! A strange, lonely woman, sharing her memories with a strange, lonely pet. I walked back down the road towards Hampstead and as I went I turned over two questions in my mind. If the Falcon had been so secretive, how come she had found out about the Maltesers? It seemed unlikely that he had told her. So who had?

The second thing was even stranger. She had telephoned me and asked to speak to Tim Diamond. I hadn't said anything on the subject of my brother. So how had she known that his real name was Herbert?

KILLER IN THE RAIN

I didn't go back to the flat that afternoon. It wouldn't have been the same without Herbert. Quieter, tidier, less dangerous and generally nicer ... but not the same. Also I was worried about him. I wouldn't want to spend half an hour with Snape and Boyle, let alone a whole day. Boyle could have killed him by now. On the other hand, if he told them about the Maltesers, I'd kill him myself. Either way he was in big trouble and the sooner I found out just what was going on, the better it would be for him.

Things might have been different if Lauren Bacardi had been able to tell me where the dwarf had been when he worked out what the Maltesers meant. If I could see what he had seen, maybe I'd be able to work it out too. But I had a nasty feeling that the only way I'd be able to talk to Lauren again would be with a

Ouija board. The people who had snatched her were playing for keeps. By now she probably had more lead in her than a church roof.

That just left the dwarf. Johnny Naples might be pushing up the daisies himself, but if I could pick up his trail I might still learn something. His book matches had led me to Lauren Bacardi. I wondered what else I might find in his room. So that afternoon I took the tube to Notting Hill and walked back down the Portobello Road to the Hotel Splendide.

I passed Hammett's newsagent on the way. The old guy who owned it was standing in the window and he saw me pass. I'm only guessing now but I reckon he must have picked up the telephone and called the hotel a moment later. And at the hotel, Jack Splendide must have made a phone call of his own. Like I say, I'm only guessing. But it took me ten minutes to walk from the newsagent to the hotel and that was just about all the time they needed to arrange my death.

The hotel was just like I remembered it, leaning carelessly against the flyover. The plain-clothes policeman and the dog had gone, of course, but the dustbins were still there, spitting their leftovers into the gutter. It was after three and already it was getting dark, the sun sliding behind the horizon like a drunk behind a bar. An old man carrying two plastic bags full of junk stumbled past, on his way from one nowhere to another. A cold wind scattered the litter across the street. Depressing? Well, it was five days to Christmas and I was pretty depressed myself.

I went into the hotel. Jack Splendide was sitting behind the counter where I'd found him on my first visit. He was reading a dirty paperback. It was so dirty, you couldn't read half the words. It looked like somebody had spilt their breakfast all over it. He was still sucking a cigar-probably the same cigar, and he hadn't changed his shirt either. The last time he'd changed that shirt I probably hadn't been born.

"Hello," I said.

"Yeah?" He really knew how to make a guy feel welcome.

"I want a room."

"How long for?"

"One hour."

He frowned. "We only rent by the night. Fifteen pounds. Sixteen pounds with a bed."

I'd managed to grab all Herbert's cash before we parted company and now I counted out the money on to the counter. Splendide took it, then stood up, reaching for the key.

"I want Room 39," I said.

"Suppose it's taken?"

I gestured at the hooks. "The key's there," I said. "Anyway – who needs it? The room doesn't have a lock."

"This is a class hotel, kid." He was offended. The cigar waggled between his teeth like a finger ticking me off. "You don't like it, you can book in someplace else."

I didn't like it. But I had to go through with it. "Just give me the key," I said.

He argued a bit more after that. I thought he was holding out for more money, but of course he was keeping me waiting on purpose. That was what he had been told to do. In the end he let me have the key – like he'd been intending to all the time. I should have been smart enough to see right through his little act, but it had been a long day and I was tired and ... OK, maybe I wasn't as smart as I thought.

Anyway, he gave me the key and I climbed up the stairs to the fifth floor, then along the corridor to Room 39. It was only when I'd opened the door and gone in that I began to think that maybe this wasn't such a good idea after all. It was unlikely that the room had been cleaned since the dwarf's death – it was unlikely that the rooms at the Hotel Splendide were ever cleaned – but the police would have been through it with a fine-tooth comb. But now that I was here, it wouldn't hurt to have a look. And I had paid.

I began with the drawers. There was a big, asthmatic chest of them. They groaned when I pulled them open and the brass rings rattled. But apart from a bent safety-pin, a mothball and a moth it had killed, they were empty. Next I tried the table. That should have had two more drawers but somebody had stolen them. That just left the bed. I went and sat on it, remembering how Johnny Naples had lain there with that red carnation blossoming in the button-hole of his shirt. He had sat in this room. He had lived in it. He had worked out the location of a three and a half million pound fortune in it. And he had died in it.

The traffic thundered past about two metres away from the window. It was still a mystery how he had ever managed to sleep in it.

My eye was drawn to a dustbin in one corner. It was a green plastic thing, so broken and battered that it should have been in a dustbin itself. I leant across and flicked a hand through the rubbish that lay in the bottom.

There wasn't much: two crisp packets, the wrapper from a bar of chocolate, a couple of dud batteries and an empty packet of cigarettes. I was about to leave it when I remembered. It wouldn't have meant anything to the police – that was why they'd overlooked it – but it meant something to me. Back in the office, the day it had all started, the dwarf had smoked Turkish cigarettes. And this was a Turkish cigarette packet. It had belonged to Naples.

I plucked it out of the dustbin and opened it, hoping … I don't know … for a telephone number scrawled on the inside or something like that. What I got was even better. It was a shower of paper: little white squares that had been neatly torn up. I knelt down and examined the scraps. Some of them had writing on them, parts of words written in blue ink. I slid them across the carpet with a pointed finger, putting the jigsaw back together again. It didn't take me long before I had it: five words in English with what I guessed were the Spanish translations written beside them.

DIGITAL
PHOTODETECTOR
LIGHT EMITTING DIODE

Frankly, they were a disappointment. Why had Johnny Naples written them down? I was certain they had to be connected with the Maltesers. That would explain why, after he'd torn the paper up, he'd taken the extra precaution of hiding them in the cigarette packet. He'd have flushed them down the toilet if the hotel had toilets. It was the Spanish translations that helped me figure it out. Suppose Johnny Naples had come across the five words in his search for the diamonds. His English was good, but it wasn't that good. He might not have understood them. So he'd have written them down to look up later.

The only snag was, I didn't understand them

either. Obviously, they were something to do with science, but science had never been my strong point. If you met my science teacher, I think you'd know why. I don't think science was his strong point either.

I scooped the pieces up and put them in my pocket. I'd searched the drawers, the table and the bin. That just left the bed. I tried to look underneath it but a wooden rim running down to the carpet made that impossible. It was one of the oldest beds I had ever seen, a monster of thick wood and rusty springs with a mattress half a metre thick and about as comfortable as a damp sponge cake. It took all my strength to heave the thing up on its side but I was determined to look underneath. Not that there was much to discover: a yellowed copy of the *Daily Mirror*, one slipper and about ten years' worth of accumulated dust.

But it was the bed that saved my life.

I was just about to pull it down when I heard the window shatter and at the same time a car roared away.

Something dark green and about the size of a cricket ball flew into the room. It took me about one second to work out that it wasn't a dark green cricket ball and another second to throw myself to the ground. The grenade hit the bed and bounced back towards the window. Then it exploded.

I should have been killed but I was already

hugging the floor and there was this great wall of springs and mattress between me and it. Even so it was like being inside a Rainbow Screecher on Guy Fawkes' Night. Suddenly it seemed that the whole room was on fire – not just the room, the very air in the room. The floor buckled upwards like a huge fist, pounding me in the stomach. The explosion was so loud I thought it would crack open my skull. All this happened at once and at the same time I was seized by the shock wave and hurled back, twisting in the air, and finally thrown out of the room, my shoulders slamming into the door and carrying it with me. I was unconscious by the time I hit the floor. I don't know how long I stayed like that. Maybe ten minutes. It could have been ten days.

I woke up with a mouth full of splinters and two hysterical opera singers screaming in my ears. Actually, there weren't any opera singers, but that's what it sounded like. My clothes were torn to ribbons and I could feel the blood running from a cut above one eye. Other than that, I seemed to be in remarkably good health for someone who had just been blown up. There would be plenty of bruises, but there were no broken bones. I stood up – one bone at a time – and leant against a wall for support. The wall slid away. There was too much dust and smoke in the air to see. I stood where I was, waiting for things to settle down a bit before I made any sudden move.

Which was just as well. The Hotel Splendide had been waiting for an excuse to fall down for twenty years or more. The grenade had been all it needed. The whole of the back wall, the one that faced the flyover, had simply collapsed and I was now standing on a piece of floor that stretched into thin air. I shivered as the breeze whipped the smoke up around me. The traffic roared past, a blur of brightlycoloured metal whirling endlessly into the night. I was surprised that nobody had stopped ... but how could they? It was a flyover. Doubtless the police would shut it down soon enough but anyone stopping right now would only add a multiple pile-up to the evening's entertainment.

I stepped back, looking for the staircase or whatever might be left of it. This looked like being the hotel's last night. It was on fire, the flames spreading rapidly, the wood snapping, water hissing out of broken pipes. My hearing still wasn't back to normal but I could just about make out the sound of people shouting. In the distance, police cars or fire engines or something with sirens were drawing nearer. A naked man ran past, his face half-covered in shaving foam. I followed him. We'd both had a close shave that day.

My guardian angel must have been working overtime just then. Lucky it didn't belong to a trade union. The iron bar narrowly missed my head and didn't even notice it until it smashed into the wall, spraying me with plaster. I wheeled round and there was Jack Splendide, lifting the bar to try his luck again. His shirt was in shreds and his stomach wasn't a whole lot better. Both his trouser legs had been blown off at the knee. I realized he must have been close to the dwarf's room when the explosion happened – perhaps in the room next door. And he didn't seem too happy that I'd survived.

He swung the bar again and this time I dodged. He was about twenty kilograms overweight and that made him slow. On the other hand, he didn't need to be too fast. He was between me and the staircase. I had the flames on one side of me and a five-storey fall right behind me. I wondered if I could jump across on to the flyover. It was only about two metres, but the way I was feeling right now it was about a metre too far. I leapt back, avoiding a fourth blow. Now I was in the ruins of what had been Room 39. The flames were getting nearer. So was Jack Splendide.

He was shouting at me. What with all the din and the screaming in my ears, it was difficult to make out what he was saying but I gathered that he blamed me for the destruction of his hotel. He must have really liked that place. There were tears running down his cheeks and he was holding that iron bar (part of a towel-rail) with genuine affection. I wanted to explain that it wasn't my fault that a passing motorist had decided to hurl a bomb at me, but he wouldn't listen to reason. Jack Splendide had flipped. And he wanted me dead.

The iron bar came curving up over his shoulder as he swung it with both hands, but then the top got snarled up in a loop of wire. As it came down, it tore the wire out of the wall and for a few seconds electric sparks danced in the air. That distracted him just long enough for me to grab hold of a piece of table and bring it crashing into his stomach. He howled and dropped the bar. I hit him again, this time propelling him forward right to the edge of the floor.

He flailed at the air with his hands. There was a fall of at least fifteen metres to the cold, hard concrete below and I thought that was just where he was heading. Unable to regain his balance, he yelled and plunged forward, his body lunging out into the night. But at the last moment he managed to grab hold of the very edge of the fly-over. And that was how he finished up: a human bridge. His feet were on the floor in what was left of Room 39. His hands were desperately clutching a piece of metal jutting out of the side of the flyover. His body sagged between the two.

I looked behind me. The flames were closing in. I wouldn't even make it through the shattered doorway now. But I didn't fancy jumping across to the flyover. Jack Splendide was the only answer. A human bridge. I took two big steps. One foot in the small of his back and I was across – safely standing on the edge of the road.

"Kid … hey kid!" I heard him and walked back over to him. He was a big, strong man but he couldn't stay like that much longer. "Help me!" he hissed, the sweat dripping off his forehead. The wind jerked at my shirt. The cars roared by, only inches away now. Some of the drivers hooted at me but they couldn't see Jack Splendide. I crouched down close to him. By now I'd been able to put a few things together.

"Who was it, Splendide?" I asked. "Who threw the grenade?"

"Please!" His hands tightened their hold as his body swayed.

"You must have told them I was here. Who was it?"

There was no way he could stall me. He was getting weaker by the minute and across the gap the flames were creeping up on him. He could probably feel them with the soles of his feet. "It was the Fat Man," he gasped. "He guessed you might go back to the hotel. He paid me … to call if you did."

"Why?"

"You insulted him, kid. Nobody insults the Fat Man. But I didn't know he was going to try and kill you. I mean … the grenade. Honest, kid. I thought he was just going to take a shot at you – to scare you."

Yeah, I thought. And you came up to the fifth floor to watch.

"Help me!" he whimpered. "Give me a hand up, kid. I can't hold on much longer."

"That's true," I said, straightening up.

"You can't leave me here, kid. You can't!"

"Wanna bet?"

I walked away, leaving him stretched out between the flames and the flyover with a long, long way to fall if he let go. Maybe the police or firemen reached him in the end. To be honest, I don't really care. Jack Splendide had set me up to be killed. He might not have been expecting a grenade, but he'd known the Fat Man didn't play games.

It had begun to rain. Pulling the remains of my shirt closer to my shivering skin, I walked down the flyover and forgot about him.

THE PROFESSOR

I was woken by the smell of lavender. Lavender? Yes – perfume. You've smelt it before, Nick. Where? I can't remember but maybe it was mixed with the raw meat and ... I swallowed, stretched, opened my eyes.

"Blimey, you're a sight!" Betty Charlady exclaimed.

I was half stretched out on Herbert's desk in his office. I'd had to walk home the night before and by the time I'd got in I'd been too tired to go upstairs. I'd looked at the second flight of steps. They led to a bed with a crumpled sheet and a screwed up quilt. I'll never make it, I'd thought and so I'd gone into the office and collapsed there. And now Betty Charlady was standing in front of me, looking at me like I'd dropped in from another planet.

"What happened to you?" she demanded, shaking her head and sending the artificial daisies on her hat into convulsions.

"I had a bad night," I said. "How did you get in?"

"Through the door."

"It was open?"

She nodded. "You ought to lock it at night, Master Nicholas. You never know who might visit..."

I needed a hot bath, a hot meal, two Disprin and a warm bed – not necessarily in that order. Instead I went up and washed my face in the sink while Betty made breakfast: boiled eggs, toast and coffee. I looked at myself in the mirror. Somebody else looked back. His hair was a mess, there were bags under his eyes and he had a nasty cut on his forehead. I felt sorry for the guy. If he felt as bad as he looked he must be in pretty rotten shape. I wondered if he felt as rotten as me.

Ten minutes later, I was sitting down in the kitchen, eating. Betty had insisted on cutting my toast into soldiers which was pretty embarrassing. I'd been threatened, blown up, attacked – and here I was being treated like a kid again. But I suppose she meant well.

"Where's Mr Timothy?" she asked.

"Herbert?" I said. "He's in jail. Accused of murder."

"Murder!" she shrieked. "That's a crime!"

"Well ... yes."

"No. I mean accusing Mr Herbert of doing

anything like that." She sniffed. "Anybody could see he wouldn't hurt a fly."

She was right there. Herbert ran away from them. He was probably the only private detective in the country who was even scared of goldfish.

"So you're doing all the detective work for him," she said. I nodded. "Have you found out anything yet?"

Had I found anything out? Well, I'd found out that Beatrice von Falkenberg had a strange taste in pets. I'd found out that if you stood too close to an exploding grenade it made your ears hurt. I'd found out that the Fat Man still wanted to lose weight and that I was the weight he wanted to lose. But when you added up everything I'd found out, it would just about fit on the back of a postage stamp and you wouldn't even need to write in small letters.

"No, Betty," I said. "I haven't found out anything. Not unless you know what a digital detector or a photo lighter is."

"A wot?" she asked.

The scraps of paper that I had found in the dwarf's room were still safely in my shirt pocket. The trouble was, my shirt pocket was still in the hotel. It had been blown off the shirt by the blast and for the life of me I couldn't remember exactly what the words had been.

"I'm going to have a bath," I said.

"I'll run it for you," Betty volunteered.

I shook my head. Any more encouragement and she'd be offering to scrub my back. "No, thanks ... you go home. I can manage."

"But what about the cleaning?"

I reached into my pocket and pulled out one of Herbert's ten-pound notes. It hurt me to see it go, but there was no denying that Betty had done a good job. When she'd come, the flat had looked like a junk-yard. Now it was more like an industrial slum. "Here you are," I said. "Come back next week, after Christmas."

"Ooh! Ta!" She took it. "Happy Christmas, Master Nicholas," she burbled.

"Happy Christmas, Betty," I said.

Some time later, the doorbell dragged me out of a beautiful sleep. I looked at my watch. It said five to ten. It had said five to ten when I'd gone to bed. Either it had been a short sleep or I needed a new watch. I held it up to my ear and shook it. There was a dull *ping* and the second hand fell off. Well, that's what comes of buying a second-hand watch.

I pulled on a pair of jeans and a sweater and made my way downstairs. The bell was still ringing. Whoever was down there was leaning on the button. I pressed the intercom to let him in, hoping he wouldn't do the same to me. I don't like being leaned on and in the last few days I'd had more than enough of it. I went into the office and had just sat down when my client walked in.

Correction – he didn't walk, he staggered. And I smelt him before I saw him. It must have been around lunchtime but he'd been drinking since breakfast and he'd brought the stale reek of whisky as his visiting-card.

I recognized him from somewhere. He was around sixty, small, fat, unshaven, owlish, with round glasses, dressed in a crumpled grey raincoat with bottle-sized pockets.

He fumbled his way towards one of the chairs that Betty Charlady had repaired for us and sat down heavily, stretching out his legs. He was wearing green socks. I could see them through the holes in the soles of his shoes. I waited for him to say something but he wasn't in a hurry. He pulled a single cigarette out of his pocket, straightened it between his thumb and forefinger and twisted it into his mouth. He lit it with a trembling hand. The match had almost burned itself out before he found the end of the cigarette. He wasn't just a drunk. He was a short-sighted drunk. Suddenly I remembered where I'd seen him. He'd been at the Falcon's funeral, standing – swaying – next to Beatrice von Falkenberg.

"It's good to sit down," he said.

"You tired?" I asked.

"No. It's just that I keep falling over when I stand up. Or bumping into things." He sucked in smoke. "You see, sir, I got this problem..."

"Drink?" I muttered sympathetically.

"Thanks. I'll have a large Scotch."

I shook my head and slid an ash-tray towards him. He flicked the cigarette and scattered ash across the top of the desk. "Who are you?" I asked.

"The name's Quisling," he said. "Quentin Quisling."

"Your parents liked q's," I said.

"Yeah – bus queues, shopping queues ... but that's not why I'm here. You may have heard of me, sir. I used to be called the Professor."

Sure I'd heard of the Professor. That had been another of the names on Snape's blackboard. What had Snape told me? The Professor had been the Falcon's tame scientist, something of a whizz-kid. But a year ago he'd gone missing. Looking at him now, I could see where he'd been. On the skids. Professor Quisling might have been smart once but now he looked like Billy Bunter grown old and sick. He had the skin of a five-year-old cheese and he spoke with a wheezy, grating voice. He puffed smoke into the air and coughed. Cigarettes were killing him while booze was arranging the funeral.

"I wanted to see your brother," he said.

"He's not here."

"I can see that, sir. I don't see much. But I can see that." He pulled a half-bottle of whisky out of his pocket, unscrewed it, squinted and tilted it towards his throat. The liquid ran down the side of his neck. He groped for the cigarette and found it. "All right," he said. "I'll split it with you. Fifty-fifty."

"The cigarette?" I asked.

"That's very funny, sir. I can see you have a sense of humour." He screwed the cigarette between his lips and coughed. It was a horrible cough. I could hear the marbles rattling in his lungs. "You know who I am?" he asked.

"You just told me."

"I used to be the Falcon's brains." He stabbed at his chest with a bent thumb. "He wanted something fixed, I fixed it."

"Light bulbs?" I asked.

"Oh no, sir. I invented things for him. Things you wouldn't understand."

"So what happened to you?" I asked.

"This happened to me." He waved the bottle. "But I know what you've got, sir. Indeed I do. I saw you at the funeral and I figured it out. A packet of Maltesers, would it be? Well ... I know what to do with them. Together we could make money."

"What are you suggesting, Professor?" I said.

"You give them to me and you wait here." He smiled at me with crooked, sly eyes. "I'll come back tomorrow with half the money."

I nodded, pretending to consider the offer. In fact I was amazed. Here was a guy who was killing himself as sure as if he had a noose around his neck. He couldn't afford a decent pair of shoes and he was dressed like a dummy in an Oxfam shop. But he thought he could pull a fast one on me just because I was a kid and he was a so-called adult. For a moment he reminded me of my maths teacher. You know the sort. Just because they can work out the angles in an isosceles triangle, they think they rule the world. I decided to play him along.

"I give you the Maltesers," I said. "And you come back with half the loot?"

"That's right, sir," Quisling said. He finished the half-bottle and lobbed it towards the dustbin. It missed and smashed against the wall. He didn't seem to notice.

"But what do the Maltesers do?" I asked.

"They open the..." He stopped himself just in time. "I'll tell you when I bring the money," he said.

I knew that once I'd given him the Maltesers I'd never see him again. But I'd had an idea. I pulled open the drawer of the desk and took out the box that I'd hidden there a few days before. "This is what you want," I said. He reached forward hungrily but I didn't let go. "You will come back?" I queried.

"Sure, sir. I'll come back. On my mother's grave."

The old girl probably wasn't even dead. "When?" I asked.

"Tomorrow morning," he said.

I lifted my hand and he snatched the box away.

"In the morning," he repeated.

The door slammed shut behind him.

I waited thirty seconds before I followed him. He wouldn't see me behind him. With his eyesight he wouldn't see me if I stood next to him. And if Quentin Quisling really did know where the Falcon's diamonds were hidden, he would lead me to them. The box of Maltesers I'd given him would, of course, be useless. But perhaps I'd let him keep them – after he'd led me to the end of the rainbow. That was the way I'd planned it but of course that was far too easy, and when nothing can go wrong that's when everything always does. I'd reached the front door. I'd turned round to lock it behind me. I could hear an engine turning – a van parked close by. There was a movement in the street. I glanced up just in time to see something short and unpleasant come thudding down. It hit me behind the ear. I was out like a light.

FAIRY CAKES

I wish somebody had told me it was Knock Out Nick Diamond Week in London. It had happened to me twice in two days and I was getting a bit tired of it. Being knocked out isn't so bad. It's waking up that's the real problem. Your head hurts, your mouth is dry and you feel sick. And if it's pitch dark and you're locked up in the back of a van that could be going anywhere, it's pretty scary too.

I was still in London. I could tell from the sound of the traffic and from the number of times we stopped. Once – when we were at a traffic light or something – I heard vague voices outside and thought of hammering on the side of the van. But it probably wouldn't have done any good and anyway, by the time I'd made up my mind, the van had moved off. A few minutes later, we stopped. The door was pulled open. There wasn't a lot of light left in the day but what there was of it streamed in and punched me in the eyes.

"Get out," a voice said. It was a soft voice, the sort of voice you'd expect to float on the scent of violets. It had a slight German twang. I'd heard that voice once before.

I got out.

The first thing I saw was a road sign. It read: Bayly Street SEl which put me somewhere on the south bank of the river, opposite the City. I looked around me. This was warehouse territory. The old brick buildings rose up five storeys high on both sides of the road, the narrow gap of sky in between criss-crossed by corrugated iron walkways, hooks and chains, pipes and loading platforms. A hundred years ago, Bayly Street would have been on its feet. Twisted coke cans, broken slates and yards of multicoloured cables spilled out of the deserted buildings like entrails. The street was pitted with puddles that seemed to be eating their way into the carcass.

Another sign caught my eye, bright red letters on white: McAlpine. It was a death warrant in one word for Bayly Street. There's nothing more destructive than a construction company. They'd gut the warehouses and build fancy apartments in the shell. Each one would have a river view, a quarry-tiled garage and a five-figure price tag. That's the trouble with London. The rich have got it all.

There was a man standing beside the van, holding a silenced gun which he was pointing in my direction. He might have been a gangster, but he went to a smart tailor. He was dressed in a pale grey suit with a pink tie. His shoes were as brightly polished as his smile. A moment later, the driver's door opened and a second man got out. He was dressed identically to the first, except that his tie was a powder blue. They were both short and thin and both wore their hair parted down the middle – one dark, one blond. They were both approaching fifty and had spent a lot of money trying to back away again. Their slightly plastic faces had to be the work of a slight plastic surgeon. Know what I mean? Cut out the fat, take up the wrinkles, re-tone the flesh, thank you sir, and make sure you don't sneeze too violently. I had a feeling the two men were fond of each other.

"This way," Blondie said, gesturing with the gun.

"After you," I replied.

"I don't think so."

There had to be men at work on a construction site nearby. I could hear them now, their hydraulic drills jabbering away in the distance, the mechanical grabbers churning up the mud. I thought of making a break for it. But there was no chance. There was nobody in sight and they'd have shot me down before

I'd gone five metres. The driver had walked across to a heavy wooden door and unlocked a padlock the size of a soupplate. It led into a room like an abandoned garage: bare concrete floor, burnt-out walls, junk everywhere. For a nasty minute I thought that this was it and that I was about to reach the last full-stop, but there was a staircase in one corner and Blondie steered me towards it. We went up five flights. Each floor was the same – derelict and decaying. But then we came to another door and another padlock. The fifth floor was different.

It was open-plan and about as big as a tennis-court, only it would be difficult to have a game – not with a grand piano parked in the middle. It had a large, wide window – more like a French door really – reaching from floor to ceiling, but being five storeys up it didn't lead anywhere. The room was furnished with a grey carpet, grey silk curtains and a silvery three-piece suite arranged around a white marble table. There was an open-plan kitchen with a tray loaded with cups and plates for tea.

The dark-haired man went into the kitchen while Blondie waved me over to the sofa.

"And who are you?" I asked, although I already had a good idea.

"I'm William," Blondie said. "And that's Eric." He gestured.

"Gott and Himmell," I muttered. The two German schoolboys from Eton. That gave me a complete score on Snape's blackboard.

"We thought it was time we invited you to tea," Gott went on. "I do hope you like fairy cakes."

The kettle boiled. Himmell filled the pot and brought the tray over to the table. "Who's going to be mother?" I asked. They both raised their eyebrows at that. I couldn't believe it. These were meant to be the Falcon's two right-hand men but they looked about as dangerous as my two maiden aunts. But then I remembered the way they'd brought me here and the fact that there were two dead bodies to be accounted for. They might look like a joke. But they could still make you die laughing.

Himmell poured the tea into china cups decorated with roses interlaced with swastikas, and then handed round the fairy cakes. I didn't feel like eating but it looked like he'd made them himself and I didn't want to hurt his feelings.

"Who plays the piano?" I asked. Polite conversation seemed like a good idea.

"We both do," Gott said. "But now, my friend, it's your turn to sing." Himmell laughed at that. I didn't. I've found funnier lines in a Latin dictionary. "You have something we want," Gott went on. "Let me explain, Nicholas ... if I may call you Nicholas? A charming name."

I bit into the fairy cake. It tasted like Fairy Liquid.

"We were following the dwarf the day he visited you and your brother. We didn't know then what he was carrying. We searched your apartment that evening but we found nothing. Then we ran into Miss Bacardi."

"Is she here?" I asked.

"You'll see her soon enough. She told us about the Maltesers. Most ... unusual. So we went back to your flat for a second time. That was the day of the Falcon's funeral. We were certain that we would find the Maltesers then. But after we'd broken in, we were surprised. Who was the man waiting for us?"

"His name was Lawrence," I said. "He was the chauffeur of the Fat Man. He was after the Maltesers too."

"It was unfortunate for him." Gott sighed. "He said some very hurtful things. So Eric hurt him. In fact, he killed him. I have to tell you, Nicholas. Eric is a lovely person. Lovely. But he gets moody sometimes. And when he's moody, he shoots people."

I smiled at Himmell. "Nice fairy cakes," I said.

"We still want the Maltesers," Gott said. "We know your brother is in prison. And we know you know where they are. So either you tell us now or..."

"Or what, Gott?" I asked.

"It would be a terrible shame," he replied. "You're a very nice boy. Really very sweet. How old are you?"

"Thirteen."

"Yes – far too young to end up in a plastic bag with six bullets in your chest. Would you like some more tea?"

Himmell filled my cup. He didn't seem to have quite such a good grasp of the English language as his friend. They were still both smiling at me with their plastic smiles and I wondered if, after the face-lifts, they were capable of anything else. Gott finished his tea and smacked his lips.

"Thank you," he said. "You do make a lovely cup, Eric."

"Anudder cup?"

"*Nein danke.*" He turned to me. "So where are they?"

I'd been thinking. I'd have been happy to tell them if I thought it would get me out of there. But somehow I didn't believe it. Once they'd got what they wanted, they wouldn't need me and I'd be in that plastic bag like a shot. And I mean shot. I had to buy time. Given a bit of time, maybe I could find my way out of this jam.

I coughed. "Well, it's a bit tricky…" Himmell's face fell. He was still smiling, but I reckon his nose and chin must have sunk a good centimetre or two. "I mean, I do have them. They're at Victoria Station. In a left luggage locker. But Herbert has the key."

"The number?"

"Um ... one hundred and eighty!" I'd been making it up as I went along and I sang out that number like a darts commentator on finals night.

"At Victoria Station?"

"Yes. But you can't open it."

He lifted the gun. "I think we can."

Gott got to his feet and strolled over to the piano. Then he sat down on the stool and rubbed his hands over the keys. I stood up. "Thanks for the tea," I said. "If that's all you wanted to know..."

"You're not going anywhere." Gott played a chord. "Eric!"

Himmell had a few cords of his own. I don't know where he'd got the rope from but there was nothing I could do. While Gott played a tune on the piano, Himmell tied me up. He did it very professionally. My hands went behind my back where they were introduced to my feet. By the time he'd finished, I couldn't even twitch in time to the music and I could feel my fingers and toes going blue as the blood was cut off. Gott finished his little recital and stood up.

"Well, Nicholas," he said. "We're going to Victoria Station." He looked at his watch. "We'll be back around five. And if you've been lying, we'll bury you around five thirty."

I tried to shrug. I couldn't even manage that with all the ropes. "If this is what they teach you at public school," I said, "I'm glad I went comprehensive."

"Take him into the back room," Gott snapped. "It's time he met our other guest."

Himmell picked me up and carried me across the room. I'm not heavy but he was still stronger than I thought. There was a door at the far end, beyond the piano. He drew back a metal bolt with one hand and opened it.

"When are you going to let me out of here?" a voice demanded. A voice I knew.

Himmell threw me down on the floor. I found myself sitting opposite Lauren Bacardi. She was tied up just like me.

"Company for you," Gott said.

He closed the door and locked it behind him. A minute later I heard the two Germans leave for Victoria Station. I wondered what they'd find in Locker 180. I wondered if there even was a Locker 180. I just knew that I had until five to get out of here. I'd bought myself time OK. But I didn't fancy paying the price.

With an effort, I tried to put them out of my mind. I looked round at Lauren. "Hi," I said. "I know you," she said.

"Yeah. Nick Diamond. We met at the Casablanca Club – the night they came for you."

She nodded. "I remember. Thanks a bunch, Nick. I was enjoying my life until you came along."

She was still dressed in the glitzy clothes she had worn for her singing act but the fake jewellery was gone and she had washed off some of the make-up. She looked better without it. She was sitting in the corner with her knees drawn up, a plate and a mug on the floor beside her. There was no furniture in the room, which was about as big as a large store cupboard. It was lit by a single small window which would have been too high up to reach even if we hadn't been tied up. I gave a cautious tug at the ropes. In the movies, there would have been a piece of broken glass or something for me to cut them with. But it looked like I was in the wrong movie.

I gave up. "I'm sorry about this," I said. "But I didn't lead them to you."

"No? Then who did?"

It was a good question. How had they found out about her? "You told them about the Maltesers?" I said.

She sniffed. "Why else do you think I'm still alive?"

"Enjoy it while you can," I said. "They're going to be back at five and they're not going to be very happy. I strung them a line out there. When they get back, I reckon they're going to want to string me up with one."

"Then we'd better move."

"Sure. If I can just get across to you, maybe you can get at my ropes with your teeth and..."

I stopped. Lauren Bacardi had wriggled. That was all she had done but now the ropes were falling away from her like over-cooked spaghetti. It was incredible. I tried it myself. But while she got to her feet, unhooking the last loop from her wrist, I stayed exactly where I was.

"That's a real trick," I said. "How did you do it?"

"Before I became a singer I worked in cabaret," she told me. "I was the assistant to an escapologist ... Harry Blondini. I spent two and a half years being tied up. Harry loved ropes. He used to wear handcuffs in bed and he was the only guy I ever knew who took his showers hanging upside-down in a straitjacket. He taught me everything he knew."

By now she was kneeling beside me, pulling the knots undone. "Why didn't you escape before?" I asked.

"There was no point. The door's barred from the outside. There's nothing I can do about that. And even if I could reach the window, it's too small for me to get through."

Too small for her, but when she gave me a leg-up about fifteen minutes later, I found I could just squeeze through. Gott and Himmell hadn't bothered to lock it. Why should they have? They'd left me tied up and anyway, it didn't lead anywhere. It was five storeys up and just too far below the roof for me to be able to scramble up there. I paused for a moment on the window ledge, my legs dangling inside, my head and shoulders in the cold evening air. I could see men working on a construction site in the distance and I shouted, trying to attract their attention. But they were too far away and anyway, there was too much noise.

I looked down. It made my stomach heave a little. The pavement was a long, long way below. I could see the French windows that led back into the main living-room about three metres away. If I could break in through them, I could open the door and let Lauren out and at least we'd be on the way to safety. But the windows were too far away and although they had a narrow ledge of their own, there was no way I could reach it. Unless...

This was a warehouse and like all the other warehouses it had a hook on a metal arm jutting out of the wall – in this case exactly halfway between the two windows and about a metre above them. In the old days it would have been used to hoist goods up from the street on a rope. The rope was gone, of course. But rope was at least one thing we had in plenty.

I squeezed myself back into the room.

"No way out – eh?" Lauren muttered.

"There might be." I explained what I had in mind.

"You're crazy," she said. "You can't do it."

"I've got to do it," I said. "Better crazy than dead."

Ten minutes later I was half-in and half-out again, but this time with a length of rope around my waist. We'd taken the rope that Himmell had used to tie us up and knotted it into a single length. There was a good four metres of it. I held the slack in my hand and now I began to swing it a bit like a lasso. Then I threw it, holding on to the end. The loop flew out towards the hook, missed and fell. I pulled it in and tried again. I hooked it on the fourth attempt.

So there I am, five storeys up, leaning out of a window. There's a rope leading from me to a hook and then back again and I tie the end around my waist too. Remember that isosceles triangle I mentioned? Well, it's a bit like that. The two windows are the lower corners. The hook is the point at the top. All I have to do is jump and the rope will swing me across like a pendulum from one side to the other. At least that's the general idea.

I didn't much like it. In fact I hated it. But I was running out of time and there didn't seem to be any other way.

I jumped.

For a giddy second I swung in the air, one shoulder scraping across the brickwork. But then my scrabbling hands somehow managed to grab hold of the edge of the French windows. I pulled, dangling in mid-air, supported only by the rope, my legs kicking at nothing. I pulled with all my strength. And then I was crouching on the ledge, trying hard not to look down, my heart beating in my chest like it would rather be someplace else.

I stayed where I was until I'd got my breath back, afraid of falling back into space. The ledge could only have been twenty centimetres wide and my whole body was pressed against the window panes. Without looking back into the street, I reached down and pulled off my shoe. Slowly I lifted it up. It was cold out there, but the sweat was running down inside my shirt. My eyes were fixed on the grand piano on the other side of the window. Somehow looking at it made me forget where I was and what I was doing. I held the shoe firmly in one hand, then brought it swinging forward. The heel hit the window, smashing it. I dropped the shoe into the room then, avoiding the jagged edges of broken glass, slipped my hand through, found the lock, turned it. The window opened. With a sigh of relief I eased my way inside, then untied the rope and pulled it in after me.

I hadn't got very far, but at least I was still alive.

Gott and Himmell had left the tea things out. I put my shoe back on and took a swig of milk out of the jug. Then I went over to the door and drew back the bolt.

Lauren raised an eyebrow when she saw me. "So you made it?" she said.

"Yeah," I said. I would have said more but for some reason my teeth were chattering at about one hundred and fifty miles per hour. It must have been even colder out there than I'd thought.

Lauren tried the door that led to the stair case. It was locked. Then she strolled across to the broken window and looked out.

"That's great, Nick," she drawled. "We're out of the cupboard but we can't get out of the room. There's nobody near enough to hear us shouting for help. You've sent our German friends on a wild goose chase and when they get back they're going to string you up and use you for target practice. We don't have enough rope to climb down with and we don't have any guns."

"That's about it," I agreed.

"Then you'd better think up something fast, kid." She pointed out of the window. "Because here they're coming now."

THE LAST CHORD

I ran back over to the window. Lauren was right. The blue van was at the end of Bayly Street. It would have reached us already if a lorry hadn't backed out of the construction site, blocking its path. Now it was stuck there while some guy in a yellow hat tried to direct the driver. Fortunately it was a tricky manoeuvre. They'd be stuck there for maybe another couple of minutes. How had they got back from Victoria so quickly? I played back what had happened in my mind and realized that my great escape had probably taken about an hour. It's amazing how time flies when you're enjoying yourself.

Lauren was in the kitchen, rummaging through the drawers. "What are you doing?" I asked.

"I'm looking for a knife." She held up an egg-whisk.

"This is all I can find."

"They've got guns," I reminded her. "You're not going to get very far with an egg-whisk."

"I know. I know." She threw it over her shoulder. "So what are we going to do?"

What were we going to do? If we yelled for help, the only people who would hear us would be Gott and Himmell. The noise from the construction site would see to that. Even if we found a knife, it would be no defence against automatic pistols. There was no way out and any minute now they'd be coming in. I looked out of the window. The lorry seemed to be pinned at an angle across the road. The man in the yellow hat was frantically giving directions, swatting at invisible flies. I heard the lorry grind into gear. It began to edge back wards. Soon the road would clear and the blue van would come. It would come right underneath the window. I tried to remember where it had stopped when they brought me here. That time they'd parked in front of the door. Would they park there again? Perhaps.

"Lauren," I said.

"Yes?" She'd found a corkscrew and a dessert spoon.

"Quickly..."

The window that I'd broken in through was, like I said, a French window. It came all the way down to the floor. I looked out again. The lorry had almost completed its turn. The man in the yellow hat was walking away, his job done.

"The piano," I said.

"The piano?"

"Come on!"

"Nick – this is no time for a concert."

"That's not what I have in mind."

I got my shoulder down to the piano and began to push. It was on castors which helped, but even so it must have weighed a ton. It was a Bechstein, a great chunk of black wood with a gleaming white ivory smile. God knows how much it had cost but if this is what you needed to be a pianist, it made a good argument for taking up the triangle. Lauren had twigged what I was doing and now she stood there, staring.

"Honey," she said. "You can't be serious."

"Deadly serious," I said.

"Deadly," she agreed.

She came over and joined me. With the two of us pushing, the piano moved more easily. Inch by inch we drew closer to the open window. It was going to be a close fit but the piano would just about slide through the frame. It occurred to me that that was probably how they'd got it in here in the first place. How long had it taken them to hoist it up? The return journey was certainly going to be a hell of a lot faster.

"Are you ready?" I asked.

"Yes."

I gazed over the top of the piano. The lorry was in the clear now, rumbling quickly away. The blue van slid forward towards us. I flexed myself. There was a bust of Beethoven or someone on the piano. He was frowning as if he knew what was about to happen. The blue van drew closer, slowing down as it prepared to park.

We pushed with all our strength. The piano shot forward. Its back leg went over the ledge and with a hollow jangle it teetered on the brink, the pedals digging into the carpet. The van was almost level with us now. I pushed again. The piano resisted. Then, with a wave of relief, I felt it topple over backwards. I can tell you now, Bechstein grand pianos are not built with any consideration for aerodynamics. It must have been a bizarre sight as it plummetted through the air: a huge black beast with three rigid legs and no wings. It flew for all of two seconds. Then it crashed fair and square into the van.

It was the Bechstein's last chord, but it was a memorable one. If you imagine someone blowing up an orchestra in the middle of Beethoven's Fifth, you'll get the general idea. It was an explosion of music – or a musical explosion. A zing, a boom and a twang all rolled into one and amplified a hundred times.

They heard it at the construction site. I doubt if there was anywhere in London that they didn't hear it.

It was the Bechstein's last chord and I some how doubted that the van would be doing much more travelling either. It hadn't been completely crushed but it must have been disappointed. Steam was hissing out of the radiator and two of the tyres were spinning away like giant coins. Black oil formed a sticky puddle around the wreckage. The exhaust pipe had shot away like a rocket and was lying about forty metres down the road. The whole twisted carcass of the van was covered in splinters of wood and wires. One of the piano's legs had shattered the front window. I didn't like to think what it had done to the driver.

"Quite a performance, honey," Lauren said.

"Concerto for piano and van," I muttered. And now people did come running. Suddenly it was as if Bayly Street had become Piccadilly Circus. They came from the construction site, from left, from right, from just about everywhere. They looked at the carnage. Then they looked up. I leant out of the window and waved.

It was about twenty minutes later that one of the construction workers appeared in the Germans' living-room. He was carrying a pair of industrial pliers which he must have used to cut through the two padlocks. Lauren and I were sitting on the sofa waiting for him.

"The piano..." He gaped at us. "Was it yours?"

"Sure," I said. "But don't worry. I wasn't much good at it anyway."

We walked out of the room leaving him standing there. Well, what was he expecting? An encore?

We managed to slip away in the crowd, but not before I'd heard that – miraculously – nobody had been killed.

Apparently the driver of the v.an would have to be cut away from the steering wheel while the passenger had managed to impale himself on the gear-stick. A doctor had already arrived but Gott and Himmell were more in need of a mechanic. We got a taxi back to the office where I picked up the real Maltesers and then we went straight on to Lauren's place. There were too many people looking for me in Fulham. From now on I'd have to keep my head down and my raincoat collar up. She lived in a mansion block in Baron's Court – about a ten-minute drive away. It was one of those great brick piles with fifty doorbells beside the front door and fifty people who don't know each other inside. She had a basement flat which must have been all of ten centimetres above the main Piccadilly tube line. Every time a train went past the floor rumbled. Or maybe it was my stomach. I hadn't had a decent meal in twenty-four hours and I was hungry.

She left me in the living-room while she went into the kitchen to fix supper. It was a cosy room in a theatrical sort of way, with a gas fire hissing in the grate, a kettle on the floor and odd bits of clothes thrown just about everywhere. The furniture was old and tired, with a sofa that looked like it was waiting to swallow you up whole.

The walls were plastered with posters from theatres and music halls where Lauren had appeared, either as a singer or as an escapologist's assistant. It was a room with a past but no future. A room of rising damp and fading memories.

When she came back in she had changed into some sort of dressing-gown and had brushed her hair back. For a woman old enough to be my grandmother she looked good. But then you should see my grandmother. The food she was carrying looked even better. She had it on a tray: omelettes, salad, cheese, fruit, a bottle of red wine for her and Coke for me. We didn't say much while we ate. We were just glad to be there. Glad to be alive.

"Thanks," I said when I finished the omelette.

"I should thank you, Nick." Lauren poured

herself some more wine. Her hand was trembling a little. "If it hadn't been for you ... hell ... they were going to kill me."

"You were the one who got out of the ropes," I reminded her. I glanced at the poster above the gas fire. It showed her with a flashy guy in a sequinned straitjacket. He had greasy black hair, a moustache and a toothpaste advertisement smile. "Is that Harry Blondini?" I asked.

"Yes." She stood up and turned the record-player on. There was a click and a solo saxophone slithered through the room. She'd lit herself a cigarette and the smoke curled in time to the music. Her eyes told me everything I needed to know about the escapologist. But she told me anyway. "I loved him," she said. "For two years we worked together in the theatre and we lived together for five. We were going to get married. But then, at the last minute, he ran off with a snake-charmer. What did she have that I didn't – apart from two anacondas and a boa constrictor? That was the day before our wedding – the day before we were meant to tie the knot." She smiled a half-smile. "Well, what should I have expected from an escapologist? He escaped. And he broke my heart.

"That was when I took up singing. I've been singing for twenty years, Nick. The same old songs. And in all that time I've only met two decent people. Johnny Naples and you. You're a nice kid, Nick. If I'd ever had a son, I'd have liked him to be like you.

"All I've ever wanted is a place of my own – maybe somewhere in the sun, like the South of France. Look at this place! Ten metres underground – I never get to see the sun. And the Casablanca Club's the same. When they finally bury me, I'll actually be going up in the world. But it's a lousy world, Nick. Lousy..."

Maybe she'd had too much wine. I don't know. I'd asked her a simple question and she'd given me her life history. It was lucky I hadn't asked her anything tricky. We could have been there all night. I'd had enough. I was tired and I was dirty.

"I need a bath," I said.

She shook her head. "Of all the baths in all the towns in all the world, you have to walk into mine. There's no hot water."

"Then I'll just turn in."

"You can sleep on the sofa."

I took the tray back into the kitchen while she got me a couple of blankets. It was after she'd said goodnight and I was about to leave that I remembered the one question I'd meant to ask her. It was the whole reason I was there.

"Lauren," I said. "Back in the Casablanca Club ... you were about to tell me something. You told me that you were out with Johnny when he saw something. It made the Maltesers and everything else make sense."

"That's right."

"Well ... where were you?"

She paused, silhouetted in the doorway. "We were buying sausages," she said. "In Oxford Street. In Selfridges. In the food department."

SELFRIDGES

I don't like Oxford Street on the best of days – and let me tell you now, December 24th isn't one of them. Bond Street Station had been doing a good impersonation of the Black Hole of Calcutta and Lauren and I were glad to get out. But there was little relief outside. The Christmas rush had turned into the Christmas panic and the season seemed to have run pretty short of good will. Taxi drivers blasted their horns. Bus drivers leant out of their windows and swore. You couldn't blame them. The traffic probably hadn't moved since December 22nd. There were so many people clawing their way along the pavement that you couldn't see the cracks. And everyone was carrying bulging bags. Of food, of decorations, of last-minute presents. I sighed. Herbert was still in prison.

He'd been there almost a week now. It

looked like Christmas for me was going to be the Queen's speech and two frozen turkey croquettes.

But there was Selfridges with its white pillars, gold clocks and flags fluttering across the roof. Somewhere inside the department store – in the food section – Johnny Naples had seen something that could have made him three and a half million pounds. The thought cheered me up. I clutched the Maltesers. Lauren had lent me a sort of shoulder-bag and I had brought them with me. I wouldn't have felt easy without them.

We crossed the road, weaving between the traffic, and went in the front entrance. We were greeted by a cloud of sweet, sickly scent. This was the perfume hall. They stocked all the perfumes in the world – and you could smell them all at once.

"Do you want to try this one?"

A pretty girl leant over a counter, holding out a bottle of aftershave towards me. I shook my head. She had a nice face. But she was a couple of years early.

It was hot in Selfridges. The air had been chewed up by air-conditioning machines and spat out again. That was how it smelt. Second-hand. We went into the menswear department, following the signs that read "food".

"Come along and meet Father Christmas

on the third floor in the magical grotto." The voice came out of invisible speakers, floating above the heat and the crowd.

"See all your favourite nursery rhymes. On the third floor. It's open now."

The food department was even worse than perfume and menswear. It was like nuclear war had just been announced. The shelves were being stripped, the shop assistants bullied. I felt Lauren put her hand round my arm.

"This way," she said.

"I'm with you." But it was an effort. Relax for a minute and I'd have been swept away on a river of rampant consumerism, drowned in a lake of last-minute shopping.

"If we get separated, we can meet outside Marks and Spencer," she said. "It's just across the road."

We made our way round the centre section of the food department, which was more or less like any supermarket. There were separate bars here and there – juice, sandwiches and cookies – but most people were ignoring them. The meat counter was at the back. There was a number in what looked like a car headlamp, hanging from the ceiling. Every few seconds there was a loud buzzing and the number changed. "Now serving 1108" it read when we got there. It buzzed again – 1109. A clutch of housewives stared up at it. They were all clutching tickets like they'd just gone in for some sort of raffle.

So Selfridges sold sausages. I could see them through the glass front of the cabinet. They looked very nice. I'm sure they tasted great. But I didn't see what that had meant to Johnny Naples. What did sausages have to do with the Falcon?

"Lauren..." I began.

"He was standing here," she said. "Then he suddenly turned round and went that way." She pointed.

"You mean he went straight on?"

"No. We'd come from that way. He retraced his steps."

I followed in the footsteps of the dead dwarf. They took me further round the central supermarket, past the nuts and into the fruits where some fancy items nestled amongst the plums and Granny Smiths. "Brazilian Loquats, £3.50 kg" a sign read. That was probably a bargain if you knew what to do with a loquat. After that it was chocolates and then cash-tills. There was a row of six of them – with six women in brown coats and white straw hats. Five of them were ringing up prices on their tills like they were typing a novel. The sixth was just passing the purchases over a little glass panel in the counter and the prices were coming up automatically.

But I still hadn't seen anything that made me any the wiser. As far as I could see, Selfridges didn't even sell Maltesers.

"It was here," Lauren said.

"Here – what?" I sounded tired and depressed. Maybe that was because I was. It had been a wild goose chase and I didn't even have enough money to go back to the meat counter and buy a wild goose.

"He knew," Lauren insisted. "He was standing where you were. And he suddenly smiled..."

I looked around and suddenly I wasn't smiling at all. There was a door opposite, leading into the street. Two men had just come in with the crowds. I think I saw them a few seconds before they saw me.

"Lauren," I hissed.

"What?"

I gestured. They'd changed since our first encounter but I'd have recognized Gott and Himmell anywhere. They were still wearing identical suits – pale green with embroidered waistcoats this time. But Himmell (with the blond hair) now had his left arm in plaster. Gott was walking with a stick. Both men had so many plasters on their face that I could hardly see any skin. But the skin I could see wasn't looking too healthy.

"You told them about the sausages," I said.

"Of course I told them," Lauren growled. "They were going to give me some more of their fairy cakes."

She'd told them. They'd come to look at the food department for themselves. And now they'd seen us.

"Let's move," I said.

We moved.

We ducked to the left – through an archway and down a flight of stairs past wines and spirits. Looking over my shoulder, I saw Gott giving Himmell some hurried instructions. A moment later I collided with a pair of little old ladies. With a little old screech they flew into a pile of crystallized fruit which collapsed all around them. I didn't stop to apologize. Manners maketh man, my father used to say. But Gott and Himmell weren't far behind. And they had every good reason to unmaketh me.

"Which way?" Lauren asked.

I stopped. There was a door leading out to Orchard Street but it was blocked with about a dozen people fighting their way in. That left us a choice of three or four directions.

"Wait a minute, Lauren..." I said.

I was about to say that this was ridiculous. Gott and Himmell might be crazy, but there was no way they were going to try anything. Not in the middle of Selfridges on Christmas Eve. I was going to say that they'd wait for us outside and that we'd have to give them the slip when we left. I was going to say...

But right then a cabinet of watches behind my head exploded. Just like that. Glass flew out in glittering fragments. A shop assistant screamed. I spun round. Gott was standing at the top of the stairs. He was holding a gun. It was silenced so there had been no bang. But it was smoking. And nobody had noticed. They hadn't heard anything and they were too busy with their shopping to stop anyway.

"That way!" I cried.

Lauren went one way. I went another.

She must have missed the way I was pointing. She ran down a corridor back into menswear while I made for the escalator. There was no time to hesitate. And perhaps it was for the best. We had more chance of getting away if we split up.

"The meeting place for customers who have lost their companions is on the lower ground floor..." The voice poured soothingly out of the speakers. Lauren had certainly lost me. But unless I lost the Germans, our only meeting-place would be the morgue.

The escalator was slow. Impossibly slow. And I couldn't run up it – I was hemmed in by shoppers on both sides. I squatted down and looked back, wondering if Gott and Himmell had missed me. They hadn't. There was no sign of Gott but Himmell was standing there, taking aim. This time I think I heard the *phutt* as the bullet came out. Just above my head, a white box with the figure "1" on it suddenly shattered and the light went out inside.

I reached the top of the escalator and swung round past a collection of hats, then on to a second escalator with a third after that. On the third floor, not even knowing if Himmell was still behind me, I ran forward – through the children's clothes department and on.

I stopped to catch my breath at another of the archways. There were fewer people up here. After all, who buys children clothes for Christmas except relatives who should know better? I couldn't see Himmell and I thought I'd lost him, but then a plastic dummy about twelve centimetres away from me suddenly lurched over backwards with a hole in its forehead and fell with a clatter of broken plastic. Gott had gone after Lauren. But Himmell was still after me. I turned and ran.

And now there were more people. I didn't mind that. The more the merrier as far as I was concerned. It took me a few seconds to realize where I was heading and by then it was too late to go anywhere else. There was a sign:

To Santa's Grotto

Now I remembered the loudspeaker announcement. Father Christmas and my favourite nursery rhymes. I'd almost prefer to spend the afternoon with Himmell.

The straggle of people had become a queue. I ignored it. A few people protested as I ran past them but most of them had little children with them and they weren't going to start a fight. I ran on, past a red screen and down a brightly-lit corridor. It led into a pram park and there was a woman standing behind a desk, gently controlling the crowd. She called out to me but I ignored her, sliding down a ramp to crash into a brick wall. Fortunately, the brick wall was made out of cardboard. I glanced back, hoping that I'd at last shaken Himmell. But there he was, one arm in white plaster jutting out of his body as if he'd been caught in the middle of a karate chop. His other arm was jammed into his pocket. I knew what it was holding.

I dived into Santa's grotto. I didn't like it. But I had no choice.

It was packed inside with everyone talking in low voices while nursery rhymes played on the loudspeaker system. There were a lot of models – Elizabethan villages and that sort of thing, illustrating the rhymes. They'd fixed them up with those little dolls that do jerky movements. They didn't fool me. Jack and Jill looked slightly ill while Miss Muffet seemed to be having convulsions. The models were arranged so that the passage swerved round with dark sections and light sections. I moved as quickly as I could, pushing aside anyone who got in the way. Nobody complained. With their arms full of little kids asking inane questions, they had more than enough to worry about.

So had I. I felt trapped in Santa's grotto. I needed an exit. I saw one, but it was blocked by a security guard. I turned another corner past Little Jack Horner and stopped again next to Humpty Dumpty. There was no sign of Himmell. Perhaps he was waiting for me outside. Some of the children were more interested in me than in the models. I suppose I must have looked pretty strange, panting and sweating – the way you do when you're running for your life. I took a couple of steps further into the grotto. At the same moment, Humpty Dumpty exploded in all directions, his arms and legs soaring into the air. All the King's soldiers and all the King's men certainly won't be able to put that one together again, I thought as I forced my way through the crowd.

And still nobody knew anything was wrong. It was incredible. But it was also gloomy. And if you've got your eyes on a ship with thirty or so white mice, maybe you won't notice when a private detective's younger brother is being murdered behind you. I looked round. Himmell had been held up by a tough-looking gang of seven-year-olds. Still walking backwards, my eyes fixed on him, I turned a corner. Somebody seized me. I was jerked off my feet. I twisted round again. I couldn't believe it. I'd bumped into Santa Claus and he'd pulled me on to his lap.

Now he looked at me with cheerful eyes and a white-bearded smile. He really was the complete department store Santa: red hat, red trousers and tunic, bulging stomach and bad breath.

"You're a bit big for Santa, aren't you?" he asked in a jolly Santa voice.

"Let me go," I said, squirming on his lap. But he clung on to me. I got the feeling he was enjoying himself. "And what do you want for Christmas?" he asked.

"I want to get away from a guy who wants to kill me."

He laughed at that. There were a whole lot of people in Santa's chamber and if I hadn't been so angry I'd have been red with embarrassment. A little girl – she can't have been more than six – pointed at me and laughed. Her parents took a photograph.

"Ho ho..." Santa boomed out.

He didn't make the third "ho".

There was another quiet *phutt* and he keeled over. I threw myself on to the floor. Himmell was on the other side of the chamber, reloading his gun. Nobody was looking at him. They were looking at Santa, at the body twitching on the chair, at the red stuff that was staining his beard. The little girl began to cry.

"Don't worry," I said. "Santa's OK."

Santa died. I fled.

I got out of the grotto just as the people began to scream in earnest. I could still hear them as I ran across a floor of women's clothes, searching for a way out.

"Security to third floor, please. Security to third floor." The calm, unruffled voice came over the loudspeakers as I spotted a fire exit, pulled it open and found myself in a quiet stairwell. I wanted to go back down to street level but even as I stood there, I could hear the tramp of feet coming up. They didn't sound like shoppers. They were too fast, too determined. It had to be the security guards. I looked up. The stairway was clear. I made for the fourth floor.

Through a door, along a corridor, through another door and suddenly I'd burst into the toy department. I was tired now. I couldn't run much more. And the noise and the colour of the toys somehow drained away the last of my strength. Robots buzzed and clicked. Electric organs played hideous tunes. Computer games bleeped and whined. Something whipped past my head. I thought it was another bullet and jerked back, sending a whole pile of robots flying. But it was only a sales assistant with a paper glider. The robots writhed on the floor. I shrugged and staggered off into the toys.

I was sure I'd lost Himmell now. From toys I went into sports – first the clothes, then snooker tables, weights, golf clubs and hockey sticks. I rested against a counter that had been set up for a special promotion. There was a sign reading:

Discover the delights of deep-sea diving

A young salesman was showing an American couple the latest equipment: masks, wetsuits, harpoons.

"The harpoon works on compressed air," I heard him say. "You just pull the lever here, load it like this and then—"

And then Himmell appeared. He'd come from nowhere. He was only about three metres away from me. I had nowhere else to run. He had his hand in his pocket and now he brought it up, the jacket coming with it. He smiled. He was going to shoot me through the pocket. Then he would just walk away. And no one would know.

I lunged to one side, grabbed the harpoon gun, then wheeled round. The salesman shouted. I pressed the trigger.

The gun shuddered in my hands. The harpoon shot out, snaking a silver rope behind it. For a moment I thought I'd missed. The harpoon seemed to sail over Himmell's shoulder. But then I saw that one prong had gone through his suit, pinning him to the wall. The American stared at me.

"Good gun!" I said. And dropped it. Himmell lunged forward but he wasn't going anywhere. He was stuck there like a German calendar.

"You little...!"he began.

I didn't want to hear him. I found another fire exit and this time I managed to get out of Selfridges without being stopped. I crossed the road and made my way around the front of Marks and Spencer. I was relieved to find Lauren waiting for me.

"What kept you?" she said.

"You got away OK?" I asked.

"Sure. Gott could hardly walk, let alone run. Himmell was in better shape."

"Yeah," I agreed. "He was."

Lauren sighed. "Well, that was a waste of time," she said. "We didn't learn anything."

I thought back to the food department, to the things I had seen. And suddenly I understood. It was as if I'd known all along, only someone had to sock me on the jaw to make me realize it. I smiled. Johnny Naples must have smiled that way. Lauren saw it. "Come on..." I said.

The same taxis and the same buses were jammed in the same place as we crossed Oxford Street again. We got back on the tube. It would take us to South Kensington where we'd get a bus.

I knew. But I had to be sure.

INFORMATION

"The bar-code," I said.

"The what?"

"Those little black and white lines you get on the things you buy."

"What about them?"

I pulled the Maltesers out of the shoulder-bag and showed them to Lauren. "Look," I said. "You see? It's got a bar-code."

"So what?"

"That's what they were using in Selfridges. The girl was passing her products over a scanner and the scanner was telling the cash-till how much the products cost." Lauren looked blank so I went on. "Maybe if you pass *this* bar-code over a scanner, it'll do something different."

"Like what?"

"I don't know. That's what we're going to find out."

I needed a science lesson in a hurry and for once in my life I was sorry school had shut for the holidays. But I had another idea. Journalists write about technology and things like that. They know a little bit about everything. And I knew a journalist: Clifford Taylor, the guy who'd interviewed Herbert and me. He'd been at the Falcon's funeral too, so I figured he must still work on the same newspaper, the *Fulham Express*. That was where we were heading now. I had to be sure that I was right.

Nobody reads the *Fulham Express* but everybody who lives in Fulham gets it. They don't have any choice. It's one of those free newspapers that come uninvited through the letterbox in a shower of plumbers' business cards, minicab telephone numbers and special offers from the *Reader's Digest*. It's delivered every Wednesday in the morning. And you can see it every Wednesday, in the afternoon, stuffed into litter bins or drinking up the dirt in the gutter.

We took a bus all the way down the Fulham Road, past Herbert's flat, to the bottom – Fulham Broadway. This was the Fulham Road at its worst: dirty in the rain, dusty in the sun, always run-down and depressing. I'd occasionally walked past the office of the *Fulham Express* but I'd never been inside before. It was on the main road, next to a bank. Lauren and I climbed up a flight of stairs and found ourselves in a single, rectangular room with a printing press at one end and a photocopying machine at the other. In the middle there were two tables, piled high with newspaper clippings. The room must have been a dance studio at one time because it had mirrors all the way down one wall, making it seem twice as big as it was. Even so, it was small.

Clifford was there, feverishly working on a story that in a few days someone would use to wrap their fish and chips. I coughed and when he didn't respond, I walked up to him. He was the only person there.

"Clifford..." I said.

"Yes?" He looked up.

"You don't remember me?"

"If you're from the dance class, you're too early. The newspaper has the room until five—"

"I'm Nick Diamond."

He took his glasses off and wiped them. There were sweat patches under his arms and his acne had got worse. He was a mess. I doubted if he could even spell personal hygiene. "Nick who?" he asked.

"Diamond." I glanced at Lauren who shrugged. "You interviewed me," I reminded him. "My brother's a private detective."

Now he did remember. "Of course! Absolutely! How's it going? There's not much call for private detectives in Fulham—"

"I know," I interrupted. Clifford liked talking. When he'd interviewed us, he'd talked more than we had. "I wondered if you could help me," I said.

"Sure. Sure."

"It's a sort of scientific question. Do you know anything about shopping?"

"Shopping?" He frowned. "I don't think I know anyone called Shopping. There's Chopin ... but he's a composer, not a scientist."

"No." I sighed. "I'm talking about shops. And about bar-codes. I want to know how they work."

Clifford ran a hand through his hair. There wasn't that much left for him to run it through. In fact, he had more dandruff than actual hair. "OK." He leant back and put his feet up on the desk. "Technology is mainly about one thing: information. The electronic storage and transmission of information. Computers store information. Satellites send information. But all this information isn't written out like a book. No way. It's turned into what's known as digital information."

"What does digital information look like?"

"Well, in the old days it would have been a hole punched into a computer tape. There are holes in the modern compact disc too – although they're too small to see. And a bar-code is another form of digital information.

It's as simple as that.

"All products have a bar-code on them these days. If you look at them, you'll see that there's a number with thirteen digits underneath it. That's all a bar-code is. A number – a unique number that can tell the computer everything it needs to know."

I'd taken out the box of Maltesers again while he talked. Clifford's eyes lit up when he saw it. He leant forward and took it.

"Take this box," he said. "Here's the bar-code on the bottom." He pointed to the strip of blue and white lines in the left-hand corner. "Part of it would tell the computer that this is a product made by Mars. Another part of it would tell the computer that it's a box of Maltesers, that it weighs so much and costs so much. It could even remind the shopkeeper to stock up."

"How does the computer read the bar-code?" I asked.

"Well, that's all done with lasers," Clifford explained. "There's a sort of little window built into the counter near the cash-till. The person who's sitting there passes the box of Maltesers – or whatever – over it. Now, behind the window there's a laser scanner. The shop assistant could use a light-emitting diode which is the same sort of thing, but either way, the light hits the bar-code. Are you with me so far?"

I wasn't sure, but I nodded anyway. If I'd learnt one thing from science lessons at school it was this. When scientific types start explaining things, it's hard enough to follow. But when they start explaining the explanations, that's when you really get lost.

"All right." He nodded. "The light beams hit the bar-code. Now, the dark lines don't reflect light. Only the white ones do that. So only some of the light gets reflected. And somewhere inside that little window there's a photodetector which is a clever machine that produces a pulse of electricity whenever you shine a light on it. Do you see? As you slide the bar-code over the window, the shining light hits the lines. Some of it is reflected back on to the photodetector which gives out a 'bleep' for every white line. It's the 'bleep' that's the digital information sent to the computer. Almost like Morse code. And that's how the computer knows what the product is!"

He stopped triumphantly and sneezed. Lauren reached out for the Maltesers and he gave them to her. She turned them over and examined the bar-code.

"Could you use the bar-code like a … key?" I asked. That was the word the Fat Man had used. He had said he was looking for a key.

"Absolutely!" the journalist said. "That's just what it is, really."

"But could it open something – like a safe?"

"It depends how you programmed your computer. But the answer's yes. It could open a safe. Play Space Invaders. Make the tea..."

"They open the..." I'd asked the Professor what the Maltesers did and that was what he'd said before he caught himself. It was all clicking together. A key. A code known only to the Falcon. A safe. Johnny Naples had guessed the day he went to Selfridges. Now I remembered the words he'd written down on the scraps of paper I'd found in his room. Digital ... photodetector ... light-emitting diode. Clifford Taylor had used them all in his explanation.

I'd always thought that it was the Maltesers themselves that were the answer to the riddle. But I'd been wrong and I could have guessed. When Johnny Naples had bought the envelope at Hammetts, he'd done something else. He'd bought a pair of scissors. Why? To cut out the bar-code. That was all he needed. He just had to feed it into... But that was one thing I still didn't know.

"I do hope I've been helpful," the journalist said.

"Sure," I said. "More helpful than you'd guess."

"Is there a story in it?"

I nodded. "An international master-criminal, a gang of crooks, a fortune in diamonds? There's a story OK."

Clifford Taylor sighed. "I'm afraid I can't

use it. It's much too exciting for the *Fulham Express*. But look out for the next edition. I'm doing a very interesting piece on the effectiveness of one-way traffic systems in Chelsea."

"I can hardly wait," I said.

We left him at his desk and went back down the stairs. It was only when we got to the bottom that Lauren's hand flew to her mouth. "I've left the Maltesers upstairs!" she exclaimed. "Hang on, honey…"

I watched her run up the stairs and into the newspaper office. About a minute later, she reappeared, waving the Maltesers. "I must be out of my mind!" she said. "How could I leave them?"

I thought no more of it. That was definitely a mistake.

We were near Herbert's flat so I decided to go in and get some fresh clothes. It was easier for Lauren to take the tube straight to Baron's Court, so we parted company outside Fulham Broadway Station. It was a beautiful day. Cold but with a brilliant sun. Lauren stopped outside the station almost like she was afraid to go in.

"Nick…" she said.

"Yes?"

"What I said that night – I want you to know that I meant it. You're a nice boy. You deserve the best."

I stared at her, then laughed uneasily.

"What is this?" I said. "I'll only be an hour or so. You're talking like I'm never going to see you again."

"Sure." She shook her head. "Forget it."

She went into the station.

I walked all the way up the Fulham Road, past the cemetery and on to the flat. As I walked, I thought. I understood so much now. What the Maltesers meant and why everybody wanted them. The only trouble was, if the Maltesers really were a sort of digital key, how was I to find the digital door? And there was something else that puzzled me. Who had shot Johnny Naples in the first place? My money was on the Fat Man. If it had been Gott and Himmell, they'd have told me when I was their prisoner. After all, they'd told me about Lawrence without blinking an eye. But at the same time, I couldn't believe it. I just couldn't see the Fat Man getting his hands dirty that way. It wasn't his style. So if not him – who?

I checked the bag. At least the Maltesers were safe. Right now that was all that mattered.

It was around three when I reached the flat. I slipped in as quickly as I could. The fewer people who saw me go in the better. I didn't mean to stay there long – just long enough to pull on a fresh shirt and a new pair of socks and make a clean getaway. I went up the stairs. The office door was open. I went in.

There were four thugs in there waiting for me. One was behind the door. He kicked it shut after I'd gone through it so when I turned round there was no way out. I'd have given my right arm for a way out. If I hung around there much longer they'd probably tear it off anyway. The four thugs were all wearing extra large suits. That was because they were extra large thugs. I was once taught at school that Man evolved from the ape and all I can say is that these four had a long way to catch up. They were big, heavy and brutal with unintelligent eyes and thick lips. They were all chewing gum, their lower jaws sliding up and down in unison. "Are you Nick Diamond?" one of them asked.

"Me?" I said. "No ... no! I'm not Nick Diamond. I'm ... er ... the delivery boy."

"What are you delivering?" a second demanded.

"Um..." I was having to think on my feet. Any minute now I'd be thinking on my back. If I was still conscious. "I'm a singing telegram!" I exclaimed, brilliantly. "Happy birthday to you, happy..." I tried to sing but the words died in my throat. The four thugs weren't convinced. "Come on, guys," I pleaded. "Gimme a break."

"Yeah – your legs," the third one said.

They all laughed at that. I'd heard more cheerful sounds on a ghost train. They were still laughing as they closed in on me.

"You're making a big mistake," I said.

The man behind the door was the first to reach me. He grabbed my shoulder with one hand and lifted me clean off my feet. "There's no mistake, sunshine," he said. "The Fat Man wants to see you."

IN THE FOG

I discovered that the four thugs were called Lenny, Benny, Kenny and Fred. Lenny was in charge. He was the one with the driving licence. They'd parked the car outside the flat. It was a Morris Minor. After we'd all piled in it I was surprised it was able to move. I certainly wasn't. I was on the back seat between Benny and Kenny. Things were so tight that if they'd both breathed in at the same time, I'd have been crushed. The Maltesers were still in my shoulder-bag but now the shoulder-bag was on Fred's lap. Lenny was driving. I was being "taken for a ride" as they say. And I had a nasty feeling I'd only been given a one-way ticket.

We drove out of town, west towards Richmond. Lenny had made a telephone call from the flat before we left so I knew the Fat Man would be waiting for me. It looked like he was going to have a long wait. These heavies really were heavy and the Morris Minor could only manage thirty miles an hour on the level. Not that I was in any hurry. In fact, my only hope was that the engine would finally explode under the pressure. I could hardly see them "taking me for a ride" on a bus.

"You can't do this to me," I protested. "I'm under-age. I'm only a kid. I've got my whole life ahead of me."

"That's what you think," Lenny sneered.

"But I've got money," I said. "I could make you guys rich."

"Sure." Lenny swung the steering wheel. "You can leave it to us in your will."

The car turned off the main road and began to follow a winding lane through what looked like the remains of an industrial complex. It was still pretty complex but I reckoned it hadn't been industrial for a hundred years. It was a network of Victorian buildings, most of them burnt out. Another bit of London that was falling down. The lane led down to the river. Suddenly we came to the end of the tarmac and I could hear gravel crunching underneath the tyres. The Morris Minor bounced up and down. The four thugs bounced in their seats. The springs screamed for mercy. We drove right up to the edge of the river. Then Lenny put on the handbrake. We'd arrived.

"Out," he ordered.

He'd produced a gun from somewhere and I don't need to tell you what it was pointing at. If you've ever looked into the single eye of a gun barrel, you'll know it's no fun. The devil must have an eye like that.

"Walk," Lenny said.

I walked. We'd stopped in a space about the size of a car-park, only the Morris Minor was the only car parked there. It was another building site, more luxury houses for the Thames. But they'd only got as far as the foundations and a few pieces of the framework. The iron girders hemmed us in like we were on the stage of a Greek amphitheatre, only there was no audience. The light was fading and to complete the picture – or maybe to obliterate it – the fog had rolled in across the water. It carried the smell of salt and dead fish in its skeleton fingers and when it touched my neck I shivered. I couldn't see across to the other side of the Thames. Which meant that anyone on the other side couldn't see me. I was alone with just about the four nastiest customers you could ever hope not to meet.

There was a low hiss as one of them lit a paraffin lamp. It threw a circle of hard, white light. They'd set it all up in advance. I didn't understand it – but somehow I didn't like it much. There was a wooden chair about four metres away from the edge of the river and an old iron bathtub right in front of it. The bathtub was quite deep. It came to about the same level as the chair. Nearby, there was a pile of brown paper sacks. Kenny picked one up and tore it open. Grey powder flooded out. At the same time, Benny walked forward carrying a hose. Water was already spluttering out, liquid mercury in the strange, harsh light. Cement, water, a bathtub, a chair and the River Thames. Now I understood it – and I liked it even less.

"Sit down," Lenny said.

He waved the gun towards the chair. I walked forward, the soles of my shoes squelching on the wet gravel. The four men never stopped watching me. They weren't getting any pleasure out of this. They were just doing a job. Mind you, I wasn't getting any pleasure out of it either – and I wasn't being paid. But there was nothing I could do. I sat down on the chair. It was so close to the bathtub that my legs had to go in it. Out of the corner of my eye I could see Kenny and Benny mixing the cement. If I ever get out of this one, I thought to myself, I'll take the first flight to Australia. My parents might not have been ideal company, but they'd never tried to kill me. At least, not so you'd notice.

"Look, Lenny…" I began, trying to be reasonable.

"Button it, kid," he snapped.

Kenny and Benny came over, each carrying

a large bucket of wet cement. They glanced at Lenny. He nodded. As one, they tipped them up. The stuff poured out sluggishly, like cold porridge. It splattered down into the bath, covering my shoes and rising about fifteen centimetres up my legs. I could feel it seeping through my socks. It was icy. And it was heavy, too. My shoes were pressing against my toes. They were only sneakers and already the cement was oozing through them. I wiggled my toes. Lenny pressed the gun against the side of my neck. "Keep still," he said.

"But it's wet..." I complained.

"Don't worry, kid. It's quick-drying. You keep still and it'll set in no time."

Two more buckets followed the first and two more went after them. By the time Kenny and Benny had it finished, the cement came all the way up to my knees. If anyone had seen me – sitting there with my legs in a bath staring out across the Thames – they'd have thought I was mad. But nobody would see me. It was dark now. And the fog had got thicker. Like the cement.

Lenny wasn't even bothering to massage my neck with his gun any more. The cement had almost set. I experimented. Carefully I tried to lift my right foot. I couldn't do it. That was when I began to get really afraid. Talk about having one foot in the grave – I had both feet and most of my legs. I was glued to the bathtub and I knew that any minute now they'd pick it up and drop it into the river. I – it – we would sink like a stone. I'd spend the rest of eternity in an upright position.

They say that when a man drowns, his whole life flashes before him. Mine did that now but it was all over in about five seconds. That made me sad. It had been a short life and I'd spent far too much of it at school.

I heard a sort of glugging sound coming from the Thames. That made my ears prick up. A boat. It was getting closer. For a moment I was hopeful. It might be a river police boat. Or perhaps a dredger of some sort. But Fred had been waiting for it. The grey curtains of fog were pushed aside by the bow of a sleek, white cruiser. A rope was thrown out of the darkness. A gangplank was slid over the edge and made steady on the bank. The Fat Man walked down it.

He was dressed in a dinner jacket with a mauve bow tie and a white silk scarf hanging loose around his neck. He nodded at Fred and the others and then strolled over to me. Without saying a word, he leant down and tapped the concrete with his knuckles. That made my heart lurch. The stuff was already solid. I couldn't even feel my feet. He straightened up. The four thugs formed a rough circle around us. And I can tell you now, circles just don't come any rougher.

"No wisecracks today, Nicholas?" the Fat Man demanded. "Nothing funny to say?"

"You're a loony, Fat Man," I said.

"And you, my boy, are a fool. You were lucky to escape alive from the Hotel Splendide. But now your time has run out."

"What have you got against me?" I asked. "What did I ever do to you?"

"You lied to me," the Fat Man said. "Worse still, you defied me. I gave you forty-eight hours to find something for me. Find it you did not."

"Well..." I said. "How about a second chance?"

He sniffed. At the same time, Fred moved forward. He'd opened the shoulder-bag and taken out the Maltesers. He handed them to the Fat Man. The Fat Man looked at the bottom, holding them to the light so that he could read something. "Perfect!" he whispered. That threw me. How had he found out about the Maltesers? He'd never mentioned them before. He must have read the expression in my face because he smiled. "You're wondering how I discovered what was inside the dwarf's package?" he asked. He turned round to the boat. "Professor!"

I peered through the swirling fog. A second figure appeared at the top of the gangplank and made his way unsteadily down. He stood at the edge of the circle of light, blinking at me.

Quentin Quisling, the Professor. He shook his head. "You gave me the wrong box, sir," he said in an accusing tone of voice.

"So the Professor came to me," the Fat Man continued. "A wise decision. A very wise decision. Did you know that the Professor designed them in the first place? You see, the Falcon needed a key – but a key that didn't look like a key. He had too many enemies. The Professor created the bar-code—"

"But why Maltesers?" I asked. The information wasn't going to be much use to me, but I wanted to know.

The Professor shrugged. "I like Maltesers," he said.

"And now I have them." The Fat Man smiled. The smile stretched his skin across his cheekbones like an elastic band. "And soon, very soon, the Professor will tell me what they open—"

"And then you'll kill him too," I interrupted. I had nothing to lose. I was only minutes away from the end. I could feel the chill of the cement spreading through my entire body. I turned to the Professor. "You don't think the Fat Man will share the money with you, do you?" I said. "Once you tell him your secret, you'll be joining the queue at the bottom of the Thames."

"It's fifty-fifty..." the Professor mumbled but I could see he had his doubts.

"I'll see you in Hell, Professor," I said.

The Fat Man was furious. His face had gone white and the veins in his neck were standing out so far they were threatening to snap his bow tie. "Throw him in!" he yelled.

He stepped back. At once, Lenny, Benny and Kenny moved in on me. They bent down and a moment later I was in the air, bath and all, being carried towards the Thames. Don't let me kid you. I like to think I'm smart. Sometimes I act older than I am. But right then I would have screamed and cried and torn my hair out if I'd thought for a single second that screaming and crying and tearing my hair out would do any good.

The river drew closer. The Fat Man watched. The three men shuffled forward.

They were about two metres from the edge of the water when the spotlight cut through the fog and the darkness. It came from high up, somewhere behind me. It was hard to tell. The night seemed to rip apart, torn into shreds by the beam. The fog boiled furiously in its grip. The gangsters stopped as if frozen.

There was a crackle in the air. Then a voice boomed out, amplified by a loudhailer.

"This is the police. Stay where you are. You're surrounded."

Lenny, Benny and Kenny dropped me. I crashed to the ground but remained standing up. The Fat Man ran for the boat. He still had the Maltesers. The Professor stumbled after him. Lenny took out his gun and fired in the direction of the spotlight. I tried to dive for cover but I was about as capable of that as an oak tree. There was an answering shot. Lenny was blown off his feet. His gun clattered to the ground.

"Don't move," the voice commanded. "We're armed." It was a bit late to be telling Lenny that.

The Fat Man had reached the boat and turned round, stretching out a hand for the Professor. But the Professor was nowhere near him. Half-drunk and short-sighted he ran forward, missed the gangplank and dived into the Thames. Benny, Kenny and Fred scattered and ran for cover. But now the whole area was swarming with men. They were throwing black shadows as they sprinted through the glare.

The Professor couldn't swim. He was floundering in the water, shouting for help. But the Fat Man couldn't wait. The police had almost reached the boat.

The boat's engine roared and it swung away from the bank. At the same moment the Professor let out a ghastly scream. He'd been in the water. He'd been close to the propellors. Too close. I was glad I couldn't see what the Fat Man had accidentally done to him.

Benny, Kenny and Fred were arrested. I saw

them thrown to the ground. The whole building site was lit up. And I was still standing in the middle of it all, knee-deep in cement.

And then I felt the bathtub being dragged slowly towards the river. I couldn't believe it. There was a figure squatting, struggling, pulling the bathtub along the gravel. With me in it.

But then I heard a familiar voice. Snape's voice.

"No, Boyle," he said. "You can't push him in. We've come here to rescue him. Go to the car and get a chisel."

IN THE BATH

Snape and Boyle drove me back to the flat. I was cold. I was wet. And I was fed up. My trousers, shoes and socks were ruined and my legs weren't feeling much better. My throat was sore and my nose was blocked. They'd got my feet out of the cement but I could still feel the cement in my blood and there was nothing they could do about that. And I'd lost the Maltesers. It had been a bad day. I was glad it was over. If I'd known it was going to be a day like that, I'd have stayed in bed.

They came in with me and I made them some coffee. While the kettle was boiling, I tried to call Lauren. I thought she might be worried about me. But there was no answer. I flicked on the hot-water tank for a bath and went back downstairs. Snape and Boyle had made themselves comfortable in the office. I fixed us three cups of coffee and took them in. I didn't like them and they didn't like me. But like it or not, they'd saved my life. The least I could do was give them a cup of coffee.

"All right," I said. "How did you find me?"

"We were watching the flat," Snape told me. "We saw you go in and we saw you taken out. Lucky for you. We followed you to the Thames. When we saw what was going on, Boyle here called for back-up on the radio."

"Why were you watching the flat?" I asked.

Snape let out a sniff of laughter. "Why do you think? In the last few days we've been receiving some of the craziest reports I've heard in thirty years. A young boy blows up a hotel in the Portobello Road. A young boy pushes a grand piano out of a fifth-floor window. A young boy goes berserk in Selfridges and leaves forty hysterical children and a dead Santa Claus behind him. You'd think London was crawling with lethal young boys. Except they all fit the same description. Yours."

"I can explain," I said.

"I'm delighted to hear it. You've been making life very difficult for me. You've upset Boyle..."

"I'm upset," Boyle agreed.

"...and you've done more damage than the Germans managed in two world wars. And I thought your brother was a menace!"

"Where is Herbert?" I asked.

Snape's eyes narrowed at that. "We released him at lunchtime. We couldn't hold him. To be honest, we didn't want to."

"Well, I haven't seen him."

I wasn't particularly bothered just then. It was strange that Herbert should have just disappeared, but I could understand it. He'd probably gone to Aunty Maureen in Slough. He'd hide out there until the heat was off. I shivered. Herbert hadn't paid the gas bill for the flat. The heat had been off for two weeks.

"Did he tell you everything?" I asked.

"Well ... Herbert and canaries have a lot in common."

Snape held out a hand. "I want the Maltesers," he said.

"I don't have them," I said. "The Fat Man took them." Snape's eyes narrowed a little more. "If you don't believe me, you can search my bag."

"I already have," Boyle muttered.

"The Fat Man took them," I repeated. "When you arrest him you can get them from him."

"Arrest him?" Snape twisted his neck until the bone clicked. "That may not be so easy."

"Why not?"

"It's a question of evidence, lad. We haven't got anything on him. Nothing concrete—"

"What about the stuff he was burying me in?"

"You don't understand!" Snape was distressed. "He'll deny he was ever there. He'll say it was a case of mistaken identity ... in the fog. He'll have an alibi."

I shook my head in disbelief. "So that's it, then," I said. "If the Fat Man goes free, he'll find the diamonds and that'll be the end of it."

"You should have given us the Maltesers in the first place," Boyle said.

"Sure." I nodded. "And if the Fat Man had come strolling in and claimed them as lost property I suppose you'd have handed them over."

That made Boyle scowl again. But Snape stood up. "You've got a lot of questions to answer," he said.

"Are you arresting me?"

"No. You've had enough for one day. We'll talk to you next week. Like you say, the Fat Man has the Maltesers and that's the end of it. We'll be in touch."

I showed them to the door. Snape stopped in the doorway and turned round. "Happy Christmas," he said.

I'd forgotten until then. It was Christmas Eve. "Yeah ... Happy Christmas, Chief Inspector," I said. "And to you, Boyle."

Boyle grunted. He probably didn't even know what Christmas was.

An hour later I was lying in the hot water with

the soap bubbles up to my neck and Herbert's plastic duck floating around my feet. My body wasn't a pretty sight just then. What with the ropes, the cement and the general manhandling, I had more bruises than I cared to count. But it felt good in the bath. I needed to relax. It was time for some serious thinking.

What did the Maltesers unlock?

I knew the answer. I knew I knew the answer.

It had to be something near Herbert's flat. Johnny Naples had left Notting Hill Gate with the Maltesers and a pair of scissors. By then he'd found the answer. He knew where he was going and he went to Fulham. But he'd been followed – and rather than lead anyone to his destination, he'd come to us. So it had to be something near. But what was there near the flat connected with the Falcon?

Four days later we'd found Naples dying. He'd managed to say two things: "The Falcon" and "the sun". I assumed it was sun. Henry von Falkenberg didn't have a son ... at least, not one that we'd heard about. But what had the sun got to do with the Falcon? Nothing ... unless he'd been talking about another falcon. Maybe not a man. A bird. Or a statue of a bird.

And then I thought about the Maltesers themselves and about a phrase that Clifford Taylor had used. The journalist had described the laser as "the shining light". The sun was a shining light, too. But the phrase bothered me. I'd seen those words somewhere before. The Maltesers.

When the Fat Man had taken them, he'd looked on the bottom. I'd already tricked the Professor once. He'd told the Fat Man to find something, to check that they were the real ones. Henry von Falkenberg would have had to mark them in some way. And there was an easy way.

"You'll see that there's a number with thirteen digits underneath."

That was what the journalist had said. And I knew that number. I'd read it so many times that I'd learnt it off by heart: 3521 201 000000. That number was the final clue.

I pulled the plug out with my toes and wrapped a towel round my body. Then, still dripping water, I went downstairs. It took me an hour before I found what I was looking for but there it was – a piece of paper with another number on it. I'd written that number myself on the day of the Falcon's funeral.

There were thirteen digits on the Maltesers box – but the last six of them were all zeroes. Cross those out and you'd be left with seven digits.

A telephone number. And I knew which telephone it rang.

That was when our own telephone rang.

The noise of the bell was so sudden, so loud, that I almost dropped the towel. I went into the office and picked it up.

"Nick Diamond?"

The voice was ugly with hatred. I didn't believe a voice could hate that much.

"Gott," I said.

"We have your brother."

That took me by surprise. Herbert? But that was the way Gott worked. He'd snatched Lauren, then me. Why shouldn't he add Herbert to his list?

"If you don't give us what we want," Gott snarled, "he dies."

I didn't have what they wanted, but I wasn't going to say that. Because suddenly I knew everything. It all made sense. I should have seen it a long, long time before.

"Come to the cemetery," I said. I was talking even before I knew what I was saying. "I'll meet you at the Falcon's grave. Tomorrow at twelve o'clock." I hung up.

I didn't want to get into any arguments.

Then I opened the drawer of Herbert's desk. On the day we had first met the Fat Man, he had given us a card with his telephone number. I called it now, hoping there would be someone in.

"Yes?" It was a flat, neutral voice.

"I want to talk to the Fat Man," I said.

"He's not here."

"It's important I get a message to him."

"Who is this?"

"Nick Diamond."

There was a pause. Then the voice said, "What is the message?"

"I know what the key opens," I said. "And I'm willing to do a deal. Tell the Fat Man to be at Brompton Cemetery tomorrow. At the Falcon's grave at five to twelve exactly. Alone. Have you got that?"

"Yes."

"Good." I hung up on him too.

After that I made one last call. That was the hardest to make. It cost me three and a half million pounds. But the way I looked at it was like this. The Fat Man had the Maltesers. Gott (and maybe Himmell) had Herbert. And I had the answer. If I'd planned things right, it would all sort itself out the next day at noon.

If I hadn't ... well, we were meeting in a cemetery. At least they wouldn't have to carry me far.

I just hoped it would be a sunny day.

THE SHINING LIGHT

There are only about three or four days in the year when the Brompton Cemetery is more or less empty – and Christmas Day, of course, is one of them. That would suit my plans. Witnesses were one thing I could do without. It was eleven forty-five when I walked up to the Falcon's grave. There was nobody in sight. Fortunately it was another crisp, cloudless day. The sun had no warmth, but it was bright. At least the weather was on my side.

I stood beside the Falcon's grave. The earth was still fresh where they'd buried him, like a sore that hasn't healed. It would take the grass time to grow over it – but where better to find time than in a cemetery? I looked at the memorial, that Victorian telephone box with the stone falcon perched on top. There's an old saying. I thought of it now. "You can't take it with you." But the Falcon had – or at least, he'd tried his best to. I read the inscription on the memorial. I'd read it before.

THE PATH OF THE JUST IS AS SHINING LIGHT,
THAT SHINETH MORE AND MORE
UNTO THE PERFECT DAY.

The Falcon must have smiled when he had that cut in. I wondered if he was still smiling in his grave.

I heard the gate grind open down at the Fulham Road. That had to be the Fat Man. Sure enough, he appeared a few moments later, wearing a camel-hair coat with real humps. He carried a shooting stick and walked at a jaunty pace, for all the world like a man taking a little exercise before his Christmas lunch.

He saw me standing by the grave, raised the shooting stick and sauntered over. He was smiling, but only with his lips. His eyes didn't trust me.

"Happy Christmas, Fat Man," I said.

"I hope so," he replied. "And I hope you're not wasting my time, my boy. You should know by now that I don't take kindly to—"

"Have you the Maltesers?" I cut in.

He nodded. "In my pocket."

"Let me see them."

He took them out but held on to them like he was afraid I was going to grab them.

"Read me the number on the bottom," I said.

He turned the box over. "3521 201 000000." It was the right number. "You say you know what these chocolates meant to the Falcon," he said in a graveyard voice. "You say you want to make a deal. What deal?"

"We'll split the money," I said. "Fifty-fifty."

"Eighty-twenty."

"Sixty-forty."

We were juggling figures. It didn't matter to me. I knew that once I showed the Fat Man what to do with the Maltesers, I'd be dead. But it was important that he hung on to them. They had to be out in the open.

"Seventy-thirty," the Fat Man said. "It's my last offer."

It was his last offer. There was a movement on the path behind him, and when he turned round there were Gott and Himmell with Herbert between them. It had been a week since I'd last seen him and Herbert had lost weight.

I smiled at him. "Hello, Herbert," I said.

He looked at me reproachfully. "The name is Tim," he muttered.

There are times when my brother really amazes me. I'd been kidnapped, tied up, chased around London, threatened and half killed. He'd been arrested for murder and kidnapped himself. We were unarmed and surrounded by three psychopathic killers. And he was worried about Christian names. "How are you ... Tim?" I asked.

"I'm OK," he said. He considered. "Actually I've got a runny nose and—"

"All right," the Fat Man interrupted. "What is this?"

"It's a cemetery," Herbert said.

The Fat Man gritted his teeth.

"Do you know them?" I asked him.

He glanced at Gott and Himmell. "I know them," he said.

"If that little swine is trying to trick us—" Gott began.

"I'm doing what I said I would," I cut in. "I promised I'd lead you to the Maltesers in return for Herbert – I mean – Tim." I pointed at the Fat Man who was still holding them. "There they are. And I promised the Fat Man that I'd tell him their secret. If you'll let me, I will."

Nobody said anything. The wind ruffled my hair. I was wearing a body-warmer but my body was far from warm. I just wanted the whole thing to be over.

"Go ahead," Gott said.

"Yes, go ahead," the Fat Man repeated. "And it had better be good."

"All right," I said. "This is how it goes. Henry von Falkenberg was a very careful man, a man who trusted no one. He had three and a half million pounds in diamonds stashed here in England. It was in a safe that had been specially built for him. Even the key to the safe was special. It was designed so that nobody would even know it was a key. Only the Falcon knew. It was the only way he could feel safe himself.

"The Professor built the safe for him – the late Quentin Quisling. I guess we'll never know, but I suppose he built in some sort of device so that Henry von Falkenberg could choose his own combination. That wouldn't have been difficult. The key was a bar-code. It could be on a tin of baked beans, a pack of playing cards – a box of Maltesers. The Falcon brought the key with him every time he came to England. If he was searched by the police, he had nothing to fear. Who would suspect that a few black lines on the bottom of a box of sweets could open up a fortune?

"There was one thing, though. One fail-safe device. There was a number written on the box. I don't know why. Maybe it appealed to the Falcon's sense of humour. Or maybe it was a clue-a puzzle for his heirs to fight over. But that number was 352 1201 with a few zeroes added to stretch it out. I wrote that number down for my brother on the day of the Falcon's funeral. It's the phone number of this cemetery."

I walked forward to the monument. Nobody

spoke but their eyes followed me like so many gun barrels. I stood on tip toe and wiped the cuff of my shirt across the eyes of the falcon. As I had guessed, they weren't made of stone. They were glass.

"And where is this ingenious safe?" I asked.
"You're looking at it. The Falcon had it designed like a memorial. You see the inscription? The 'shining light' it's referring to is the light beam that opens it. Johnny Naples tried to tell me about that – the sun.

"I won't try to explain to you how a bar-code works. I only half understand it myself. But what you're looking at here is the first solar-powered bar-code reader. You've got to hand it to the Professor. He may have been crooked. He may have been a drunk. But he was clever.

"The sunlight goes in through the eyes of the stone falcon. You run the bar-code – at a guess – across the open beak. Somewhere inside all this there's a photodetector, a small computer and an opening device – all solar-powered. If you've got the right bar-code, it'll open the safe." I pointed at the Maltesers, still clutched in the Fat Man's hand. "That's the right bar-code," I added. "It's as simple as that."

I stopped. Nobody spoke. Only Herbert looked puzzled. He obviously hadn't understood a single word I'd said.

I wasn't exactly sure what was going to

happen next, but I'll tell you the general idea. The Fat Man isn't going to share the diamonds with Gott and Himmell. Gott and Himmell clearly have no intention of sharing the diamonds with the Fat Man. But now everybody knows the secret. Herbert and I are forgotten. Nobody cares about us any more. We slip away to live happily ever after, leaving our three friends to sort themselves out as best they can. That was the general idea. But obviously I'd been talking to the wrong general.

It all happened at once.

Almost casually, the Fat Man had lifted his shooting stick so that the end was pointing at Himmell. At the same time, Gott's hand had slid quietly into his jacket pocket. The two shots were almost simultaneous. Himmell looked down. There was a hole in his chest. The Fat Man lowered his shooting stick. And it was a shooting stick. The smoke was still curling out of the hole at the bottom. He smiled. The smile faded. He frowned. He raised a hand. He'd only just realized that he'd been shot in the neck. This time Gott hadn't used a silencer.

The Fat Man and Himmell slid to the ground together. The Maltesers fell on the grass. The last of the chocolates rolled out.

"Pick it up," Gott said.

I picked up the box. Something was chattering. I was just thinking that it was a bit cold for grasshoppers when I realized what it was. It was Herbert's teeth.

"Give me the box," Gott said.

I gave it to him, then stepped back a pace. Now Herbert and I were standing close together. Gott's gun was out of his jacket. There were too many plasters on his face to be sure, but I think his smile had grown even wider.

"I'm going to enjoy this," he said.

There were two gunshots.

Herbert's hands came up to his stomach. He groaned and lurched forward. "Nick..." he whispered. He pitched on to the grave.

I stared at him.

"Get up, Tim," I said.

"But I've been shot."

"No you haven't."

He held his hands up to his face. There was no blood. He lifted up his shirt and looked underneath. There were no bullet holes. Now he was blushing. "Sorry..." he muttered.

Gott had watched this performance with strange, empty eyes. Suddenly, he toppled forward. There were two holes in the back of his jacket. He hadn't had time to fire his own gun.

A figure appeared behind him, moving towards us. And that was the biggest surprise of the day.

It was Betty Charlady.

"Ello, Mr Nicholas," she gurgled. She was

still in her fluffy bedroom slippers, with a forest of artificial flowers on her head. "Wotcha, Mr Timothy. Blimey! What a turn-up ... innit.

"Betty!" Herbert exclaimed. "What are you doing—" But then he plugged his mouth with his thumb, stopping himself in mid-sentence.

Betty was holding a gun. The gun had just killed Gott.

With a smile, she pulled off her hat and threw it on to the grass. Her wig, with the electric curls, went next. Once more her hand reached up and this time it pulled at the very skin of her face. It stretched, then tore loose, carrying the wrinkles and make-up with it. The gun in her other hand remained steady but otherwise, in front of our eyes, she was changing.

Betty Charlady was gone. Another woman stood in her place.

"Who is she?" Herbert whispered.

"Beatrice von Falkenberg," I said. "The Falcon's widow. Snape told us that she used to be a great actress. It looks like Mrs Charlady was one of her performances."

"That's right, boys," Beatrice said.

I took a quick look round the cemetery. The way things were going, I wouldn't have been surprised if the alligator had turned up – perhaps disguised as a hedgehog.

"But ... but why?" Herbert asked.

"I had to find the diamonds," she said. "My late husband's fortune. When the dwarf gave you the package, I had to get close to you – to find out what you knew. Then I saw your advertisement for a daily. That gave me the idea."

"And Gott and Himmell were working for you," I said.

"That's very clever of you, Nicholas," she muttered. "How do you know?"

I shrugged. "I told you we were going to the Casablanca Club. You were the only person who knew. But somehow Gott and Himmell managed to turn up just in time to snatch Lauren Bacardi. We led them to her."

Herbert looked at me in astonishment. "That's brilliant," he said.

"There's more. They learnt about the Maltesers from Lauren and they told you. That's how you knew what to ask for when I visited you in Hampstead. You were all in it together."

"Until their use ran out," Beatrice said.

"It's incredible," Herbert said.

"Not really," I said. "I almost guessed when I visited Beatrice. She knew your real name. She called you Herbert – not Timothy. And she was wearing the same perfume as Betty. Lavender. That was something she forgot to change."

"You're very clever," Beatrice said.

"Maybe. But there's one thing I don't get. Why did you kill Johnny Naples in the first place?"

She shrugged. "It was an accident. Gott and Himmell had tracked him down to the Hotel Splendide. They were going to snatch him, but I went to see him first. I walked in as Betty Charlady. Nobody looked twice. I wanted to persuade him to share what he'd found with me. I told him I was his only hope. I could keep Gott and Himmell off his back. And I could use them to stay ahead of the Fat Man. But he was greedy. He wouldn't listen. He had a gun. There was a fight. Like I say, it was an accident." She sighed. "There can't be any more accidents. You two can't leave the cemetery. No witnesses." For a moment she slipped back into her Betty Charlady voice. "Cheerio then, Mr Nicholas. Ta, ta, Mr 'erbert."

She lifted the gun.

"Oh, no!" Herbert whimpered.

"I don't think so, Beatrice." I said.

She looked beyond me and her face jerked back like she'd been slapped. But then she lowered the gun and laughed. Suddenly, the cemetery was full of uniformed policemen. They were springing up everywhere – out of the long grass and from behind the gravestones. At their head, running to be the first one to reach us, were Snape and Boyle.

"Well ... that's a lucky coincidence,"

Herbert said.

"What do you mean – coincidence?" I said. "I called Snape last night. I told him everything." Herbert's mouth fell open. "Well, I wasn't going to come here alone."

By this time Boyle had reached Beatrice von Falkenberg. She stretched out her hands elegantly for the cuffs but he threw himself at her anyway – a flying rugby tackle that sent her crashing to the ground.

"You could have come out sooner, Chief Inspector," I said as Snape arrived. "We were nearly killed."

"That's true, laddy," Snape agreed. "But ... well, it was Boyle. He wanted to see what would happen. He asked me to hold back. And as it's Christmas..."

The policemen began to clear away bodies. Snape leant down and picked up the Maltesers box.

"Now, let's see about this," he said.

The three of us gathered around the memorial. The stone falcon waited, its wings spread, its beak open, its glass eyes blinking in the sun. Carefully, Snape tore off the bar-code. He threw the rest of the box away. Then he laid the strip face up in the falcon's beak and pulled it through.

Behind the eyes, inside the falcon's head, a lens focused the sun's beams on to the bar-code. The white stripes reflected some of them back on to a photodetector hidden inside the falcon's body. We heard the click as a connection was made. There was a soft hum. A solar-powered generator had sprung to life. It activated a motor. There was another click and the entire front of the memorial – along with the inscription – swung open to reveal a solid metal container.

And that was the last surprise of the day. There was to be no Christmas bonus for Snape, no reward for us. Because there weren't any diamonds. There wasn't even a lump of coal. The container was empty. We were looking at three and a half million pounds worth of nothing.

THE FALCON'S MALTESER

"But Nicholas, I still don't understand."

"I've gone through it all twice, Herbert."

"Well, if you wrote it all down... That would help."

"Maybe I will."

It was the second day of the New Year. It didn't feel much different to the old year. It was cold. There wasn't any gas in the flat. And, as usual, we were down to the last handful of change. We'd had a great Christmas, Herbert and me. Two frozen turkey croquettes and the Queen's speech-only we'd missed the Queen's speech. Mum and Dad had sent us a card and a couple of presents but they hadn't cheered us up. The card showed two koalas in a Christmas tree. The presents were a boomerang for me and a hat with corks for Herbert.

I threw the boomerang away. It came back.

There were still a couple of weeks until term began and I'd have liked to have gone skiing. A lot of the guys in my class had made it to Switzerland or Austria or wherever and they'd be full of it when they got back. It didn't seem fair. After all I'd been through I couldn't even afford the bus fare to the travel agent.

And then the parcel came. Special delivery. From the South of France. It was addressed to me.

I think I knew who it was from before I opened it. There was only one reason I could think of why the Falcon's safe had been empty. I hadn't mentioned it to Snape or Boyle. I hadn't even mentioned it to Herbert.

"What is it?" he asked.

"I don't know."

"Well, open it."

I opened it. Inside the brown wrapping-paper there was a carton about the same shape and size as a film-box. It was filled with tissue paper but nestling in the centre was a round ball of milk chocolate...

"A Malteser!" Herbert said. The colour walked out of his face. Herbert didn't much like chocolates any more. And he hated Maltesers.

There was a card attached to the box. The message was short and not so sweet. It was written in a flowing, looping hand.

No hard feelings?

L.B.

No hard feelings? I wasn't so sure. Lauren had sold me the sob story of her life – and OK she hadn't had the breaks – but then she'd double-crossed me. All along she'd known more than she'd let on. Maybe she'd worked it out for herself or maybe Johnny Naples had told her. But she'd known about the cemetery and she'd known about the Falcon's memorial. I'd given her the last piece of the jigsaw when I told her about the bar-code. And that day, in the office of the *Fulham Express*, she'd made up her mind to steal the diamonds. She'd accidentally left the Maltesers upstairs. And when she'd gone up to get them, she'd made a simple copy of the key: photocopy.

She'd never gone into Fulham Broadway Station – at least, not down to the trains. The moment I'd left, she'd doubled back to the cemetery. Perhaps she'd overtaken me in a taxi. The sun had been shining that day. She'd slid her photocopy through the falcon's beak. And the diamonds had been hers.

I reached down and squeezed the Malteser between my finger and thumb. I was angry. I wanted to see it shatter. But it wouldn't. There was something hard in the centre.

"Herbert..." I said.

He looked. The chocolate had squashed. It

wasn't a Malteser at all. There was something sparkling inside. "What is it?" he asked.

"What does it look like?" I said.

The last of the chocolate had crumbled away. I was left holding a diamond the size of a peanut. What would it be worth? Ten thousand pounds? Twenty thousand? Certainly not peanuts.

So we would go skiing after all. And Herbert would break his leg as he got on to the plane and we'd blow all the money we got from the diamond before we'd even got round to paying the gas bill. But what did I care? It was the New Year and we'd come out of it all alive, and although diamonds may be for ever, you've got to grab every good minute and enjoy it while it's there.

Photograph © Jon Cartwright

Anthony Horowitz is the author of the number one bestselling Alex Rider books and The Power of Five series. He has enjoyed huge success as a writer for both children and adults, most recently with the latest adventure in the Alex Rider series, *Russian Roulette*, and the highly acclaimed Sherlock Holmes novel, *The House of Silk*. His latest novel, *Moriarty*, is also set in the world of Sherlock Holmes and was published in October 2014. Anthony was also chosen by the Ian Fleming estate to write the new James Bond novel which will be published this year. Anthony has won numerous awards, including the Bookseller Association/Nielsen Author of the Year Award, the Children's Book of the Year Award at the British Book Awards, and the Red House Children's Book Award. In 2014 Anthony was awarded an OBE for Services to Literature. He has also created and written many major television series, including *Injustice*, *Collision* and the award-winning *Foyle's War*.

You can find out more about Anthony and his work at:
www.alexrider.com
@AnthonyHorowitz